FIRST LORD'S FURY

FIRST LORD'S FURY

BOOK SIX OF THE CODEX ALERA

JIM BUTCHER

ACE BOOKS, NEW YORK

THE BERKLEY PUBLISHING GROUP
Published by the Penguin Group
Penguin Group (USA) Inc.
375 Hudson Street, New York, New York 10014, USA
Penguin Group (Canada), 90 Eglinton Avenue East, Suite 700, Toronto, Ontario M4P 2Y3, Canada
(a division of Pearson Penguin Canada Inc.)
Penguin Books Ltd., 80 Strand, London WC2R 0RL, England
Penguin Group Ireland, 25 St. Stephen's Green, Dublin 2, Ireland (a division of Penguin Books Ltd.)
Penguin Group (Australia), 250 Camberwell Road, Camberwell, Victoria 3124, Australia
(a division of Pearson Australia Group Pty. Ltd.)
Penguin Books India Pvt. Ltd., 11 Community Centre, Panchsheel Park, New Delhi—110 017, India
Penguin Group (NZ), 67 Apollo Drive, Rosedale, North Shore 0632, New Zealand
(a division of Pearson New Zealand Ltd.)
Penguin Books (South Africa) (Pty.) Ltd., 24 Sturdee Avenue, Rosebank, Johannesburg 2196,
South Africa

Penguin Books Ltd., Registered Offices: 80 Strand, London WC2R 0RL, England

This is an original publication of The Berkley Publishing Group.

FIRST EDITION: December 2009

Library of Congress Cataloging-in-Publication Data

Butcher, Jim, 1971–
    First lord's fury / Jim Butcher.—1st ed.
      p.   cm.—(Codex Alera ; bk. 6)
    ISBN 978-0-441-01769-0
    1. Imaginary places—Fiction.   2. Imaginary wars and battles—Fiction.   I. Title.
    PS3602.U85F57 2009
    813'.6—dc22

                                                                    2009037610

PRINTED IN THE UNITED STATES OF AMERICA

10   9   8   7   6   5   4   3   2

For our own Knights and legionares,
the men and women of the United States Armed Forces.
If you didn't do what you do, I couldn't do what I do. Thank you.

ACKNOWLEDGMENTS

This one owes deep debts of gratitude to my editor, Anne Sowards, who deserves something for having to put up with me. Another big thank-you goes out to Priscilla, for going above and beyond the call of fandom in helping make the map of Alera, finally. Thanks also to the many fans at the jim-butcher.com forums, whose efforts helped us to refine and create the map by providing us with multiple reference points upon the maps they have made.

And, as ever, thank you, Shannon and JJ.

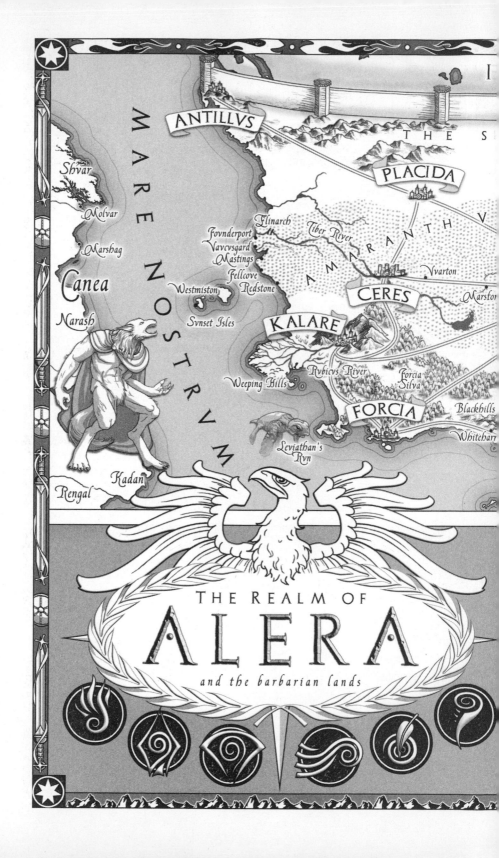

ANTILLVS

PLACIDA

THE S

MARE NOSTRVM

Shvar

Molvar

Marshag

Canea

Narash

Kadan

Rengal

Flinarch

Fovnderport
Vavcvsgard
Mastings
Fellcove
Redstone

Westmiston

Svnset Isles

Tiber River

A M A R A N T H V

Vvarton

Marstor

CERES

KALARE

Rvbicvs River

Forcia
Silva

Weeping Hills

FORCIA

Blackhills

Whitehar

Leviathan's
Ryn

THE REALM OF

ALERA

and the barbarian lands

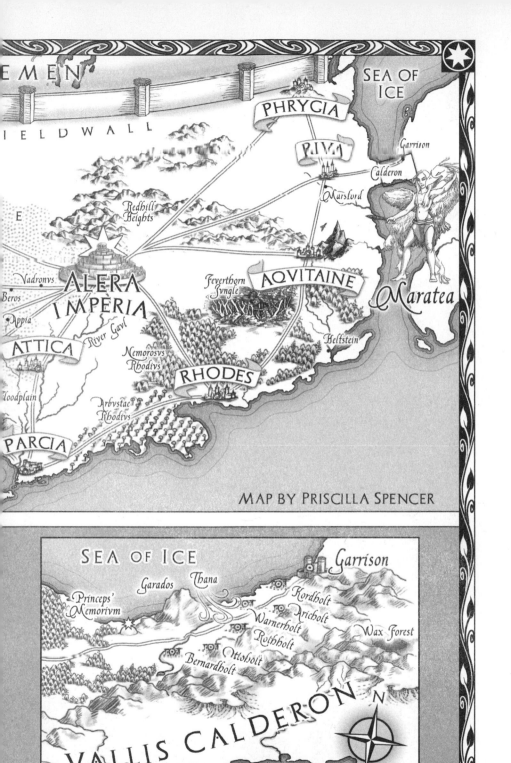

EMEN

FIELDWALL

SEA OF
ICE

PHRYGIA

RIVA

Garrison

Calderon

Marslord

Redhill
Heights

ALERA
IMPERIA

Vadronvs

Beros

Appia

Feverthorn
Syngle

AQVITAINE

Maratea

ATTICA

River Gavl

Nemorosvs
Rhodivs

Heltstein

loodplain

RHODES

Arbvstae
Rhodivs

PARCIA

MAP BY PRISCILLA SPENCER

SEA OF ICE

Garrison

Garados   Thana

Princeps'
Memorivm

Kordholt

Aricholt

Warnerholt
Rotholt

Wax Forest

Ottoholt

Bernardholt

VALLIS CALDERON

N

PROLOGUE

The steadholt was located several miles south of the ruined wasteland that had once been Alera Imperia, and it was an old one. Windmanes had not been sighted there in more than six centuries. Furystorms had been absent for even longer than that. The land, for miles about, had been a patchwork of farmlands, steadholts, villages, and roads for hundreds of years. Wild furies had been so few and so feeble that they were all but extinct.

As a result, the little steadholt had not been built with stone walls surrounding it, or with a heavy stone central hall for shelter from fury-inspired weather. It was instead a collection of cottages and small houses, where each family had lived in its own home, separate from the others.

But all that had been before the vord came.

Invidia Aquitaine stood at the outskirts of the little steadholt, hidden in the shadows.

Shadows were abundant these days, she reflected.

The newborn volcano that stood as a gravestone for Gaius Sextus, the final First Lord of Alera, had continued to spew forth clouds of dark smoke and ash in the days and weeks after its creation. Even now, the sky was covered with low clouds that would release spring rain in fitful sputters or maniacal bursts. Sometimes the rain was yellow, or red, and sometimes green. The clouds themselves were dimly lit, even at night, by an angry scarlet light from the fire-mountain to the north—and in every other direction by the steady, haunting green glow of the *croach*, the waxy growth that covered the ground, the trees, the buildings, and every other feature of the land the vord had claimed for their own.

Here the vord had driven their presence the deepest. Here, at the heart of what had once been Alera, they had taken the most. The *croach*, the living presence of the vord, covered everything for a hundred miles in every direction, choking all other life from the land.

Except here.

The little steadholt was green. Its kitchen gardens were well under way despite the fact that summer had not quite arrived. Its modest-sized field already promised a fine crop of grain. Wind sighed in the leaves of its enormous old trees. Its animals grazed upon the grass of a rich pasture. In the darkness, if one ignored the eerily lit sky, the green glow of *croach* stretching to the horizon in every direction, and the occasional alien shriek of one of the vord, it looked like a normal, prosperous Aleran steadholt.

Invidia shuddered.

The parasite on her torso reacted to the motion with an uncomfortable ripple of its own. Since its dozen awl-tipped legs were wrapped around her, their sharp tips sunk inches into her flesh, it caused pain. It was nothing compared to the agony she suffered as its head twisted, its eyeless face and branching mandibles sunken into the flesh between two of her ribs, burrowed invasively into her innards.

Invidia loathed the creature—but it was all that kept her alive. The poison upon the balest bolt that had nearly taken her life had spread all through her body. It had festered there, growing, devouring her from within, so swiftly and perniciously that even her own ability to restore her body via furycraft had been overwhelmed. She had fought it for days as she stumbled away from civilization, certain that she was being pursued, barely conscious as the struggle in her body raged. And when she had realized that the struggle could end in only one way, she found herself lying upon a wooded hillside and knew that she was going to die.

But the vord Queen had come to her. The image of that creature, staring down at her without an ounce of pity or empathy, had been burned into her nightmares.

Invidia had been desperate. Terrified. Delirious with poison and fever. Her body had been so knotted with shivering against the fever-cold that she literally had not been able to feel her arms and legs. But she *could* feel the vord Queen, the creature's alien presence *inside* her thoughts, sifting through them one by one as they tumbled and spun in the delirium.

The Queen had offered to save Invidia's life, to sustain her, in exchange for her service. There had been no other option but death.

Though they sent a wave of agony washing through her body, she ignored the parasite's torturous movements. Like shadows, there was, of late, also an abundance of pain.

And a small voice that whispered to her from some dark, quiet corner of her heart told her that she deserved it.

"You keep coming back here," said a young woman at her elbow.

Invidia felt herself twitch in surprise, felt her heart suddenly race, and the parasite rippled, inflicting further torment. She closed her eyes and focused on the pain, let it fill her senses, until there was no semblance of fear remaining in her mind.

One never showed fear to the vord Queen.

Invidia turned to face the young woman and inclined her head politely. The young Queen looked almost like an Aleran. She was quite exotically lovely, with an aquiline nose and a wide mouth. She wore a simple, tattered gown of green silk that left her shoulders bare, displaying smooth muscle and smoother skin. Her hair was long, fine, and white, falling in a gently waving sheet to the backs of her thighs.

Only small details betrayed her true origins. Her long fingernails were green-black talons, made of the same steel-hard vord chitin that armored her warriors. Her skin had an odd, rigid appearance, and almost seemed to reflect the distant ambient light of the *croach*, showing the faint green tracings of veins beneath its surface.

Her eyes were what frightened Invidia, even after months in her presence. Her eyes were canted up slightly at the corners, like those of the Marat barbarians to the northeast, and they were completely black. They shone with thousands of faceted lenses, insectlike, and watched the world with calm, unblinking indifference.

"Yes, I suppose I do," Invidia replied to her. "I told you that this place represents a risk. You seem unwilling to listen to my advice. So I have taken it upon myself to monitor it and ensure that it is not being used as a base or hiding place for infiltrators."

The Queen shrugged a shoulder, unconcerned. The movement was smooth but somehow awkward—it was a mannerism she had copied but clearly did not understand. "This place is guarded ceaselessly. They could not enter it undetected."

"Others have said as much and been mistaken," Invidia warned her. "Consider what Countess Amara and Count Bernard did to us last winter."

"That area had not been consolidated," the Queen replied calmly. "This one has." She turned her eyes to the little houses and tilted her head. "They gather together for food at the same time every night."

"Yes," Invidia said. The Aleran holders who dwelt in the little steadholt in cobbled-together households had been working the fields and going about the business of a steadholt as if they were not the only ones of their kind living within a month's hard march.

They had no choice but to work the fields. The vord Queen had told them that if they did not, they would die.

Invidia sighed. "Yes, at the same time. It's called 'dinner' or 'supper.'"

"Which?" the Queen asked.

"In practice, the words are generally interchangeable."

The vord Queen frowned. "Why?"

She shook her head. "I do not know. Partly because our ancestors spoke a number of different tongues and—"

The vord Queen turned her eyes to Invidia. "No," she said. "Why do they eat together?" She turned her eyes back to the little houses. "There exists the possibility that the larger and stronger would take the food of the weaker creatures. Logic dictates that they should eat alone. And yet they do not."

"There is more to it than simple sustenance."

The Queen considered the cottage. "Alerans waste time altering their food through various processes. I suppose eating together reduces the inefficiency of that practice."

"It does make cooking simpler, and it is partly why it is a practice," Invidia said. "But only in part."

The Queen frowned more deeply. "Why else eat in such a fashion?"

"To be with one another," Invidia said. "To spend time together. It's part of what builds a family."

Great furies knew that was true. She could count on her fingers the number of meals she had taken with her father and brothers.

"Emotional bonding," the vord Queen said.

"Yes," Invidia said. "And . . . it is pleasant."

Empty black eyes looked at her. "Why?"

She shrugged. "It gives one a sense of stability," she said. "A daily ritual. It is reassuring to have that part of the day, to know that it will happen every day."

"But it will not," the Queen said. "Even in their natural habitat, it is not a stable circumstance. Children grow and leave homes. Routines are disrupted by events beyond their control. The elderly die. The sick die. They all die."

"They know that," Invidia said. She closed her eyes and for an instant thought of her mother, and the too-brief time she had been allowed to share her table, her company, and her love with her only daughter. Then she opened her eyes again and forced herself to look at the nightmare world around her. "But it does not seem that way, when the food is warm and your loved ones are gathered with you."

The vord Queen looked at her sharply. "Love. Again."

"I told you. It is the primary emotion that motivates us. Love for others or for oneself."

"Did you take meals like this?"

"When I was very young," Invidia said, "and only with my mother. She died of disease."

"And it was pleasant to have dinner?"

"Yes."

"Did you love her?"

"As only children can," Invidia said.

"Did she love you?"

"Oh, yes."

The vord Queen turned to face Invidia fully. She was silent for two full minutes, and when she finally spoke, the words were spread apart carefully for emphasis—it gave the question a surprisingly hesitant, almost childlike, quality. "What did it feel like?"

Invidia didn't look at the young woman, the young monster that had already destroyed most of the world. She stared through the nearest set of windows at the dinner being set down at the table.

About half of the people inside were Placidans, taken when the vord had completed their occupation of Ceres and moved forward over the rolling plains of that city's lands. They included an old man and woman who were actually a couple. There was a young mother there, with two children of her own and three more that the vord had deposited in her care. There was a man of early middle age who sat beside her, an Imperian farmer who had not been wise enough or swift enough to avoid capture when the vord came for Alera Imperia and the lands around her. Adults and children alike were tired from a day at work on the steadholt. They were hungry, thirsty, and glad of the simple meal prepared for them. They would spend some time together in the hearth room after the meal, take a few hours of time to themselves with full stomachs and pleasantly weary bodies, then they would sleep.

Invidia stared at the little family, thrown together like a mass of driftwood by the fortunes of invasion and war and clinging to one another all the more strongly because of it. Even now, here, at the end of all things, they reached out to one another, offering what comfort and warmth they could, especially to the children. She nodded toward the candlelit table, where the adults actually shared a few gentle smiles with one another, and the children sometimes smiled and even laughed.

"Like that," she said quietly. "It felt like that."

The young Queen stared at the cottage. Then she said, "Come." She strode forward, graceful and pitiless as a hungry spider.

Invidia ground her teeth and remained where she stood. She did not want to see more death.

The parasite writhed in agonizing reproof.

She followed the vord Queen.

The Queen slammed the door open, disdaining the doorknob, to shatter its entire frame. Though she had displayed it on rare occasions before, her raw physical might was unbelievable from such a slender figure—even to Invidia, who was well used to seeing earthcrafters perform feats of superhuman strength. The Queen strode over the splinters and into the kitchen, where the little family took their dinner at a table.

They all froze. The youngest of the children, a beautiful male child perhaps a year old, let out a short wail, which the young mother silenced by seizing the child and placing her hand over his mouth.

The Queen focused on the mother and child. "You," she said, pointing a deadly, clawed fingertip at the young woman. "The child is your blood?"

The young holder stared at the vord Queen with wide, panicked eyes. She nodded once.

The vord Queen stepped forward, and said, "Give him to me."

The woman's eyes filled with tears. Her eyes flicked around the room, haunted, seeking the gaze of someone else—anyone else—who might do something. None of the other holders could meet her gaze. The young mother looked up at Invidia pleadingly, and she began to sob. "Lady," she whispered. "My lady, please."

Her stomach twisted and rebelled, but Invidia had learned long ago that retching sent the parasite into convulsions that could all but kill her. She ate seldom, of late. "You have another child," she told the young mother in a calm, hard voice. "Save her."

The man sitting beside the young mother moved. He gently took the boy from her arms, leaned forward to kiss his hair, and held him out to the vord Queen. The child wailed in protest and tried to go back to his mother.

The vord Queen took the child and held him in front of her. She let him kick and wail for a moment, watching him with her alien eyes. Then, quite calmly, she held the boy close to her body with one arm and twisted his head sharply to one side. His wails ceased.

Invidia found herself about to lose control of her stomach, but then she saw that the child still lived. His neck was twisted to the breaking point, his breaths coming in small, labored gasps—but he lived.

The vord Queen stared at the sobbing mother for a moment. Then she said, "She feels pain. I have not harmed her, yet she feels pain."

"The child is hers," Invidia said. "She loves him."

The Queen tilted her head. "And he loves her in return?"

"Yes."

"Why?"

"Because it is the nature of love to be answered in kind. Especially by children."

The Queen tilted her head to the other side. Then she stared down at the child. Then at the young mother. Then at the man seated beside her. She leaned down and touched her lips to the child's hair and paused for a moment, as if considering the sensation.

Then, moving slowly and carefully, she released the child from her hold and passed him back to the weeping mother. The young woman broke down into shuddering sobs, holding the child close.

The vord Queen turned and left the cottage. Invidia followed.

The young Queen walked up a nearby hillside and, once they had crested the hill and moved into sight of a vord landscape stretching out before them, stood with her back to the little steadholt for a time. "Love is not always returned among your kind."

"No," Invidia said simply.

"When it is not," she said, "it is a kind of pain to the one who has loved."

"Yes."

"It is irrational," the vord Queen said—and to Invidia's shock, there was a quiet heat to the words. An anger. The vord Queen was angry.

Invidia felt her mouth go dry.

"Irrational," the Queen said. Her fingers flexed, the nails lengthening and contracting. "Wasteful. Inefficient."

Invidia said nothing.

The vord Queen spun abruptly, the motion so swift that Invidia could barely track it. She stared at Invidia with unreadable, alien eyes. Invidia could see a thousand tiny reflections of herself in them, a pale, half-starved woman with dark hair, clad only in a suit of vord-chitin carapace that fit her as closely as her own skin.

"Tomorrow," the vord Queen said, smoldering anger filling the normally empty tones of her voice, "you and I will have dinner. Together."

Then she turned and vanished in a blur of green silk into the endless rolling waves of *croach*.

Invidia fought the sense of terror spreading through her stomach. She stared back down at the collection of cottages. From her place on the hillside, the steadholt looked lovely, furylamps glowing in its little town square and inside the cottages. A horse nickered in a nearby pasture. A dog barked several times. The trees, the houses, they all looked so perfect. Like dollhouses.

Invidia found herself suppressing a laugh that rose up through the madness of the past several months, for fear that she would never be able to stop.

Dollhouses.

After all, the vord Queen was not quite nine years old. Perhaps that was exactly what they were.

Varg, Warmaster of the fallen land of Narash, heard the familiar tread of his pup's footsteps upon the deck of the *Trueblood*, flagship of the Narashan fleet.

He peeled his lips back from his teeth in macabre amusement. Could it be the flagship of a Narashan fleet when Narash itself was no more? According to the codes, it was the last piece of sovereign Narashan territory upon the face of Carna.

But could the code of law of Narash be truly considered its law without a territory for it to govern? If not, then the *Trueblood* was nothing more than wood and rope and sailcloth, belonging to no nation, empty of meaning as anything but a means of conveyance.

Just as Varg himself would be empty of meaning—a Warmaster with no range to protect.

Bitter fury burned inside him in a fire-flash instant, and the white clouds and blue sea he could view through the cabin's windows abruptly turned red. The vord. The accursed vord. They had destroyed his home and murdered his people. Of millions of Narashans, fewer than a hundred thousand had survived—and the vord would answer to him for their actions.

He got hold of his temper before it could goad him into a blood-rage, breathing deeply until the normal colors of daylight returned. The vord would pay. There would be a time and a place to exact vengeance, but it was neither here nor now.

He touched a claw tip to the page of the book and carefully turned it to the next. It was a delicate creation, this Aleran tome, a gift from Tavar. Like the young Aleran demon, it was tiny, fragile—and contained a great deal more than its exterior suggested. If only the print wasn't of such a diminutive size. It was a constant strain on Varg's eyesight. One had to read the thing by daylight. With a proper, dim red lamp, he couldn't make it out at all.

There was a polite scratch at the door.

"Enter," Varg rumbled, and his pup, Nasaug, entered the cabin. The younger Cane bared his throat in respect, and Varg returned the gesture with slightly less emphasis.

Pup, Varg thought, as he looked fondly upon his get. *He's four centuries old, and by every reasonable standard should be a Warmaster in his own right. He fought the accursed Aleran demons on their own ground for two years and made good his escape despite all of their power. But I suppose a sire never forgets how small his pups were once.*

"Report," he rumbled.

"Master Khral has come aboard," Nasaug rumbled. "He requests an audience."

Varg bared his teeth. He carefully placed a thin bit of colored cloth into the pages of the book and gently closed it. "Again."

"Shall I throw him back into his boat?" Nasaug asked. There was a somewhat wistful note to his voice.

"I find myself tempted," Varg said. "But no. It is his right under the codes to seek redress for grievances. Bring him.

Nasaug bared his throat again and departed the cabin. A moment later, the door opened again, and Master Khral entered. He was nearly as tall as Varg, closer to nine feet than eight when fully upright, but unlike the warrior Cane, he was as thin as whipcord. His fur was a mottled red-brown, marked with streaks of white hairs born from scars inflicted by ritual and not by honest battle. He wore a demonskin mantle and hood, despite Varg's repeated requests that he not parade about the fleet in a garment made from the skins of the creatures who were presently responsible for keeping them all alive. He wore a pair of pouches on cross-body belts, each containing a bladder of blood, which the ritualists needed to perform their sorcery. He smelled like unclean fur and rotten blood, and reeked of a confidence that he was too foolish to see had no basis in reality.

The senior ritualist stared calmly at Varg for several seconds before finally baring his throat just enough to give Varg no excuse to rip it out. Varg did not return the gesture at all. "Master Khral. What now?"

"As every day, Warmaster," Khral replied. "I am here to beg you, on behalf of the people of Narash and Shuar, to turn aside from this dangerous path of binding our people to the demons."

"I am told," Varg rumbled, "the people of Narash and Shuar like to eat."

Khral sneered. "We are Canim," he spat. "We need no one to help us attain our destiny. Especially not the demons."

Varg grunted. "True. We will take our destiny on our own. But obtaining food is another matter."

"They will turn on us," Khral said. "The moment they have finished using us, they will turn and destroy us. You know this is true."

"It is true," Varg said. "It is also tomorrow. I am in command of today."

Khral's tail lashed in irritation. "Once we have separated from the ice ships, we can pick up the pace and make landfall within a week."

"We can make ourselves into meals for the leviathans, you mean," Varg replied. "There are no range charts of the sea this far north. We would have no way to know when we entered a leviathan's territory."

"We are the masters of the world. We are not afraid."

Varg growled low in his chest. "I find it remarkable how often amateurs confuse courage with idiocy."

The ritualist's eyes narrowed. "We might lose a vessel here and there," Khral acknowledged. "But we would *not* owe our lives to the charity of the demons. A week, then we can begin to rebuild on our own."

"Leave the ice ships," Varg said. "The same ships that are carrying more than half of our surviving people."

"Sacrifices must be made if we are to remain true to ourselves," Khral declared, "if our spirits, our pride, and our strength are to remain pure."

"I have noticed that those who speak as you do are rarely willing to include themselves among those sacrificed."

A furious snarl burst out of Khral's throat, and one paw-hand flashed toward the hip bag at his side.

Varg did not so much as rise from his crouch. His arms moved, shoulders twisting with sinewy power as he flung the Aleran book at Khral. It sailed through the air in a blur of spinning motion, and its hard spine struck the master ritualist in the throat. The impact knocked Khral's shoulders back against the door to the cabin, and he rebounded from it to fall to the cabin's deck, making gagging sounds.

Varg got up and walked over to the book. Its leaves had opened, and some of the delicate pages had been harshly folded. Varg picked it up carefully, smoothed the pages, and considered the Aleran creation again.

Like Tavar, he mused, it was apparently more dangerous than it appeared.

Varg stood by for a moment, as Khral's gagging gradually transformed to labored breathing. He hadn't quite crushed the ritualist's windpipe, which was disappointing. Now he'd have to suffer the fool again tomorrow. After surviving today's conflict, Khral would be unlikely to allow Varg another such opportunity to remove him.

So be it. Some ambitious underling might turn a dead Khral into a martyr. It was entirely possible the ritualist would be more dangerous dead than alive.

"Nasaug," Varg called.

The pup opened the door and considered the prostrate form on the floor. "Warmaster?"

"Master Khral is ready to return to his boat."

Nasaug bared his throat, not quite hiding his amusement. "Immediately, Warmaster." He leaned down, seized Khral by his ankle, and simply dragged him out of the cabin.

Varg gave Nasaug a few minutes to get Khral back into his boat, then strode out onto the *Trueblood*'s deck.

The ship was painted black, as most Narashan vessels were. It offered a stealth advantage when moving at night, and during the day it collected enough heat to enable the adhesive sealing the hull to remain flexible and watertight. It also lent them an air of menace, particularly to the Aleran demons. They were nearly blind at night and painted their own ships white so that they could see a little more clearly during darkness. The very idea of a black ship was alien to them, and darkness was a primal fear for the species. While their blindness and fear might not stop them from attacking, especially with their sorcery at hand, it *did* prevent any independent individual or small group from attempting to board a Narashan vessel for whatever mad reason it might concoct.

The Alerans were many things, but not stupid. None of them liked the idea of stumbling around in the darkness while the night-wise Canim came for them.

Varg went to the ship's prow and stared out over the sea. They were in waters hundreds of leagues north of any he had sailed before, and the sea was choppy. The weather had remained clear, either as the result of fortune or Aleran sorcery, and the fleet had made the long, slow trek from Canea without serious incident—something Varg would have considered the next best thing to impossible only months before.

The voyage from Canea to Alera was a month's worth of sailing with a moderately favorable wind. It had taken them over three months to get this far, and there were still three weeks' worth of ocean in front of them at their current pace. Varg turned his eyes to the south and studied the reason for their crawl.

Three almost unbelievably enormous ships rode squarely in the center of the fleet, rising like mountains from the sea and dwarfing even the *Trueblood* into insignificance—but their size was not the most remarkable thing about them.

The ships had been built from ice.

The Alerans had used their sorcery to reshape icebergs calving from a glacier into seaworthy forms, with multiple decks and a vast capacity for their precious cargo—all that remained of once-proud Canea. Makers, females, and pups filled the three ships, and the Narashan captains of the vessels escorting her had orders to spill their crews' blood like seawater if that was what it required to protect the civilians.

The ships had enormous, flat decks, and no mast could stretch high or broad enough to hang enough sail to move the vessel, but the Alerans had managed to overcome the problem with their typical ingenuity. Hundreds of poles with crossbars had been placed on the topmost deck of the ship, and they billowed with every form of cloth one could imagine. They alone would not propel the ice mountains, but Tavar was, correctly, of the opinion that even a small contribution would prove significant over time. Then, too, the wind demons with the Aleran fleet had been tasked with bringing up enough of a breeze to lighten the load on the water demons who truly drove the vast ships.

Propelled primarily by Aleran sorcery, the ice ships had proved to be steady in the water. If the quarters for his people were a bit cold—albeit less so than one would have imagined—their discomfort was a small price to pay for survival. Some of the sick and elderly had been transferred to Varg's transports to get out of the cold, but for the most part matters had proceeded with relative simplicity.

Varg looked up and down the length of his ship, watching his sailors tending to their work. His warriors and sailors were painfully lean, though not cadaverous. Gathering rations had been a hurried affair during the escape, and there were thousands of mouths to feed. Priority for food went to the Aleran wind and water demons, then sailors, with civilians close behind. The demon Legions followed, thanks to the necessity of maintaining their fragile forms, and last came Varg's warriors. The order might have been reversed during lean times in a land campaign, but here, on the open water, those most vital to the fleet's progress and purpose had priority.

Varg watched as a hunting ship sailed into the fleet from outside the formation. It moved sluggishly, even under full sail, but its speed was adequate to catch the ice ships. A massive form floated in the water behind the hunting ship—the corpse of a medium-sized leviathan.

The demons' work, again. Leviathans were fiercely territorial, but they hated the cold of the chilled sea surrounding the ice ships. Hunting vessels would sail out of the bitterly cold water and draw the attention of a leviathan. Then air and water demons would work together to slay it, somehow drowning the creatures on air even while they were in the water.

It was a dangerous business. Two out of ten hunting ships never returned—but those that did brought enough food with them, in the form of the leviathans, to feed the entire fleet for two days. The taste of leviathan meat and blubber was indescribably foul, but it kept a body alive.

Nasaug came to his side and watched the hunting ship with Varg. "Warmaster."

"The good Master is gone?"

"Yes," Nasaug said. "And surly."

Varg bared his teeth in a grin.

"Father," Nasaug said. He paused to choose words carefully. Varg turned to face him and waited. When Nasaug did that, what he had to say was generally unpleasant—and worth listening to.

"In three weeks we will reach Alera," Nasaug said.

"Yes."

"And fight the vord beside the demons."

"Yes."

Nasaug was silent for a long moment. Then he said, "Khral is a scheming fool. But he has a point. There is no reason for the Alerans to keep us alive once we have won the war."

Varg's ears twitched in amusement. "First we must win the war," he rumbled. "Many things can happen in the passing of time. Patience."

Nasaug flicked his ears in agreement. "Khral is building a following. Speaking to gatherings on the ice ships. Our people are afraid. He is using that fear."

"It is what bloodspeakers do," Varg said.

"He could be dangerous."

"Fools often are."

Nasaug did not gainsay him, but then he rarely did. The younger Cane straightened his shoulders in resignation and looked out to sea.

Varg put a hand on his pup's shoulder. "I know Khral. I know his like. How they think. How they move. I have dealt with them before, as have you when you fed Sarl to the Tavar."

Nasaug showed his fangs in a grin of remembrance.

Varg nodded. "If necessary, we will deal with them again."

"This problem might be better removed now than later."

Varg growled. "He has not yet stepped outside the code. I will not kill him improperly."

Nasaug was quiet for a moment more. Then he looked back behind them at the tiny, cramped cabin built just behind the forecastle, the smelliest and most uncomfortable quarters on the ship.

It was where Varg's Hunters lived.

"Hunters do not exist to circumvent the code," Varg growled, "but to preserve its spirit against its letter. Of course they could do the job. But it would only give Khral's ambitious underlings additional fire—and a genuine grievance to rally their followers behind. We may need the ritualists before all is done." He leaned his paw-hands on the rail and turned his nose into the wind, tasting the sky and the sea. "Master Marok is the brother of one of my finest enemies, and seniormost of the followers of the Old Path. I have his support within the ritualist camp."

Nasaug flicked his ears in acquiescence and seemed to relax a bit. He stood with his sire for a moment, then bared his throat and departed back to his duties.

Varg spent an hour or so on deck, inspecting, offering encouragement, snarling at imperfection. All was quiet, otherwise, which he mistrusted. There hadn't been nearly enough adversity during this crossing. Ill fortune must be holding its balest bolt until it could be sure it was lethal.

Varg returned to his book, an ancient Aleran writing apparently handed down since their people's prehistory. Tavar had said that they were not sure how much of the material was original and how much had been added in over the centuries—but if half of it was truth, then the Aleran warmaster described in its pages had been competent, if a shade arrogant. It was easy to see how his memoirs had influenced the strategies and tactics of the Aleran Legions.

Though, Varg mused, he was not at all convinced that this Julius person, whoever he was, would have had a very great deal to teach Tavar.

Sir Ehren ex Cursori walked toward the tent at the heart of the vast Legion camp outside the ancient city of Riva. He looked up the hill toward the walled city and felt uncomfortable for what must have been the hundredth time in a few days. The walls of Riva were high and thick—and offered him a conspicuous lack of comfort, considering that he and the surviving Legions under the command of First Lord Aquitaine were on the *outside* of them. Traditionally, when attacking a city, that was where the enemy tended to congregate.

Oh, certainly, the palisade walls around each Legion were a perfectly defensible barrier, he knew. But the modest earthworks and wooden walls were not enough to stop the vord.

Then again, the walls of Alera Imperia herself hadn't stopped them, either.

Ehren shook his head and brushed off the heavy thoughts with a sigh. There was no good in dwelling over what even the true First Lord of Alera, Gaius Sextus, had been powerless to stop. But at least in dying, Gaius had given the people of Alera a fighting chance to survive. The fire-mountain that had arisen as the vord closed their jaws on the heart of Alera had all but wiped out their horde, and the Legions brought down against all hope from the far northern cities by Gaius Isana had savaged the survivors.

Against any other foe the Alerans had faced, that would have been quite sufficient, Ehren reflected. It seemed quite unfair that such an enormous act of wanton destruction should prove to be nothing more than a moderate setback, regardless of who the enemy might be.

A quiet and rational part of his mind, the part that did all of his mathematics when he was faced with columns of figures, told him that the vord would be Alera's last foe. There was no way, none at all, to defeat them with the forces Alera had remaining. They were simply breeding too swiftly. Most wars, in the end, came down to the numbers. The vord had them.

It was as simple as that.

Ehren firmly told that part of his mind to go to the crows. It was his duty to serve and protect the Realm to the best of his ability, and he would not better attend to that duty by listening to such demoralizing naysaying, regardless of how correct it might be in a historical—and literal—sense.

After all, even driven to her knees, Alera was still a force to be reckoned with. The greatest gathering of Legions in a thousand years had congregated on the open plain around the city of Riva—the vast majority of them made up of veterans from the continually warring cities of Antillus and Phrygia. Oh, true, some of the troops were militia—but the militia of the sister cities of the north were quite literally as formidable as any of the active Legions of the south, and smithies were turning out weapons and armor for the Legions more rapidly than at any time in Aleran history. In fact, if they could have produced even more equipment, the Realm had volunteers enough for a dozen more Legions to add to the thirty already encamped.

Ehren shook his head. Thirty Legions. Just over two hundred *thousand* steel-clad *legionares*, each one part of a Legion, a living, breathing engine of war. The lower ranks of the Citizenry had been distributed among the Legions, so many that every Legion there had a double-sized cohort of Knights ready to do battle. And, beyond that, a full bloody Legion Aeris, its ranks consisting solely of those with the skills of Knights Aeris, led by the upper ranks of the Citizenry, had been harassing the foe for months.

And standing by beyond even that force was the First Lord and the High Lords of the Realm, each a furycrafter of almost unbelievable power. There was strength enough in that camp to rip the earth to its very bones, to set the sky on fire, to draw down the hungry sea from the north, to raise the winds to a killing scythe that would destroy any caught before it, all protected by a seething sea of steel and discipline.

And yet refugees, fleeing the destruction spreading from the heart of the Realm, continued to flood in. There was a desperate edge to the voices of centurions driving their troops to drill. Couriers, riding the winds, went roaring into the skies on thunderous columns of fury-guided air, so many that the Princeps had been forced to establish a policy for lanes of approach to prevent the fliers from collisions. Smithies burned their forges day and night, creating, preparing, repairing, and would continue doing so until the vord overran them.

And Ehren knew what was driving all of it.

Fear. Unmitigated terror.

Though the gathered might of all Alera spread for miles around Riva, the fear was a scent on the air, a shadow hovering at the edges of vision. The vord were coming, and calm, quiet voices whispered in every mind with the capacity for thought that even the power gathered there would not be enough. Though Gaius Sextus had died like a rogue gargant brought to bay, crushing his foes as he fell, the fact remained that he *had* fallen. There was an unspoken thought lurking behind everyone's eyes—if Gaius Sextus could not survive the vord, what chance did anyone else possess?

Ehren nodded to the commander of the score of guards surrounding the command tent, spoke the current passphrase, and was admitted to the tent without needing to so much as slow his steps. Nothing much really slowed Ehren's steps these days, he reflected. Gaius Sextus's letter to then–High Lord Aquitaine had apparently seen to that—among other things.

"Five months," snarled a rumbling voice, as Ehren entered the tent. "Five *months* we've been sitting here. We should have been moving south against the vord weeks ago!"

"You're a brilliant tactician, Raucus," replied a deeper, quieter voice. "But long-term thinking was never your strongest suit. We can't know what surprises the vord have in store for us on ground they've had time to prepare."

"There's never been evidence of any defenses," Antillus Raucus, High Lord Antillus retorted, as Ehren brushed aside the second tent flap and entered the tent proper. Raucus faced the Princeps across a double-sized sand table in the center of the tent that bore a map of all Alera upon it. He was a big, brawny man with a craggy face long used to winter winds, and he wore the scars of a soldier upon his face and hands, the reminders of nicks and cuts that had been so numerous and frequent that not even his considerable skills at furycraft could smooth them away. "In all of our history, this is the most powerful force ever assembled. We should take this army, ram it right down their throats, and kill that bitch of a Queen. Now. Today."

The First Lord was a leonine man, tall and lean, with dark golden hair and black, opaque eyes beneath the simple, undecorated steel band of his coronet, the traditional crown of a First Lord at war. Dressed in his own colors of scarlet and black, still, Aquitainus Attis—Gaius Aquitainus Attis, Ehren supposed, since Sextus had legally adopted the man in his last letter—faced Raucus's insistent statement with total calm. In that, at least, he actually *was* like Sextus, Ehren thought.

The First Lord shook his head. "The vord are obviously alien to us, but just as obviously intelligent. We have prepared defenses because it is an intelligent measure that even fools realize increases our ability to defend and control our land. We would be fools ourselves to assume that the vord cannot reach the same conclusion."

"When Gaius led our forces against the vord, you advised him to attack," Raucus pointed out. "Not retreat. It was the correct course of action."

"Given how many vord came to the final assault on Alera Imperia, apparently not," the First Lord replied. "We had no idea how many of them were out there. If he'd taken my counsel, our assault would have been enveloped and destroyed—and the vord were expecting us to do so."

"We know their numbers now," Raucus said.

"We *think* we do," Aquitaine shot back, heat touching his voice for the first time. "This is our *last chance*, Raucus. If these Legions fall, there is *nothing* left to stop the vord. I will *not* waste the blood of a single *legionare* if I cannot be sure to make the enemy pay a premium for it." He folded his hands behind his back, took a breath, and released it again, reassuming his air of complete calm "They will come to us, and soon, and their Queen will be compelled to accompany them and coordinate the attack."

Raucus scowled, his shaggy brows lowering. "You think you can mousetrap her."

"A defensive battle," Aquitaine replied, nodding. "Draw them to us, endure the assault, wait for our moment, and counterattack with everything we have."

Raucus grunted. "She's operating with furycraft now. And on a scale equal to anyone alive. And she's still got a guard of the Alerans she took before Count and Countess Calderon ruined that part of her operation."

Not even Antillus Raucus, Ehren noted, was willing to point out openly to the new Princeps that his wife was among those who had been compelled to take up arms with the vord.

"That's unfortunate," Aquitaine said, his voice hard. "But we'll have to go through them."

Raucus studied him for a few seconds. "You figure on taking her yourself, Attis?"

"Don't be ridiculous," Aquitaine said. "I'm a Princeps. It's going to be me, and you, and Lord and Lady Placida and every *other* High Lord and Lord and Count who can raise a weapon and the entire Legion Aeris and every *other* Legion I can arrange to be there besides."

Raucus lifted his eyebrows. "For one vord."

"For *the* vord," Aquitaine replied. "Kill her, and the rest of them are little more than animals."

"Bloody dangerous animals."

"Then I'm sure hunting fashions will become all the rage," Aquitaine replied. He turned around and nodded. "Sir Ehren. Have the reports come in?"

"Yes, sire," Ehren replied.

Aquitaine turned to the sand tables and swept a hand in invitation. "Show me."

Ehren calmly walked to the tables and took up a bucket of green sand. Raucus winced when he did. The green sand marked the spread of the *croach* across Alera. They'd run through several buckets already.

Ehren dipped a hand into the bucket and carefully poured green sand over the model of a walled city on the sand table that represented Parcia. It vanished into a mound of emerald grains. It seemed, to Ehren, an inadequate way to represent the ending of hundreds of thousands of Parcian lives, both the city's population and the vast number of refugees who had sought safety there. But there could be no doubt. The Cursors and aerial spies were certain: Parcia had fallen to the vord.

The tent was silent.

"When?" Aquitaine asked quietly.

"Two days ago," Ehren said. "The Parcian fleet was continuing the evacuation right up until the very end. If they stayed near the coastlines, they could have employed much smaller vessels as well and loaded all of the ships very heavily. They may have taken as many as seventy or even eighty thousand people around the cape to Rhodes."

Aquitaine nodded. "Did Parcia unleash the great furies beneath the city on the enemy?"

"Bloody crows, Attis," Raucus said quietly, reproof in his voice. "Half the refugees in the entire south were at Parcia."

The First Lord faced him squarely. "No amount of grieving will change what has happened. But prompt action based upon rational thought could save lives in the near future. I need to know how badly the enemy was hurt by the attack."

Raucus scowled and folded his heavy arms, muttering beneath his breath.

Aquitaine put a hand on the other man's shoulder for a moment, then turned to face Ehren. "Sir Ehren?"

Ehren shook his head. "There was nothing to indicate that he did so, Your Highness. From what we have heard from the survivors, High Lord Parcius was assassinated. The vord didn't assault and breach the walls until after he had fallen." He shrugged. "The reports indicate widespread incidents with wild furies in the aftermath, but that was to be expected given the number of deaths."

"Yes," Aquitaine said. He folded his arms and studied the map in silence.

Ehren let his eyes drift over it as well.

Alera was a land of vast stretches of sparsely settled or uninhabited wilderness between the enormous cities of the High Lords. Furycrafted roads between the great cities, and a great many waterways, provided lifelines of trade and created a natural support structure for smaller cities, towns, and villages that spread out into the countryside around them. Steadholts, farming hamlets, were scattered into the areas between the towns and cities, each supporting between thirty and three hundred or so people.

All that had changed.

The green sand covered the core of Alera, sweeping most thickly up from the uninhabited wasteland that had once been the city of Kalare, through the rich, productive lands of the Amaranth Vale, over the gutted corpse of the city of Ceres, and up to the smoldering slopes of the volcano that now loomed over what had once been Alera Imperia. Strands, like the branches of some alien tree, spread out from that vast central trunk, swelling into larger areas that surrounded several of the other great cities—cities that had settled in to fight until the bitter end and were stubbornly withstanding months of siege. Forcia, Antillus, Rhodes, and Aquitaine had all been besieged and currently fought the invaders at their gates. The rolling plains around Placida had fared better, and the *croach* had not managed to close within twenty miles or so of the city's walls—but even so, the stubborn Placidans had lost ground slowly and inexorably, and would be in the same position as the others in a matter of weeks.

Antillus and Phrygia, in the far north, had been spared attack thus far—but columns of the *croach* had swollen and sprouted, growing steadily and mindlessly toward them, just as it did toward the northeastern city of Riva—and, by extension, toward Ehren ex Cursori. Though he admitted it was possible that he was taking it a little personally.

"The refugees from Parcia are going to put more strain upon Rhodes's food supply," Aquitaine murmured, finally. "Raucus, send out a call for volunteers. We'll send Rhodes every earthcrafter willing to go in and help produce more food."

"We can't keep that up, Attis," Raucus said. "Oh, the earthcrafters can bring in a season's crop once a month, if they need to, maybe faster. But there just isn't enough soil inside the city's walls. They're depleting it of what the crops need to grow far more quickly than it can restore itself."

"Yes," Aquitaine said. "They can only maintain that kind of production for a year. Eighteen months at the outside. But even with every rooftop and avenue in Rhodes converted to grow crops, it will be a strain to fill another eighty thousand bellies. Once starvation sets in, disease will follow, and with the city so crowded, they will never recover." He shrugged elegantly. "This will all be decided in well under eighteen months, after which we will break the sieges. We will keep as many as possible alive until then. Send the earthcrafters."

Raucus put his fist to his heart in a Legion salute and sighed. "I just don't get it. These fields where they're growing new vord. The Legion Aeris is burning them to ash before they can get more than a crop or two of their own out. How can there be so crowbegotten *many* of the bastards?"

"Actually," Ehren said, "I think I know the answer to that, my lords."

Aquitaine looked up and arched an eyebrow at Ehren.

"I've gotten a report from an old business acquaintance of mine outside of Forcia. He's an aphrodin smuggler who used to use furycraft to grow crops of hollybells in caverns beneath the ground." Hollybells, the lovely blue flower from which the drug aphrodin was made, could thrive without sunlight in certain conditions. The smugglers who manufactured the drug for recreational use, despite laws against such activity, had taken advantage of the fact. "He says that the areas where the vord seem to be most populous coincide almost exactly with parts of the land that have a large number of such suitable caverns."

Aquitaine smiled thinly. "The fields on the surface were a ruse," he murmured. "Something to keep our attention, to make us feel as if we were succeeding—and to prevent us from searching for the true source of the enemy's numbers until it was too late to do any good." He shook his head. "That's Invidia's influence. It's the way she thinks."

Ehren coughed into an awkward silence.

"Attis," Raucus said, evidently choosing his words carefully, "she's helping the vord Queen. Maybe of her own will. I know that she is your wife, but . . ."

"She is a traitor to the Realm," Aquitaine said, his voice calm and hard. "Whether or not she has turned against Alera of her own will is irrelevant. She is an enemy asset that must be removed." He slashed a hand gently at the air. "We're wasting time, gentlemen. Sir Ehren, what else have you to report?"

Ehren focused his thoughts and kept his report concise. Other than Parcia's loss, little had changed. "The other cities are holding. None report a sighting of a vord queen."

"Are there any signs that the *croach* has invaded the Feverthorn Jungle?" the First Lord asked.

"None as yet, sire."

Aquitaine sighed and shook his head. "I suppose whatever the Children of the Sun left behind has kept us out for five hundred years. Why should the vord be any different?" He glanced over at Raucus. "If we had more time, we could use that against them, somehow. I'm sure of it."

"If wishes were horses," Raucus rumbled back.

"Being a trite cliché makes it no less true," Aquitaine said. "Please continue, Sir Ehren."

Ehren took a deep breath. This was the moment he'd dreaded all morning. "Sire," he said, "I think I know how to slow their advance toward Riva."

Raucus let out a startled huff of a laugh. "Really, boy? And you just now thought of mentioning it?"

Aquitaine frowned and folded his arms. "Speak your mind, Cursor."

Ehren nodded. "I've been running calculations of the rate of the vord advance in various stages of their campaign, and I've isolated where they moved slowest and most rapidly." He cleared his throat. "I can show you the figures if—"

"If I didn't trust your competence, you wouldn't be here," Aquitaine responded. "Continue."

Ehren nodded. "The vord moved most quickly during their advance through the Amaranth Vale, sire. And their slowest advance came when they crossed the

Waste of Kalare—and again when they advanced through the region around Alera Imperia." He took a deep breath. "Sire, as you know, the vord use the *croach* as a sort of food. It's mostly a gelatinous liquid, underneath a very tough, leathery shell."

Aquitaine nodded. "And they can somehow control the flow of nutrients through it. It's something like an aqueduct; only instead of water, it conveys their food supply."

"Yes, sire. It is my belief that, in order to grow, the *croach* needs to consume other forms of life—animals, insects, grass, trees, other plants, and so on. Think of them as the casing around a seed. Without that initial source of nutrients, the seed can't grow, can't extend roots, and can't begin its life."

"I follow you," Aquitaine said quietly.

"The Waste of Kalare was virtually lifeless. When the *croach* reached it, its rate of advance dropped precipitously. It did so again when it was crossing the region that had been blasted by the forces Gaius Sextus unleashed—another area that had been virtually emptied of life."

"Whereas in the Vale, the richness of the soil and land fed the *croach* very well, enabling it to spread more quickly," Aquitaine murmured. "Interesting."

"Frankly, sire," Ehren said, "the *croach* is an enemy just as dangerous as any of the creatures the vord queen creates. It chokes off life, feeds the enemy, serves as a sentinel to them—and who knows, it may do even more that we aren't yet aware of—and we know that the main body of their troops does not advance without the *croach* to supply them. The only time they've done so—"

"Was in the presence of the vord queen," Aquitaine said, his eyes glinting.

Ehren nodded and exhaled slowly. The First Lord understood.

"How much time might this give us?"

"Assuming my calculations are correct and that the rate of progress is slowed to a comparable degree, four to five weeks."

"Giving us time enough to equip at least four more Legions, and a high probability of forcing the vord Queen to appear to lead the horde over the open ground." Aquitaine nodded, his expression pleased. "Excellent."

Raucus looked between the pair of them, frowning. "So . . . if we can keep the *croach* from coming up, the vord Queen has to attend to fighting us in person?"

"Essentially, yes," Aquitaine said. "The extra time to prepare will hardly hurt, either." He glanced over at Ehren and nodded. "You have the full authority of the Crown to recruit the necessary firecrafters, evacuate anyone left in that corridor of approach, and deny its resources to the enemy. See to it."

"See to *what*?" Raucus said.

"In order to slow the *croach* and compel the Queen to reveal herself," Ehren said quietly, "we'll need to starve it. Burn out anything that grows. Salt the fields. Poison the wells. Make sure that it has nothing to help it set down roots between the current line of advance and Riva."

Raucus's eyes widened. "But that means . . . bloody crows. That's nearly three hundred *miles* of settled, arable land. Some of the *last* such in Alera that's still free. You're talking about burning down the best of the croplands we have left. Destroying thousands of our own people's steadholts, cities, homes. Creating tens of thousands of additional refugees."

"Yes," Aquitaine said simply. "And it will be a great deal of work. Best get started at once, Sir Ehren."

Ehren's stomach twisted in revulsion. After all that he had been through since the vord had come, he had seen more than enough of destruction and loss inflicted by the enemy. How much worse would it be to see more of Alera destroyed—this time at the hands of her own defenders?

Especially when, deep down in his guts, he knew that it wouldn't make any difference. Whatever they did, this war could end in only one way.

But they had to try. And it wasn't as though the vord would destroy those lands any less thoroughly, when they came.

Ehren put his fist to his heart in a salute and bowed to the First Lord. Then he turned and left the tent, to arrange the greatest act of premeditated destruction ever perpetrated by Aleran forces. He only hoped that he wasn't doing it for nothing—that in the end, the desolation he was about to create would serve some sort of purpose.

As such things went, Ehren thought, it was a rather small and anemic hope, but the slender little Cursor decided to nurture it anyway.

After all.

It was the only one he had left.

Gaius Isana, the theoretical First Lady of Alera, wrapped her thick traveling cloak about her a little more securely and stared out the window of the enclosed wind coach. They must be very close to her home now—the Calderon Valley, once considered the farthest, most primitive frontier in all of Alera. She looked down at the landscape rolling slowly by, far beneath them, and felt somewhat frustrated. She had only infrequently seen Calderon from the air, and the countryside beneath her stretched out for miles and miles and miles all around. It all looked the same—either wild forest, with rolling mountains that looked like wrinkles in a tablecloth, or settled land, marked by broad, flat swaths of winter fields being prepared for spring, its roads running like ruler lines between steadholts and towns.

For all that she knew, she could be looking at her home at that precise moment. She had no reference point with which to recognize it from this high.

". . . which has had the effect of reducing the spread of sickness through the refugee camp," said a calm young woman's voice.

Isana blinked and looked at her companion, a slender, serious-looking young woman with wispy, white-blond hair that fell in a silken sheet to her elbows. Isana could feel the girl's patience and gentle amusement, tainted with an equally gentle sadness, radiating out from her like heat from a kitchen oven. Isana knew that Veradis had doubtlessly sensed her own bemusement as Isana's thoughts wandered.

Veradis looked up from a sheaf of notes and arched a faint, pale eyebrow. The barest hint of a smile haunted her mouth, but she maintained the fiction. "My lady?"

"I'm sorry," Isana said, shaking her head. "I was thinking of home. It can be distracting."

"True enough," Veradis said, inclining her head. "Which is why I try not to think of mine."

A spear of bitter grief flashed from the young woman, its base fashioned from guilt, its tip from rage. As quickly as it appeared, the feeling vanished. Veradis applied her furycraft to conceal her emotions from Isana's acute watercrafting senses. Isana was grateful for the gesture. Without a talent for metalcrafting to balance the empathic sensitivity native to any watercrafter of Isana's skill, strong emotions could be as startling and painful as a sudden blow to the face.

Not that Isana could blame the young woman for feeling it. Veradis's father was the High Lord of Ceres. She had seen what happened to her home when the vord came for it.

Nothing human dwelt there now.

"I'm sorry," Isana said quietly. "I wasn't thinking."

"Honestly, my lady," Veradis said, her voice calm and slightly detached, a telltale sign of the use of metalcrafting to stabilize and conceal emotion. "You've got to get over that. If you try to avoid every subject that might remind me of Cer . . . of my former home, you'll never speak another word to me. It's natural for me to be feeling pain right now. You did nothing to cause it."

Isana reached out to touch Veradis's hand lightly for a moment, and nodded. "But all the same, child."

Veradis gave her another small smile. She glanced down at her papers, then back to Isana. The First Lady straightened her spine and shoulders and nodded. "Excuse me. You were saying? Something about rats?"

"We had no idea that they might be carrying the disease," the young woman said. "But once the security measures were put in place to guard three camps against the vord takers, the rat populations in them were severely reduced. A month later, those same camps had become almost completely free of the sickness."

Isana nodded. "Then we'll use the remaining security budget from the Dianic League to begin implementing the same measures in the other camps. Priority will be given to those who are hardest hit by the disease."

Veradis nodded and withdrew a second paper from her sheaf. She passed it to Isana, along with a quill.

Isana scanned the document and smiled. "If you already knew how I was going to respond in any case, why not proceed without me?"

"Because I am not the First Lady," Veradis said. "I have no authority to dispense the League's funds."

Something in the young woman's tone of voice or perhaps in her posture raised an alarm in Isana's mind. She'd felt a similar instinctive suspicion when Tavi had been withholding the truth from her, as a child. A very small child. As Tavi grew, he'd become increasingly capable of avoiding such discoveries. Veradis's skills of evasion simply did not compare.

Isana cleared her throat and gave the young woman an arch look.

Veradis's eyes sparkled, and though her cheeks didn't become pink, Isana suspected it was only because the younger woman was using her furycraft to prevent it. "Though, my lady, since lives were at stake, I *did* issue letters of credit to the appropriate contractors, so that they could go ahead and begin their work, beginning at the worst camps."

Isana signed the bottom of the document and smiled. "Isn't that the same thing as doing it without me?"

Veradis took the document back, blew gently on the ink to dry it, and said, in a satisfied tone, "Not anymore."

Isana's ears suddenly pained her, and she frowned, looking back out the window. They were descending. Within a minute, there was a polite tap at Isana's window, and a young man in gleaming, newly made steel armor waved a hand at her from outside. She rolled down the window, letting in a howl of cold air and the roar of the columns of wind that kept the coach aloft.

"Your Highness," the young officer called, touching his fist to his heart politely. "We'll be there in a moment."

"Thank you, Terius," Isana called back. "Would you see to it that a messenger is sent for my brother as soon as we land, please?"

Terius saluted again. "Of course, my lady. Be sure to fasten your safety straps."

Isana smiled at him and closed the coach's window, and the young officer banked up and away, to move back to his place at the head of the formation. The sudden lack of roaring sound made the inside of the coach seem too still.

After a silent moment spent rearranging her wind-tossed hair, Veradis said, "It is possible that he knows, you know."

Isana arched an eyebrow at her. "Hmmm?"

"Aquitaine," Veradis said. "He might know about the fortifications your brother has been building. He might know why you came here today."

"What makes you say that?"

"I saw one of Terius's men entering Senator Valerius's tent this morning."

Valerius, Isana thought. *A repulsive man. I'm really rather glad Bernard found it necessary to break his nose and two of his teeth.*

"Really?" Isana asked aloud. She mused for a moment, then shrugged. "It doesn't matter if he knows, really. He can say what he wishes and wear anything on his head that he likes—but he isn't the First Lord, and he never will be."

Veradis shook her head. "I . . . my lady . . ." She spread her hands. "Someone must lead."

"And someone will," Isana said. "The rightful First Lord, Gaius Octavian."

Veradis looked down. "If," she said, very quietly, "he is alive."

Isana folded her hands in her lap and looked out the window as the valley below began to grow larger, the colors brighter. "He is alive, Veradis."

"How can you know that?"

Isana stared out the window and frowned, faintly. "I . . . I'm not sure," she said, finally. "But I feel certain of it. It *feels* to me as if . . . as if it is nearly suppertime, and he is about to come in from tending the flock." She shook her head. "Not literally, of course, but the *sense* of it, the emotion, is the same."

Veradis watched Isana with calm, serious eyes, and said nothing.

"He's coming home," she said quietly. "Octavian is coming home."

There was silence. Isana watched the walls of Garrison, the fortress-town her brother commanded, grow larger and more distinct. They changed from lines to sharp-edged ridges to constructions of seamless, furycrafted stone. The flag of the First Lord, a scarlet eagle on a blue field, fluttered in the breeze, and beside it flew her brother's banner—a brown bear on a field of green.

The town had grown *again*, even though Isana had been there only two weeks before. The shantytown originally erected just outside of Garrison's walls had been replaced with solid buildings of furycrafted stone, and a new wall had been raised to protect them. Then a second shantytown had gone up at the base of *that* wall, and Isana had been there the day Bernard's engineers had brought up the third one, another layer of concentric half circles that enfolded the growing town.

The shanties were gone, replaced by more buildings of stone—rather square, blocky buildings with very little to distinguish one from the next, but Isana was sure that they were perfectly functional and practical.

And outside the *third* wall, still another shantytown was growing, like moss on the northern side of a stone.

Veradis's eyes widened as she saw the place. "My. This is rather a large town for a Count to have in his keeping."

"There are many people without homes these days," Isana said. "My brother will probably give you some perfectly logical explanation as to why they are here, if you should ask. But the truth is that he's never turned anyone away from his door. Anyone who made it this far . . ." She shook her head. "He'd do whatever he could for them. And he would make sure they were taken care of. Even if all he could do was give them the cloak off his own back. My brother finishes what he begins."

Veradis nodded thoughtfully. "He raised Octavian, did he not?"

Isana nodded. "Especially the last several years. They were close."

"And that is why you feel that Octavian will return. Because he finishes what he begins."

"Yes," Isana said. "He's coming home."

Veradis was quiet for a moment more as the coach soared over the outer walls of Garrison. Then she bowed her head, and said, "As you say, my lady."

Isana pushed away the ugly worry that had been ripping its way into her thoughts since her son had left with the Canim armada.

Tavi was coming home.

Her son *was* coming home.

Gaius Octavian, son of Gaius Septimus, son of Gaius Sextus, and the uncrowned First Lord of Alera, lay quietly on his back, staring up at the stars.

Given that he was lying on the floor of a cavern, it probably wasn't a good sign.

He searched his alleged memory for an explanation as to why he might be doing such a thing, and why the stars were so brilliant and swirling around so quickly, but he seemed to have misplaced that fact. Perhaps the bump he felt swelling on his skull had dislodged his memory. He made a mental note to ask Kitai if she'd seen it lying around on the floor somewhere.

"A reasonably educational attempt, child," murmured a woman's voice. "Do you see now why it is important not only to maintain a windstream beneath you but a windshield in *front* of you?"

Ah, that was right. Lessons. He was taking lessons. Cramming for an examination, really, with a particularly astute tutor. He struggled to remember which subject they'd been working on. If he was pushing things this hard, final examinations must be soon, and the Academy had very little sympathy for its students during the grueling chaos of final exams.

"We're doing history?" he mumbled. "Or mathematics?"

"I know that you find it counterintuitive to project wind both ahead of you and behind," his tutor continued in a calm tone. "But your body was not designed for high-speed flight. If you do not take measures to protect yourself, especially your eyes, even relatively minor amounts of particulate matter in the air could blind you or otherwise bring your flight to a . . . terminally instructive conclusion. Adept fliers accomplish it so naturally that they have no need to consciously think about creating the shield."

The stars had begun to wink out. Perhaps there was weather moving in. He'd have been concerned about rain if he wasn't already in a cave—which again brought up the question about where the bloody stars had *come* from.

"Ow," Tavi said. His head throbbed as the stars faded, and he suddenly remembered where he was and what he was doing. "Ow."

"I doubt that you will die, child," Alera said calmly. "Let us repeat the exercise."

Tavi's head pounded. He sat up, and the throbbing pressure eased somewhat. He'd clipped his head on a hanging icicle nearly three feet around at its base, and the thing had been harder than stone. He looked blearily around the cavern, which was lit by a dim glow emanating from the thirty-foot circular pool in its center, the water coming up to just below the level of the floor. Light and shadow danced and rippled around the ice cave, separated into bands of various colors by the water.

Ice groaned and crackled all around them. The floor of the cave swayed and rolled in a steady motion, though the size of the ice ship above and around them meant that it moved far more gently than the deck of any vessel.

"Maybe we shouldn't call it a cave," he said thoughtfully. "It's really more of a cargo hold."

"It is my understanding," Alera said, "that the occupants of a vessel are generally aware of the presence of a cargo hold. This space is secret to everyone but me, you, and Kitai."

Tavi tried to shake some of the ringing out of his ears and looked up at his tutor. Alera appeared to be a tall young woman. Despite the cold of the cavern, she wore only a light dress of what at first seemed to be gray silk. A closer look would show that the dress was made from cloudy mist as dark as a thunderhead. Her eyes constantly swirled with bands of color, endlessly cycling through every imaginable hue. Her hair was the color of ripe wheat and long, her feet were bare, and she was inhumanly beautiful.

Which was appropriate, Tavi supposed, since Alera wasn't human at all. She was the embodiment of a fury, perhaps the greatest fury upon the face of Carna. Tavi didn't know how old she was, but she spoke of the original Gaius Primus, the half-legendary founder of the Realm, as though she had been having a conversation with him just the other day. She had never displayed what sort of power she might have—but under the circumstances, Tavi had decided that treating her with courtesy and polite respect was probably a wiser action than trying to elicit some sort of display from her.

Alera arched an eyebrow at him. "Shall we repeat the exercise?"

Tavi stood up with a groan and brushed fine, soft snow from his clothing. There was better than a foot of powder on the ground. Alera said she had put it there in order to increase his chances of surviving his training.

"Give me a second," Tavi said. "Flying is hard."

"On the contrary, flight is quite simple," Alera said. Her mouth had curved into an amused smile. "Surviving the landing is less so."

Tavi stopped himself from glaring at her after a second or so. Then he sighed, closed his eyes, and focused on his windcrafting.

Though the air of the cavern did not contain any discrete, manifest furies, such as windmanes or Countess Calderon's fury, Cirrus, it was full to bursting with furies nonetheless. Each individual was a tiny thing, a mite, with scarcely any power whatsoever; but when gathered together by the will and power of a windcrafter, their combined strength was enormous—a mountain made from grains of sand.

Gathering the numbers of ambient furies necessary for flight was a tedious process. Tavi began to picture the furies in his mind, visualizing them as motes of light that swirled through the air like a cloud of fireflies. Then he began to picture each individual mote being guided toward him by a featherlight breath of wind, one by one at first, then two at a time, then three, and so on, until every single one of them had gathered in the air around him. The first time he had successfully called the wind furies to him, it had taken him half an hour to accomplish the feat. Since then, he'd cut that time down to about three minutes, and was getting faster, but he still had a considerable way to go.

He knew when he was ready. The very air around him crawled eerily against his skin, pressing and caressing. Then he opened his eyes, called to the furies in his thoughts, and gathered them into a windstream that swirled and spun, then lifted him gently from the cavern's snowy floor. He guided the furies into lifting him until the soles of his boots were about three feet from the floor, and hovered there, frowning in concentration.

"Good," Alera said calmly. "Now redirect—and do not forget the windshield this time."

Tavi nodded and twisted the angle of the windstream, so that it pressed against him from behind and below, and he began to move slowly across the cavern. The required concentration was enormous, but he made the attempt to split that focus into a separate partition in his thoughts, maintaining the wind-stream while he focused on forming a shield of solidified air in front of him.

For a second, he thought it was going to work, and he began to press ahead with more force, to move into speedier flight. But seconds later, his concentration faltered, the wind furies flew apart like so much dandelion fluff, and he plunged down—directly into the center of the thirty-foot pool.

The shock of the cold of near-freezing water sucked the breath out of his lungs, and he flailed wildly for a second, until he forced himself to use his mind rather than his limbs. He reached out to the furies in the water, gathering them to him in less than a quarter of a minute—he was more adept with watercrafting—and willed them into lifting him from the water and depositing him on the snowy floor of the ice cavern. It did not particularly lessen the bitter, biting pain of the cold, and he lay there shuddering.

"You continue to improve," Alera said, looking down at him. She considered his half-frozen state calmly. "Technically."

"Y-y-you are n-n-not b-b-being h-h-helpful," Tavi stammered through his wracking shivers.

"Indeed not," Alera said. She adjusted her dress as if it were any other cloth and knelt beside him. "That is something you must understand about me, young Gaius. I may appear in a form similar to yours, but I am not a being of flesh and blood. I do not *feel* as you do, about any number of things."

Tavi tried to focus on a firecrafting that would begin to build up the heat in his body, but there was so little left that it would be a lengthy process, assuming he could manage it at all. He needed an open source of flame to make it simple, but there wasn't one. "W-what d-do y-you m-mean?"

"Your potential death, for example," she said. "You could freeze to death on this floor, right now. It wouldn't particularly upset me."

Tavi thought it a fine thing to keep focusing on his firecrafting. "Wh-why not?"

She smiled at him and brushed a strand of hair back from his forehead. It crackled, and a few bits of ice fell down over his eyelashes. "All things die, young Gaius," she said. Her eyes went distant for a moment, and she sighed. "All things. And I am old—far, far older than you could comprehend."

"H-how o-old?"

"You have no frame of reference that is useful," she said. "Your mind is exceptionally capable, but even you could scarcely imagine a quantity of one million objects, much less the activity of a million years. I have seen thousands of millions of years, Octavian. In a time such as that, oceans swell and die away.

Deserts become green farmlands. Mountains are ground to dust and valleys, and new mountains are born in fire. The earth itself flows like water, great ranges of land spinning and colliding, and the stars themselves spin and reel into new shapes." She smiled. "It is the great dance, Aleran, and the lifetime of your race is but a beat within a measure."

Tavi shivered even harder. That was a good sign, he knew. It meant that more blood was getting to his muscles. They were slowly getting warmer. He kept up the firecrafting.

"In that time," she said, "I have seen the deaths of many things. Entire species come and go, like the sparks rising from a campfire. Understand, young Gaius. I bear you no ill will. But any given single life is a matter of such insignificance that, honestly, I have trouble telling one of you from the next."

"I-if that's true," Tavi said, "th-then wh-why a-are you h-here with me?"

She gave him a rueful smile. "Perhaps I am indulging a whim."

"P-perhaps you aren't t-telling the whole tr-truth."

She laughed, a warm sound, and Tavi abruptly felt his heartbeat surge, and his muscles slowly began to unlock. "Clever. It is one of the things that make your kind appealing." She paused, frowning thoughtfully. "In all my time," she said at last, "no one had ever spoken to me. Until your kind came." She smiled. "I suppose I enjoy the company."

Tavi felt the warmth beginning to gather in his belly as the firecrafting finally gained momentum. Now he'd just have to be careful not to let it build too much. He might be tired of the cold, but he didn't think that setting his intestines on fire would be any more pleasant in the long term. "But i-if I died, would you have anyone to talk to?"

"It would be bothersome, but I suppose I could find and keep track of some other bloodline."

The shuddering finally—finally!—abated. Tavi sat up slowly, and reached up to rake his wet hair back. His fingers felt stiff and partially numb. Bits of ice fell from his hair. He kept the firecrafting going. "Like Aquitainus Attis?" Tavi suggested.

"Likely," she said, nodding. "He's a great deal more like your predecessor than you are, after all. Though I understand his name is Gaius Aquitainus Attis now. I'm not sure I understand why a legal process would alter his self-identity."

Tavi grimaced. "It doesn't. It's meant to alter how everyone else thinks of him."

Alera shook her head. "Baffling creatures. It is difficult enough for you to control your own thoughts, much less one another's."

Tavi smiled, his lips pressed tightly over his teeth. "How much longer before we'll be able to send them a message and let them know that we're coming?"

Alera's eyes went distant for a moment before she spoke. "The vord seem to have realized how waterways are used for communications. They are damming many streams and have placed sentry furies to intercept messenger furies within all the major rivers and tributaries. They have almost entirely enveloped the coastlines of the western and southern shores of the continent. As a result, it seems unlikely that it will be possible to form a connection via the waterways until you have advanced several dozen miles inland from the coast, at the very least."

Tavi grimaced. "We'll have to send aerial messengers as soon as we're close enough. I assume that the vord know we are coming."

"That remains unclear," Alera said. "But it seems a wise assumption to make. Where will you make landfall?"

"On the northwest coast, near Antillus," Tavi replied. "If the vord are there, we will assist the city's defenders and leave our civilians there before we march inland."

"I am sure High Lord Antillus will be filled with pleasure at the notion of tens of thousands of Canim camping on his doorstep," Alera murmured.

"I'm the First Lord," Tavi said. "Or will be. He'll get over it."

"Not if the Canim devour his resources—his food stores, his livestock, his holders . . ."

Tavi grunted. "We'll leave several crews of leviathan hunters behind us. I'm sure he won't mind if a few dozen miles of his coastline are cleared of the beasts."

"And how will you feed your army on the march inland?" Alera asked.

"I'm working on it," Tavi said. He frowned. "If the vord aren't stopped, all of my species is likely to be destroyed."

Alera turned her glittering, shifting gemstone eyes to him. "Yes."

"If that happens, who would you talk to?" Tavi asked.

The expression on her beautiful face was unreadable. "It isn't an eventuality that concerns me." She shook her head. "The vord are, in their way, almost as interesting as your own kind—if far more limited in flexibility of thought. And variety is nonexistent among them, in most senses of the word. They would likely grow quickly tiresome. But . . ." She shrugged. "What will be, will be."

"And yet you're helping us," Tavi said. "The training. The information you can provide us. They are invaluable."

She bowed her head to him. "It is a far cry from taking action against them. I am helping you, young Gaius. I am not harming them."

"A very fine distinction."

She shrugged. "It is what it is."

"You tell me that you acted directly at the battle of Ceres."

"When Gaius Sextus invoked my aid, he asked for prevailing conditions that would affect everything present with equal intensity."

"But those conditions were more beneficial to the Alerans than the vord," Tavi said.

"Yes. And they were within the limits I set forth to the House of Gaius a thousand years ago." She shrugged. "So I did as he requested—just as I have moderated the weather for the fleet for the duration of this voyage, as you requested." She tilted her head slightly. "It appears that you have survived your previous lesson. Shall we try again?"

Tavi pushed himself wearily to his feet.

The next attempt at flight lasted all of half a minute longer than the first, and he managed to come down in nice, soft snow instead of the icy water.

"Broken bones," Alera said. "Excellent. An opportunity to practice watercrafting."

Tavi looked up from his grotesquely twisted left leg. He ground his teeth and tried to push himself up, but his left arm gave out on him. The pain was unbelievable. He sank back into the snow and fumbled at his belt until his hand found the hilt of his dagger. A moment's concentration, transferring his focus and his thought into the orderly crystalline matrix of high-grade steel, and the pain receded into the calm, detached lack of feeling that came with metalcrafting.

"I'm tired," he said. His own voice felt unfastened, somehow, separate from the rest of him. "Bonesetting is taxing work."

Alera smiled and began to answer when the pool of water exploded into a cloud of flying droplets and angry spray.

Tavi shielded his face against the sudden, icy deluge, and blinked at the pool as Kitai rose out of the water on a furycrafted column of liquid and dropped neatly to the cavern's floor. She was a tall young woman of exotic beauty and extraordinary grace. Like that of most of the Marat, her hair was a soft, pure white. She had shaved it close to her skull on the sides while leaving a long, single mane running down the center of her head, after the fashion of the Horse tribe of the Marat. She was dressed in close-fitting blue and grey flying leathers. The clothes quite admirably displayed a slim physique, significantly more well muscled than an average Aleran girl's. Her canted eyes were a brilliant green identical to Tavi's own, and they were bright and hard.

"Aleran!" she snapped, her voice ringing back from the frozen walls. Her anger was a palpable thing, a fire that Tavi could feel inside his own belly.

He winced.

Kitai stalked over to him and placed her fists upon her hips. "I have been speaking to Tribune Cymnea. She informs me that you have been treating me like a whore."

Tavi blinked. Several times. "Um. What?"

"Don't you *dare* play innocent with me, Aleran," she spat. "If anyone is in a position to know, it is Cymnea."

Tavi struggled to make sense of Kitai's statements. Cymnea was the Tribune Logistica of the First Aleran Legion—but before circumstance and emergency had forced her into becoming Tribune Cymnea, she had been Mistress Cymnea, proprietor of the Pavilion, the finest house of ill repute in the camp following the Legion.

"Kitai," Tavi said, "I don't understand."

"Augh!" she said, and flung her hands in the air. "How can such a brilliant commander be such an idiot?" She turned to Alera, pointed an accusing finger at Tavi, and said, "Explain it to him."

"I feel I am hardly qualified," Alera replied calmly.

Kitai turned back to Tavi. "Cymnea tells me that it is custom, among your people, that those who wish to be wed to one another do *not* lie together before they make their vows. This is a ridiculous custom—but it *is* the way of the Citizenry."

Tavi glanced at Alera and felt his cheeks warm a little. "Um. Yes, well, that's the *proper* way to go about it, but it isn't what everyone always *does* . . ."

"She informs me," Kitai continued, "that those of your rank commonly take courtesans to your bed for simple pleasure—and set such baubles aside once you have found a proper wife."

"I . . . some young Citizens do that, yes, but—"

"We have been together for *years*," Kitai said. "We have shared a bed and pleasured one another on a daily basis. For *years*. And you are finally becoming competent."

Tavi thought his cheeks might actually burst into flame. "*Kitai!*"

"I am informed that the fact that we have been together for so long will be the source of much mockery and outrage among the Citizens of Alera. That they universally regard me as the Princeps' *whore*." She scowled. "And for some baffling reason, that is considered to be a very bad thing."

"Kitai, you aren't—"

"I will *not* be treated that way," she snarled. "You idiot. You face problems enough in assuming the Crown without giving your enemies in the Citizenry such an obvious weakness to exploit. How *dare* you allow me to be a means by which you are brought to harm?"

Tavi just stared at her helplessly.

The anger faded from her expression. "Of course," she said, her voice very quiet, "this all assumes that you intend me to be your wife."

"Honestly, Kitai, I hadn't . . . I hadn't even thought about it."

Her eyes widened. Her mouth dropped open in an expression of something almost like horror. "You . . . you hadn't?" She swallowed. "You plan to take another?"

Tavi felt his own eyes widen. "No. No, crows, no, Kitai. I hadn't considered it because I never thought it would end any other way. I mean, it wasn't even a *question* to me, *chala*."

For an instant, her uncertainty was replaced with relief. And then that expression gave way to another in turn: Kitai narrowed her eyes dangerously. "You just assumed I would do it."

Tavi winced. Again.

"You assumed I would have no other option. That I would be so desperate that I would be *forced* to become your wife."

Clearly, anything he said would only make things worse. He kept his mouth shut.

Kitai stalked over to him and seized him by the front of his tunic, lifting him several inches, despite the difference in their sizes. The young Marat woman was far stronger than an Aleran her size, even without employing furycraft. "This is what is going to happen, Aleran. You will no longer lie with me. You will treat me in exactly the fashion that you would any proper young lady of the Citizenry. You will court me, and do it *well*, or so help me I will strangle the *life* from you."

"Um," Tavi said.

"And," she said, a massively threatening quality in her tone, "you will court me properly after the ways of *my* people. You will do so with legendary skill and taste. And only when *that* is done will we share a bed once more."

She spun on a heel and stalked back toward the pool.

Tavi stammered for a second, then blurted, "Kitai. It might help if you *told* me what the customs of your people involved."

"It might have helped had you done me the same courtesy," she replied tartly, without turning around. "Find out for yourself, as I did!" She stalked out onto the surface of the pool as if it had been solid ground, spun, and gave him one last indignant look, her green eyes flashing, and vanished into the water.

Tavi stared after her numbly for a few seconds.

"Well," Alera said. "I'm hardly a good judge of the intricacies of love. But it seems to me that you have done the young woman a grave disservice."

"I didn't *mean* to!" Tavi protested. "When we got involved with one another, I had no idea who my father was. I was a *nobody*. I mean, I never even considered that a proper courtship might be necessary." He waved a hand at the water. "And it wasn't as if she wasn't willing, bloody crows! She was more eager than I was! She barely gave me a choice in the matter!"

Alera frowned thoughtfully. "In what way is that relevant?"

Tavi scowled. "You're taking her side because she's a girl."

"Yes," Alera said, smiling. "I may be no expert, but I have learned enough of your ways to know which side of this debate I am obliged to support."

Tavi sighed. "The vord are on the verge of destroying the Realm and the world. She could have picked a better time for it."

"It is entirely possible that there might not *be* another time," Alera said.

Tavi fell quiet at that, staring at the rippling waters of the pool. "I'd better figure something out soon, then," he said, finally. "I'm fairly sure she won't accept the end of the world as a valid excuse."

Alera let out another laugh. "Let us continue," she said, mirth coloring her tone. "We will begin with proper bonesetting, after which we will resume flying lessons."

Tavi groaned. "How much longer do we keep at this?"

"Another half dozen flights or so," Alera said calmly. "For tonight, at any rate."

Half a dozen?

Tavi suddenly felt very tired. His imagination provided him with a sudden image—himself, lying in the snow like a sea jelly, every bone in his body smashed to powder, while a furious Kitai squishily strangled him.

Alera looked at him with a serene smile. "Shall we continue?"

⊡⊡⊡⊡ CHAPTER 1

There was a quick rap on the cabin door, and Antillar Maximus entered the cabin. One of Tavi's oldest friends, Maximus had shared a room with Tavi for the better part of three years at the Academy and was one of the few people in the fleet who would have opened the door without being bidden to.

"Thought you should know," Max began, but then he stopped and blinked at Tavi. He shut the door behind him before blurting out, "Bloody crows, Calderon. Are you sick or something?"

Tavi looked blearily at Max from where he sat at the cabin's small writing desk, poring over maps. "Didn't sleep well last night."

Max's rough, handsome face flashed into a quick, boyish grin. "Aye. Tough to go back to a cold bunk once you get used to a warm one."

Tavi gave him a steady look.

Max's smile widened. "Don't get me wrong. I think it's always a good thing when your Legion's captain is more relaxed and calm than he might be otherwise. I'm all in favor of the captain having a woman. I could see about maybe finding some kind of replacement if you aren't too terribly particular, Captain."

Tavi picked up his cup of tea. "If you don't finish before I've drunk this, I'm throwing this mug at your fat head."

Max folded his arms and leaned back against the door with a serene smile. "Of course, Your Highness."

The honorific stole whatever faint amusement Max had brought with him. Tavi knew that his grandfather was dead, but he had not spoken to the others about it. He had no way to prove it, after all—and Alera had made clear that she had no intention of displaying herself to others in the fleet.

Besides, there was a considerable difference between being the rightful heir and actually assuming the office of the First Lord.

Tavi pushed the thoughts from his mind. Those problems would attend to themselves in time. First, survive today.

"You came in here for a reason, Max?"

Max's smile faded as well. He nodded, his neck slightly stiff. "Crassus is on the way back in. He should be on deck in the next few moments."

Tavi rose and gulped down the rest of the strong tea. He doubted the mild stimulants in it would help him much after yet another grueling night of lessons with Alera, but he was willing to try. "Get me Magnus and the First Spear. Signal the *Trueblood* and invite Varg to come to the *Slive* at his earliest convenience."

"Already done," Max said. "Finish your biscuit, at least."

Tavi frowned at him but turned to pick up his breakfast, a plain square of ship's biscuit, a stiff and greyish bread made with some of the last of their flour and some of the less noxious portions of a taken leviathan. "I am not going to miss these," he said, but he tore into it with a will. If things went badly that day, he might not get a chance to eat later on.

"I've been thinking," Max said. "Kitai might have a point."

Tavi shook his head. "If so, I don't see it."

Max grunted. "Look, Tavi. You're my friend. But you've got some of the most crowbegotten blind spots."

"What do you mean?"

"You're the bloody Princeps of *Alera*, man," Max replied. "You're the bloody role model—or at least, you're supposed to be."

"It's ridiculous," Tavi said.

"Of course it is," Max returned. "But like it or not, that's what the office demands. That you comport yourself in all ways and at all times as the most honorable and dignified young Citizen of the Realm."

Tavi sighed. "And, so?"

"And so the Princeps of the Realm can't afford things running around to embarrass him," Max said. "Mistresses are one thing. Bastards are another."

Max's mouth twisted up at the word. His own father, High Lord Antillus, had conceived Max with a dancing girl he had favored. His second son, Crassus, had been born legitimately, leaving Max bereft of any sort of title or claim. Tavi knew that Max's entire life, including his very limited acceptance from the Citizenry of the Realm, had been powerfully shaped by his lack of legitimacy.

"That really isn't an issue, Max," Tavi said. "There's never been anyone but Kitai."

The big Antillan exhaled heavily. "You're missing the point."

"Then maybe you should explain it to me."

"The point is that things like who the Princeps is sleeping with *matter*," Tavi's friend replied. "Rival claims to the Crown have caused wars before, Tavi. And worse. Crows, if old Sextus had left a bastard child or two running around Alera, great furies know what might have happened after they killed your father."

"I'll give you that," Tavi said. "It matters. But I'm still waiting for the point."

"The point is that the Realm didn't know you were Septimus's son until last year—and even then, you were way out in the hinterlands, fighting a campaign. You didn't exactly attract a lot of visitors."

"No, I didn't."

"When we get back home, that's going to change," Max said. "Everyone's going to be watching you like hawks. They're going to pry into your life in every way you could possibly imagine, and probably in some that you can't—and every Citizen with a daughter even vaguely close to the right age is going to be hoping to turn her into the next First Lady."

Tavi frowned.

"You want to marry Kitai," Max said. It wasn't a question.

Tavi nodded.

"Then you're going to make a lot of people upset. And they're going to pry up every little piece of information they can get against her. They're going to try to bring pressure to bear against her, any way that they can—and if you just carried on with her the way you have been, you'd make it *easy* for them to begin rallying support against you."

"I really don't care what they think, Max," Tavi said.

"Don't be an idiot," his friend replied, his voice tired. "You're to be the First Lord of Alera. You've got to lead a nation filled with powerful Citizens with mutually conflicting interests. If you can't build up enough support to accomplish that leadership, a lot of people are going to suffer because of it. You'll try to send relief to a Count's holding that's been devastated by a flood but find that it's been blocked by the Senate, or maybe choked off somewhere in the communications or financial chain. You'll issue rulings in disputes between Lords and High Lords which they bring to you and find out that both sides were setting you up to look bad, regardless of what you did—and eventually, because that would be the *point* of the whole thing, someone will try to take the crown away from you."

Tavi rubbed at his chin, studying Max. His friend's words were . . . not what he'd really expected of him. Max had a fantastic instinct for analyzing tactical and strategic situations, a gift that his training at the Academy had sharpened and honed—but this kind of thinking was out of character for his old friend.

Tavi inhaled deeply, understanding. "Kitai came to you to talk about it."

"Couple of weeks ago," Max said.

Tavi shook his head. "Bloody crows."

"I don't know if it will work," Max said. "Making your courtship a semi-public event, I mean."

"Do you think it might?"

Max shrugged. "I think it will give the people who *do* support you a way to counter anyone who tries to start using Kitai to drum up some opposition. If you've courted her with the same consideration that would be expected of a young Aleran lady highly placed in the Citizenry, it lends her a certain amount of status by association." He frowned. "And besides . . ."

Tavi sensed his friend's sudden reluctance to speak. He shook his head, feeling a smile tug wearily at the corners of his mouth. "Max," he said quietly, "just say it."

"Bloody crows, Calderon." Maximus sighed. "I'm the one who treats girls like disposable pleasures. You've always been the smart one. The capable one. The one who went to every class and studied and did well. You're the one coming up with ways to use furycraft that no one's ever dreamed of before, and you can barely *use* it. You've gone up against Canim and Marat and vord queens alike, and you're still in one piece." He met Tavi's eyes, and said, "I know that you don't think of Kitai the way I thought of my lovers. She's not a playmate. You see her as your equal. Your ally."

Tavi nodded, and murmured, "Yes."

Max shrugged and dropped his eyes. "Maybe she deserves some romance, too, Calderon. Maybe it wouldn't hurt you to go out of your way to make her feel special. Not because she can fight, or because she's practically a princepsa of her own people. But just because you want to *show* her. You want her to *know* how much you care."

Tavi stared at Max for a moment and felt somewhat thunderstruck.

Max was right.

He and Kitai had been together for a very long time. They had shared everything with one another. Whenever she had been gone, it had left an enormous, restless hole somewhere inside him that adamantly refused to be filled. So many things had happened to them together—but he hadn't ever really spoken to her about the depth of his feelings. She'd known, of course, just as he had been able to sense her devotion to him through the odd link the two of them shared.

But some things needed to be said before they could be truly real.

And some things couldn't be said. They had to be done.

Bloody crows. He'd never asked her what the marriage customs of her people were. He'd never even *thought* to ask.

"Crows," Tavi said, calmly. "I . . . Max, I think you have a point."

Max spread his hands. "Yeah. Sorry."

"All right," Tavi said. "Then . . . I suppose that while I'm finding a way to get the rest of Alera to accept the Canim's help, and figuring out how to defeat the vord, and coming up with enough support to actually *be* the First Lord, I'll have to work an epic romance into the schedule."

"That's why you're the Princeps, and I'm just a humble Tribune," Max said.

"I . . . I don't really know much about being romantic," Tavi said.

"Neither do I," Max said cheerfully. "But look at it this way. It won't need to be much to improve on what's gone before."

Tavi made a growling sound and reached for his empty mug.

Max opened the door and saluted, banging his right fist against his armored chest, grinning openly at Tavi. "I'll see to the incoming boats, Your Highness, and make sure everyone finds his way to your cabin."

Tavi held on to the mug. It wouldn't do to throw it at Max in plain view of everyone on deck. He put the mug down, gave Max a look that promised eventual repayment, and said, "Thank you, Tribune. Shut the door on your way out, please."

Max departed and shut the door, and Tavi sank tiredly back onto his chair. He looked at the maps spread out on his desk—and drew out the one he hadn't shown the others. Alera had helped him with it. It showed the spread of the vord *croach* over the face of Alera, like gangrene oozing into the body from an infected wound.

The vord had to number in the hundreds of thousands by now, perhaps even in the millions.

Tavi shook his head ruefully. It said something about the world, he thought, that the vord threat was arguably the *second* most perplexing problem he had. He wasn't sure *what*, but it definitely said something.

CHAPTER 2

"Gentlemen, Warmaster," Tavi said. "Thank you for coming." He looked around his cabin at the gathering of what he'd come to think of as his campaign council. "In the next few hours, your troops will be learning what I'm about to tell you. You'll need to know it first."

He paused to take a steadying breath and to make sure that his expression and body language were calm. It wouldn't do to let them see him nervous, given the gravity of what he was about to explain. And it wouldn't do to let the Canim see him nervous under any circumstances.

"The vord have already attacked Alera," Tavi said. "The first assault was beaten back, but not broken. Ceres has fallen. As has Alera Imperia. In the time we've been sailing home, other cities may have fallen as well."

Dead silence settled on the ship's cabin.

Nasaug turned his dark-furred head to Varg. The Canim Warmaster twitched an ear and kept his blood-colored eyes on Tavi.

"What's more," Tavi continued, "the First Lord, my grandfather, Gaius Sextus, was slain while fighting a holding action to give the folk of the capital a chance to escape."

No one spoke, but an almost-silent chorus of moans of shocked disbelief went up from the Alerans present. Tavi didn't want to keep his tone brisk and businesslike. He wanted to scream his outrage and grief that the vord had taken his grandfather from him before he'd had a chance to get to know Sextus better. But his anger, no matter how hot it burned, wouldn't change anything.

Tavi forged ahead into the silence. "The Amaranth Vale is completely lost. The vord have somehow suborned Alerans into their service, and now furycraft meets furycraft in battle. In addition, most of the causeways have been cut, to prevent the vord from making use of them, so they cannot be factored into our planning." He turned to a map of Alera that was tacked up on the back of the cabin door. The spread of the *croach* was marked in pips of green ink. "As you can see, the vord have filled the valley and stretched out their *croach* along the causeways—even if rendered inert of furycraft, they still are, after all, passable roads. They hold most of the coastline of the continent, and they have laid siege to most of the cities of the Realm.

"But their hold is far from complete. These stretches of countryside between the lines of the causeways and the cities are as yet unoccupied, probably because the vord deem them lower-priority areas. Our people, though, are cut off. Anyone isolated behind the lines of the *croach* is trapped. Our best estimates say that they have, at the most, another eight or ten months before the *croach* fills in the empty areas."

He turned to them with a cold little smile. "So. We have that long to destroy the vord threat."

"Bloody crows," Max breathed. "As long as it isn't too difficult a chore or anything."

"Our work is cut out for us," Tavi acknowledged.

Crassus raised a hand. Max's younger half brother bore a resemblance to Max, but everywhere Max was rough, the more slender young man was refined. Crassus was an inch shorter and thirty pounds of muscle lighter than his brother, and he had the noble profile of a Citizen of the blood that could have leapt straight from any number of old statues, paintings, or coins. "If the First Lo— If Sextus perished during a holding action, that implies that there was still organized resistance, and that it might still be there. What do we know of the Legions and their strength?"

"That Aquitainus Attis, who had been serving as Gaius's battle captain, at the First Lord's request, has been legally adopted into the House of Gaius—as my younger brother."

Max let out a snort. "He's thirty years older than you."

Tavi smiled slightly. "Not according to Gaius Sextus. It seems that he knew that his death was coming for him. He didn't know if I would be returning, and someone had to lead the Realm in my absence. He selected the man most fit for the duty." Tavi put the tips of his first and second fingers on Riva and Aquitaine, separately. "Depending on the state of our troops during his withdrawal, he will have retreated either to Aquitaine or Riva with the Legions, and will presumably be gathering more to him." He moved his finger two thousand miles to the west and rested it on Antillus. "As you can see, Antillus is free of the *croach* for now. Our mission will be to land here, make contact with Aquitaine, if possible, then join him."

Valiar Marcus, the grizzled First Spear of the First Aleran Legion, rubbed at his jaw with one hand. The blocky old centurion squinted at the map. "Two thousand miles. On no supplies but some dried leviathan meat. And no cause-ways to use. That could take us all spring and half the summer."

"I think we can arrange something somewhat more timely than that," Tavi said. "In fact, unless I miss my guess, we'll need to."

Varg growled. "The vord Queen."

Tavi nodded. "Exactly. She'll almost certainly be overseeing the next conflict between the vord and the Aleran main body. She is our primary target, gentlemen."

Valiar Marcus shook his head. "One bug. In all that."

Tavi showed his teeth. "If it were easy, we wouldn't need Legions to get things done. If possible, we're going to slide in behind the vord and catch them between our forces and Aquitaine's. We'll make sure that the Queen doesn't go scampering out the back door."

"Bold and stupid aren't the same thing," Marcus said. "But sometimes they're pretty close, sir." Marcus frowned. "Sorry. Sire."

Tavi waved his hand. "I haven't been recognized by the Senate and the Citizenry yet. Until we've solved our problems, let's just keep on the way we have been."

"Tavar," Varg growled, "your huntmaster makes a good point. Two thousand miles is a fair walk. If it is to be done at speed, there must be food. Armies can't move like that when they're hungry."

Durias, the First Spear of the Free Aleran Legion, lifted his head and met Tavi's eyes. The quiet young man didn't speak until Tavi acknowledged him; though the brawny former slave was as solid as stone in the face of danger, he still wasn't comfortable associating with Citizenry. "We'll need more than merely food," he said in a deep, soft voice. "We've worn through all kinds of equipment. Can Antillus supply us?"

Tavi swung his gaze to Crassus.

The young Antillan frowned before saying, cautiously, "To some degree. But if the vord are getting ready to lay siege to the place, they won't be eager to part with supplies."

Varg growled, "Take them."

Crassus turned to blink at Varg.

"We have numbers and your crafters. I could take the city with what forces I have here. So could you demons. Make sure they know we can take them. Don't dither around with Aleran customs. Make it clear that they are obligated to cooperate."

Tavi raised a hand. "We'll solve that problem when we come to it. We still don't know much about the internal situation at Antillus. Crassus?"

"My father's banner isn't flying there," Crassus replied, his expression still showing his disturbance at Varg's proposed diplomacy. "His seneschal, Lord Vanorius, is probably running the city. I think it would be wise for me to arrive ahead of the fleet, Your Highness, and let him know what's happening."

Tavi grimaced. "It's easier to ask forgiveness than permission," he said. "I'll send you up as the fleet begins to debark, but a city full of frightened people might not react reasonably. I want to be on land with the Legions and the Canim warriors in good order by the time they're able to respond."

Crassus exhaled through his nose and nodded stiffly. "As you wish."

Tavi turned back to the map. "Let's see," he said. "Vord are winning. Two-thousand-mile march. No supplies. Ten months to go before the survivors are wiped out." He turned back to them. "I think that's about it. Any questions?"

The last member of the campaign council wore the blue-and-red tunic of a Legion valet. His wispy white hair drifted around his mostly bald pate, his eyes were watery, and his hands, though covered with liver spots, were steady. "Ah. Your Highness?"

"Yes, Maestro Magnus?"

"As your de facto commander of intelligence, I . . ." He shrugged diffidently. "Believe that it's just possible that I should be aware of the source of your information."

He spoke the last several words through clenched teeth.

Tavi nodded soberly. "I can see why you'd feel that way." He looked around at the rest of them. "Crassus and his Knights Aeris have found us a decent patch of ground to land upon. We'll move in with the Legions and warriors first and debark the civilians as time allows." Tavi turned to Varg, and said, "We'll have to move quickly. I'll do everything I can to make sure that your folk have whatever shelter is available."

"So that the vord overrun them in a few days?" Nasaug asked.

Varg turned slightly toward his get with a faint, low growl of reproof. He faced Tavi without blinking. "His point is valid."

Tavi inhaled deeply and nodded. "You're right, of course. They'll need the protection of the city's walls."

Max shook his head gravely. "Old Vanorius is *not* going to like this."

"He doesn't need to like it," Tavi said bluntly. "He just needs to do it." He paused and softened his tone. "Besides, I can't imagine he'll be too upset about gaining several thousand Canim militia to help him defend the walls."

Varg let out an interrogative growl, his head tilting slightly.

Tavi regarded him steadily. "Did you think I'd expect you to leave your civilians here alone and unguarded?"

"And if you get us to do some of the fighting for you," Varg said, "so much the better for your folk."

"You aren't the vord," Tavi said, simply. "We can work out our problems later."

Varg stared at him for a moment, then tilted his head slightly to one side. "Tavar," he rumbled, rising. "I will see to the preparations as you suggest."

Tavi returned the Canim-style bow, careful to use exactly the same degree and duration as Varg. "It is appreciated, Warmaster. Good day. And to you, Nasaug."

"Tavar," the younger Cane growled. The pair of them left the cabin, almost seeming to fold in on themselves to fit through the door. The others took that as their cue to be about their own duties and also filed out.

"Magnus," Tavi said quietly. "A moment."

The old Cursor paused and looked back at Tavi.

"The door," Tavi said.

Magnus shut the door and turned to face him. "Your Highness?"

"I'm sorry I cut you off earlier. I hope I didn't entirely sever both legs."

"Your Highness." Magnus sighed. "This is no time for levity."

"I know," Tavi said quietly. "And I do need your help. My intelligence is . . . incomplete. I'll need you to speak to whoever Lord Vanorius has bringing in information and sort out exactly where Aquitaine is and how we might contact him."

"Your Highness—"

"I can't tell you, Magnus," Tavi said in a calm, quiet voice. "I'm quite certain my grandfather never revealed all of his sources to you."

Magnus regarded Tavi thoughtfully for a few moments. Then he bowed his head, and said, "Very well, Your Highness."

"Thank you," Tavi said. "Now. You've been giving Marcus odd looks for weeks. I want to know why."

Magnus shook his head. After a moment, he said, "I'm not sure I trust him."

Tavi frowned. "Crows, man. Valiar Marcus? Why not?"

"He . . ." Magnus sighed. "It's nothing I can quantify. And I've been trying for weeks. There's just . . . something off."

Tavi grunted. "Are you sure?"

"Of course not," Magnus replied, automatically. "Nothing's sure."

Tavi nodded. "But you haven't let go of it, either."

"It's my gut," Magnus said. "I know it. I just can't figure out *how* I know it." He lifted a hand and pushed white hair back from his eyes. "It's possible I'm going senile, I suppose." He peered at Tavi suddenly. "How long have you known about Sextus?"

"Since a few days after we escaped Canea," Tavi said quietly.

"And you said nothing."

Tavi shrugged. "What would it have changed except to frighten everyone and make us appear more vulnerable to the Canim?" He shook his head. "Everyone sitting on slow ships with nothing to do but chew on bad thoughts—we'd have had blood on the decks in a week. This way, by the time word gets around, we'll be in the middle of operations. Everyone will have work to turn his hand to."

Magnus sighed. "Yes. I suppose it was necessary to keep it quiet." He shook his head, his eyes gleaming faintly for a moment. "But please, Your Highness. Don't make a habit of such things. My heart can only take so much."

"I'll do what I can," Tavi said. He nodded to Magnus and turned back toward his desk. "Oh, Maestro."

"Hmm?"

Tavi looked up from a weary slump on his chair. "Valiar Marcus has saved my life. And I, his. I can't imagine that he would ever turn against the Legion. Or against me."

Magnus was silent for a moment. Then he said, quietly, "That's what everyone always thinks about traitors, lad. It's why we hate them so."

The old man left the cabin.

Aquitainus Attis, the man who had been striving to take the Crown of Alera for most of his lifetime, was now only a heartbeat away from taking it incontestably. Could there be one more knife lurking, awaiting the right moment to strike?

Tavi closed his eyes. He felt fragile. He felt frightened.

Then he rose abruptly, stalked across the room, and began donning his armor, a suit taken from a *legionare* who had perished of his wounds after the evacuation to replace the one he'd lost in the harbor city of Molvar. The familiar weight of Aleran lorica settled upon him, cold and solid. He slung his sword at his hip and felt the cold power of the steel singing quietly down the length of the blade.

There was work to be done.

Best be about it.

CHAPTER 3

"Keep your back straight," Amara called. "Turn your heels out a little more!"

"Why?" called the girl on the pony. She was riding in the practice ring the small detachment of Garrison's cavalry troopers had set up. It was, in essence, a four-foot-deep pit lined with soft earth, about two hundred yards long and half that across.

"It will help you maintain your balance," Amara called from the side of the pit.

"My balance is good already!" the girl insisted.

"It is right now," Amara said. "But when Ajax does something you weren't expecting, you might find differently."

The little girl had dark, curly hair and muddy hazel eyes, and was eight years old. She lifted her head and sniffed in a gesture that Amara found reminded her rather intensely of Kalarus Brencis Minoris. She folded her arms over her stomach and shivered a little. "Try to use your legs more, Masha," she called. "Keep your head level. Pretend you've got a cup of water balanced on it, and that you don't want to spill any."

"That's silly," Masha called back, smiling at Amara as she went past. She shouted merrily, over her shoulder, "Why would I take a cup of water on a pony ride?"

Amara found herself smiling. Smiles had been a rare enough thing over this long and quietly heartless winter. Between all the great and terrible things that had been happening to the Realm, it was all too easy to lose track of one life lost, even if it had been lost in an act of courage and dedication to the Realm. One life balanced against all those lost was not a measurable fraction.

But that detail hadn't mattered to Masha when Bernard had told the little girl that her mother wouldn't be coming back to her.

The child's wants were simple: She wanted her mother. That single lost life had turned a little girl's world into bleak desolation. Masha hadn't spoken for more than a week and was still plagued with nightmares. At first, Amara and Bernard had tried to calm her down and send Masha back to her own bed, but the trip down the hall was simply too far to walk for the fourth time in an evening when one hadn't slept properly for several days. Now, as often as not, the child simply stumbled down the hall and into their bed for the comfort and warmth offered by someone who cared, and slept snuggled up firmly between them.

Great furies knew that Masha deserved a chance to smile and to feel joy.

Even if it might not last.

The quiet morning was broken by the distant roar of windstreams being raised to carry multiple flights of either couriers or Knights Aeris into the bright spring skies. Amara frowned back at Garrison, then murmured to her wind fury, Cirrus, and held up her hands before her face. The fury bent the light passing between her hands to give Amara a better field of view, and she saw several distant, dark shapes against the blue skies, racing northwest, southwest, and east.

She frowned. Anyone flying east from Garrison passed out of the lands of Alera altogether and into the wild country where the barbaric Marat held dominion. In the general direction of the southwest lay the vast encampment at Riva. To the northwest lay the Shield city of Phrygia, now all but empty of her native defenders and groaning under the weight of the refugees from the vord-taken portions of the Realm—which made it little different than Calderon.

Amara took a moment to sweep her gaze down the valley, once more surveying the acres and acres and acres and acres of tents, lean-tos, converted carts and wagons, stone domes crafted directly up from the earth, and other makeshift shelters. There had not been room at Riva for more than a tithe of the folk displaced by the invasion. They had been shuffled out to cities lying between Riva and Phrygia, including up to the Shield city herself, and the Calderon Valley had willingly taken up its fair share of the burden. And then the acting First Lord had promptly tripled that burden.

It had been mildly nightmarish to come to terms with what the invasion meant. With the ground frozen by winter, scanty supplies, and practically nonexistent medical care, the very old and the very young had suffered terribly. Pyres for the dead had burned every single night. With the advent of the spring thaw, fury-accelerated crops had begun to alleviate the food shortage—but for many Alerans, the food had come weeks, or only *days*, too late.

Masha's original pony had been left behind when she had been evacuated from the leading edge of the vord invasion, as a means to convince the child's mother, Rook, to undertake a mission for the Crown. Ajax had arrived only days before, a gift for the child from Hashat, the leader of the Horse Clan of the Marat. Had the horse come but a fortnight sooner, it would almost certainly have been stolen, slaughtered, and eaten by starving refugees.

Bernard had undertaken the refugee problem with the practical energy typical, as far as Amara could tell, among the longtime residents of the Calderon

Valley. A lifetime spent fending for themselves on a savage frontier had given them a sense of self-sufficiency, confidence, and independence that was unusual among freemen. To her husband, the sudden influx of Alerans had not merely been a problem: It was also an opportunity.

Within weeks, the effort to provide shelter for every soul in the valley had become an organized drive, assisted by Bernard's squad of Legion engineers and the holders of the valley, who seemed to regard the incoming tide of strangers as a challenge to their sense of hospitality. And once *that* drive was done, Bernard used the structure he'd established among the refugees to turn their hands to improving Calderon's defenses and vastly widening the lands that could be cultivated for food crops.

It was incredible, what people could do when they pulled together.

The sudden thunder of hooves jerked Amara from her reverie as a large man rode up on a muscular bay gelding. The horse protested being drawn to a halt and complained loudly as it lashed the air with its front hooves. That scream, in turn, flickered down to little Ajax in the training ring. The pony promptly hopped up into the air and twisted his body with the sinuous ease of a cat. Masha let out a shriek and went flying.

Amara whipped a hand forward, sending Cirrus out to slow and cushion the child's fall, and a sudden geyser of wind erupted from near the ring's floor. Between Amara's effort and the soft earth (intentionally prepared for just such an occasion as this), the child landed more or less safely.

Ajax, clearly pleased with himself, went running around the ring at full speed, tossing his mane, his tail held high.

"Bernard." Amara sighed.

The Count of Calderon scowled at the big gelding as he calmed the animal, dismounted, and tied his reins to one of a long row of hitching posts. "Sorry," he said, and gestured to the horse. "This idiot is practically quivering for someone to sound the charge. I don't even want to think about what he was like *before* he was gelded."

Amara smiled, and the two of them descended into the ring, where Masha lay sniffling. Amara examined the girl for injuries, but she'd received nothing more than bruises. Amara helped her up with her hands and with kind, gentle words, while Bernard narrowed his eyes and focused his earthcrafting on Ajax, slowly bringing the proud little horse to a halt. Bernard pulled a lump of honeyed wax from his pocket and fed it to the horse, speaking quietly as he took up Ajax's reins again.

"Back straight," Amara told the child. "Heels out."

Masha sniffled a few times, then said, "Ajax should be more careful."

"Probably," Amara said, fighting off a smile. "But he doesn't know how. So you need to practice proper form."

The girl cast a wary glance at the pony, docilely eating his treat from Bernard's hand. "Can I practice it tomorrow?"

"Better if you get on right now," Amara said.

"Why?"

"Because if you don't, you might not ever get back on," Amara said.

"But it's scary."

Amara did smile, then. "That's why you have to do it. Otherwise, instead of controlling your fear, your fear is controlling you."

Masha considered this gravely for a moment. Then she said, "But you said fear is good."

"I said it was normal," Amara replied. "Everyone feels afraid. Especially when something bad happens. But you can't let that scare you into quitting."

"But you quit doing Cursor stuff for the First Lord," Masha pointed out.

Amara felt her smile fade.

Behind Masha, Bernard rubbed studiously at his mouth with one hand.

"That was different," Amara said.

"Why?"

"For a lot of reasons you might not understand until you're older."

Masha frowned. "Why not?"

"Come on," Bernard rumbled, stepping in. He lifted the child into the air as lightly as a piece of down and put her on the pony's saddle. He was a big man with wide shoulders, his dark hair and beard streaked with threads of silver. His hands were large, strong, and scarred with a lifetime of work—but for all of that, he was as gentle with the child as a mother cat with her kittens. "One more time around the ring, like before," he said calmly. "Then we'll need to go get some lunch."

Masha gathered up the reins and bit her lower lip. "Can I go slow?"

"That's fine," Bernard said.

Masha clucked her tongue and began walking Ajax along the outside wall of the ring, her back practically bending backward in its efforts to stay straight. Her toes rested on the pony's ribs.

"Well?" Amara asked quietly, once the child was several yards away.

"Isana's coming."

"Again? She was here three days ago."

"Senator Valerius has managed to put together a quorum of the Senate," Bernard said. "He's planning on challenging the legitimacy of Septimus's marriage."

A bad taste went through Amara's mouth at the words, and she spat on the ground. "There are times when I wish you'd hit that egomaniac quite a bit harder."

"There was a lot of confusion during the rescue," Bernard said. "And Valerius wouldn't shut up. Interfered with my thinking." He pursed his lips, and mused, "I'll do better next time we're in that situation."

Amara let out a small snort and shook her head, watching Masha ride. "Bloody crows," she growled a moment later through clenched teeth. "Even *now*, with everything at stake, these idiots are playing their games. They'll still be doing deals under the table when a bloody vordknight tears them to shreds—as if the vord are some kind of transitory inconvenience!"

"They have to pretend that," Bernard said. "Otherwise, they'd be forced to admit that they were fools not to listen to the warnings we tried to give them five bloody years ago."

"And that would be terrible," Amara said. She thought about the situation for a moment. "If Valerius is successful, it gives Aquitaine every excuse he needs to keep the crown, even i . . . even when Octavian returns."

Bernard grunted agreement.

"What are we going to do?"

"Talk to my sister," Bernard said. "Figure out which Senators might be swayed to our side." Masha and Ajax had nearly completed their slow circuit of the ring. "How is she?"

"She was smiling earlier," Amara said. "Joking. Almost laughing."

Bernard let out a rumbling sigh. "Well. That's something good today, at least. If we could win that much every day, it would add up."

"It might," Amara said.

He looked at her obliquely, then gently covered her hand with his. "How are you doing?"

She tightened her fingers on his, feeling their gentle strength, the rough texture of his work-hardened skin. "A woman whose death warrant I practically signed has charged me with protecting and rearing her child. Less than a day after she did, I killed Masha's father. And every night, when she has nightmares, the little girl comes running to me to make her feel better." Amara shook her head. "I'm not sure how I'm supposed to feel about that, love."

Masha looked up at Amara as she came closer. She made sure her back was straight, and her smile was in equal measure chagrined and proud.

Amara found herself smiling back. She couldn't help it.

In the face of looming terror, the child's smile was a victory banner of its own.

Bernard looked between the two of them and nodded, his eyes bright. "Why don't you fly her back to Garrison? I'll lead Ajax, and we'll meet 'Sana in my office."

Amara looked at her husband and gave him a slow and gentle kiss on the mouth. Then she started walking toward Masha, tugging on her leather flying gloves as she went. The little girl noticed, and cheered.

Amara thought about her husband's words and pursed her lips thoughtfully. *Maybe he's right. Maybe enough of the little victories really will add up.*

CHAPTER 4

"Then you bloody well cut *down* trees enough for your section," Valiar Marcus bellowed. "The bloody amateur Legion has got two-thirds of its palisade up already, and you fools sit around here whining about how you had to leave your camp stakes back in Canea?" He strode down the line of laboring *legionares*, smacking his baton against armor plate and the occasional lazy skull. After the long and idle time spent on the ships, discipline was sadly lacking, the men unused to the weight of their armor. "If the Free Aleran has its camp up before we do, great furies help you miserable bastards, what I do to you will send you crying to the vord for shelter!"

Marcus kept up the steady tirade as he marched up and down the First Aleran's chosen campsite ashore. They held two neighboring hilltops, rocky rounded old nubs of mountains covered in thorns and brush. The wide valley between was for the Canim, who had set to establishing their own camp with a will. The massive, inhuman troops were well supplied with hand tools, and while they lacked the Aleran skills of furycraft, they more than made up the difference in raw physical power— and numbers.

Marcus paused to stare down at the valley below. Bloody crows, but there were a lot of Canim down there. Every one a fighter, too. Varg wasn't willing to risk bringing his noncombatants ashore until basic fortifications had been established. Marcus could hardly blame him. If he'd been landing in Canea with the last survivors of all Alera, he wouldn't have debarked them on open ground only five miles from the most warlike city on the continent, either.

From the hilltop, Marcus could stare north at Antillus, rings of massive, grey-white stone that sat piled atop one another upon the bones of another ancient mountain. In the afternoon light, its stones almost shone blue, reflecting the colors of the sky and the cold sea. Whoever Antillus Raucus had left in charge of his home city, most likely one of his more conservative, trusty old cronies, was almost certainly chewing his own guts out in consternation just then.

Marcus took a moment to consider the placement of the Canim camp. Any force traveling out from the city would have to pass one of the Aleran camps before it could engage the wolf-warriors. Not only that, but positioned as they were in the valley, the Canim camp could not be seen from the city walls. Oh, a small wing of Knights Aeris had overflown them within moments of their landing, but with the slightest amount of caution, the custodian of Antillus could keep quiet and prevent his civilian population from panicking until there was time to sort things out.

Not only that, but—assuming the fools could get the hilltops secured in good order—the two Aleran Legions commanded a far-more-potent advantage of terrain than did the Canim. Assaulting an Aleran Legion in a prepared position was a game that could only be won by paying the bloodiest of prices. Yet the Canim's sheer advantage of numbers meant that an Aleran assault upon *them* would be an equally foolish proposition. And, by camping south of the city, the landing Legions and Canim horde alike had placed themselves squarely between Antillus and the oncoming vord. No matter how thick the commander at Antillus might be, he'd have to appreciate *that* little fact.

Any number of things could have gone badly wrong—but the timing and relative positioning of the various troops had all fallen into place so smoothly that it seemed that fortune had smiled upon them all.

Nothing could be less true, of course. The entire business had been planned, and shrewdly. But then, Marcus had come to expect nothing less of the captain. That was something Octavian's grandfather had never been. Sextus had been a grandmaster of political machinations—but he'd never led a Legion in the field, never stood and fought beside them, risked himself along with them and won his place in the eyes of the *legionares*. Sextus had commanded loyalty, even respect, from his subordinates. But he had never been their captain.

Octavian was. The men of the First Aleran would die for him.

Marcus continued along the circuit of the camp, bellowing imprecations and curses, snarling at every single flaw while giving perfection only stony silence. It was what the men expected of him. Rumors were flying wildly as word of the state of affairs in Alera spread among the troops, and the men were nervous. The curses and snarls of the blocky old First Spear and the other centurions were touchstones, a constant fact of life whether the Legion was at rest or about to clash with the foe. They settled the men more surely than any amount of encouragement or reassurance.

But even the tough, capable centurions gave Marcus speculative glances, as if seeking out his thoughts on their predicament. Marcus returned the glances with nothing but crisp salutes, letting them see the First Spear proceeding with business as usual.

As evening wore on, Marcus stopped at the southernmost point of the defenses and stared out at the gathering darkness. According to Octavian, the body of vord slowly advancing on Antillus was still forty miles away. According to too many years spent in the field, Marcus knew that you never really knew where the enemy was until he was close enough to touch with a blade.

It was, he realized, partly why he had preferred his life as Valiar Marcus to the one he'd followed as a Cursor. A soldier might not know *where* his enemy was, but he nearly always knew *who* the enemy was.

"Thinking deep thoughts?" said a quiet voice behind him.

The First Spear turned to find Maestro Magnus standing behind him, less than a long step away. He had approached in perfect silence to within range of a killing stroke. Had Magnus chosen, he could have struck with the *gladius* at his side, or a knife he'd concealed on his person. Given Marcus's armor, the first choice of targets would have been the back of the neck—a thrust down, at the proper angle, could sever the spine, cut one of the large blood vessels in the neck, and shut off the windpipe all at the same time. Done properly, it resulted in a certain, silent kill of even a heavily armored target.

Marcus remembered practicing it, over and over and over, back in his days at the Academy, until the motion was ingrained into the muscles of his arms and shoulders and back. It was one of the standard techniques taught to the Cursors.

Magnus had just used him for practice.

It was one form of gamesmanship among student Cursors, though Marcus had never participated himself—a way to tell the other Cursor that you could have killed him, had you wished it. Magnus's stance, relaxed and nonchalant to the casual observer, was centered and ready for motion, a subtle challenge. Anyone trained at the Academy would have recognized that.

So. The older Cursor was fishing.

The First Spear grunted as though nothing had happened. The nearest group of laboring *legionares* was a good forty feet off. There was no need to guard his speech if he lowered his voice. "Wondering how long before the vord get here."

Magnus stared at him for a silent minute before easing out of the stance and walking up to stand beside the First Spear.

Marcus noted the slight protrusion of a knife's handle, where it was hidden up the old Cursor's sleeve. Magnus might be long in the tooth, and his dueling days were long behind him. But that wouldn't make him any less deadly should he choose to act. It was never the enemy's muscle or weapons or furies that made him a true threat. It was his mind. And Magnus's mind was still razor-sharp.

"Quite a while, one would think," Magnus said. "The Antillans don't expect them to make their first assaults for another two weeks or more."

Marcus nodded. "They're talking to us, eh?"

The old Cursor's mouth twitched at one corner. "It was that or fight us. They didn't seem eager to do that if they could avoid it." He, too, stared to the south, though Marcus knew his watery eyes were nearsighted. "Octavian wishes to speak with you."

Marcus nodded. Then he squinted at the other man, and said, "You been giving me looks, Magnus. What's wrong with you? I steal your favorite boots or something?"

Magnus shrugged his shoulders. "Between the time you retired from the Antillan Legions and the time you came back to service with the First Aleran, no one recalls where you were."

The First Spear felt his stomach begin to burn. Acid made a belch rise up through his throat. He covered it with a rough snort. "And that's got your knickers in a twist? One old soldier goes back to life on a steadholt. It ain't surprising that he don't stand out, Magnus."

"It's perfectly reasonable," Magnus acknowledged. "But not many old soldiers are named to the House of the Valiant. There are—were, when we left—five such men in the entire Realm. Each of them is currently a Citizen. Three Steadholders and a Count. None of them went back to life as a freeman."

"I did," the First Spear said easily. "Wasn't hard."

"There were many veterans who helped found the First Aleran," the Cursor continued in a calm voice. "Many of them from Antillan Legions. Every one of them recalls you, at least by reputation. None of them had heard anything about what happened to you after you retired." He shrugged. "It's unusual."

Marcus barked out a laugh. "You been sucking down too much leviathan liver oil." He let his voice grow more serious. "And we've got plenty enemies enough without you looking for more where there ain't none."

The old Cursor regarded Marcus with mild, watery eyes. "Yes," he said politely. "Where there ain't none."

Marcus felt his throat constrict. He *knew*. Knew something. Or thought he did.

Marcus doubted that the old Cursor had worked out that he was, in fact, Fidelias ex Cursori, accomplice to Attis and Invidia Aquitaine, traitor to the Crown. Certainly, he wasn't aware that Marcus had, at the end, turned on High Lady Aquitaine, assassinating her with a poisoned balest bolt—or coming damned close to it, at any rate. And he had no way of knowing how much more

the name of Valiar Marcus, First Spear of the First Aleran Legion, had come to
mean to a weary, jaded old killer named Fidelias.

But the knowledge was in Magnus's eyes. He might not have all of his facts
lined up yet—but it was plain in his manner, his actions, his words.

He knew enough.

For an instant, Fidelias felt a mad impulse to try something he'd rarely found
useful in his lifetime: He thought about telling the old Cursor the truth. Whatever happened, afterward, at least the uncertainty would be gone.

His mouth opened. Fidelias noted, with a bemused sort of detachment, that
he hadn't actually decided to speak. But some part of him—the Marcus in him,
likely—had proceeded without his approval.

He said, "Magnus, we should talk," then the vord exploded out of the gathering shadows.

There were three of them, low to the ground and moving fast. They were
long beasts, six legs on lean, sinuous bodies, with slender, lashing tails stretched
out behind them. They were covered in fine scales of black chitin, shining and
glossy, reflecting the bloody light of the failing sun. Fidelias had an instant to
observe that they moved like garim, the great lizards of the southern swamps,
then he was in motion.

His *gladius* would be all but useless. So he reached out through Vamma, his
earth fury, drawing power from the adamant bones of the old mountain beneath
him. He seized a thick, heavy wooden pole, laid ready to be planted in the earth
as part of the palisade.

Fidelias whirled on the nearest vord and swung the heavy pole up and
down in a vertical arc, like a man wielding an axe. The length of wood must have
weighed eighty pounds, but he swung it as lightly as a child would a walking
stick and struck the leading vord with grisly, shattering power. Green-brown
blood sprayed out everywhere, spattering Fidelias and Magnus alike.

The pole snapped in half, one end suddenly a mass of shards and splinters.
Fidelias turned to the next vord and drove that end forward like a spear tip. The
shock of impact lanced viciously up through his arms and shoulders, and even
with Vamma's influence to buttress him, Fidelias was knocked back from his
feet as the pole shattered beneath the strain. He hit the ground hard. The
stricken vord thrashed wildly, dying, with several shards of wood too large and
wickedly pointed to be properly called "splinters" protruding from the back of
its skull.

Then the third vord was on him.

Its teeth hit his calf, snapping down with terrifying force. He heard his leg
break, but such was the power of the thing's jaws that sensation vanished completely. Its tail lashed forward, and Fidelias struggled, his fury-enhanced strength

letting him slam the vord around before it could settle a grip on him with its claws or tail, and preventing it from bracing itself firmly with all of its six claw-tipped legs. It had incredible physical power. If it was able to plant its feet, it would simply rip Fidelias's leg off at the knee.

The vord's long, slender tail suddenly whipped around his thigh, and Fidelias saw, in an instant of frozen horror, that hundreds of sharp, tiny ridges, like the teeth of a serrated knife, had suddenly extended along its length. The vord would simply lash its tail free, cutting the muscles of his thigh from the bone in one long spiral, like carving the meat from a ham.

Magnus let out a shriek and swept his *gladius* down. Though the old man's arms were lean, they were backed by the power of his own earthcrafting, and the famous sword of the Legions severed the vord's tail at its base.

The vord released Fidelias and whirled on Magnus with unnerving speed and precision, and the old Cursor went down under its weight.

Fidelias pushed himself back up and saw Magnus holding the vord's jaws away from his face with both hands. Magnus wasn't as strong an earthcrafter as Fidelias was. He was unable to dislodge the vord, and the thing had managed to begin raking at him with its claws as it struggled to clamp the incredible power of its jaws over Magnus's face.

For an instant, Magnus's eyes met his.

Fidelias saw the branches of logic in his mind, unfolding as calmly and cleanly as if he'd been performing a theoretical exercise.

The situation was ideal. The vord was already badly wounded. The nearest *legionares* were already taking up their weapons and charging forward—but they would never arrive in time to save Magnus. Fidelias himself was badly wounded. The shock was keeping him from feeling it, but he knew that even with the attentions of a Legion healer, he'd be off his feet for a few days.

Magnus knew.

No one would be able to blame him for only killing two and a half of three vord. Fidelias would remain hidden. Valiar Marcus's position would be secure. And to accomplish it, all Fidelias would need to do was . . . nothing.

Nothing but let one of *them*, the vord, the foe of every living thing on Carna, rip a trusted confidant of the rightful First Lord of Alera to quivering bits of meat.

And suddenly he was consumed with rage. Rage at the lies and selfish ambition that had poisoned the heart of Alera ever since the death of Gaius Septimus. Rage at Sextus's stubborn pride, pride that had driven him to turn the Realm into a venomous cauldron of treachery and intrigue. Rage at the things he had been forced to do in the name of his oath to the Crown, and then in supposed service to the greater good of all Alera, when it seemed clear that the man to whom he had sworn his oath had abandoned his own duty to the Realm. Things that boy at the Academy, all those years ago, would be horrified to know were in his future.

It had to stop.

Here, before the greatest threat any of them had ever known, *it had to stop*.

Valiar Marcus let out a roar of furious defiance and threw himself onto the vord's back. He jammed an armored forearm between the vord's jaws, and felt the terrible pressure of its teeth as they clamped down. He ignored it and ripped savagely at the vord's head with his shoulders, twisting and worrying at the thing like a man trying to rip a stump from the earth.

The vord let out a hiss of rage. It was too sinuous and flexible to let him snap its neck.

But as he strained and pulled, Valiar Marcus saw its scales pulled up, extending slightly from the skin of its neck, baring the tender flesh beneath to a blow struck from the proper angle.

Maestro Magnus saw it, too.

He produced the knife from his sleeve with a single flicking motion of his hand, as smoothly and swiftly as a skilled conjurer. The blade was small but bright, its edge deadly keen.

The Cursor drove it to the hilt into the vord's neck. Then, with a ripping twist, he opened the thing's throat. The vord bucked, muscles straining in sudden agony—but its jaws had suddenly lost their power.

Then the *legionares* arrived, swords hacking, and in a moment, it was over.

Marcus lay on his back on the earth in the aftermath. One of the *legionares* had gone running to find a healer and raise the alarm. The others had spread out in a line, putting their armored bodies between the gathering night outside and the two wounded old men behind them.

Marcus lay there panting and turned to look at Magnus.

The old Cursor was just staring at him, his watery eyes blank with shock, his face and white beard stained with vord blood. He stared at Marcus and stammered out a few sounds that had no meaning.

"We got to talk," Marcus growled. His own voice sounded rough and thin. "You're getting a little paranoid, old man. Jumping at every shadow. You need to relax."

Magnus looked at him. Then he turned and stared at the three dead vord on the ground around them. One of them, the second to die, was still twitching, its tail fluttering randomly in the low brush.

Magnus wheezed out a laugh.

Marcus joined him.

When the healers came up with reinforcements, they eyed the pair of wounded old men as if they'd gone completely mad.

They could only laugh harder.

⬡⬡⬡⬡⬡ CHAPTER 5

Running boots hammered the ground outside the command tent, and Antillar Maximus shouted the password at the sentries stationed there as if he intended to bowl them out of his way with sheer volume. Tavi looked up from his reports immediately, lifting a hand, and Maestro Magnus stopped speaking. The old Cursor gathered together loose pages from the table, resorting to holding the last several down with one hand. An instant later, Maximus flung the tent's door flap aside, letting in a rush of wind scented heavily with spring rain.

Tavi smiled at Magnus's forethought. No pages went flying. The old Cursor had been wounded only two days before—but he'd taken only a single night's rest after Tribune Foss had released him for duty, and though battered and obviously stiff, he had returned to the command tent the next morning.

"Tavi," Max said, panting, "you need to see this. I've had them bring your horse."

Tavi arched an eyebrow at Max's use of his first name and rose. "What's happening?"

"You have to see it," Max said.

Tavi checked the fittings on his armor to make sure they were tight, slung the baldric of his *gladius* over his shoulder, and followed Max out to the horses. He swung up, waited for Max and the two *legionares* currently on guard duty to mount up as well, then gestured for Antillar to lead the way.

In the days since the landing, the Canim and the Alerans had settled down into their camps in good order. Only one sticking point was any cause for concern—the little stream that fed the well in the valley between the two Aleran camps ran so deeply that there was no way to reroute it to within reach of either Legion camp. As a result, all three groups had to use the wells Tavi's engineers had sunk into the rocky ground in the valley, and a series of shallow pools in the approximate center of the Canim camp had been the results.

So far, they had shared the water without serious incident—which meant that no one had been killed, though one Canim and two Alerans had been injured. Tavi followed Maximus to the southernmost gate of the Canim camp. Two of the warrior-caste guards were on duty there, one in the scarlet and black steel armor of Narash, the other in Shuaran midnight blue and black. The Narashan lifted a paw-hand in greeting, and called, "Open the gate for the Warmaster's *gadara*."

The gate, made from leviathan hide stretched over a frame of enormous leviathan bones, swung open wide, and they entered the Canim fortifications.

"It started about ten minutes ago," Max said. "I told a *legionare* to stay with it and write down anything he heard."

Tavi frowned ahead of them, idly keeping his horse from sidestepping as they entered the Canim camp, and the wolf-warriors' scent filled the beasts' nostrils. There was a crowd gathered ahead of them, and more were heading that way. Even mounted on a tall horse, Tavi could barely see anything over the craning heads of the Canim in front of him, most standing to their full eight feet or more to peer ahead.

The press of traffic became too much, and Tavi and his men halted, the air around them full of the snarled vowels and growled consonants of the Canim tongue. Max tried to get them moving through the crowd again, but even his *legionare's* bellow could make no headway against the ferocious, roaring buzz of the Canim crowd.

Deep, brassy Canim horns brayed, and a small phalanx of red-armored Canim warriors came marching stolidly through the crowd like men walking against the current of a quick-running stream. Tavi recognized Gradash, the silver-furred huntmaster—a rank of warrior roughly equal to that of centurion—guiding the warriors. He directed them to fan out around the Alerans, then tilted his head slightly to one side, a gesture of respect. Tavi returned it.

"Tavar," Gradash called. "With your consent, I will take you forward."

"Thank you, huntmaster," Tavi replied.

Gradash bared his throat again and began shouting more commands. In short order, gawkers found themselves savagely shoved aside, and the Alerans' horses begun moving forward once more.

They drew near the central watering pool within a moment, and found dozens of Alerans there, mixed in among the Canim to gather around the pool. Tavi saw why, and sucked in a breath through his teeth.

No wonder everyone had come to stare.

A cloaked form stood upon the surface of the water. The cloak was made of rich, grey fabric with a deep hood. Tavi couldn't see any of the features of whoever was beneath the cloak, except for dark lips and a pale, delicate chin. His heart lurched in his chest, even so.

It was the vord Queen.

The troop of Canim soldiers led Tavi and his party to the far side of the pool, where Varg and Nasaug were standing, together with a grey-furred old Cane wearing sections of vord chitin that had been fashioned into armor. He wore a red mantle and hood over that, the cut of which was identical to the garments worn by Canim ritualists—but this was the first time Tavi had seen such a garment made of anything but the pale, supple leather of human flesh.

The vord Queen never moved. Tavi glanced down the line of pools and saw what seemed to be identical images standing upon each of them. Crowds continued to gather.

"Bloody crows," Max swore. "That's a *watersending*."

Tavi felt his jaw tighten. Projecting an image through a watercrafting was a relatively difficult use of furycraft. Projecting *several* of them was impossi— Well, not impossible, clearly . . . but very, very improbable. Tavi wasn't sure if Gaius Sextus himself could have managed it.

"She's just standing there," Max said, frowning. "Why is she just standing there?"

"Ferus," Tavi said to one of his guards. "Go back to the camp. Tell Crassus I want every Knight Aeris we have immediately flying reconnaissance out to fifty miles. I want our Knights Terra to patrol out to ten miles and make sure nothing is tunneling toward us. Cavalry is to ride escort, no group smaller than twenty, back before nightfall."

Ferus slammed his fist to his chest and turned his mount to begin working his way out of the Canim camp.

Max grunted. "You think it's supposed to be a distraction?"

Tavi gestured at the crowds. "If it isn't, it's doing a crowbegotten good job of it. No reason to take chances. Come on." Tavi nudged his horse forward until he was standing next to Varg and Nasaug.

"Morning," Varg said, studying the watersending.

"Good morning," Tavi replied.

"I ordered my fastest ships put out to sea already," Varg replied. "Borrowed some of your witchmen to go along and keep an eye on the ocean."

Many of the watercrafters who professionally used their talents to conceal ships from leviathans had grown used to the Canim during the pair of voyages over the past six months. Canim in general were not disposed to admiration of furycrafting, but their ships' crews had been more than mildly impressed with the skills of the witchmen. "You think they're coming in by sea?"

Varg's ears twitched in an ambivalent motion, a Cane gesture that meant more than a shrug but less than "no." "I think that the Queen had to come back here after she went to Canea. I think she did not use one of our ships. They have carried out operations in all terrain. No reason to take chances."

Tavi nodded. "I sent scouts by land and air."

"Expected you would," Varg said, showing his teeth in a gesture that might have been meant to be an Aleran smile of approval—or a Canim gesture of threat. Given Varg's personality, Tavi decided it was probably both. Varg knew Tavi well enough to anticipate his reaction and had wanted him to know it. Such ability was an invaluable asset in an ally. In an enemy, it was terrifying.

Max snorted out a breath, and observed, to Nasaug, "You fellows throw out the most complimentary threats of anyone I ever met."

"Thank you," Nasaug said gravely. "It will be an honor to kill one so courteous as you, Tribune Antillar."

Max barked out a belly laugh and bowed his head slightly to one side, showing his throat to Nasaug. The younger Cane's mouth lolled open in a small Canim grin.

They waited in silence for several more minutes as the crowd continued to grow.

"Ah," Tavi said.

Varg glanced at him.

"That's why the Queen hasn't spoken," Tavi explained. "She's causing her image to appear. And she's waiting for word to spread about it, so that there's time for an audience to gather." He frowned. "Which means . . ."

"Means she can't see through it," Varg rumbled. "She isn't gaining intelligence this way."

Tavi nodded. It would explain how the vord Queen was making multiple images appear. Sending the projection forth wasn't the difficult part of the watersending. Bringing light and sound *back* from the other side was the difficult part. "She wants to speak to us," Tavi said. "Everyone, I mean. Crows, she must be causing this image to appear in every body of water large enough to support it." Tavi shook his head. "I wish I'd thought of that."

Varg grunted. "Handy, in time of war. Issue orders to the populace. Alert them to enemy movements. Keep your makers from being taken by surprise. Tell them what you need produced, save the time lost to waiting on messengers." Varg narrowed his eyes. "Vord Queen doesn't need any of that, though."

"No," Tavi said. "She doesn't."

"The vord are orderly. Logical. She must have an objective in this."

"She does," Tavi said. He felt his mouth harden into a line. "It's an attack."

The image stirred, and silence fell over the gathering.

The vord Queen lifted her hand in a gesture of greeting. There was something unnatural in the gesture that made it look like a formal motion, as if she was consciously forcing the movements of her joints to adhere to constraints to which she was not accustomed.

"Alerans," she said, and her voice rang out loudly, amplified to be heard for hundreds of yards in every direction. The Canim nearest the pool folded their ears back against their skulls and erupted into a chorus of snarls in reaction to the explosion of sound.

"I am the vord. I have taken the heart of your lands. I have laid siege to your strong places. I have slain your First Lord. You cannot destroy me. You cannot withstand me."

Silence fell for long heartbeats. The vord Queen let the words sink in.

"The vord are eternal. The vord are everywhere. Among the stars, between the worlds, we conquer. We grow. Against us, no victory is possible. You may withstand us for a time, but in ten years, in a hundred years, in a thousand years we will return, stronger and wiser than before. We are inevitable. Your kind is doomed."

Another silence. Tavi looked around at the crowd. Every face was fixed upon the image of the vord Queen. The Alerans looked pale, or sickened, or simply stared in fascination. Canim body language was more difficult to read, but even the wolf-warriors seemed subdued. This was the face of the creature who had all but wiped out their entire civilization—millions upon millions of Canim, entire nations, the smallest of which was nearly half as large as Alera herself.

But regardless of the individual reaction, every person there watched.

They listened.

"I bear you no personal hatred or animosity. I have no desire to inflict pain or suffering upon any individual. I do what I do to protect my children and allow them to prosper. This world is their legacy. They will have it."

The image moved, deliberately lifting her slender, pale hands. She drew back her hood, slowly, to reveal the exotically beautiful face of a young woman— one who looked, in fact, very like Kitai. She had the same high cheekbones, the same long, fine white hair, the same sharp cleanliness of features softened by full lips and wide, canted eyes. But where Kitai's eyes were brilliant green, the vord Queen's eyes were black, faceted like an insect's reflecting the light in a mesmerizing, alien glitter of colors.

"But I am willing to offer you this chance, Alerans. There need not be war between our peoples. I will take your cities. But for those with the wisdom to bow before the tide of history, I will provide places of safety in which you will be permitted to govern yourselves, to support your families, and to live out the natural course of your lives in complete autonomy, save for this: You will not be permitted to bear children. This is within my power.

"The war can end. The fighting can end. The death and famine and suffering can end. I will open the Amaranth Vale to be resettled by your people. And while you are there, you will have my protection. No outsider will be permitted to harm you. The full might of the vord will shield you. My power will allow you to live long lives, free of every pestilence and plague known to your kind.

"I beg you to see reason, Alerans. I offer you peace. I offer you health. I offer you safety. Let the strife between us end. Your leaders have not protected you. Your Legions have been laid waste. Millions of lives have been lost to no purpose. Let it end.

"I make you this offer. Any Aleran who wishes to enter my protection must do only this: Come, unarmed, to any part of the world within the sphere of our control. Tie a band of green cloth around your arm. This will be the signal to my children that you have bowed to the natural order. You will be fed, given care, and transported to places of safety, freedom, and peace."

There was nothing but silence.

Bloody crows, Tavi thought. *That's brilliant.*

"Fail to set aside your irrational need to continue this conflict, and you will leave me no other choice." Her hands rose to replace the hood, veiling her alien beauty again. Her voice dropped to a quiet, calm, uninflected murmur. "I *will* come for you."

Tavi stopped himself from shuddering, but only barely. Max didn't bother to try.

"Tell your neighbors. Tell your friends. Tell any who were not here to see that the vord offer you peace and protection."

Silence reigned. No one moved.

Max said, very quietly, "Peace and protection. You think she's serious?"

"No children," Tavi murmured back. "A stranglehold takes longer to kill than does a clean thrust—but it makes you just as dead."

"You don't feel it when you go, either," Max replied.

"At least now I know why," Tavi said.

"Why what?"

"The vord Queen is keeping a steadholt of Alerans captive, near Alera Imperia. Like animals in a zoo. It was an experiment, to see if it could be made to work."

Max blinked at him. "How did you know about that?"

"Crown secret."

Max grimaced. "If everyone heard this, in all Alera . . . Tavi you know that there are going to be people scared enough to do anything."

"I know."

"If we lose even part of our people to desertion or surrender, it could kill us. We're at the brink."

"That's why she's doing it. I said it was an attack, Max."

Varg looked over at Tavi with narrowed eyes, his ears pricked forward. The Cane was close enough to have heard even their lowered voices.

"What are we going to do about it?" Max sighed. "Crows, look at them."

Everyone, Canim and Aleran alike, stared at the image of the vord Queen. Their fear and uncertainty filled the air like woodsmoke.

"Tavar," Varg growled suddenly. "Your helmet."

Tavi glanced at the Cane. Then he drew his helmet off and passed it over to Varg.

The Warmaster of the Canim leapt up onto the low stone wall on the edge of the pool, helmet in hand. He stalked through the shallow water until he stood before the image of the vord Queen.

Then he swept the helmet in a horizontal arc, catching the water that formed the hooded head of the vord Queen, decapitating the watery image.

Then he flung back his head and drank the helmet empty in a single draught.

Varg rose to his full nine feet in height before roaring, his basso voice a challenge to the volume of the watersending itself, "I AM STILL THIRSTY!" His sword rasped clear of his scabbard as he lifted it high and faced the Canim soldiers. "WHO WILL DRINK WITH ME?"

Thousands of eyes focused on the Warmaster. The silence became something brittle and crystalline, something that was on the brink of shattering, changing. Fear and rage and despair surged in the air, like the confused, shifting winds that preceded a storm or the currents that could rip swimmers in any direction when the tides began to change.

Tavi dismounted and strode forward to stand beside Varg. His hobnailed boots clicked on the stone of the wall and splashed through the water. He took back his helmet from Varg's grasp, swept it through the watery heart of the image of the vord Queen, and drank deeply.

Steel rasped on steel as ten thousand swords sprang free of their sheaths. The sudden, furious roar of the Canim shook the air with such force that the water of the pools danced and jumped as if under a heavy rainstorm. The watersendings could not maintain their integrity in the face of that disruption, and they collapsed, splashing back down into the pools, shaken to bits by the enraged howls of Canim and Aleran alike.

Tavi joined them, shouting in wordless anger, and drew his sword, lifting it high.

The storm of approval from the Canim redoubled, making the plates of Tavi's lorica vibrate and rattle against one another, resolving into a thundering chant of, "VARG! TAVAR! VARG! TAVAR!"

Tavi exchanged a Canim salute with Varg, then turned and went back to his horse. He mounted up on the dancing, nervous animal and beckoned Max and his second guard. As they rode from the Canim camp, the crowd, still howling his Canim name, parted before and around them in an armored sea of swords and fangs and wrath.

Tavi kicked his mount into a run and headed back to the First Aleran's camp.

"What are we going to do?" Max called as they rode.

"What we always do when the enemy attacks us," Tavi said. He bared his teeth in a wolfish smile. "We're going to hit back."

CHAPTER 6

Invidia entered the massive, dome-shaped structure where the vord Queen took a daily meal and shuddered as she always did. The walls were made of faintly glowing green *croach*. There were swirls and mounds of it everywhere, splayed into abstract shapes that were both beautiful and revolting. The ceiling stretched fifty feet overhead, and Invidia could have used the massive space beneath it to teach a class in flying.

Spiderlike creatures, the keepers, swarmed over the *croach*, their many-legged, translucent bodies fading eerily into the ambient glow of the walls, floor, and ceiling. If a keeper wasn't moving, one could all but stumble over it, so well did they blend with the massive construction. Hundreds of the creatures swarmed through the place, climbing smoothly up the walls and across the ceiling, a constant and irritating motion.

In the center of the dome was the high table from the banquet hall of the High Lord of Ceres along with its chairs. It was a gorgeously carved, massive construct of Rhodesian oak, a gift to the current High Lord's great-grandfather. One could have seated half a cohort of *legionares* along its length without once hearing armored shoulder plates click together.

The vord Queen sat at one end of the table, her hands folded primly upon its tablecloth. The tablecloth was grimy, stained with the great furies only knew what fluids, and had not been cleaned.

The Queen made a gesture with one pale hand to the seat on her left.

Invidia's customary seat was at the Queen's right hand.

If Invidia had, for some reason, been replaced, she knew it was unlikely that she would leave the dome alive. She controlled an urge to moisten her lips and focused upon her body, preventing her heart from racing faster, her skin from breaking into a cold sweat, her pupils from contracting.

Calm. She had to remain calm, confident, and competent—and most of all, *useful*. The vord had never heard of such a thing as a retirement. Unless one counted being buried alive and dissolved by the *croach*.

Invidia walked across the floor, nudging a slow-moving keeper out of her way with one foot. She sat down beside the Queen. She had to survive the meal. Always, survive. "Good evening."

The Queen stared down the table and was silent for a moment, her alien eyes unreadable. Then she said, "Explain the gestures Alerans make to show respect to their superiors."

"In what sense?" Invidia asked.

"Soldiers do this," the Queen said, lifting her fist to her heart and lowering it again. "Citizens bend at the waist. Mates press their mouths together."

"The last isn't quite a gesture of respect," Invidia said, "though the others are. They are an acknowledgment of the other's status. Such an acknowledgment is considered to be necessary and favorable to the order of society."

The Queen nodded once, slowly. "They are gestures of submission."

Invidia did arch an eyebrow this time. "I had never really considered them such. However, that is a valid description, if an incomplete one."

The Queen turned her unsettling eyes to Invidia. "Incomplete in what sense?"

Invidia considered her answer for a moment before saying, "Gestures of deference and respect are far more than simply acknowledging the greater power of another. By accepting such a gesture, the person who receives it also acknowledges an obligation in return."

"To do what?"

"To protect and assist the person making the gesture."

The Queen's eyes narrowed. "He who holds the greatest power has obligation to none."

Invidia shook her head. "But no matter how powerful an individual may be, he is only a part of a greater whole. Gestures of respect are a mutual acknowledgment of that fact—that both the giver and the receiver are part of something greater than they, each with his role to play within the whole."

The vord Queen frowned. "It . . . acknowledges the need for structure. For order. That for the good of all, that which must be, will be. It signifies acceptance of one's part of that order."

Invidia shrugged. "At its core, yes. Many Alerans never give such gestures any serious consideration. They are simply a part of how our society functions."

"And if such a gesture is not given, what results?"

"Unpleasantness." Invidia replied. "Depending upon the person who has been slighted, there could be repercussions ranging from retaliatory insults to imprisonment to a challenge to the *juris macto.*"

"Justice by combat," the Queen said.

"Yes," Invidia replied.

"The rule of strength over the rule of law. It seems to reject the ideals of Aleran social order."

"On the surface. But the fact of the matter is that some Alerans are a great deal more powerful, in a direct and personal sense, than nearly all of the rest. Attempting to force a particular behavior out of such individuals by any direct means could lead to an equally direct conflict, in which a great many people could be harmed."

The Queen considered that for a moment. "Thus, indirect means are used to avoid such situations. The lesser are encouraged to avoid provoking a direct confrontation from one of greater power. Those of great power must consider the possibility of direct conflict with someone who is their equal before taking action."

"Precisely," Invidia replied. "And the safest way to manage conflicts is through the rule of law. Those who too often ignore the law in favor of the *juris macto* become outcasts within the society and run the risk of another Citizen taking matters into his own hands."

The Queen folded her hands on the tabletop and nodded. "Among the vord," she said, "we rarely contemplate indirect means of conflict resolution."

Invidia frowned. "I had not realized that any internal conflict existed among your kind."

The Queen's expression flickered with something that was both chagrined and sullen. "It is rare." Then she straightened, cleared her throat—an artificial sound, since as far as Invidia could tell, she never did it at any other time—and asked, "How was your day?"

It was the signal to begin the ritual of dinner. Invidia never grew any more comfortable with it, despite the repetition. She replied politely and made inane, pleasant conversation with the Queen for a few moments as the wax spiders, the keepers, trooped toward the table bearing plates, cups, and cutlery. The insectlike vord swarmed up the table's legs in neat ranks, setting a place for the Queen, for Invidia . . .

. . . and for someone who was apparently to sit at the Queen's right hand.

The empty chair with its empty plate setting was unnerving. Invidia covered her reaction by turning to watch the rest of the keepers bringing forth several covered platters and a bottle of Ceresian wine.

Invidia opened the bottle and poured wine into the Queen's glass, then into her own. Then she looked at the glass in front of the empty seat.

"Pour," the Queen said. "I have invited a guest."

Invidia did so. Then she began uncovering platters.

Each platter bore a perfectly square section of the *croach*. Each was subtly different than the next. One looked as if it had been baked in an oven—badly. The edges were black and crisp. Another had sugar sprinkled over its surface. A third was adorned with a gelatinous glaze and a ring of ripe cherries. A fourth had been coated with what had once been melted cheese—but it had been scorched dark brown.

Invidia sliced each piece into quarters, then began to load the Queen's plate with a single square from each platter. After that, she served herself the same.

"And our guest," the Queen murmured.

Invidia dutifully filled the third plate. "Whom are we entertaining?"

"We are not entertaining," the Queen replied. "We are consuming food in a group."

Invidia bowed her head. "Who is to be our companion, then?"

The Queen narrowed her insect eyes until only glittering black slits were visible. She stared down the length of the enormous table, and said, "She comes."

Invidia turned her head to look as their guest entered the glowing green dome.

It was a second queen.

It shared its features with the Queen: Indeed, it might have been her twin sister—a young woman little older than a teenager, with long white hair and the same glittering eyes. There, the similarities ended. The younger queen prowled forward with alien grace, making no effort at all to mimic the motion of a human being. She was completely naked, and her pale skin was covered in a sheen of some kind of glistening, greenish mucus.

The younger queen walked forward to the table and stopped a few feet away, staring at her mother.

The Queen gestured to the empty chair. "Sit."

The younger queen sat. She stared across the table at Invidia with unblinking eyes.

"This is my child. She is newly born," said the Queen to Invidia. She turned to the young queen. "Eat."

The younger queen considered the food for a moment. Then she grasped a square in her bare fingers and stuffed it into her mouth.

The Queen observed this behavior, frowning. Then she took up her fork and began cutting off dainty bites with it, eating them slowly. Invidia followed the elder Queen's lead and ate as well.

The food was . . . "revolting" fell so far of the mark that it seemed an injustice. Invidia had learned to eat the raw *croach*. The creature keeping her alive needed her to ingest it in order to feed itself. She had been startled to learn that it could taste even worse. The vord had no grasp of cooking. The very notion was alien to them. As a result, they couldn't really be expected to do it very well—but that evening they had perpetrated nothing short of an atrocity.

She choked the food down as best she could. The elder Queen ate steadily. The younger queen was finished within two minutes and sat there staring at them, her expression unreadable.

The younger queen then turned to her mother. "Why?"

"We partake of a meal together."

"Why?"

"Because it might make us stronger."

The younger queen absorbed that in silence for a moment. Then she asked, "How?"

"By building bonds between us."

"Bonds." The younger queen blinked slowly, once. "What need is there for restraints?"

"Not physical bonds," her mother said. "Symbolic mental attachments. Familiar feelings."

The young queen absorbed that for half a dozen heartbeats. Then she said, "These things do not improve strength."

"There is more to strength than physical power."

The young queen tilted her head. She stared at her mother, then, unnervingly, at Invidia. The Aleran woman could feel the sudden heavy, invasive pressure of the young queen's awareness impinging upon her thoughts. "What is this creature?"

"A means to an end."

"It is alien."

"Necessary."

The young queen's voice hardened. "It is alien."

"Necessary," repeated the elder Queen.

Again, the young queen fell silent. Then, her expression never changing, she said, "You are defective."

The enormous table seemed to explode. Splinters, some of them six inches long and wickedly sharp, flew outward like arrows. Invidia flinched instinctively, and barely managed to get her chitin-armored forearm between her and a flying spear of wood that might have plunged through her eye.

Sound pressed so hard against Invidia's eardrums that one of them burst, a wailing thunderstorm of high-pitched, shrieking howls. She cried out at the pain and reeled out of her chair and back from the table, borrowing swiftness from her wind furies as she went, embracing the weirdly altered sense of time that seemed to stretch instants into seconds, seconds into moments. It was the only way for her to see what was happening.

The vord queens were locked in a fight to the death.

Even with the windcrafting to aid her, Invidia could barely follow the movements of the two vord. Black claws flashed. Kicks flew. Dodges turned into twenty-foot bounds that ended at the nearest wall of the dome, whereupon the two queens continued their struggle while crouched on the wall, bounding and scuttling up the dome like a pair of dueling spiders.

Invidia's eyes flicked to the ruined table. It lay in pieces. A ragged furrow was torn through one corner, where the younger queen had surged forward, plunging *through* the massive hardwood table as if it had been no more a hindrance than a mound of soft snow. Invidia could scarcely imagine the tremendous power and focus that would be required for such a thing to happen—from a creature who had been born, it would seem, less than an hour before.

But swift and terrible as the young queen might have been, the match was not an even one. Where claws struck the elder Queen, sparks flew from her seemingly soft flesh, turning the attack aside. But where the younger queen was hit, flesh parted, and green-brown blood flew in fine arcs. The vord queens fought a spinning, climbing, leaping duel at a speed too swift to be seen clearly, much less interfered with, and Invidia found herself tracking the motion simply to know when she might need to leap out of the way.

Then the elder Queen made a mistake. She slipped on a slickened spill of the younger queen's blood, and her balance faltered for a fraction of a second. There was not time enough for the young queen to close in for a more deadly blow—but it was more than time enough for her to dart behind the elder Queen and seize the fabric of the dark cloak. With a twisting motion, she wrapped the cloak around the elder Queen's throat and leaned back, pulling with both frail-seeming arms, tightening the twisted fabric like a garrote against her mother's neck.

The elder Queen bent into a sinuous bow, straining against the strangling cloth, her expression quite calm as her dark eyes fell with a palpable weight upon Invidia.

The Aleran woman met her eyes for a pair of endless seconds before she nodded once, rose, lifted her hand, and with an effort of will and furycraft caused the air within the nose, mouth, and lungs of the young queen to congeal into a nearly liquid mass.

The response was immediate. The younger queen twisted and writhed in sudden agony, still holding on desperately to the twisted cloak.

The elder Queen severed it with a slash of her claws, slipped free, turned, and with half a dozen smoothly savage movements tore the younger queen open from throat to belly, removing organs along the way. It was calmly done, the work of an old hand in a slaughterhouse more than the intense uncertainty of a battle.

The young queen's body fell limp to the floor. The elder Queen took no chances. She dismembered it with neat, workmanlike motions. Then she turned, as if nothing at all had happened, and walked back to the table. Her chair remained in its place though the table had been ruined.

The Queen sat down in her chair and stared forward, at nothing.

Invidia walked slowly over to her side, righted her own fallen chair, and sat down in it. Neither of them spoke for a time.

"Are you hurt?" Invidia asked, finally.

The Queen opened her mouth, then did something Invidia had never seen before.

She hesitated.

"My daughter," the Queen said, her voice a near whisper. "The twenty-seventh since returning to Alera's shores."

Invidia frowned. "Twenty-seventh . . . ?"

"Part of our . . . nature . . ." The vord shivered. "Within each queen is an imperative to remain separate. Pure. Untainted by our contact with other beings. And to remove any queen that shows signs of corruption. Beginning several years ago, my junior queens have universally attempted to remove me." Her face was touched by a faint frown. "I do not understand. She did no physical harm to me. Yet . . ."

"She hurt you."

The Queen nodded, very slowly. "I had to remove their capacity to produce more queens lest they gather numbers to remove me. Which has hurt us all. Weakened us. By all rights, this world should have been vord five years ago." Her eyes narrowed, and she turned her faceted gaze upon Invidia. "You acted to protect me."

"You hardly needed it," Invidia said.

"You did not know that."

"True."

The vord Queen tilted her head, studying Invidia intently. She braced herself for the unpleasant intrusion of the Queen's mind—but it did not come.

"Then why?" the Queen asked.

"The younger queen clearly would not have permitted me to live."

"You might have struck at both of us."

Invidia frowned. True enough. The two queens had been so intent upon one
another, they would hardly have been able to react to a sudden attack from Invidia. She could have called up fire and obliterated them both.

But she hadn't.

"You could have fled," the Queen said.

Invidia smiled faintly. She gestured to the creature latched upon her chest.
"Not far enough."

"No," the vord said. "You have no other place to go."

"I do not," Invidia agreed.

"When something is held in common," the Queen asked, "is it considered
a bond?"

Invidia considered her answer for a moment—and not for the benefit of the
Queen. "It is often the beginning of one."

The vord looked at her fingers. Their dark-nailed tips were stained with the
younger queen's blood. "Do you have children of your own?"

"No."

The Queen nodded. "It is . . . unpleasant to see them harmed. Any of them.
I am pleased that you are not distracted by such a thing at this time." She looked
up and squared her shoulders, straightening her spine—mirroring Invidia herself.
"What is the proper Aleran etiquette when an assassination interrupts dinner?"

Invidia found a small smile on her mouth. "Perhaps we should repair the
furniture."

The vord tilted her head again. "I do not have that knowledge."

"When my mother died, my father apprenticed me to all the finest master
artisans of the city for a year at a time. I think mainly to be rid of me." She rose
and considered the broken table, the scattered splinters. "Come. This is a more
demanding discipline than flying or calling fire. I will show you."

They had just sat back down at the repaired table when the whistling, trilling
alarm shrieks of wax spiders filled the air.

The Queen came to her feet at once, her eyes opening very wide. She stood
perfectly still for a moment, then hissed, "Intruders. Widespread. Come."

Invidia followed the Queen outside into the moonlit night, onto the gently
luminous *croach* that spread around the enormous hive. The Queen started
downslope, pacing swiftly and calmly, as the trilling alarm continued to spread.

Invidia heard angry, high-pitched buzzing sounds unlike anything she had encountered. The creature on her chest reacted to them uneasily, shifting its many limbs and sending anguish pouring through her body in a fire that threatened to rob her of breath. She fought to continue walking in the Queen's shadow without stumbling, and finally had to put her hand to her knife and draw upon a pain-numbing metalcrafting to let her continue.

They came to a broad pool of water that had gathered at the center of a shallow valley. It was no more than a foot deep and perhaps twenty across. The shallow waters teemed with the larval forms of the takers.

Standing upon the waters in the center of the pool was a man.

He was tall, half a head over six feet at least, and was dressed in gleaming, immaculate *legionare's* armor. His hair was dark, cropped short in a soldier's cut, as was his beard, and his eyes were intensely green. There were fine scars visible on his face, and upon him they looked as much like a military decoration as the scarlet cloak secured to his armor with the blue-and-scarlet eagle insignia of the House of Gaius.

Invidia found herself drawing in a sharp breath.

"Who?" the Queen demanded.

"It . . . it looks like . . ." Septimus. Except for the eyes, the man at the center of the pool was almost identical to her onetime fiancé. But it could not be him. "Octavian," she said finally, all but snarling the word. "This must be Gaius Octavian."

The vord Queen's claws made a quiet, sickly-stretchy sound as they elongated.

The watery image was in full color, an indicator of excellent control of furycraft. So. The cub had grown into a wolf after all.

The strange buzzing sounds continued, and Invidia could see something striking the watery image, small splashes of water leaping up as if a boy had been throwing stones. Invidia called upon her windcrafting to slow the motion of the objects, to focus more closely upon them. Upon closer inspection, they appeared to be hornets. They were not hornets, of course, but seemed to be of the same general wickedly swift and quietly threatening appearance. Their bodies were longer, and sported two sets of wings, and they flew faster than any hornet and in perfectly straight lines. As she watched, one of the hornet-things struck at the water image, its abdomen bending forward to expose a gleaming, serrated spear of vord chitin as long as Invidia's index finger. It hit the water image with an explosion of force and came tumbling out the other side to fall stunned into the water.

Invidia shivered. There were dozens, if not hundreds, of the things swarming out from innocuous lumps in the *croach*.

"Enough," the Queen said, raising a hand, and the series of impacts came to an abrupt halt. The buzzing hums ceased, as did the trilling shrieks of the wax spiders, and silence fell. The surface of the pool rippled as thousands of larval takers came up to tear at the bodies of the stunned hornets.

The Queen stared at the image in silence. Minutes passed.

"He copies us," the Queen hissed.

"He understands why we chose to appear this way," Invidia replied. She looked down the shallow valley, focusing upon her windcrafting to magnify her sight of the next larval pool. An image of Octavian stood there as well. "He means to address all of Alera, as we did."

"He is that strong?" the Queen demanded.

"So it would seem."

"You told me his gifts were stunted."

"It would appear that I was mistaken," Invidia replied.

The Queen snarled and stared at the image.

A moment later, it finally spoke. Octavian's voice was a resonant, mellow baritone, his expression calm, his posture confident and steady. "Greetings, Alerans, freemen and Citizens alike. I am Octavian, son of Septimus, son of Gaius Sextus, the First Lord of Alera. I am returned from my journey to Canea and have come to defend my home and my people."

The vord Queen let out a rippling hiss, an utterly inhuman sound.

"The vord have come, and have dealt us a grievous wound," Octavian continued. "We mourn for those who have already perished, for the cities that have been overrun, for the homes and lives that have been destroyed. By now, you know that the enemy has overrun Alera Imperia. You know that all of the great cities still standing face imminent attack if they are not besieged already. You know that the vord have cut off tens of thousands of Alerans from retreat to safety. You know that the *croach* is growing to devour all that we know and all that we are."

Octavian's eyes flashed with sudden fire. "But there are other things that you do not know. You do not know that the Legions of the Shield cities have united with those gathered from other cities into the largest, most experienced, battle-hardened force ever fielded in the history of our people. You do not know that every Knight and Citizen of the Realm has banded together to fight this menace, under the leadership of my brother, Gaius Aquitainus Attis. You do not know that not only is this war not over—it has not yet begun.

"For two thousand years, our people have worked and fought and bled and died to secure the safety of our homes and families. For two thousand years, we have persevered, survived, and conquered. For two thousand years, the Legions have stood as our sword and shield against those who would destroy us."

Octavian threw back his head, his eyes harder than stone, his expression as calm and fixed as the granite of a mountain. "The Legions are *still* our sword! They are *still* our shield! And they *will* defend us from this threat as they have all the others. In a thousand years, when the histories are read, they will mark this season as the deadliest of our time. And in a thousand years, they will *still* know of our valor, our strength. They will know that the House of Gaius gave their lives and blood, fought with sword and fury against this foe, and that all of Alera stood with us! They will know that we are *Alerans*! And that this land is *ours*!"

A surge of emotion rolled over Invidia, so intense that she staggered to one knee. It combined exaltation and hope and terror and rage, all bound together so inextricably that they could not *be* separated from one another. She fought to strengthen her metalcrafting, to blunt the impact of the emotions, and realized with some dull, dazed corner of her mind that the tide was flowing over her from the direction of the little captive steadholt.

Octavian continued, his voice harder and quieter than before. "Like you, I saw the face of the enemy. I saw her offer you peace. But be sure, my country-men, that all she offers is the peace of the grave; that she offers nothing less than the utter destruction of all of our kind, both those living today and those who have gone before us. She asks us to lie meekly upon the earth and wait for our throats to be cut, to bleed painlessly to the death of our entire race."

His voice turned gentle. "I say to you this: The freemen of Alera are free. They are free to do as they think best. They are free to take what measures they wish to ensure the safety of their loved ones. Especially for those folk caught behind the lines, it is understandable that some of you may seek the safety of surrender. That is a choice you must make within your own hearts. When the vord are defeated, no recrimination will be levied, regardless of your decision.

"But as for you, Citizens of the Realm, who have for so long enjoyed the power and privilege of your station, the time for you to prove your worth has come. Act. Fight. Lead those who would stand beside you. Any Citizen who surrenders to the vord will, in the eyes of the Crown, be considered a traitor to the Realm.

"I can promise you only this: Those who fight will not fight alone. You are not forgotten. We *will* come for you. My grandfather fought the vord tooth and nail. He fought until he died to protect the lives of his people. Gaius Sextus set the standard by which our posterity will judge us all. I will not accept less from any other Citizen of the Realm. Not from you. Not from myself.

"Our foe is mighty but not invulnerable. Tell your friends and neighbors what you have heard here tonight. Stand. Fight. We will come for you. We *will* survive." The image fell silent for a moment—and then, unnervingly, turned to stare directly at the vord Queen. "You."

Invidia took a short breath and checked the other pools.

The water images had disappeared.

"That's him," Invidia hissed. "It is Octavian's sending."

"You," Octavian said, staring at the vord Queen. "You killed my grandfather."

The vord Queen lifted her chin. "Yes."

"I offer you this chance," Octavian said, and his voice was cold, calm, and all the more menacing for it. "Leave Alera. Flee back to Canea. Take with you any of your kind you wish to survive."

The Queen smiled with the tiniest twitch of a single corner of her mouth. "Why should I do that?"

"Because I'm coming," Octavian's image said, very quietly, "for you."

The Queen stood as unmoving as stone.

"When I'm finished," Octavian promised, "nothing will be left of your kind but stories. I will burn your homes. I will bury your warriors." His voice grew even softer. "I will blacken your sky with crows."

Gaius Octavian's image sank with perfect, controlled grace into the water.

And then he was gone.

The pool was very still.

The vord Queen lifted her hands and slowly drew up her hood. Then she resettled her cloak around her though Invidia knew perfectly well that she was all but unaffected by temperature. The vord didn't move for several moments—then, abruptly, she let out a hiss and turned, bounding into the air and summoning up a gale of wind to bear her aloft, streaking toward the little steadholt.

Invidia called upon her furies to race after the Queen and caught up to her by the time they had reached the steadholt. They descended together, landing in the central yard. The Queen streaked toward one of the homes, smashed the door to splinters, and darted inside.

Invidia braced herself, her stomach twisting in agonized anticipation. She wished those poor holders no ill—but she could do nothing to save them from the Queen's wrath.

Crashing sounds came from inside the house. Then a wall exploded outward, and the Queen smashed her way into the cottage next door. Again came the sounds of furious destruction. Then the Queen smashed her way into the next cottage. And the next. And the next, moving so swiftly that there was no time for screams.

Invidia drew a deep breath. Then, deliberately, she forced herself to walk to the first house—the one with the little family they had visited weeks before. Invidia could have killed the Queen earlier that evening. If she had, those holders might not have died. The least she could do for them was force herself to look upon what she had wrought by her inaction.

Stones crunched beneath the chitin armoring her feet as she approached, smelling the woodsmoke of the makeshift family's fire. She steeled herself for a moment against what she would see, then stepped through the front door.

The kitchen table was smashed. Pots were strewn everywhere. Broken dishes littered the floor. Two windows had been shattered.

And the little house was empty.

Invidia stared in incomprehension for a moment. Then, in dawning realization, she rushed back out the door and went to the next house.

As empty as the first.

She left the cottage and studied the ground. The stones that crunched beneath her feet were not stones. They were the bodies of hundreds of the vord hornets, their stingers still extended in death, shattered, bent, and twisted.

The vord Queen let out a furious wail, and redoubled sounds of destruction came from inside another home. Within seconds, the place simply collapsed in on itself, and the Queen emerged from it, her alien eyes strange in her furious features, tossing aside a crossbeam as thick as her thigh and several hundred pounds of stone with a flick of one arm.

"Tricked," hissed the Queen. "*Tricked.* While I listened to his words, he *took* my steadholt away from me!"

Invidia said nothing. She fought to keep herself calm. She had never seen the vord Queen so angry. Not while she was disemboweling her traitorous child. Not when Gaius Sextus had all but annihilated her army at Alera Imperia. Never.

Invidia was well aware that she was one of the most dangerous human beings on the face of Carna. She also knew that the vord Queen would tear her apart without growing short of breath. She focused on being silent, calm, and part of the background. The raid had been flawless. Octavian had not only let his image stand there to give Alerans time to gather—he had used it to trigger any defenses around the little steadholt, revealing them to the raiders. Once aware of the vord hornets, his men had evidently been able to circumvent them.

She'd sensed the rescue attempt when it had begun. The surge of hope from the other side of the hill. And she'd assumed it was a result of his speech and actually spent effort blocking it out.

She thought it would be best not to mention that fact to the near-berserk Queen. Ever.

"He took the dogs," the Queen snarled. "He took the cat. He took the *livestock.* He left me *nothing!*" She looked around her, at the empty shell of the steadholt, and with a gesture of one hand disintegrated a cottage in a sudden sphere of white-hot fire.

Pieces of molten stone flew everywhere. Some of it arched high enough to come raining down like falling stars, several seconds later.

Then the Queen went still again. She stayed that way for a moment and turned abruptly to begin stalking toward the nearest edge of the *croach*. She made a curt gesture to the Aleran woman as she went.

Invidia fell into step behind the Queen. "What will you do?"

The vord looked over her shoulder at Invidia, her fine white hair in wild disarray, her pale cheek smudged with soot and dust and earth. "He has taken from me," she hissed, her voice quavering with alien rage. "He has hurt me. He has *hurt* me." Her claws made that stretching-tearing sound again. "Now I will take from *him*."

⌐□⌐□⌐□⌐□⌐CHAPTER 7

Valiar Marcus entered the command tent and saluted. Octavian glanced back and nodded at him, beckoning Marcus to come in. The captain looked weary and ragged after the effort he'd expended to send forth the watercrafting he'd used to address all of Alera, but he had not slept since then. He'd spent the night in the command tent, reading reports and poring over maps and sand tables. A small pool, crafted into existence by Legion engineers, occupied one corner of the tent.

The Princeps stood before the little pool, looking down at a shrunken image of Tribune Antillus Crassus, which stood upon the water's surface. "How many holders did you get out of there?"

"Eighty-three," Crassus replied. His voice was very distant and dim, as if coming down a long tunnel. "All of them, sire—and their beasts and livestock, too."

The captain barked out a short laugh. "You had fliers enough for that?"

"It seemed a good statement to make to the enemy, sire," Crassus replied, one corner of his mouth turning up in a small smirk. "We had to drop them off within a few hours, but at least they won't go to feeding the *croach* anytime soon."

Tavi nodded. "Casualties?"

Crassus's expression sobered. "Two so far."

Marcus saw steely tension stiffen Octavian's shoulders. "So far?"

"You were right. The vord had defensive measures in place—this kind of hornet thing. They came flying up out of the *croach* like balest bolts when your image appeared in the pool." Crassus's expression remained calm, but his voice sounded ragged. "They had stingers that could drive right through lumber or mail. We were able to stiffen the plates of the lorica with battlecrafting, enough to keep the little bastards from punching through. If we hadn't been able to prepare for it . . . crows, sire, I don't want to think about it. We did well enough, but their stingers were poisoned, and wherever they hit flesh instead of steel, our folk got hurt. I lost two men last night, and another dozen who were hit are getting sicker."

"Have you tried watercrafting?"

Crassus shook his head. "Hasn't been time. We had a sky full of vordknights to worry about. I'm nearly certain that some of the windcrafters the vord turned are spooking around on our back trail. We had to stay ahead of them."

Octavian frowned. "You're out of occupied territory?"

"For now."

"Do you have time to make the attempt at a healing?"

Crassus shook his head. "I doubt it. The vord are still trying to find us. I think the best chance for the wounded is to get them back to the Legion healers."

Marcus saw the captain debating with himself. A commander was always tempted to involve himself too much in whatever mission was under way. But to lead, one had to maintain a rational perspective. Octavian couldn't assess the men's condition himself or the disposition or skills of the enemy. Yet he did not want more of his men's lives to be needlessly lost. The temptation to override the judgment of a field commander had to have been very strong.

The captain sighed. "I'll have the healers ready for you the moment you land."

Crassus's image nodded. "Thank you, sir."

"That much pursuit," the captain mused. "The vord Queen was upset?"

Crassus shuddered. "Sir . . . we were at least ten miles away from her hive, and we *heard* her screaming. Believe me, I didn't have any trouble convincing the men to fly all night without resting."

"She has handles, then," the captain mused. "We can make that work for us. I'm sure of it." He frowned at the Tribune. "What is your plan?"

"I'm going to give the men a couple of hours rest, then we'll start again. We'll cross two more bands of *croach* before we get back. I'm expecting more vordknights to be in position to intercept us."

"Don't let them."

"No, sir," Crassus said.

The captain nodded. "Good work, Tribune."

Crassus's eyes flashed at the compliment, and he slammed a fist to his heart in a sharp salute. The captain returned it, then passed his hand over the image. Within seconds, the water from which it had formed returned smoothly and silently to the pool.

The captain sank onto a camp stool and pressed the heels of both hands against his forehead.

"Sir," Marcus said. "You should rest."

"Presently," the captain replied wearily. "Presently."

"Sir," Marcus began, "with all due respect you sound just like—" He barely caught himself in time to avoid betraying himself. *Just like your grandfather.* Valiar Marcus hadn't been a close professional colleague of Gaius Sextus. He *couldn't* know what the First Lord had been like in private. "Just like a new recruit trying to tell me he'll be able to finish the march just fine, even though the soles of his feet are one big blister, and he's got a broken ankle."

A faint smile touched the captain's mouth. "Right after we're done, then."

"Very good, sir. How may I help you?"

The captain lowered his hands and eyed Marcus. "What do you know about Marat courtship customs?"

Marcus blinked slowly. "Excuse me?"

"Courtship among the Marat," Octavian said wearily. "What do you know about it?"

"I'm sure Magnus would know more than me, sir."

The captain waved an irritated hand. "I asked him already. He said once he'd learned about how they would occasionally devour their enemies, he knew all he needed to want nothing to do with them."

Marcus snorted. "Certain amount of sense in that, sir. The Marat can be dangerous."

The captain scowled. "Tell me about it. After you tell me what you know about their courtship."

"You figuring on keeping the Ambassador, then?"

"It's not that simple," the captain replied.

"Should say not. Lot of Citizens aren't going to like that idea."

"The crows can have them," the captain replied. "The only people making this decision are me and Kitai."

Marcus grunted. "I've heard stories."

"Like what?"

Marcus shrugged. "The usual. That they mate with their beasts. That they participate in blood rites and orgies before battle." He suppressed a shudder. He'd seen that last with his own eyes, and it was the material of nightmare, not fantasy. "That their females are beaten until they submit to the will of a husband."

The captain let out a loud snort at this last.

Marcus nodded slowly. "Aye. If the Aeldenwalde is any indication, that last one is just so much dandelion fluff."

"Anything else?"

Marcus pursed his lips and debated with himself. Valiar Marcus couldn't be expected to know much of the Marat or their customs. On the other hand, a well-connected, respected northern soldier knew a lot of folk. Some of them would travel. Some of them would return with stories. And . . .

And, Marcus realized, he wanted to help the captain.

"I served with a fellow who became the chief of armsmen for a fairly large merchant family," he said finally. "He told me something about a contest."

The captain frowned and leaned forward intently. "Contest?"

Marcus grunted in the affirmative. "Apparently a Marat woman has the right to demand a trial by contest of her prospective groom. Or maybe it was a trial by combat. He wasn't real clear on the point."

Octavian arched a raven black eyebrow. "You're kidding."

The First Spear shrugged. "All I know." That much was true. Even the Cursors had known little apart from the barbarians' military capabilities. Information on Marat society was fairly scanty. The two peoples had, for the most part, practiced avoiding one another. It had been sufficient to know the threat that they represented, so that the Legions could counter them effectively.

Certainly, no one had ever ordered a Cursor to find out how to propose to a Marat woman.

"Trial by combat," Octavian muttered darkly under his breath. Marcus thought he might have said, "Perfect."

Marcus kept a straight face. "Love is a wonderful thing, sir."

Octavian gave him a sour look. "Did you get the reports from Vanorius?"

Marcus opened up a leather case on his belt and passed a roll of papers to the captain. "Thanks to Magnus, yes, sir."

The captain took the papers, leaned his hip against a sand table, and started reading. "You've read them?"

"Aye."

"Your thoughts?"

Marcus pursed his lips. "The vord exist in overwhelming numbers, but they don't appear to be all that bright without a queen to guide them. There's always some fighting at the city sieges, but the besieged High Lords' problems and solutions more closely resemble being trapped in a heavy blizzard than waging war."

Octavian flipped a page, his green eyes rapidly scanning the next. "Go on."

"The enemy has a large force on the move, toward Riva. They should have gotten there already, but Aquitaine burned all the ground between Riva and the old capital right down to the bloody dirt. It appears to have slowed them down."

The captain grimaced and shook his head. "How long before they engage Aquitaine?"

"Tough to say. Assuming their pace remains as slow as it is now, another twelve to fourteen days." Marcus frowned, and said, "Even if they assault the Legions and lose, they could strike us a death blow unless we've taken out the Queen. If she tells them to, they'll fight to the last wax spider. They'll take the lion's share of our strength with them."

"And she'll simply make more," Octavian said.

"Yes, sir."

"I'd say our best option is to be there in twelve to fourteen days, then. Wouldn't you?"

Marcus felt his eyebrows try to climb up to his hairline. "That isn't going to happen. We don't have causeways. We'll never cover that distance in time to join the battle. We don't have enough fliers to shuttle in a viable number of ground troops."

Octavian's eyes glittered, and he smiled. The expression transformed the features of the normally serious young man. It was the grin of a boy with a good prank in mind. "Did you know," he said, "that Alera reached a peace agreement with the Icemen?"

"Sir? I heard something about it, but you hear a lot of things in a Legion rumor mill."

Tavi nodded. "You know Lord Vanorius?"

"Aye, somewhat. We spoke regularly when I was serving Antillus. Always on Legion business."

"Go to him," Tavi said. "We need woodcrafters. I want every Knight Flora, every Citizen with woodcrafting, and every professional woodworker in Antillus to report to this camp by dawn."

"Sir?" Marcus said. "I'm not sure I understand."

"Really?" Octavian said, that smile flickering to life again, if briefly. "Because I'm quite certain that you don't."

"Woodcrafters."

"Yes," said the captain.

Marcus lifted an eyebrow warily as his fist rose to his heart in salute. "What do you want me to tell Vanorius when he asks why you need them?"

"Operational security," the captain said. "And if that doesn't work, inform him that disobeying a lawful order of the Crown in time of war is considered treason." His eyes hardened. "I am not making a request."

"Yes, sir," Marcus said.

Outside the tent, a sentry challenged a halfling, and a rumbling basso voice replied in snarling tones. A second later, one of the sentries leaned into the tent, and said, "Pair of messengers from the Canim, Captain."

Octavian nodded and beckoned with one hand. "Show them in, please."

Marcus wasn't familiar with the two Canim who entered the tent a moment later, stooping slightly to keep their ears from brushing the ceiling. One, a dark-furred brute, was dressed in battered old warrior-caste armor that was missing two or three pieces. The other, a lean and golden-furred individual with beady eyes, wore the riveted-steel jacket that had become the main armor for the now-veteran Canim militia.

Marcus felt a little shock of realization go through him. Varg would never send a warrior on courier duty at all, much less one who presented such a slipshod appearance as this one. And the golden-furred Cane was, most likely, a Shuaran, the only Canim any Aleran had ever seen with that shade of fur. The Shuaran Canim had not come to Alera with Sarl's invasion force. They had never left Canea. They could therefore never have become members of Nasaug's war-trained militia—and it would have been as good as asking to be torn to pieces for a nonmilitia Cane to falsely claim membership in those ranks. Canim pride was ferocious, jealous, and bloodily decisive.

Perhaps a shoddily armored warrior could have been sent on a message run. Perhaps the golden-furred Cane had been in the ranks all along, and Alerans had simply never noted his presence. Either of those things was remotely possible.

But both of them?

Marcus scratched at his nose with a fingertip, and when he lowered his hand again, it came to rest within an inch of his sword's hilt. He flicked a glance at Octavian, hoping to warn him.

There was no need. The captain had evidently reached the same conclusions as Marcus, and though he remained outwardly calm, he surreptitiously hooked a thumb through his belt, which placed it in close proximity to the handle of the dagger sheathed at the small of his back.

"Good morning," Octavian said politely, tilting his head very slightly to one side in a salute of superior to subordinate. "Did you gentlemen have something for me?"

The armored Cane shuffled forward a few steps, reaching into a pouch at his side.

His paw-hand emerged clenching a stone knife. The armored Cane roared, in Canish, "One people!"

And slashed at the captain's throat.

Marcus felt his heart leap into his mouth. The captain was a capable opponent when he employed his metalcrafting, but that ability would do him no good against a stone weapon. Without the forewarning of his metalcrafting of the weapon's approach, he would be forced to pit his raw physical ability against the Cane's—and without furycraft to aid them, no Aleran could match the power of a Cane, and only the fastest could match their speed.

Octavian jerked his head back and the slash missed by a hair. He dropped back, taking a pair of spinning steps as he drew the dagger from his belt and flung it. The weapon tumbled one and a half times and sank into an unarmored portion of the Cane's thigh. The Cane howled in sudden pain, stumbling.

"Sir!" Marcus shouted, drawing and lofting his *gladius* in a single motion. He didn't stop to see if Octavian caught it. He charged the second Cane, who had produced a slender wooden tube. As Marcus approached, the Cane lifted the tube to his mouth and exhaled, and a little flash of color and steel flew out the end. Marcus ducked his head and felt the missile ping against the good Aleran steel of his helmet. Then he called out to his earth fury as he barreled into the would-be assassin.

The Cane was viciously strong, but inexperienced. The two of them went to the ground hard, and instead of immediately attempting to escape, the Cane started thrashing his limbs in a useless attempt to sink claws or fangs into Marcus. There was no time to capture the opponent. He had to remove the gold-furred Cane from the fight and go to Octavian's aid. Marcus seized one of the Cane's wrists in a bone-pulverizing grip, then slammed his other fist down onto the Cane's head, shattering his foe's skull with the power of the fury-enhanced strike.

Marcus looked back up to see the captain break the Cane's crude stone blade with a swift move of his *gladius* and go on to deliver four lightning-fast slashes to the armored Cane. Any two of them would probably have been fatal, but the captain was nothing if not thorough. He struck until he was sure the attacker was completely incapacitated, and whirled toward Marcus and the second Cane, sword lifted in his hand to strike.

The two men faced one another as the armored Cane toppled slowly and limply to the ground behind the captain, and Marcus had a startling realization: Octavian's reasoning had been identical to his own. He had struck to dispatch his opponent swiftly and immediately so that he could go to the other man's aid.

Octavian's eyes scanned Marcus and the Cane with the broken head. Then he turned back to his own dead opponent, scowling. "Crows," he growled. "Bloody crows."

The sentries burst in. Without hesitation, they both plunged swords into the Cane Marcus had downed. Like captain, like *legionare*, Marcus supposed. When they approached the second downed Cane, the captain waved a hand at them. "Finished." He looked up. "Marcus. Are you hurt?"

"I'll manage," Marcus said, panting. He was in shape enough to keep pace with the Legion, but he had been on a ship for months, and there had been no real way to remain in proper Legion condition.

And face it. You're getting old.

Octavian wiped Marcus's *gladius* clean of blood on the dark fur of the dead Cane, then offered the weapon back to him, hilt first. Marcus nodded his thanks, inspected the weapon for stains or damage, found it serviceable, and slid it back into its sheath.

Octavian glanced at Marcus, and said, simply, "Thank you." Then he strode from the tent, rigid with anger, or perhaps in simple reaction to the attempt on his life.

The three *legionares* stared after him. "What happened?" asked one of the sentries. "I thought we were supposed to be allies."

Marcus grunted and sent them on their way to follow the captain with a slap on an armored shoulder. "So did I, soldier. So did I."

CHAPTER 8

"For goodness sake, my lady," Veradis said in a tranquil tone. "You must calm yourself."

Isana cast a mildly irritated glance over her shoulder at the younger woman as she paced back and forth across her quarters, the largest room in Riva's finest inn. "How can I relax, knowing the kind of men I'm about to be dealing with?"

"Not every man in the Senate is some kind of masterful schemer, exerting all his energies to acquire more power and influence at the expense of all others."

"No," Isana agreed. "Some of them are *incompetent* schemers."

Veradis arched an eyebrow, her expression taking on a quality of mild disapproval.

Isana exhaled. She folded her hands before her and took a deep breath, making an effort to still her emotions. "I'm sorry. Now that we know my son is back, they're going to push that much harder to take away his birthright. I shouldn't be pushing that burden onto your thoughts, Veradis."

"Of course you should, my lady," Veradis replied. "That is one of the things an aide is for. That, and to suggest that you might take a different kerchief with you to the Senate hearing. You've all but shredded that one." The young woman rose and paced solemnly to stand before Isana, offering a folded white handkerchief. Isana took it with a faint smile.

"Only a man with a certain frame of mind does well as a Senator," Veradis told her quietly. "He has to be able to speak well. He has to be able to convince others to follow his point of view. He has to be willing to negotiate and make compromises. And most of all, he has to protect the Citizens who voted him into the office—his own interests. That before all. So long as his constituents are pleased, he is safe in his position." Veradis moved her shoulders in an elegant shrug. "Senators go to great lengths to protect the interests of those who voted for them. Some of them tiptoe along the boundaries between legitimate representation and criminal enterprise. Some of them dance gleefully back and forth over the line."

The young Cerean met Isana's eyes, and said, "But in their own way, you can rely upon them more than almost any man in the Realm. They *will* act to protect their interests. Which means that they make enemies among their peers. You can rely upon them to settle up old debts or compound them, my lady."

Isana smiled faintly. "Senator Theoginus said almost the same thing."

Veradis smiled. "Uncle Theo is an incorrigible old horse trader. But he knows that room, my lady."

"Can he be trusted?" Isana asked.

Veradis considered that gravely. "Under the circumstances, I believe so. Valerius is from Aquitaine, after all—one of the cities most separated from the vord threat. Uncle was one of the men who most wanted action taken on Count Calderon's warning about the vord, and Valerius all but crucified him for it. If Uncle Theo says he has strong support among the Senators of those areas most harmed by the vord, I'd say he's almost certainly honest, and that it is highly probable that he is also correct."

Isana shook her head. "You had to stop to consider whether or not your own uncle might be lying to you."

"My uncle the Senator," Veradis said, her serious eyes sparkling for a moment. "Yes, my lady. I love him. And I know him."

"I suppose it's rather late to be revisiting that concern," Isana said. "They must have convened by now."

Veradis nodded. "My lady . . . regardless of today's outcome, you should know that there are a great many people to whom you will always be the true First Lady of Alera."

Isana held up a hand. "No, Veradis. Too much is at stake. The one thing certain to destroy us is division. Despite recent history, I believe that Alera is a Realm of law. If its lawmakers so decide . . ." She shook her head. "To attempt to hold on, to defy them openly, would only hurt the Realm. We absolutely *must* avoid turning our focus upon fighting one another instead of keeping it where it should be."

There was nothing to betray it in her face, but Isana sensed the sudden sharpening of Veradis's interest. "If Valerius has his way, you will be nothing but a Steadholder again. Your son would be but one more bastard child of the Citizenry. And Aquitainus Attis, the man responsible for the Second Battle of Calderon, and the deaths of your friends and neighbors, will rule the Realm."

"Exactly," Isana replied. "The Realm. Which will still be here." She shook her head and sighed. "I haven't forgotten what he's done. But we won't survive what's coming unless we stand together. If that means that I must . . ." She shrugged. "If I must accept that I will return to my home, the richer by many enemies, and that Aquitaine will never need to answer for what he did to the Calderon Valley, so be it."

Veradis nodded slowly. Then she asked, "And Octavian. Will he see it the same way?"

Isana considered the question for a moment. Then she nodded. "I believe so. Yes."

"Even though," Veradis said, "you know that should Alera prevail against the vord, Aquitaine could not possibly afford to leave Octavian alive and at liberty, after."

Isana grimaced. Then she lifted her chin, Aquitaine's strong, appealing face appearing in her mind's eye, and told Veradis, "Should Aquitaine become First Lord, he would be well-advised to choose his battles—and his enemies—with great care."

Veradis stared at her intently, then slowly shook her head.

Isana tilted her chin to one side, frowning inquisitively.

"My father used to speak to me often of the nature of power," Veradis said. "One of the things he often lamented was that the only folk truly worthy to hold it were those who did not seek it."

Isana frowned. "I don't understand."

Veradis smiled, and for a moment there was nothing solemn or sad in her face. Isana was struck by the young woman's delicate beauty. "I know you don't," she said. "Thus proving my father's point." She bowed her head, a stately and formal gesture, and said, "I will abide by your wishes, my lady."

Isana was about to reply when there was a quick rap at the door, and Araris leaned inside. "My lady," he murmured, bowing his head, "you have a visitor."

Isana arched an eyebrow as she turned toward the door and smoothed her dress. Whatever the Senate decided, they would send a representative to bring her before them—but her senses told her that Araris's usual steady calm was shaken to one degree or another. The Senate's choice in escorts would say much about the outcome of the debate.

"Thank you, Araris. Please send him in."

Isana wasn't sure whom she had been expecting, but Aquitainus Attis hadn't been featured on her mental list. The High Lord entered, resplendent in scarlet and black, though he had affixed the official Crown heraldry for the House of Gaius, the scarlet-and-azure eagle, to his tunic's breast. His dark golden hair was immaculate, even weighted down by the slender steel circlet of the Aleran crown, and his dark eyes were as intense and focused as every other time Isana had seen the man.

Aquitaine bowed his head politely, if very slightly. "Lady," he murmured.

"Lord Aquitaine," Isana replied, holding her tone to neutrality. "What an unexpected . . ." She smiled, faintly. ". . . visit."

"The timing was important. With all the Senators in chambers, their informants are neglecting their duties. I would speak with you alone if you are willing."

"You are a married man, sir," Isana replied, with no trace of accusation anywhere in the phrase. It was considerably more damning that way, she thought. "I think it would be highly inappropriate."

"In truth," Aquitaine replied, "I have already certified my divorce from Invidia, effective as of today."

"What a terrible burden has been lifted from your shoulders," Isana said.

Aquitaine inhaled slowly, through his nose, and exhaled the same way. Isana felt the faintest trace of frustration from the man. It was rapidly walled away behind a metalcrafting.

"I would prefer," Aquitaine said, "to have this discussion privately."

Isana regarded him as though waiting for him to finish his sentence.

"Please," Aquitaine added, his voice not quite a growl.

Veradis cleared her throat, and said, "I will wait outside, my lady."

"As you wish," Isana said. "But Araris stays with me."

Araris came through the door at a pace that suggested he'd begun moving before Isana had finished the sentence. He held it open for Veradis, then closed it behind her as she left.

Aquitaine smiled. "You don't trust me, lady?"

Isana smiled at him and did not answer.

Aquitaine let out a brief, rather harsh laugh. "There are few who would behave in such a manner toward me, Isana, and with good reason. I do not regard myself as an unreasonable man, but neither do I react well to discourtesy and disrespect."

"If you were the First Lord," she replied, "that might be a problem. But you aren't."

He narrowed his eyes. "Aren't I?"

"Not yet," Isana said in a tone that stopped just short of being belligerent. She met the man's eyes calmly for a full minute of silence, then dropped her voice into a more conversational register. "Unless the Senate has already told you how the outcome of the hearing would fall out, I suppose."

Aquitaine shook his head and responded in kind. "Valerius, of course, assures me that it will all happen precisely the way he intends. Lamentably, I am aware of the value of such promises."

She gave him another sharp look, and his mouth spread into a leonine smile. "You thought I'd come here to gloat over your dismissal, lady?"

"The possibility had occurred to me," she admitted.

He shook his head. "I don't have the time to waste on such a petty gesture."

"Then why have you come?"

Aquitaine crossed to the room's sideboard and poured wine from a bottle into a waiting glass. He took it up and swirled it lazily around the inside of the glass. "The Senators are, of course, in a frenzy. They sense a chance to reduce the powers of the office of First Lord, despite the ugly realities before us. And, if they have their way—and Alera survives, of course—then they will succeed. And we already saw what happens after a weakening of the office of the First Lord of Alera. Regardless of how things play out in the future, you and I have a common interest in defending it."

Isana studied him as he cautiously took a sip of wine. Then she said, "Let's assume for a moment that I agree. What are you proposing?"

"Marriage," Aquitaine said calmly.

Isana found herself sitting in a chair with no clear recollection of how she had gotten there. She just stared at Aquitaine while her lips took their time to form her next words, as a flash of blazing-hot, blindly jealous rage flashed forth from Araris, who stood rock-still with his back to the door. He bottled it quickly, moving one hand to the hilt of his sword as he did, but all the same that single searing surge of emotion left Isana feeling off-balance, as if she'd come out of a dark cellar to stare directly into the sun. After a moment, she managed to choke out a few words. "Are you insane?"

Aquitaine's teeth flashed again. "It's an insane line of work," he responded.

"But it actually is a viable solution. I would retain the crown, with the line of succession passing to your son upon my death or retirement. And, given the nature of our relationship, his personal safety would become my responsibility, lest I lose the respect of the Citizenry for not being able to protect my own heir."

"And what about your children?" Isana asked.

"I have none," Aquitaine replied. "None of which I am aware, in any case—and I certainly have no legitimate heirs. And since your watercrafting will enable you to control completely whether or not I *do* manage to sire a legitimate heir, you can choose never to bear me children—in which case Octavian ascends smoothly to the Crown when he is older, wiser, and more ready to lead the Realm."

Isana narrowed her eyes in thought. "Of course," she said, "if something should happen to me, you would be free to take another wife. In that event, the child she bore you would have a claim upon the throne—a claim blocked by my son."

Aquitaine let out a rueful chuckle. "Invidia was ever an artist of treachery," he said. "I see that you did not survive your association with her by happy accident."

"Additionally," Isana continued, "how could you ever be certain that I was not plotting to remove *you*, once your guard was down?"

"Because you won't," Aquitaine said simply. "You aren't that kind of person."

"The kind of person willing to kill to protect her child?"

"The kind who stabs another in the back," he said. "You'd be looking into my eyes. I can live with that."

Isana just stared at the man. Aquitaine, to her, had always been simply the male counterpart of Invidia, a partner in her ruthless political enterprises. She would never have guessed that he might be the sort to understand that not every person was plotting against all the others, capable of murder and treachery when it provided enough gain. Though perhaps it should have come as no surprise. Invidia had been capable of seeing fidelity in others, an essential core of . . . of honor, Isana supposed, that made their word worth more than a few seconds of warm breath.

She had certainly exploited that trait in Isana.

"Tell me," Isana said. "What possible reason I could have to pursue this plan instead of supporting the lawful succession of the Realm?"

"Three reasons," he responded without pause. "First, because doing so would obviate the need for the current struggle in the Senate, pulling the teeth of the various Senators involved. Valerius has driven this conflict forward predicated on the notion that this is a time of war and we need an immediate, settled chain of command. Our union would steal Valerius's thunder, prevent the Senate from gathering into separate factions over the issue, and avoid setting a dangerous precedent of the Senate dictating terms to the office of the First Lord."

"Second?"

"Because it would mean that I would have neither reason to harm your son nor need to defend myself against him. Octavian is capable, I freely acknowledge. But by dint of experience and advantage of position, I am more so. Any struggle for power between us would be disastrous for him, personally, and for the Realm as a whole."

It would have been easier to sneer at Aquitaine's remark, Isana thought, if she hadn't just pressed that same point upon Veradis so emphatically.

"And third," Aquitaine said, "because it's going to save lives. The vord are coming. Too much time has already been wasted precisely because there are lingering doubts about who truly wears the crown. Each day, our enemy grows stronger. Whether Octavian wears the crown or I, these days of doubt are paralyzing us. I am here. He is not."

Isana quirked an eyebrow at him. "I wonder, Lord Aquitaine, if you happened to be standing near a pool last night. Or any other body of water."

Aquitaine lifted a hand palm up in a gesture of concession. "Granted, he is most likely alive and back from Canea. Granted, his display of power was impressive . . ." Aquitaine shook his head, his expression reminding Isana of a man preparing to eat something he found distasteful. "Not impressive. Inspiring. His words to our own people meant more than a simple declaration of his presence. He brought them courage. He brought them hope."

"The way a First Lord should," Isana said.

"He must still be on the west coastline, somewhere. It is a long march from there to here, Lady Isana. If our folk are allowed to remain uncertain of who leads them until he arrives, it may already be too late for any of us to see another spring. I believe that we can avoid that by openly working together. The willing union of our houses will put the minds of the Citizenry and people alike at rest. If we allow the Senate to decide, there will always be doubts, questions, cadres, and conspiracies, no matter which of us has the throne."

Aquitaine stepped forward and held out his hand. "I will not live forever. I may well fall in the coming war. Either way, in the end, the crown will be his. We will have no need to test one another. Lives will be saved. Our people will be given their single greatest chance to survive."

Another flash of rage slapped against Isana's senses, as Araris took half a step forward from his position by the door. This time it was sharp enough that

Aquitaine felt it, too. He turned to blink at Araris several times. Then he looked back and forth between them, and said, "Ah. I hadn't realized."

"I think you should leave, Attis," Araris said. His voice was quiet and very, very even. "It would be better for all of us."

"What's happening outside these walls is more important than you, Araris," Aquitaine said calmly. "It is more important than I. And while your penchant for defending women for the wrong reasons remains undimmed, your emotions are completely irrelevant to the problem at hand."

Araris's eyes flashed, and another surge of anger pressed against Isana. She fancied she could feel it bending back her eyelashes. "Odd," Araris said. "I don't see it that way."

Aquitaine shook his head, a precise and meaningless smile on his mouth. "We aren't a pack of schoolboys anymore, Araris. I have no particular desire for any intimacy beyond that which is required for the sake of appearance," he said. "As far as I am concerned, I would be well pleased for you to live your private life in whatever manner you chose, Lady Isana."

"Araris," Isana said quietly, and held up her hand.

His eyes remained on Aquitaine for another hot second. Then he glanced at her, frowning, as she silently urged him to understand what she was going to do. After an endless number of heartbeats, Araris visibly relaxed and returned to his position by the door.

Aquitaine watched the swordsman withdraw and turned back to Isana, frowning thoughtfully. He stared at her for a long moment, then slowly lowered his hand, and said, "Your answer is no."

"Your offer is . . . reasonable, Lord Aquitaine," she said. "Very, very reasonable. And your arguments are sound. But the price you ask is too high."

"Price?"

She smiled slightly. "You would have me give my world to this plan. Abandon things it has taken a lifetime to build. Embrace deceits and empty ideas. It would leave my mind and heart a wasted heath, as burned and empty and as useless as all those farms you destroyed to slow the vord."

Aquitaine looked thoughtful for a moment. Then he nodded, and said, "I do not understand. But I must accept your answer."

"Yes. I think you must."

He frowned. "Octavian knows he must protect himself against me. And I, for my part, must similarly protect myself against him. If it is possible, I will avoid a direct confrontation. I have no particular desire to do him harm." He met Isana's eyes. "But these things have a way of taking on a life of their own. And I *will* see the Realm whole, strong, and ready to defend itself."

She inclined her head to him, very slightly, and said, "Then your wisest course will be to accept the will of Gaius Sextus, Lord Aquitaine."

"Gaius Sextus is dead, lady." He bowed just as slightly in reply. "And look where accepting the will of that old serpent has brought us."

Aquitaine nodded once to Araris and strode from the room.

Araris shut the door behind the High Lord and turned to Isana. He exhaled slowly, and only then did he lift his hand from his sword.

Isana padded over to him and their arms slid around one another. She held him very close to her, leaning her cheek against his chest. She stayed there for several moments, closing her eyes. Araris's arms tightened around her, holding her without pressing her too hard against the steel links of his armor. As they stood close, Isana felt the cool reserve of the metalcrafting he'd been using to contain his emotions as it receded.

For some time, there was only his presence, the warmth of his love, as steady as any rock, and Isana let that warmth push back the cold of her worries and fears.

After a little while, she asked, "Did I do the right thing?"

"You know you did," he replied.

"Did I?" she asked. "He had a point. He had several."

Araris made a growling sound in his throat. After a moment, he said, "Maybe. So ask yourself something."

"What?"

"Could you live a lie?"

She shuddered. "I've done it before. To protect Tavi."

"So did I," he said. "I was there." He gestured at his scarred face. "Paid a price for it. And when . . . when I got out from under that burden, it was the best thing that had happened to me since Septimus died."

"Yes," Isana said quietly. She lifted a hand and laid it on his scarred face, on the old coward's brand burned there. She leaned in and kissed his mouth gently. "No. I can't do that anymore."

He nodded and rested his forehead against hers. "There it is, then."

They were still for a while, and Isana finally asked, "What did Aquitaine mean about defending the wrong woman?"

Araris made a thoughtful sound. "Something that happened after Seven Hills," he said. "Septimus had led one of the cavalry wings personally, in the pursuit of the enemy after we'd taken the field. The rebel command staff had fled to half a dozen different steadholts where . . . where they hadn't used their slaves kindly."

Isana shivered.

"One in particular . . . I forget his name. Tall, lanky fellow, a Count. He was good with a blade, and his retainers fought to the death to defend him. It took me, Aldrick, Septimus, and Miles to break their last line of defense. And we barely managed it." He sighed. "It was ugly before it was done. And this Count had kept a number of body slaves in his chambers. One of them had killed herself when she saw him die. The others weren't in much better shape. Wasn't one of them older than sixteen, and they'd all been fitted with discipline collars."

Isana felt suddenly sick.

"We took the steadholt's staff alive, mostly. One of them had put the collars on them. So we got them off three of the girls, but the fourth one . . ." Araris shook his head. "She might have been fourteen. She'd been wearing the collar since she was ten. And she was . . ."

"Wrong?" Isana suggested gently.

"Broken," Araris replied. "She had no idea how to relate to other people unless it was to offer herself. She could barely dress herself. She'd been regularly given wine and aphrodin. A beautiful child, really, but you could see it in her eyes. She'd been damaged, and she wasn't coming back.

"Of course, the Princeps extended his protection to her. But she was getting more upset and desperate every day. Like her world had been inverted. She didn't know where she fit, or what to do. By the time we got back to Alera Imperia, she just shivered and screamed a lot." He glanced up at Isana. "She was a watercrafter, a strong one."

Isana inhaled sharply. "But . . . that means that as her gifts were blooming . . ."

Araris nodded. "She got to feel exactly what those men felt when they took her. The poor child. Death would have been kinder than what she went through." He cleared his throat. "So. She wouldn't stop screaming and crying until one night she did. Septimus sent Miles to check on her—he'd been making moon eyes at her ever since he first saw her. He wasn't more than a year or two older than she was. Miles followed the Princeps' orders and walked in on the girl and Aldrick."

"Oh, crows," Isana sighed.

"Miles was jealous, and furious that Aldrick should use her so—though the girl didn't seem to mind. So he challenged Aldrick to the *juris macto* on the spot."

"The famous duel in Alera Imperia," Isana said.

Araris nodded. "Miles was going to get himself killed, so I nudged him out in front of a wagon. That's where he got his bad knee. And I took his place in the *juris macto*."

Isana frowned up at him. "Why?"

"Because what Aldrick was doing was wrong. Regardless of whether or not it reassured her." He gave her a brief, wan smile. "There are some things you just can't ignore."

She nodded slowly. "Go on."

"Not much more to it," Araris said. "I beat Aldrick, but I couldn't kill him. He was one of the Princeps' *singulares*. Like a brother to me. But while he was still on his knees, Septimus walked up to him and castigated him, in front of half of the capital. Cast him out of his company and made it clear in no uncertain terms that Aldrick was to stay out of his sight if he wanted to keep breathing."

"What happened?"

"No one in Alera Imperia would have let him wash their dishes for free after what Septimus said. So he took the girl and left."

"Odiana," Isana said. The image of the tall, dour Aldrick and the sweetly curved dark-haired woman always to be found in his company sprang into her thoughts.

Araris nodded. "I tried to be kind to her, for my part. Helped her eat. Gave her my blanket one cold night, on the way to the capital. I suppose that's why she helped me at Second Calderon. But afterward, I thought that it would have been better if I hadn't fought him once Miles was safely in a healing tub. The duel made the events that provoked it public knowledge. Septimus had no choice but to dismiss Aldrick, and as harshly as possible. If I hadn't handled it that way, maybe Aldrick would have been at First Calderon. Maybe it would have made a difference. Maybe a lot of things would be different."

"Do you believe that?" Isana asked.

Araris smiled faintly. "I don't know. I think about it often, what I might have done differently. But I suppose we all do that with the important choices."

A knock sounded at the door.

"Ah," Isana said. "The escort from the Senate, I suppose." They broke their embrace, and Isana carefully smoothed her dress. "Would you care to open the door, please."

Araris drew himself back up into flawless military posture and inclined his head to her. Then he went to the door, reached out a hand—

And the door *itself* flew from its hinges with a squeal of tearing metal, struck Araris full on in the chest, and flung him across the room to crash into the opposite wall.

Men in black armor entered the room, moving swiftly, precisely. One of them flung the door from Araris's prostrate body. Two more held weapons on the downed swordsman. Two pointed gleaming blades at Isana, who froze, staring wide-eyed.

The men weren't dressed in black armor.

They were covered in vord chitin. The gleaming steel bands of discipline collars shone upon their throats.

There was a light tread in the hall, and a slender figure covered in a great, dark cloak entered the room. A slender, feminine, snow-white hand rose to point a single, green-black fingernail at Isana. "Yes," hissed an alien, buzzing voice. "Yes. I recognize the scent. That is she."

"Lady," urged a quiet voice from the hall. "We cannot circumvent the sentry furies much longer."

The vord Queen—for she could be no one else—prowled across the room to Isana and seized her wrist in a crushing grip. Isana bit down on a cry of pain as something broke with a quiet *crack*.

"Bring them both," the Queen all but purred. "Oh, yes. Now it is my turn."

⊡⊡⊡⊡CHAPTER 9

"Tribune Antillar," Tavi said. "I need you."

Max looked up from his lunch, blinking in confusion at the tone of Tavi's voice. But though Max was Tavi's friend, he was also Legion. He rose at once, banged a fist to his chest in salute, and fell into step beside Tavi before he'd finished chewing his last bite of food. As Tavi stalked out of the mess hall, he spotted Crassus pacing across the camp, speaking earnestly to one of the Legion's centurions.

"Tribune Antillus!" Tavi barked. "Centurion Schultz! With me."

Crassus and Schultz reacted in almost precisely the same way Max had. Tavi never slowed his steps, and they hurried to fall into pace behind him and Maximus. Tavi headed for the Canim encampment without speaking further, but they hadn't gone a hundred yards before hooves thundered over the ground, and Kitai swung herself down from her horse, her expression dour. She stared intently at Tavi for a moment, then started walking next to him.

A surge of relief and pleasure at seeing her face briefly suppressed the anger and calculation that drove his current steps. "When did you get back?" he asked.

"Just now, Aleran. Obviously." She looked at him again, as though to reassure herself that he was still there. "I felt something."

"Two Canim just tried to kill me."

Kitai's lips peeled back from her teeth. "Varg?"

"No way to know for certain. But it isn't like him."

Kitai growled. "His people. His responsibility."

Tavi grunted, neither agreeing nor disagreeing with her. "Were you successful?"

She eyed him, and said, not without a measure of scorn, "Aleran."

Tavi bared his teeth in a fierce grin. "Of course. I apologize.".

"As well you should," Kitai said. "What do you hope to accomplish?"

"I will get answers from Varg," Tavi said.

"What?" blurted Max. "The *Canim* tried to *kill* you?"

"About five minutes ago," Tavi said.

"Then why the crows are we walking toward their camp?"

"Because I need to move fast before this becomes something bad," Tavi said. "And because that's where Varg is."

"And if he *did* send them to kill you, what's going to stop him from finishing the job when you get there?"

"You are," Tavi said.

Max scowled. "Oh. I am."

"Don't be a hog about it," Tavi said. "Crassus and Schultz deserve to contribute, too."

Max let out a growling sound. "Bloody Legions," he muttered, under his breath. "Bloody Canim. Bloody crazy First Lords."

"If you want to stay here . . ." Tavi began.

Max glowered at him. "Of course not." He glanced over his shoulder. "Schultz is competent. But it would all go to the crows if my little brother was in charge, and he outranks Schultz."

"Technically speaking," Crassus said, "I also outrank you."

"Do not," Max said. "We're both Tribunes."

"I got there first."

"We got there at the same time. Besides, I got assigned to the First Aleran six months before it formed," Max replied.

Crassus snorted. "As a centurion. A fake centurion."

"Doesn't matter. Seniority's mine."

"Children," Tavi chided. "You don't see Schultz bickering about such things, do you?"

"If it please the captain, sir," the plain-faced Schultz said, "I am not a part of this."

Kitai grinned, showing her canine teeth. "Schultz has the best sense among them. He merits command for that alone."

Schultz ignored the comment with noncommissioned stoicism.

They strode out from the camp on the hill and went down toward the larger Canim encampment. The gate guards saw Tavi and the others coming. One of the guards, a Cane with whom Tavi was not familiar, held up a hand, signaling for Tavi to halt and be identified, standard procedure for the Canim camp.

Tavi took a deep breath and reminded himself that he was not making a standard visit.

Instead of halting, he called strength from the earth, leaned back, and kicked the wooden palisade gates open with a resounding crash. The two Canim on guard, caught behind the gates as they opened, were flung to the ground on either side—and every set of black and scarlet Canim eyes in view turned to focus on what had happened.

"I seek my *gadara*, Varg," Tavi stated in the snarling tongue of the wolf-warriors, loudly enough to be heard by the watching Canim. "Let any who wish to stand in my way step forth now."

The way toward the center of the Canim camp was abruptly vacated.

Tavi stalked forward, trying to appear as though he longed for nothing so much as an excuse to vent his rage upon any Cane luckless enough to draw his attention. He had enough experience with them to know how important body language and confidence was to communicating effectively with them. His main worry was that some young warrior might believe his stance and attitude were bravado, a bluff, and decide to call him on it.

He had already killed two Canim. Given how implacable Varg and the warrior caste had become about protecting what remained of their people, it might already be too late to salvage anything out of the situation. Once blood was spilled, the Canim could become less than rational.

Come to think of it, Alerans weren't much different.

Kitai fell into place beside Tavi, her green eyes narrowed, her expression hard. "You do not believe Varg is behind this," she said beneath her breath.

"No. If he wanted me dead, he'd bring a sword and do it himself."

Kitai nodded. "Therefore, someone else sent the killers."

"Yes," Tavi said.

Kitai frowned thoughtfully for a moment. Then she said, "I see. You fear that whoever sent the killers knew that they would die."

Tavi nodded. "Likely, they are already working to spread word among the Canim."

Kitai narrowed her eyes. "They will accuse you of murder."

"I've got to get to Varg first," Tavi said. "Before word has time to spread."

Kitai glared at a pair of warriors in blue-and-black steel armor, golden-furred Shuarans who had never faced Aleran Legions on the battlefield and who might therefore be more willing to challenge the Aleran party. One of the pair looked like he might—but his companion, a larger Cane, flicked his ears in amusement and watched the Alerans pass with unconcealed interest.

Kitai grunted in satisfaction. "And before word has time to spread among the Alerans, too."

Tavi nodded. "That's why we're doing this the noisy way."

She cast him a single worried glance. "Not all enemies are like Varg. Be cautious."

Tavi snorted out a breath through his nose and fell silent again as they finished their march through the camp uncontested.

As Tavi approached the center of the camp, he spotted a dozen of the most senior of the Canim warrior caste, their armor covered in so many scarlet patterns that little, if any, black steel could be seen. They were all resting in nonchalant poses around the entrance to the dugout shelter Varg used as a command post.

Several were sitting on their haunches, as if loitering in groups of two and three, passing the time. Two more were playing *ludus* on an oversized board with enlarged pieces. Another pair were facing one another with wooden practice swords. The two Canim did not engage their blunt blades. One was posed in a defensive stance, blade held across his body. His opposite held his own blade gripped over his head, parallel to the line of his spine.

As Tavi grew closer, the positions of each warrior shifted at what appeared to be precisely the same time. The first Cane slid a step to one side and shifted the angle of his blade. His partner eased half a step forward in dancelike synchronization, turning his body, and brought his own blade down and forward to a full extension, the sword's wooden tip stopping just short of the other Cane's blade. They both froze again, only to change positions once more a few breaths later. As the positions settled, the first Cane dropped his jaws open in an easy grin. The second let out a rumbling snarl of disappointment. The two lowered their blades, inclined their heads to one another in a Canim bow, and turned to observe the approaching Alerans as if their contest had concluded when it did by pure coincidence.

Tavi stopped a few feet beyond the range of a long lunge from one of the Warmaster's guardians, growled under his breath, and called, "*Gadara!* I would speak with you!"

Silence yawned for a moment, and the dozen guards faced the Alerans calmly, relaxed. Every one of them had a paw-hand on a weapon.

Varg emerged from the dugout in his crimson steel armor, prowling deliberately into the light. Nasaug followed his sire, his eyes focused on the Alerans. Varg came forward, toward Tavi, and stopped a fraction of an inch outside of his own weapon's reach.

Tavi and Varg exchanged a Canim-style salute, though it was barely detectable, heads tilting very slightly to one side.

"What is this?" Varg said.

"It is what it is," Tavi replied. "Two Canim just attempted to kill me in my command post. They entered posing as your messengers. One wore the armor of a Narashan warrior. The other wore the equipment of Nasaug's militia."

Varg's ears swiveled forward and locked into position. For a Cane, it was an expression of polite interest, but the stillness of the rest of Varg's body amounted to the equivalent of an expressionless mask, meant to give nothing of his thoughts away.

"Where are they?" Varg asked.

Tavi felt himself tense at the question but forced his body to remain confident, calm. "Dead."

Varg's throat rumbled with a low growl.

"I cannot let such a thing pass unchallenged," Tavi replied.

"No," Varg said. "You cannot."

"I would face the Cane responsible."

Varg's eyes narrowed. Several seconds of silence passed before he spoke. "Then you would face me. I lead my people. I am responsible for them."

Tavi nodded slowly. "I thought you'd say that."

Nasaug let out a low, rumbling growl.

"Peace," Varg rumbled, glancing over his shoulder.

Nasaug subsided.

Varg turned back to Tavi. "Where and when."

"Our forces must leave in two days," Tavi said. "Is that time enough to prepare such a thing?"

"In addition to what is already under way?" Varg asked. "No."

"Then we will meet as soon as you have made preparations. Single blade, open field, until one falls."

"Agreed," Varg said.

The two exchanged another barely detectable bow. Tavi took several slow steps back, never turning his eyes from Varg. Then he turned, made a gesture with one hand to his companions, and started back the way he had come.

Rumors were already flying among the Canim. Hundreds, if not thousands, of them came to stare at the Alerans as they returned. Though the mutter of basso voices speaking Canish was never a friendly, soothing sound, Tavi imagined that their general tone was considerably uglier than any he had heard before. He walked through the crowd of towering wolf-folk, his eyes focused ahead of him, his expression set in a clenched-jaw snarl. He was peripherally aware of Kitai at his side, of Max, Crassus, and Schultz at his back. They were all walking in time with him, boots striking the ground at the same time—even Kitai, for once.

The Canim did not try to stop them although Tavi spotted a large mob coming their way as they reached the edge of the camp, led by half a dozen ritualists in their mantles of pale human leather. He tracked it from the corner of his eye but did not alter their pace. If the Aleran party appeared to the Canim around them to be fleeing, it could trigger an attack—and no matter how powerful the individuals with him might be, they were only a handful of people, and there were hundreds of Canim around them. They would be torn to pieces.

Tavi went back through the broken gates and past the two guards there, both of whom were on their feet again and looking surly. Neither met Tavi's gaze or attempted to challenge him, though, and the ritualist-led mob was still a hundred yards off when Tavi went through and started back up the hill. It wasn't until they were out of range of a Canim-thrown stone or spear that he allowed himself to begin to relax.

"Bloody crows," breathed Schultz, from behind him.

"Crows and bloody furies," agreed Max. "Did you see that group with the ritualists? They'd have jumped on us in a heartbeat."

"Aye," Crassus said. "That would have gotten ugly."

"Which is why the captain broke the gates on the way in," Kitai said. "Obviously."

"I've never regretted making sure I had a quick way out," Tavi said. "Centurion."

"Sir," Schultz said.

Tavi nodded to the *legionares* on duty at the gate to the First Aleran's camp as they passed through. "I want you to speak to your Tribune. Let him know that I want the Battlecrows for detached duty. That's all he needs to know."

"Sir," Schultz acknowledged.

"Pack them up for a mounted march and take them up to the engineering cohort's position. It's on a beach north of Antillus. Secure the engineers and keep an eye out for any suspicious Canim. If they're going to make trouble for us, it will be at the staging area, so I want your men on station before nightfall."

"I have no idea what you're talking about, sir," Schultz said seriously. He saluted and turned to start walking. "On my way."

"Max, take the cavalry with him. Keep one wing ready to respond to an attack at all times. Don't be subtle about it, either. I want anyone who thinks about interfering with the engineers to know what they're in for if they try it."

Max nodded. "Got it. What are we guarding again?"

"You'll figure it out," Tavi said. "Crassus, I know they aren't going to like it, but I need the Knights to pretend they're engineers again. The next couple of days are going to be difficult. Go with Max and Schultz and report to the senior engineering staff."

Crassus sighed. "At least it won't be more ice ships."

Tavi glanced over his shoulder and smiled. "Not . . . exactly, no."

Max and Crassus traded a look.

"Does he know how annoying that is?" Max asked.

"Oh, absolutely," Crassus said.

"You think we should say anything about it?"

"The burden of command is heavy," Crassus said soberly. "We should probably let him have his sick fun."

Max nodded. "Especially since he's going to do it anyway."

"He is the mighty First Lord," Crassus said. "We are but lowly *legionares*. We obey without question."

"We do?"

"That was a question. You're questioning."

"Right," Max said. "Sorry."

"Just get up there, both of you," Tavi said. "The vord will be here in force in two days. We need to be on the move by then. I need you to help make it happen."

The brothers rapped fists to breastplates and marched off, continuing to bicker lightly with one another as they walked.

Kitai watched them for a moment and smiled. "They have become friends. I like that."

"They're brothers," Tavi said.

She looked at him, green eyes serious. "It is not the same for everyone. Blood draws some together. Their blood came between them."

Tavi nodded. "They weren't always this way, no."

Kitai smiled faintly. "They are your friends as well. They went when you asked them to go."

"They know what is at stake. They're afraid. Schultz, too. That's why they're joking."

"They're joking because they just followed you into a horde of angry Canim and walked back out again in one piece," she replied. "The battle energy had to go somewhere."

Tavi grinned. "True."

She tilted her head. "I'm curious. What did you accomplish, other than arranging a duel with one of the more dangerous beings we have encountered?"

"I started a conversation," Tavi said.

Kitai eyed him for a moment, then said, "They are right. It is annoying when you do that."

Tavi sighed. "It'll work, or it won't. Talking about it can't help."

She shook her head. "And your other plan. Will it work? Will we get there in time?"

Tavi stopped walking and regarded her. "I think there's a chance. A good chance." He turned to her, bowed formally, and asked, "Ambassador, would you do me the pleasure of joining me for a late dinner this evening?"

Kitai arched a white eyebrow. A slow smile spread over her lips. "Dinner?"

"It is the way things are properly done," he said. "You might wear your new gown."

"Gown?"

"I had it delivered to your tent while you were gone. I think it's lovely. Tribune Cymnea assures me it is elegant and tasteful."

Both her eyebrows lifted now. "In all of this, amidst everything you are doing, you made time to get me a gift."

"Obviously," Tavi said.

Kitai's mouth curved up into another slow smile. She turned and sauntered away, hips swaying a little more than was necessary. She paused to say, "There is hope for you yet, Aleran." Then she continued on her way.

Tavi frowned after her. "Kitai? So . . . you're coming to dinner?"

She didn't answer, except to laugh and keep walking.

CHAPTER 10

Amara suppressed an irrationally intense urge to have Cirrus choke off Senator Valerius's supply of air. She supposed she didn't absolutely *need* to choke him. Not fatally, anyway. She might be satisfied enough with merely watching him turn purple and collapse—but the man was so detestable that she scarcely trusted herself. So instead of murder, or a pleasant near murder, she folded her hands calmly into her lap and forced herself to remain calm.

Bernard leaned over, and murmured, "If I asked you politely, do you think you could strangle that smug idiot from all the way up here?"

She tried to suppress the giggle that surged up out of her belly at his words but was only partly successful. She covered her hand with her mouth but nonetheless earned a number of irritated glances from those in the amphitheater's audience.

"Tonight's script is for a tragedy," Bernard scolded her quietly, leaning close to put a restraining hand on her arm. "Not a comedy. Contain yourself before you upset the audience."

She fought down another laugh and punched his arm lightly, turning her attention back to the ancient Senator Ulfius's quavering recitation of obscure lineage. "—son of Matteus, whose title did *not* pass to his eldest, illegitimate son, Gustus, but to his younger and properly invested son, Martinus. Thus, is the precedent established, my fellow honored Senators, my lords in attendance."

Senator Valerius, a saturnine man of middle years and tremendously digni-fied appearance, began to applaud with long, elegant hands, and there was ir-regularly spread support of the gesture. "Thank you, Senator Ulfius. Now if there are no further—"

One of the seventy or so men seated on the floor of the amphitheater cleared his throat loudly and rose in place. His hair was a thicket of white spikes, his nose was laced with red from drinking too much wine, and his knuckles were swollen almost grotesquely from repeated brawling. A bandage on his right hand testified that not all of it had been in his youth, either.

Valerius adjusted the drape of purple cloth that denoted his status as Sena-tor Callidus and eyed the other man. "Senator Theoginus. What is it?"

"I thought I might exercise my right as a member of this Senate to voice my thoughts," Theoginus drawled, his slow Ceresian accent coming through with broadly overdone exaggeration—a deliberate counterpoint to Valerius's classi-cally trained, firmly northern intonations. "Assuming the Senator Callidus still intends to chair this august body in accordance with the rule of law, of course."

"Every moment wasted is a moment that could have been used preparing ourselves to face the enemy," Valerius responded.

"Indeed," Theoginus said. "Does that include the moments spent on your quite excellent manicure, Senator? I'm sure the shine of your nails will dazzle the vord before they can get anywhere near us."

A low laugh, as scattered as the previous applause, went through the audi-ence. Amara and Bernard both added their own voices to it. The bandages on Theoginus's knuckles made an even more stark contrast to Valerius's appear-ance. "I think I like him," Amara murmured.

"Theoginus?" Bernard replied. "He's a pompous ass. But he's on the right side, today."

Valerius was far too polished to show any reaction to the laughter. He waited for it to vanish, and for another quarter minute after that before answering. "Of course, Senator, we will hear what you have to say. Although I ask, for the sake of the brave young men preparing to face the enemy, that you keep your commentary concise and to the point." He bowed his head slightly, gestured with a single hand, and seated himself gracefully.

"Thank you, Valerius," Theoginus replied. He hooked his thumbs in the folds of his robes, thus ensuring that the bandages on his right hand remained highly visible. "With all due respect to Senator Ulfius for his prodigious knowledge of Aleran history and Aleran law, his argument is specious and deserves to be laughed out of this amphitheater."

Ulfius rose, making spluttering sounds, his bald, speckled pate turning bright red.

"Now, now, Ulf," Theoginus said, giving the other Senator a broad, jowly smile. "I meant to go about that more gently, but Valerius says we've got no time to spare for your feelings. And you know just as well as I do that Parciar Gustus was a slobbering madman who murdered half a dozen young women, while Parcius Fidelar Martinus was the first serving Citizen to be named to the House of the Faithful after the Feverthorn Wars—and that was only after he *twice* declined Gaius Secondus's invitation to join the House of the Valiant."

Senator Theoginus snorted. "Trying to compare those two to Gaius Octavian and Gaius Aquitainus Attis strikes me as pure desperation—especially given that you have no evidence to prove that Octavian's birth was illegitimate."

Valerius rose to his feet, raising a hand. "A point of order, honored Theoginus. The burden of proof to establish legitimacy falls upon the parents, or if they are not living and able to do so, upon the child. Legitimacy, especially among the Citizenry, must be established."

"Which it has been," Theoginus said. "With the signet ring of Princeps Septimus, the eyewitness testimony of Araris Valerian, and by the signed hand of Princeps Septimus himself." Theoginus paused as a low mutter ran through the amphitheater, among Senators and observers alike, then eyed Valerius, waiting.

"Gaius Sextus never formally presented Octavian to the Senate," he replied smoothly. "By law, he has not been legally recognized."

"As a Citizen in his own right," Theoginus countered. "Which has no bearing whatsoever on Gaius's choice of an heir—which is a clear matter of public record."

"It is to be hoped," Valerius replied, "that the First Lord of the Realm should have the grace to be a Citizen as well."

"Semantics, Senator. We have all seen ample demonstration of Octavian's evident skills with our own eyes. The proof was, after all, good enough for Gaius Sextus. Why should it not be good enough for the rest of us?"

"The testimony of Gaius Sextus's personal physician has established that Sextus had been a victim of long-term poisoning by means of refined helatin,"

Valerius said soberly. "Helatin damages the entire body, including the mind. It is entirely possible that Gaius Sextus was non compos mentis during the last year of his life—"

Valerius's voice was lost in a sudden uproar of protest, and Amara found herself wanting to strangle the weasel again. First, he made everyone languish through Ulfius's argument, then attempted to press and close the issue in a rush, citing the need for prompt action. Granted, such tactics had been successful in the Senate before, though generally not in the face of any serious opposition. But this . . . calling Gaius's mental competency into question was a masterful stroke. If enough of the Senate was willing to go along with the idea, it would mean that nearly anything Gaius had done during the vord invasion could be found an illegal action, invalidated by the power-thirsty Senate. After all, Sextus could hardly defend his actions now.

There was a way to head off Valerius's true thrust, though, if Theoginus was clever enough to see it.

Theoginus raised a hand, a silent call for order, and the noise diminished to a susurrus of rapid whispers. "Honored brother of the Senate," Theoginus said, scorn open in his voice, "nearly every Lord and High Lord of the Realm worked in Gaius Sextus's presence during the entire campaign last year. Surely you do not suggest that so many Citizens of the Realm, the majority of them gifted watercrafters, could have simply failed to notice madness when they saw it?"

"Brother—" Valerius began.

"And if he *was* gone to his dotage," Theoginus continued, "then surely his adoption of Aquitainus Attis into his house must be viewed in a manner every bit as suspect as his declaration of Octavian's legitimacy."

"Hah," Amara said, baring her teeth in a grin and pounding her fist on Bernard's thigh. "He *saw* it."

Bernard enfolded her fist in his hands. "Easy, love, you'll leave bruises."

"Aquitainus Attis," Theoginus continued, turning to speak to the seated Senate at large, "is without a doubt one of the finest examples of talent, ability, and effective leadership that the Citizenry has to offer. His skill and personal courage in battle against the vord cannot be questioned." He drew in a deep breath, and spoke in a voice like thunder. "But those facts give no one the grace to defy the law of the Realm! Not Aquitaine. Not the Citizenry. And not the Senate." He turned in a slow circle to face each of the seated Senators. "Make no mistake, honored Senators. To defy the will of Gaius Sextus now is to betray the laws that have guided the Realm since its founding—laws that have allowed us to overcome centuries of turmoil and war."

"For tradition's sake," interrupted Valerius, "we ought to needlessly throw away the lives of our fighting men. Is that what you're saying, Senator?"

Theoginus faced Valerius squarely. "Half of our Realm is gone, sir. Lives beyond counting have been lost. Alera Imperia herself has fallen and been devoured by earth and fire. But most of what is left of the Realm is beyond the reach of any foe. It is curved into the intangible bedrock of the mind and heart—the law. It is within the good steel of those Legions outside the city walls, ready to give their lives in Alera's defense. It flows within the veins of her Citizenry, called to arms and ready to face whatever foe should try to harm her people." He swept his hand in a dramatic gesture, to the west. "And it is out *there*, in the living monument of the House that has guided the Realm since time immemorial. It is in Gaius Octavian."

True silence had fallen on the amphitheater. Theoginus knew how to speak to a crowd. He knew how to draw upon their emotions—and the constant hum of low fear that permeated all of Alera in these desperate months left them primed for just such an approach.

Theoginus's eyes raked the gathered Senate again. "Remember that, when you vote. Remember the oaths you have sworn. Remember the simple truth—that Sextus's lawful heir is coming to defend our lands and our peoples. Turn aside from the law, from what the Realm has always been, and Alera will be no more. Whether we stand, whether we fall, Alera will be gone. And we here will have murdered her: murdered her with quiet words, loud speeches, and raised hands. *Remember.*"

Theoginus gave the Senator Callidus a glare that might have set the man on fire. Then he took his seat once more and folded his arms.

Valerius stared at his opponent for a long, silent moment. Then he gazed at the rest of the Senate. Amara could practically read his thoughts. Theoginus had employed a dangerous gambit. One could never be sure that an impassioned speech would move an audience in the intended direction—but the Ceresian senator had spoken well. The power of his words still resonated in the room. Any opposition Valerius raised, at this point, would earn him nothing but angry glares. His best course of action was almost certainly to move ahead and count upon the support he'd gathered in the days previous to this confrontation. It was a close vote. He might already have done enough to tip the scales.

Valerius nodded slowly and raised his voice. "I call the vote of the Senate upon the issue of the legitimacy of Gaius Septimus's alleged marriage to one freeman Isana of the Calderon Valley. A vote of yes will confirm the legal status of the marriage. A vote of no will deny it."

Amara found herself holding her breath.

"All those who would vote no?" Valerius asked.

Hands began to rise, scattered throughout the seated Senators. Amara found herself counting them furiously.

"How many?" Bernard whispered.

"They need thirty-six," she replied, still counting. *Thirty-two. Thirty-three. Thirty-four.*

Valerius added his hands to those raised.

"Thirty-*five*," she hissed.

"Those who would vote yes?" Valerius asked.

Hands began to rise—and trumpets began to howl.

A wave of worried whispers washed up around Amara. Heads began to turn. One distant trumpet was joined by another, and another, and another. The whispers became a murmur.

"What is that?" asked a matron seated behind Amara of her husband. "The signal?"

The old gentleman patted her arm. "I'm not sure, dear."

Amara turned to Bernard, her eyes grave. He met her gaze, his own face calm but resigned. He recognized the standard Legion trumpet call just as well as she did.

The Legions outside the southern wall of the city of Riva were sounding a call to arms.

"They can't be here," Amara said. "Not already."

Bernard gave her a half smile and rose. Around her, other Citizens were doing the same thing, moving with brisk, worried efficiency toward the amphitheater's exits, the matter before the Senate forgotten. "They seem to have formed a habit of surprising us. Let's prepare for the worst and hope for the best."

She took his hand and rose. They were just leaving the theater when a young woman came rushing toward them through the crowd, being jostled roughly several times in her haste. She was a slender young woman, with a long, rather serious face and long, cobweb-fine hair of pale gold. "Count Calderon!" Lady Veradis called. "Count Calderon!"

Bernard caught sight of her waving hand and waded through the crowd, moving through it easily enough by dint of pure mass. Amara stayed close to him, in his wake, avoiding the minor collisions that would otherwise have rattled her.

"Veradis!" Bernard called. He took the girl by the shoulders, a supportive, steadying gesture. She was clearly shaken, her face pale, her eyes wide. "What happened?"

"The First Lady, Count," she sobbed. "It's chaos over there, and I can't find the Placidas, and I don't know whom to trust."

Bernard looked around for a moment, and followed Amara's pointed finger to an alley between two buildings, an eddy in the stream of humanity flowing around them. Bernard moved them over into the relatively quiet space, and said, "Slow down, Veradis. Slow down. What happened?"

The girl gained control of herself with a visible effort, and Amara remembered that Veradis was an extremely gifted watercrafter. The emotions of the frightened crowd were probably an ongoing torment to her. "Your sister, sir," she said, her voice steady. "Your sister's been taken. Araria, too."

"Taken," Amara asked sharply, "Taken by what?"

The horn signals continued to blow, growing louder and more numerous.

"I don't *know*," Veradis said. "When I got back to her chamber, the door had been broken down. There was blood—probably not enough of it to have killed anyone. And they were gone."

Amara heard, among the other calls, the trumpets of High Lord Riva's Legion sounding the assembly, from deeper in the city. As Citizens in service to Riva, Bernard and Amara had been assigned to the support of the First Rivan Legion. Bernard glanced up. He'd heard the sound, too. "I'll go," he said. "See what you can find out."

Amara bit her lip but nodded and turned back to Veradis. "Lady, can you fly?"

"Of course."

Amara turned back to her husband, took his face in her hands, and kissed him. He returned it with brief, fierce intensity. When they broke off the kiss, he touched her cheek with the back of one hand, then turned and vanished into the crowds.

Amara nodded to Lady Veradis. "Show me," she said.

The two of them lifted off into the night, two small shapes among many who were flitting through the skies over Riva, while the Legion horns continued to blare.

CHAPTER 11

"You have no idea of the potential for destruction in the forces you are tampering with," Alera said calmly. "None whatsoever."

Tavi stood in his command tent, looking down at a large map of the Realm spread out across an entire tabletop, its corners weighted with small white stones. The air hummed with the tension of a windcrafting that would prevent their voices from carrying outside. His dress-uniform tunic was folded neatly on the cot in the corner, ready for his dinner with Kitai. "Then perhaps you should educate me," he murmured.

Alera looked as she always did—serene, remote, lovely, garbed in grey, her eyes shimmering through one metallic or gemstone hue after the next. "It would be difficult to truly explain, even to you. Not in the time that remains."

Tavi arched an eyebrow at that remark and studied Alera more closely. The human-appearing fury folded her hands before her, the posture of a proper Aleran matron. Had they been trembling? Did the nails look . . . uneven? Ragged, as if she'd been chewing upon them?

Something, Tavi decided, was definitely off about the fury tonight.

"If it isn't too much trouble, perhaps you could explain what sorts of problems I might be letting myself in for if I go through with the plan."

"I don't see why," Alera responded. "You're going to do it in any case."

"Perhaps."

She shook her head. "What you are asking is going to set certain cycles into motion. The ultimate result of those cycles could be the slow freezing of the world. Glaciers that grow and grow each year, slowly devouring all the land before them."

Tavi had just picked up a glass of watered wine and taken a drink. He half choked on it. "Bloody crows," he croaked. "When?"

"Not in your lifetime," Alera said. "Or in the lifetimes of your children, or their children. Perhaps not in the lifetime of your entire people. Almost certainly, beyond the length of time your written memory will survive you. A thousand years, or two thousands, or three or twenty. But it will come."

"If I do not act," Tavi said, "the vord will destroy my people before the snow flies *this* year." He shook his head. "The Alerans of thousands of years in the future will never have the chance to exist—and you'll never get to tell anyone that you told them so. The theoretical Alerans of tomorrow will have to look out for themselves."

He half expected her to smile at his commentary. It was the sort of quiet, cerebral humor that the fury seemed to appreciate. She did not respond.

"You'll help us?" he asked.

She inclined her head slowly. "Of course."

Tavi stepped closer to her abruptly, reached down to her folded hands, and lifted them. His heart went up into his throat as he did. The fury before him was a being of almost unthinkable power. If she took exception to his actions . . .

But she only stood there regarding him with a calm expression. He moved his eyes from hers to her fingertips.

They looked ragged, the material of them frayed, somehow, chewed. Tavi had once seen the bodies of soldiers who had fallen into a river during a battle. The men had drowned, and their remains had not been recovered for more than a day. The fish and other creatures of the river had been at them, biting and snipping off tiny bits of flesh. The wounds had not bled. They had remained cold, inert, grey, as if the bodies had somehow become sculptures of soft clay.

Alera's fingers looked like that—like a wax sculpture an industrious mouse had been nibbling upon.

"What is this?" he asked her quietly.

"Inevitability," the fury replied. "Dissolution."

He frowned for a moment, both at her hands and at her reply. The meaning sunk in a few seconds later. He looked up at her, and whispered, "You're dying."

Alera gave him a very calm, very warm smile. "A simplistic way to view what is happening," she replied. "But I suppose that from your perspective it does share certain superficial similarities."

"I don't understand," Tavi said.

Alera considered her hands in his for a moment. Then she gestured down the length of her body, and said, "Know you how this form came to be? Why it is that I speak to your family's bloodline?"

Tavi shook his head. "No."

She gave him a chiding glance. "But you have conjectured."

Tavi inclined his head to her. "I hypothesized that it had something to do with the mural in the First Lord's meditation chamber."

"Excellent," Alera said, nodding. "The mosaic in the chamber floor is made from pieces of stone brought there from all over the Realm. Through those pieces, the original Gaius Primus was able to communicate with and command furies all across the land to bring him information, allow him glimpses of places far away, and to do his will." She pursed her lips. "That was when I first began to become aware of myself, as a discrete entity. Over Primus's lifetime, I continued to . . . congeal, I suppose, would be the best word for it. He sensed my presence and, in time, I understood how to speak with him and how to manifest a material form." She smiled, her eyes distant. "The first words I remember actually hearing with my own ears were Primus's: *Bother, I've gone mad.*"

Tavi let out a short, choking laugh.

She smiled at him. "The mosaic was the focus upon which this form was predicated. It was what drew thousands upon thousands of furies with no individual identity into something more." She put a hand flat to her own chest. "Into Alera."

"And when my grandfather destroyed Alera Imperia, the mosaic was destroyed with it," Tavi said.

"Unavoidable, from Sextus's perspective. Had it remained intact, the vord Queen would have possessed it. She would almost certainly have understood what it meant and attempted to control me through it. She might even have succeeded."

"And that's why the First Lords never spoke of you to anyone," Tavi said quietly. "Why there's not a word of you in any of the histories."

"No foes of the House of Gaius could attempt to usurp control of me if they did not know of me."

"But they could kill you," Tavi said quietly.

"Indeed." She drew in a deep breath and let it out in a sigh. "In a very real sense, I have been killed by the vord invasion—but it took a certain length of time for me to form. It will likewise take time for me to return to my original state."

"I hadn't . . . I didn't realize," Tavi said. "I'm so sorry."

She arched an eyebrow. "But why? I do not fear what is to come, young Gaius. I will feel neither loss nor pain. My time in this form is almost done. All things must come to an end. It is the way of the universe."

"After so long helping my family and the Realm, you deserve better."

"In what way is that relevant? What one deserves and what one experiences are seldom congruent."

"When they are, it is called 'justice,'" Tavi said. "It's one of the things I'm supposed to help provide, as I understand the office."

Alera's smile took on a bitter undertone. "Bear in mind that I have not always helped your family or your people. I am unwilling to place any creature before any other. And every action I take mandates a reaction, a balance. When Sextus wished me to moderate prevailing weather in the Vale, it would cause half a dozen furystorms elsewhere in the Realm. When he would ask me to lend strength to the great currents of wind, it would spin off cyclones hundreds of miles away. Until the vord came, I and my kin had killed more Alerans than any foe your folk had ever faced." Her eyes glinted with something savage and cold. "The argument could be made, young Gaius, that what is happening to me *is* justice."

Tavi took that in for a moment, mulling it over in his mind. "When you are gone . . . Things will change."

Her eyes went unreadable. "Yes."

"What things?"

"Everything," she said calmly. "For a time. The forces so long bound up in this form must settle out to a balance once more. The countryside of all the Realm will become more active with wild furies, more turbulent, and more dangerous. Weather patterns will shift and change. Animals will behave oddly. Plants will grow at unnatural rates, or wither for no apparent reason. Furycrafting itself will be unstable, unpredictable."

Tavi shuddered, imagining the chaos that would grow from such an environment. "Is there no way to prevent it?"

Alera looked at him with something almost like compassion. "None, young Gaius."

Tavi sank down onto a camp stool and put his elbows on his knees, his head bowed. "Nothing. You're sure."

"All things end, young Gaius. One day, you will, too.

Tavi's back hurt. Some motion during the fight with the Canim assassins had pulled a muscle. It would be simple to ease the pain in a tub, a mild water-crafting. Even if he didn't have a tub, the discomfort was minor enough to alleviate with a few moments of intense focus. But at the moment, he wasn't sure he was capable of that. His back hurt.

"You're telling me," he said, "that even if we somehow overcome the vord, it won't be over. Someday soon, the land itself is going to turn against us. We might overcome this nightmare only to drown in chaos."

"Yes."

"That's . . . a lot to have in front of me."

"Life is unfair, uncaring, and painful, young Gaius," Alera said. "Only a madman struggles against the tide."

She didn't make a whisper of sound, but Tavi lifted his eyes to find Alera kneeling, facing him, her face level with his. She reached out and touched his cheek with her frayed fingertips. "I have always found the particular madness of the House of Gaius singularly intriguing. It has fought the tides for more than a thousand years. It has often failed to attain victory. But it has never conceded the struggle."

"Has it ever faced something like this?" he asked quietly.

"When the first Alerans came here, perhaps," Alera said, her eyes distant. "My memories of it are very distant. It would be centuries before I knew your people. But they were few. So very few. Eleven thousand lives, perhaps."

"About the same size as a Legion and its followers," Tavi said.

She smiled. "And so it was. A Legion from another place, lost, and come here to my lands." She gestured toward the entrance to the tent. "The Canim, the Marat, the Icemen. All lost travelers." She shook her head sadly. "The others, too. Those that your people exterminated, over the centuries. So much lost to fear and necessity."

"When they came here, they had no furycrafting?" Tavi asked.

"Not for years."

"Then how did they do it?" he asked. "How did they survive?"

"With savagery. Skill. Discipline. They came from a place where they were unrivaled masters of war and death. Their enemies here had never seen anything like them. Your forebears could not return whence they had come. They were trapped here, and only victory gave them survival. So they became victors—no matter the cost."

She met his eyes calmly. "They did things you would scarcely believe. They committed the most monstrous and heroic deeds. The generations of your people in that time became a single, savage mind, death incarnate—and when they ran short of foes, they practiced their skills upon one another."

Tavi frowned. "Are you saying that I and my people must do the same if we are to survive?"

"I am not the one making a choice. I have no opinion. I only share facts."

Tavi nodded slowly and gestured with one hand. "Please continue."

Alera frowned pensively. "It was not until the original Primus threw down all who opposed him, carrying out brutal war in the name of establishing peace, that they began to come to their senses. To build something greater. To lay the foundations of the Realm as you know it today." She put a hand on his shoulder. "Laws. Justice. Art. The pursuit of knowledge. It all came from a single source."

"The ability to kill," Tavi whispered.

"Strength is the first virtue," Alera said. "That is not a pleasant fact. Its distastefulness does not alter the truth that without strength to protect them, all other virtues are ephemeral, ultimately meaningless."

She leaned forward slightly. "The vord have no illusions. They are willing to destroy every living thing on this world if that is what it takes to ensure the survival of their kind. They are death incarnate. And they are strong. Are you prepared to do what may be necessary for your people to survive?"

Tavi lowered his eyes and stared at the ground.

There was more he could do to help the war effort. Much more. There were steps he could take that he would have believed utterly unthinkable a year before. His mind had always been a steady fountain of ideas, and now was no exception. He hated himself for giving birth to such monstrous concepts, but the Realm was fighting for its life. In the dead of night, when he could not sleep, when he was most afraid of the future, the steps would come to him.

Those steps could only be taken upon the broken bodies of the dead.

Principles were shining, noble things, he thought. Those who worked hard enough to keep them polished them lovingly—but the simple fact was that if he wanted any Alerans at all to survive, he might have to sacrifice others. He might have to choose who lived and who died. And if he was to truly be the First Lord of the Realm, the leader of its people, he would be the one to make that choice.

It would, in fact, be his duty.

A flood of emotions he rarely permitted himself to feel flowed over him. Grief for those already lost. Rage for those who might still die. Hatred for the enemy who had forced the Realm to its knees. And pain. He had never asked for this, never wanted it. He did not want to be the First Lord—but neither could he walk away.

Necessity. Duty. The words sounded vile in the lonely vaults of his mind.

He closed his eyes, and said, "I will do what is necessary." Then he looked up at the great fury, and his words sounded hard and cold to his own ears. "But there is more than one kind of strength."

Alera stared at him for a long moment, then slowly inclined her head. "And so there is, young Gaius," she murmured. "And so there is." With that, she was gone.

Tavi sat on his camp stool, feeling exhausted, limp and tired as a wrung-out dishrag. He struggled to see the path before them all, to imagine its twists, turns, and forks. There were times when an odd kind of certainty suddenly blossomed in his thoughts, a sense of crystalline understanding of the future. His grandfather, like the First Lords before him, was rumored to have the gift of foreknowledge. Tavi didn't know if it was true.

The vord had to be stopped. If Alera could not throw them down, their path would end, abruptly and in total silence. No one would know that they had ever been.

But even if they somehow won through, the havoc inflicted by the war, the horrible price in pain and grief and loss paid by the people of Alera would leave them in no condition to do battle with the chaos of the great fury's dissolution. A people already steeped in violence and war would still be drunk on rage and blood, blind to any other path.

When they ran short of foes, they practiced their skills upon one another. Of course they had. It was all they knew.

How to stop it? Provide his people with another enemy, to focus their wrath outside of themselves? Tavi glanced toward the Canim camp and shivered. He thought of Doroga and Hashat—and Kitai. His stomach turned in slow, revolting knots.

It couldn't be allowed to happen. Such a struggle would not be quick. The blood-thirst of a generation of Alerans at war would be only temporarily slaked, and in the end it would change nothing. They would turn upon themselves.

Gaius Octavian, the young First Lord of Alera, sat alone and followed the possible paths in his mind. He clenched his fists, hoping in vain for an answer to come, for certainty to suddenly flow through him.

But it didn't.

With a word and a savage slash of his hand, he darkened the tent's furylamps.

No one should see the First Lord weep.

CHAPTER 12

Amara and Lady Veradis descended onto the forward command center of the Legions surrounding Riva, where the banners of multiple High Lords declared the presence of the most potent powers of the Realm. A nervous young Placidan Lord in charge of aerial security nearly roasted them almost before they had a chance to give him the appropriate password. Amara had been forced to redirect the full force of her windstream into the young man's face, all but scattering him and the squad of Knights Aeris accompanying him from the sky. It was a flier's traditional means of communicating extreme displeasure at the stupidity of a fellow flier, providing a humiliating and discomforting but generally harmless rebuke.

"You're really quite amazing with windcrafting, Countess," Veradis said. The young healer had always seemed to be a woman of great self-possession to Amara, but there was something nervous and quick to the rhythm of her speech tonight. "Honestly. I don't think even my father controls his power that precisely."

"I'm a flier. Your father has several other furycrafts to practice and a city to administrate."

Veradis made no reply, and Amara cursed her thoughtless words. High Lord Cereus certainly had no city anymore. Ceres was a memory, its people a band of scattered and widely dispersed refugees—where they survived at all. "What I meant to say," Amara said quietly, "is thank you, lady."

Veradis gave her a strained nod as they moved out of the circled furylamps of the landing area. Other fliers were streaming in. Amara saw Lord and Lady Placida descending, an unlikely-looking couple: He was stout, plain, and blocky, a man who looked more like a blacksmith or woodworker than a High Lord of Alera. She was tall, regal, a fiercely beautiful woman with long red hair barely constrained by a long braid and an aura of fiery intensity. Both wore Legion armor and carried swords. She carried a slender dueling blade, while Lord Placida bore a great monster of a sword on a belt over one shoulder, a weapon suitable for felling gargants and medium-sized trees with a single stroke.

"Countess Calderon," Lady Placida said. She hurried off the landing area as other fliers descended, nodding to Amara and to Veradis. "Veradis, hello, child. Countess, do you have any idea what's going on?"

"Lady Aria, Lady Isana has been taken," Veradis said. "Men came to her quarters at the inn. They circumvented the furies watching it and took her and Sir Araris."

"What?" Lady Placida asked, her face growing darker.

"In the middle of all of this?" Lord Placida said, waving a hand around at the Legions. He looked up at his wife, and said, "She doesn't have significant strategic value. Could it be personal?"

"You're assuming it was the enemy who took her," Lady Placida said, glancing up at the banners overflying the command tent, foremost among them Lord Aquitaine's. "As the focus of Octavian's support here at Riva, she has a great deal of political value." Her hand strayed to her sword, and she smiled, "I'm going to—"

Placida frowned, staring at nothing, and put his hand over hers before she could draw the blade. "No," he said. "Temper, my love. Think. Attis is cold-blooded, not stupid. Raucus would take his head off." He paused, and allowed, "Or you might."

"Thank you," Lady Placida said, stiffly.

"Or I suppose I might," he mused, taking his hand from hers and drumming his fingers on the baldric of the greatsword. He narrowed his eyes in thought. "Which . . . could be what the enemy had in mind. Especially now that we know Octavian is on his way."

"Sow division among us? Could these creatures understand us that well?" Lady Placida asked. Some of the anger seemed to ease out of her.

"Invidia could," Placida pointed out.

"I should have called her out years ago," Lady Placida said, scowling.

Lord Placida harrumphed, uncomfortably. "It wouldn't have been very lady-like of either of you."

"There's no way to know what's happened yet," Amara said, cutting across them. "And no, Lady Placida, I don't know what's going on. I was hoping you would."

"The pickets must have seen an approaching force," Placida said confidently. "Our forces are already moving to man the outer palisades. That's the only thing that would have raised this much racket from the Legion captains."

"I thought they were more than a week away," Amara said.

"If it's any consolation, Countess, so did I," Lady Placida said. She glanced at the command tent again as more trumpet signals came drifting on the wind, clearly torn. "Our Legions are in the center of the defenses. We must be there to stand with them, Countess."

Amara nodded. Crafters with the power of the Placidas would be integral components of any battle plan. There was no one to substitute for them. "I'll keep you informed as to what I find."

"Do," Lady Placida said. She put a hand on Amara's shoulder and squeezed. "As soon as I'm free, I'll do whatever I can to help you."

Amara managed not to wince. It might have been a measure of how much pressure Lady Placida was under that she had misjudged the fury-enhanced strength of her own fingers.

Placida took his wife's arm and gestured toward the command tent. "We'll find out whatever we can from Attis. Dear?" The two of them nodded to Amara and Veradis and strode toward the command tent, passing a squad of heavily armed *legionares*.

"Should we go, too?" Veradis asked.

"Unfortunately, I don't have permission to be inside command," Amara said. "Something about being considered Gaius Sextus's personal assassin, I suppose." Indeed, the *legionares* on duty outside the tent were watching Amara closely. "And I doubt that you have permission, either."

"No. I'm supposed to be remaining here as a civilian watercrafter when the Legions enter battle." She frowned at the guards, and said, "If we wait here doing nothing, it may be hours before anyone can be sent to Lady Isana's aid."

"That's true."

Veradis frowned more severely. "I suppose we might go in anyway." She eyed the guards. "They seem like perfectly decent soldiers to me, though. I'm not sure I could do it without injuring them, and they haven't earned that. And I dislike the notion of creating work for some poor healer."

Amara's imagination treated her to the image of what havoc might result from a strongly talented young Citizen determined to bypass a group of stubbornly resistant guards, outside a much larger group of High Lords with a good many reasons to be nervous. She shuddered. "No. I'm sure we can find an alternative."

The curtain to the command tent opened, and a small, slender figure emerged, innocuous among the armored forms crowding the night. The sandy-haired young man slipped into the shadows and walked away calmly, effectively invisible amidst the bustle of the stirring camp.

"There," Amara said. "There's our option." She dodged a pair of Phrygian Lords and pursued the unobtrusive young man.

Two steps before she reached him, he turned, blinking, his expression mild, even anxious to please. Amara, however, recognized the subtle centering of his balance and took note of the fact that she couldn't see one of his hands, which was quite likely touching the hilt of a dagger concealed beneath his rather loose and travel-worn coat.

"Ah," Amara said, spreading her hands at her sides, to show them empty. "Sir Ehren."

The young man blinked up at her, his gaze flicking over her, then over Veradis, who came hurrying up behind her. "Ah. Countess Calderon. Lady Veradis. Good evening, ladies. How may I serve you?"

Amara reflected that it had quite probably been Sir Ehren, who was serving as one of Aquitaine's primary intelligence agents, who had both added her to the no-admittance list around Lord Aquitaine and managed to see to it that she received a copy of the list, a pride-preserving courtesy that had prevented an unpleasant scene. She liked Ehren, though in the wake of Gaius Sextus's death, she was uncertain of where his loyalties ultimately lay—but as a classmate of Octavian's, she judged it unlikely that he would have mild, passive inclinations about the succession, regardless of whom he decided to support.

"Well," Amara said. "That's a more complicated question than it would at first seem."

Sir Ehren arched an eyebrow. "Ah?"

"Gaius Isana has been abducted," Amara said, and watched the young man's reaction very closely.

Ehren had been trained to school his reactions, just as she had. He had also been trained to falsify them. She knew the signs to look for, which would mark a reaction as genuine or false. He would, of course, know that she knew it, and could potentially modify his response to take advantage of the fact—but she judged that it would take someone with more experience in life than Sir Ehren currently possessed to deceive both her own trained eyes and ears *and* the watercrafting senses of someone as skilled as Veradis. Particularly if she clubbed him over the head with the news rather than taking a more subtle approach.

Sir Ehren's reaction was a complete *non*reaction. He simply stared at her for a moment. Then he pinched the bridge of his nose between his thumb and forefinger. "She's been . . . bloody *crows*." The voice that emerged from the young man was a great deal more strident—and frustrated—than she would have expected to accompany his face and bearing. "Abducted. Of *course* she has been. Because obviously there isn't *enough* going wrong tonight." He glared at her. He had a rather effective glare, Amara thought, despite the muddy hazel color of his eyes and the fact that he stood nearly half a foot shorter than she did and was thus compelled to glare *up* at her. She had to make a conscious effort not to take a step back. Veradis *did* step back from him. "And I suppose," he said, "you want me to help."

Amara faced the young man mildly. "You . . . do seem to be having that sort of evening, Sir Ehren."

"Crows," he said wearily. The word betrayed a wealth of exhaustion. He hid it well, but Amara could see the signs of strain on his young face. If he'd been any older, she suspected, the past weeks would have aged him ten years. He closed his eyes for a moment and took a deep breath. The change in the young man was nearly magical. His expression became mild again, his posture diffident, nearly servile. "I'm not sure how you could trust anything I did to help you, Countess."

"She couldn't," Veradis said quietly, and took a step closer to the young man, extending her hand. "But I could."

Ehren eyed Veradis. A skilled watercrafter's ability to sense the truth in another, when it was freely shared, was the bane of all manner of deceptive enterprise—and if trusted too casually, was a wellspring of fresh deceptions in its own right. As someone who had spent years becoming skilled in that particular expertise, he probably regarded it with almost as much distrust and wariness as Amara did.

"How could this possibly harm the Realm, Cursor?" Veradis asked, smiling slightly.

Ehren warily took her hand. "Very well."

"One question," Veradis said quietly. "Whom do you serve?"

"The Realm and people of Alera, and the House of Gaius," Ehren replied promptly. "In that order."

Veradis listened with her head tilted slightly to one side. As the young man spoke, she shivered slightly, withdrew her hand, and nodded to Amara.

"I note," Amara said drily, "that your choice of loyalties, Cursor, is not quite the Academy standard."

Ehren's mild eyes flickered with something hard, and he began to say something but seemed to think better of it. Then he said, "One should bear in mind that at the moment, there are two scions of the House of Gaius in the Realm. I'm working with the one that's actually here."

Amara nodded. "Isana was taken from—"

"I know where she was staying," Ehren said. "And I know the security precautions protecting her. I designed them."

Amara arched an eyebrow. If that was the case, then it seemed likely that Ehren was serving as Aquitaine's de facto minister of intelligence. That he was, in effect, the spymaster of what remained of the entire Realm.

He watched her reaction and grimaced. "Gaius sent me to Aquitaine with his last letters. In them, he commanded me to serve him to the best of my conscience, or to inform him that I could not do so and depart, and to do him no harm. And he recommended me to Aquitaine as the most trustworthy Cursor he could pass on, at the moment."

Amara felt a small pang in her chest at that.

But then, Gaius *hadn't* been able to trust her. She'd walked out on her oath.

With good reason, perhaps, but the fact remained that she had turned away from his service.

"The same went for Sextus's physician, by the way," Ehren said. "Not as though Aquitaine needs one, but you never know. He's around here somewhere." The young man shook his head. "I'm sorry, I'm wandering. Too many things going on." He scrunched up his eyes, and said, "Right. The First Lady. The attack had to be aerial. Any other approach would have garnered too much of a reaction from the furies protecting the inn."

"How could they have done it at all?" Veradis asked.

"We don't have unlimited furypower at our disposal," Ehren said, his voice carrying a slight edge. "The enemy has furycraft, too. We thus have a finite number of secure furies. Many of them had been diverted to protect the majority of the political and military resources of the Realm, which were at the Senate meeting."

"What are the odds they could have brought the First Lady down anywhere inside the city or encampment without being seen?" Amara asked.

"Bad," Ehren replied frankly. "She's been everywhere since the capital. Helped a lot of people. She's better known on sight among the populace than Sextus ever was." He sighed and faced Amara squarely. "Aquitaine wasn't behind it. He couldn't have done it without me finding out."

Amara grimaced. "You're sure?"

"Very."

"Then it was the enemy," Amara said.

"It seems likely," Ehren said. "We know that the vord Queen still controls a cadre of skilled Knights Aeris and Citizens."

"If the vord have her . . . if they flew out, they could be miles from here by now," Veradis breathed.

"Aquitaine is occupied," Amara said. "And the temptation for him to remain occupied is going to be great."

Ehren tilted his head to one side, a gesture of allowance, while spreading the fingers of one hand. He looked torn.

"Help us," Amara said.

"There is a lot more at stake here than one woman's life," Ehren replied quietly.

"Cursor," Amara said, "you learned from my example that it was wrong to blindly follow a First Lord. That you could find yourself used. So it is time to ask yourself whether you serve the Realm first—or the people who *are* the Realm. Gaius Isana was Steadholder Isana first. And freeman Isana before that." She smiled tightly, and delivered the next sentence flat, without the coating of gentleness that would have made it slide home like a well-honed knife. "And she was your friend's mother before that."

Ehren gave her a sour look but leavened it with a nod of thanks, that she hadn't driven that last home in the properly manipulative Academy fashion.

"Aquitaine has all that remains of the Realm to stand with him tonight," Veradis said. "Who does the First Lady have?"

Ehren tapped a toe several times on the ground and nodded once, sharply. "Come with me."

They followed him as he started through the encampment, moving at a quick walk. "Where are we going?" Amara asked.

"Every scrap of battlecraft we have is being focused right now," Ehren said. "There's a force of better than five hundred thousand vord closing on us. They'll reach the defenses within the hour."

"How did they get here so swiftly?"

"We're not sure," Ehren said. "But logic suggests that they repaired the severed causeways."

"*What?*" Veradis demanded. "Could they possibly have *done* that in the time they've had? It would take our own engineers months, maybe years."

"The work isn't complicated," Ehren said. "Just heavy and repetitive. If they had enough gifted earthcrafters focused on the task it could be done relatively quickly. The causeways weren't built by Citizen-level skills. For healing over the cuts, a powerful Citizen with the proper knowledge could theoretically repair several miles a day."

Amara let out a blistering curse. "That's what that little slive meant." At Ehren's glance, she clarified. "Kalarus Brencis Minoris. The vord Queen's slave-master. Before I killed him, he said he'd been focusing on recruiting more earth-crafters, as ordered."

Ehren hissed between his teeth. "I remember the report now. We should have put it together."

"Hindsight is always better," Amara said, walking beside him.

"But isn't that a good thing?" Veradis asked. "If the roads are restored, per-haps Octavian's forces can get here more quickly."

"It's unlikely they've repaired all the causeways," Amara replied. "Most prob-ably they've rebuilt a single artery for their own use, to move an attack force here rapidly. They're coming up from the south, mainly, near the capital. Octavian is far west and a bit north of us."

"And he's only got two Legions." Ehren sighed. "Assuming he got back from Canea with everyone and all those freed slaves stuck to their banners. Maybe fifteen thousand men, total."

"Sir Ehren," Amara repeated. "Where are we *going?*"

"Gaius Attis," Ehren said, pronouncing the name without the hesitation of unfamiliarity, "retained a certain number of skilled individuals for his personal use. I have the authority to dispatch them as needed."

"*Singulares?*" Veradis asked.

"Assassins," Amara said, without emphasis.

"Ah. A little of both," Ehren replied. "Attis felt a need to be sure he had a hand ready to move quickly, if necessary."

"To strike at Octavian if it seemed possible," Amara said.

"I rather think they were primarily intended for his ex-wife," Ehren replied. "Primarily."

Amara gave him a sharp glance. "And you are in charge of them? You know when they are to be used? And you have the authority to send them to help us?"

Ehren bowed to her from the waist, without slowing down.

Amara watched him steadily. Then she said, "You are either a very good friend, Sir Ehren—or a very, *very* good spy."

"Ah," he said, smiling. "Or a little of both."

They walked to the rear corner of the camp, where the tents that were usually reserved for critical noncombat personnel were pitched, according to the standard format for a Legion camp. They usually housed smiths, farriers, valets, cooks, mule skinners, and the like. Ehren walked straight to an oversized tent that displaced four of the regulation-sized structures, opened the flap, and walked in.

A dozen swords leapt from their scabbards in slithering, steely whispers, and Amara straightened from ducking into the tent to find a blade not six inches from her throat. She looked down its length, to the oft-scarred hand that held it in a steady grip, and let her gaze track up the arm of the swordsman to his face. He was enormous, dark of hair, his beard clipped in a short, precise cut. His eyes were steely and cold. It didn't seem that he held the sword so much as that the weapon seemed to grow from his extended hand. Amara knew him.

"*Aldrick,*" hissed a woman's voice. A small, richly curvaceous woman wearing a plain linen gown with a tight-fitting leather bodice stepped out from behind the swordsman. Her hair was dark and curly, her eyes glittering, darting left and right at odd intervals. The smile on her face did not match the eyes at all. Her hands opened and closed in excitement, and she licked her lips as she slid closer to Amara and pushed the end of the blade very gently down. "Look, lord. It's the nice wind girl who left us to die naked in the Kalaran wilderness. And I never thanked her for it."

Aldrick ex Gladius, one of the deadliest swordsmen in Alera, hooked a finger down into the back of the woman's bodice and dragged her close to him, leaving his sword extended. She leaned against his pull. He didn't seem to notice. He slid a hand around her waist, when she was close enough, and pressed her shoulders back against his mailed torso. "Odiana," he rumbled. "Peace."

The fey-looking woman twitched several more times, her smile widening, and subsided. "Yes, lord."

"Little man," Aldrick rumbled. "What's she doing here?"

Ehren smiled up at Aldrick, standing diffidently, as though he weren't bright enough to notice all the naked steel in the room and too innocent of the ways of violence to understand how much danger he was in. "Ah, yes. She's here to, ah, there's a special mission for you all, and you're to do it."

Amara glanced around the tent. She recognized some of the men and women in it, from long before, during her graduation exercise from the Academy. Back before her mentor had betrayed her. Back before the man she'd pledged her life to support had done the same. They were the Windwolves—mercenaries, the long-term hirelings of the Aquitaines. They were suspected in any number of dubious enterprises, and though she could not prove it, Amara was certain that they had killed any number of Alerans during their employers' various schemes.

They were dangerous men and women one and all, strongly gifted at furycraft, known as an aerial contingent, Knights for hire.

"Hello, Aldrick," Amara said calmly, facing the man. "This is the short version: As of now, you are working with me."

His eyebrows climbed. His eyes went to Ehren.

The little man nodded, smiling and blinking myopically. "Yes, that's correct. She'll tell you what you need to know. Very important, and I've other messages to deliver, good hunting."

Ehren nodded and bumbled out of the tent, muttering apologies.

Grimacing, Aldrick watched him go and eyed Amara. A moment later, he put his sword away. Only then did the others in the room lower and put away their weapons.

"All right," he said, staring at Amara with distaste. "What's the job?"

Odiana stared at her with what Amara could only describe as malicious glee. Her smile was unsettling.

"The usual," Amara said, smiling as though her innards hadn't spent the last moments shimmying and twisting in fear. "It's a rescue."

CHAPTER 13

"You've barely touched the meal," Kitai said quietly.

Tavi glanced up at her, a stab of guilt hitting him quickly in the belly. "I . . ." The sight of Kitai in the green gown hit him even more heavily, and he lost track of what he'd been about to say.

The silken gown managed to satisfy propriety while simultaneously placing every one of the young woman's beautiful features on display. With her pale hair worn up in an elegant coil atop her head, the rather deep neckline of the gown made her neck look long and delicate, giving the lie to the slender strength he knew was there. It left her shoulders and arms bare as well, her pale skin smooth and perfect in the glow of the muted furylamps inside the pavilion he'd had set up on a bluff overlooking the restless sea.

The silver-set emeralds she wore at her throat, upon a gossamer-thin wire tiara, and on her ears flickered in the light, gleaming with tiny inner fires of their own. A subtle firecrafting had been worked into them by a master artisan at some point in their past. The second firecrafting that went with them, an aura of excitement and happiness, hung around her like a fine and subtle perfume.

She arched one pale brow in challenge, her lips curving up into a smile, waiting for an answer.

"Perhaps," he said, "I've developed a hunger for something other than dinner."

"It is improper to have one's dessert before the meal, Your Highness," she murmured. She lifted a berry to her lips and met his eyes as she ate it. Slowly.

Tavi considered sweeping the tabletop clear with one arm, dragging her across it and into his arms, and finding out what that berry tasted like. The notion struck him with such appeal that he had lifted his hands to the arms of his chair without even realizing it.

He took another slow breath, savoring the image in his mind, and the desire running through him, and with a moment's struggle, sorted out which were his own ideas and which were hers. "You," he accused, his voice coming out much lower and rougher than he'd intended, "are earthcrafting me, Ambassador."

She ate another berry. More slowly. Her eyes sparkled as she did. "Would I do such a thing, my lord Octavian?"

It became a real effort of will to remain seated. He turned to his plate with a growl and took up a knife and a fork to neatly slice off and devour a piece of the beef—real, honest Aleran *meat*, none of that leviathan-chum they'd been forced to choke down on the voyage—and washed it down with a swallow of the light, almost transparent wine. "You might," he said, "if it suited you."

She took utensils to her own roast. Tavi watched her, impressed. Kitai generally took to a good roast with all the delicacy of a hungry lioness and often gave the impression that she would respond in a similar vein should anyone attempt to usurp her share. Tonight, if she did not move with the perfect smoothness of a young woman of high society, her behavior was nonetheless not too terribly far off the mark. Someone, presumably Cymnea, had been teaching her the etiquette of the Citizenry.

When had she found the *time*?

She ate the bite of meat as slowly as she had the berries, still watching his eyes. She closed her own in pleasure as she swallowed, and only a moment after did she open them again. "Are you suggesting that I would prefer it if you tore this dress from me and ravished me? Here? On the table, perhaps?"

Tavi's fork slipped, and his next piece of roast went flying off the table and onto the ground. He opened his mouth to reply and found himself saying nothing, his face turning warm.

Kitai watched the roast fall and made a clucking sound. "Shame," she purred. "It's delicious. Don't you think it's delicious?"

She ate another bite with the same, torturously slow, relaxed, elegantly restrained sensuality.

Tavi found his voice again. "Not half so delicious as you, Ambassador."

She smiled again, pleased. "Finally. I have your attention."

"You've had it the whole time we've been eating," Tavi said.

"Your ears, perhaps." She cleared her throat, resting her fingertips upon her breastbone for a moment, drawing his gaze there involuntarily. "Your eyes, certainly," she added drily, and he let out a rueful chuckle. "But your thoughts, *chala*, your imagination—they have been focused elsewhere."

"My mistake," Tavi said. "Obviously."

"Obviously," Kitai replied with a rather smug smile. Her expression grew more serious. "Though not solely for the immediate reasons."

He frowned and rolled a hand, inviting her to continue.

She folded her hands in her lap and frowned, as if gathering her words together before releasing them. "This enemy is a threat to you as your others are not, *chala*."

"The vord?"

She nodded.

"In what way?"

"They threaten to unmake who you are," she said quietly. "Despair and fear are powerful foes. They can change you into something you are not."

"You said something like that last winter," he said. "When we were trapped atop that Shuaran tower."

"It is no less true now," she said in a quiet voice. "Remember that I can feel you, *chala*. You cannot hide these things from me. You have tried to, and I have respected your desire. Until now."

He frowned at her, troubled.

She slid her hand across the table, palm up. His own hand covered it without the need for a conscious decision on his own part.

"Talk to me," she urged quietly.

"There was always someone nearby on the ships. Or else we were in lessons and . . ." He shrugged. "I . . . I didn't want to burden you. Or frighten you."

She nodded and spoke without rancor. "Was it because you think I am insufficiently strong? Or because you find me insufficiently brave?"

"Because I find you insufficiently . . ." he faltered.

"Capable?" she suggested. "Helpful?"

". . . replaceable," he finished.

Her eyebrows lifted at that. She returned his earlier gesture, rolling her hand for him to continue.

"I can't lose you," he said quietly. "I can't. And I'm not sure that I'm able to protect you. I'm not sure anyone can."

Kitai stared at him for a moment without expression. Then she pressed her lips together, shook her head, and rose. She walked around the table with that same severe expression on her face, but it wasn't until she was standing beside Tavi's chair that he realized that she was shaking with unreleased laughter.

She insinuated herself onto his lap, lovely in the green grown, wrapped her pale arms around his neck, and kissed him. Thoroughly. Her gentle laughter bubbled against his tongue as she did. When she finally drew away, moments later, she put her fever-warm hands on either side of his face, looking down at him fondly.

"My Aleran," she said, her voice loving. "You idiot."

He blinked at her.

"Are you only now realizing that forces greater than ourselves might tear us apart?" she asked, still smiling.

"Well . . ." he began. "Well . . . well no, not exactly . . ." He trailed off weakly.

"But that was always true, Aleran," she said, "long before the vord threatened our peoples. If they had *never* done so, it would still be true."

"What do you mean?"

She shrugged a shoulder. Then she took up his knife and fork and cut another slice of roast as she spoke. "Many things can end lives. Even the lives of Aleran Citizens. Disease. Fires. Accidents. And, in the end, age itself." She fed him the piece of roast and watched him begin to chew before nodding approval and beginning to cut another. "Death is certain, Aleran—for all of us. That being true, we know that all of those we love will either be torn away from us, or we will be torn away from them. It follows as naturally as the night after sundown."

"Kitai," Tavi began.

She slipped another piece of roast into his mouth, and said, quietly, "I am not finished."

He shook his head and began to chew, listening.

She nodded approval again. "In the end, the vord are nothing special, Aleran, unless you allow them to be. In fact, they are less threatening than most."

He swallowed, and said, "How can you say that?"

"How can I not?" she replied smoothly. "Think on it. You have a reasonably good mind when you choose to use it. I am certain it will come to you eventually." She arched and stretched, lifting her arms straight overhead. Tavi found his left hand resting on the small of her back, left bare by the gown. He couldn't seem to stop himself from stroking that soft skin in a slow circle, barely touching. "Mmmm. That pleases me. And this gown pleases me. And the jewels, too—though I couldn't wear them on a nighttime hunt. Still, they are beautiful."

"And *expensive*," Tavi said. "You wouldn't believe."

Kitai rolled her eyes. "Money."

"Not everyone uses obsidian arrowheads as the basic standard of trade," he told her, smiling.

"No," she replied tartly. "Though if it cost an Aleran money every time he wanted to kill something, it might have helped make your people's history much less interesting reading." She looked down at him for a moment, smiling, then asked, "Do you think the jewels are beautiful, Aleran?"

Tavi touched her cheek. "I'd like to see you in nothing else."

Her smile widened. "That," she said, "would be wholly inappropriate, my lord Octavian." But her hands very slowly rose to the nape of her neck, and the clasp of the gown. Tavi let out another low, growling sound, and felt his hand curling possessively on the line of her waist.

Hoofbeats came rapidly thudding toward the isolated pavilion. The guards, who were stationed in a loose line forty yards down the hill at Magnus's insistence, against the possibility of further vord infiltrators, began exchanging passwords with the messenger, whose voice was pitched high with excitement.

Tavi groaned and rested his forehead against Kitai's . . . gown for a moment. "Of course. Something happens now."

Kitai let out a low, wicked laugh, and said, "We could just keep going, if you like."

"Bloody crows, no," Tavi said, flushing again. He rose, lifting her as he did, and set her gently down on her feet. "Do I look all right?"

She leaned up and licked the corner of his mouth, eyes dancing, then wiped it with a napkin. She straightened the lines of his dress tunic slightly, and said, "You look most proper, my lord Octavian."

He growled beneath his breath, something about remembering not to kill the messenger, and walked to draw aside one of the cloths that veiled the pavilion's interior. A Legion valet was hurrying up the slope beside a messenger in the armor of an Antillan militiaman. The Antillan strode up the hill in the precisely spaced stride of an experienced *legionare*, stopped before Tavi, and saluted crisply. "Your Highness."

Tavi returned the salute. The messenger was a senior centurion of the force defending the city, come out of retirement for the task, and was closer to fifty than forty. "Centurion . . . Ramus, isn't it?"

The man smiled and nodded. "Aye, sir."

"Report."

"Compliments of the Lord Seneschal Vanorius, sir, and there's been word from Riva."

Tavi lifted his eyebrows. "A watersending?"

"Yes, si—" The centurion's eyes had flicked past Tavi to Kitai, and the words choked in his throat. He coughed sharply, then inclined his head and saluted again. "Ah. Please excuse the intrusion, lady Ambassador."

Tavi checked, just to be sure the gown was still on. It was. But with Kitai, you never really knew. He couldn't blame Ramus for faltering, though. She looked stunning. "Word from Riva, centurion?" Tavi prompted.

"Yes, sir," the man said. "Lord Aquitaine reports that the city is under attack."

Tavi blinked and arched an eyebrow, permitting himself no further sign of surprise. "Really?"

"How?" Kitai demanded sharply.

"The message wasn't a long one, sir," the centurion replied. "My lord Vanorius said to tell you that some kind of interference ended it almost before it had begun. Just that Aquitaine appeared, in his visage and voice, having somehow driven through the interdiction the vord have kept on watersendings until, um, recently, Your Highness."

"Well, then," Tavi said. He inhaled once, nodded to himself, then glanced sharply over his shoulder at Kitai.

She nodded, already drawing on a dark traveling cloak. "I will speak to her immediately."

"Thank you," Tavi said. As Kitai left he said, to Ramus, "Centurion, please give the Lord Seneschal my compliments and inform him that our plans to depart have just been moved up by thirty-six hours. I'll be moving the troops tonight. The city must be prepared to receive the auxiliaries and refugees a little sooner than we expected."

"Yes, sir," Ramus said, but his eyes were hard with suspicion.

Tavi eyed him. Ramus was only one man—but he was the kind of man other *legionares* listened to. The Antillans and the Canim were about to be left alone with one another in hideously dangerous proximity. This was an opportunity to plant a useful seed, one he'd sown as often as possible over the past days. "Centurion," Tavi said. "I'd appreciate it if you'd speak your mind."

"They're *Canim*, sir," the *legionare* spat. "They're animals. I fought their raiders in my time in the Legions. I've seen what they do to us."

Tavi considered his answer for a moment before giving it. "I could say that the Legions make use of animals in war on a daily basis, Ramus," he said, finally. "But the truth of the matter is that they are their own people. They are our enemies, and they make no pretense otherwise." He smiled, baring his teeth. "But we both have a bigger problem today. I've fought with the Canim personally, both against them and beside them, centurion, and I've got the scars to prove it. I've spent more time in the field against them than any Aleran commander in history. They're vicious, savage, and merciless. And they keep their word."

Tavi put a hand on the centurion's shoulder. "Follow orders, soldier. They'll follow theirs. And if we're smart and lucky, maybe we'll all get to cut one another's throats next year."

Ramus frowned. He began to turn, and hesitated. "You . . . you really think that, son? Er, sir?"

"No two ways about it. They're in the same corner we are. And there's some of them I'd sooner trust at my back than a lot of Alerans I've known."

Ramus snorted. "Ain't that the crowbegotten truth." He squared his shoulders and slammed a fist to his chest. "I'll take word to my lord Vanorius, sir."

"Good man," Tavi said. He drew the dagger from the centurion's belt, turned, and speared what remained of his roast onto the end of it. Then he passed the knife back to the man. "For the ride back. No sense in letting it go to waste. Good luck to you, centurion."

Ramus took the dagger back with a small, quick grin. "Thank you, Your High—"

A wind suddenly screamed down out of the north, a wall of cold air thirty degrees colder than the still-chilly northern night. One moment, the night was quiet, and the next the wind threatened to rip the pavilion from the ground.

"Bloody crows," Ramus cried, lifting a hand to shield his face. Whipped by the wind, the sea below almost seemed to moan protest as its surface was lashed into a fine spray, "What's *this*?"

Tavi lifted his own hand and faced north, peering at the sky. Clouds were being swallowed by a grey darkness spreading from north to south. "Well," he said, baring his teeth in a snarling smile, "it's about bloody time."

He put a hand to his mouth and used a couple of fingers to let loose a whistle piercing enough to carry even over the sudden roar of cold wind, a trick his uncle Bernard had taught him while shepherding. He made a quick signal to the line of guards, who gathered in on him with alacrity.

"That's enough vacation, boys," he said. "Break out your extra cloaks. It's time for us to save the Realm."

⬦⬦⬦⬦CHAPTER 14

Valiar Marcus became aware that he was being stalked before he'd passed the fourth row of Legion tents in the first quadrant of the First Aleran's camp. At night, the silent rows of bleached, travel-stained canvas were silent except for the occasional snore. Walking among them could be an eerie experience, like walking in a graveyard, the tents falsely aglow with the light reflected from the standard-issue bleached canvas. It was not easy to slip through a Legion's grid of white tents without presenting a conspicuous dark profile against the fabric—which was by and large the reason every Legion used white canvas in the first place. But it could be done by one patient and skilled enough.

Marcus wasn't sure what had tipped him off to the presence of his tail. He had long since ceased to question his knowledge of such things. He'd been in the business his entire life, and his mind seemed to assemble dozens of tiny, nearly unconscious cues into a tangible realization of his surroundings without any particular intent to do so on his part.

Upon reaching his tent, instead of entering he abruptly stopped in his tracks and went completely still. He reached into the earth and sent a portion of his awareness into the ground around him. The beating hearts and deep breathing of a couple of hundred *legionares* flowed up into him through his boots, tangible sensation that somehow *felt* like the background noise of waves breaking upon a shore *sounded*. The hasty stutter step of someone caught moving, somewhere nearby, stood out from that background like the cry of a nearby gull.

Marcus couldn't pinpoint the exact location of his pursuer, but he did get a good general sense of the direction. He turned to face whoever it was, and said, quietly, "If your intentions are peaceful, show yourself."

After a moment of silence, Magnus stepped out from between two tents and faced the First Spear.

"We can speak inside your tent," Magnus murmured.

"The crows we can," Marcus growled back, as quietly, letting his annoyance show in his voice. "I'm going to my bloody cot. And I don't like being followed like that. A mistake in judgment on anyone's part could make things turn ugly."

Magnus walked closer. The old Cursor looked weary and stiff, and he studied Marcus with watery eyes. "Only if you get spotted by the mark. I'm getting old for this kind of work, First Spear. But I've got no one else to do it."

Marcus tried to sound annoyed. "To spy on me?"

"You don't add up," the old Cursor said. "There are some mysteries hanging around you. I don't like that."

"There's no mystery." Marcus sighed.

"No? There's some reason you are apparently so skilled in Cursor fieldcraft?"

Marcus ground his teeth. One wouldn't absolutely have had to be a Cursor to notice old Magnus following him—but he hadn't made any mistakes, and there were few others who would have sensed Magnus's presence. In the absence of other factors, it wouldn't be suspicious for a veteran centurion to have done so. But with Magnus's suspicions aroused, the First Spear had provided him with one more point of confirmation that Valiar Marcus was not who he appeared to be.

"After all we've been through," he said quietly, "do you really think I'm out to harm the captain?"

"I think the captain has too high an opinion of his own cleverness," Magnus replied. "He's young. He doesn't know how the world works. Or how cold-blooded it can be."

"All right." Marcus sighed again. "Assume you're right. I've had plenty of chance to do something bad before now. And I haven't."

Magnus gave him a brittle smile. "If your intentions are peaceful, show yourself."

Marcus stared at him, tempted again to confess. But that wouldn't serve the best interests of the First Aleran or the Princeps. If he revealed himself to Magnus, he would certainly be arrested, assuming he was not executed immediately once his true identity was known. Of course, if Magnus worked things out, that would happen anyway.

But he hadn't done it yet.

Marcus growled a well-used obscenity beneath his breath. "Good night, Magnus."

He stalked into his tent and tossed the flap back with unnecessary force. It was as close as he could come to slamming a door. Then he kept his attention on the ground and waited until the old Cursor's footsteps had retreated.

He reached for the lacings of his armor with a sigh and was startled half out of his wits when a Cane's basso voice rumbled quietly, from the blackness at the back of his tent, "It is good that you did not let him in. It would have been awkward."

Marcus turned and muttered his lone little furylamp to life at its weakest intensity. By its dim golden glow, he made out the massive form of a Canim Hunter, crouching on his cot, making the suspended canvas mattress sag with his weight. Marcus's heart was racing at the surprise, and he stood with one hand on the hilt of his *gladius*. He faced the Cane for a few seconds, then asked, quietly, "Sha, isn't it?"

The reddish-furred Cane inclined his head. "The same."

Marcus grunted. Then he started unlacing his armor again. If Sha had meant to do him harm, it would have happened already. "I take it you aren't here on a hunt."

"Indeed," the Cane said. "There are facts it would be advantageous for Tavar to have."

"Why not go tell him then? Or write a letter."

Sha flicked his ears casually to one side, a gesture reminiscent of an Aleran's shrug. "They are of an internal nature. No Cane of honor could, in good conscience, reveal them to an enemy." The Hunter's teeth showed in a sudden flash of white. "And I could not reach the Tavar. He was engaged in a mating ritual and heavily guarded."

"And you've passed sensitive information through me before," Marcus said.

Sha nodded his head again.

Marcus nodded. "Tell me. I'll be sure he knows."

"How much do you know of our bloodspeakers?"

"The ritualists?" Marcus shrugged. "I know I don't like them much."

Sha's ears twitched in amusement. "They are important to our society in that they serve the makers."

"Makers," Marcus said. "Your civilians."

"They make food. Homes. Tools. Weapons. Ships. They are the heart and soul of my people, and the reason that warriors like my lord exist. It is they whom the warriors like my lord truly serve, they whom he is pledged to nurture and protect."

"A cynical man," Marcus said, "would make mention of how much serving your people seems to resemble ruling them."

"And a Cane would call cynicism in this context nothing but a form of cowardice," Sha replied without rancor, "a decision to think and react without integrity based upon the assumption that others will do the same. When have you seen Varg do anything but strive to protect his people?"

Marcus nodded. "True."

"The warriors live by a code of conduct. It is how they judge the worth of their lives. When one warrior veers from the code, it is the duty of others to call him to task on it—and, if necessary, to kill him rather than allow him to overstep his authority. Varg honors the code."

"What relationship do the ritualists have with the makers?" Marcus asked.

Sha showed his fangs again. "For the most part, a cowardly one. They, too, are meant to be the servants of the makers. Their skills are meant to safeguard the makers against disease and injury. To guard our children as they are born. To offer counsel and comfort in times of loss. To mediate disputes fairly and to discover the truth when it is unclear."

"I've only seen them using their skills at war."

Sha let out a low growl. "The bloodspeakers' abilities depend upon blood. They are fueled by it. This you know already."

"Yes," Marcus said.

"There was a time when it was considered something monstrous for a bloodspeaker to use any blood but his own—just as it is repellent for any warrior to order other warriors into battle without being able and willing to fight himself."

Marcus frowned. "That would rather sharply limit what a given ritualist could do, I take it?"

"Except in times of great need," rumbled Sha. "Or when he was willing to die to do what he believed needed to be done. As such, the powers of the bloodspeakers were greatly respected. Their acts and sacrifices were deeply honored, even by their enemies. The depth of commitment and sincerity of a bloodspeaker was unquestionable." Sha was silent for a moment. Then he spoke in a more detached, businesslike tone. "Some generations ago, the bloodspeakers discovered that they could greatly expand their powers by using the blood of others—the more individuals, the more potent the blood. At first they asked for volunteers—a way for makers to share in the honor and sacrifice of the bloodspeakers' service. But some of them began to do so in war, taking the blood of their enemies and turning the power gained from it to the service of their own war powers. It was argued that the Canim had thus outgrown the need for warriors. For many years, the bloodspeakers attempted to control the warriors—to use them to frighten and intimidate others where possible, and to serve as blood gatherers in times of war. In some ranges, the bloodspeakers were successful. In some, they were less so. In some, they were never able to gain power."

"Why didn't the warriors simply act against them?"

Sha looked shocked at the very suggestion. "Because they are the servants of the makers, as we are, demon."

"Apparently not," Marcus said

Sha waved a hand. "The code forbids it, unless they are guilty of the grossest excesses. Many bloodspeakers did not embrace the New Way. They remained faithful to their calling, their limits. The followers of the Old Way continued to serve the makers and do great good. They worked to convince their brothers of the integrity of their point of view."

"I take it that didn't go well," Marcus said drily.

"A bloodspeaker remaining faithful to his calling has little time left to spend upon politics, especially in these days," Sha replied. He leaned forward slightly. "Those who scorn the Old Way have all the time they need to scheme and plot and speak half-truths to the makers to gain their support."

Marcus narrowed his eyes. "I take it that one of these followers of the New Way is behind the attack on Octavian."

"Likely," Sha said. "Two makers were convinced to make the attempt." His lips peeled away from his fangs in what looked to Marcus like revulsion and anger. "It is an inexcusable offense."

Marcus shucked out of his armor, stacking the four shell-like pieces of it upon one another and tucking it under his cot. "But Varg cannot act on it?"

"Not while honoring the code," Sha replied. "There are still followers of the Old Way among the bloodspeakers, worthy of respect. But they are few, and do not have the power necessary to call their own to task—assuming the person in question would stand for what he has done instead of denying it."

"If this person died, what would result?" asked Marcus.

"If his killer were known, it would cause outrage among the makers, who do not clearly see how he has betrayed them. One of his lickspittles would likely take his place."

Marcus grunted. "Interchangeable corruption is the worst kind of problem of any office. We know that here, as well." He thought on it for a moment. "What does Varg wish of Octavian?"

"My lord does not wish anything of his enemy," Sha said, stiffly.

Marcus smiled. "Please excuse my unfortunate phrasing. What would be an ideal reaction, for someone like Varg, from someone like Octavian in this situation?"

Sha inclined his head in acknowledgment. "For now, to ignore it. To carry on as if the threat was of no particular concern. More demon-slain Canim, no matter how guilty or well deserved, would only give the bloodspeakers more wood for their fires."

"Hmmmm," Marcus mused. "By doing nothing, he helps to undermine this bloodspeaker's influence while Varg looks for an internal solution."

Sha inclined his head again and stepped off the cot. The enormous Cane moved in perfect silence. "It is good to speak with those who are perceptive and competent."

Marcus found himself smiling at the compliment without any apparent source or object and decided to return it in kind. "It is good to have enemies with integrity."

Sha's ears flicked in amusement again. Then the Hunter raised the hood of his dark grey cloak to cover his head and glided out of the tent. Marcus felt no need to make sure that he had a safe route out of the First Aleran's camp. Sha had gotten in easily enough—which was, in its own way, proof that Varg had not been behind the attempt on Octavian's life. Had Hunters managed to get that close to Octavian, their past performance suggested that he would not have survived the experience, despite all the furycraft he'd managed to master in the past year. Odds were excellent that Marcus wouldn't have survived it, either.

He sighed and rubbed a hand over his close-cropped hair. He'd been looking forward to a relatively lengthy night's sleep, as compared to what he'd been getting lately. Sha's visit had neatly assassinated that possibility, if nothing else.

He muttered to himself and donned his armor again, something a great deal more easily done with help than alone. But he managed. As he dressed, the weather shifted with abrupt intensity, a cold wind that came howling down out of the north. It set the canvas of his tent to popping, and when Marcus emerged from it, the wind felt as if it had come straight down the slope of a glacier.

He frowned. Unseasonal, for this late in the year, even in the chilly north. The wind even smelled of winter. It promised snow. But it was far too late in the year for such a thing to happen. Unless . . .

Unless Octavian had, somehow, inherited Gaius Sextus's talents in full measure. It was impossible. The captain had not had time to train, nor a teacher to instruct him in whatever deep secrets of furycraft had allowed Gaius Sextus to readily, frequently, and casually exceed the gifts of any other High Lord by an order of magnitude.

Furycraft was all well and good—but no one man could turn spring into bloody winter. It simply was not possible.

Pellets of stinging sleet began to strike Marcus's face. They whispered against his armor like thousands of tiny, impotent arrowheads. And the temperature of the air continued to drop. Within a few moments, frost had begun to form upon the grass and upon the steel of Marcus's armor. It simply could not be happening—but it was.

Octavian had never been an able student where impossibilities were concerned.

But in the name of the great furies, *why* would he do such a thing?

As he turned onto the avenue that would lead to the Legion's command tent, he met up with Octavian and his guards, walking briskly toward the command tent.

"First Spear," the captain said. "Ah, good. Time to roust the men. We're leaving for the staging area in an hour."

"Very good, sir," Marcus replied, saluting. "I need to bend your ear for a moment, sir, privately."

Octavian arched an eyebrow. "Very well. I can spare a moment, but after that I want you focused on getting the First Aleran to our departure point."

"Yes, sir," Marcus responded. "Which is where, sir?"

"I've marked a map for you. North."

Marcus frowned. "Sir? North of here there's nothing but the Shieldwall and Iceman territory."

"More or less," Octavian said. "But we've made a few changes."

By noon the next day, the entire First Aleran, together with the Free Aleran Legion and the Canim warriors, had reached the Shieldwall, which lay ten miles to the north of the city of Antillus. Snow lay on the ground, already three inches deep, and the steady fall of white flakes had begun to thicken. If it had been the midst of winter, they would have promised a long, steady, seasonal snowfall.

But that single impossibility had evidently not been enough for the captain.

Marcus had served in the Antillan Legions for years. He stared in mindless, instinctive horror at the sight before him.

The Shieldwall had been broken.

A gap a quarter of a mile wide had been opened in the ancient, furycrafted fortification. The enormous siege wall, fifty feet high and twice as thick, had stood as unchangeable as mountains for centuries. But now, the opening in the wall gaped like a wound. In years gone by, the sight would have raised a wild alarm, and the shaggy white Icemen would already have been pouring into it by the thousands.

But instead, everything seemed calm. Marcus took note of several groups of wagons and pack animals who traveled on a well-worn track through the snow, leading to the gaping opening. Unless he missed his guess, they were carrying provisions. Tribune Cymnea's logistics officers appeared to be loading up supplies for a march.

Without signaling a halt, the captain continued riding straight toward the hole in the wall, and the Legions of Canim and Aleran soldiers followed him.

Marcus shivered involuntarily as he passed through the opening in the Shieldwall. The men were complaining to one another when they thought they wouldn't be overheard. Orders had come back from the captain: No one was to utilize the simple firecrafting that would have done more to insulate the men against the cold than any cloak.

On the other side of the Shieldwall was . . . a harbor.

Marcus blinked. The open plain before the Shieldwall was perfectly flat for half a mile from the wall's base, as it was along the entire length of the wall. It made it easier to shoot at targets if they weren't constantly bobbling up and down on varying terrain and helped to blind the enemy with his own ranks when the Icemen attacked. It was, simply, an open patch of land.

It was packed with the tall ships of the armada that had returned from Canea, a forest of naked masts reaching up to the snowy sky. The sight was bizarre. Marcus felt thoroughly disoriented as the Legions turned right down the length of the Shieldwall. They eventually had the entire force in a column parallel to the wall. The captain ordered a left face, and Marcus found himself, along with thousands of other *legionares* and warriors, staring at the out-of-place ships.

Octavian wheeled his horse and rode to approximately the midpoint of the line. Then he turned to face the troops and raised a hand for silence. It was rapid in coming. When he spoke, his voice sounded calm and perfectly clear, amplified by an effort of windcrafting, Marcus was certain.

"Well, men," the captain began. "Your lazy vacation to sunny Canea is now officially over. No more recreation for you."

This drew a rumbling laugh from the Legions. The Canim did not react.

"As I speak," the captain continued, "the enemy is attacking all that remains of our Realm. Our Legions are battling them on a scale unmatched in our history. But without our participation, they can only postpone the inevitable. We need to be at Riva, gentlemen, and right now."

Marcus listened to the captain's speech, as he outlined the situation on the far side of the Realm—but his eyes were drawn to the ships. He didn't see as clearly as he used to, but Marcus noted that the ships had been . . . modified, somehow. They rested on their keels, but instead of plain, whitewashed wood, the keels had somehow been replaced or lined with shining steel. Other wooden structures, like arms or perhaps wings, spread out from either side of the ships, ending in another wooden structure as long as the ship's hull. That structure, too, sported a steel-lined keel. Between the ship's keel and those wings, it stood perfectly straight, its balance maintained. Something about the design looked vaguely familiar.

"With decent causeways," the captain was saying, "we could make it there in a couple of weeks. But we don't have weeks. So we're trying something new."

As he spoke the words, a ship flashed into sight. It was a small, nimble-looking vessel, and Marcus immediately recognized Captain Demos's ship, the *Slive*. Like the other ships, she had been fitted with a metal keel. Like the others, she sported two wing structures. But unlike the other ships, she had her sails raised, and they bellied out taut, catching the power of the northerly winds.

That was when Marcus realized what the modifications reminded him of: the runners of a sled. He took note of another detail. The ground before the wall wasn't covered in inches of snow. It was coated in an equal thickness of ice.

The *Slive* rushed along the icy ground, moving swiftly, far more swiftly than she ever could at sea. A cloud of mist sprayed out from its steel runners in a fine, constant haze, half-veiling the runners, creating the illusion that the ship was sailing several inches above the ice, unsupported by anything at all. In the time it took Marcus to realize that his jaw had dropped open and to close it again, the *Slive* appeared, rushing down upon him, its runners making the ice beneath them crackle and groan, then soared on by, its sails snapping. Less than a minute later, it was better than a mile away, and only then did it begin to heave to, swinging around into a graceful turn. It took a few moments for the ship to rerig its sails to catch the wind from the opposite quarter for the return trip, and they bellied out for almost a minute before the *Slive* lost her momentum and began to return toward them.

"I'm afraid it's back to the ships," the Princeps said into the shocked silence. "Where we will sail the length of the Shieldwall to Phrygia and take the remaining intact causeways south to the aid of Riva. Your ship assignments will be the same as they were when we left Canea. You all know your ships and your captains. Fall out by cohorts and report to them. We'll leave as soon as the road ahead is ready for us."

"Bloody crows," Marcus breathed. If all the ships could sail so swiftly over the ice—though he somehow doubted that the *Slive*'s performance was typical—they could sail the entire breadth of the Realm in . . . bloody crows. In hours, a handful of days. Phrygia and Riva were the two most closely placed of the great cities of the Realm—a fast-moving Legion on a causeway could make the journey in less than three days.

If it worked, if the winds held, the ice held, and the newly designed ships held, it would be the swiftest march in Aleran history.

Stunned, Marcus heard himself giving orders to his cohort and coordinating with the First Aleran's officers to make sure the embarking went smoothly. He found himself standing in silence beside the captain as men, Canim, and supplies were loaded.

"How?" he asked quietly.

"My uncle used to take me sledding during the winter," Octavian said quietly. "This . . . seemed to make sense."

"The snow was your doing?"

"I had help," the captain said. "From more than one place." He lifted a hand and pointed to the north.

Marcus looked and saw movement among the trees to the north of the Shieldwall. Faint, blurred shapes with pale, shaggy fur flickered here and there among them.

"Sir," Marcus choked. "The Icemen. We can't possibly leave Antillus unprotected."

"They're here at my invitation," he replied. "Managing snow in springtime is one thing. Turning it into ice quickly enough to suit our need is another thing entirely."

"The reports at Antillus were true, then? That the Icemen have power over the cold?"

"Over ice and snow. A form of watercrafting, perhaps. That was my mother's theory." He shrugged. "We certainly don't have the ability to coat the ground in ice from here to Phrygia. The Icemen do. That's where Kitai's been the past few days. Their chiefs are on good terms with her father."

Marcus shook his head slowly. "After all those years of . . . they agreed to help you?"

"The vord threaten us all, First Spear." He paused. "And . . . I gave them an incentive."

"You *paid* them?"

"In property," Octavian replied. "I'm giving them the Shieldwall."

Marcus began to feel somewhat faint. "You . . . You . . ."

"Needed their help," the captain said simply. He shrugged. "It *is* Crown property, after all."

"You . . . you gave them . . ."

"When this is all over, I think I'll see if I can get them to lease it to us."

Marcus's heart was actually lurching irregularly. He wondered if it was the beginning of an attack. "Lease it, sir?"

"Why not? It isn't as if they've got much use for it, except for keeping us away from them. If we're leasing it, we'll be responsible for upkeep, which they couldn't do in any case. A tangible, fixed border will exist between us, which might help lower tensions on both sides if we can avoid incidents. And since it's their own property, generating revenue, I think they might be considerably less likely to attempt to demolish it on a weekly basis."

"That's . . . sir, that's . . ." Marcus wanted to say "insane." Or perhaps, "ridiculous." But

But a blizzard was coating the land with ice in the middle of what should have been a pleasantly warm spring day.

The analytical part of Marcus's mind told him that the logic of the idea was not without merit. If it didn't work, in the long term the Realm would certainly be no worse off than it was now—barring a major invasion, which was already under way, if from a different direction.

But what if it *did* work?

He was thoughtfully staring at the ships and the distant Icemen when Magnus approached and saluted the captain. He studied Marcus's expression for a moment and frowned slightly.

"This wasn't your idea, I take it?" the old Cursor asked.

Marcus blinked at him. "Are you barking mad?"

"Someone is," the older man growled.

Octavian gave them both an oblique look, then pretended to ignore them.

Marcus shook his head and tried to regain his sense of orientation and purpose. "Times," he said, "are changing."

Magnus grunted sour, almost offended, agreement. "That's what they do."

⊢□□□⊣CHAPTER 15

Their kidnappers had bound Isana and covered her head with a hood before taking her from the room. Her stomach dropped from beneath her as they took to the air again, two windcrafters combining their skills to summon a single wind column to support the weight of three people. Isana was not clothed for such travel. The wind was making her skirts billow out and putting her legs on display.

She had to stop herself from laughing. The Realm's deadliest foe had just taken her from the heart of the most heavily defended city in the world of Carna, and she was worried about impropriety. It was laughable—but hardly funny. If she let the laughter start, she was not sure she would be able to stop it from becoming a scream.

Fear was not something she had ever become comfortable with. She had seen others who had—and not simply metalcrafters, either, who could cheat—walling away all of their emotions behind a cold, steely barrier of rational thought. She had known men and women who felt the fear every bit as intensely as she did, and who simply accepted its presence. For some of them, the fear seemed to flow through them, never stopping or finding purchase. Others actually seemed to seize on it, to channel it into furious thought and action. Countess Amara was an excellent example of the latter. Whereas, even closer to her, Araris had always stood as an example of the former . . .

Araris. She had seen him fly limply across the room. She had seen men dropping a hood over his lolling head. They had, apparently, taken him with her when they left. They wouldn't have hooded him if he was dead, surely.

Surely.

Isana flew on in her fear, and it neither gave her strength nor poured around her leaving her untouched. She felt like a bar of sand that was slowly and steadily being eaten away by the currents of terror around her. She felt sick.

Well enough, she chided herself sharply. If she vomited in the hood, she'd have a considerably humiliating situation to add to her danger and discomfort. If she could neither use nor coexist with the fear, she could at least force herself to carry on—refusing to let the fear make her stop using her mind to do everything within her power to resist her enemies. She could at least do as much as she had in the past.

She had been blinded before, and been forced to rely upon other senses to guide her. She could not see through the hood, nor hear over the roar of the wind, or feel with her cold-numbed, bound hands, nor smell nor taste anything but the slightly mildewed scent of the hood over her head. But that did not mean she was unable to learn anything about her captors.

Isana braced herself and opened up her watercrafter's senses to the emotions of those around her.

They came at her in a mind-searing burst of intensity. Emotions were high among the enemy, and intensely unpleasant to experience. Isana fought to sort out the various impressions, but it was like trying to listen to individual voices within a large chorus. A few high notes stuck out, but by and large they blended into a single whole.

The most intense sensations came from the two men holding her arms—and the primary emotion she felt in them was . . . confusion. They proceeded in a state of bewilderment and misery so acute that for a few seconds Isana could not distinguish her own emotions from theirs. Years of living with her gift had given her an ability to distinguish the subtle weave and flow of emotions, to make reasonably educated guesses at the thoughts that accompanied them.

The men knew that something was badly wrong, but they couldn't focus on what it might be. Every time they tried, waves of imposed sensation and emotion swept over the thought and washed it away. The only time anything solid held was when Isana heard an inhuman shriek drift up from somewhere ahead of them. Both men immediately concentrated with a ferocious intensity, their emotions perfectly synchronized, and Isana felt one of them rise slightly, the other sink, and guessed that they had just been ordered to bank into a long turn, changing their course in the air.

Isana shivered. They were most likely collared slaves, then, forcibly converted to the service of the vord through the use of slaver's collars. Once she'd determined that, she was able to feel more from the two men—their hearts overflowed with sadness. Though their minds had been rendered incapable of reason, on some level they must have known what had been done to them. They knew that their skills and power had been turned against their own people by an enemy, even if they could not consciously assemble the disparate pieces of the concept. They knew that they used to be something more but could not remember what it was, and that denial, that inability to reason, caused them enormous emotional pain.

Isana felt herself begin to weep for them. Kalarus Brencis Minoris had collared these men. Only he could free them—and he had been dead for more than half a year. They could never be freed, never be restored, never be made whole.

She made them a silent promise that she would do everything in her power to ensure that neither would live as a slave. Even if she had to kill them with her own hands.

As she pressed her awareness out past her two captors, she sensed other men. Not all of them were as badly disoriented as her escorts. Those who retained a greater capacity for reason harbored their own eidolon of raw terror. Fear so intense and so savage that it was practically a living *thing* had been forced into their thoughts, and it ruled their decisions utterly, like a watchdog placed within each of their minds. Some of them had lesser degrees of terror—and those men's emotions made Isana shudder with revulsion. In them, the darker portions of human nature, a lust for violence and blood and power, had been encouraged to grow and had overrun their thoughts like rampant weeds devouring a garden. Those men were nothing less than mortal monsters, terrors held on a psychic leash.

And there was . . .

Isana hesitated over this last sensation, because it was so faint, and came to her as a trembling vibration that she could barely be sure was real. She could *feel* the presence of . . . an innocent heart, one that felt emotions with the purity and depth and passion of a young child.

Then another shriek floated to her, and that sense of the child abruptly sharpened—and beneath the simple surface lurked alien currents of feeling, so strange and varied that Isana found herself wholly unable to tell one from the next, much less fit an accurate name or description to the emotion. They were cold things. Dry things. As they pressed against her, Isana was reminded of the rippling legs of a centipede that had once slithered up her calf.

She realized, with revulsion, that the being she sensed was the vord Queen.

Her two escorts began to descend, and her ears popped several times under the changing pressure.

Wherever her captors were taking her, it had not taken them long—and it seemed that they had arrived.

They landed roughly, and Isana would have fallen without the support of both guards. She was propelled forward, being dragged every few steps, and she stumbled upon a slight rise in the ground, as if their path had taken them over a flat stone a few inches high.

But instead of stony earth beneath her feet, the ground gave slightly with a kind of rubbery tension. Isana forced herself to keep breathing slowly and steadily.

She was walking on the vord's *croach*.

None of her captors spoke, and the surface beneath their feet deadened their footfalls to silence. Eerie sounds drifted in the air around her, muffled by the hood. Clicks. Chitters. Once, there was an ululating call that raised the hairs on the back of her neck. Very faintly, she could hear booming reports, like distant thunder. She swallowed. Somewhere far away, Alera's firecrafters had begun their work, filling the skies with their furies.

The ground suddenly sloped down, and a rough hand pushed her head forward, her chin to her chest. She bumped her head against what felt like a rocky outcropping in any case, and it stung momentarily. Then the sounds all faded to silence, and the noise of her captors' breathing changed subtly. They must have brought her inside or underground.

One of her guards pushed her roughly to her knees. A moment later, he removed the hood, and Isana blinked her eyes against the sudden invasion of soft green light.

They were in a cavern, a large one, its walls too smooth to have been formed by nature. The walls, the floor, and a pair of supporting pillars were all covered in the *croach*. The waxy green substance pulsed and flowed with unsettling light. Liquids flowed beneath its surface.

Isana craned her neck, trying to find Araris, her heart suddenly hammering against her ribs.

A second pair of guards dragged him into Isana's line of view. They jerked the hood from his head and dropped him in a heap to the cavern floor. Isana could see that he'd suffered a number of abrasions and contusions, and she felt a physical burst of pain in her heart to see the bruises, the blood—but he had sustained no obvious critical trauma. He was breathing, but that was no guarantee of his safety. He could be bleeding to death internally even as she stared at him.

She never made a conscious decision, but she found herself suddenly straining against her captors, trying to go to Araris. They pushed her brutally to the floor. Her cheekbone dimpled the *croach*.

It was humiliating, how casually, how easily they had taken away her choice. She felt a blaze of anger, suffered a sudden urge to respond in earnest through Rill. She fought the impulse down. She was in no position to resist their strength. Until she had a better chance—until she and *Araris* had a better chance—to succeed in escaping, it would be wisest not to resist. "Please!" she said. "Please, let me see to him!"

Footsteps, softened by the *croach*, approached her. Isana lifted her eyes enough to see a young woman's bare feet. Her skin was pale, almost luminous. Her toenails were short, and the glossy green-black of vord chitin.

"Let her up," the Queen murmured.

The men holding Isana down withdrew at once.

Isana didn't want to look farther up—but it seemed somehow childish not to, as if she was too frightened to lift her face from her pillow. So she pushed herself from the floor until she was kneeling, sitting back on her heels, composed her wind-raveled dress along with her own equally frayed nerves, and lifted her gaze.

Isana had read Tavi's letters describing the vord queen he had encountered beneath the now-lost city of Alera Imperia, and had spoken to Amara regarding her own experience with the creature. She had expected the pale skin, the dark, multifaceted eyes. She had expected the unsettling mixture of alien inconsistency with everyday familiarity. She had expected her to bear an unsettling resemblance to the Marat girl, Kitai.

What she had *not* expected, not at all, was for another achingly familiar face to appear, contained within the canted eyes and exotic beauty of Kitai's visage. Though the Queen resembled Kitai, she was not identical. There was a subtle blending of the features of her face, as parents' faces would combine in the face of their child. The other face within the Queen's was one Tavi had never seen—that of his aunt, Isana's sister, who had died the night he was born. Alia.

Isana saw her younger sister's face in the vord Queen, muffled but not subsumed, like a stone lying quietly beneath a blanket of snow. Her heart ached. After all this time, she still felt Alia's loss, still remembered the moment of awful realization as she stared at a limp bundle of muddy limbs and ragged clothing on the cold stone floor of a low-roofed cavern.

The vord Queen's distant expression suddenly shifted, and she jerked her head back from Isana as though she had smelled something vile. Then, an instant later, seemingly without crossing the space in between, the vord Queen's eyes were immediately in front of hers, her nose all but brushing Isana's. She took a slow, seething breath, then hissed, "What is it? What is that?"

Isana leaned back, away from the Queen. "I . . . I don't understand."

The Queen let out a low hiss, a boiling, reptilian sound. "Your face. Your eyes. What did you see?"

Isana struggled for a moment to slow her racing heart, to control her breath. "You . . . you looked like someone familiar to me."

The Queen stared at her, and Isana felt a terrible, invasive sensation, like a thousand worms writhing against her scalp.

"What," the vord Queen hissed, "is Alia?"

Rage struck Isana without warning, cold and biting, and she flung the memory of that cold stone floor against the sensation upon her scalp as though she could crush the worming caress with the very image. "No," she heard herself say, her voice flat and cold. "Stop that."

The vord Queen twitched, a motion that moved her entire body, like a tree swaying in a sudden wind. She twitched her head to one side and stared at Isana, her mouth open. "Wh-what?"

Isana *felt* the creature abruptly, her presence coalescing to her watercrafting senses like a suddenly rising mist. There was a sense of complete, startled surprise in her, coupled with a child's flinching pain at rejection. The vord Queen stared at Isana in wonder for an instant—an emotion that segued rapidly toward something like . . .

Fear?

"That is not yours to take," Isana said in a hard, firm tone. "Do not try to do so again."

The vord Queen stared at her for an endless moment. Then she rose with another eerie hiss and turned away. "Do you know who I am?"

Isana frowned at the vord's turned back. *Do you?* she wondered. *Why else would you ask?*

Aloud, she said only, "You're the first Queen. The original, from the Wax Forest."

The vord Queen turned to give her an oblique look. Then she said, "Yes. Do you know why I am here?"

"To destroy us," Isana said.

The vord Queen smiled. It was not a human expression. There was nothing pleasant in it, no emotion associated with it—only a movement of muscles, something performed in imitation rather than truly understood. "I have questions. You will answer them."

Isana returned her smile with as blank and calm an expression as she could find. "I fail to see why I should do so."

"If you do not," the vord Queen said, "I will cause you pain."

Isana lifted her chin. She found herself smiling, very slightly. "It would not be the first time I have felt pain."

"No," the Queen said. "It would not."

Then she turned, took two long strides, seized Araris by the front of his mail coat, and lifted him into the air. With a motion of perfectly unfiltered speed and violence, she spun and slammed his back against the *croach*-covered wall. Isana's heart caught in her throat, and she waited for the Queen to strike him, or rake him with her gleaming, green-black nails.

But instead, the vord Queen simply leaned into the unconscious man.

Araris's shoulders slowly began to sink into the glowing *croach*.

Isana's throat tightened. She had read reports, spoken to holders who had seen their family or loved ones trapped beneath the *croach* in a similar fashion. Those so entombed did not die. They simply lay passively, as if they had drifted into a light sleep in a warm bath. And, as they drowsed, the *croach* slowly, painlessly ate them down to bones.

"No," Isana said, shifting forward into a crouch, lifting one hand out. "Araris!"

"I will ask questions," the vord Queen said slowly, as if chewing the words to test them for flavor, while Araris sank into the gelatinous substance. She released him after a few moments, though he continued to be drawn slowly into it, until only his lips and nose remained free of the *croach*. She turned, and her alien eyes glittered with something that Isana could sense as a kind of raw, uncaring fury. "You will speak with me. Or I will cause him pain you cannot imagine. I will take him away from you, little by little. I will feed his flesh to my children before your eyes."

Isana stared at the vord Queen and shuddered, before lowering her eyes.

"You are a momentary curiosity," the vord Queen continued. "I have other concerns. But understand that your fate is mine to decide. I will destroy you. Or I will allow you to live out your days in peace with those other Alerans who have already seen reason. Live it with your intended mate—or without him. It means little to me."

Isana was silent for a long moment. Then she said, "If what you say is true, young lady, then I cannot help but wonder why you are so angry."

She saw the vord Queen move—a blur of motion that she did not register in time to allow her to so much as flinch before the blow fell across her face. Isana fell back to the floor, fire burning her forehead, and wet, hot blood flowed down over her face, into one eye, half-blinding her. She did not cry out—at first because she was simply too startled to respond to the sheer speed of the assault, then because she forced herself to remain silent, to show no sign of pain or weakness before the alien being before her. She ground her teeth as fire spread over her forehead and face, and she made no sound.

"I will ask the questions," the vord Queen said. "Not you. As long as you answer them, your mate will remain whole. If you refuse, he will suffer. It is that simple."

She turned away from Isana, and a radiant green glow filled the chamber. Isana hunched her body uselessly against the agony as she lifted her hand to her forehead. A single cut perhaps four inches long ran along her brow, in an almost precisely straight line. The cut was open nearly all the way to her skull and bled freely.

Isana drew several deep breaths, focusing her effort through the pain, and called upon Rill. The work was harder, much harder than it would have been with even a modest basin of water, but she was able to watercraft the wound closed. A few moments later, she was able to reduce the pain somewhat, and between that and the cessation of bleeding, she felt dizzy, mildly euphoric, her thoughts clogged into muddled clumps. She must have looked a horror, half her face a sheet of red. Her dress was ruined. There was no reason not to use the sleeve to try to wipe some of the blood away, though her skin was tender, and she thought she probably succeeded in nothing but smearing it around a little more.

Isana swallowed. Her throat burned with thirst. She had to focus, to find a way to survive, for Araris to survive. But what could she do, here, with this creature facing her?

She looked up to find the cavern transformed.

Green light swirled and danced through the *croach* covering the cavern's ceiling. Bright pinpoints of light, many of them, stood in slowly swaying ranks. Other lights darted and flowed. Others pulsed at varying rates of speed. Waves of color, subtle variations of shades, washed across the ceiling, while the vord Queen stared up at it, utterly motionless, her alien eyes reflecting pinpoints of green like black jewels.

Isana felt slightly nauseated by the seething, organic motion of the luminous display, but was struck by the impression that there was something about it, a kind of link between the luminosity and the vord Queen that she could not fathom.

Perhaps, she thought, her eyes simply were not complex enough to see what the vord Queen saw.

"The attack progresses well," the vord Queen said, her tone distracted. "Gaius Attis, if that is what he is to be called now, is a conventional commander. An able one, but he shows me nothing more than I have seen already."

"He's killing your forces, then," Isana said quietly.

The vord Queen smiled. "Yes. He has increased the efficiency of the Legions remarkably. The soldiers who escaped me last year are blooded now. He spends their lives well." The vord Queen watched for a moment more before asking, calmly, "Would you give your life for him?"

Isana's stomach twisted as she thought of Aquitaine wearing the First Lord's crown. She remembered the friends of the entirety of her adult life she had buried because of his machinations.

"If necessary," she said.

The vord Queen looked at her, and said, "Why?"

"Our people need him," Isana said.

The vord Queen's head tilted slowly to one side. Then she said, "You would not do it for his sake."

"I . . ." Isana shook her head. "I don't think so. No."

"But you would do it for them. For those who need him."

"Yes."

"But you would be dead. How would that serve the attainment of your goals?"

"There are things more important than my goals," Isana said.

"Such as the survival of your people."

"Yes."

"And that of your son."

Isana swallowed. She said, "Yes."

The vord Queen considered that for a time. Then she returned her eyes to the ceiling, and said, "You answered me clearly and promptly. As a reward, you may go to your male. Assure yourself of his health. See that I have not yet taken his life. If you attempt to escape or attack me, I will prevent you. And tear off his lips as punishment. Do you understand?"

Isana ground her teeth, staring at the Queen. Then she rose and walked to Araris. "I understand."

The Queen's glittering eyes flicked to her once more, then turned back to the ceiling. "Excellent," she said. "I am glad that we have begun learning to speak to each other. Grandmother."

⌑⌑⌑⌑⌑CHAPTER 16

Amara watched the battle with the vord unfold from the air.

She had seen battles before, but mostly those joined between Alera's Legions and her more traditional foes—the forces of rebel Lords and High Lords, smaller-scale conflicts with armed outlaws, and of course, the Second Battle of the Calderon Valley, fought between multiple factions of the Marat and the hideously outnumbered defenders of Garrison, at the valley's easternmost end.

This battle bore little resemblance to those.

The vord approached, not like an army in the array of battle but like an oncoming wave, a tide of gleaming green-black darkness beneath the light of a weak moon. It was like watching the shadow of a storm cloud roll forward over the landscape—the vord moved with the same steady, implacable speed, with the same sense of impersonal, devouring hunger. It was an easy matter to track their progress: There was little light upon the lands of Riva, but where the vord walked, they consumed it all.

By contrast, the Legions were clothed in light. All up and down the Aleran lines, the standards of the individual centuries and cohorts blazed with fury-crafted fire, each in the signature colors of their Legions and home cities. In the center of the lines, the Crown Legion was a blaze of scarlet-and-azure light, flanked by First and Second Aquitaine in a shroud of crimson fire. The right flank was centered upon the veteran forces of High Lord Antillus, burning with cold blue-and-white light, the left around the similarly veteran Legions of High Lord Phrygius, its standards sheathed in glacial green-and-white fire.

Other Legions, some from cities that no longer remained standing, all of them far less experienced than the northern veterans, had been interspaced between those three points and spread across the rich fields surrounding the plain south of Riva in a wall of solid steel and light.

Behind them, hidden from the vord by a wall of illumination, Amara could see the ranks of cavalry waiting for direction for the battle captains of their Legions to decide where they could best be used. Rangy, long-legged coursers from the plains of Placida stood beside the hulking, heavily muscled chargers of Rhodes, who in turn stood next to the shaggy, hardy little northern horses that were barely taller than ponies.

Aquitaine was not content to rest behind the massive fortifications built around the city. The invaders had driven Aleran forces from one defensive position after another, and he had been strongly against Gaius Sextus's defensive strategy from the beginning. Supported by the experienced Legions of the north, he was determined to carry the battle to the enemy.

The Aleran forces were in motion, moving forward.

From high above, Amara could sometimes see entire cohorts of Knights Aeris, black spots of shadow, far below, sharply outlined against the lighted columns of Legions on the ground. There were fewer than there should have been relative to the forces on the move. The Knights Aeris of Alera had taken hideous casualties in the battle to defend Alera Imperia. Their sacrifice had been one of the factors to help convince the enemy to commit the lion's share of its forces to the final assault on the city itself—an assault that had resulted in annihilation for the attacking vord.

Gaius Sextus's final, suicidal gambit had bought Alera the time the Realm needed to recover and prepare for *this* battle, but the cost had been grievous—and Amara feared that their comparative weakness in the skies would leave the Legions with a deadly weak point in their order of battle.

The leading edge of the vord tide rushed to within a quarter mile of the front ranks of the advancing Legions, and a flare of scarlet-and-blue light leapt skyward from the Crown Legion, Aquitaine's signal to commence. Alera's Knights and Citizens, after months of preparation and fear, after enduring more than a year of humiliation and pain inflicted by the invaders, were ready, at last, to give them an appropriate reply.

Even though she'd heard of the general theory behind the opening salvo of furycraft, Amara had never seen anything quite like it. She had witnessed the utter destruction of the city of Kalare by the wrath of the great fury Kalus, and it had been a horrible, hideous sight, vast beyond imagining, uncontrolled, horrible in its beauty—and completely impersonal. What happened to the leading wave of vord was every bit as terrible and even more frightening.

The lords of Alera spoke in a voice of fire.

The standard assault of a skilled firecrafter was the manifestation of a sudden and expanding sphere of white-hot fire. They were generally large enough to envelop a mounted rider. Anything caught inside them would be charred to ashes in an instant. Anything within five yards would generally be melted or set aflame—and anything living within another five yards of *that* would be scorched beyond the capacity of a human being to sustain hostilities. The fire came with an ear-piercing hiss and vanished with a hollow boom. It would leave secondary fires and smooth depressions of molten earth in its wake.

Manifesting such an attack was extremely draining upon the furycrafter involved. Even those with the talents of Lords and High Lords counted the number of spheres he could manifest without resting in the dozens, and not many of those. Given how many vord were on the field, even with the gathered might of all Alera's firecrafters, they could not inflict instant, significant losses upon the mass of the enemy body.

Gaius Attis had considered a way to improve on that.

Instead of the roar of full-blown fire-spheres, a flicker of tiny lights, like thousands of fireflies, sprang up ahead of the oncoming vord. A moment later, Amara began to hear a tide swell of tiny reports, *pop pop pop*, like the celebratory fireworks crafted by children at Midsummer. The sparkling lights thickened, redoubling, creating a low wall in front of the enemy, who charged ahead without slowing.

No single one of the little firecraftings was a deadly threat to a human being, much less to an armored warrior form of the vord—but there were *hundreds of thousands* of them, each one an almost-effortless crafting. As the little flowers of fire continued to blossom, the air around them began to shimmer, turning the sparkling line of lights into strip of hellishly molten air that almost seemed to glow with its own fire.

The leading elements of the vord plunged into the barrier and agonizing destruction. Their screams came up to Amara only distantly, and with a little help from Cirrus, she could see that the vord had not moved more than twenty feet across the killing oven Gaius Attis had prepared for them. The warriors staggered and collapsed, roasted alive, bits of flesh and armor cooking away and being flung up into the gale of rising hot air as ash. Tens of thousands of vord perished in the first sixty seconds.

But they kept coming.

Moving with frantic energy, the vord flung themselves in utter abandonment at the barrier, and thousands more died—but each vord that perished absorbed some of the furycrafted flame. Amara was reminded uncomfortably of a campfire in a thunderstorm. Certainly, no single drop of water could extinguish the flame. It would be boiled to steam as it tried—but sooner or later, the fire would go out.

The vord began to push through, bounding over the charred corpses of those who had come before, using as shields the bodies of their companions who were collapsing from the heat, each successive vord pushing a few feet farther than the one ahead of it.

Signals from the Crown Legion pulled the line of deadly heat back toward the Legion lines, forcing the enemy to pay the full price for those last yards of ground, but they could not bring the band of superheated air too close to the Aleran lines without exposing their own troops to the flame—which also blinded the Aleran battle commanders to the movements of the enemy. So, as the vord began to break through, another signal went up from the Crown Legion, and the massive firecrafting ceased. Seconds later, the vord joined battle with the Legions.

"They have no thought for their own lives," said Veradis, staring down as Amara did. "No thought at all. How many of them died just now, simply so that they could *reach* the battle?"

Amara shook her head and didn't answer. She hovered upon her windstream, high up in the night sky, where the air was cold and bitter. Three wind coaches carrying Aldrick and his swordsmen hovered a few yards off.

"When will the scouts return?" Veradis asked anxiously. The young Ceresian woman was only a moderately good flier, and her long hair and dress were hardly ideal for the circumstances, but she handled herself with composure. "Every moment we wait here, they could be taking her farther away from us."

"It won't do the First Lady any good to go charging off in the wrong direction," Amara called back. "I don't like them, but Aldrick's people know their business. When one of their fliers reports in, we'll move. Until then, we're smartest to wait here, where we can get anywhere we need to be the most quickly." She pointed a finger. "Look. The cyclone teams."

Small, dark clouds of fliers swept down in ranks over the meeting of the opposing forces. As Amara watched, she saw them seizing the air, made treacherously turbulent by the extended fury of the slow-motion firecrafting the Alerans had held before the vord. Citizens and Knights Aeris seized upon that motion in the air, focusing and shaping it, each team adding its own momentum as they wheeled in a caracole down the lines, spinning the furious winds and spinning them again.

It took them only a few moments, working together—and then in half a dozen places just behind the frontmost ranks of the vord, great whirling columns of ash and soot and scorched earth writhed up from the ground. The cyclones roared, howling out a ground-scorching wail of hunger, and began to rush rampantly through the vord ranks, seizing the creatures like ants and tossing them hundreds of feet through the air—when they didn't drive tiny bits of detritus through their carapaces like so many diminutive arrowheads, or simply rend them limb from limb on the spot. Each cyclone was shepherded by its own team of windcrafters, each of which kept its own massive, deadly vortex from turning back upon Aleran lines. Windmanes, glowing white forms, like skeletal human torsos trailing a shroud of smoke and mist where their legs should have been, began to glide out of the cyclones and swept down to attack anything within their reach upon the earth.

Amara shook her head. She'd been trapped without shelter in a furystorm that had called up windmanes once before—and the deadly, wild wind furies had nearly torn her to pieces. Gaius Attis was creating hundreds more of the creatures with the cyclones he was harnessing, and they would haunt the region for decades, if not centuries to come, posing a threat to holders, cattle, wildlife—

Amara forced herself to abandon that line of thought. In this respect, at least, she thought Aquitaine was quite right—if the vord weren't stopped, here, now, there wouldn't *be* any holders. Or cattle. Or wildlife.

We aren't just fighting for ourselves, she thought. *We're fighting for everything that lives and grows in our world. If we do not throw down the vord, nothing of what we know will remain. We will simply cease to be—and no one will be left to remember us.*

Except, she supposed, for the vord.

Amara clenched her hands hard and restrained herself from calling upon Cirrus and flinging her own skills into the battle being fought below.

"Countess?" called Veradis in a shaking voice.

Amara looked around until she spotted the younger woman, hovering several yards farther south and slightly lower than Amara was. She altered her windstream until she had maneuvered into position beside the Ceresian Citizen. "What is it?"

Veradis pointed wordlessly at the causeway leading up from the southwest.

Amara frowned and focused Cirrus upon the task of bringing the road into clearer visibility. At first, in the dim light of the weak moon, she could see nothing. But then flickers of light farther down the road drew her attention, and she found herself staring at . . .

At a moving mass, on the road. That was all she could be certain of. It was different from the stream of still-coming vord warrior forms in that there was no gleam of wan light on vord armor, no regular, seething mass of creatures moving as many bodies under the control of a single mind. There were flickers of light moving amidst that body, irregular in shape, spacing, and color, or she wouldn't have been able to see anything at all.

Amara concentrated, murmuring to Cirrus to draw the distant road even closer in her sight. It was difficult to do so while maintaining her windstream, but the far road sprang into focus after a moment of effort and showed Amara the last thing that she had been expecting in the vord's train.

Furies.

The road was *filled* with manifest furies. Thousands, tens of thousands, of them.

The variety of the furies in sight was dizzying. Earth furies showed themselves as hummocks of stone in the road, rumbling along through the earth. Some were vaguely shaped like animals, but most were not. The largest of them pushed the entire causeway up into a single hummock as they cruised forward, moving as fast as a running horse. Wood furies bounded along the causeway, their shapes never quite matching that of any single animal or creature, but blending the traits of many—others, invisible in the trees and plants at either side of the road, could only be seen as a ripple of forward motion amidst the living things. Water furies bounded or slithered forward, some shaped like great serpents or frogs, while others were simply amorphous shapes of pure water, held together by the will of the fury inhabiting it. Fire furies rushed among them, mostly in the form of predator animals, though others were flickering forms of fire, changing from one instant to the next—it was they whose light Amara had seen. And from three to twenty feet above the surface of the road rushed a horde of wind furies. They were mostly windmanes, though Amara could see far larger wispy shapes ghosting among them, the largest in the form of a truly enormous shark that cruised through the air as if it were the sea.

So *many* furies. Amara felt slightly dizzied.

She dimly noted forms moving along the outer edges of the road, or flying slightly above it—captured Alerans. She realized, after a moment's thought, that they were *herding* the furies below, using furycraft of their own to keep the mass of furies moving along the causeway. The driven furies were not pleased about it either. Their aggressive anger was something that Amara could practically feel pressing against her teeth.

But if they were doing *that* it meant . . .

"Bloody crows," Amara swore. "Those are feral furies."

Veradis stared at her with wide eyes, her face pale. "All of them? Th-that's impossible."

But it wasn't. Not after months of warfare against the vord. The enemy had been indiscriminate in its slaughter. And every Aleran killed meant more furies suddenly bereft of human restraint and guidance. Somehow, the vord had gathered together bloody *legions* of the deadly things. And this was no problem like that of dealing with windmanes in a furystorm, easily solved by taking shelter in a building of earth and stone. If someone tried that against *this* mob, the earth furies would crush him in his own shelter, assuming the wood furies didn't simply follow them in, or the fire furies turn what should have been a haven into a murderous furnace.

Feral furies were not easily intimidated or dissuaded from their violence. It required the skills of a full-blown Citizen to deal with them. It had taken Aleran Citizens centuries to pacify the settled lands of Alera, then the routes followed by the causeways.

And now several centuries' worth of danger and death were racing toward the Aleran lines.

The Legions would never be able to stand before the hammerblow those feral furies would deliver. Simply surviving them would require all of the focus and furycraft at their command—which would mean that they would *not* be able to direct it toward the vord. And in a purely physical contest, the invaders would grind the Alerans to dust.

And should the feral horde shatter the Legion lines and rush through to Riva and the freemen and refugees now living there . . . their deaths would be violent and horrible, the loss of life enormous.

The enemy had just transformed Riva from a stronghold into a trap.

Amara felt herself breathing harder and faster than she needed. To the best of her knowledge, there were no Aleran fliers operating as high as her group. The teams covering the lower altitudes wouldn't be able to see the oncoming threat until it was far too late to react.

Amara shivered and suppressed a desire to scream in frustration.

"Aldrick," she snapped. "Take the Windwolves back to Riva, directly to the High Lord's tower. Stand there to cover Lord and Lady Riva, and to respond to any emergency requiring your team's support." Her eyes flicked to Veradis. "Lady Veradis will explain."

Aldrick stared at her, but only for a second. His eyes shifted down and back up, then he nodded once. He made a short series of hand gestures to one of his men, and seconds later, the Windwolves' fliers and the coaches they carried were banking into a turn, to descend toward the embattled city at their best possible speed.

"Amara," Veradis said.

"There is no time," Amara replied calmly. "The enemy has those furies channeled and moving in the proper direction, but they don't have anything like real control over them. They must have modified the causeway, somehow. Once they turn those furies loose, everything is going to change."

"What do you mean?" Veradis asked.

"We won't be able to hold the city," Amara spat. "Not in the face of so many hostile furies. They'll rip the city to shreds around us, killing our people along the way. The only thing we can do is withdraw."

The younger woman shook her head dazedly. "W withdraw? There's nowhere left to go."

Amara felt a surge of fierce pride rush through her. "Yes," she said. "There is. You will follow Aldrick and his people. Explain to him about the feral furies. Make sure Lord Riva knows, as well."

"B-but . . . what are you going to do?"

"Warn Aquitaine," she snapped. "Stop hovering there like an idle schoolgirl and go!"

Veradis nodded jerkily, turned, and began accelerating to catch up with the Windwolves. Amara watched for a few seconds, to be sure Veradis wasn't about to fly off in the wrong direction in sheer confusion. Then she turned, called to Cirrus, and dived, rushing down toward the far-distant earth with all the speed that gravity and her fury could give her. There was a thunderous explosion all around her as her speed peaked, and she realized that she had none of the operating passwords for the battlefield below. She would just have to hope that the combat teams patrolling the air were too slow to stop her or kill her before she could speak to Aquitaine.

Besides, that was the least of her worries.

How was she going to be able to face Bernard and tell him that for the sake of the Realm, she had chosen to leave his sister's fate in enemy hands?

CHAPTER 17

Tavi stood at the prow of the *Slive* and stared ahead of the fleet as it raced across the long strip of ice laid out upon the north side of the Shieldwall. The ride was not a gentle one. Extra ropes and handholds had been added all over the ship, and Tavi only stayed standing by virtue of holding on to one supporting rope with each hand.

He had grown used to the sound of the runners screaming as they glided over the ice, a sort of endless squeal-hiss that went on and on and on. The ship juddered and shook as it raced before the unnaturally steady northwestern wind, sails rigged to catch it to best advantage. The *Slive* creaked and groaned with every shudder and thump. Those of her crew not terrified for dear life were frantically running up and down the ship, making constant efforts of woodcrafting to keep her timbers from shivering apart under the strain.

"There it is," Tavi called back, pointing ahead to where a Legion javelin with a green cloth tied across its butt had been thrust into the ice. Crassus and his windcrafters had been racing ahead of the fleet, ensuring that the frozen path the Icemen had created for them remained smooth and safe.

Well. Relatively safe. The pace of the ships was faster than any travel Tavi had ever heard of, short of actual flight. They had covered the full day's marching distance of a Legion on a causeway in the first three hours. At that speed, a patch of bare earth within the ice could catch a ship's keel, and sheer momentum would send it tumbling end over end down the length of the vessel. The *Tiberius* actually *had* struck such a bare spot, where the ice hadn't had time to harden properly.

Tavi had watched in helpless horror from a hundred yards away as the vessel wavered, its wing-runners snapping off, and began to tumble, its masts snapping like twigs, its planks splintering into clouds of shattered wood—its crew being tumbled before and among the juggernaut mass of the doomed ship.

Three other ships had foundered as well, overbalanced by the wind, or by mismanagement of their sails, or by simple foul luck. Like the *Tiberius*, they had come to pieces. Tavi thought himself a bit cowardly for feeling relieved that at least he hadn't actually seen it happening with his own eyes: When an ice-sailing ship went down at full speed, no one survived the wreckage. Canim and men were simply crushed and broken like limp, wet dolls.

Now the fliers were marking any spots that might cause another such accident. It was a simple precaution that had already guided them around two more potentially lethal patches of ground. Any idiot could have thought of it ahead of time, but Tavi hadn't—and the lives of the crews of four ships, Canim and Aleran alike, now hung over him.

"The way remains smooth!" Tavi called, noting the next green-flagged javelin beyond the first. "Keep the pace!"

"Giving orders to keep doing what they're already doing," drawled Maximus from a few feet down the handrail. "Well, they say never issue an order you know won't be obeyed, I suppose."

Tavi gave Max an irritated glance and turned back to face forward. "You want something?"

"How's your stomach?" Max asked.

Tavi clenched his teeth and stared out over the land ahead of them. "Fine.

It's fine. It's that slow rolling that really does me in, I think." The ship struck a depression in the ice, and the entire vessel sank, then rose sharply into the air, its runners actually clearing the ice for a fraction of a second. Tavi's heels flew up, and only his hold on the safety ropes kept him from being slammed violently to the deck or off the ship completely.

His stomach gurgled and twisted in knots. One fine thing about being up in the prow was that the ship's sails hid him from view of the stern. He'd already lost what little breakfast he'd had over the rail with no one the wiser. And, with the *Slive* running out in front of the two columns of ships sailing in neat lines behind them, the reputation of the invincibility of the House of Gaius was neatly preserved.

"See?" Tavi choked out a moment later. "Little bumps like that pose no problem."

Max grinned easily. "Demos sent me up to tell you that he suggests we stop for a meal in the next hour or so. His woodcrafters are getting tired."

"We don't have time," Tavi said.

"There will still be plenty of time to break our ships into tiny bits of kindling before we get to Phrygia," Max said. "No sense in doing everything the first day."

Tavi glanced back at him wryly. He took a deep breath, thinking, and nodded. "Very well. At his discretion, Demos will signal the fleet to heave to for a rest." He squinted ahead against the glare of daylight on ice and snow. "How far have we come?"

Max held up his hands and crafted a farseeing before his eyes, peering at a Shieldwall tower they were passing. A number was carved into its stone side, over the entry door for the troops stationed there. "Five hundred and thirty-six miles. In seven hours." He shook his head, and said, his voice wistful. "That's the next best thing to flying."

Tavi glanced back at Max, thoughtfully. "Better, really. We're moving more troops than every flier in Alera could carry. Think of what it could mean."

"What?" Max said. "Moving troops around faster?"

"Or food," Tavi said. "Or supplies. Or trade goods."

Max lifted both eyebrows, then lowered them, frowning. "You could move freight from one end of the Wall to the other in a few days. Even on causeways, it's a six-week trip to Phrygia from Antillus. You have to go all the way down to Alera Imperia, then . . ." His voice trailed off, and he coughed. "Um. Sorry."

Tavi shook his head, forcing a small smile onto his mouth. "It's all right. No use pretending it didn't happen. My grandfather knew what he was doing. I probably would have done the same."

"Taurg crap," Max said scornfully. "No. Your grandfather killed hundreds of thousands of his own people, Tavi."

Tavi felt a hot surge of anger in his chest, and he glowered at Max.

Max faced him, one eyebrow raised. "What?" he asked in a reasonable tone. "You gonna fight me every time I tell you the truth? I'm not scared of you, Calderon."

Tavi gritted his teeth and looked away. "He died for the Realm, Max."

"Took a good many people with him when he went, too," Max replied. "I'm not saying he didn't do what needed doing. I'm not saying he was a bad First Lord. I'm just saying that you aren't much like him." He shrugged. "I'm thinking that your solutions wouldn't look much like his did."

Tavi frowned. "How so?"

Max gestured at the front of the ship. "Old Sextus never would have had his ship up front, where disaster could hit it if our fliers got sloppy or unlucky. He'd . . ." Max scrunched up his eyes thoughtfully. "He'd have positioned two or three of either his worst captains or his best up here. His worst to get rid of the deadweight if another ship went down, his best because they'd be the ones most likely to challenge his authority."

Tavi grunted. "No good. I need all my captains. And Demos *is* the best captain in my fleet."

"Don't let Varg hear you say that," Max said. "And speaking of taking pointless risks . . ."

Tavi rolled his eyes. "I had to. If the ritualists had been given time to whip the Canim into a frenzy over the two makers we killed, Varg wouldn't have dared to leave them back at Antillus for fear he'd lose control. By changing the issue to a question of Varg's personal honor, it brought the whole thing to a screaming halt. Varg is the dead makers' champion now, not the ritualists. He's still in control."

"So when he kills you, it will be orderly," Max said.

"It won't come to an actual duel," Tavi said confidently. "Neither one of us wants that. We're only doing it to force the ritualists to hold back, rather than urging other Canim to take action and maybe remove Varg from power. But if Varg can pull the ritualists' fangs, a duel won't be necessary. We'll resolve it before it comes to bloodshed." After a hesitation, he added, "Probably."

Max snorted. "What if he doesn't? He brought the ritualists with him, you know."

Tavi shrugged. "I doubt they *all* want me dead, Max. And they've got experience fighting the vord. He'd be a fool to leave them behind. He'll handle them."

"All right. But what if he doesn't?"

Tavi stared out at the path ahead of them for a silent moment, and said, "Then . . . I'll have to kill him. If I can."

They hung on to the safety lines while the *Slive* bucked and shimmied over the ice. After a moment, Max put a hand on Tavi's shoulder, then made his way carefully aft, to relay the heave-to command to Captain Demos.

⊐ЮⅠⅡ⊏ CHAPTER 18

For Amara, the next several hours were a desperate blur.

She came down square in the middle of the Crown Legion, whose *legionares* had been stationed at Alera Imperia for years, and many of whom would recognize her on sight. She nearly skewered herself on a spear, and the startled *legionare* she'd half landed on nearly gave her a killing stroke with his *gladius*. Only the swift intervention of the *legionare* beside him kept him from plunging the wickedly sharp steel into Amara's throat.

After that, it was a matter of convincing the men that only their centurion could deal with her, and that centurion's Tribune would need to do the same, and so on, all the way up to the captain of the Crown Legion.

Captain Miles was a more formal-looking version of his older brother, Araris Valerian. He had the same innocuous height, the same solid, leanly muscled build. His hair was a few shades lighter than Araris's, but then both of them were showing enough threads of silver to make the distinction a fine one these days. Sir Miles limped over to her, moving briskly, every inch the model of a Legion captain, his face darkening with wrath. No surprise, that. Amara couldn't imagine a captain worth his salt who would be thrilled to have some kind of administrative matter thrust into his hands now, when the battle was freshly under way.

Miles gave Amara one look, and his face went absolutely pale.

"Bloody crows," he said. "How bad is it?"

"Very," Amara said.

Miles gestured curtly for the *legionares* holding Amara's arms to release her. "I wish I could say it was good to see you again, Countess, but you've been a harbinger for confusion and danger a little too often for my taste. How can I help you?"

"How can you get rid of me, you mean," Amara said, grinning. "I need to see Aqui—Gaius Attis. Now. Sooner if possible."

Miles's eyes narrowed, then a small, hard grin touched his mouth. "This should be interesting. If you will follow me, Countess Calderon."

"Thank you, Captain," Amara said.

He paused, and said, "Countess. I take it that you aren't going to attempt anything, ah, ill-advised."

She smiled sweetly at him. "Would you care to take my weapons, Sir Miles?"

He huffed out an annoyed breath and shook his head. Then he beckoned for Amara to follow him.

She walked through the blazing light of Legion standards, passing from the Crown Legion proper into a space opened between the single surviving Imperian Legion and the First Legion of Aquitaine. The space between them was filled with cavalry, including, it would seem, the command group around Gaius Attis.

As Amara approached, half a dozen men with long dueling blades—Aquitaine's *singulares*, presumably—drew their weapons and immediately nudged their horses to stand between Amara and Lord Aquitaine.

"Relax, boys," growled Miles. He turned to Amara, and said, "Wait here, Countess. I'll speak to him."

Amara nodded stiffly, and Miles pressed through the *singulares* and disappeared. She did not look at the bodyguards and stood with her weight far back on her heels, her hands in plain view. The very gentle slope of the land let her look down over the heads of the *legionares* between herself and the actual battle line, and she paused for a moment to watch the battle.

From far enough away, she thought, it looked nothing like a brutal struggle. The *legionares* looked like laborers in a field, all spread out in a line, their weapons rising and falling while trumpets blew and drums pounded. The shouts of battle blended into a single vast roaring noise, like wind or surf, individual cries swallowed up and made insignificant against the aggregate sound.

Amara murmured to Cirrus for a farseeing, then swept her gaze up and down the lines.

Last year, almost all of the enemy infantry had appeared as low-slung, swift-moving imitations of the vicious lizards of the Kalaran swamps called "garim." Most of the rest had looked almost like nightmarish renditions of armored Alerans, their arms transformed into stabbing, chopping scythes, while great wings like those of beetles or perhaps dragonflies lifted them into aerial combat.

The vord had taken new forms.

Most of them, Amara saw, looked like some kind of enormous praying mantis, though squatter, more powerful-looking. They rushed across the ground on four legs, while the two lengthy forelimbs ended in more curving scythe blades. The reason for the change became apparent within seconds, when Amara saw one of thing long scythe claws flash up, then down, at the end of the vord's unnaturally long limb. Its point swept over the shieldwall of legionares of the Crown Legion, and plunged down with inhuman power, slamming through the top and rear of a luckless *legionare's* helmet, slaying him instantly.

The vord did not stop there. The creature dragged the *legionare's* body forth from the line, swinging it left and right as it did so, battering the *legionares* on either side of the dead man. Other vord rushed toward the disruption in the lines, and more men died as the creatures stabbed down with their blades, or hooked a *legionare's* shield with them, to drag another man out of the defensive advantage of the line.

The vord had developed new tactics along with their new forms, it would seem.

But then, so had Aquitaine.

Within seconds of the vord assault, a pair of men stepped out of the rear ranks wielding great mauls of preposterous size—Knights Terra. Drawing their power from the earth beneath them, they stepped forward with the heavy weaponry, shattering chitin and slaying vord with every swing. Within seconds, they had killed or driven back the vord nearby, after which they returned to their original positions. As they did, a centurion, bellowing until his face was purple, kicked his men into a semblance of order and re-formed the line.

Amara looked up and down the lines, counting heavy weaponry. She was shocked at how many Knights Terra she could see, waiting in supporting positions in the third or fourth rank of each Legion, ready to step forward and steady any weak points in the shield line. Standard tactical doctrine insisted that the power represented by Knights Terra should be concentrated in one place, hammered into a deadly spearpoint that could thrust through any foe.

Then she realized—in the current situation, standard tactical doctrine had been superseded by the desperation of the Realm's defenders. Standard doctrine was based upon the assumption that the furycrafting talent of a Knight would be in short supply, for the excellent reason that they nearly always were. But here, now, the Citizens standing to battle outnumbered the Legions' Knights by an order of magnitude. They could *afford* to place the normally rare assets into supporting positions in the line. There would be plenty of furypower left over.

The medicos labored feverishly, dragging the wounded and dead back from the line, where they would be sorted into three categories. First came the most severely wounded, who would need the attentions of a healing tub merely to survive. Next priority went to those men most lightly wounded—a visit to a healing tub and a comparatively minor effort from a watercrafter would put them back into the lines in an hour.

And then came . . . everyone else. Men with their bellies ripped open could not hope to return to the fight, but neither were they in danger of expiring from their injury within the day. Men with shattered ribs, their wind too short to permit them to scream, lay there in agony, their faces twisted with pain. They were worse off than those who had lost limbs and managed to stop the bleeding with bandages and tourniquets. A man whose eyes were a bloody, pulped ruin sat on the ground moaning and rocking back and forth. Scarlet tears streamed down his cheeks in a gruesome mask.

The dead, Amara thought morbidly, were better off than all of them: They could feel no pain.

"Countess!" Miles called.

Amara looked up to see that Aquitaine's bodyguards had opened a way between them, though they didn't look happy about it. Miles was standing in the newly created aisle, beckoning her, and Amara hurried to join him.

Miles walked her over to where Aquitaine sat on his horse beside a dozen of his furycrafting peers—High Lord Antillus, High Lord Phrygia and his son, High Lord and Lady Placida, High Lord Cereus, and a collection of Lords who, through talent or discipline, had established themselves as some of the most formidable furycrafters in the Realm.

"Countess," Aquitaine said politely. "Today's schedule is somewhat demanding. I am pressed for time."

"It's about to get worse," Amara said. After a beat, she added, "Your Highness."

Aquitaine gave her a razor-thin smile. "Elaborate."

She informed him, in short, terse sentences, of the horde of feral furies. "And they're moving fast. You've got maybe half an hour before they reach your lines."

Aquitaine regarded her steadily, then dismounted, stepped a bit apart from the horses, and took to the air to see for himself. He returned within a pair of minutes and remounted, his expression closed and hard.

Silence spread around the little circle as the mounted Citizens traded uneasy looks.

"A furybinding?" Lady Placida said, finally. "On *that* scale? Is it even possi—" She paused to glance at her husband, who was giving her a wry look. She shook her head and continued. "Yes, as it is in fact happening at this very moment, of course it is possible."

"Bloody crows," Antillus finally spat. He was a brawny man, rough-hewn, and had a face that looked as if it had been beaten with clubs in his youth. "Furies will go right through the lines. Or under them, or over them. And they'll head straight for Riva, too."

Aquitaine shook his head. "Those are entirely uncontrolled furies. Once they're set loose, there's no telling *which* direction they'll go."

"Naturally," Amara said in a dry tone. "It would be impossible for the vord to be able to give them a direction."

Aquitaine looked at her, sighed, and waved an irritated gesture of acceptance.

"If there are that many wild furies, the vord don't need to aim them," the silver-haired, aged Cereus said quietly. "Even if they could only bring the furies close and let them spread out randomly, some of them are bound to hit the city. It wouldn't take many to cause a panic. And as crowded as the streets are . . ."

"It would clog the streets and trap everyone inside," Aquitaine said calmly. "Panic in those circumstances would be little different from riots. It will force the Legions to maneuver all the way around the city walls instead of marching through. Force us to divide our strength, sending troops back to restore order. Cause enough confusion to let the vord slip agents and takers inside." He frowned, bemused. "We haven't seen any vordknights yet, in this battle." He looked back over his shoulder. "They're north and west of us, spread out in a line, like hunters. Ready to snap up refugees as they flee the city in disorder."

Amara got a sinking feeling in her stomach. She hadn't thought all the way through the chain of logic in the vord Queen's gambit, but what Aquitaine said made perfect sense. Though the vord were deadly enough in a purely physical sense, the weapon that might truly unmake Alera this day was terror. In her mind's eye, she could see panicked refugees and freemen being slaughtered by wild furies, could see them taking to the streets with all they could carry, shepherding their children along with them, seeking a way out of the death trap the walls of Riva had become. Some would manage to escape the city—only to find themselves the prey of an airborne foe. And while the rest of the city's residents were trapped and embroiled in chaos, the Legions were effectively pinned in place. They could not retreat without leaving the people of Riva to be butchered.

The great city, its people, and its defending Legions would all die together within days.

"I think we'd better stop those furies," Antillus rumbled.

"Yes, thank you, Raucus," Lord Phrygia said in an acidic tone. "What would you suggest?"

Antillus scowled and said nothing.

Aquitaine actually seemed to smile for an instant, something that surprised Amara with its genuine warmth. It faded rapidly, and his features shifted back into his cool mask again. "We have two choices—retreat or fight."

"A *retreat*?" Raucus said. "With this mob? We'd never coordinate it in the face of the enemy. Whichever Legions were the last out would be torn to shreds."

"More to the point," Lord Placida said quietly, "I think it's a good bet that they'll be expecting it. I think you're right about their circling their aerial troops into position behind us."

"Even more to the point," Aquitaine said, "we have nowhere left to go. No position that will be any stronger than this one. That being the case—"

"Your Highness," Amara interrupted smoothly. "In point of fact, that is not entirely true."

Amara felt every eye there lock upon her.

"The Calderon Valley has been prepared," she said calmly. "My lord husband spent years trying to warn the Realm that this day was coming. When no one listened, he did the only thing he could do. He readied his home to receive refugees and fortified it heavily."

Aquitaine tilted his head. "How heavily could he possibly have strengthened it on a Count's income?"

Amara reached into her belt pouch, drew out a folded piece of paper, and opened a map of the Calderon Valley. "Here is the western entrance, along the causeway. Half-height siege walls have been built across the entire five-mile stretch of land, from the flint escarpments to the Sea of Ice, with standard Legion camp-style fortresses every half mile. A second regulation siege wall belts the valley at its midway point, with fortresses and gates each mile. At the eastern end of the valley, Garrison itself has been surrounded by more double-sized siege walls, enclosing a citadel built to about a quarter of the scale of the one in Alera Imperia."

Aquitaine stared at her. He blinked once. Slowly.

Lady Placida dropped her head back and let out a peal of sudden laughter. She pressed her hands to her stomach, though she couldn't have felt it through her armor, and continued laughing. "Oh. Oh, I never thought I'd get to *see* the look on your face when you found out, Attis . . ."

Aquitaine eyed the merry High Lady and turned to Amara. "One wonders why the good Count has not seen fit to inform High Lord Riva or the Crown of his new architectural ambitions."

"Does one?" Amara asked.

Aquitaine opened his mouth. "Ah. Of course. So that Octavian would have a stronghold should he need to use one against me." His eyes shifted to Lady Placida. "I assume that the Count has enjoyed the benefit of some support from Placida."

Lord Placida was eyeing his wife with a rather alarmed expression. "I would like to think you would have, ah, informed me if that was the case, dear."

"Not Placida," she said calmly. "The Dianic League. After Invidia's defection, most of us felt foolish enough to take steps to correct our misplaced trust in her leadership."

"Ah," her husband said, and nodded, pacified. "The League, quite. None of my business, then."

Amara cleared her throat. "The point, Your Highness, is that there is indeed one more place where we might make a stand—a better place than here, it could be argued. The geography there will favor a defender heavily."

Aquitaine closed his eyes for a moment. He was very still. Then he opened his mouth, took a deep breath, and nodded. His eyes flicked open, burning with sudden energy. "Very well," he said. "We are about to be assaulted by furies of considerable strength and variety. The fact that they happen to be feral is really rather immaterial. We have neither the time nor the resources to pacify or destroy them. We'll bait them instead. Keep them focused on the Legions instead of upon the Rivan populace." He considered the gathered group pensively. "We'll divide the labor by city, I think. High Lord and Lady Placida, if you would, please summon your liegemen and divide yourselves among both Placidan Legions. Make sure the Legions maintain their integrity."

Aria nodded sharply, once, then she and her husband dismounted and launched themselves skyward.

"Raucus," Aquitaine continued, "you'll take your Citizens to the Antillan Legions, and Phrygius will cover his own troops—and yes, I know the two of you have the most Legions in the field at the moment and that your furycrafters will be spread thin. Lord Cereus, if you would, please gather together the Citizens from Ceres, Forcia, Kalare, and Alera Imperia and divide them to assist the northern Legions."

Phrygius and Antillus both nodded and turned their horses, kicking them into a run as they raced in separate directions, toward their own Legions. Cereus gave Amara a grim nod and launched himself skyward.

Aquitaine gave a series of calm, specific instructions to the Lords remaining, and the men departed in rapid succession.

"Captain Miles," he said, at the last

"Sir," Miles said.

Sir, Amara noted. *Not sire.*

"The Crown Legion will proceed to the northeast gates of Riva to escort and safeguard the civilians," Aquitaine said.

"We're ready to continue the fight, sir."

"No, Captain. After last year, your Legion was down to four-fifths of its strength before today's battle was joined. You have your orders."

Sir Miles grimaced but saluted. "Yes, sir."

"And you, Countess Calderon." Aquitaine sighed. "Please be so kind as to carry word to your own liege, Lord Rivus, that it will be his responsibility to shield the population of Riva as he evacuates them to the Calderon Valley. Have him coordinate with your husband to make sure this happens as quickly as possible."

Amara frowned and inclined her head. "And you, Your Highness?"

Aquitaine shrugged languidly. "I would have preferred to drive straight for the Queen as soon as she revealed herself. But given what's happening, she has no need to put in an appearance."

Amara began to ask another question.

"Neither does my ex-wife," Aquitaine said smoothly.

Amara frowned at him. "The Legions. You're asking them to fight wild furies and the vord alike. Fight them while a horde of refugees staggers away. Fight them while they themselves retreat."

"Yes," Aquitaine said.

"They'll be ground to dust."

"You exaggerate the danger, Countess," Aquitaine replied. "Fine sand."

Amara just stared at the man. "Was . . . was that a joke?"

"Apparently not," Aquitaine replied. He turned his face toward the lines again.

His eyes were calm, and veiled . . .

. . . and haunted.

Amara followed his gaze and realized that he was staring at the screaming casualties on the ground, the men whose proportion of agony to mortality had run too high to rate immediate attention. She shivered and averted her eyes.

Aquitaine did not.

Amara looked back to the battle itself. The *legionares* were holding the enemy tide at bay—for now.

"Yes," Aquitaine said quietly. "The Legions will pay a terrible price so that the residents of Riva can flee. But if they do not, the city will fall into chaos, and the civilians will die." He shook his head. "This way, perhaps half of the *legionares* will survive the retreat. Even odds. If we are forced to defend the city to our last man, they will *all* die, Countess. For nothing. And they know it." He nodded. "They'll fight."

"And you?" Amara asked, careful to keep her tone completely neutral. "Will you fight?"

"If I reveal my position and identity, the enemy will do everything in their power to kill me in order to disrupt Aleran leadership. I will take the field against the Queen. Or Invidia. For them, it would be worth the risk. Until then . . . I will be patient."

"That's probably best, Your Highness," Ehren said quietly, stepping forward from his unobtrusive position in the Princeps' background. "You aren't replaceable. If you were seen in action in these circumstances, it's all but certain that Invidia, or the Queen, would appear and make every effort to remove you."

Amara drew in a slow breath and looked past Aquitaine to where Sir Ehren hovered in attendance. The little man's expression was entirely opaque, but he had to realize Aquitaine's situation. His recent storm of new orders had, effectively, stripped him completely of the support of his peers in furycrafted power. The others as strong as he had been dispatched to protect their Legions.

Leaving Aquitaine to stand against his ex-wife or the vord Queen—should they appear—alone.

One gloved fingertip tapped on the hilt of his sword. It was the only thing about him that might have been vaguely construed as a nervous reaction.

"Either one of them is at least a match for you," Amara said quietly. "If they come together, you won't have a chance."

"Not if, Countess," Aquitaine said, thoughtfully. He slid his finger over the hilt of the sword in an unconscious caress. "I believe I've had my fill of 'if's. When. And we'll see about that. I've never been bested yet." He pursed his lips, staring at the battle, then gave himself a little shake, and said, "Take word to Riva. Then return to me here. I will have more work for you."

Amara arched an eyebrow at him. "You'd trust me enough for that?"

"Trust," he said. "No. Say instead that I have insufficient *distrust* of you to make me willing to waste your skills." He smiled that razor-thin smile again, and waved a hand vaguely toward the battle lines. "Frankly, I find you a far-less-terrifying enemy than our guests. Now go."

Amara considered the man for the space of a breath. Then she nodded to him, somewhat more deeply than she needed to. "Very well," she said, "Your Highness."

CHAPTER 19

In the hours that followed, Isana listened to the vord Queen assault and savage the collected military might of the Realm.

She never left the glowing green chamber beneath the earth. Instead, she simply stared upward, into the glowing light of the *croach*, and gave Isana a running commentary of the battle. In neutral, unhurried tones, the Queen reported the outcomes of maneuvers and attacks.

Isana had seen enough of the war with the vord to translate the words into images of pure horror in her thoughts. She stood beside Araris, checking every so often to be sure that his nose and mouth were still uncovered. His skin, beneath the surface of the *croach*, did not appear to be irritated or burned—yet. But it was hard to be certain. It was like looking at him through tinted and ill-shaped glass of particularly poor quality.

"I find it . . . I believe this is a form of anger, though not a particularly potent example," said the vord Queen, after several moments of silence. "There is a word for it. I find the Aleran defense to be . . . irritating."

"Irritating?" asked Isana.

"Yes," the Queen said, staring upward. She pointed with one black-clawed finger. "There. The workers and noncombatants are fleeing the city. And yet I cannot, quite, reach them. Their destruction would all but assure the end of this war."

"They are defenseless," Isana said quietly.

The vord Queen sighed. "If only that were true. Assigning nearly half the population as expendable protectors is wastefully unnecessary. Most of the time. It won't make a difference in the end, but for now . . ." She lifted a hand and let it fall again, a gesture that somehow contained her irritation, her passing annoyance, and the fate of Alera, all in the same imagined handful. "This world has been ferociously competitive since long before my wakening."

"Those are women," Isana said quietly. "The aged, the sick. Children. They are not a threat to you."

The vord Queen's eyes glinted oddly. "The women can produce more of you, and that cannot be tolerated. The aged and sick . . . there might be some merit in continuing to allow them to drain your people's resources, but their experience and knowledge might tip a balance, which would prove costly."

"And the children?" Isana said, her voice growing colder despite herself. "What harm could they possibly do you?"

The vord Queen's lips spread in a slow, bitter smile. "Your children are indeed no threat. Today." She turned her eyes from the ceiling and stared at Isana for a time. "You think me cruel."

Isana looked from Araris's slack, unconscious face to the vord Queen. "Yes," she hissed.

"And yet, I have offered your people a choice," the Queen said. "A chance to surrender, to accept defeat without losing their own lives—which is more than your people have ever offered me. You think me cruel for hunting your children, Grandmother, but your folk have hunted mine, and killed them in tens of thousands. Your folk and mine are the same, in the end. We survive, and we do so at the expense of others who seek nothing more than to do the same."

Isana was silent for a long moment. Then she asked, very quietly, "Why do you call me that?"

The vord Queen was also quiet for a time. Then she answered, "It seems fitting, as I understand such things."

"Why?" Isana pressed. "Why would you consider Tavi your father? Do you truly believe yourself his child?"

The vord Queen moved her shoulders in a shrug that did not look as though it came naturally to her. "Not in the sense that you mean. Although, like you, I did not choose those whose blood would merge to create mine."

"Why would you care?" Isana asked. "Why should it matter to you whether or not you refer to me in a way that is appropriate to Alerans?"

The Queen tilted her head again, her expression abstracted. "It should not matter." She blinked her eyes several times in rapid succession. "It should not. And yet it does."

Isana took a deep breath, sensing something vital stirring beneath the vord's cool, smooth surface. She wasn't sure if she was speaking to the Queen as she murmured, "Why?"

The vord Queen folded her arms abruptly over her chest and turned away, a motion that appeared quite human. She looked up at the glowing ceiling above her, at the other walls of the room—anywhere but at Isana.

"Why?" Isana asked again. She took a step closer. "Does the answer to the question matter, to you?"

Frustration and a desperate, unfulfilled need flared through the chamber, bright and solid against Isana's watercrafting senses. "Yes. It matters."

"And finding the answer is important to you."

"Yes. It is."

Isana shook her head. "But if you destroy us, you might never know the answer."

"Don't you think I *know* that?" the vord Queen spat. Her eyes flared wide open as she bared her teeth in a snarl. "Don't you think I *understand*? I sense as you do, Grandmother. I *feel* everything, *everything* my children feel. I feel their pain and fear. And through them, I feel *your* people as well. I feel them screaming and dying. I am so filled with it that I could almost split open down the middle."

A calm, hard voice spoke into the chamber, causing Isana to flinch in surprised reaction. "Be cautious," said Invidia Aquitaine. "You are being manipulated." The former High Lady entered the chamber, attired in the formfitting black chitin-armor apparently worn by all of the Aleran Citizens who served the vord.

The vord Queen turned her head slightly, her only acknowledgment of Invidia's words. She frowned, and swiveled her unsettling eyes back to Isana. Silence stretched for a time before she asked, "Is this true?"

Isana stared at Invidia. She had heard Amara's descriptions of the creature clinging to Invidia's torso, its bulbous body pulsing in a rhythm like a slow heartbeat. But seeing it happening, seeing the blood that seeped weakly from where the creature's head thrust into the woman's chest, was a different matter altogether. Invidia had been many things to Isana—ally and manipulator, mentor and murderess. Isana had ample reason to hate the former High Lady, she supposed. But looking at her now, she could summon forth nothing more than pity.

And revulsion.

"That is a matter of viewpoint," Isana replied to the vord Queen, her eyes never leaving Invidia. "I am attempting to understand you. I am attempting to enable you to understand us more clearly."

"Knowledge may make you more able to prevail against me," the Queen said. "It is a sensible course of action to pursue. But the reverse is also true. Why would you seek to allow me to understand your kind better?"

Invidia stepped forward. "Isn't it obvious?" she asked, her voice calm. She looked nowhere but at Isana. "She senses the emotions in you, just as I do. She hopes to draw them out of you, to use them to influence your actions."

The Queen's mouth twisted into a chill smile. "Ah. Is that true, Isana?"

"From a certain point of view," Isana replied. "I hoped to reach out to you. To convince you to cease hostilities."

"Invidia," the Queen said, "how would you evaluate her skills at watercrafting?"

"As the equal of my own," Invidia replied smoothly. "To be cautious, I would say that she was my equal at least."

The vord Queen absorbed that for a moment. Then she nodded. "In your judgment, is there anything she could directly accomplish by this method?"

"Only to learn how pointless it is to try," Invidia replied, her voice tired. "There is without question emotion like our own inside you. But you do not feel it in the same way we do. It does not influence your decisions or judgment." She stared at Isana without any emotion showing on her face or in her manner, and said, "Believe me. I've tried. It is already over, Isana. If you would reduce the pain and suffering our people experience, you should advise them to surrender."

"They would not listen," the Queen said dismissively. "And besides, I'm not letting her go."

Invidia frowned. "Then I see no value in keeping her—or her lover—alive."

"Let us say that it is for the good of the Aleran people," the Queen said.

Isana jerked her gaze from the treacherous High Lady to the Queen. "What?"

The Queen shrugged a shoulder, a gesture Isana found somehow familiar and intensely uncomfortable. "The Aleran people suffer because they fight. They will never surrender the fight so long as Gaius Octavian is alive. Gaius Attis might give them the ability to resist, for now—but he is a pretender, and your people know it. So long as the true heir to the House of Gaius walks the land, there will always be many who will fight. He must be dealt with."

The Queen pointed a clawed fingertip at Isana. "Octavian's mother is in my control. He will be forced to come to me in an attempt to preserve her life. However, by all accounts she has demonstrated irrational resolve in the past. She might destroy herself to prevent Octavian from coming after her—which is why I need the male alive and unharmed. So long as he remains so, she will retain the hope that both of them might escape this place together."

Isana tried to prevent herself from shivering at the cold, detached calculation in the Queen's voice, at the calm precision of her logic. She couldn't.

"I have her," the Queen said. "Having her will give me Octavian. When he is dead, the rest of Alera will crumble and yield. Better for me and my children. Better for them."

"Kill them both," Invidia suggested. "Revenge may draw him to you as surely as concern."

The vord Queen bared her green-black teeth in a smile. "Ah. His progenitor's progenitor waited nearly twenty-five years to take his vengeance when the time was right. That bloodline does not seek to redress such imbalances in . . . what is the phrase? In fire?"

"In hot blood," Isana said quietly.

"Exactly," said the vord Queen. She turned to Invidia. "Why are you not in the field?"

"Two reasons," Invidia said. "First, our spies in Antillus report that Octavian and his Legions marched to the north nearly two days ago."

"What?" the Queen said. "Where are they now?"

Invidia's mouth curled into a chilly little smile. "We know nothing more. Your horde arrived at Antillus several hours ago. It has enfolded the city and is taking losses at more than triple the rate of any other besieged city."

The Queen's black-jewel eyes narrowed. "Canim conscripts fighting alone cannot put up such resistance."

"Nasaug's conscripts have an unusually high degree of training and experience. They are considerably more formidable than the conscripts in Canea," Invidia said. After the slightest of pauses, she added, "As I warned you."

The vord Queen's eyes flashed with silent anger. "Octavian must have some plan for the Shieldwall. It is the only significant structure north of Antillus. I will dispatch airborne warrior forms to patrol the Wall and locate him."

"The second reason I am here," Invidia continued, "is because while you have been chatting with the woman who cannot directly harm you, your attention has wavered from the battle. The High Lord and Lady of Placida and my former husband have been freed from the press of the fight to redirect the feral furies we loosed upon them. They have nothing like overt control, but they have driven most of the ferals out of Riva and away from the fleeing civilians. Our own troops are now suffering at least as heavily from their attentions as are the Legions."

The vord Queen's eyes widened, and she whirled to stare at Isana.

"I was also hoping," Isana said mildly, folding her hands in front of her, "to distract your attention from the fight. I thought it might weaken the coordination of your creatures if you weren't constantly overseeing them."

The vord Queen's eyes blazed for a moment, flickering with odd motes of brilliant green light. Then she whirled and strode back into the area from which she had stared at the battle before. "Get back out there. Take my *singulares*. Find and destroy any High Lord or Lady you can isolate. I will see to it that their attention is directed elsewhere."

Invidia lifted her chin. "It might be better to accept our losses and plan for the next—"

The Queen whirled, her face suffused with rage, and shrieked in a voice like tearing metal, "FIND THEM!"

The sheer volume of the scream slammed against Isana like a fist, and she staggered back against the wall. She sagged there for a moment, her ears ringing, and felt a trickle of heat upon her upper lip; her nose had begun bleeding.

In the stunned seconds of silence after, she found herself blinking dully, staring at the unmoving Araris, his scarred face slack, his eyes opened and focused—

Isana froze.

Araris met her eyes for an instant, gazing through a murky half inch of *croach*. Then his eyes flicked down, and back up to hers. Isana glanced down.

She had not before noted that Araris stood with one hand behind his back—where he was, she abruptly realized, clasping the solid steel handle of the dagger secreted beneath his wide belt. Steel, which might be shielding his mind against numbness, against pain, against the disorientation of any toxins within the alien substance, just as it had utterly hidden his emotional presence from Isana's own senses—and presumably from those of the vord Queen and Invidia Aquitaine.

Araris Valerian, arguably the greatest swordsman of his generation, was not yet out of the fight.

He met her eyes for a breath, winked at her once, then closed them again.

Isana straightened her spine slowly and made sure her emotions and expression were under control as she turned back to face Invidia and the vord Queen.

Invidia was smiling at the Queen, her expression, beneath its chill veneer, balanced between terror and glee. Then she inclined her head and swept out of the chamber.

The vord Queen said, to Isana, "This will only cause more pain." Then she lifted her face again, and the walls and ceiling of the chamber began to glow once more. "In the end it will change nothing. I will kill Octavian. I will kill you all."

In the silence that followed, Isana suppressed a surge of fury. How dare she? How *dare* this creature threaten her son?

No, Isana thought to herself, grimly. *No, you won't.*

CHAPTER 20

Riva burned, illuminating the moonless night.

"There's always a fire," Amara said, her tone dull. "Why is there always a fire?"

"Fire's a living thing," Sir Ehren replied. He stared at the city as Amara did, looking up at it from the plain on its northern side. Refugees streamed past them in a dazed, shambling river, directed by elements of the Rivan civic legion, and flanked by the *legionares* of Riva. "If you don't control it, it looks for food, eats, and grows. It's in every house in the city, and it just takes a moment's carelessness to set it loose." He shrugged. "Though I imagine all the feral furies had something to do with it, too."

A windmane swept out of the night, letting out a whistling shriek as it dived toward the pair of Cursors speaking at the side of the causeway. Amara idly lifted a hand and made an effort of will. Cirrus flung himself at the hostile fury in a rush of wind, and as the two met, Amara's fury was outlined in ghostly white light, a specter of a long-legged horse. Like a dozen others in the past hour, the clash was brief. Cirrus's lashing hooves rapidly drove the windmane away.

"Countess," Ehren said. "I understand that you were in the city."

Amara nodded. She felt oddly detached from the events of the night, smooth and unruffled. She wasn't calm, of course. After what she had seen, only a madwoman would be calm. She suspected it was more like going numb. The terrified, wounded flood of humanity in front of her would have been heart-wrenching if she hadn't seen so much worse within Riva's walls as the feral furies overran them. "For a while. I was bearing messages back and forth between Riva and Aquitaine."

Ehren studied her intently for a moment. Then he said, "That bad?"

"I saw an earth fury that looked like a gargant bull knock down a building being used to shelter orphaned children," she said in a level tone. "I saw a pregnant woman burned to black bones by a fire fury. I saw an old woman dragged down into a well by a water fury, her husband holding her wrists the whole way. He went with her." She paused, musing over the placid, inflectionless calm of her own voice, and added, "The second minute was worse."

Ehren folded his arms and shivered. "I hate to think what would have happened if the High Lords hadn't been able to return to the city to drive some of the ferals away."

"True," Amara said.

"Countess. Are you sure you're all right?"

"Perfectly."

The little Cursor nodded. "And . . . the Count?"

Amara felt herself grow more distant. She thought it was likely the only reason she wasn't weeping hysterically. "I don't know. He was part of Riva's command staff. He wasn't there."

Ehren nodded. "He . . . doesn't seem the sort of man to stay indoors when something like this is happening."

"No. He isn't."

"If I had to guess," Ehren said diffidently, "I'd say he was probably assisting in the evacuation. And that you'll see him as soon as he's gotten everyone he can out of the city."

"It wouldn't be out of character," Amara agreed. She took a deep drink from a flask of water she'd forgotten she was holding. Then she passed it back to Ehren. "Thank you."

"Of course," he said. "Where are you going now?"

"I'm to help provide an air patrol over the refugee column," Amara said. "Princeps Attis thinks that their aerial troops will be in position to attack us farther down the causeway." She paused, then asked, "And you?"

"I'm consolidating the food and supplies of the column," Ehren said with a grimace. "Which closely resembles bald theft—especially to everyone whose food I order taken away."

"There's no choice," Amara said. "Without rationing, most of these people won't have the strength to reach Calderon."

"I know," Ehren said, "but that doesn't make it any more palatable." They both fell quiet and watched the refugees shuffle past. "Crows." He sighed. "Hard to believe that this could have been worse. Give the Princeps his due. He reacted quickly. He's light on his feet."

Amara felt a thought stirring, deep down beneath the numbness. She frowned. "Yes," she said. "The presence of the High Lords in the city made the difference . . ." She drew in a sharp breath as the thought crystallized in her head. "Sir Ehren. The vord will strike at them."

"I wish them good luck," Ehren snorted. "The High Lords are more than capable of handling an attack from any of the vord we've seen in this battle."

"What about from their fellow Citizens?" Amara asked. "Such as the ones who took Lady Isana."

Ehren's mouth opened slightly. "Ah," he said. "Oh dear."

Amara spun on her heel, leapt into the air, and let Cirrus lift her aloft. She gathered speed and was shortly hurtling like an arrow toward the burning city.

Amara soared up toward the High Lord's citadel, the tallest of many towers in the great city. Several times, she had to bank around columns of thick black smoke. The air was turbulent as fires spread below.

She could hear the battle raging south of the city. Drums rolled, pounding out messages. Horns blared. The huge, hollow thumps of the more traditional fire-spheres thrummed through the air, whumping irregularly against Amara's chest. Though the screams of wounded *legionares* did not reach her, the shrieks of dying vord carried through the air, the distance removing the steely menace from their high-pitched cries. They rather sounded like a distant, enormous flock of birds.

Amara wasn't far enough away to escape the pain and terror of the night, though. Human shouts and cries and screams came up from the city—the men of the civic legion, trying to rescue those trapped by fires, the wounded, the dying. She saw several vord as she overflew the city—solitary warriors, leaner and swifter-looking than those attacking the front lines, who had somehow made their way into the city during the night's confusion. Teams of three and four armored men, probably Knights Ferrous, seemed to be hunting the vord in turn, stalking through the blazing, panicked maze of Riva's dying streets.

Knights Aeris and Citizens with the ability to fly were everywhere above the city, pulling trapped civilians from the fires, and Amara fancied that from a distance they must all look like so many moths—dark silhouettes in the air fluttering around Riva's flames.

Rogue furies roamed the streets and rooftops, constantly repelled by the efforts of a single Citizen or by groups of civilians working in concert. Amara herself had bowled several more windmanes out of her path on the way to the city. At least the feral furies were not as numerous or aggressive as they had been in the hours before, though they were still deadly dangerous to any who met them without sufficient furycraft to defend themselves.

Lights moved through the streets, furylamps carried by fleeing civilians: The wounded and young and elderly piled into the few remaining wagons and their *legionare* escorts, mostly. The fires cast lights on some of the streets, but the shadows in the others were all the deeper for them.

The High Lord's tower was the sole island of order and calm within the city walls. Lights blazed all around it, reflecting from the shining armor of the *singulares* on duty there. The tower had a wide stone balcony winding around its entire exterior, from which the High Lord could look out over his city. As Amara approached, she could see Lord Riva's entourage, gathered around the man himself, as he paced a steady circle around the balcony, delivering orders to messengers who came and went with desperate haste.

Far too *much* desperate haste, Amara realized. The havoc resulting from the vord assault had thrown the entire defense of the city into chaos; there was no visible air patrol over the High Lord's tower. Doubtless, Riva was planning to leave the city within the next hour and had dispatched the majority of his fliers to escort the fleeing refugees. Most of the other fliers were even now saving the lives of those trapped behind burning buildings, much as Amara had done during a fire in the capital during her days in the Academy, starving fires of air on a small scale or using walls of wind to shield those the fires would have consumed. Any remaining fliers had doubtless been pressed into service as messengers, coordinating with Gaius Attis and the Legions.

Black shapes darted and flitted through the smoke and firelight and shadows that covered the city, seemingly moving at random through the crisis. Amara gritted her teeth. She and a class of first-year Cursors from the Academy could have flown into the city blowing trumpets and breathing fire without being noticed, much less stopped. Any of those swift-moving human forms could be enemy fliers.

Amara looked wildly around the city, struggling vainly to identify Gaius Attis or one of the High Lords or Ladies. She darted up several dozen yards to try to get a better view. Riva's lofty towers—*Great furies, what kind of crowbegotten competitive delusion infected this city's architects, to build so many of the bloody things?*—presented a dizzying aerial maze of cornices, arches, and spires. The fires below and the rising columns of smoke threw off every angle, made distances difficult to judge, and reduced every airborne figure to a featureless outline.

There, down near the street level. An avian shriek rose from below, and a falcon-shaped burst of white-hot flame soared down into an alleyway, plunging in a raptor's strike. The light from the fire fury briefly illuminated one of the vord infiltrators, lurking not thirty feet from a laboring wagon heavily loaded with wounded civilians. The fire falcon exploded into a fireball that shattered and scattered the enemy horror, leaving behind half a dozen small fires and a large, greasy stain. Campfire sparks leapt from the smaller fires, swirling into a flowing stream that rushed up through the air and gathered upon the extended wrist of a woman dressed in *legionare's* armor. The sparks congealed into the form of a small, almost delicate hunting falcon, and let out another whistling shriek that somehow conveyed a fierce sense of primal triumph.

Amara rushed down toward Lady Placida, who tossed her long braid of red hair over her shoulder and turned to face her before she had come within a hundred feet, her sword in hand.

Amara slowed, lifting both hands, until she had come close enough for Lady Placida to see her features in the light cast by the glowing falcon.

"Countess Amara," Lady Placida said. She returned the sword to her side with fluid grace. Her voice was roughened by smoke and exertion. Her eyes turned back down to the escaping wagon below, and she waved at the elderly man coaxing its overburdened mule, gesturing for him to continue. "What can I do for you?"

"Did you know that there is no longer an aerial curtain over the city?" Amara called.

Lady Placida's eyes widened, noticeable even in the half-light against her smoke-stained face. "What? No, no it's been complete madness here." She looked around her, clearly calculating. "But that would mean that . . . bloody crows. We're vulnerable."

Amara nodded. "Where is Aquitaine?"

"The southern plaza. Probably still there." Lady Placida flicked her wrist and sent the little fire falcon hurtling up into the night. "Countess, apprise the Princeps of the situation. I will warn the Citizens—*behind you!*"

Amara immediately redirected Cirrus, and shot twenty feet down, to her left, and behind her. She turned over as she went, and had a brief vision of a man in black chitin-armor, long blade in hand, plunging toward her and compensating for her dodge. She twisted and arched her back in midair, and the sword swept by not two inches from the end of her nose.

With a mental hammerblow of recognition, Amara realized that she knew the young man wearing the collar and armor of the vord. His name was Cantus Macio, a young Forcian Citizen who had attended the Academy in one of the same two-year terms she had been there. His dark blond hair was shorter than she remembered, his face and body heavier with maturity, but she remembered him. He'd shared several of her classes and been one of the minority of Citizens who would treat the relatively small number of freemen at the Academy with courtesy and respect—and had been one of the more capable furycrafters in his class.

Macio's eyes showed no similar recognition. They were wide and empty. Amara quickly changed her course to a reciprocal of his, which would buy her the largest lead before he could alter his own path of flight, dodging lightly around a column of smoke so that Macio wouldn't be able to see her immediately.

Above Amara, three more vord-armored forms had plunged down upon Lady Placida. She bobbed lightly in the air, left and right, then drew her slender sword and struck in the same motion. A shower of bright green sparks flared up, and the enemy flier she'd struck went soaring past her into an uncontrolled spin, trailing a bright scarlet spiral of blood. He slammed into a wall with sickening force, as Lady Placida shot straight upward, turning to engage the other two vord-taken Citizens.

As the leading foe closed on her, Lady Placida reached out with one hand, and a wooden banner pole thrusting from the side of a tower suddenly twisted in place and lashed out like a club, striking one of the enemy fliers in the hip and sending him tumbling. The second flier closed to sword range, and sparks lashed out in emerald fountains as his blade met Lady Placida's, chiming half a dozen times as the two swept past one another.

Lady Placida spun in the air to face Amara, blood coursing from a cut on one cheek. "Countess!" she cried. "Find the Princeps!" Then she spun again, her lips locked in a defiant snarl, as the pole-struck Citizen swept past her, blade in hand. The light and steely music of the clash of powerful metalcrafters rang through the fire-choked night.

Amara stared up at Lady Placida for a heartbeat, torn, but her duty was clear. Even more than its most capable furycrafters, the Realm needed leadership. Princeps Octavian might be on his way, but he was not *here*. Princeps Attis was. If Alera lost him now, in these chaotic circumstances, the confusion of sorting out who would take command could mean the destruction of the Legions as well as the civilians they fought to protect. They might never *reach* the fortifications at Calderon.

She turned and willed Cirrus to plunge them both into the nearest plume of smoke, the better to hide from any pursuit, and rushed southward through the city's towers. The route was treacherous, deadly. Slender stone bridges arched between some of the towers, and she nearly took her head off on one of them, concealed as it was in smoke and shadow. Banner poles and stone carvings thrust from the towers, too—but she dared not fly at street level. Below, where the refugees and lower-class civilians had dwelt in numbers, laundry lines frequently crisscrossed the streets. Hitting one at flight speed would be lethal.

She found the southern plaza within moments—a broad, wide-open space of furycrafted stone that had been used as a market practically since Riva's founding. A lone figure stood in the precise center of the plaza—and even from her elevation, Amara recognized the bearing and profile of Gaius Attis.

In a circle around him, filling most of the rest of the plaza, stood more than a dozen feral furies, the smallest of them larger than a bull gargant. A serpent, its scales made of granite and obsidian, coiled upon itself, its back broader than a large city street. The deadly, wispy form of the wind-shark Amara had seen before came next, swirling and pacing in a circle all around Attis. A bull formed of knotted roots and hardwood boughs snorted and tossed its head, each of its horns longer than a *legionare's* spear, while its cloven hooves scraped and scored the stone of the plaza.

The air fairly shimmered with power, the energies of those enormous, aggressive furies thickening it until Amara felt that she could hardly breathe. She stared down for a few seconds, stunned. Furies of that size and strength were tremendously powerful, the sorts of beings that could only be mastered by the most powerful Citizens in the Realm. If anyone had commanded even *one* of these beings, it had been someone with the skill and power of a High Lord.

And Gaius Attis was, quite calmly, holding a dozen of them in their places, like so many unruly schoolchildren.

As she watched, he lifted one arm, his hand clenched into a fist, the gesture a beckoning, like a man hauling in on a heavy rope. The fury that faced him most directly, a long, lizardlike creature made of muddy water, arched as if in sudden agony and let out a howl like a thousand boiling teakettles. Then it simply flew into individual droplets of water, driven as if before a hurricane's winds—directly toward Gaius Attis. His head dropped back and he let out a low cry of pain. Then, without a pause, he whirled toward the fire fury shaped like an animate, walking willow tree, flinging out his hand, and the water of the defeated lizard fury rushed toward the tree. As steam gushed forth, Gaius Attis jerked his arm toward him again in that same, beckoning gesture, and the steam and fire both rushed back toward him, swirling around him, and again he screamed.

It hit Amara with a sudden shock—Gaius Attis was claiming new furies.

She dared not approach him, not in that seething cauldron of raw power.

Even if Cirrus hadn't been loath to go near, she wouldn't have tried it. Claiming furies was a dangerous business. Claiming furies of such size was . . . was practically lunacy. The energies unleashed by a struggling fury could bake a man to bones, rip him to shreds, and Amara did not have Gaius Attis's formidable array of talents with which to insulate herself from harm.

Instead, she landed on a nearby rooftop, gathered Cirrus to her, and sent him forth in a farspeaking crafting. They only functioned in a direct line of sight, and she didn't know how badly the discharge of energies below would garble her message, but she could think of nothing else.

"Your Highness," she said, her voice urgent, "we've lost control of the local skies. Former Citizens are attacking the Citizens still attempting to aid the evacuation. It is imperative that you leave immediately."

Attis lifted his eyes and scanned the nearby rooftops until he spotted Amara. He grimaced and answered in a voice cut thin with strain. "A few moments more. I cannot permit these beings to run loose, Cursor. They'll leave this entire region uninhabitable for a thousand years."

"Don't be a bloody *fool*, Your Highness," Amara snarled back. "Without you, there might not *be* anyone left to inhabit it."

Attis snarled, his dark eyes smoldering for a moment with quite literal fire. "One doesn't just drop everything and walk away from a business like this, Countess. You may note the eleven rather large and irate furies trying to kill me at the moment."

"How long will it take you to disengage?"

Aquitaine gave a twitching shake of his head, then extended a hand toward the bull-shaped wood fury and ground his teeth. "Unknown," he said, his voice strained. "Not long. If there are any survivors out here when they are freed, they won't have a chance. If you would kindly cease jogging my elbow with this farspeaking . . ."

Amara grimaced and recalled Cirrus and sensed the presence coming at her back as a ribbon of ice laid over her spine. She didn't waste time looking back. She flung herself forward, off the five-story roof, and dropped like a rock.

The stone edging of the roof behind her exploded into a cloud of gravel. One stone struck her hard in the back, another in the thigh. She grimly focused through the pain, calling upon Cirrus to cushion her fall, spun her body in midair, and, supported by the fury, landed in a catlike crouch. She leapt forward into a rolling dive, and an instant later a heavy boot slammed down onto the surface of the plaza with enough force to send cracks through the stone for ten feet in every direction.

Amara drew her sword even as she came to her feet and raised it to a high guard position. She found Cantus Macio staring at her with blank eyes.

"Macio," she said, her voice shaking. "Hello. Do you remember me? From the Academy? Amara?"

He tilted his head, watching her.

Then he lifted his hand, and fire rushed at her in a swirling vortex.

Amara called to Cirrus, raising a wall of wind to stop the onrushing fire, but Macio was simply far more powerful than she. The rush of wind shoved back against her with tremendous force as it tried to slow the onrushing firestorm, and Amara found herself tossed back like a leaf.

Rather than fighting the motion, she spun into it, calling out to Cirrus again to take to the air—only to see the shimmer of something moving behind a wind-crafted veil, and to feel a shock of stunning pain as an unseen fist slammed into her jaw.

Amara staggered, her concentration upon maintaining flight shattered, and tumbled down. Fortunately, she'd had little time to gather altitude or speed, but even so, her landing upon the hard stone of the plaza was an acutely painful experience. Training let her turn her motion into a rolling one, but it still slammed her limbs brutally. Her weapon was knocked clear of her hand, and she counted herself lucky not to have wound up impaled on it.

She struggled to push herself up, panicked. Speed was her only chance. She didn't have the power she would need to confront Macio and his veiled ally directly. The only way she could survive would be to take the battle to the open skies. She found the wall of one of the buildings framing the plaza and used it to help herself stand.

She had risen to her knees by the time Macio's fist tangled painfully in her hair. He dragged her up with fury-born strength, lifting her flailing toes clear of the ground.

Her arms felt like they'd been weighted with lead. She drew the knife from her belt and drove it up and back at the arm holding her. If she could cut the tendons, it wouldn't matter how much earthcraft Macio knew—the mechanisms of his arm would be broken, and his grip would be gone. The cut slid off something rigid, probably the chitin-armor that encased Macio. Twisting her shoulders, she thrust one heel down at him, aiming for the knee. The blow struck home, but suspended as she was, it was weak. Macio grunted and shifted his weight, and her next two kicks hit what felt like this armored thigh, doing him no harm.

Amara felt Macio's arm surge with power and slam her into the stone wall behind her. Her teeth snapped together on her tongue as her back and shoulders hit the stone. The taste of blood filled her mouth. Stars clouded her vision, and her limbs hung limp and flaccid.

Move. She had to move. Speed was her only chance.

Macio drew his sword with a deliberate motion, frowning up at her as he did. Then he set the sword's tip against her ribs, just beneath her left breast. It would be a thrust to the heart.

"Amara," he said, his voice that of someone who has recognized a former acquaintance at a dinner party. He nodded to himself, then said, "There's no more Academy, you know." His fingers tightened on the sword's hilt. "I'm sorry."

┠▫▫▫▫▫▫CHAPTER 21

Amara watched Macio's eyes. They were clinically detached as he angled the blade for a thrust between the ribs and took a breath. In the instant before he pushed the weapon forward, she twisted to the side, drawing in her stomach as hard as she could. She could feel the edge of the sword burn a single hot line along her belly, but she was able to lash out with her fist and land an accurate, if weak, blow to the bridge of his nose.

Macio rocked back from the strike, blinking involuntary tears from his eyes—and then abruptly turned his upper body, his sword sweeping up and back as though it had a will of its own. There was a crack of impact as something struck the blade, and a small cloud of spinning fragments of wood rose up from it.

Wild hope surged through Amara, blazing through her body. The extra heartbeats the distraction had given her were time enough to sort out her terrified, stunned thoughts. She called upon Cirrus to lend her the fury's speed and watched the world slow around her. Even as it did, she swept the knife up again in the strike she should have used in the first place, cutting not at Macio's arm but at her own hair where he held her.

The sharp knife parted her hair without slowing, and she fell free of his grip. She dropped to the ground and dived to one side. She saw his sword moving again, lazily graceful in the expanded time sensation of her windcrafting. A long, lean arrow fletched with green and brown feathers glided toward Macio's head. The collared Citizen intercepted the arrow with his blade, and a second cloud of splinters flew out. Macio's sword continued its plane of motion, driving toward Amara with almost-delicate grace. Her own body moved just as slowly, but she was able to slap the flat of the blade with her hand as its tip drove toward her abdomen, and the sword plunged past her to bite deep into the stone wall.

Amara rolled over one shoulder, gathered her legs together beneath her as she did, and came to her feet with an explosive leap. Cirrus rushed into the air beneath her, bearing her up and away from Macio, avoiding the return sweep of his black by the width of a finger.

The plaza sat nestled deep between the high buildings of Riva, and she could feel Cirrus straining as her fury struggled to move enough stone-smothered air to take her into the open sky. The center of the plaza would have been a better location for a takeoff, but she could not possibly approach it through the ring of enormous furies still crouched there. Instead, trapped at the edge of the plaza, she lifted from the ground too slowly and was forced to stop trying to gain altitude before she struck the side of the building that was her goal.

She grabbed a windowsill with one hand, drove the toes of her left foot against another, and, bolstered still by Cirrus, began to ascend the side of the building in an almost-spiderlike fashion.

The presence of so much stone, which had limited Cirrus, would also have afflicted Macio's wind furies—and the young man must have weighed nearly a hundred pounds more than she did. A quick glance over her shoulder showed her Macio sprinting toward her—but instead of employing windcrafting to pursue her, he let out a grunt and leapt explosively, drawing upon an earthcrafter's strength to send himself hurtling up nearly three stories in a single bound. Eyes locked on Amara, he sank his fingertips into the stone as if it had been soft clay, and with earthcrafted power, he began scaling the building even more quickly than she could.

Amara reached the top barely a breath ahead of Macio, caught her belly on its edge, and struggled desperately to haul herself fully onto the roof.

An iron grip settled on her ankle.

She looked down, desperate, helpless against the power in Macio's clutching hand—and prayed that she had correctly guessed from which building the earlier shots had come. Macio found purchase for one of his feet, and Amara knew that his next move would be simply to swing her by the ankle and smash her against the building's side like an oversized porcelain doll.

The wall three feet from the top of the building exploded outward with a resounding crack of shuttering stone. A broad-knuckled hand snared the neck of Macio's chitin-armor in an iron grip, and heaved back, smashing the young Citizen's head against the side of the building. Macio let out a single, choking sound, then the hand gripping him slammed him to the stone again and again and again. Macio's fingers slipped loosely from Amara's ankle, and his blood spattered the wall. His neck snapped during the second or third impact. On the fifth, the wall actually gave way, and Macio's body vanished into the interior of the tower. There were a few more ugly, heavy sounds of impact, of tearing flesh and breaking bone.

Amara hauled herself wearily back onto the roof and lay there gasping with pain, exertion, and sheer terror. The horrible things she had seen that night came rushing back into her thoughts, and she found herself sobbing silently, clutching her belly as if to keep it from rupturing.

Bernard's hand touched her shoulder a moment later, and she opened her eyes to stare up at him. Her husband was covered in smoke stains, his face all but completely black. There was a fresh cut on one of his cheeks. Fresh blood, Macio's blood, had splattered over his tunic, face, and neck. The dust and flakes of shattered stone, mixed to a paste with more blood, covered his right arm to the elbow. His Legion-issue *gladius* was at his side, opposite a wide-mouthed war quiver, and he held his heavy-limbed bow in his left hand.

He gathered her up with his left arm and all but crushed her to his chest. Amara clutched him back, feeling the warmth and strength of him against her. "It's about time," she whispered.

"I leave you alone for an hour, woman," he said, his voice shaking. "And I find you running around with a younger man."

She let out a choking little laugh that threatened to bring out more sobs and held him for another few heartbeats. Then she pushed gently at him, and he rose, lifting her to her feet. "We c-can't," she said. "There are more of them around."

The dull cough of a nearby firecrafting thudded through the air in punctuation. There was an extended roaring sound, and a cloud of dust began to emerge from farther in the city, joining the smoke and fire.

"More of the crafters the vord took?" Bernard said. "Why are they here?"

"They came for the Citizens," Amara said. "At least one of them was nearby under a veil. He hit me hard enough to let the other catch up with me."

As she finished speaking, there was a howl of wind above them, and a pair of dark forms streaked by, firelight flickering on steel, showers of sparks exploding irregularly between them. Two others darted after the first pair, converging on them from different angles and altitudes. A few seconds later, far overhead, multiple spheres of white-hot fire burst into life in a rapid line of explosions. Distant, staccato thumps followed. Then a series of deep blue streaks answered the spheres, flashing in the other direction. A hissing drone, like a rainstorm hitting a hot skillet, followed a few moments later.

"Bloody crows," Bernard breathed. "This is not a smart place to be."

"No," Amara said. "Those are good signs."

Bernard frowned at her.

Amara gestured wearily at the sky. "The enemy crafters must have been working in stealth, picking off our Citizens as they tried to help the city. They had probably been doing it for half an hour or more before I ever arrived. If there's open battle now, it means that those stealthy operations ceased to be useful to the enemy. Lady Placida must have gotten the word out to her fellow Citizens."

Bernard grunted. "Maybe. Or maybe half of the enemy crafters are making a big show of it while the rest lurk and wait for a chance to ambush distracted Citizens."

Amara shivered. "You are a devious man." Then she glanced down at the plaza and back to Bernard. "What are you doing up here?" she asked.

"Watching Aquitaine," he said. His voice was quiet and completely neutral. "His *singulares* got torn up something terrible by that bull fury. The ones who could walk had to drag out the ones who couldn't. Left him there all alone."

"Watching him," Amara said quietly. "Not watching over him."

"That's right."

Amara bit her lip. "Despite the loyalty a Citizen owes to the Crown and its heirs."

The fingers of her husband's blood-encrusted right hand clenched into a fist. "The man's directly responsible for the deaths of more than four hundred of my friends and neighbors. Some of them my own bloody holders. According to Isana, he makes no secret of the fact that he may someday deem it necessary to kill my nephew." He stared out at the lone figure in the plaza, and his quiet voice burned with heat without growing louder, while his green eyes seemed to gather a layer of frost. "The murdering son of a bitch should count himself lucky I *haven't* paid him what he's owed." His lips pressed together, staring at Attis's motionless, focused form amidst half a dozen enormous furies. "Right now, it'd be easy."

"We need him," Amara said.

Bernard's jaw clenched.

Amara put a hand on his arm. "We *need* him."

He glanced aside at her, took a slow breath, and made a motion of his head that was so miniscule that it could hardly be recognized as a nod. "Doesn't mean I have to like—"

His head whipped around, and his body began to follow before Amara heard the light tread upon the stone roof. She turned to see a faint blur in the air, someone hidden behind a windcrafted veil and approaching with terrifying speed. Then there was a sound of impact and Bernard let out a croaking gasp, doubling over. The blur moved again, and Bernard's head snapped violently to one side. Teeth knocked loose from his jaw rattled onto the roof like a small handful of ivory dice, and he crumpled to the floor beside them, senseless or dead.

Amara reached for Cirrus and her weapon simultaneously, but their attacker flung out a nearly invisible arm and a handful of salt crystals struck her, sending the wind fury into disruptive convulsions of ethereal agony. Her sword was not halfway from its sheath before a thread of cold steel, the tip of a long, slender blade, lay against her throat.

The blade shimmered into visibility, then the hand behind it, then the arm behind the hand, and suddenly Amara found herself facing the former High Lady of Aquitaine. Invidia stood clad all in black chitin, and that same horrible, pulsing parasite-creature was locked about her torso. Her hair was dark and unkempt, her eyes sunken, and her skin had an unhealthy pallor.

"And to think," Invidia said. "I've spent the last half an hour scouring this entire plaza looking for the *singulares* I was sure Attis had hidden. Quite unlike him to use nonexistence as camouflage, though I suppose it did make them impossible to find. Hello, Countess."

Amara shot her motionless husband a glance, swept her eyes over the plaza below, and clenched her teeth. "Go to the crows, traitor."

"Oh, I have," Invidia said lightly. "They'd begun to peck at my eyes and lips when the vord found me. I am disinclined to repeat the experience."

Amara felt a chill smile stretch her lips. "Am I supposed to feel sorry for you?"

"Come, Countess," Invidia replied. "It is far too late for any of us to seek redemption for our sins now."

"Then why haven't you killed me and had done?" Amara replied, lifting her chin to bare more of her throat to Invidia's blade. "Lonely, are we? Missing the company of our fellow human beings? Needing some scrap of respect? Forgiveness? Approval?"

Invidia stared at her for a moment though her eyes looked through Amara as though she weren't there. A frown creased her brow. "Perhaps," she said.

"Perhaps you should have thought of that before you began murdering us all," Amara spat. "You aren't wearing a collar, like the others. They're slaves. You're free. You're here by choice."

Invidia let out a harsh laugh. "Is that what you think? That I have a choice?"

Amara arched an eyebrow. "Yes. Between death and destroying your own kind. You could defy the vord and die of the poison still in you—die horribly. But instead you've chosen to let everyone else die in your place."

Invidia's eyes widened, and her lips peeled back from her teeth in an unnatural grimace.

"The truly sad part," Amara said, naked contempt ringing in her voice, "is that in the end, it will make no difference. The moment you are more of a threat than an asset to them, the vord *will* kill you. You selfish, petulant child. All the blood on your hands has been for *nothing*."

Invidia's jaws clenched, and spots of color appeared high on her cheeks. Her whole body began shaking. "Who," she whispered. "Who do you think you are?"

Amara learned into the blade and met Invidia's eyes with her own. "I know who I am. I am the Countess Calderonus Amara, Cursor of the Crown, loyal servant of Alera and the House of Gaius. Though it cost me my life, I *know* who I am." She bared her own teeth in a wolfish smile. "And we both know who you are. You've chosen your side, traitor. Get on with it."

Invidia stood motionless. The many fires blew a hot wind over the rooftop. Somewhere, there was a roar of collapsing masonry as a building succumbed. Distant thumps of firecrafting pulsed irregularly through the night. The distant desperation of the trumpets and drums of the embattled Legions remained a constant, hardly noticed music.

"So be it," Invidia hissed.

And then the rooftop exploded into motion.

Amara called upon Cirrus, and the wounded fury flooded into her, lending speed and agony alike as time seemed to slow down. Amara surged forward, bobbing down, and ducked under the quick cut that Invidia flicked at her neck. Given the fury-born strength of the former High Lady, had the blow landed, Amara had no doubt that it would have killed her. She coiled her knee up against her chest as she moved, then, one hand coming down to rest lightly on the rooftop, she drove her leg out, all the strength of her hips and legs behind it, the power driven with brutally concentrated force through her heel and into Invidia's hip.

Invidia's armor absorbed much of the bone-breaking power of the blow, but it struck her with such speed that its force drove her back through the air. The incredible strength conveyed by furycraft did nothing to add to her body's mass, after all, and Amara's kick had moved with such raw speed that even had she possessed the superior strength of an earthcrafter, it would have been all but redundant.

Amara felt her ankle snap, and the pain, added to Cirrus's own agony, was enough to wash away her concentration on her windcrafting. The world returned to its usual pace, and Invidia crashed backward into the low stone rim that lined the edge of the roof. She hit with brutal force, and a cry was driven from her lungs. She shook her head and lifted a hand, her eyes blazing with sudden fury.

Then fire exploded directly upon her, the white-hot fury of a Knight Ignus's fire-sphere, intensified by an order of magnitude. The bloom of scalding heat washed back over Amara in a flood that flung her ragged-cut hair straight back from her head, and she threw herself to the ground to shield the unmoving Bernard's face from the scalding heat of that blast.

She looked back a moment later, her eyes still dazzled from the intensity, and found that half of the building's rooftop, the part where Invidia had stood, was simply *gone*. There was no rubble, no fires, no dust—the building simply ceased to be in the area of a sphere the diameter of a couple of carriages. The places where the building had been devoured were cut as neatly as if with a knife, the very edge of the original material burned black and otherwise perfectly in shape. A terrible smell filled the air.

There was no sign of Invidia.

There was the sound of a very light impact on the rooftop nearby. Amara looked up to see another veiled, nearly invisible shape, standing ten feet away, facing the sterile destruction on the rooftop. "I do hope," Gaius Attis murmured, "that you were not burned. I tried to contain the spread of the heat."

"You *used* us," Amara snarled. She jerked her furious gaze away from Attis's veiled form. Sheer pain had all but blinded her with tears, but she found Bernard's throat with her fingers. His pulse beat steady and strong, though he still wasn't moving. His own fury-born strength had enabled him to survive Invidia's blow to the jaw. Had such a strike landed on Amara, it would have broken her neck.

"It was necessary," Attis replied evenly. He turned, scanning the smoke-and-fire skies over Riva. "Invidia would never have exposed herself to me if she did not think she could kill me easily, such as when I was distracted with those furies. And if she hadn't found someone watching over me, she would have assumed my guard to be too well concealed, and not shown herself for fear of being taken by surprise. You and your Count are both capable enough that it was feasible you might have been entrusted with warning me of danger but vulnerable enough to be quickly overwhelmed by someone of Invidia's caliber."

"She might have killed us *both*," Amara said.

"Quite," Attis answered. "But not without revealing her presence."

Amara stared at him hard for a moment, blinking tears from her eyes. "Those weren't feral furies," she said. "They were yours, disguised."

"Obviously, Cursor. Honestly, do you think I would stand about completely unprotected when the slightest disturbance would result in my death? When a person with a great deal of dangerous personal knowledge about me is running about with the vord during an assault?" He paused reflectively. "I regret that I couldn't tell you or your Count what I was doing, but it would rather have defeated the point."

"You risked our lives," Amara said. "Wounded some of your own bodyguards. And you didn't even know that she would show herself."

"Incorrect," he replied. He knelt to begin picking up the unconscious Bernard. "Invidia has an acute talent for sensing weakness and exploiting it."

There was a hissing sound, and a slender sword, its blade a shaft of vord green fire, abruptly emerged from the stone beneath Attis's feet and thrust up into his groin. Attis screamed and flung himself away from the blade, which cut its way free of his body with a sizzling hissing wail. He only barely managed to stumble aside as a three-foot circle of stone roof exploded upward and outward.

A figure emerged from below, all black chitin and scorched flesh, holding the blazing green blade in its hand. It was bald, its scalp burned black. Amara could scarcely have recognized Invidia if not for the quivering, pulsing, agonized movements of the badly scorched creature that clung to her over her heart. "I do know how to exploit weakness," she hissed, her voice a rasping croak, "such as your insufferable tendency to gloat after a victory, Attis."

Attis lay on the rooftop, white as a sheet. His right hand twitched in what seemed a complete lack of controlled movement. Both legs were limp. He wasn't bleeding, but the white-hot blades the high Citizenry employed almost always cauterized wounds. Only the fact that he was propped up against the roof's stone rim prevented him from simply lying supine.

His left hand moved jerkily to his jacket, then emerged with a paper envelope. He flicked it weakly across the distance to Invidia, and it landed touching her feet. "For you. Love what you've done with your hair."

Invidia bared her teeth in a smile. Blood ran from her burned lips. Her teeth and the whites of her eyes were eerie against the unbroken black scorching of her face. "And what is this?"

"Your copy of the divorce papers."

"How thoughtful."

"Necessary. I couldn't legally be rid of you until I had served them."

Invidia's smile didn't waver as she walked forward, sword hissing as its flames caressed the cool air. "You're rid of me now."

He inclined his head in a mocking bow, his face a mask of calm disdain. "And that not soon enough."

"For either of us," she purred.

There was a raptor's cry and a small falcon of white-hot fire hammered into the rooftop at Invidia's feet, spreading in an instant into a blazing wall between her and Attis.

Amara's exhausted gaze rose to the skies, where half a dozen fliers, the weapons of each and every one of them ablaze with fire, were already stooping into a dive that would carry them down to the embattled rooftop. They dived in an irregular wedge, and Placidus Aria led the way, burning sword in hand, the hems of her skirts snapping and tearing in the speed of her flight.

Attis began to let out weak, choking, scornful laughter.

"Bloody crows," Invidia snarled. She spun and flung herself off the back side of the building, vanishing from sight even as wind began to howl, carrying her into a heavy smoke cloud.

Amara clung to Bernard as three of the new arrivals settled on the roof while the other three stayed aloft. Old High Lord Cereus, his white hair orange in the firelight, came down beside the Lord and Lady of Placida, while Phrygius, his son, and High Lord Riva stood guard in the air.

"Aria," Amara called. "The Princeps needs a healing tub, immediately."

"Hardly," Attis said, his tone calm. "That's rather the point of firecrafting the sword's blade, after all. It's all but impossible to heal a cauterized wound."

"Oh, be *quiet*," Amara snapped. After clenching her jaws for a moment, she added, "Your Highness."

Aria went to Gaius Attis, took a brief look at his injuries, and shook her head. "The city is lost. We're rendezvousing with the Legions' rear guard now. We've got to move."

"As you wish," Attis said. "Thank you, by the way, for intervening. I'd hate to give her the satisfaction."

"Don't thank me," Aria replied tartly. "Thank Amara. Without her warning, I might not be alive at all." She bent over, grunted, and hauled the wounded man up and over one armored shoulder.

"Hurry!" called one of the men above them. "The vord have breached the wall!"

Without a word, High Lord Placida picked up Bernard. Cereus slipped one of Amara's arms over his shoulders and lifted her to stand beside him, favoring her with a kindly smile. "I hope you don't mind letting me do the honors, Countess."

"Please," Amara said. She felt quite dizzy. "Feel free."

The six of them lifted off the roof in a roar of wind, and Amara saw little point in staying awake for what followed.

CHAPTER 22

The ice ships flew over the bitterly cold miles at a speed that, at times, beggared the wind that drove them. Marcus felt fairly sure that such a feat was mathematically impossible by any reasonable standard. The captain of the ship he rode upon had been to the Academy, or so he claimed. He said something about the momentum upon the slight downhill slopes gradually adding up, and that the pressure on the ships' steel runners actually turned the ice immediately beneath them into a thin layer of water.

Marcus didn't care about explanations. It all seemed awfully shady to him.

The fleet stopped every six hours, to make repairs that were inevitably made necessary by the battering the wooden hulls endured and to give ships that had been forced to stop for repairs a chance to catch up with the rest of them. Marcus savored the rests. The entire fleet had seen the wreckage of the ships that had overbalanced and failed, and there wasn't a thinking being among them who hadn't realized exactly what condition his corpse would be in should his own ship run afoul of bad fortune.

But the most recent rest period had been a mere hour ago. The next would not come until after dawn.

Marcus stood in the prow of the ship as it followed its companions east. The night sky had not yet begun to brighten with the approach of dawn, but it couldn't be far away. He watched the fleet soar over the endless ice road before them for a time, his thoughts turning in circles that slowly grew quieter and less important. A little while later, when the first blue light had begun to form in the east, Marcus yawned and turned to pace back down the deck toward the closet-sized room that was his cabin for some sleep. He didn't know if the jolting ship would allow him any rest, but at least, for a change, his own thoughts wouldn't be keeping him from his sleep.

He opened the door to his cabin, paused at a sudden scent, then scowled and stepped into the unlit room, shutting the door behind him. "Bloody crows. When did you get on the ship?"

"At the last stop," Sha rumbled in the quietest voice he could manage.

Marcus leaned his shoulders back against the door and folded his arms over his chest. In the cramped confines of the cabin, he was all but touching the lean Cane, and he had no intention of triggering a potentially violent response by making physical contact with the Hunter. "What word do you bring?"

"None," Sha said. "For there is none to bring. Our problem remains unchanged."

Marcus grunted. "Meaning that your leader and mine will be forced to duel."

"So it would seem," Sha said philosophically. "Though they have both faced such things before and survived them. The stronger will prove it upon the other."

Marcus grimaced. "That's a loss to both of our peoples, no matter who wins."

"Has a solution occurred to you?"

"Not yet," Marcus said. "But that doesn't mean that it isn't there."

Sha let out a thoughtful growl. "It may yet be possible to strike down my lord's enemy, Khral."

"I thought his proper title was Master Khral of the Bloodspeakers."

"Khral," Sha repeated.

Marcus felt himself smile in the darkness. "Gaining what, by removing him?"

"Time. There will be a delay while a new leadership is established among the bloodspeakers."

"Which could create additional problems of its own."

"Yes."

"What would be the cost of buying such time?"

"My life," Sha said simply, "offered in apology to my lord after the deed was done."

Marcus frowned in the darkness. He was about to ask if the Cane was willing to make such a sacrifice, but the question was a foolish one. If Sha said that he would go through with such a thing, he most certainly would. "Is your life yours to end?"

"If, in my best judgment, it is in the service of my lord's honor? Yes."

"Would not the loss of your service greatly hamper your lord in the long term?"

There was a brief, intense silence. "It might," Sha said, a growling undertone of frustration in his voice. "In which case, I would be neglecting my duty to him by following this path. It is hard to know the honorable course of action."

"And yet you do not serve his interests by continuing to allow Khral to hold power." Marcus narrowed his eyes in thought. "What you need to do . . ."

Sha waited in patient silence.

"You can't assassinate this Cane for fear of making him a martyr among your people. Correct?"

"Even so."

Marcus scratched at his chin. "An accident, perhaps? These ships are dangerous, after all."

"My lord would never condone the collateral loss of life that would require. Or forgive himself for it. No."

Marcus nodded. "Difficult to push him under the runners of his ship without being seen."

"Impossible," Sha said. "I spent the last two days looking for the opportunity. He hides in his cabin, surrounded by sycophants. Cowardly." He paused a beat, and allowed, "If practical."

Marcus drummed his fingertips on the cool steel of his armor. "What happens if he isn't assassinated? What if he just . . . disappears. No blood. No evidence of a struggle. No one ever sees him again."

Sha let out another rumbling growl, one that raised the hairs on the back of Marcus's neck despite the fact that he was beginning to understand it as a sound accompanying pensive moments for the Cane. "Disappear. It is not . . . common to our service."

"No?"

"Never. We serve our lords, but in the end we are his weapons, his tools. He abides by our work as if he had done it with his own hands. If my lord could best solve his problem by killing another Cane, he would do so with his own blade. When he cannot do so, for reasons of tradition or because of the code, and his Hunters are sent, it is understood that they are yet his weapons."

"And that protects him from the consequences of his actions?"

"Provided his Hunters are not caught," Sha said. "It is the proper way for a great lord to defend his honor when a foe hides behind the law. Khral speaks lies to our folk, tells them that my lord intends to destroy the bloodspeakers. Warns him that they will know he has begun when he is murdered."

"Which gives him the status of a martyr without paying the price," Marcus mused, "as well as making it impossible for Varg to act without harming himself."

"Yes. And Khral's lackeys lead many bloodspeakers, and have said that they will withdraw their support should such a thing happen. Losing their strength now would be inconvenient and embarrassing."

From what Marcus had seen of the ritualists' power in battle, their sudden absence could prove downright fatal. "You haven't answered my question," he said. "What if Khral simply vanished?"

There was a rasping sound, the Cane's stiff-furred tail lashing against the walls of the tiny cabin. "It is not our way. My lord would not be held responsible. But Khral's followers would cry that the demons had done it—and there are demons on every ship in the fleet, using their powers to hold them together."

"So it must happen where none of the woodcrafters could possibly do it," Marcus said. "And then?"

A rumbling chuckle came from Sha's chest. "It is a long-standing tradition, among the bloodspeakers, to set out upon meditative pilgrimages, alone and unannounced, to establish one's piety and devotion to the Canim people and seek the enlightenment of one's mind."

"It could work," Marcus said.

"If it was possible," Sha said. "Is it?"

Marcus smiled.

* * *

The most difficult part of the plan was getting to Khral's ship without being observed: The various vessels of the fleet had been exposed to a tremendous variation of strains. Some had encountered losses of their sails or yardarms, slowing their progress. Others had suffered fractures in their keels or rudders, requiring a lengthy halt for repairs. The original formation the fleet had assumed had been completely upset by the unpredictable nature of the voyage, and now Aleran and Canish ships alike were thoroughly intermixed.

Each ship had acquired a similar routine in two days of swift travel. At the rest stops, virtually everyone aboard, crews and passengers alike, would pile off onto solid ground. Even the saltiest hands aboard the ice ships had begun to turn a bit green around the gills (or wherever it was the Canim turned green, Marcus supposed), and they were glad of the chance to stand in place without being jolted from their feet or flung into a companion.

The Aleran woodcrafters who fought to hold the ships together were no exception. Marcus watched as the four men aboard Khral's ship staggered drunkenly down the ladders to the ground. Then they shambled away to sit on a fallen tree trunk nearby and pass among themselves a bottle of some vile concoction the amateur distillers in the Legions had created. Dazed *legionares* and limp-eared Canim warriors alike took the opportunity to stretch their legs, united by a torturous common foe—or at least by a common torture.

Khral's caution remained vigilantly in place. His ship had been brought to a halt better than eighty yards from any of the others, and sentries had been posted fore and aft, port and starboard. Against the backdrop of rippling white ice, anyone who approached would be spotted immediately.

Marcus and Sha padded down the length of an Aleran ship parked parallel to the larger Canim vessel, and Marcus waited until a gust of unseasonably chill wind had driven a cloud of snow and sleet into the air, swirling it around them in a freezing veil. Then Marcus drew his sword, grunted with effort, and hacked a hole in the sheet of ice a little larger than his own foot. He put a hand down through the ice to the bare earth beneath, called upon his earth fury, Vamma, and the ground quivered, the ice cracked, and the cold earth swallowed both him and Sha without making a sound.

The Cane clutched at Marcus's armored shoulder with one paw-hand, and the steel plates creaked in protest at the strength of the grip. Marcus gritted his teeth and tried to keep the damage to the ice sheet to a minimum as he parted the earth around them as if it had been water. He held a compact sphere of open space around them, small enough to force Sha to hunch over almost double. Marcus was acutely conscious of the Cane's hot, panting breaths sliding over the back of his neck.

"Easy," he said. "We're fine."

Sha growled. "How long will it take to reach Khral?"

Marcus shook his head. "Depends on the ground between here and there. Earth will only take a moment. If there's much stone, it will be more difficult."

"Then begin."

"Already have."

Sha let out a pensive rumble in the close darkness. "But we are not moving."

"No," Marcus said. "But the earth around us is, and carrying us with it." He took a shuddering breath. He hadn't used a tunneling crafting in fifteen years. He'd lost his appreciation for how strenuous they were. Or perhaps he was just getting old. "I need to concentrate."

Rather than make any affirmative response, Sha simply fell silent.

Crows, but it was good to work with a professional.

The ground between their entry point and Khral's ship was heavily scattered with megalithic boulders, the leavings of some long-vanished glacier, freed from the ice and sunk into the silt in the following thaw, most likely. He detoured around them. Passing directly through would have been possible, but stone was an order of magnitude more difficult to craft than earth. Though it doubled the distance the tunneling had to travel, Marcus judged that, even so, he would come out ahead in terms of energy expended—though time would be a concern. It took them nearly twenty minutes to reach their destination, which was under the safety margin he'd estimated in planning, if only barely.

It was impossible to feel the ship itself through the baffling layer of ice upon the surface, but it was easy to sense the pressure of the ship's weight, transferred through the ice and pressing down upon the soil. He guided the tunneling to the ship's aft and began to nudge slowly upward. The temperature inside the little bubble of air suddenly dropped, and the earth of its curved top was replaced with chill, dirty ice.

They couldn't afford to simply rip up through the ice. Breaking ice could cause great whip-crack bolts of sound. Sha went to work. He drew a tool from a scabbard at his side, a curving blade the shape of a crescent moon, but with its grip suspended between the moon's points, so that the outer curve ran along the wielder's knuckles. The blade was toothed like a saw, and the Cane went to work with great, ripping motions of his arms and shoulders. It took him less than a minute to slice out a hole in the ice large enough for him to fit through, and when the block of ice fell in, the black-stained hull of a Canim ship was revealed above it.

As the Cane carefully stowed the odd knife, Marcus rose, laid a hand on the wooden hull, and called upon his wood fury, Etan. As his fury surged into the ship's hull, he felt his own senses extend through its superstructure. The timbers were all under strain, of course, and the evidence of recent, heavy furycrafting was everywhere. Excellent. Amidst all of those marks of activity, a few more gentle touches would never be noticed.

Marcus murmured to Etan beneath his breath, made an effort of will, and watched as the timbers of the hull gathered and puckered like a suddenly opening mouth. Sha watched this with his eyes narrowed, then nodded once and slithered through the opening. Marcus waited for a few breaths, so that Sha would have time to give warning of any trouble. When no such warning came, he hauled himself into the ship and found himself standing in the deep shadows of the ship's aft cargo hold.

Sha went to the edge of the hatch, centered himself in the hold, and took seven quick silent paces directly toward the stern. He turned directly to his right, took two more paces, then reached up to put his fingers on the hold's ceiling. He glanced at Marcus, to be sure the Aleran had seen the spot.

Marcus nodded and slid up to stand in the indicated position. Sha turned to interlace his fingers, creating a stirrup of his hands. Marcus stepped up into the Cane's grip and found himself lifted lightly upward until he could touch the Canim-scale ceiling. He focused on the planks, narrowed his eyes, and with a sudden spreading motion of his hands, forced the thinner deck planking apart just as he had the hull. Even as the opening gaped, Sha heaved, and Marcus found himself shooting upward through the hole. The stench of rotten blood and musky Cane flooded his nostrils. He landed on one knee, oriented rapidly, and found a lean, reddish-furred Cane sitting on his haunches at a low table, a dozen rolls of leathery parchment spread out before him over its surface. Khral.

Marcus took two swift steps and smashed into Khral, overbearing the Cane by sheer surprise and momentum. Fangs raked at his face, until he drove a hard fist upward, slamming the Cane's muzzle closed just as Khral began to let out a cry.

Surrounded by wood and far from the earth below, Marcus had no way to call upon Vamma again, to borrow of the fury's power, and as a result he was at a lethal disadvantage in close combat with an adult Cane. He delivered a quick, hard strike to Khral's throat. The blow wasn't nearly strong enough to be lethal, but it did turn a second attempted shout into a croaking sound, then the Cane grabbed hold of Marcus's armor and flung him halfway across the cabin.

Khral looked around wildly until his eyes lit upon one of the pale leather pouches the ritualists all carried, hanging from a peg on a wall. The Cane lunged for it.

Marcus lifted a hand and made a sharp beckoning gesture, willing Etan into motion, and the peg wavered and dropped the pouch just as Khral reached for its strap. It hit the deck with a sludgy, sloshing sound, and droplets of blood spattered the wall.

Sha came slithering up through the small hole in the floor like an eel racing from its burrow. The Hunter soared across the cabin in a single bound and landed atop the struggling Khral. Sha's arms moved in a lashing motion, and Khral's eyes bulged even farther as a leather cord whipped tight around his throat. Sha rode Khral down to the deck, leaning back against the strangling cord as they went.

Marcus strode across the room and replaced the pouch upon the peg on the wall. He touched the wall and coaxed Etan into absorbing the droplets of gelatinous blood into the wood, drawing it deep into the grain, where it would not be seen from the surface. He turned to Sha, who was holding tight to the strangling cord, pulling with just as much strength though Khral had stopped moving several seconds before.

When Sha saw that Marcus was finished, he glanced at the wood, gave Marcus a respectful nod, then twisted the strangling cord so that he could keep it looped around Khral's throat while gripping it in one hand. He used it like a boat hook, dragging the senseless ritualist over to the hole in the floorboards, and made his silent way back down into the hold.

Marcus replaced several pieces of the fine, pale hide upon the table, examining his memory to be sure they were returned to the same spot they had been when he entered. Then he checked the cabin door, finding it bolted from the inside, and finally made his way back to the entry point.

Marcus smiled. No one within the ritualist camp was going to know what to make of this.

As he was about to descend, he saw Khral's bunk and stopped to stare at it in fascinated horror.

The bunk was covered with a heavy hide blanket, its fur still upon it. For a moment, Marcus couldn't think of what kind of beast would leave such a mottled, mismatched, patchy coat behind. Then he understood what he was looking at.

There were perhaps a hundred human scalps in the grisly blanket. Many of them sported hairs so fine that they could not possibly have come from an adult. Some of the scalps were, in fact, quite small.

Marcus fought down his gorge and made his way almost blindly into the hold. Up on the deck of the ship, he heard a trumpet blow, a call that was taken up generally, the quarter-hour warning. The fleet was preparing to move again.

Marcus and Sha went back to the opening in the hull and leapt down into the open pocket beneath it, dragging Khral with them. Marcus called up Vamma with a snarl, and within a moment, they were enclosed in earth once more.

"Is he alive?" Marcus demanded a moment later.

"In the strictest sense of the word," Sha replied.

"Wake him."

Sha was silent in the darkness. Then he growled something beneath his breath. There was the sound of several sharp blows. Khral began to make sputtering sounds.

"He speak Aleran?"

"No," Sha said.

"Translate for me, please."

"Yes."

Marcus reached out a hand and felt blindly until he encountered Khral's hide. Then he shot out a hand, seized the Cane by the ear, and dragged him forward with all the strength Vamma could give him.

"I am about to kill you," he said quietly, and Sha echoed him in rumbling Canish. "In a moment, we will leave. And I'm going to leave you here. Ten feet beneath the earth and the ice. The dirt is going to press against you, press into your mouth, your nose, your eyes." He gave the ear a savage twist. "You're going to be crushed to death, slowly, Khral. And no one will so much as know whether you are alive or dead."

Marcus waited for Sha to finish speaking, then shoved Khral roughly away, releasing his ear. Khral babbled incoherently in Canim, and it sounded like he was trying to cling to Sha.

Marcus heard Sha's saw-toothed tool leave its sheath, heard it strike with a meaty thump. Khral let out a scream. An instant later, Marcus smelled bile and sewage. Sha had gutted the ritualist.

Marcus put his hand on the earthen wall again and willed the tunneling to begin moving again. Khral began to babble in greater panic as the sphere of air moved away from him, left him behind. He kept on babbling and screaming until, a few seconds later, his voice abruptly vanished.

Sha let out a satisfied growl but otherwise made no comment.

They emerged where they had entered the tunneling, with Marcus checking warily before they climbed out—but he found that no one was paying any attention. The horns were still blowing. Marcus swept his gaze around as best he could and spotted winged black forms high overhead, flying up from the south. Vordknights.

"Come on!" Marcus growled to Sha as he clambered back up onto the sheet ice.

Sha came out hard on Marcus's heels and let out a snarl.

"Aye," Marcus said in reply. "We're under attack."

CHAPTER 23

Marcus hadn't run twenty feet when Antillus Crassus came soaring out of the open sky on a roaring column of cold wind, landing beside him and dropping into a run with him. "First Spear! Captain wants you!"

"Where?" Marcus called back. Drums and horns continued sounding, and everywhere Canim and Alerans alike were running back toward their ships. Flags were being run up masts—the green pennants that were the signal to continue on course at full speed.

Instead of answering, Crassus dragged one of Marcus's arms over his shoulders, clamped onto him with an iron grip, and both of them were lifted off their feet by a surge of gale winds. The ice below receded as they arched sharply into the air, and Marcus found himself fighting not to cling to the young Tribune for dear life. He hated flying, hated being utterly at the mercy of another's talent and judgment. They swept over two dozen tall-masted ships swarming with activity, and all the while, the distant forms of the flying vord grew closer.

The flight was a brief one—more like an excessively long jump than Marcus's previous experiences with flight. They came down directly onto the deck of the *Slive*, sending a pair of coiled lines slithering over the deck and earning a glare of reprimand from Captain Demos. Crassus clapped Marcus on the shoulder and bounded back into the air, soaring up to join the fliers of the Knights Pisces already in the air. They were spread out into a covering formation around the *Slive*.

Marcus spotted the captain up near the prow, speaking intently with Maestro Magnus. The Ambassador stood with him, wearing a mail shirt, the only armor he'd ever seen her wearing. Maximus and two of the First Aleran's Knights Ferrous loitered nearby, and Marcus noted that all of the *Slive*'s most skilled swordsmen, some of them capable of being Knights Ferrous themselves, were doing their jobs in the areas nearest the captain.

Marcus strode to the front of the ship, stepping over a pair of heavy, loose poles on the way—replacement spars for the rigging, probably—and banged his fist to his heart in salute. "Captain."

"Marcus," the captain replied. He frowned and nodded down at Marcus's armor. "What happened?"

Marcus glanced down. He hadn't seen any blood splatter on his armor aboard Khral's ship. It must have happened during the tunneling, when Sha had gutted the scheming ritualist. The speckles of blood had been smeared by the wind of his short flight, but fortunately that helped to thin it out, disguising its true color. Canim blood was darker than Aleran, but spread thin over the surface of his armor, it looked almost the same. "Just one crowbegotten thing after another, sir," he answered.

"Tell me about it," the captain said. He squinted up into the grey sky and nodded at the incoming enemy. "Tell me what you see, First Spear."

Marcus grunted and turned to look as well. His eyes weren't what they used to be, but he could make things out well enough to understand what the captain meant.

"That's not an attack force, sir," he said after a moment. "There's not enough of them, and they're spread too thin."

The captain grinned as the wind began to gust harder than it had all morning. "That was my thought as well."

"Scouts," Marcus said.

The captain nodded. "Maybe spread all up and down the Shieldwall."

With a grinding sound, the vessel nearest the *Slive* began to move, her sails bellying out before the cold wind. Up and down the line, other ships were getting under way, though the *Slive*'s sails were still furled.

"Why?" Marcus asked.

"Looking for us, naturally," the captain replied. "I think odds are good that the vord knew we left Antillus marching north. And even though this idea has worked out, it wouldn't take a genius to deduce that the only major structure north of Antillus might play a role in whatever we had planned."

Marcus grunted. It made sense. The vord could spare a few thousand fliers for scouting duties, and barring the windcrafters enslaved by the enemy, the vordknights were the fastest troops they possessed. More ships passed the motionless *Slive*. "What is the plan, sir?"

"Oh, we run," the captain said offhandedly. "They're flying against the wind, and we're with it. They can't maintain the pace as easily as we can. They'll tire, and we should lose them within a few hours."

Marcus nodded. "Yes, sir." He cleared his throat. "I'm not a sailor, sir, but don't we need to use the sails if we're going to leave the vord in our wake?"

Behind the captain, Ambassador Kitai grinned wolfishly.

"I don't want to take unnecessary losses in a general skirmish," the captain said. "We are going to remain behind. If they see a lone ship, potentially unable to run, I believe the vordknights will see it as an opportunity to attack."

"You want to stop them from running off to tell their Queen about us," Marcus said, nodding.

The captain spread his hands. "That, and I need to explore a few theories. It might be better to test them now than when we reach the enemy's main body. I'd like you to coordinate efforts with Captain Demos and make sure he has someone who can advise him on how he and his crew can best work in tandem with our Knights."

Marcus saluted. "Of course, sir."

"Thank you," the captain said. "Demos is on the aft deck, I believe."

Marcus checked his weapon and armor as he marched down the length of the ship to Demos, an old soldier's habit long since become something very near a reflex action. As he walked, he watched the ships of the fleet gliding gracefully around the *Slive* and proceeding to the east. He went up several short, steep stairs to ascend from the deck to the raised afterdeck, and noticed his legs shaking with fatigue. The tunneling had taken a great deal more out of him, physically, than he had anticipated. The realization seemed to spark a general revolt of his limbs, with muscles and joints each voicing distinct and unique complaints.

Marcus gritted his teeth and exchanged nods with Demos and the bosun.

"First Spear," Demos drawled. As usual, the sword-slender captain of the *Slive* was dressed in plain, well-made clothing, all of it in black. He wore a long dueling blade at his side, its handle plain and worn. "You all right?"

Marcus grunted. "Starting to think that maybe I'm getting too old for all this running around."

"Maybe you should retire," Demos said.

"Soon as the work is done."

"Work's never done," Demos said.

"Hngh. Maybe I'll get lucky and catch an arrow in the eye."

Demos's bland face barely showed a shadow of a smile. "That's the spirit." He turned his eyes to the sky and pursed his lips. "Octavian was right."

Marcus squinted up to see that the scattered line of vordknights were gathering into a more cohesive swarm. "How many?"

"Ninety, maybe a hundred," Demos said.

Marcus drummed his fingers on the hilt of his sword. "And how many on your crew?"

"Twenty-seven," he replied calmly. "And me. And you. And the Princeps. And Antillar. Plus young Antillus and his flyboys overhead. Enough."

"Assuming the enemy isn't bringing something new to the fight."

Demos showed his teeth. "Don't go all giddy on me."

"If the world were a giddy place, it wouldn't need men like me," Marcus said.

Demos nodded. "Me, either." He squinted speculatively. "Wonder if Octavian's going to stretch his muscles."

"As far as I know, his talents are still rather limited."

Demos gave Marcus a deadpan look. "We're sailing down a smooth, flat sheet of ice, which is staying cold in the middle of spring, running in front of a wind coming in from a good angle to move us that hasn't wavered or fluttered for two days." He looked back up at the oncoming vord. "That isn't luck. There isn't that much of it in the whole world."

Marcus had long suspected that the captain's talents had begun to blossom, and Demos had a point. If he was unsure of his abilities, the captain might well decide to test them upon a real foe in some controlled fashion—somewhere out of sight of the rest of the fleet, in the event that things did not proceed well.

The last of the fleet's ships went gliding past, and Demos watched its stern speculatively. "There they go."

"Might want to get your men out of the rigging," Marcus said. "Vord'll be here shortly. The flyboys will be making it too breezy for them to come down on us all at once."

Demos nodded laconically and gestured to the bosun. He started bellowing sailors down out of the rigging. Though they often went about armed with knives, today Demos's crew were all wearing armored jacks and carrying blades and other instruments of martial mayhem. Demos ordered the sails furled, taken down, and stowed, so that they would not become victims of combat. He'd also ordered the decks wetted, and the crew had been slopping laboriously melted water over the entire ship for the past quarter of an hour. Despite the wind and cold air from the north, the temperature was not quite sufficient to refreeze the water on the deck, and the *Slive*'s timbers soaked it up as if the ship herself was thirsty to return to the sea.

Marcus could hardly fault Demos's caution. Firecrafting could be dangerously unpredictable in a battle, even when used by experts. If the captain had decided to try his hand at it, Demos's precaution was entirely sensible. They had just finished when one of the sailors cried out, "Here they come!"

Marcus turned his head to see the group of vordknights alter course and go into a steep dive toward the motionless ship. As they came down, perhaps a score of them split off from the main body, diving ahead of the rest to engage Antillus Crassus and his Knights Aeris.

Tribune Crassus made a broad circling motion over his head with his left arm to gain his Knights' attention, and flashed a quick series of hand signals. Half a dozen of the Aleran fliers streaked up to meet the contingent of vordknights, falling into a v-shaped formation as they went. The others, including Crassus, remained behind to guard the ship.

Marcus had time to see the enemy vanguard engage the Knights. The six men of the First Aleran simply bowled through their more numerous opponents, with the lead flier diverting his windstream, slewing it around in wide arcs that scattered the vordknights like dandelion fluff. The two men on either side of the leader closed in to catch his arms and prevent him from falling, while the other three struck at a number of vordknights whose efforts to regain control of their flight had brought them within striking distance of a weapon. One of the Alerans' blades struck home, and a vordknight went spiraling off on an odd angle, leaking a spray of green-brown blood, a severed wing fluttering down more slowly above him.

Then the main body of the vord drove through the Aleran vanguard to fall upon the ship.

At another signal from Crassus, tempest winds suddenly howled, and vordknights began to veer off, forced away from the ship by the violence of the gale. The first thirty or forty of the enemy were driven off, but there were simply too many of them for the Knights Aeris to reach them all. A few managed to wing down through the winds, and as the attack went on, the vord forced away earliest began to circle and fall upon the ship from every direction. Weapons flashed in the light, and someone screamed.

A vordknight landed on the deck not six feet from Marcus, and sent a lightning flash of terrified energy through his body.

The enemy was a few inches shorter than he, and roughly man-shaped. Its body was covered in chitinous armor, layered in bands that almost seemed to resemble a *legionare's* lorica. Its head was roughly the shape of a helmeted Aleran's though there was no opening where the mouth should have been—only smooth skin. Its eyes were multifaceted and greenly reflective, like a dragonfly's, an impression echoed by the four broad, translucent wings upon its back, now slowing from the blurring shape they had been in flight and folding in upon the vordknight's back.

Those alien eyes turned to Marcus, and the vord rushed him. Both of its arms ended in scything blades rather than hands, and its weapon-limbs were upraised and ready to strike.

Marcus sidestepped the first double blow of the deadly appendages, drawing his blade as he did. His first stroke clove into the chitin on the vord's shoulder, and was nearly trapped there as the vord's momentum carried him past. Marcus managed to jerk the weapon clear in time, leaving an ugly wound hacked into the vord's flesh. The weapon came away stained with green-brown blood.

The vord spun to return to the attack—but there was a flash of steel and angry scarlet sparks, and the vordknight's head jumped up off its shoulders as if propelled by the blood that jetted up in a fountain behind it.

The headless vordknight turned in place as if the blow had done nothing to inconvenience it, blades slashing. Captain Demos, long blade in hand, was forced to leap back from the foe, though his sword spat angry scarlet sparks again as it met one of the enemy scythes, and cut it cleanly from the vord's body. Demos regained his balance, hacked the vord's other scythe away with casual efficiency, then stepped forward and drove his heel into the thrashing creature's belly. The kick sent it tumbling over the side of the ship.

Two more of the vordknights landed on the aft deck, rapidly followed by a third. Demos raised his left hand and made a twisting motion, and the railing around the stern side of the deck suddenly bowed, as if made of a supple willow switch, and snared one of the vordknights around the ankle.

Marcus charged the other pair before they could orient themselves and attack. He drove his blade into a gleaming eye, released it, and shoved the wounded vord away with all his strength. He ducked beneath the second vord's blow and came in low, hitting the thing around the waist and getting his own body in too close to the vordknight's to allow the creature to use its scythes on him. He was heavier than the vord by a very great deal. It weighed no more than a large sack of meal, and as his armored body slammed the vordknight to the deck, it crunched audibly.

He heard Demos's light steps as the ship's captain went past him, and sparks flared several more times somewhere at the edge of his vision. Marcus concentrated on the vord beneath him—the creature was tremendously powerful, easily more than a match for his own physical strength, and Marcus could not enhance it with furycraft this far from the earth beneath the ship, even if it hadn't additionally been coated in six inches of ice.

Marcus stayed atop the vord, relying upon his weight instead of his strength, keeping as close to the vord's body as possible, denying it any small bit of leverage with which it could employ the full power of its body. Marcus began to slam his helmeted head against the vord's, one blow after another. After several such strikes, his own ears were ringing, but the vord's struggles had lost cohesion.

A second later, Demos's blade hissed somewhere near Marcus's back, and red sparks fell all around his head and bounced up from the vordknight's face. Marcus rolled to one side as swiftly as he could and looked up to see Demos behead the scytheless vord. He carried Marcus's *gladius* in his left hand and shifted his grip upon it to offer it back to him. Marcus took the sword with a nod and looked around, his heart pounding.

The crew had engaged the enemy. Evidently, Demos hadn't chosen them

first and foremost for their nautical skills. Though they fought in bands of two
and three and four, they cooperated against the enemy with the tactical discipline of elite *legionares*. Several vordknights already lay dead on the *Slive's* deck,
most of them dismembered to boot. As Marcus watched, a grizzled sailor pitched
a fishing net over a landing vordknight, entangling its wings in the net's cords.
Then he hauled the vord from its feet, while two other members of the crew
went to work on the creature with axes.

Elsewhere, the burly bosun flailed desperately at three of the vordknights
with his back to the mainmast, his short-handled bill keeping them back but
doing them no harm. Marcus elbowed Demos, who stood at his back, and nodded toward the embattled bosun.

Demos growled under his breath and lifted his left hand again. The mainmast itself groaned and bent, and its two lowest spars swept down like a giant's
fist, hammering two of the three vordknights flat in a spray of disgusting fluids.
The third vordknight leapt back in alarm, beginning to unfurl its wings, but the
bosun didn't give the creature time to flee. He closed in with the bill and all but
split the vordknight in half with a single, downward-sweeping blow. The bosun
kicked the stunned and dying vord over the side of the ship, glanced at Demos,
and touched the brim of an imaginary hat.

"Too bad he ran out of whiskey on the way home," Demos commented judiciously. "He fights better when he's drunk."

The ongoing gale had churned up a thickening curtain of ice crystals, and
Marcus couldn't see the front of the ship. More vord continued to land, singly
and in pairs, and everyone he could see was rushing to hack them down as
quickly as possible, anxious to keep the weight of numbers in the Alerans' favor.
Another vord landed on the port side, and Demos glided forward to dispatch it
before it could be joined by others.

Marcus found himself faced with a foe on the starboard side, but reacted too
slowly to force it off the ship and found himself fighting simply to remain alive.
His sword matched the scythes of the vordknight, turning one blow after another,
and his experience offset the creature's power and fearless aggression, allowing
him to stay just outside the critical distances that would allow it to close and cut
him to bits.

But he knew that he couldn't keep it up for long. His foe was both stronger
and faster than he, and it would only be a matter of seconds before he found
himself unable to deny the vord an opportunity for a lethal onslaught. Terror
gave him strength enough for the moment, but if the fight didn't change in the
next few seconds, he was a dead man.

Marcus's hand found the ship's rail behind him, and he retreated a few steps along it, the vord pursuing. His open hand hit a smooth shape, and he drew a heavy belaying pin from its rack on the rail and flung it at the vordknight's head.

The vord's scythes snapped up to block the missile an instant too late, and it struck the creature between its eyes. The vordknight staggered, and before it could recover, Marcus charged the foe, barreling it off the aft deck and falling six feet to the main deck, all of his armored weight coming down atop the vord. There was a loud popping sound, and vord blood flew out in a nauseating burst. The vordknight collapsed beneath Marcus like an emptied wineskin.

Marcus was shocked silent for an instant by the pain of the fall—and then howled in triumph as he realized that he was still alive. He came to his feet painfully, blinking gore from his eyes, and just as he'd reached them, a warning voice screamed, "Fidelias, behind you!"

Fidelias whirled, half-blinded with vord blood, his blade lifted to a defensive guard to find himself faced with . . .

Maestro Magnus.

There were no vord in sight.

Fidelias stared at Magnus for a second that seemed an eternity. He watched as the other man's eyes hardened and narrowed. He watched as he saw his own acknowledgment of the truth reflected in the old Cursor's eyes.

He'd just given himself away.

He stood there like that, staring at Magnus, as the gale winds began to ebb. The cloud of icy spray died away to the sounds of the defiant jeers of the *Slive*'s crew. The vord were retreating, but he and Marcus stood frozen.

"I admired you," Magnus said quietly. "We all admired you. And you betrayed us."

Fidelias lowered his sword, slowly. He stared down at it. "How did you know?"

"Accretion of evidence," Magnus replied. "There are a limited number of individuals, by talent, training, and nature, who could accomplish the things you have. Given what you've done, how you've operated, I knew you had to be a Cursor. I made a list. But there aren't many of us old *Cursori Callidus* left alive, after Kalarus's Bloodcrows were through with us. It was a very short list."

Fidelias nodded. It had only been a matter of time before he was discovered. He'd known that for quite a while.

"You are a traitor," Magnus said quietly.

Fidelias nodded.

"You killed Cursor Serai. One of our own."

"Yes."

"How many?" Magnus asked, his voice shaking with rage. "How many have you murdered? How many deaths can be laid at your feet?"

Fidelias took a deep breath, and said quietly, "I stopped counting back when I still worked for Sextus."

Fidelias wasn't sure when Octavian and the others arrived, but when he looked up, the Princeps was standing beside Magnus, his retinue behind him. His eyes were hard, green stones.

"I watched you murder men not five feet from me on the wall at Garrison," Octavian said quietly. "I watched you try to hang Araris. I watched you stab my uncle and throw him off the wall. You killed people I'd known my whole life in the Calderon Valley. Neighbors. Friends."

Fidelias heard the strangled tone in his voice as something distant and unconnected to his thoughts. "I did those things," he said. "I did them all."

The Princeps' right hand closed into a fist. The pop of his knuckles was like the crackling of ice.

Fidelias nodded slowly. "You knew I could lie to a truthfinder. You needed to elicit the reaction under pressure. This was a trap all along."

"I told you I wanted to test a theory," the Princeps said, his words clipped. "And when Magnus reported his suspicions to me, including word of your covert activities with Sha, it forced me to take action."

The Princeps looked away, squinting out into the distance.

Fidelias said nothing. The silence was profound.

When the Princeps spoke, it was in a near whisper, thick with anger and grief. "I thought I would be proving your innocence."

The words sent a pain through Fidelias's guts as sharp and real as any sword's thrust.

"Do you have anything to say for yourself?" the Princeps asked.

Fidelias closed his eyes for a moment, then opened them and drew in a slow breath. "I made my choices. I knew the consequences."

Octavian stared at him in cold silence, and Fidelias suddenly realized that the posts he'd seen on the deck of the *Slive* were not replacements for broken spars.

Gaius Octavian turned his back and began to walk away, rigid with anger and pain. Each strike of his boots on the deck was distinct, final. He did not look back when he said, "Crucify him."

CHAPTER 24

Tavi watched as Magnus and the execution detail left the ship. It included each of the Knights Ferrous on board and a pair of Demos's most combat-capable sailors. They took Fidelias ex Cursori and the spars for the crucifixion with them.

"Tough to believe," Max said quietly. "I mean . . . Valiar Marcus."

"People lie, kid," Demos said. "Especially about who they are."

"I know, I know," Max said quietly. "I'm just . . . just surprised, that's all. He was always so solid."

"All in your head," Demos said calmly. "He was what he was. You're the one who made him solid."

Max glanced at Tavi. "Sir, are you sure you . . . ?"

Tavi grimaced, and said, "Max, he betrayed my grandfather after swearing to serve him. He gave his own student, back at the Academy, to the Aquitaines to be tortured. He is the only surviving member of the senior Cursori who could possibly have provided details about the organization to Kalarus's Bloodcrows. I personally witnessed him kill half a dozen *legionares* defending the battlements at Second Calderon, and the plan he helped execute killed hundreds more. Any one of those crimes merits execution. In time of war, they merit summary execution."

Max frowned and did not look at Tavi. "Do we know if he's done anything since he assumed the identity of Valiar Marcus?"

"It doesn't matter what he's done since, Max," Tavi replied, keeping his voice level, completely neutral. "He is guilty of treason. There are a host of crimes a First Lord can choose to be lenient about. There is one he absolutely cannot."

"But . . ."

Crassus cut in, overriding his brother's protest. "He's right, Max. You know he's right."

Demos folded his arms and nodded at Max. "Be glad the fellow did some good before he got caught. It doesn't give the dead back to their families. The man chose to kill. He crossed a line. He knew his own life might be forfeit because of it." He nodded in the guard detail's general direction. "Fidelias knows that. He knows that Octavian doesn't have any choice in the matter. He's made his peace with it."

"How could you possibly know that?" Max asked.

Demos shrugged. "When Magnus spotted him, Fidelias didn't kill the old man. He could have, easily, and for all he knew, it might have kept his secret. He could have tried to run before the battle was over. He didn't."

Tavi listened to it all without paying much attention. Marcus, a traitor. Marcus, who had saved his life only days ago, at considerable risk to his own. Marcus, who had done his best to murder members of Tavi's family.

Not Marcus, he told himself. *Fidelias. There was no Marcus. There never was a Marcus.*

There were too many lies. They were starting to make his head hurt. The sun seemed too bright.

"As soon as the execution detail is back on board, please get under way, Captain," Tavi said. "I'll be in my cabin." He turned before anyone could acknowledge him and walked back to his cabin with his head bowed. The curtains were already drawn, leaving the space fairly dark, and he sank down onto his bunk, shaking with postbattle adrenaline.

He had only been there for a few moments when the door opened, and Kitai entered. She walked across the little room, her steps brisk, and Tavi felt the gentle pressure of an aircrafting come up around them, to make their conversation a private one.

"Why are you being an idiot?" she demanded.

Tavi opened his eyes and looked at her. She stood over him with her legs planted in a wide, confident stance "*Chala,* do the Marat have a word for 'diplomacy'?"

Her green eyes began to look almost luminous as her anger grew. Tavi could feel the heat of it pressing against him, simmering inside him. "This is not a time for humor."

Tavi narrowed his eyes at her. "You disagree with what is happening to M— To Fidelias."

"I do not know Fidelias," she replied. "I know Marcus. He does not deserve this."

"Perhaps. Perhaps not. Either way, he *is* guilty of treason, and the law is clear."

"Law," Kitai said, and spat on the deck as if the word had carried a bad taste. "He has fought loyally for you for years."

"He has *lied* to me for years," Tavi replied, and considerable heat burned in his own reply. "He has betrayed the trust of the Realm. He has murdered innocents, Citizens and loyal freemen."

"And risked his life countless times on the field with us," Kitai snapped back.

Tavi found himself hurtling up off the bed, his voice rising unbidden to a bellowing roar so loud that it made him see stars. "HE TRIED TO MURDER MY FAMILY!"

They both stood there for a moment, Tavi breathing heavily. Kitai looked him up and down, then slowly arched an eyebrow. "Of course. Your judgment is clearly unbiased, Your Highness."

Tavi opened his mouth to reply, then forced himself to stop. He sat back down on the bunk, still breathing heavily. He stayed that way for a full minute. Then he looked back up at Kitai, and said, "Yes. He hurt me personally. But he did that to a lot of people. Even if the law didn't mandate an execution, it would be a form of justice to allow him to be sentenced by those he had wronged."

"No," Kitai said. "It would be a needlessly bureaucratic form of revenge." She paused, and added, with a faint wisp of wry humor, "Which, now that I think on it, is a functional description of Aleran law in any case."

Tavi rubbed at his forehead with one hand. "It had to be this way. If he had run, I could have let him go. But he didn't."

"So you will waste him."

Tavi frowned. "I don't understand."

"He knew what would happen to him if he stayed," Kitai said. "Therefore, he wanted the outcome."

"He wanted to die?"

Kitai frowned pensively. "I think . . . he wanted balance. Order. He knew that the things he has done were wrong. Submitting himself to sentencing, to justice was . . ." She shook her head. "I cannot remember the Aleran word."

"Redemption," Tavi said thoughtfully. "He wanted to confess. He knew he would not be forgiven for his crimes, but by choosing to act as he did . . ."

"He gained a sense of order," Kitai said. "Of peace. He creates a solid Realm in his thoughts and pays a just penalty for the things he has done." Kitai reached into a pocket and tossed him something underhand.

Tavi caught it. It was a triangle of chitin as long as his smallest finger—the tip of a vordknight's scythe.

"Things have changed, my Aleran. The vord are here, and they will kill us all. It is madness to labor on their behalf." She moved forward and put a hand on his arm. "And he has saved your life, *chala*. For that, I am in his debt."

"Crows." Tavi sighed and sagged back down, staring at the deck.

Kitai moved quietly to sit down on the bunk beside him. She put her wrist to his forehead. Her skin felt pleasantly cool.

"You have a fever, *chala*," she said quietly. "You've been holding the weathercrafting too long."

Tavi gritted his teeth. "Have to. Won't be much longer. We should reach Phrygia by morning."

"You told me that Sextus did this," she said. "Pushed himself to do what he saw as his duty—even though it cost him his health, even though it put the Realm at risk of losing its First Lord." She slid her hand down his arm to twine her fingers with his. "You said it was shortsighted of him. You said it was foolish."

"He did it for weeks on end," Tavi said.

"But not continually," she countered. "Only at night, during his meditations."

"It doesn't matter," Tavi said. "If the ice melts, there's no getting it back with spring coming on. I just have to hold it for a few more hours."

She frowned, clearly unhappy, but did not gainsay him.

"You think I'm wasting Fidelias's life."

"No," Kitai said. "He is there because he wanted to be there. You are wasting his death."

He frowned at her for a moment, then her meaning sunk in. "Ah," he said.

"He should be given the choice," Kitai said. "If nothing else, you owe him that."

Tavi leaned over and kissed her hair gently. "I think," he said, "you may be right."

Tavi walked carefully over the ice to the execution party. They were gathering up their tools and preparing to return to the ship. As he approached, they saluted.

"Leave us," Tavi said. The men saluted again and hurried to return to the ship.

There were a number of allowable variants for crucifixion, ranging from the practical to the downright sadistic. Which one was used was mostly determined by how much anguish the authorities felt the offender had earned. Many were designed to contain and circumvent specific furycrafting talents.

For Fidelias, they had used steel wire.

He hung upon the crossed spars, his feet dangling two feet above the ground. His arms had been bound to the outthrust arms of the cross with dozens of circles of steel wire. More wire bound his waist to the trunk of the cross. That much steel would virtually neutralize his woodcrafting. Being suspended from the earth would prevent him from employing earthcrafting. He was dressed only in his tunic. His armor, weapons, and helmet had been taken from him.

Fidelias was obviously in pain, his face pale. His eyes and cheeks looked sunken, and the grey in his hair and stubbled face was more prominent than at any other time Tavi had seen him.

He looked old.

And weary.

Tavi stopped in front of the cross and stared up at him for a moment.

Fidelias met his eyes. After a time, he said, "You should go. You should catch up to the fleet before the next stop."

"I will," Tavi said quietly. "After you answer one question."

The old Cursor sighed. "What question?"

"How do you want to be remembered?"

Fidelias let out a dry, croaking laugh. "What the crows does it matter what I want? I know what I will be remembered for."

"Answer the question, Cursor."

Fidelias was silent for a moment, his eyes closed. The wind gusted around them, cold and uncaring.

"I never wanted a civil war. I never wanted anyone to die."

"I believe you," Tavi said quietly. "Answer the question."

Fidelias's head remained bowed. "I would like to be remembered as a man who tried to serve the Realm to the best of his ability. Who dedicated his life to Alera, even if not to her lord."

Tavi nodded slowly. Then he drew his sword.

Fidelias did not look up.

Tavi stepped around to the back of the crossed poles and struck three times.

Fidelias abruptly dropped to the ground, cut free from the coils of wire by Tavi's blade. Tavi took a step and stood over Fidelias, staring down at him.

"Get up," he said quietly. "You are condemned to die, Fidelias ex Cursori. But we are at war. Therefore, when you die, you will do so usefully. If you truly are a servant of the Realm, I have a better death for you than this one."

Fidelias stared up at him for a moment, and his features twisted into something like pain. Then he nodded in a single jerky spasm.

Tavi extended his hand, and Fidelias took it.

CHAPTER 25

The fleet reached Phrygia in the false light of predawn, when the eastern sky had just begun to turn from black to blue. Starlight and moonlight on the snow made it easy to see, and Antillus Crassus and a handful of Knights Pisces had flown ahead to bring official word of the fleet to Phrygius Cyricus, Lord Phrygius's second son and seneschal of the city while his father was in the field.

"Times are changing," Fidelias said. "I don't think anyone's ever outrun the wall's grapevine without flying."

"What makes you say that?" Tavi asked him.

The Cursor gestured up at the wall, where a surprisingly sparse number of faces looked out from the battlements. "If they'd gotten wind of something like this, the whole city would have turned out."

Tavi glanced back behind him, at the seemingly endless river of masts and sails gliding over the ice. It had been an impressive sight when he'd first taken it in, even to someone who had sailed with a veritable armada over the deeps. To the folk and *legionares* of Phrygia, most of whom had never seen a tall ship, much less the open sea, it must be awe-inspiring, scarcely believable.

He glanced aside at Fidelias, who stood beside him in the tunic, breeches, and cloak of a civilian. He was unarmed. Two Knights Ferrous stood within sword reach of him, their weapons sheathed, their hands hovering near the hilts. Maximus stood on Tavi's other side and kept track of Fidelias's movements with an oblique eye.

Tavi studied him for another reason. Fidelias looked different than Valiar Marcus. Oh, his features hadn't changed, though Tavi supposed they might do so gradually, should Fidelias wish to reassume his former appearance. It was something subtler than that, and much deeper. The way he spoke was part of it. Marcus had always sounded like an intelligent man, but one who had been given little education, a hard-nosed and capable soldier. Fidelias's voice was smoother and more mellifluous, his inflections elegant and precise. Marcus had always held himself with parade-ground rigidity, and moved like a man carrying the extra weight of Legion armor, even when he wasn't wearing any. Fidelias looked like a man coming near to the end of an exceptionally vigorous middle age, his movements both energetic and contained.

Then Tavi hit on it, the real thing that separated Valiar Marcus from Fidelias ex Cursori.

Fidelias was smiling.

Oh, it wasn't a grin. In fact, one could hardly tell it was a smile at all. But Tavi could definitely see it in some subtle shift of the muscles in his face, in the scarcely noticeable deepening of the lines at the corners of his eyes. He looked . . . content. He looked like a man who had made his peace.

Tavi had no intention, however, of removing the guards tasked with watching him. For that matter, Tavi himself would be watching the man like a hawk. Fidelias ex Cursori had lived a lifetime in an exceptionally dangerous, treacherous line of work. It had made him into an exceptionally dangerous—and treacherous—individual.

"Our next step," Tavi told him, "is to gather whatever information Cyricus has that we don't. We'll use it to plan our next movement."

"That would seem logical," Fidelias said.

Tavi nodded. "I'd like you to be present."

Fidelias arched an eyebrow and glanced up at him. "Is that an order?"

"No," Tavi said. "It would be meaningless. What would I do if you refused? Put you to death?"

Fidelias's eyes wrinkled at their corners. "Ah, true."

"It is a request. You have more field experience than Magnus, and you may have some insight into the thinking behind the current leadership of the main Aleran forces. I would value your advice."

Fidelias pursed his lips. "But would you trust it?"

Tavi smiled. "Naturally not."

The older man let out a quick bark of a laugh. He shook his head, and said, "It would be my pleasure, Your Highness."

Phrygius Cyricus, Seneschal of Phrygia and commander of its defending Legions, was sixteen years old. He was an almost painfully thin young man, dressed in the white-and-green livery of the House of Phrygius, and his dark hair was untidy enough to merit an assault from some kind of elite barbering strike force. His dark eyes peered out from behind his hair as he bowed to Tavi.

"Y-your Highness," Cyricus said. "W-welcome to Phrygia."

Tavi, accompanied by Maestro Magnus, Fidelias, and Kitai, stepped over the threshold of the High Lord's citadel and into the cramped courtyard beyond. "Master Phrygius," he replied, bowing slightly in return. "I'm sorry I couldn't arrange to arrive at a more convenient hour."

"Th-that's all r-right," Cyricus replied, and Tavi realized that the boy was not stammering in nervousness. He simply had a stammer. "If y-you would come w-with me, m-my lord father's staff has prepared a r-report of the latest news from the f-front."

Tavi lifted his eyebrows, impressed. "Straight to business, eh?"

"Th there's f food and wine waiting for you and your . . . Cyricus paused and swallowed, glancing past Tavi to the hulking form of Varg, who had entered the courtyard last. "G-guests."

"That is well," Varg said. "I am hungry."

Cyricus swallowed again. Then the boy lifted his chin and marched over to face Varg, meeting his gaze. "Y-you are w-welcomed as a guest, sir. B-but if you hurt anyone under my lord f-father's p-protection, I will kill you myself."

Varg's ears quivered. He bowed from the waist to the youth. "It will be as you say in your house, young Master." Then he glanced at Tavi, and rumbled, in Canish, "Does the pup remind you of anyone, Tavar?"

Tavi answered him in kind. "As I recall, I had a knife to your throat at the time."

"It did give you a certain credibility," Varg admitted.

Tavi carefully kept himself from smiling, and said, "Master Cyricus, I assure you that Warmaster Varg has had extensive experience as a guest of Aleran Citizens and that he has always displayed admirable courtesy."

Varg's ears twitched in amusement.

Cyricus inclined his head to Tavi. "V-very well, Y-your Highness. This way please."

The young man and an escort of "honor guards," all of whom stared warily at Varg, led them into a small reception hall within the citadel. A dozen men were waiting there around a large sand table, presumably the young seneschal's staff and the commanders of the city's defenses. As Tavi entered, they offered a crisp salute as a group. Tavi returned the gesture and nodded. "Gentlemen."

Cyricus made introductions for his people and Tavi did likewise, leaving Fidelias entirely out of the matter. Then he said, "Let's get an idea of the larger picture so far. Who can summarize the current position of our forces at Riva?"

Canto Cantus, a steely-haired man in Legion armor, glanced at Cyricus, as if for permission. The young man's nod was barely perceptible but very much there. Cantus didn't speak until after he'd gained approval. "The short version is that Riva has fallen. Completely. In a single night."

Tavi stared at Cantus for long seconds, and his heart began pounding harder in his chest. He limited his reaction to digging his fingernails into the heel of his right hand, then forced himself to relax. "Survivors?"

"A great many," Cantus said. "Princeps Attis realized what was happening in time to evacuate most of the civilians from Riva. But the Legions took a bloody beating covering the retreat of the refugees. They're still sorting out what's left."

"Tell me what happened."

Cantus gave a cold, concise summary of the tactics used by the vord.

"That isn't much," Tavi said.

Cantus shrugged. "Bear in mind that we're putting this together from garbled watersendings and reports from refugees who were running for their lives and were not trained observers. The reports all seem to conflict with one another."

Tavi frowned. "All right. They're retreating. To where?"

"The C-calderon V-valley, Your Highness," Cyricus said. "A-allow me." The young man touched a finger to the sand table, and the smooth white grains shifted into ripples that settled into the shapes of mountains and valleys, displaying causeways as flat rectangular strips. A miniature walled city, representative of Riva, appeared and began crumbling almost immediately. Rippling motion along the causeway north and east of Riva showed the position of the refugees. Solid rectangular blocks following in their wake represented the Legions. A series of menacing triangles, representing the spread of the vord, followed after the Legions.

Tavi frowned down at the map for a long moment. "What do we know about enemy numbers?"

"There appear to be quite a few of them," Cantus replied.

Tavi looked up from the table, arching an eyebrow.

Cantus shook his head. "It's hard to get within sight of the horde during daylight, even for fliers. There is a constant battle for control of the air with those wasp-men they've got. I can spare only a handful of fliers to use for reconnaissance, and they've returned reports varying from three hundred thousand to ten times that number. So far, none of them have turned north for Phrygia. They seem to be intent on pursuing Princeps Attis."

"They don't dare do anything else," Tavi said. "If the High Lords get a chance to catch their breath, they can still be very, very dangerous to the vord."

Fidelias cleared his throat. He pointed a finger toward the far end of the northeastern causeway, the one that ended at Garrison. "Offhand, I'd say your pessimistic scout was the most likely to have been correct in his observations."

"Why?"

"The geography," Fidelias said. "Princeps Attis is seeking advantageous ground. Calderon may suit his purposes."

"Why say that?" Varg rumbled.

Tavi began to ask Cyricus to expand the sand table's view of the Calderon Valley, only to find that the stuttering young man was already in the process of doing it. Tavi made a mental note to himself: If he survived this war, he simply *had* to offer the young man a job. Initiative like that was uncommon.

"Ah, thank you, Master Cyricus," Tavi said. "Princeps Attis is leading the vord into a funnel," Tavi said. "Once they've passed the western escarpments and entered the Calderon Valley, they're going to be forced to crowd in closer and closer. Sea on the north, impassable mountains in the south."

"Neutralizing the advantage of numbers," Varg growled.

"In part. But he's also going there because my uncle has turned the place into a bloody fortress."

Fidelias glanced up at Tavi, frowning.

"You saw the holders of the Calderon Valley throw up a siege wall in less than half an hour at Second Calderon," Tavi said. "Now consider that my uncle's had the next best thing to five years to prepare."

The Cursor lifted his eyebrows and nodded. "Still. If the numerical disparity is that great, the Shieldwall itself might not be enough. And if he's leading the vord into a trap, he's going to be stuck in it as well. There won't be any way for him to retreat any farther. There's nowhere else he can go."

"He knows that," Tavi said, frowning. "And the vord know it, too. Which is why he did it."

Cyricus frowned. "Y-your Highness? I d-don't understand."

"He isn't so much leading them into a trap as he is playing the anvil to our hammer." Tavi touched the sand table, made a minor effort of will, and added multiple rectangles to the landscape, representing his own forces. Then he began to shift the pieces as if they'd been part of a game of *ludus*.

As the Legions fell back into the Valley, the vord crowded in behind them. As they pushed back the Legions, bit by bit, the frontage of the horde continued to contract—and the pieces representing his forces and Varg's came rushing up behind to pin them into the valley. "We hit them here."

Varg grunted. "Few score thousand of us, and millions of them. And you want us to ambush them."

Tavi bared his teeth when he smiled. "This isn't about killing the vord host. This is about finding and killing the vord Queen. She'll likely be somewhere at the rear of the horde, guiding them forward and coordinating their attack."

Varg's tail swished pensively, and his eyes narrowed. "Mmmm. A bold plan, Tavar. But if you do not find and kill her, our forces will be left facing the vord in the open field. They'll swallow us whole."

"We aren't getting any stronger. If we don't neutralize the vord Queen here, we might never have such an opportunity again. They'll swallow us whole in any case."

Varg growled low in his chest. "True enough. I have seen the end of my world. If I'd had the opportunity to make a choice like this one when they were ravaging my own land, I would not have hesitated."

Tavi nodded. "Then I want boots on the causeway by midmorning. We'll have to move fast if we're going to plug them into the bottle. Master Cyricus—"

"I've had logistics p-preparing p-provisions and supplies for your forces since Tribune Antillus arrived yesterday after-n-noon. They are w-waiting for you at the southern gate of the city, next to the causeway. It's only a week's w-worth, but it was the best we could do f-for the time being."

"Oh my," Kitai said in Canish, her eyes sparkling. "I may be in love."

Tavi replied in the same tongue. "I saw him first."

Varg's ears quivered again.

Tavi turned to Cyricus, and said, "You may have noticed that we have a number of Canim with us. They aren't able to use the causeways."

Cyricus nodded rapidly. "Would supply wagons do, Your Highness?"

"Admirably," Tavi said.

"I will requisition as m-many as can be f-found."

Tavi met the young man's eyes and nodded. "Thank you, Cyricus."

Cyricus bowed again, and began giving stammering orders to Phrygia's command staff. None of the men seemed to react adversely to Cyricus's youth or to the confident manner in which he issued orders. The men obviously trusted the young Citizen's competence, which suggested that he had given them good reason to do so. Tavi was even further impressed.

"Two days to Riva," Kitai murmured, looking at the map. "Two more days up to Calderon. Four days total." She looked up at him from across the sand table, green eyes intent. "You are going home, Aleran."

Tavi shivered. He drew his knife from his belt and thrust it into the sand table at the western mouth of the Valley. That was where it would all be decided. That was where they would find the vord Queen; or else see his Realm and his people consigned to oblivion.

The dagger stuck there, quivering.

"Home," Tavi said quietly. "It's time to finish what we started."

Chapter 26

Sir Ehren sat beside the driver of the supply wagon. Though the causeways were smooth, all in all, once enough speed and momentum had been gathered, he felt sure that every single divot and crack in the road's surface would hammer directly through the wagon's structure and into his rear end and lower back. Though the unseasonable chill of the past several days had ended, it had been replaced by steady, relentless rain.

He looked back over his shoulder at two hundred and fourteen wagons like the one he currently endured. Most of them were barely half-full, if not completely empty. Beyond the wagons trudged refugees from Riva, many of them taken sick because of the rain and the lack of food and shelter. Legions marched ahead of them and behind, though individually the *legionares* were little better off than the civilians.

Combat continued at the rear of the column, where Antillus Raucus had taken command of the defense. Great thumping bursts of basso sound marked Aleran firecraftings. Lightning frequently crackled down from the weeping skies, always to strike along their backtrail. The least-battered Legions took turns at breaking up the enemy's momentum, supported by the weary cavalry. Wounded men were brought up from the rear and handed to overworked healers in their medical wagons. Several of the empty supply wagons had already been filled with the wounded who could not walk for themselves.

Ehren looked back ahead of them, to the Phrygian Legion marching in the vanguard. Just behind them came the command group of the highest-ranking Citizens, including the covered wagon bearing the wounded Princeps Attis. Technically, he supposed he could always go up to the Princeps and report in person on the status of the supplies. If that happened to get him out of the bloody rain for a few moments, it would be a happy coincidence.

Ehren sighed. It had been a perfectly fine rationalization, but his place was at the head of the supply column. Besides, it was better that Attis had as few reminders of Ehren ex Cursori as possible.

"How much farther, do you think?" Ehren asked the teamster beside him.

"Bit," the man said laconically. He had a broad-brimmed hat that shed rain like the roof of a small building.

"A bit," Ehren said.

The teamster nodded. He had a waterproofed cloak as well. "Bit. And a mite."

Ehren eyed the man steadily for a moment, then sighed, and said, "Thank you."

"Welcome."

Running horses approached, their hooves a drum of muffled thunder. Ehren looked back to see Count and Countess Calderon riding toward him. The Count had a bandage on his head, and one side of his face was so deeply bruised that it looked like a frenzied clothier had dyed his skin to complement a particularly virulent shade of purple. The Countess bore a number of smaller, lighter marks, souvenirs of the battle with the former High Lady of Aquitaine.

She and her husband reined in as their horses drew even with Ehren's wagon. "Sir Ehren."

"Countess."

"You look like a drowned rat," she said, giving him a faint grin.

"Drowned rat would be a step up," Ehren said, and sneezed violently. "Feh. How can I help you?"

Amara frowned. "Have you heard anything about Isana?"

Ehren shook his head gravely. "I'm sorry. There's been no word."

Count Calderon's expression turned bleak at this, and he looked away.

"Your Excellency," Ehren said, "in my opinion, there is every reason to believe that she is still alive."

Count Calderon frowned, without looking back. "Why?" He spoke between clenched teeth. Ehren winced in sympathy. The Count's swollen jaw obviously made it painful for him to speak.

"Well . . . because she was abducted to begin with, sir. If the vord wanted her dead, there was no reason for them to go to the trouble to arrange a covert entry into a secured building. They would have killed her on the spot."

Count Calderon grunted, frowned, and looked at Amara.

She nodded to him and passed along the question she could evidently see in his face. "Why would they want her alive, Sir Ehren?"

Ehren winced and shook his head. "We have no way to know that. But the vord went to a lot of trouble to secure her. We can hope that she is valuable enough to the enemy that they will not have harmed her. At least, not yet. There's hope, sir."

"I've seen what the vord do to those they take alive," Calderon growled, the words angry and hardly intelligible. "Tell me that my sister is alive and in the hands of those *things* . . ."

Amara sighed. "Bernard, please."

The Count looked back at her. He nodded once and pulled on his horse's reins, guiding the beast a few paces away. He stood with his back to them.

Amara bit on her lower lip for a few seconds. Then she turned to Ehren, her composure regained. "Thank you, Sir Ehren," she said, "for trying. We need to speak to Princeps Attis."

Ehren chewed on his lower lip. "I'm not sure . . . he's seeing any visitors."

"He's seeing us," Bernard said roughly. "Now."

Ehren arched an eyebrow. "Ah?"

"Before we arrive, we need to discuss in detail how best to employ the defenses of the Valley," Amara said. "No one knows them better than we do."

Ehren wiped rain out of his eyes and raked his hair back on his head. "That seems reasonable enough to me. I'll ask him. I can't promise anything."

"Please," Amara said.

Ehren nodded to her, then swung down from the wagon and ran ahead, toward the command group. It was not difficult. The entire group could travel no faster than its slowest members, and as a consequence they hadn't been pushing half as fast as a Legion on the move. Half a dozen *singulares* recognized him on sight, and one of them waved him past the invisible barrier their presence represented.

Ehren knocked on the rear door to the covered wagon, still jogging to keep up. Lady Placida opened the door a moment later and offered Ehren her hand. He took it and clambered up into the wagon. "Thank you, Your Grace."

"It was no trouble, Sir Ehren."

Ehren's glanced past her, to where a nearly motionless form lay on a rough mattress beneath a wool blanket. "How is he?"

Lady Placida grimaced. "Not well. I was able to restore some of the proper blood flow, but . . . with cauterization like that, there are limits. He's well beyond them."

Ehren's stomach twisted. "He's dying."

"He's also lying right here, listening to you," came Attis's voice, weak and amused. "I'd ask you to quit speaking over my head, but in my current condition you have little choice."

Ehren tried to smile. "Ah. Apologies, Your Highness."

"What Aria means to tell you," Attis said, "is that the backstabbing bitch filleted me. The lower half of my body has been sliced open from groin to ribs. My guts are an unholy mess and will doubtless begin to stink in short order. My heart is laboring too hard because apparently being bisected does terrible things to one's blood pressure. The injuries are too severe and extensive to be healed.

"I can't eat anything. Without all the proper tubes in my belly, the food would simply rot in any case. I can drink a little, which means that I will die of starvation a few weeks from now instead of from thirst a few days from now. Unless, of course, an infection takes me first, which seems likely."

Ehren blinked several times at that. "Y-your Highness. I'm sorry, I didn't realize."

"There's hardly a need for you to apologize, Cursor. Life ends. You can hardly blame yourself for that."

Ehren regarded him for a moment, then lowered his eyes and nodded. "Yes, Your Highness. Are . . . are you in pain?"

Attis shook his head. "I am managing it for now."

"Maybe you should rest."

"I'll have a vast surplus of rest, presently. For now, I have a duty to perform."

"Your Highness," Ehren protested. "You are in no condition—"

Attis waved a dismissive hand. "I am in no condition to fight. But in a conflict of this scale, I will contribute the most to our cause by coordinating the efforts of others and determining sound courses of action. I can do that very nearly as well from this wagon as I can from my horse."

Ehren frowned and glanced up at Lady Placida.

She shrugged one shoulder. "Provided his thoughts remain clear, I believe he is correct. He's the best we have when it comes to tactical and strategic decisions, his staff are already in place, and his structure and methods are already established. We should use him."

Are you sure you didn't mean, "use him up," Your Grace? Ehren thought. *There is little love lost between you.*

Not that Ehren had any right to be casting stones. He inhaled deeply and guarded his tongue. "I . . . see. Your Highness, Count and Countess Calderon came to me. They urgently request that you meet with them to discuss how best to utilize the Calderon Valley's defenses."

"No rest for the wicked," Attis murmured. "Yes, I suppose they're right. Please send them to me, Sir Ehren."

Ehren bowed his head. "As you wish."

One of the *legionares* in the rear guard collapsed when the long column of refugees and soldiers were within sight of the entrance to the Calderon Valley. Instantly, vord warriors rushed into the break in the Aleran defenses, not pausing to attack. They only pushed ahead, bringing ever more of their numbers into the weak point of the broken Aleran line.

Ehren realized what had happened when he heard refugees begin to scream.

He stood up on the wagon's seat and stared back behind them. They were

currently moving up a gentle grade, and he could clearly see the mantislike warrior forms plunging left and right through the column, scythe-arms whipping
about to sprinkle blood and death on the defenders. Horns called wildly. *Legion
was marching on the column's flanks formed up to engage the enemy.*

The vord were not executing their typical, gruesomely enthusiastic assault.
They never stopped moving, even when they struck a badly aimed blow. Casualties
were far lighter than they might have been—but the sheer, screaming presence of
the creatures among the refugees was doing something far more deadly. Terrified
refugees scattered, racing for the shelter of the tree line.

Horns cried out in answer from the vanguard, and High Lord Phrygius
turned his Legion in its tracks to begin marching double time back to the battle.
An instant later, several forms leapt skyward from the command tent. Ehren
thought he recognized the Placidas, old Cereus, and a figure that might well
have been Countess Amara. The High Lords and Lady went west. The lone flier
turned east, and shot off like an arrow from the bow.

"Rally!" Ehren cried. "Sound the rally here! Get those people out of the
forest!"

The teamster on the cart fumbled with his bullhorn for a moment, then
lifted it to his mouth and blew three long, surprisingly mellifluous notes, before
pausing and repeating the process. The wagons immediately began hurrying to
catch up with Ehren, forming into a double column to compact them into as
little space as possible as the First Phrygian went by. Once they were clear,
Ehren and his driver completed the maneuver, the carts peeling off from the
road and forming an enormous circle, a makeshift fortress of dubious wooden
walls.

Refugees had been repeatedly instructed how to react to a given horn signal,
in the event of a moment just such as this. It had probably done a minimal
amount of good. Even perfectly simple tasks were sometimes difficult or impossible under the conditions of an actual life-threatening situation. It was why
soldiers trained and drilled endlessly—so that when they were numb with terror,
they could, nonetheless, do everything they needed to do.

Once the wagons had stopped, the teamster sounded the rally call again on
his horn. Some of the nearest refugees cried out and ran for the dubious shelter
of the circled wagons. Others saw them and followed. Ehren supposed it was
even possible that some of them had understood the signal. He saw dozens of
the refugees who had run for the trees come running back. Some, but not all
of them. Ehren shivered. Anyone who believed that the forest would provide any
haven from the vord was going to be rudely surprised. He had already seen at
least a dozen mantis warriors go gliding into the trees.

The Legions and the vord hammered at one another, while Citizens and vord-knights streaked back and forth overhead in the rain. Drums rumbled, and men died. The Aleran order of battle had been swallowed by pure chaos, but the vord seemed to have no such difficulty. In absolute terms, the number of warriors they'd slipped through the gap in the Legion lines was not sizeable—but those vord, rushing wildly up and down through the column, had an effect on the Aleran troops entirely disproportionate to their numbers. They shrieked and rushed around, striking randomly as targets presented themselves, panicking men and animals alike.

So many horn signals were blowing that Ehren could not possibly tell one from another, the net result being a meaningless cacophony.

And then Ehren heard the drums.

He had never heard their like before—big, basso, ocean-deep drums whose voices rumbled so low that they were more felt than heard. But if the drums' voices were strange to him, their tone and rhythm were perfectly clear: Their voices were angry.

Perhaps thirty of the mantis warriors came rushing toward the circled wagons in a cohesive pack, following a trail of screaming refugees who ran in vain toward their fellows. The vord cut them down as they fled, despite the efforts of a mismatched group of horsemen from three different cities' Legions, who tried to force the vord off the Aleran civilians.

"Spears!" Ehren screamed, and teamsters and carters began tugging spears from their racks on the side of the wagon. They armed themselves, then started passing extras out to any refugee willing to fight, and the ring of wagons suddenly bristled with martial thorns.

The mantis-form vord let out shrieks of eager hunger, and the foremost of them bounded into the air and came with its limbs extended. Ehren got to watch it fall toward him, and only barely had time to brace his spear on the bottom of the wagon, then to crouch down beneath it. The vord came down on the spear, which punched its way through the armor on the creature's belly and partially emerged from its back. The vord wailed in pain, and its legs thrashed viciously. One scythe plunged through the floor of the wagon. Ehren, crouched down, received several blows against his own shoulders and flanks—and then the teamster let out a bellow and shoved the vord off Ehren and back onto the ground outside the circle of wagons, with Ehren's spear still thrust through it.

Ehren seized the first weapon that came to hand, a gunnysack loaded with turnips. As another vord attempted to climb onto the wagon, he spun the bag of vegetables and struck hard at the vord's face. His blow didn't harm the mantis warrior, but it did distract the creature long enough for the teamster to hit it with a sizeable piece of lumber—in fact, Ehren realized, it was the handle to the wagon's brakes. The vord reeled back under the blow, shaking its head, stumbling drunkenly on its slender legs.

And the drums grew louder.

Ehren will never know how much time went by during that desperate struggle in the rain. He noted several hollow squares of *legionares*, facing outward, with groups of refugees taking shelter behind a wall of muscle and steel. More *legionares* were on the move, but for the moment, at least, the circled wagons were on their own.

Twice Ehren watched wagon horses panic and break out, trying to escape. The vord brought them down and tore them to pieces. One luckless teamster found himself in the back of the wagon when his horse bolted. The vord made no distinction between him and his draft animal. Half a dozen men were dragged from the wagons. Several smaller mantis warriors rushed forward and under the wagons entirely and tore into the refugees gathered inside, spilling more Aleran blood before they could be brought down.

And all the while, the drums grew louder.

Ehren ripped a sleeve from his shirt and used it to swiftly wrap his teamster's leg after the man had received a badly bleeding wound. More men had fallen. The screams of terrified children rang shrilly in the air. Ehren took up the broken haft of a spear and used it as a club, striking out at heads and eyes, though he knew the weapon would be useless for anything but a mild deterrent. The vord seized the wagon next to his own and dragged it out of the circle, opening a gap in the frail defensive formation. Ehren screamed in fear and protest, as a detached, calm portion of his mind noted that once the vord were inside the circle, the rest of his life would be numbered in seconds.

And the ground began to shake.

A bestial, massive bellow rose from a basso rumble to a whistling shriek. Ehren whipped his head around in time to see a large black gargant crash into the vord attacking the circled wagons. The beast was a monster, even for its breed, the top of its hunched back standing at least twelve feet above the ground. Its stocky, rather squat body was vaguely reminiscent of its cousin, the common badger, though its thick neck and broad head clearly distinguished it from the far smaller beast, especially when one considered the three-foot tusks thrusting forward and curving slightly up from the gargant's jaw.

This particular beast was a battle-scarred old brute, with the white seams of hair indicating the presence of scars upon the beast's flesh—a veteran brawler. The swiftest of the vord scattered from the gargant's path. The slower or less lucky vord did not get clear in time, and the gargant's hammering paws and sheer mass smashed them to a disgusting, gelatinous paste.

Seated atop the gargant's enormous back was the largest Marat Ehren had ever seen. His broad shoulders were so heavily sloped with muscle that it almost seemed a deformity. A faded red Aleran tunic looked as though the sleeves had been cut away from it to make room for arms thicker than Ehren's thighs, and a heavy, braided plait of the same material bound his long hair back from his face. In his right hand he carried a long-handled cudgel, and as Ehren watched, the Marat leaned far over the side of the gargant, clutching a braided leather rope to keep from falling, bracing his feet on the gargant's flanks like a man climbing down a cliff face on a line. The club swept through the air in a graceful arc, and quite literally knocked a mantis warrior's head from its chitin-armored shoulders.

"Good day!" boomed the Marat in cheerful, heavily accented Aleran. A sweep of his club smashed a leaping mantis warrior from the air before it could touch him, then he hauled himself lightly back up onto the gargant's back. He shouted something and tapped the gargant with the handle of his cudgel, and the beast bellowed again, batting another vord away from the wagons with its clawed paws.

Ehren stared, stunned.

The huge black gargant and his rider had not come alone.

There were at least a thousand of the great creatures within sight, and more coming down the causeway from the Calderon Valley, each bearing one or more Marat riders. They smashed through the vord that had penetrated the Aleran lines like a stone hurtling through a spider's web. The noise was indescribable, as was the heavy, musky odor of gargant on the air. The beasts went by like a thunderstorm, like a tide of muscle and bone, leaving smashed and broken vord scattered over the earth.

There was a howl of wind, and Countess Calderon streaked by no more than twenty feet from the ground, rushing along the trail of destruction left by the lead gargant and his iron-thewed rider. The hem of her cloak snapped and cracked like a dozen whips in the speed of her passage. She vanished as rapidly as she had appeared.

Ehren found himself standing over the wounded teamster, makeshift club in hand, panting for breath, his ears ringing. The world suddenly seemed to be a very quiet place.

"What . . ." The teamster coughed. "What just happened?"

Ehren stared dazedly back down the road to the west, toward the main body of the troops, where the angry bugling of the gargants drowned out all other sound. Several pockets of humanity remained along his line of sight, where desperate refugees had banded together to pit their inadequate furies against the foe, and where *legionares* had formed a shield around groups of civilians and withstood the onslaught. There were many dead and wounded on the ground.

But there wasn't a living vord warrior in sight.

"Doroga," Ehren breathed. "That was Clan-Head Doroga. Must have been." He turned to the teamster and began to more thoroughly see to the man's leg. "I think we just got reinforcements."

⌷⊞⌷⊞⌷ CHAPTER 27

Travel with the vord Queen was, Isana felt, an extremely unsettling experience—not so much because of the alien nature of the environment as because of all the small, familiar things that appeared, here and there.

Enough of the enslaved Knights Aeris had survived the Battle of Riva to lift a wind coach, though there were precious few others. Each evening, when dark lay on the land, Isana would accompany the vord Queen to the wind coach. She would emerge directly from the Queen's hivelike lair to climb aboard the coach. The coach would soar up into the sky, just as every other coach she had ridden in. After a time, it would descend again, depositing them at the entrance to another hive.

The Queen would lead Isana back down into the new hive. Dozens of wax spiders would cooperate to carry Araris, still virtually entombed in a coffin-sized slab of *croach*, down to the new hive, where they would seal him to the wall as before.

Once that was finished, they sat down at a table (one always waited to receive them) to take a meal together. Genuine candles would light the table, though the eerie glow of the *croach* was more than enough light to see by. The food was . . . Isana wasn't sure she could justly call it a form of torture, any more than she could have ascribed malevolence to Tavi's disastrous first effort at cooking griddle cakes when he was a child. But whether ignorance or malice was to blame, the food twisted unpleasantly in her stomach. Eating sliced sections of the *croach* inexpertly prepared in the imitation of one dish or another was an experience Isana could have done without.

Several days after the Battle of Riva, Isana descended into the evening's hive and watched the spiders settling Araris into the *croach*.

"I have a surprise for you," the vord Queen said.

Isana had to keep herself from flinching. She hadn't realized the Queen was standing at her elbow. "Oh," she said, her tone neutral. "A surprise?"

"I have given consideration to your reasons for desiring properly prepared implements for the dinner ritual."

"Clean dishes," Isana said. "A clean tablecloth? Clean cutlery?"

"Your species is young and weak," the vord Queen said. "Disease is no enemy of the vord. We have lived longer than most diseases. We have survived them. The hygienic concerns of the dinner ritual are unnecessary."

"And yet," Isana said, "if you do not follow them, you are not doing it properly."

"Just so," the vord Queen said. "There are . . . intangible factors at work here. Things that make your kind difficult to predict." The petulant tone of a sulking child entered the Queen's voice. "Their backs should have been broken at Riva. But they fought more tenaciously than at any time in my observation."

"And they will only grow more determined," Isana said. "Not less."

"That is irrational," the Queen said.

"But true."

The Queen stared at Isana sullenly. "I will permit you to observe the proper forms of the dinner ritual. Water will be brought to you in containers. You may use salt and water to clean the implements. You have one hour. Prepare three places."

She turned abruptly and stalked over to the *croach*-lined dome she used to command her creations.

The wax spiders began carrying in silverware, plates, and cups. Isana felt sure that basins of water and salt would not be far behind.

She sighed and rolled up her sleeves, wondering as she did how many First Ladies of Alera had found themselves playing scullion to an invading enemy.

It was slightly more than an hour later when, for the first time since the Battle of Riva, they were joined at the meal by Lady Invidia.

Isana stared at the other woman in shock. Invidia had been burned. Horribly. Though portions of her face and neck showed the fresh pink skin indicative of flesh that had been watercrafted whole, they only served to create a contrast against the thick scarring of flesh burned beyond the ability of any healer to make whole. Invidia had been considered one of the great beauties of Alera. One could still see the faint echoes of that beauty, but they only made the melted-wax scarring of her features that much more horrible. One of her eyes drooped at the outer corner, as if the flesh had melted and run down a bit before hardening again. Her lips were twisted into a permanent sneer. Her hair was all but gone, replaced by burn-scarred skin and a close-shaved stubble. The creature on her chest showed similar scars, but it still pulsated and stirred from time to time.

"Good evening, Isana," Invidia said. The words were slurred very slightly, as if she'd had a little too much wine. "Always a pleasure to see you."

"Great furies," Isana breathed. "Invidia . . . What happened?"

The former High Lady's eyes flickered with something satisfied and ugly. "A divorce."

Isana shivered.

Invidia picked up her spoon and examined it thoughtfully. She did the same with her plate. She looked at Isana and arched an eyebrow before looking at the Queen. "I take it she convinced you to see reason?"

"I decided to experiment," the Queen replied, "on the theory that by doing so, I might gain additional insight into Alerans."

Invidia's eyes went back to Isana, and her lips peeled back from her teeth. "I see. Though there seems little point for you in continuing the exercise. Dinnertimes are about to become a matter of historical record. Along with plates and silverware."

"Part of my duty to my kind is to learn from and absorb the strengths of those beings we displace," the Queen replied. "The emotional bonding between homogenous bloodlines seems to be the foundation of a wider sense of bonding among the species. Study is warranted."

Isana felt a sudden stirring of emotion from the Queen as she spoke—a brief spike of sadness and remorse, as slender and cold as a frost-covered needle. Isana did not look up at Invidia, but in her watercrafting senses, the simmering cauldron of pain, fear, and hate that comprised Invidia's presence did not change.

The former High Lady had not sensed the instant of vulnerability in the vord Queen.

The burns, the injuries, the trauma of suffering so much pain, had doubtless left her weakened, of furycraft, of body, and, most importantly, of mind. Now was the time to pressure her, to see what information she might give away, what weaknesses she might reveal.

From somewhere outside the hive, there was a high, ululating shriek or whistle. The Queen's head snapped around toward the entrance—turning an unsettling half circle to do so—and she rose from the table at once to stalk over to the glowing dome.

Isana watched her go and toyed with her food. She was starving, but this particular dish—intended to be some sort of marinade and roast combination, perhaps?—tasted singularly vile.

"Terrible, isn't it?" Invidia said. She cut herself a small bite, impaled it on a fork, and ate it daintily. "On a scale of one to ten, ten being the most revolting and one being almost edible, I believe that rating this recipe would require the use of exponents."

Isana ate the largest bite she thought she could stand. It was not large. She chased it down to her stomach with several swallows of water. There was no point in starting an attack too soon. Even in her diminished state, Invidia would surely notice anything truly overt. "I suppose food does not absolutely need to taste good in order to keep one alive."

"But to keep one from committing suicide, it *does* need to taste better than *this*," Invidia said. She fixed her eyes on Isana and smiled. It was a grotesque expression. "Why, First Lady. What do you see that disturbs you so?"

Isana cut another bite from the rectangular brick of roasted *croach*. She ate it very slowly. "I'm sorry to see you so harmed, Invidia."

"Of course you are," she said, her voice dripping acid. "After all we've done for one another, of course you feel sympathy for me."

"I think you should hang from the neck until dead for what you've done, Invidia," Isana replied gently. "But that isn't the same thing as seeing you in such pain. I don't like to see anyone suffer. That includes you."

"Everyone wants someone to suffer, Isana," the former High Lady replied. "It's simply a matter of finding a target and an excuse."

"Do you really believe that?" she asked quietly.

"That is the truth of the world," Invidia said harshly. "We are selfless when it suits our purposes, or when it is easy, or when the alternative would be worse. But no one truly wishes to be selfless. They simply desire the acclaim and good-will that comes from being thought so."

"No, Invidia," she said quietly, firmly. "Not everyone is like that."

"They are," Invidia said, her voice shaking with unsteady intensity. "You are. Under the lies you tell yourself, part of you hates me. Part of you would love to pluck out my eyes while I screamed."

"I don't hate a serpent for being a serpent," Isana said. "But neither will I permit it to harm me or those I care about. I will kill it if I must, as quickly and painlessly as possible."

"And that's what I am to you?" Invidia asked. "A serpent?"

"That's what you were," Isana said quietly.

Invidia's eyes shone with a feverish intensity. "And now?"

"Now, I think you might be a mad dog," Isana said quietly. "I pity such a poor creature's suffering. But it changes nothing about what I must do."

Invidia dropped her head back and laughed. "What you must do?" she asked. She put her fingertip on the table, still smiling, and smoke began rising in a thin, curling thread. "Exactly what do you think you could possibly do to me?"

"Destroy you," Isana said quietly. "I don't want to do it. But I can. And I will."

"If you go shopping for a hat, darling, be sure to get one several sizes larger than the one it's replacing." She glared at Isana. "So you were the choice of the flawless Princeps Septimus, over every woman in the Realm actually qualified to be his wife. So your child by him was recognized by Gaius. It means nothing, Isana. Don't think for an instant that your strength can compare to mine."

"Oh," Isana said, "I'm quite sure it doesn't. It doesn't need to." She stared at Invidia for a quiet moment, her expression calm, then she picked up her knife and fork again. "When have you gone too far, Invidia? At what point do the lives your new allies take begin to outweigh your own?"

The expression drained out of the former High Lady's scarred face.

"When does your own life become something you don't want to live anymore?" Isana said in that same quiet, gentle voice. "Can you imagine another year of living this way? Five years? Thirty years? Do you want to live that life, Invidia?"

She folded her hands in her lap and stared at Isana, her scarred face bleak and expressionless.

"You could change things," Isana said quietly. "You could choose another path. Even now, you could choose another path."

Invidia stared at her, not moving—but the creature on her chest pulsed horribly, its legs stirring. She closed her eyes, stiffening in pain, which Isana could all but feel lance through her own body. She remained that way for a long moment, then opened her eyes again.

"All I can choose is death." She gestured bleakly to the creature that still grasped her. "Without this, I would die within hours. And if I do not obey her, she will take it from me."

"It isn't a very good choice," Isana said. "But it *is* a choice, Invidia."

That rictus of a smile returned. "I will not willingly end my own life."

"Even if it costs others theirs?"

"Have you never killed to protect your life, Isana?"

"That isn't the same."

Invidia arched an eyebrow. "Isn't it?"

"Not at all."

"I am what the Realm and my father and my husband have made me, Isana. And I will *not* simply lie down and die."

"Ah," Isana said quietly. "Quite."

"Meaning what, precisely?"

"Meaning," Isana said, "that whether you realize it or not, you've already made your choice. Probably quite some time ago."

Invidia stared at her. Her lips quivered once, as if she would speak, but she withdrew into a shell of silence again. Then she took up her fork with a deliberate movement, cut another bite of the hideous *croach* concoction, and ate it with measured, steady motions.

Now, while she was retreating from the conversation. It was time to push. "For what it's worth, I'm sorry, Invidia. I'm sorry that it came to this for you. You have so much power, so much talent, so much ability. You could have done great things for Alera. I'm sorry that it went to waste."

Invidia's gaze turned cold. "Who are you?" she asked quietly. "Who are you to say such things to me? You're no one. You're nothing. You're a camp whore who happened to be favored by a man. The fool. He could have had his choice of any woman of Alera."

"As I understand it," Isana said, "he did." She let the simple statement hang silent in the air for a moment. Then she took a breath, and said, "If you will excuse me." Isana rose from the table and turned as though to walk as far away from Invidia as the chamber would allow. But she listened as she walked. There was no chance whatsoever that Invidia would allow her to have the last word on the matter of Septimus.

"Yes. He chose you." Invidia bared her teeth. "And see what it earned him."

Isana stopped in her tracks. She felt as if someone had struck her a hard blow in the belly.

"The contracts were drawn. Sextus was agreed. Everything had been arranged. After he'd shown his power at Seven Hills, it would have been the perfect time for him to take a wife. A wife of breeding, of power, of skill, of education. But he chose . . . you."

Isana felt her hands clench into fists.

"Septimus was a fool. He imagined that those he bested would react with the same grace he thought he possessed. Oh, he never went forth to humiliate anyone, but it always seemed to work out that way. In school. In games. In those ridiculous duels the boys used to find excuses to engage in. Little things he didn't bother to remember would fester in others."

Isana turned, very slowly, to face Invidia.

The former High Lady stood with her chin lifted, her eyes bright, the unmarred portions of her face flushed and rosy. "It was easy. Rhodus. Kalarus. It barely took a whisper to put the idea in their minds."

"You," Isana said quietly.

Invidia's eyes flashed. "And why *not* me? The House of Gaius has earned its hatreds over the centuries. Sooner or later, someone would break it to pieces. Why *not* me?"

Isana faced Invidia and stood perfectly still for a long moment, looking at the other woman's eyes. Isana smoothed her worn dress down carefully, considering her words and the thoughts behind them, and the burning fires of her own grief and loss that colored all of her mind the color of blood.

Then she drew in a deep breath, and said, "For my husband's memory, for my child's future, for those whose blood is upon your hands, I defy you. I name you Nihilus Invidia, Invidia of Nusquam, traitor to the Crown, the Realm, and her people." She drew herself up straight and spoke in a hard tone barely louder than a whisper. "And before I leave this place, I *will* kill you."

Invidia lifted her chin, her lips quivering. A little hiccuping laugh drifted around in her throat. She shook her head, and said, "This world is not for such as you, Isana. Wait a few more days. You'll see."

CHAPTER 28

"Crows take it," Tavi muttered. He tried to mop the rain from his face with a corner of his sopping cloak. "We've got another thirty miles to make today."

"It's going to be darker than a Phrygian winter in another hour, Captain," Maximus said. "The men will keep going. But I hate to think what might happen to us if the vord hit us while we're setting up camp in the dark."

Tavi looked back at the column behind them. It was a mixed and disorganized sight. The First Aleran and Free Aleran Legions were managing fairly well, especially given how long they'd been cooling their heels on ships in the last few months. They moved ahead at a loping run, their endurance and footsteps bolstered by the earth furies in the causeway. At normal pace, they would be moving as quickly as a man could sprint across open ground. Tavi had been forced to reduce their speed, in part because the men were out of practice. At least they maintained their spacing with acceptable discipline.

Behind them came a long double column of supply wagons, cargo wagons, farm carts, town carriages, rubbish carts, vegetable barrows, and every other form of wheeled conveyance imaginable. Phrygius Cyricus had, in under two hours, provided them with enough carts to bear more than two-thirds of the Canim infantry. The carts themselves were not being drawn by horses—the Legion simply did not have enough personnel to care for the army of beasts that would be needed, nor did they have enough cartage to haul their feed. Instead, the vehicles were being pulled by teams consisting largely of whichever *legionares* had most recently earned their centurion's displeasure.

Canim warriors overflowed the carts in a fashion that was little short of comical. Those who couldn't fit in the carts came behind them, galloping along swiftly enough to keep pace with the reduced speed of the Legions. They could only maintain that pace for two hours or so, then the entire force would halt and allow the rested Canim in the carts to exchange places with those who had been running, rotating between them in turns throughout the day. By this time, even the Canim who had been in the carts the longest looked hungry, miserable, and exhausted, though Tavi supposed that might largely be due to the way the rain was plastering their fur to their skin.

Behind them rode the cavalry. First came the mounted alae of the Legions, eight hundred horses and their riders, then the Canim cavalry. Composed almost entirely of Shuaran Canim riding the odd-looking Canean creature called a "taurg," they each massed two or three times the weight of a *legionare* on a horse. The horned, hunchbacked taurga, each considerably larger than a healthy ox, kept pace with the column without difficulty, the muscles in their heavy haunches flexing like cables of steel. The taurga didn't look tired. The taurga looked impatient and short-tempered and as though they were giving serious consideration to eating their riders or fellow herd members. Possibly both. Tavi had ridden a taurg for weeks in Canea, and in his judgment it would not be out of character for the war beasts.

He sighed and looked aside and up at Maximus, who was riding a particularly ugly, mottled taurg of his own. "Crows, Max. I thought you'd killed and eaten that thing."

Max grinned. "Steaks and New Boots, Captain? I hate this critter like no other on Carna. Which is why I decided he could be miserable carrying me all this way in the rain instead of inflicting it on some perfectly decent horse."

Tavi wrinkled up his nose. "It stinks, Max. Especially in the rain."

"I have always found the odor of wet Aleran to be slightly unsavory," Kitai said, from where she rode on Tavi's right.

Tavi and Max both gave her an indignant look. "Hey," Max said, "we don't smell when we're wet."

Kitai arched an eyebrow at them. "Well, of course you don't smell *your-selves*." She lifted a hand and waved it daintily at the air by her nose, an affectation of gesture that Tavi thought she must have studied from some refined lady Citizen. "If you'll excuse me, gentlemen." She nudged her horse several paces to one side and let out a sigh of relief.

"She's joking," Max said. He frowned and looked at Tavi. "She's joking."

"Um," Tavi said, "almost certainly."

Kitai gave them an oblique look and said nothing.

There was a muffled roar of wind as Crassus came soaring down out of the rainy skies. He hit the water-slickened surface of the causeway with his shoulders parallel to the road, his legs spread solidly. A sheet of water sprayed up from his boots as he slid along the causeway for twenty yards before slowing to a couple of skipping steps, then came to a halt in front of Tavi's horse. He threw Tavi a crisp salute and began running alongside the horse. "Captain. Looks like we'd better get used to the idea of getting rained on. There's a fairly rocky patch about half a mile ahead. It won't be comfortable, but I don't think anyone will get sucked into the mud there."

Tavi grunted and peered up at the weeping sky. He sighed. "All right. There's no sense in pushing through in the dark. Thank you, Crassus. We'll make camp there. Please spread the word to the Tribunes. Maximus, please inform the Warmaster that we'll halt in half a mile."

The Antillan brothers both saluted, then left to follow their orders.

Tavi eyed Kitai, who continued to ride facing straight ahead, not looking at him. Her expression was unreadable. "You *were* joking, weren't you?"

She lifted her chin, sniffed, and said nothing.

For the first time in history, Alerans and Canim pitched a camp together.

Tavi and Varg walked about the camp together as their respective countrymen labored to set up the camp's defenses after a hard day's marching, in the rain, with night coming on rapidly.

"Should be interesting tonight," Varg rumbled.

"I thought that the Free Aleran Legion had done this sort of thing many times," Tavi said.

Varg growled in the negative. "Nasaug was already pushing the letter of the codes by training makers to fight. Bringing *demons* into a warrior camp? He would have been forced to kill some of his own officers to keep his place." Varg squinted at a team of Aleran engineers who were using earthcrafting to soften the stone so that they could drive the posts of the palisade into it.

Tavi watched them for a moment, considering. "There was more to it than that."

Varg inclined his head slightly. "Can't just tell a soul it is free, Tavar. Freedom must be done for oneself. Important that the slaves created their own freedom. Nasaug gave them advisors. They did everything else on their own."

Tavi glanced up at Varg. "Are you going to be forced to kill some of your officers tonight?"

Varg was silent for a moment. Then he shrugged. "Possible. But I think unlikely."

"Why?"

"Because their opposition would be based upon tradition. Tradition needs a world to exist. And the world has been destroyed, Aleran. My world. Yours, too. Even if we could defeat the vord tomorrow, nothing would change that."

Tavi frowned. "Do you really think that?"

Varg flicked his ears in the affirmative. "We are in uncharted waters, Tavar. And the storm has not yet abated. If we are still alive when it is over, we will find ourselves on unknown shores."

Tavi sighed. "Yes. And then what?"

Varg shrugged. "We are enemies, Tavar. What do enemies do?"

Tavi thought about it for a moment. Then he said, "I only know what they did in the old world."

Varg stopped in his tracks. He eyed Tavi for several seconds, then shook his ears and began walking again. "Wasted breath to talk about it now."

Tavi nodded. "Survive today. Then face tomorrow."

Varg flicked his ears in agreement. They had crossed into the Canim side of the camp as they spoke. Varg came to a halt outside a large, black tent. There was an odd smell of incense in the air, and the stench of rotting meat. From inside the tent, a deep-bellied drum kept a slow, reverberating cadence. Deep voices chanted in the snarling tongue of the wolf-warriors.

Varg stopped outside the tent and drew his sword in a long, slow rasp of steel on brass. Then he hurled it point down into the earth before the tent. It sank into the ground with a thump, and the bubbling whisper of its quivering went on for several seconds.

The chanting voices inside the tent stopped.

"I am here regarding the matter of the dead makers at Antillus," Varg called.

There was a low murmur of voices. Then a dozen of them spoke in ragged concert. "Their blood cries out for justice."

"Agreed," said Varg in a very hard voice. "What wisdom have the blood-speakers to give such justice a shape?"

Another swift and murmured conference followed. Then they answered together again. "Blood for blood, life for life, death for death."

Varg flicked his tail impatiently. "And if I do not do this?"

This time they all answered at once. "Call to the makers, call to the warriors, call for strength to lead us."

"Then let Master Khral come forth to see it done!"

There was a long silence from the tent.

Tavi arched an eyebrow and glanced at Varg. The big Cane looked intent.

"Master Khral speaks for the bloodspeakers, and for the makers! So he has assured me for many months! Let him come forth!"

Again, silence.

"Then let one of honor and experience come forth to witness it! Let Master Marok come forth!"

Almost before Varg was finished speaking, the opening of the tent parted, and a tall, weathered old Cane emerged. He wore a mantle constructed from sections of vord chitin, and a misshapen warrior-form's chitinous skull served as his hood. More plates of chitin armored his torso and legs. His fur was, like Varg's, midnight black, though both of his forearms were so heavily laden with layer upon layer of scars that almost no fur grew there at all. He wore a sling bag across his chest. The band had been woven from what looked like the legs of many wax spiders. The bag, too, was a black chitin skull from some vord form Tavi had never seen—but instead of carrying blood, it held multiple scrolls and what might have been some sort of flute carved from bone. The old Cane also had a pair of daggers stored side by side on his belt. Their bone handles looked old and worn.

"Master Marok," Varg rumbled. He bared his throat very slightly, the Canim version of a bow. Marok returned the gesture only a shade more deeply, acknowledging Varg's leadership without quite recognizing his superiority.

"Varg," Marok replied. "Has no one killed you yet?"

"You are welcome to try your luck," Varg replied. "The bloodspeakers allowed *you* to speak for them?"

"They're all afraid that if one of them steps up to the head of the pack, Khral will have them killed when he returns."

"Khral," Varg said, amusement in his voice.

"Or someone." Marok eyed Tavi. "This is the demon Tavar?"

Varg's ears flicked affirmation. "*Gadara*, this is Marok. I respect him."

Tavi lifted his eyebrows and gave Marok a Canim bow, which was returned in precisely equal measure. The old Cane watched him through narrowed eyes.

"You killed two of my people," Marok said.

"I've killed more than that," Tavi replied. "But if you mean the two false messengers who attacked me in my tent, then yes. I killed one, and a soldier under my command killed another."

"The tent was the Tavar's," Varg said. "He did not seek the makers out for murder. They trespassed upon his range."

Marok growled. "The code calls for a blood answer when an outsider kills one of us, regardless of the circumstances."

"An outsider," Varg growled. "He is *gadara*."

Marok stopped to eye Varg thoughtfully. In a much quieter, quite calm voice, he muttered, "That might work. If we can make it stick."

Tavi took his cue from Marok and lowered his voice as well. "Varg. If Lararl had done what I did, what would be the proper reply?"

Varg growled. "My people on his range? Simple defense of his territory. They would be in the wrong, not Lararl. Though I would consider it clumsy and wasteful, under the circumstances, since Lararl could quite likely have rendered them helpless without killing either of them."

Tavi grimaced. "That wasn't what I wanted. There were only two of us. Each of us was trying to dispose of his opponent so that he could help the other. I would much rather have had them alive and answering questions about who sent them."

Marok grunted. He looked at Varg. "You believe him?"

"*Gadara*, Marok."

The old Cane tilted his head slightly to the side in acknowledgment. "Khral's pack of scavengers are going to raise a whirlwind of howls if you give one of the demons status as a member of the people. Naming him *gadara* is a warrior concern, and your rightful prerogative. Establishing a demon as one of our people under the codes is another matter entirely."

Varg growled. "Without this demon, there would be no people for the codes to guide."

"A fact that does not escape me," Marok replied. "But it does not alter the codes."

"Then there must be a blood answer," Varg said.

"Yes."

Varg flicked his ears in thoughtful agreement and turned to Tavi. "Would you be willing to trade two Aleran lives for those you took?"

"Never," Tavi said quietly.

Marok made a rumble of approval in his chest.

"The poor dead fools," Varg growled. "This was a blade well sunk. Give Khral credit for that much."

"Blood," Tavi said abruptly.

The two Canim eyed him.

"What if I pay a blood price for the two dead makers? Their weight of blood?"

Marok narrowed his eyes again. "Interesting."

Varg grunted. "A Cane has twice the weight in blood of an Aleran, *gadara*. We could bleed you to a husk, and you would have paid back only a quarter."

"What if it were done slowly?" Tavi replied. "A little at a time? And the blood entrusted to, say, Master Marok here, to use for the protection and benefit of the families of the two dead makers?"

"Interesting," Marok said again.

Varg mused for a moment. "I can think of nothing in the codes to hold against it."

"Nothing in the codes," Marok said. "But it sets a dangerous precedent. Others might use it to kill as well and escape the consequences in this fashion."

Tavi showed his teeth. "Not if the party who has been wronged does the bloodletting."

Marok huffed out a harsh bark of Canim style laughter.

Varg's jaws lolled open in a smile. "Aye. That would stand up to usage." He tilted his head and eyed Tavi. "You would trust me with the blade, *gadara?*"

"If anything happened to me, your people would be finished," Tavi said soberly. "We would kill them all. Or the vord would kill them all. And there would never again be such an opportunity for us to build mutual respect."

Varg watched Marok as Tavi spoke. Then he spread one paw-hand open, as though he had just proved something to the older Cane.

Marok nodded slowly. "As the observer sent by the bloodspeakers, I will consider this payment an offering of honor and restitution—and I will see to it that the makers know that it has been concluded according to the codes. Wait here."

Marok went back into the black tent. When he returned, he held what would be a rather small vial, for a Cane, made of some kind of ivory. To Tavi, it looked nearly the size of a canteen. Marok handed the container to Varg.

Varg took it with another, deeper bow, this time reversing the roles of accorded respect with Marok. The old Cane said, "From the left arm."

Tavi steeled himself as he pushed the arm of his tunic up past his elbow and extended it to Varg.

The Warmaster drew his dagger, an Aleran *gladius* that had once belonged to Tavi. Varg carried it for use when he needed a keen-edged knife. Moving with quick, sure motions, he laid a long, shallow cut across Tavi's forearm, along a diagonal. Tavi gritted his teeth but made no other reaction to the pain of the injury. He lowered his arm to his side, and Varg bent to place the vial beneath his fingertips, catching the blood as it spilled. It slowly began to fill.

The entrance to the black tent flew open again, and a burly Cane in a pale leather mantle strode out, his fangs bared, his ears laid back. "Marok," the Cane snarled, "You will cease this trafficking with the enemy!"

"Nhar," Marok said. "Go back in the tent."

Nhar surged toward Marok, seething. "You cannot do this! You cannot so bind us to these creatures! You cannot so dishonor the lives of the fallen!"

Marok eyed the other ritualist for a moment, and said, "What were their names, Nhar?"

The other Cane drew up short. "What?"

"Their names," Marok said in that same, gentle voice. "Surely you know the names of these makers whose lives you defend so passionately."

Nhar stood there, gnashing his teeth. "You," he sputtered. "You."

"Ahmark and Chag," Master Marok said. And without warning one of his hands lashed out and delivered a backhanded blow to the end of Nhar's muzzle. The other Cane recoiled in sheer surprise as much as pain, and fell to the ground. The blood in the pouch at his side sloshed back and forth, some of it splashing out.

"Go back into the tent, Nhar," Marok said gently.

Nhar snarled and plunged one hand into the blood pouch.

Marok moved even more quickly. One of the knives sprang off his belt into his hand and whipped across his own left forearm.

Nhar screamed something, and a cloud of blue-grey mist formed in front of him, coalescing into some kind of solid shape in response. But before it could fully form, Marok flicked several drops of his own blood onto the other Cane. Then the old master closed his eyes and made a calm, beckoning gesture.

Nhar convulsed. At first Tavi thought that the Cane was vomiting, but as more and more substance poured out of Nhar's mouth, it only took a few seconds for Tavi to realize what was really happening.

Nhar's belly and guts had just been ejected from his body, as if an unseen hand had reached down his throat and pulled them out.

Nhar made a number of hideous sounds, but within seconds he was silent and still.

Marok eyed the tent, and said, "Brothers, would anyone else care to dispute my arbitration?"

A Cane's hand appeared from the black tent—but only long enough to pull the entrance flap closed again.

Varg let out a chuckling growl.

Marok reached into his own pouch and drew out a roll of fine cloth. He wrapped it around his arm with the ease of long, long practice, tearing it off with his teeth when he'd used enough. He then offered the roll of cloth to Tavi.

Tavi inclined his head to the master ritualist and accepted the cloth. When Varg nodded to him, he bent his arm and began to wind the cloth over it, though he did not do it nearly so smoothly as Marok.

Varg capped the vial and offered it back to Marok with another bow. Marok accepted the vial, and said, "This will continue when you are recovered, Tavar. I will keep the accounting. It will be accurate."

"It was an honor to meet you, sir," Tavi replied.

They exchanged parting bows, and Tavi and Varg continued their rounds of the camp. He stumbled twice, before Varg said, "You will return to your tent now."

"I'm fine."

Varg snorted. "You will return to your tent now, or I will take you there. Your mate expressed to me in very clear terms her strong desire to see you back safely."

Tavi smiled tiredly. "I do feel a bit less than myself, I suppose. Will this end our trouble with the ritualists?"

"No," Varg said. "They will embrace some new idiocy tomorrow. Or next week. Or next moon. But there is no escaping that."

"But for today, we're quit of them?"

Varg flicked his ears in assent. "Marok will keep them off-balance for months after today."

Tavi nodded. "I'm sorry. About the makers who died. I wish I hadn't had to do that."

"I wish that, too," Varg said. He looked at Tavi. "I respect you, Tavar. But my people are more important to me than you are. I have used you to help remove a deadly threat to them—Khral and his idiocy. Should you become a threat to them, I will deal with you."

"I would expect nothing less," Tavi said. "I will see you in the morning."

Varg growled assent. "Aye. And may all of our enemies be in front of us."

⋊⋉⋊⋉⋊ CHAPTER 29

Tavi lay on his cot in the command tent while the Tribune Medica of the First Aleran, Foss, argued with everyone.

"I don't care if he can eat sand and crap gold!" Foss snarled, his black beard bristling. "He's a crowbegotten *Cane*, and he's bloodied up the captain!"

"Is the captain in any danger?" Crassus asked, his voice calm.

"Not at the moment," Foss said. "But you can't expect me to stand around and say nothing while those heathen dogs bleed our bloody First Lord to be!"

"Sure he can," Max growled. "Back off, Foss. Captain knows what he's doing."

"Of course! We're charging headlong into a fight where we're outnumbered a bloody thousand to one, and he's bleeding himself before the fighting! Presumably to save the enemy the bother!"

"Necessary," Tavi said tiredly. "Leave it alone, Foss."

"Yes, sir," Foss responded, scowling. "Maybe you can answer me a question, then. Like why the crows the First Spear of the Legion is staying in a guarded tent, walking around in a civilian tunic, and not speaking to anyone."

Tavi inhaled and exhaled slowly. "Why do you think, Foss?"

"Grapevine says he took sick. His heart gave out on him in that last fight. He's near sixty, seems likely. Except that if that had been the case, I would know, because I would have been the man treating him."

Tavi sat up on his elbows carefully, and met Foss's eyes. "Listen to me very carefully, Tribune," he said. "You *were* the man who treated him. It *is* his heart. He's still recovering and won't be himself for a few days. You took him off active duty. The guard is there to make sure the stubborn old goat gets enough rest and that he doesn't relapse."

The ire faded from Foss's expression, replaced by incomprehension followed by deep concern. "But . . ."

"Did you *hear* me, Tribune?" Tavi asked.

Foss saluted at once. "Yes, sir."

Tavi nodded and sank back down onto the bunk. "I can't explain it to you, Tribune. Not yet. I need you to trust me. Please."

Foss's face sobered even more. He frowned, and said, "Yes, sir."

"Thank you," Tavi said quietly. "Are you finished with me?"

Foss nodded and seemed to gather himself, focusing on his job. His voice reclaimed its confidence and strength as he did. "I cleaned the wound and closed it. You'll need to drink plenty of water and get plenty of food. Red meat is best. Get a good night's rest. And I'd rather see you on a wagon than a horse tomorrow."

"We'll see," Tavi said.

"Sir," Foss said, "this time you need to trust me."

Tavi eyed him and found himself smiling. He waved a hand. "All right, all right. If it will stop you from nagging. Done."

Foss grunted in satisfaction, saluted, and departed the tent.

"Crassus," Tavi said, "we're near enemy territory. Make sure the earth furies have been positioned to spot any takers. And get those Canim pickets out as far as you can. Their night vision is invaluable right now."

"I know," Crassus said. "I know, Captain. Get some rest. We'll make sure we survive until morning."

Tavi started to give Crassus another string of warnings and instructions but forced himself to close his mouth. He was tired enough to make it remarkably easy. He and Max and the rest of the Legion would do their jobs properly even without Tavi telling them all how to do it. After all, what was the point in all that training and discipline if they didn't get the chance to display their capability once in a while?

He sighed, and said, "Fine, fine. I can take the hint. Make sure I'm awake by first light."

Max and Crassus both saluted and departed the tent.

Tavi sat up enough to drain the large mug of cold water from the stand beside the cot, but the thought of eating the meal beside it was revolting. He settled back down again and closed his eyes. A moment's concentration, and he drew together a windcrafting to ensure private conversation. Steady rain drummed on the tent's canvas roof. "How much of this is the loss of blood?" he asked the empty tent. "And how much of it is the result of holding that weathercrafting?"

One moment the tent was empty, and in the next Alera stood over the sand table at its center post. She chuckled warmly. "It took Sextus more than a year to be able to recognize my presence. How is it that you have learned the trick of it so quickly?"

"I've spent most of my life without any furycraft to help me," Tavi said. "Perhaps that's had something to do with it."

"Almost certainly," Alera said. "Very few of your people realize how much furycraft happens without their knowledge."

"Really?" Tavi asked.

"Certainly. How would they? Watercrafters, for example, gain a sensitivity to others that becomes a part of their very being. They have few, if any, memories of what it was like to exist *without* that sense. Nearly everyone in Alera has their senses expanded in some way, to some degree. If they suddenly lost access to their furies, for whatever reason, I expect that they would feel quite disoriented. I should think it would be something like losing an eye."

Tavi winced at the image. "I notice," he said, "that you haven't answered my question."

Alera smiled. "Haven't I?"

Tavi eyed her for a moment. Then he said, "You're saying that I'm crafting without realizing it?"

"Without feeling it," Alera corrected. "You make clear to me what it is you wish to accomplish, and I set about ordering it, within my limitations. But the effort for it still comes from you, as with any other furycrafting. It's a steady and gradual process, one you don't feel happening. You only become aware of it when physical symptoms begin to trouble you." She sighed. "It killed Sextus; not as much because he pushed too hard—though he did—as because it made him dismiss the symptoms of his poisoning, incorrectly, as part of this process."

Tavi sat up and studied Alera more closely. She held her hands in front of her, folded inside the opposite sleeve of her misty "gown." More of the gown was gathered over her head in a hood. Her eyes looked sunken. For the first time since Tavi had seen the great fury manifest, she did not look like a young woman.

"The weathercrafting," he said. "It was a strain on you as well. It's hastening your . . . your dissolution, isn't it?"

"It was a strain upon all of Alera, young Gaius," she replied, her voice quiet. "You upset natural order on a scale that is rarely seen—in concert with the eruptions of two fire-mountains, to boot. You and your people will feel the aftereffects of these few days for centuries to come."

"I sincerely hope so," Tavi said.

The great fury glanced at him and smiled, briefly. "Ah, there it is. I sometimes think that if one cut open the scions of the House of Gaius, they would find well-chilled pragmatism flowing in their veins instead of blood."

"I have provided abundant evidence to the contrary, today, I believe."

"Have you?" she replied.

"And again," he said, "you have avoided answering my question."

Her smile widened, briefly. "Have I?"

"Infuriating habit," he said. "My grandfather must have learned it from you."

"He picked that one up very quickly," she acknowledged. "Sextus was strongly devoted to the idea of being as mysterious as possible when it came to his capabilities of furycraft. He would have looked at his staff and shrugged when they wondered how such a thing as an unthinkably late freeze and a steady breeze for several thousand miles' worth of travel would be possible."

"When in fact, anyone with a High Lord's talent could manage it," Tavi murmured. "If he had, as his partner, someone such as you, who could direct his power to precisely when and where it needed to be to have the greatest effect, however widely dispersed those places might be."

"I suspect the scions of Gaius did not wish the notion to become widespread," she said, "for fear that all of those folk with a High Lord's talent would immediately set about creating such partners of their own."

"Could such a thing be done?" Tavi asked, curiously.

"Almost certainly—to one degree or another. It is also nearly certain that they would not be able to create a . . . shall we say, a balanced being."

"Someone like you," Tavi mused, "only mad?"

"I suspect the results of such an effort would make the current definitions of madness somewhat obsolete."

Tavi shivered. "The potential for conflict on that scale . . . It's . . . unimaginable."

"The House of Gaius is many things," Alera said. "But never stupid."

Tavi sighed and settled back down on the cot again. He rubbed wearily at his eyes. "Where is the main body of the vord now?"

"Closing on the mouth of the Calderon Valley," Alera replied.

"Aquitaine is still trying to draw them all there?"

"It would appear so."

"Playing the anvil to our hammer," Tavi mused. "With all those cohorts at trail, behind his lines, I'm not sure if he's brilliant or a bloody fool."

"His foolishness has been limited to a fairly narrow spectrum, all in all," Alera replied. "His tactical ability in the field has been sound. If he can force the vord Queen to oversee the assault on Calderon, he effectively pins her in place for you. My suspicion is that he expects you to lead a team of Citizens to find and neutralize the Queen."

"Of course. That's how he would do it," Tavi mused. "But he doesn't know about Varg and his warriors."

"Indeed not. And I think it possible that the vord do not, either. The path ahead of us is empty of anything but token enemy forces."

Tavi grunted. "The Queen is laying a trap of her own. Expecting me to march in with a pair of Legions and drive straight toward her, find her, and send all our finest furycrafters after her. So she'll let me through in order to know where the strike is coming from. And she'll have something in mind to counter it. Once she's destroyed me, she'll be able to finish Calderon at her leisure."

Alera opened her mouth to speak, paused to consider, then simply nodded.

Tavi grunted. "Have you been able to locate her any more precisely?"

Alera shook her head. "The *croach* remains . . . foreign, to me."

"Impenetrable?" Tavi asked.

She mused over the question for a moment. "Imagine the way your skin feels when aphrodin paste is applied to it."

Tavi grunted. It was often used upon cattle, minor injuries, and in certain cases of the healer's craft. "It goes numb. You can't feel it at all."

"Just so," Alera said. "I can guide you to within a mile or so, if she holds position for any length of time. But where the vord have claimed the territory . . . I am too numbed to be of use in any task so fine and focused."

"I'll find her," Tavi said quietly.

"I expect that you will," Alera said.

He looked over at her. "Can I defeat her?"

Alera considered the question for a time, her face looking more sunken. "It . . . seems doubtful."

Tavi frowned. "She's that strong?"

"And growing stronger by the day, young Gaius. In a way, every vord is nothing but an extension of her body, her mind, and her will. So is the *croach*."

Tavi assembled several thoughts into a logical order. "As the *croach* grows, so does her furycraft."

Alera inclined her head. "What I lose, she gains. When she fought the campaign against Sextus last year, she was already his equal in raw power. By now, she is stronger still. Considerably so. When one adds that to her native strength, speed, resilience, and intelligence, she becomes a formidable opponent. More so than anyone in your kind's history has seen, much less defeated."

Tavi inhaled deeply and blew his breath out very slowly. "And you cannot help me."

"I was created to advise and to support, young Gaius," Alera said. "Even when I was at the height of my strength, I could not have helped you in that way. I can and will help you find her. I can and will support your efforts to close to grips with her, as I already have since you landed at Antillus. But that is the limit of my power. You will prevail, or not, on your own."

Tavi was quiet for several moments before he said, "I've been doing that my whole life. This is no different."

Alera lifted her chin, a small smile on her strained mouth. "He used to talk about you, you know."

Tavi frowned. "You mean . . . my grandfather?"

"Yes. When you were at the Academy. After. He would watch over you, though you never knew it. Often, he would look in on you while you slept. Making sure that you were safe seemed to give him . . . a kind of satisfaction I never saw in him, otherwise."

Tavi frowned quietly up at the ceiling of the tent. Alera said nothing and let him think. She had, literally, inhuman patience. If it took him a week to consider his answer, she would be there waiting when he was ready. It was a portion of her personality that was both reassuring and annoying. One simply couldn't employ stalling tactics against her.

"I . . . We didn't speak to one another very often," Tavi said.

"No," she replied.

"I never understood . . . if all that time he *knew* who I was, then why didn't he ever . . . ever want to talk to me? Reach out?" Tavi shook his head. "He must have been lonely, too."

"Horribly," Alera said. "Though he never would have acknowledged such a thing openly, of course. He was, perhaps, the most isolated Aleran I have ever known."

"Then why?" Tavi asked.

Alera turned to one side, frowning thoughtfully. "I know your family well, young Gaius. But I cannot say that I knew his thoughts."

Tavi squinted at her and thought he had picked up on what she was hinting at. "If you were to guess?"

She smiled at him in approval. "Sextus had the gift of many of your bloodline, a kind of instinctive foreknowledge. You yourself have demonstrated it, now and then."

"I had rather assumed that was you," Tavi said.

She smiled whimsically. "Mmmm. I've already noted tonight how much your folk do without being aware of it. Since I am created by them, perhaps it follows that I am just as blindly unperceptive. I suppose it is possible that I am somehow unaware of knowledge I am inadvertently sending you."

"Sextus?" Tavi prompted.

Alera nodded and lifted a hand to draw a fallen lock of her hair back from her face, a very human gesture. The nails of her hand had turned black. Veins of darkness had progressed over her fingers and wrists. Tavi steeled himself against the further evidence of the fury's decay.

"Sextus had the gift more strongly than any scion of the House I have served," Alera said. "I think he sensed the storm coming years ago, since shortly after Septimus's death. I think he thought that he would be the one to guide your folk safely through the troubled times—and that you would be safer kept at a distance, until matters had calmed down." She sighed. "If not for the poisoning, he might have been right. Who can say?"

"He wanted to protect me," Tavi said quietly.

"And your mother, I think," Alera said. "Whatever Sextus may have thought of her personally, he knew that Septimus loved her. It carried weight with him."

Tavi sighed and closed his eyes. "I wish I'd known him better. I wish he were here now."

"As do I," Alera said quietly. "I've taught you all that I can in a limited time—and you've been an able pupil. But . . ."

"But I'm not ready for this," Tavi said.

Alera said nothing for a long moment. Then she said, "I think he would be proud of what you have done. I think he would have been proud of you."

Tavi closed his eyes quickly against a sudden irritating heat that flowed into them.

"You should rest, young Gaius. Regain your strength." Alera walked close and touched his shoulder lightly with one hand. "You will need it all in the days to come."

CHAPTER 30

Amara eyed the Knight standing guard outside the Princeps' command tent, and said, "I don't understand why you can't at least go in and ask."

The young man stared coldly over Amara's head at the Marat clan-head, and said, "No barbarians."

Amara fought down her irritation and remained expressionless, neutral. Doroga, for his part, returned the young man's stare steadily, leaning one elbow on the head of his cudgel. The massively muscled Marat showed no reaction at all to the half dozen very interested *legionares* commanded by the young Knight. He exuded a sense of patient confidence and let Amara do the talking—thank goodness.

"Was that your specific order, Sir . . ."

"Ceregus," the young Knight spat.

"Sir Ceregus," Amara said politely. "I must inquire if you are acting on a specific order from your lawful superiors."

The young Knight smiled woodenly. "If you recall what happened to the last Princeps who came into the presence of the barbarians in this valley, Countess, you'll find all the reason you need."

Doroga grunted. "Gave him a ride on a gargant and saved him and his people from being eaten by the Herdbane. Then your First Lord, old Sextus, gave me this shirt." Doroga plucked at the fine but worn old Aleran tunic, with its radical alterations to fit his frame.

Ceregus narrowed his eyes and began to speak.

"The good clan-head forgets to mention the retreat from Riva," Amara cut in, interrupting the young Knight. "At which time, Doroga and the other members of his clan saved the lives of tens of thousands of fleeing civilians and prevented a division of forces, which might have killed hundreds or thousands of *legionares*."

"You *dare* to suggest that the Legions—" the young Knight began.

"I suggest, Sir Ceregus, that you are going to be sorely disappointed in your officers' reactions to your decision, and I advise you to seek their advice before you find yourself in an unpleasant situation."

"Woman, I don't know who you think you are, but I do not take kindly to threats."

"I am Calderonus Amara, whose husband's walls you are currently sheltering behind," she replied

Sir Ceregus narrowed his eyes. "And I am Rivus Ceregus, whose uncle, High Lord Rivus, gave your husband his title."

Amara smiled sweetly at him. "No, boy. That was Gaius Sextus, if you'll recall."

Ceregus's cheeks gained spots of color. "The matter is closed. The barbarian doesn't go inside."

Amara looked steadily at him for a moment. The nephew of a High Lord could potentially have a great deal of clout, depending upon how favored he was by Lord Rivus. It might be worth it to give way for the time being and gain specific orders to admit Doroga next time around.

But there really wasn't time for that kind of foolishness. The vord had not assaulted the first wall as yet, but it wouldn't be long before they did. Already, their scouts, skirmishers, vordknights, and takers were haunting the western edge of the Valley.

Footsteps sounded behind her, and Senator Valerius, along with a pair of civilian-clothed bodyguards, approached the tent. He beamed at Ceregus, and said, "Good evening, Sir Knight. Would you be so kind?"

Ceregus inclined his head to the Senator, smiling in reply. He jerked his head to his fellow sentries to tell them to move aside, and waved the Senator and his men by without so much as taking note of the group's sidearms. Valerius glanced over his shoulder, just before disappearing into his tent, and gave Amara a smug and venomous glance as he did.

Ah. So that's how things stand.

Amara took a deep breath, closed her eyes, and calmed her mind. Then she opened them again, and said, "I believe I have had enough of this sort of partisan idiocy. It's what got us into this mess in the first place."

"You are welcome to the Princeps' Council, Countess," Ceregus said, his voice cold. He pointed a finger at Doroga "But *that* creature goes nowhere near the Princeps."

When she spoke, her voice was very calm, and perfectly polite. "Are you sure that's how you want to do this?"

"Did all that skulking around murdering people damage your hearing, Countess?" His eyes blazed. "Kalarus Brencis Minoris was my friend. And you killed him. So that is *exactly* how this is going to happen."

"I won't go into the details about how many deaths we can confidently lay at that young maniac's feet, Sir Ceregus. There isn't time." Amara met his eyes. "Lives are at stake, and we need the Marat. That means Doroga needs to be a part of our planning. So if you don't get out of my way, Sir Knight, I am going to move you. You will not find it a pleasant experience. Stand aside."

Ceregus lifted his chin and sneered down at her. "Is that a thr—"

Amara called upon Cirrus, surged toward the young Knight with all the violent speed her fury could lend her, and slammed the heel of her left hand across the idiot's jaw.

Rivus Ceregus went down like a poleaxed ox.

The *legionares* on sentry duty all stared in silence at the unconscious man, their eyes wide and stunned.

Doroga burst into a full-bellied laugh. He smothered it a second later and bowed his head as if pretending to unravel a loose thread from his tunic—but his shoulders quivered and jerked with his muffled amusement.

Amara would have been tempted to join him if her left wrist hadn't felt as though she had broken it. Human hands weren't meant to deliver blows with that kind of speed and force. She clenched the fingers of her right hand into a tight fist to channel the pain elsewhere, made a mental note to stop abusing her limbs like that, then turned a calm gaze on the sentries and nodded at the youngest. "You. Go into the command tent. Find a senior officer and ask whether or not the clan-head is welcome to attend."

The *legionare* threw her a sketchy, hasty salute, and hurried into the tent.

"You," Amara said, nodding at another one. "Fetch the nearest healer for the idiot."

"Y-yes, ma'am," the *legionare* said. He hurried away, too.

"I apologize for the delay," Amara said to Doroga. "I'm sure we'll have things cleared up in a moment."

"No hurry," Doroga said, a wide grin on his ugly face.

Bernard emerged from the bustle of the camp, threading his way between several sets of smith's apprentices, pairs of whom were carrying multiple suits of newly made Legion lorica on stout poles. Bernard nodded to Doroga and clasped forearms with the Marat, then turned to Amara.

His jaw hadn't been pulverized to powder by Invidia's blow, but it had apparently broken into half a dozen shards. The healers had only just been able to fuse the bones back together, including replacement teeth for the ones that had been knocked out, but there was still considerable swelling. It would take multiple sessions and simple time to repair his jaw entirely, and in the face of the battle at hand, the healers had neither to spare. When Bernard spoke, the words came from between clenched teeth, slightly misshapen. "Doroga. My lady. Have they started yet?"

"I've no idea," Amara said. "One of Valerius's dogs was in charge of the sentries and barred Doroga. We're working things out."

Bernard looked gravely down at the unconscious man. "My wife. The diplomat."

"Don't start," Amara said.

Within a minute, the *legionare* returned from the command tent, nodding to Amara. "Countess, the Princeps sends his compliments and extends his gratitude to the clan-head for coming to us in our hour of need. He is by all means welcome to attend."

She glanced at her husband and rolled her eyes. "*Thank* you, *legionare*. Doroga, if you please?"

Doroga joined Bernard in looking down at the unconscious man and scratched his jaw thoughtfully. "Maybe even if I didn't."

They proceeded inside and found Gaius Attis waiting for them. He was seated at a chair on a small platform overlooking a sand table configured to represent the Calderon Valley. A heavy blanket covered his legs, and he looked pale. Sir Ehren stood in attendance at his side and a bit behind him, and Placida Aria stood in a similar position opposite Ehren.

Gathered in the tent were most of the highest-ranking Citizens of the Realm, a group of tired, bloodied, travel-stained men and women with proud bearing and grim expressions. Every surviving High Lord was present, along with most of the High Ladies. The captains of the Legions were also there, along with representatives from the Senate—who, Amara felt sure, were there mostly in a ceremonial function. All things considered, the tent was quite crowded.

Amara spotted Lady Veradis standing beside her father, the silver-haired Lord Cereus.

"Amara," Veradis said, and hurried over, her expression concerned. "What happened?"

"Oh, I bumped my hand into something obstinate," Amara replied.

Veradis took her by the left arm and lifted Amara's hand in tandem with her own eyebrow. "This is broken."

"In a good cause. I'll have someone see to it when we're finished."

Veradis made a clucking sound with her mouth, and said, "Oh, you're impossible. Just give it to me."

"There's no need to—"

Veradis lifted her left hand and quite calmly snapped her stiffened fingers and thumb together, as if in the motion of a closing mouth, then cradled Amara's wrist gently and murmured something to herself. The pain eased over the next several seconds, and Amara let out a breath of relief.

"That's him, huh?" Doroga asked Bernard.

"Yes."

Doroga shook his head, studying Gaius Attis. Then he said, "Be right back."

The broad-shouldered barbarian calmly approached the Princeps. As he got close, both Ehren and Lady Placida seemed to grow tenser. Lady Placida slid half a step forward, to place herself between Doroga and Attis.

"Take it easy, woman," Doroga drawled. "Just want to talk to the man."

"Your weapon, sir," Aria said stiffly.

Doroga blinked, then seemed to remember his cudgel. He offered it to Lady Placida by its handle, and released it as soon as she had it. The cudgel fell with a heavy thump, and Lady Placida grunted. She had to make a visible effort of furycraft to lift the weapon again and set it calmly aside.

Doroga nodded, then stepped up onto the platform to stand over Attis, staring down at him, his hands on his hips.

"You would be the Clan-Head Doroga?" Attis asked politely.

"Yes," Doroga said. "You are the man whose people convinced Atsurak to lead thousands of my people to a bloody death."

Attis stared at Doroga, then swept his gaze around the room. Finally, he looked down at his own blanket-covered lap and smiled, rather bitterly. "It wasn't difficult."

The buzz of conversation in the room simply stopped. Everyone stared at Attis, Amara included. Oh, certainly, everyone had known who was behind the events preceding Second Calderon, but there was what everyone knew, then what they could *prove*. Lord and Lady Aquitaine had gotten away with it without leaving any concrete proof to connect them to the Marat invasion. No one had spoken of it openly—such a charge, made without proof, would have been instant and undeniable reason for the Aquitaines to call the speaker to the *juris macto*.

And yet, Attis had just admitted to his part in the plot, in front of the most powerful Citizens of the Realm.

Doroga grunted, nodding, evidently unaware of what he had just done. "Lot of people died. Yours and mine."

"Yes," Attis said.

"If there was time," Doroga said, "you and I might have an argument about that."

"Time is something of which I am in short supply," Attis replied.

Doroga nodded. "It is done. Dealing with the vord is more important. But I will have your promise not to do any such thing in the future."

Attis looked bemused. "Yes. You have it."

Doroga nodded and extended his hand. Attis reached out, and the two traded grips of one another's forearms.

"Thank you for your help today," Attis said. "You saved the lives of many of my people."

"That is what good neighbors do," Doroga said. "Maybe no one ever taught you Alerans about that."

"Entirely possible," Attis said, a smile still touching his lips. "I must ask you if any more of your people might be willing to help us."

Doroga grunted. "I have called. We will see who answers. But I and my Clanmates are here. We will stand with you."

The Princeps nodded. "I welcome you."

"Be a fool not to," Doroga said. "After this is done, you and I will talk about balancing scales."

"I would be pleased to discuss it," Attis said.

Doroga grunted, faint surprise plain on his features. "Right. Good."

"We should begin, I think," the Princeps said.

Doroga folded his arms on his chest, nodded to Attis, and ambled back over to Amara and Bernard.

"Citizens, Senators, Captains," Attis said, raising his voice. "If you would give me your attention, please. We will discuss the defense of the Valley. Our host, the rather farsighted Count Calderon, will describe his defensive structures to you."

Bernard looked at Amara and gestured in irritation at his jaw.

"Ah," she said. "Your Highness, my husband has injured his jaw and will have difficulty speaking. With your permission, I will brief everyone about our defenses."

"By all means," said the Princeps.

Amara stepped forward and up onto the platform with the sand table. Everyone gathered around to look. "As you can see," Amara said, "the Calderon Valley is divided into three separate sections by the new walls. We are currently just behind the westernmost wall. It is by far the longest and the lowest, running approximately five miles, from the escarpments to the shores of the Sea of Ice and standing at an average height of ten feet. The second wall is approximately twenty miles from here. It is just over three miles long and runs from this salient of the escarpments to the sea. It is of standard construction at twenty feet, with gates flanked by towers every half mile. The final defensive wall is situated here, at the far end of the valley, protecting the town of Garrison and the refugee camps of those who have already arrived."

"I'm curious," interrupted Senator Valerius, "how a Count of the Realm managed to fund all of this construction—and then to conceal its presence, as well."

"With a great deal of support, sir," Amara replied calmly. "The sections of wall within sight of the causeway were raised only a few days ago. The rest went unobserved thanks to the generous use of camouflage to hide them from the view of fliers and the fact that few visitors to the Valley stray far from the causeway."

"It seems odd to me," Valerius said. "That's all. Such a project must have cost you hundreds of thousands of golden eagles."

Amara eyed Valerius calmly. "Is there anything else, sir?"

"I find myself reluctant to trust your word, Countess—or the word of the Count who built these unauthorized and illegal fortifications—"

"Oh bloody crows, man!" Antillus Raucus abruptly snarled. "What the crows does it *matter* where they came from as long as we have them at hand when we need them?"

"I merely point out that this is a legal matter that can hardly be ignored once the current crisis is abated. If we are to entrust the security of the Realm to the loyalties of this . . . questionable pair of individuals . . ."

Lord Placida didn't speak. He simply turned to Valerius, grabbed the man's tunic, and with a grunt flung him out of the tent to sprawl in the mud outside. The motion was so sudden that Valerius's bodyguards were caught frozen. Placida turned to face them with narrowed eyes, then pointed at the door.

They went.

"Ass," muttered Raucus.

"Thank you, Placida," the Princeps murmured in a dry voice. "Countess, please continue."

Amara smiled at Lord Placida, nodded to the Princeps, and returned to her narrative. "We have been studying the potential defenses of the Valley for some time," she said. "This is the plan we believe will best accomplish the goals the Princeps has specified . . ."

CHAPTER 31

Gaius Octavian's host came down upon the vord-occupied city of Riva like a thunderstorm.

Though I'm not sure anyone's ever done it quite this literally, Fidelias mused.

As the Legions and their Canim allies swept down from the hills above Riva, the low-hanging clouds and curtains of rain seemed to cling to the banners of Aleran troops and Canim warriors alike, bound by a myriad of misty, intangible scarlet threads that stretched out into the air all around. The leashed clouds engulfed the entire force, concealing their numbers and identity from outside observation, courtesy of the Canim ritualists, led by their new commander, Master Marok.

Within the cloud, Crassus and the fliers of the Knights Pisces hovered over the heads of the marching forces. The Knights Aeris had gathered up the swirling energy of a dozen thunderbolts from a storm that had come through before first light. The strokes of lightning rumbled and crackled back and forth between the Knights, blue-white beasts caged in a circle of windcrafting. Their growling thunder rolled out ahead of the advancing host, concealing the sound of marching troops and cavalry alike.

"This all looks quite stylishly ominous," Fidelias commented to the Princeps. "And appearances can be quite important. But I can't help but wonder why we're doing this, Your Highness."

Octavian waited for a crash of thunder to roll by before he answered. "There just aren't many ways to disguise the identity of a force on the move," he called back, his voice confident. "And I want our full strength to come as a surprise to the vord."

"I see," Fidelias said. "For a moment I thought that you'd effectively blinded and deafened us all for the sake of making a memorable entrance."

The Princeps grinned, showing Fidelias his teeth. "We have eyes outside the mist—Varg's Hunters and the Knights Flora of both Legions."

"You're still creating an information delay. They'll have to come running in here to tell you anything. If a large force arrives unexpectedly, that could be fatal."

The Princeps shrugged. "There won't be any such force," he said with a confidence so perfectly familiar that Fidelias was almost violently reminded of Sextus.

Fidelias lowered his voice. "You can be sure of that?"

The Princeps looked at him for a moment, pensive, and nodded. "Yes."

"Then why not bypass Riva completely?"

"First, because we need to be tested in an actual battle," he replied. "We've never coordinated in offensive operations before, at least not on this scale. It's important that we know what we can do against these particular vord forms."

"And second?"

The Princeps gave Fidelias a bland look that had something granite-hard lurking under the surface. "It's not their city. Is it." He looked out at the mist, as though focusing on whatever was beyond. "Besides, Riva could conceal legions of vord behind her walls. Better to find out now and deal with them rather than waiting for them to come marching up our spines when we reach Calderon."

There was the sound of approaching hoofbeats, and Kitai appeared out of the mist. She pulled in on the Princeps' right side and matched her mount's pace to his, her green eyes intent. "The gates were not destroyed when the city was taken," she said. "They are currently closed and guarded. There are vord on the battlements and in the sky above the city."

"There's a problem," Fidelias said. "We don't have siege equipment."

The Princeps shook his head. "We won't need it." He drew a deep breath, as if bracing himself for something unpleasant, and said, "I'm going to take them down."

Fidelias found himself lifting both eyebrows. The siege gates of the great cities of Alera were more than simple steel and stone. They were wound through and through with furycraftings of every kind imaginable, and more craftings were laid upon them every year, so that they built one upon another like layers of paint. It was done that way for the specific purpose of making the gates almost entirely resistant to the influence of hostile furycraft. A High Lord of the Realm would be daunted by such an obstacle.

"You think you're strong enough to manage *that*, sir?"

The Princeps nodded once. "Yes, I do."

Fidelias studied Octavian's confident profile. "Be wary of hubris, Your Highness."

"It's only hubris if I can't do it," he replied. "Besides, I need to be tested, too. If I'm to step into my grandfather's shoes, I can't keep on concealing my abilities forever. I need to prove myself."

Kitai snorted quietly. "About bloody time," she said. "Does this mean I'm free to be more obvious as well, Aleran?"

"I don't see why not," said the Princeps.

Fidelias lifted his eyebrows. "Your Highness? I knew she could manage minor furycraftings, lights and such, but . . ."

"But?" He smiled faintly.

"But she's a *Marat*, sir. Marat don't *use* furies."

The Princeps feigned an astonished expression. "She is? Are you sure?"

Fidelias gave him a sour look.

The Princeps let out a warm laugh. "You may have noted that our dear Ambassador has very little regard for the proprieties."

"Not when they're ridiculous," Kitai sniffed.

The two sentences came out one after the other, so close together that they might have been uttered by actors following a script or spoken by the same person. Fidelias peered at their identically colored eyes as if for the first time, feeling somewhat stupid. "The way Marat operate in tandem with their clan animals. It's more than just their custom, isn't it?"

"There's a bond," the Princeps said, nodding. "I scarcely understand it myself—and she honestly gives me no help whatsoever when I try."

"That is because knowledge given freely to another is not really knowledge at all, Aleran," Kitai replied. "It is rumor. One must learn for oneself."

"And this bond . . . it allows her to furycraft as you do," Fidelias said.

"Apparently," the Princeps said.

Kitai rode for a moment, frowning. Then she said, "He's stronger. Better focused. But I can manage more things simultaneously."

The Princeps lifted his eyebrows. "You think so?"

Kitai shrugged her shoulders.

Fidelias frowned. "Ambassador . . . did you just ride up to the city gates under a veil and try to craft them down?"

Kitai shot Fidelias an annoyed scowl and said nothing.

The Princeps looked back and forth between the pair of them, his expression unreadable. Then he said, "That was thoughtful of you, Kitai."

"We want the gates down," she said. "What matter who brings them down or when?"

Octavian nodded. "Most considerate," the Princeps said.

Kitai's scowl darkened. "Do not say it."

"Say what? It's the thought that counts?"

She slapped his leg lightly with the ends of her reins.

A Marat with furycraft in the same general vicinity as the Princeps of the Realm. A Princeps who had never demonstrated his skills beyond the most basic, rudimentary uses of the craft—except when he had apparently executed furycraftings so large that they could hardly be recognized as such. Fidelias himself, a proven and confessed traitor to the Crown, an assassin for the Princeps' enemies, riding openly at the Princeps' left hand, under an assumed face and a sentence of death, willingly staying where he was. Meanwhile, in the host behind them, following the Princeps' banner were thousands of the finest troops of Alera's oldest enemies—never mind *another* enemy, Ambassador Kitai, who quite clearly shared a great deal more than affection with Octavian. And all of them were about to assault an Aleran city overrun by a foe no one had even heard of ten years ago.

The world had become a very strange place.

Fidelias smiled to himself.

Strange, yes. But for some reason, he no longer felt like a man too old to face it.

* * *

It was not long before horns began to blow, and Aleran scouts appeared in the mists ahead, woodcrafted veils unraveling around them as they approached the column. The Princeps pointed at one of the men, and said, "Scout, report!"

"They're coming, sir!" the man reported. "Skirmish line, maybe a cohort's worth, coming at us hard, sir! And they're ugly, big as they were in Canea, not those swamp-lizard things. Looks like they've got a hell of a reach on them, too."

Octavian grunted. "Looks like the Queen changed them to better handle a shieldwall."

Fidelias nodded. "Like you said she might. I'm impressed."

The Princeps coughed. "It was a guess. I wasn't certain about it. Just seemed reasonable."

Fidelias frowned, and said quietly, "Piece of advice, sir?"

"Hmm?"

"Next time, just nod. People like it better when the Princeps seems to know something they don't."

The Princeps made a quiet, snorting sound and raised a hand, signaling the trumpeter waiting nearby. "Sound advance to the Canim. Let's see what these vord think about meeting a few thousand Narashan warriors instead of a Legion shieldwall."

"And see if the Canim will be willing to take your orders, eh?" Fidelias murmured, beneath the clear notes of the signal trumpet.

Octavian grinned, and responded, quietly, "Nonsense. I have no doubts whatsoever in the solidity of our alliance."

"Excellent, sir," Fidelias said. "That's more like what I was talking about."

The shrill, brassy cries of vord warriors came drifting through the mist, different than any Fidelias had heard before but unmistakable. He had to keep himself from shuddering. For the sake of the rest of the Legion, he was still playing the part of Valiar Marcus, relegated to the role of advisor to the young captain by advancing age. Valiar Marcus would not show fear before the enemy. No matter how bloody terrifying they were to anyone with half a mind.

A double column of Canim warriors, several hundred strong, came rolling up to the front of the host, led by Varg himself. Their loping pace was swift, and Varg stopped to confer briefly with the Princeps. He nodded to Octavian, then gave a few orders in the snarling tongue of the wolf-warriors, and his troops fell into a curved double line that arched out in front of the rest of the host like a *legionare's* shield.

Fidelias could clearly see only the nearest of the Canim, at the center of the line—Varg and the warriors closest to him. The lean, powerful bodies of the Canim moved in a fashion that was both completely nonuniform and fluidly coordinated, each armored warrior occupying precisely enough space to move and use his weaponry, with his companions on either side maintaining a precise distance, seemingly without any conscious effort.

The Canim were soldiers, sure enough, clearly moving in coordinated discipline, but their methods and tactics were utterly alien to those used by Aleran *legionares*. Fidelias didn't even want to think of the pure shocking power of a Canim shieldwall. If they used such infantry tactics, an Aleran Legion would not be able to survive the clash of close combat.

Then again, the few times Alerans had clashed with Canim of the warrior caste, the battle had never gone in their favor in any case. At best they had attained a draw, during several brief clashes during the two years of combat around the Elinarch and in the Vale. In the worst cases, the warrior caste had handed the Alerans their heads.

The vord shrieked their alien cries again, this time from closer, and Fidelias felt his heart laboring harder. He straightened his back and forced his expression to Marcus's closed, prebattle discipline. He heard the Princeps giving rapid orders beside him—sending the scouts back out to the army's flanks and front, and ordering Maximus's cavalry to come up to anchor both ends of the Canim lines, to be ready to help if needed.

One Canim element to one Aleran, Fidelias noted. Even when fighting together, the Princeps was showing caution against his allies, who would see it as a reassurance and a mark of respect. The Princeps had been the first to understand the way the wolf-warriors thought, and he had applied that knowledge ably to both the battlefield and the conference table with undeniable success. Rarely had Octavian attained an overwhelming victory against the Canim, and yet at day's end, he had always managed to hold the most vital terrain or gain another mile of ground—and now his former enemies let out a howl and engaged the vord as they appeared out of the mist.

The battle was brief, elemental, and savage.

The vord warrior forms slowed for a few steps upon seeing the Canim ready to meet them, but then hurtled forward with shrill wails and whistles. Horrible scything limbs plunged at the wolf-warriors with the kind of power that would leave Aleran *legionares* screaming or dead without extraordinary skill or luck.

Against the battle line of Canim in full armor, it was . . . insufficiently impressive.

Varg simply struck the scythes from his opponents' limbs as they swept toward him, his red steel blade flashing in the strobes of blue-white light from the powers leashed above them. A third strike took the head from the vord, and a heavy kick both crumpled the black chitin of its armored torso and sent it sprawling back to die on the ground, thrashing uselessly. Varg's sword whipped one way and struck a supporting limb from one vord, then reversed itself and removed a scythe from the vord on the other side, which had been wetted in Canim blood, saving a stunned warrior's life.

Varg let out a roar of rage and what seemed to Fidelias like pure, joyous enthusiasm, struck down a second vord, and covered the fallen warrior as he rose and retrieved his weapon. Varg then broke to his right, while the recovered Cane went to his left. Both darted through the line of battle, and the Canim in the second rank followed them, so that the vord on either side of the hole Varg had created found themselves surrounded by warriors, cut down from the front and from behind.

The gap in the vord line widened, as each fallen vord's opponent pushed through and went after the flanks and rear of another foe, so that the battlefield in front of Fidelias and the rest of the command group seemed to break into two halves and part to the left and right, like two curtains opening onto a stage—one littered with the bodies of broken vord warrior forms. The battle raged off into the mist to the left and right, and out of their immediate view.

At some point, the vord shrieks turned to a new, urgent pitch—a retreat?— and Maximus's cavalry horns began to sound the charge, already receding into greater distance.

"Ah, they've broken," said the Princeps, his teeth bared in a wolfish smile. He clenched one hand into a fist. "Max is after them. They're running. By the great furies, they're *running!*"

He never turned or raised his voice above simple conversational volume— nor could he, as the image of the calm, controlled Princeps of the Realm—but Fidelias judged that Valiar Marcus would be more than happy to do it for him. "They're running, boys!" he bawled out in a training-ground bellow. "Varg and Antillar were too much for 'em!"

A thunder of cheers and Canim roars bellowed out for several seconds be- fore Fidelias passed a cutoff signal back through the line to the cohorts, where Aleran centurions and Canim huntmasters began snarling and growling orderly quiet back into the ranks.

Moments later, the first returning Canim began to appear, walking back toward the ranks in the same arching battle line in which they'd begun the fight. Several were walking only with assistance—but there were no breaks in the line. On the flanks, the Aleran cavalry was returning to its original position in the order of battle. Antillar Maximus came riding in a moment ahead of Varg and saluted the Princeps, slamming his fist into his armor, over his heart.

Varg rolled to halt in front of them and nodded to the Princeps as well. "Not much of a fight."

"It seems that they *do* have a breaking point, if the will of their Queen isn't driving them," the Princeps said. "Your warriors found it."

Varg let out a pleased growling sound of agreement.

"I hope you will do us the honor of allowing our healers to treat your wounded. There's no sense in having them out of action when we can put them back into top condition."

"That would please me," Varg replied. "I will request it of them."

Octavian inclined his head to the Canim leader and returned Antillar's salute. "Let's have it."

"A few of them managed to get out of the close fight," Antillar Maximus said. "None of them made it out of the fog. The scouts reported other vord like these falling back to the city. They went right up the wall. They're inside now, maybe a thousand."

"And those are just the ones we saw," Octavian said. "We can't leave them in a fortress at our backs, growing a supply of *croach* to feed reinforcements they move into the area. This one will be up to us, I believe. Signal the Prime Cohort and the Battlecrows. I want them to be the first through the gates. Both cavalry elements are to take up positions around the city, to catch any others who try to run."

Antillar blinked. "Those gates aren't exactly made of paper and glue, Calderon," the Tribune said. "The High Lords were probably reinforcing them for months, this winter. You know how to run the figures. Any idea of the kind of power it will take to bring them down?"

The Princeps considered Antillar's words. Fidelias eyed Antillar and Varg alike, but he didn't think either of them could see how nervous Octavian was. Then the Princeps nodded, and said, "A considerable amount of force."

"I don't think we have it," Max said.

"I think you're wrong, Max," Octavian said calmly.

The Ambassador's eyes narrowed in anticipation, all but glowing green, and her smile somehow made Fidelias take more note of the points of her canine teeth than any of the others.

The Princeps grinned at her in reply, almost unsettlingly boyish, and said, "Let's find out."

CHAPTER 32

Tavi wondered if he was about to make a very large, very humiliating, potentially fatal mistake.

He frowned, and spoke to that doubting part of himself in a firm tone of thought: *If you didn't want to take the big chances, you shouldn't have started screaming about who your father was. You could have moved quietly across the Realm and disappeared among the Marat, if you had wanted to. You decided to fight for your birthright. Well, now it's time to fight. It's time to see if you can do what you have to do. So quit whining and bring down that gate.*

"Warmaster Varg will have operational command while I deal with the gate," Tavi said.

The Legion command staff had been briefed on Tavi's intention the day before. They hadn't liked it then. Today, though, they simply saluted. Good. Varg's part in the opening skirmish of the battle (itself but a skirmish for what was to come), had convinced them of the Cane's ability.

"Tribune Antillus!" Tavi called.

After several signals were exchanged, Crassus came cruising down to the ground and landed beside Tavi's horse. They exchanged salutes, and Tavi said, "I'll be moving forward with the Prime and the Battlecrows. I want you and the Pisces hovering over my shoulders."

"Aye, sir," Crassus said. "We'll be there."

"On your way," Tavi said.

Crassus took off, and there was nothing left but for Tavi to break down a defensive structure prepared for decades if not centuries to resist precisely what he was about to attempt. He glanced over his shoulder, at Fidelias. Valiar Marcus would have been waiting stolidly, his expression hard and sober. Though his features hadn't changed whatsoever, Tavi could feel the differences in the man, the more flexible, somehow leonine nature of him. To any casual observer, Fidelias would have appeared exactly like Valiar Marcus. But Tavi could sense that the man was aware, somehow, of his fear.

His perfectly reasonable fear. His very well-advised fear. His quite mature and wise fear, even.

Shut up and get to work, he thought firmly.

Acteon, the long-legged black stallion Tavi rode, tossed his head and shook his mane. The horse had been his, and in the care of the First Aleran Legion, since shortly after he had been forced to take command— a gift from Hashat, the Marat clan-head of the Horse. The Marat stallion had greater agility and endurance than any Aleran horse Tavi had ever seen, but he wasn't a supernatural beast.

He wouldn't save Tavi from anything he didn't handle himself.

"Standard-bearer," Tavi said quietly. "Let's go."

Hoofbeats came up beside him, and Tavi looked aside at the dappled grey mare Kitai rode. His eyes went up to her rider, and he smiled faintly at Kitai, who was wearing her Legion-issue mail. It didn't offer the same protection as the heavier steel plates of his own lorica, but though she was more than strong enough to wear the heavier armor, she disdained it, preferring the greater flexibility of the mail.

"I suppose you're going to ignore me if I tell you to wait here," he said.

She arched an eyebrow at him and settled her grip on the standard. The misty wisps of faint scarlet, drifting outward from the standard like strands of seaweed, seemed to whisper to the mists around them, gathering them closer. Kitai had not picked up the royal standard of the Princeps, the plunging eagle, scarlet upon blue. Instead, she bore the original standard of the First Aleran. It had once been a blue-and-scarlet eagle, wings spread as if in flight, its background also scarlet and blue, halved, contrasting the colors of the eagle. The first battle the Legion faced had left the eagle burned black, and the First Aleran's "battlecrow" had never been replaced.

Tavi had carried the standard into an extremely dangerous situation himself . . . had it been only three, almost four years since the Elinarch? It felt like a hundred.

Kitai met his eyes and lifted her chin, a small smile on her mouth. Her message was clear. He had triumphed at that meeting. He would do so again at this one. Something quivering and tight went out of him, and his hands and mind felt a great deal steadier.

"I suppose so," he said.

He made no gesture, but the pair of them started out together at the same instant.

Tavi rode through the fog. Acteon's hooves clopped on the ground. The track to the nearest of the city's gates was obvious before him, littered here and there with the remains of the battle the rest of Alera had fought there days before. Here a splash of scarlet Aleran blood, now brown and buzzing with flies. There, a *gladius*, broken six inches from the hilt, the results of hasty construction or shoddy maintenance. A *legionare's* bloodstained helmet lay on its side, its crown bearing a puncture mark shaped much like the profile of a scythe of a new warrior-form vord they had fought that very day.

But there were no corpses, either of fallen *legionares* or of any vord beyond those slain that very hour. Tavi shivered. The vord did not let fallen meat go to waste—not even that of their own kind.

The leashed thunder of the storm came with them. Tavi could hear the steady windstreams that kept the Knights Pisces aloft nearby, within a couple of hundred yards, above and behind them. The nearest of their number, probably Crassus, hovered almost directly overhead, only just visible in the cloud.

The walls of Riva loomed suddenly out of the mist, along with the city gates. They stood forty feet high, with the towers on either side rising twenty feet beyond that. Tavi felt the muscles in his back tightening, and his heart began to beat faster.

He was about to announce his identity to anyone who was watching.

And then something, he was sure, would happen—and he doubted it would be anything he would enjoy.

Tavi focused on the gates. They were made of stone sheathed and woven with steel. They weighed tons and tons, but they were balanced so perfectly on their hinges that a single man, unassisted by furies, could push them open when their locks were not engaged. Even so, they were stronger than the stone siege walls that framed them. Fire would not distress them. A steel ram could batter them for days with no effect, and the swords of the finest Knights Ferrous in the Realm would shatter upon them. The thunderbolts held ready by the First Aleran's Knights would do little more than scar the finished steel surface. The earth itself could not be shaken around them.

In Tavi's experience, though, very few people had sufficient respect for the destructive capacities of the gentler crafts.

Wood and water.

He had a come a long, long way from the Calderon Valley, from being the scrawny apprentice shepherd without the ability to so much as operate a furylamp or an oven. In that time, he had known peace and war, civilization and savagery, calm study and desperate application. As a boy, he had dreamed of finding a life in which he proved himself despite the fact that he had no furycraft at all—and now his furycraft might be all that kept him alive.

Life, Tavi reflected, seldom makes a gift of what one expects or plans for.

But some part of him, the part that was little enamored of walking the more prudent avenues of thought, was quivering with excitement. How many times had he suffered at the hands of the other children at Bernardholt for lacking furies of his own? How many childhood nights had he lain awake, attempting simply to *will* himself the ability to furycraft? How often had he shed private, silent tears of shame and despair?

And now, he *had* those abilities. Now he knew how to use them. Fundamentally speaking.

No matter how much danger he knew he was in, there was a part of him that wanted simply to throw back his head and crow defiant triumph at those memories, at the world. There was a part of him that wanted to dance in place, and was wildly eager to show his strength at last. Most of all, there was a part of him that wanted to face his enemies for the first time upon his own talent and strength and no one else's. Though he knew he was untested, he *wanted* the test.

He had to know that he was ready to face what was to come.

So it was with both wary tension and absolute elation that Tavi reached out to the furies spread about the world before him.

Almost immediately, Tavi could feel the craftings seething over and through the great gates, running like living things within the great constructs— fury-bound structures, as potent as gargoyles but locked into immobility, focused into stasis and into maintaining that stasis absolutely. Tavi had as much chance of commanding those furies to cease their function as he had of commanding water not to be wet.

Instead, he turned his thoughts down, beneath them. Far, far below the surface, beneath the immeasurable mass of the furycrafted walls and towers of Riva, he felt the flowing water that sank into the rocks beneath the city, that had seeped through them year after slow, steady year, and pooled into a vast reservoir far below. Originally intended as an emergency cistern for the lonely little outpost of Riva, it had sunk beneath year after year of added construction as the city grew, until it had been forgotten by everyone but Alera herself.

By now, the little cistern had become something far larger than its creators—probably Legion engineers, back in the days of the original Gaius Primus—had ever intended.

Tavi focused his will upon that long-forgotten water and called out to it.

At the same time, he reached out to the earth beneath his feet, to the soil and dust lying before the city's walls. He felt through the soil, felt the grass growing beneath his horse's hooves. He felt clover and other weeds and flowers, beginning to grow, not yet brought down by the groundskeepers of Riva. There was a plethora of different plants there, and he knew them all. As an apprentice shepherd who had grown up not far from Riva, he'd been made familiar with virtually every plant that grew in the region. He'd had to learn which the sheep could eat safely and which he should avoid: which plants might trigger problems in a member of the flock and which might be used to help support the animal's recovery from illness or injury. He knew Rivan flora as only someone who had been raised there could.

He reached out to all of them and extended his thoughts to the plants, the seeds, numbering and sorting them in his thoughts. He focused his will and whispered, beneath his breath, *"Grow."*

And beneath him, as if the earth were letting out a long breath, the grass began to grow, to surge with green life. Blades lengthened, and were suddenly outstripped by the quick-growing weeds and flowers. They opened in a mute riot, sudden color flushing along the surface of the earth, and within a few seconds more, grass and flowers alike burst into seed.

Joy and fierce pride assaulted him in a distracting surge, but Tavi let the emotions wash by him and focused upon his task.

Such growth could not happen without plenty of water to nourish it, and as the sudden growth began to leach all the water from the ground, the water from the deep well began to arrive, rising through the layers of earth and stone. At an absentminded motion of his hand, a gentle stream of wind curled along the ground and sighed up over the gates and towers beside it.

Tavi opened his eyes long enough to see tiny seeds, some of them little larger than motes of dust, begin to drift up through the air, to where a thin film of water had begun to cling to the surface of the gates, the towers, courtesy of the cloud around them.

He closed his eyes again, focusing on those seeds. This would be much harder, without the gentle nourishment of the soil around them, but again he reached out to the life before him, and whispered, *"Grow."*

Again, the earth around him sighed fresh green growth. Weeds and small trees began to rise above the grass—and the walls of the great city began to flush a steady shade of green. Bits of grass grew from cracks so tiny they could barely be seen. Moss and lichen spread over the surface as quickly as if they had been spread by raindrops in a steady shower.

He was breathing harder, but could not stop now. *"Grow,"* he whispered.

Trees as tall as a man arose around him, before the wall. The air grew heavier and heavier with a damp coolness. The flawless shine on his armor began to cloud over with fine, cold mist. Green subsumed the gates and the walls alike. Ivy wound up over the walls as rapidly as a snake could slither up a branch.

Tavi clung to his saddle with one hand, refusing to slump, his teeth clenched, and snarled, "Grow!"

From the gates and walls of Riva erupted a chorus of snaps, cracks, of the snarl of tearing stone. Green swallowed the walls, lapping up from the earth beneath in a tangled, living tide, a wave of growth. Small trees sprang from cracks in the walls, and from one upon the gates. More ivy wound everywhere, along with every other form of wild growth one could imagine.

Tavi nodded in satisfaction. Then he lifted his fist and snarled, to the water coming up from below, "Arise!"

There was the sound of an ocean wave crashing onto a rocky shore as the water leapt up and washed over the walls, over the green, sank into the minute cracks in the walls—and in that instant, Tavi reached out for fire, for the little warmth that remained in the frigid water from far below, and yanked it clear of the water.

There was a hiss, and a cloud of heavy mist and puffing vapor swallowed the gates and the walls. Ice crackled and screamed.

Panting, Tavi slid off Acteon's back. He tossed the reins back up over the saddle's crest and slapped the beast on the flank, sending him running back toward the Legion, crashing through the heavy brush and small trees that had grown up behind him. He heard Kitai's mare let out a squeal, then follow the big black.

Tavi did not let go of the craftings in front of him. This would be the hard part.

He reached out to the water again and called to fire, sending it coursing back *into* the ice with a wordless cry. Steam exploded from the walls, from the cracks, in screaming whistles.

"Arise!" he called again, and again the water crashed up from the ground.

And again, he pulled the warmth from the water that had sunk even deeper into cracks that were slightly wider. And he sent heat washing back in a few seconds later.

"Arise!" he called, and began the cycle again.

"Arise!" he called again.

And again.

And again.

And *again*.

Ice and steam hissed and cracked. Stone screamed. Thick white vapor billowed out from the walls, denser than the veiling cloud, all but opaque.

Tavi fell to one knee, gasping, then slowly lifted his eyes to the gates, his jaw set.

They were coated in a layer of ice six inches thick.

Metal groaned somewhere in the gates, a long moan that echoed from empty buildings and through the mists.

"Right," Tavi panted. He pushed himself back to his feet, looked over his shoulder, and nodded at Kitai. "Here we go."

She smiled at him, and said, "Clever, my Aleran."

He winked at her. Then he slowly drew his sword. He extended it deliberately to his side and concentrated.

The metal seemed to hum—and then fire kindled and rushed down the length of the blade, a white-hot wreath. Tavi reached down into himself, focusing, using the fire along the blade as a starting point, gathering heat and preparing to unleash it.

He extended the sword toward the gate with a scream, and fire and a sudden hammer of wind rushed forth toward the frozen gates. The white-hot firebolt slammed into the gate with a force as real as any ram, the ice sublimating in an instant to steam, and the gates, strained beyond measure by the flexing of water and ice and new life growing within them, shattered.

So did the towers beside the gate.

And a hundred feet of the city's wall, on either side of the towers.

All of them roared away from the fury of that fiery blast, screaming as they flew into pieces, bursting into their own heat and wild motion as the overstrained furies within were finally pushed past the limits of the physical materials they inhabited and vented their frustrated rage on the matter about them. Stone and metal—some of the pieces were the size of a Legion supply wagon, or as long and as sharp as the largest sword—went flying and spinning away, sent crashing through half-burned buildings and crushing the bases of the outer ring of towers by the will of Gaius Octavian.

Secondary collapses followed, buildings that were torn to shreds by the destruction of the gates falling in beneath their own unsupported weight. And when *those* structures fell, they claimed others that stood alongside them.

All told, it was nearly four full minutes before the roar of collapsing stone and masonry quieted.

Tavi winced. The damage had been . . . a little more widespread than he had expected. He'd have to pay Riva for the blocks he'd ruined.

"*Aleran,*" Kitai breathed in awe.

He turned to face her and tried to look as though he'd meant to do that. He focused on the positive; at least the duration of the collapse had given him a little time to catch his breath and somewhat recover from the effort to cause it.

The silence that settled around them was oppressive, pregnant with anticipation. "Ready," Tavi told her. "Stand ready."

"You still think she will respond?" she asked quietly.

He nodded tightly and resettled his grip on his fiery blade. "She has no choice."

Within heartbeats, as though driven by his words, the vord gave them an answer.

A strange cry began to rise from dozens of points around the city—it was a sound Tavi had never heard from the vord before, a particular, ululating wail that flickered from its lowest tone to its highest in a swift, chattering trill.

And the city exploded with vord

Chapter 33

In an instant, Kitai was at his back, and a glance up showed him Crassus hand-signaling frantically, requesting permission to attack. Tavi flashed him the sign to stay in place and turned just as the nearest vord mantis flung itself at him.

There was no time for thought, or for fear. A series of thoughts so rapid that they seemed almost a flowing, single idea within his mind's eye gathered furies of the earth, of fire, of steel, and Tavi's flaming blade split the creature cleanly into two frantically twitching parts in a single diagonal, upward-sweeping stroke.

Another mantis came hard on the heels of the first—metaphorically speaking, anyway, since Tavi wasn't sure that the things actually had *feet*, much less heels. A flick of his wrist sent a howling column of wind and fire into its center of mass with such violence that the crafting tore two of the creature's long legs from its body.

Tavi checked over his shoulder. Kitai had been rushed by no less than *four* mantises. One was frantically trying to tear itself from the grasp of a pair of slender young trees, a side product of Tavi's crafting, which had bent in place at a gesture from Kitai and trapped the vord. The other three were struggling to surge forward through tall grass that writhed like serpents and seized their every limb in a thousand soft green fingers—more of Kitai's crafting.

Tavi turned back and left them to her. The sudden, focused, coordinated attack, its strength doubled upon what would appear to be the weaker of the pair to most observers, suggested the appearance of some sort of guiding intellect—perhaps even the Queen herself. The vord had moved with direction and purpose, not with the blind aggression of a creature defending its territory, as the first group of mantis-forms had done.

Or maybe they were getting smarter.

An instinct drew his face up and to one side in time to see a pair of vord-knights blurring toward him. They swept past, scythe-limbs positioned to sweep his head from his shoulders as if he'd been a dandelion and they the groundskeepers. He ducked beneath it, his hand seizing the hem of Kitai's mail shirt with a jerk, warning her, and she dropped into a low crouch that took her safely beneath the passing scythes.

He turned and pointed his sword. A lance of fire burst from it, swelling to engulf the two vordknights as they passed, burning their wings to shriveled, blackened strands. The two crashed to the ground with horrible force, their chitin-armor snapping and cracking audibly, even over the noise. His head whipped around toward the city as he rose again, and saw more vord rushing over the fallen rubble, hundreds of mantis-forms and thousands of the wax spiders with their eerie, semitransparent bodies, all of them trilling the new wail of alarm.

The real attack, the one he had dreaded, the one that had truly compelled him to come forward all but alone, came in the instant after he turned to see the enemy numbers, the river of deadly foes rushing his way, while his eyes were still widening.

He heard it, a rippling set of crackling snaps, as if a thousand mule skinners had begun popping their whips in rhythm.

"Kitai!" he called.

There wasn't time for anything more. He raised his arms and called to the wind, and it answered him with a howl, spinning into a sudden, hysterically powerful circle around him and Kitai. The vord-wasps began to hammer into that whirling shield, their chitin-stings like tiny scalpels and arrowheads at the same time. They collided with the nearly solid air in half a dozen angry swarms, each striking from a slightly different direction, their arrow-straight flight suddenly becoming a wild spin as they were thrown aside.

By some chance of fate or pure luck, a few of the wasps made it through. Tavi dispatched them with swift, sure movements of his sword, using its fire to brush them out of the air just as he had the vordknights.

The stream slackened for a breath, and Tavi looked up through the open roof of the whirling column of wind and flashed signals to Crassus. *Six targets, attack them.*

Crassus dropped a swift gesture of affirmation toward Tavi and began signaling his men. A pair of seconds later, the first caged lightning bolt was loosed, and flashed across the sky from the cloud above Tavi and Kitai to the city. A large green-and-black lump, where a patch of the *croach* high upon a wall seemed to bulge with some half-formed hulk of armor, suddenly exploded into white light and fury. Fragments went flying in every direction, and the half shape that was left seemed to gout fire for several seconds before settling into a more conventional bonfire.

And the stream of deadly arrow-wasps from that horrible hive abruptly vanished.

Tavi swatted several more wasps down, and noted that Kitai had manipulated the spinning force of the winds Tavi held around them, directing several thousand arrow-wasps into the vord still trapped in the grasses. Tavi doubted that the poison coating the wasps' stingers would prove dangerous to the mantis-forms, but their stingers punched through vord chitin with great effectiveness, and each drew its individual trickle of blood. In very short order, no mantis-forms remained standing. Kitai turned her attention to the spiders and mantis-forms rushing from the city, and the vord arrow-wasps sliced and cut into their own kind, helpless before the vast winds.

Thunder rolled overhead, accompanied by blinding-bright flashes of light. Three, four, five, six. Each time Crassus brought one of the captured bolts forth, he destroyed another hive—and after the sixth, the flow of arrow-wasps rushing into the wind shield abruptly ceased, just as the mass of the enemy body came rushing toward Tavi and Kitai.

"I think that went well," Kitai called.

"I'll take it," Tavi said. Then they both leapt upward, and the whirling shield compressed and gathered beneath them, lifting them both up into the skies and out of the reach of the vord below.

Either Crassus had been passing information by hand signal back to the command group, or else Varg had had his fill of waiting. Drums sounded, and the Legion came into sight. Varg had placed Tavi's leading cohorts in the center and flanked them with the taurg cavalry, while a fresh group of warriors stood ready to support any weak points in the line.

"Sir?" Crassus shouted toward him, gesturing at what lightning remained. "What do we do with the rest of it?"

Tavi pointed a finger at the collapsed section of wall, where the vord were pouring out.

Crassus nodded and over the next several minutes dumped all the energy they'd captured from the morning's thunderstorm into the relatively narrow opening. Lightning bolts blew craters in the earth and left the smoldering wreckage of vord forms lying on the blasted ground.

The Legion closed in, with taurga simply crushing down vord that had spread out to the sides of the opening. Their riders never needed to lift their weapons. The Battlecrows and the Prime plugged the hole in the wall and began methodically slaughtering the vord. They were aided by a thin line of Varg's warriors armed with balests, the heavy, steel-bowed, shoulder-fired weapons of the Canim. The warriors' height allowed them to shoot over the Aleran lines without striking an allied *legionare*, and when one of the steel projectiles struck a vord, the creature fell, screaming, or simply expired outright.

The mantis-form vord were dangerous opponents: So were the most experienced and decorated cohorts in the First Aleran. Tavi watched as their centurions assessed the threat of the mantis-form scythes. The weapons really weren't terribly different from the long-handled sickle-swords used by the Canim militia during the last battles against Nasaug's forces in the Vale, but if adjustments weren't made, they could take a toll on the cohorts.

Centurions all along the line came to similar conclusions at almost the same moment. At their roaring orders, the first rank dropped to fight in a low, defensive crouch while the second shifted to their spears, their shields held high and tilted up, to deflect or reduce the effect of any downward-plunging scythes toward themselves or their fighting partners in the first rank. The spearmen made long thrusts over the front rank's shoulders and helmets to discourage the vord from pressing in too close, and any vord that seemed to gain an advantage was swiftly introduced to a heavy steel balest bolt.

Tavi watched the leading cohorts take light casualties. *"Light" casualties,* he thought. *Only someone who has never cleaned the lifeblood from a fallen* legionare's *armor thinks that "light" casualties are insignificant.*

Men died, fighting at his command far below. But, he thought to himself, not nearly as many of them as if they had walked into the deadly hailstorm of arrow-wasps.

After half of a desperate hour, horns sounded again, and, with a roar, the warrior Canim went pounding toward the gap in the walls. Cohorts hastily re-formed their lines, opening gaps enough for the warriors to come through. Done in the heat of combat, the maneuver wasn't as smooth as it might have been. Dozens of Canim wound up bowling straight through the ranks of a cohort, and dozens more who all kept to the narrow lanes between them wound up stumbling into one another in the narrow spaces. Still, the Canim hit the vord lines like an avalanche of dark red and blue steel. They hammered a salient into the mass of the enemy, and with a roar, fresh *legionares*, brought up from the Free Aleran, came marching to relieve their brother soldiers.

"Bloody crows," Crassus called to Tavi. The young Antillan was staring at him. "I've never seen anyone do that much in one morning."

"I've been practicing," Tavi called back. He winked at Crassus.

The other man chuckled wearily and shook his head. "I was beginning to wonder if you had it in you, Your Highness."

"Today was nothing, Tribune," Tavi responded. "Nothing." He inhaled deeply through his nose and nodded. "Nothing but a good start. The real test comes in a few more days."

Crassus's expression sobered, and he nodded. "Orders, sir?"

"The vord will have turned Riva into a larder for the dead," Tavi replied. "You'll probably find it in the citadel, but they could have put it anywhere. Take a fire team into the city, find the larder, and burn it."

"Sir? Our dead, too?"

"None of them wanted to feed the vord," Tavi replied. "Yes. We can't leave them a food supply here."

"The *croach*," Crassus said.

"Aye," Tavi said. "As we head for Calderon, I want sweeps out five miles on either side to spot any patches of *croach* that are forming. We're going to burn it out between here and the Valley. All of it. But start with Riva. Move."

Crassus banged out a rapid salute. "Yes, sir."

"Crassus," Tavi added. He hesitated, then said, "Be careful, all right? They like to leave surprises. And there might be more of those arrow-wasp nests."

"If there are, I'll burn them out, too, sir." Crassus started signaling to the other Pisces in the air around him, and they all streaked back down toward the Legion lines.

Tavi watched the fight at the wall for another moment or two, but it was over. The vord were beginning to break, and the Aleran ranks moved forward with a steady, professional rhythm that silently declared their expectation of victory.

"Aleran?" Kitai asked quietly.

"I'm all right," Tavi said.

She shook her head. "You succeeded today."

"Hmmm?" He glanced at her. "Oh. The furycrafting."

"Yes. Does this not make you happy?"

He nodded. "Oh, yes. I suppose. But now . . . Now it's all on my shoulders. There's no escaping that."

"It always was, my Aleran," Kitai said. "You were just too stupid to realize it."

Tavi snorted out a laugh and smiled at her.

Kitai nodded in satisfaction. "Come. You need to get back to your wagon and rest. Varg has things well in hand."

"I should stay," Tavi said. "Watch. Who knows, there might be something here, some clue as to their weakness."

Kitai looked at him with what looked like enormous patience that was nonetheless clearly being tried. "Aleran," she said between her teeth, "you should rest. In your wagon. Your enclosed, covered wagon. While nearly everyone else is busy with the battle."

Tavi blinked at her owlishly, then his eyes widened. "Oh," he said. A sudden smile lifted his mouth. "*Oh.*"

And Kitai was suddenly pressed against him. There was a limited amount of sensuality available, given all the steel that was between them, but her kiss was so searing that Tavi felt in danger of having the armor melt from his back. She drew back from him, green eyes bright behind heavy lids. "You were smart today. You were *strong*. It suits you." Her eyes smoldered brighter. "I like the way it looks on you."

They kissed again, slow and heated. Then he smiled, and said, his lips brushing hers, "Race you there."

Kitai's eyes danced. Then she elbowed him aside, sending him into a brief, tumbling spin as she kicked out her own windstream behind her and dived for the camp.

Tavi laughed and sent himself rushing after her.

Chapter 34

Isana had all but fallen asleep when she was awakened by a trilling vord cry she had never heard before. The ululating wail rose and fell so swiftly that it almost seemed a chattering sound. Odder still, it rang through the quiet green light of the hive with ear-piercing intensity.

Isana sat on the floor at Araris's feet, leaning back against the cushionlike warmth of the *croach*. Both the wall and the floor sank gently beneath her as she sat reclined, essentially forming a couch under her. In point of fact, it was actually quite comfortable as long as one did not dwell upon the fact that it might at any time engulf and dissolve one's flesh.

Isana opened her eyes only enough to be able to see, and remained silent and still.

The Queen came out of her little sunken bower-alcove in a darting motion that reminded Isana of a spider, rushing out of its funnel-shaped web to seize helpless prey. She crouched at the side of a shallow pool of water—or what Isana assumed was water—on the opposite side of the hive. Her rigid-looking lips peeled back from black chitin teeth, and she let out a furious hissing sound, staring down at the pool.

The Queen was looking at a watercrafted image, Isana thought. Which meant that the pool wasn't simply a water-filled dimple in the floor. It was connected, somehow, to the water system of the surrounding area, where furies would be able to bring images and sounds.

Quiet footsteps sounded, and Invidia entered. She made some irritated gesture at one of the walls, and the ear-tearing wail ended. "What has happened?"

"My progenitors have arrived," the Queen murmured softly.

"That's impossible," Invidia said. "The attack is about to begin. You cannot divert your attention now."

"Not impossible, obviously," the Queen said, a very faint tinge of displeasure in her tone.

The creature on Invidia's chest rippled. She closed her eyes, and her cheeks lost all color for a moment.

"I suppose he could have been flown from Antillus in that time," Invidia said, much more quietly. "Where is he?"

"In Riva," the vord Queen said distantly. "Destroying the food stores."

Invidia lifted her eyebrows. Or rather, where her eyebrows should have been, had they not been seared off. Her skin was still a patchwork of burned flesh. The scars, Isana thought, would surely be permanent. Not even a watercrafter of Invidia's skill could remove them now, days after she received the burns. "The larder . . . but we needed the supply line from Riva to feed the warriors."

The Queen lifted her dark, multifaceted eyes and stared coldly at Invidia.

Invidia folded her arms. "Your anger does not change the fact that the horde cannot possibly find enough food to support active operations."

The Queen's expression darkened more. Then she raised a hand and waved it vaguely at the air. "I will send a portion of the force into sleep. They will not require food. I will mark out the smallest warrior in every group of ten."

Invidia looked slightly ill. "You're feeding them upon their own?"

The Queen went back to staring at the pool. "It is necessary. They are the least useful soldiers at the moment. It will be done before the assault, so that they can maintain their activity levels." Her mouth twitched a tiny bit at one corner. "And after, there will be other sources available."

"You cannot sustain a campaign without supplies," Invidia said.

"I do not need to sustain a campaign," the Queen replied calmly. "All I need to do is break them, here, in this valley. Once the Alerans are broken here, they are broken forever. If I lose every warrior, drone"—she paused to glance at Invidia—"and slave under my command but accomplish that, it will be well worth it."

"I understand," Invidia said, frost edging her words.

The Queen remained calm and remote. "Anger will not change the fact that the most intelligent course of action, in your position, is to go forth and position your fellow slaves in such a fashion as to maximize the cost for the Alerans to neutralize the warriors with furycraft."

Invidia was silent for a long moment before she said, calmly, "Of course." She turned to leave.

"Invidia," the Queen said.

The burn-scarred woman paused.

"You are not replaceable," the Queen said quietly. "I will therefore sacrifice you the most reluctantly. I would prefer it if you took whatever action you could to avoid becoming the victim of chance."

"Since we are being candid," Invidia said, "I must tell you that my motivations for cooperation are somewhat diluted by the fact that I am fully aware that when you no longer have a use for me, you will dispose of me."

The vord Queen tilted her head, her expression pensive. Then she nodded slowly. "Nearly one million freemen have come to me wearing the green," she said. "They are being sheltered and fed, and I will honor the bargain I offered them. It might reduce the amount of disruption if, when the organized Aleran resistance is broken, they are governed by one of their own. Someone who understands reality." She paused, and added, "I suppose it might prevent needless suffering. Preserve lives that would otherwise be lost. If that matters to you."

Invidia narrowed her eyes. "Are you making me that offer?"

The Queen nodded. "I am. Our partnership has been mutually profitable. I see no reason why it should not continue at the conclusion of hostilities. Survive, serve me well, and it will be so."

Invidia was silent for a moment. She looked away from the Queen, and Isana saw her bow her head. There was a flash of emotion from the burned woman, of fear and elated hope and bitter shame.

"Very well," she whispered.

The vord Queen nodded. "Go."

Invidia left the hive.

Several moments later, the vord Queen said, "I know you didn't sleep through that noise, Isana."

"I thought it would be more polite not to disturb you," Isana said.

"You thought you might gain information covertly," the Queen said. "It was a sensible attempt to attain some small measure of advantage." She stared down at the pool for a moment, and murmured, "Your son has grown."

Isana's heart seemed to skip a beat as a sudden pang went through her chest. "I assume you do not mean physically."

"His tactical furycraft is impressive. Less subtle and complex than Sextus's talents, but applied with greater flexibility and intelligence."

Isana swallowed. "You're trying to hurt him."

The Queen looked back at Isana, her expression surprised. "Of course."

Isana carefully did not grind her teeth or show the vord fear or rage. "But you have not succeeded."

"Yet," said the Queen, "there was a very low order of probability that this attempt would succeed. That was not its purpose."

"A sensible attempt to attain some small measure of advantage," Isana said.

"Precisely." She studied the pool's surface. "Thus far, I estimate my own strength to be the greater by a considerable margin."

"Unless he's holding something back," Isana said, primarily to plant doubt in the Queen's mind.

The Queen smiled. "Always a possibility."

Isana chewed on her lower lip for a moment, then asked, "May I see him?"

"If you wish."

Isana rose carefully. Her dress was beginning to smell almost as untidy as it looked. No, she decided. *She* was beginning to smell almost as bad as the dress looked. Her hair must look a fright. How many days had it been since she had bathed or changed clothes? There was no way for her to tell.

As she approached the pool, she saw a ghostly image appear deep within it, one that grew brighter and clearer as she drew closer to the Queen. It showed a large field of fallen stones and ruined buildings. There were warrior-vord corpses all over it. The Queen waved a hand, and suddenly the vord sprang back to life and were surrounded by the blurred form of *legionares*. An instant later, the wall rose up again, colored oddly green, then a slender young man stood before the city gates of Riva.

"This is what he did no more than an hour ago," the Queen murmured. "The image becomes too indistinct to be useful as his Legion closes to battle. These events transpired just prior."

Isana watched in awe as her son, tall and proud, tested his will against the furycrafted fortress and reduced it to rubble. She watched as the enemy came forth to kill him and found only death instead. She watched as the Legions marched up to the city and hammered into the vord. She watched her son cast his defiance into the teeth of the enemy who had all but destroyed Alera—and emerge victorious. Her heart pounded hard with terrified pride, with worry, with hopeful anxiety.

Her child. Septimus's child.

"If only you could see him, my lord," Isana whispered, closing her eyes against sudden tears.

"Was it difficult?" the Queen asked a moment later.

Isana willed her tears away with a simple watercrafting and opened her eyes again. "Was what difficult?"

"Rearing the child without the aid of your mate."

"At times," Isana said. "I had help. My brother. The other folk at his stead-holt."

The Queen looked up from the foggy haze that had enveloped the pool's image. "It is a collective effort, then."

"It can be," Isana said. "Was it difficult for you?"

The Queen tilted her head inquisitively.

"Bringing forth this horde without the aid of subordinate queens," Isana clarified.

"Yes."

"Would it not make it easier to use your warriors effectively if you had the help of more queens?"

"Yes."

"And yet you have not created more."

The Queen turned her young-seeming face back to the pool, troubled. "I have tried," she said.

"But you cannot?"

"I can create them." The Queen's face became puzzled, wounded. It was a child's expression. "They all try to kill me."

"Why?" Isana asked.

For a moment, she thought the Queen wasn't going to answer. When she spoke, her voice was very small. "Because I have been changed. Because I do not function in the manner which their instincts tell them I should."

A slow wave of sadness and genuine pain washed out of the vord Queen. Isana had to fight to remind herself of the destruction and death brought by this creature to all of Carna.

"That's why you left Canea and returned here," Isana said suddenly. "Your junior queens turned upon you, so you escaped them."

As she sat beside the pool, the Queen drew her knees up to her chest, wrapping her arms around them. "I did not escape them," she replied. "I merely postponed the confrontation."

"I don't understand," Isana said.

"The continent across the sea called Canea has been overrun," the Queen said in a quiet monotone. "But it will take decades, perhaps centuries, for my children to consolidate and fully exploit their new territory—to make it impregnable. Once that is done, and they have a secure base of operations, they will come here to destroy me and everything of my creation. Already their forces have grown to an order of magnitude beyond mine."

The Queen turned her eyes to Isana. "That is why I am here. That is why I must destroy you, I must create my own stronghold if I am to survive. That, too, is a task requiring many years." She rested her chin upon her knees, closed her eyes, and whispered, "I wish to live. I wish for my children to live."

Isana stared down at the monstrous child's genuine sorrow and fear, and fought against the pity the sight and sense of her evoked. She was a monster, nothing less—even if she might also be something more.

The Queen rocked back and forth, a tiny and distressed motion. "I wish to live, Isana. I wish for my children to live."

Isana sighed and turned to walk back to her place beside Araris. "Who doesn't, child," she murmured. "Who doesn't."

CHAPTER 35

From the beginning of the Vord War, the enemy had, time after time, attacked positions that were not ready to defend against a threat of the magnitude they represented. Despite the desperate attempts to warn Alera of what was coming, no one listened, and as a result, the vord had driven the Alerans from their fortresses and cities alike, one after the next. Time after time, the lightning-swift advance of the vord or the inhuman tactics they used had overwhelmed the insufficiently prepared defenders. Time after time, the light had dawned upon a world more and more thoroughly dominated by the invaders—but this dawn was different.

The Calderon Valley was ready to fight.

"There's a dent in it somewhere," growled Antillus Raucus, slapping one paw back at the ornate lorica covering his right shoulder. "It isn't moving right."

"You're imagining things," High Lord Phrygius answered. "There's no bloody dent."

"Well, something's not right."

"Yes," said High Lord Placida in a patient tone. "You slept in it again. You aren't young enough to keep doing that, Raucus. You've injured your shoulder joint, likely."

"I'm young enough to toss your short ass right off this wall," Raucus snapped back. "We'll see whose joint gets injured."

"Boys, boys," Placidus Aria said. "Please don't set a bad example for the other children."

Ehren, standing well behind the High Lords, was too self-contained to smile. But he rocked back and forth on his heels in silent amusement before turning his head to cast a wink at Amara.

She rolled her eyes at him in response and stepped up to stand beside Lady Placida. They stared out at the wide-open plain rolling out of the mouth of the Calderon Valley, a sea of gently rising and falling green. The sun had risen bright, the day fair. Crows had been wheeling overhead for days, first in dozens, then hundreds, and now in thousands. They cast a steady stream of flickering shadows over the earth. The enemy had used them to drop takers into Aleran defensive positions before—now any such attempt would be thwarted by the earth furies on constant patrol among the Aleran forces, which had created a side benefit of all but exterminating the rats, slives, and other vermin that tended to haunt garbage piles around a Legion position.

Let the vord try to use the crows against them again. Calderon was ready.

"Countess," Lady Placida said. "I believe I heard Lady Veradis tell you to sleep for at least twelve hours."

"Which is ridiculous," Amara replied. "It was just a broken wrist."

"And several injuries from Riva, I believe," Lady Placida said.

"She only told me twelve because she knew I needed six," Amara said.

"A most excellent rationale."

"Thank you," Amara said gravely. After a moment, she said, "I have to be here. He still can't talk very clearly. Interpreting for him could be important."

"I understand," Lady Placida said. She turned to face Amara, her lovely face calm and hardly showing the weariness Amara knew she had to be feeling. "Countess . . . should we win this battle, not all of us are going to survive it. Should we lose, none of us will."

Amara glanced away, out at the plain, and nodded.

Lady Placida took a step forward and put a hand on Amara's shoulder. "I am just as mortal as anyone else. There is something I would say to you, in case there's not another chance."

Amara frowned and nodded.

"I owe you my life, Countess," Aria said, simply. "It has been my honor to have known you."

Tears stung Amara's eyes. She tried to smile at the High Lady, stepped closer, and embraced her. "Thank you. I feel the same way."

Lady Placida's hug was nearly as strong as Bernard's. Amara tried not to wheeze.

Lord Placida had approached as they spoke, and he smiled briefly as they both turned to him. "In point of fact, dear, all of us owe her our lives."

Aria arched an imperious eyebrow. "You are not going to hug the pretty little Parcian girl, you goat."

Placida nodded gravely. "Foiled again."

From perhaps twenty feet down the battlements, a *legionare* pointed to the southwest, and cried, "Signal arrow!"

Amara turned to see a tiny, blazing sphere of light reaching the top of its arc and beginning to fall. Thousands of eyes turned to follow the firecrafting on the arrow, blazing so bright that it could be seen clearly even under the morning sun. No one spoke, but sudden tension and controlled fear lanced up and down the length of the wall like a lightning bolt.

"Well," Antillus Raucus said. "There it is."

"Brilliant last words," Phrygius said beside him. "We'll put them on your memorium. Right next to, 'He died stating the obvious.'"

"Ah," Lord Placida said. "It begins."

"See?" Phrygius said. "Sandos knows how to go out with style."

"You want to go out with style, I'll strangle you with your best silk tunic," growled Antillus.

Amara found herself letting out a breathless laugh, very nearly a giggle, despite the fear running through her. The fear didn't go away, but it became easier to accept. Her husband, his holders, the *legionares* assigned to him and, over the last months, some of the most powerful members of the Dianic League had been working to prepare this place for this very morning.

Time, then, to make it all worthwhile.

"I must join my husband," Amara said firmly. "Good luck, Aria."

"Of course," Aria replied. "I'll try to keep the children here from fighting each other instead of the vord. Good luck, Amara."

Amara called upon Cirrus, stepped off the wall, and rose into the air. She glided a swift mile down the wall, over a river of men clad in steel, morning light flashing off the polished metal as surely and brightly as if from water. Drums below began rattling the signal to stand ready, so many of them that it sounded to Amara like the rumble of a distant thunder.

Other couriers and messengers were darting up and down the wall, in the air and mounted upon swift horses. Amara narrowly avoided a collision with another flier, a panicked-looking young Citizen in armor too large for him, who called a hasty apology over his shoulder as he struggled to maintain his own windstream. She did not think he looked old enough to attend the Academy, much less serve as a courier in a war.

But he could fly, and the vord had taken away the Alerans' ability to spare their young from the deadly realities at hand. At least he'd been given a duty he could perform rather than simply being relegated to the ranks of Knights Aeris.

Amara arrowed neatly down to the command group, positioned at the center of the wall's north–south axis. Her landing hardly stirred the capes of the elite Knights Ferrous and Terra serving as bodyguards for the command staff. Evidently, word of how she had dealt with the young idiot outside the Princeps' tent had spread, at least enough to ensure that she would be readily recognized. The leader of the contingent was waving her past before she'd settled her weight completely onto her feet again.

Amara brushed past them with a nod, settling her own sword a little more comfortably on her hip. She had declined the offer of a suit of lorica. A body had to be conditioned to bear its weight over the course of months of effort, and Amara had not had that kind of time to spare. Instead, she wore a far-more-comfortable leather coat lined with small plates of light, strong steel. It would almost certainly preserve her hide against an arrow or the slash of a scalpel-edged dueling blade.

Pity the vord didn't fight with either of those weapons.

Amara strode forward to the low observation platform built upon the wall in lieu of an actual tower and mounted the steps to it rapidly.

"I'm simply saying that it's the sort of thing that one can't take too seriously," High Lord Riva was saying. The rather dumpy Lord of Riva looked a bit out of place in Legion lorica, finely made as it might be. "Bloody crows, man," he sputtered. "You've built a bloody campaign fortress right in my own backyard!"

"Good thing I did, too," Bernard said mildly, through his stiffened jaw.

Lord Riva scowled, and said, "I never even appointed you. Bloody Sextus did it, interfering old busybody."

"Mmhmm," Bernard agreed. "Good thing he did, too."

Riva gave him a harsh look that faded quickly as he let out an exasperated sigh. "Well. You tried to warn us about the vord, didn't you?"

"We're all trying to do our best to serve the Realm and our people, sir," Bernard said. He turned and smiled at Amara as she joined them. "My lady."

She smiled and touched his hand briefly. "Shouldn't we sound battle positions?"

"Enemy isn't here yet," Bernard said, his voice placid. "Men stand around with swords in their hands for a few hours, they get nervous, tired, start wondering why some fool gave the order for no reason." He winced and touched his fingertips to his jaw as the effort of so many words pained him. "Won't hurt to wait. Excuse me."

Bernard turned to walk down the wall to the elderly man in Legion armor and a centurion's helmet, his trousers emblazoned with not one, but two scarlet stripes of the Order of the Lion. He muttered a couple of words, and old Centurion Giraldi, out of retirement and back in his armor, nodded stolidly and began dispatching couriers.

"Countess," Riva greeted her, "when a lord raises a great fortress in his liege lord's hinterlands, it's perfectly reasonable to be suspicious. Look what happened at Seven Hills. I don't think I'm out of line, here."

"Under most circumstances, you wouldn't be, Your Grace. But given our situation, I'd say that this is something we can discuss when this is all over. We can even have a hearing over it. Assuming any legates survive."

Riva grunted, rather sourly, but conceded the point with a nod. He stared out to the southwest, his gaze following the line of the causeway that led back to Riva. "My city taken. My people fleeing for their lives, dying. Starving." He looked down at his armor, at the sword on his belt, and touched it gingerly. When he spoke again, he sounded like a very tired man. "All I've ever wanted for my lands was justice, prosperity, and peace. I'm not much of a soldier. I'm a builder, Countess. I was so pleased with how many folk were moving through the lands to trade, with how much good work you and your husband had done in Calderon. Increasing trade. Building goodwill with the Marat." He looked at her mildly. "I assumed that you were saving the money you were making, after taxes. Or investing it, perhaps."

"Oh, we *were* investing it, my lord," Amara said, smiling faintly. "In this morning."

Riva pursed his lips and nodded. "I suppose I can hardly argue with that. How did you do all this? How did you keep it hidden?"

"The walls?" Amara shrugged. "Most people who pass through the valley never leave the causeway. Anything out of sight of the causeway is not difficult to conceal. For the walls, most of the work, as I understand it, is preparing the earth beneath, first. Gathering the proper stone and so on. Once that is done, the raising of the walls is much simpler."

Riva frowned and nodded. "True. So you aligned the proper stone over time and only brought them up as you needed them."

"Yes. The Dianic League was most useful in helping us with that, as well as with some of the more serious stone-moving craftings." She gestured out at the land before them. "And the walls are only the beginning of the defenses, of course. A skeleton, if you see what I mean."

Lord Riva nodded. "It's . . . all quite irregular."

"My lord husband and his nephew have been exchanging ideas for it by letter for quite some time. Gaius Octavian has a rather irregular turn of mind."

"So I have gathered," Riva said. He looked at Bernard, and said, "I have to admit, I think he's probably the right choice for running the defenses here. He knows them better than anyone else in the Realm, after all."

"Yes, he does," Amara said.

"Rather remarkable man, really. Do you know, he's never once said, 'I told you so.'"

"He isn't the sort to think such things are important," Amara said, smiling. "But, Your Grace . . . he told you so."

Lord Riva blinked at her, then let out a rueful chuckle. "Yes. He did, didn't he?"

"Riders!" cried a lookout at the corner of the tower, pointing.

The Aleran pickets who had been watching for the approach of the vord appeared at the top of a distant hill, riding their horses hard down its slope and onto the open plain. Vordknights swarmed over them like night insects around a furylamp, sweeping down to strike and rake, while arrows leapt up from the scouts, with only limited success in warding away the attackers.

"Those men are in trouble," Riva said.

Bernard raised his fingers to his lips and let out a piercing whistle. He lifted his hand to the Knights Aeris waiting behind the wall and gave them the flier's hand signals for "lift off," "escort," and with a slashing movement of his wrist indicted the direction they were to travel.

In a roar of wind, thirty Knights Aeris swept into the sky and shot toward the riders, to begin herding the vordknights from the fleeing horses with the blasts of their windstreams. They sent the enemy fliers tumbling for a moment or two, not closing to weapons range when they could simply scatter the enemy through the sky like so many dry leaves. They took up position over the scouts, circling protectively above them in an airborne carousel.

Bernard grunted satisfaction. "Like what Aquitaine did at Ceres. No reason to fight the bloody things and lose valuable Knights Aeris. Just get them out of the bloody way."

The vordknights retreated after a desultory pursuit in which they were simply cast back and completely neutralized by the windstreams of the fliers. The riders came thundering in through a gate crafted into the wall near the command platform. The leader of the riders, a man wearing a woodsman's green and brown and grey leathers, swung down from his horse and moved with quick purpose toward Bernard, throwing him a crisp Legion salute though he wore neither armor nor sword. Rufus Marcus had been part of the cohort of *legionares* who had first encountered the vord, years ago, as well as being a survivor of Second Calderon. Like Giraldi, he wore two stripes of the Order of the Lion on his breeches, though they had been so thoroughly muddied that one could hardly tell that they had originally been red.

Bernard returned the salute. "Tribune. What are we looking at?"

"Flyboys had it pretty well, sir," Rufus replied. "I make it better than three million of their infantry coming, and they aren't being subtle about it. They're in close order, sir, not like the packs they move in out in the countryside."

"That means . . . that means that this Queen of theirs is present," Riva said, looking back and forth between them. "Correct?"

"Aye, milord," Bernard said. "Or so we think."

"Sir," said the scout, "they've also got a good many of those giants they used for wall work during the campaign last year."

Bernard grunted. "Figured they would. Anything else?"

"Aye. We couldn't work around to the back, but I'm sure they had something coming along behind the main body. They weren't kicking up any dust with all the rain we've had of late, but they were drawing crows."

"Second force?" Bernard said, frowning.

Amara said, "A guess—a pack of prisoners that they plan to feed to their takers and use to counter our crafting, the way they did at Alera Imperia."

Tribune Rufus nodded. "Could be. Or it could be they called their fliers back together to have them in numbers. We've only seen a few. Maybe they're keeping them on the ground to prevent us spotting them."

"We'll be able to handle vordknights," Bernard said tightly. "It's probably best to assume that they're coming with something we haven't seen before."

The scout took a swig of water from a mostly empty skin. "Aye. Almost always a solid bet. I don't think the vord have much of a bluff. The way they're coming on, they think they've got themselves a good hole card."

"Do you still play cards, Tribune?" Amara asked, idly amused.

"Oh, aye." Rufus grinned. "Mostly why I stay in the Legions, Countess. When those townies and wagon guards lose, they figure they don't want to scuffle with me and five thousand other fellas."

Rufus finished the water in his skin, his eyes on the horizon from which he had recently appeared. A moment later, he grunted as if someone had punched him in the belly, and said, "Time to place our bets."

Amara turned to see the vord pour over the horizon.

Again she was struck by how much it was like watching the shadow of a cloud wash over the land. There were so many of the mantis-form warriors, moving together, that they seemed like a single entity, a carpet of gleaming green-black armor, of slashing edges and piercing points. Amara almost felt that she would cut her finger if she pointed at them.

The leading vord poured down over the hilltop—and the horde began to spread. More forms came rolling over *every* hilltop Amara could see, from horizon to horizon, all moving together, dressing their line as they went until, in the last mile, they all came rushing forward together, in a vast and single wall of terrible purpose. More eerie still, it happened in complete silence. There was not a shriek or a cry, no rattle of drum, no blaring of horns. They simply came on like the shadow of a cloud, and every bit as unstoppable. The silence was horrible. It made them seem somehow unreal in the bright light of morning.

Bernard stared at them intently, then nodded. Beside him and slightly to one side, old Giraldi raised his voice in a parade-ground bellow. "Draw steel!"

His voice carried up and down the wall in booming clarity in that perfect silence—and then more than one hundred and fifty thousand swords whispered from their sheaths. The sound of it, far more deadly than any rustling of leaves in the wind, which it resembled, flowed up and down the wall. Amara realized, with faint surprise, that her own weapon was in her hand.

They were ready, she realized.

They were *ready*.

She never consciously decided to shout, but she suddenly felt her voice rising, trumpet-clear in the morning light, as she cried out her scorn and defiance toward the enemy, a simple howl of, "Alera!"

The echoes of her voice rolled over the silent land.

Sudden thunder shook the stones of the wall, shook the ground itself, as every soul on the wall, every single defender now standing against that dark tide, added their own terror and fury to the air. There was no one theme to the shout, no one word, no single motto or cry—but the Legions spoke in a single *voice* that sent a violent elation through Amara's limbs and made the sword in her hand feel lighter than the air she mastered.

That shout of defiance crashed into the vord lines like a physical blow, and for an eyeblink the enemy advance slowed—but then it was answered with a mind-splitting storm of shrieking vord cries, painful to the body, the mind, and the soul. The enemy rushed forward at a full sprint over the last several hundred yards of ground before the wall, blackening the earth as far as the eye could see, their cries answering the defenders.

And born of that primal, furious thunder, the last battle of the war, perhaps the last of the Realm, began.

CHAPTER 36

The Legions screamed their defiance of the vord, and Ehren couldn't keep himself from joining them, out of nothing but raw reflex and naked terror. On some level, he was fairly sure that not many of the vord would be intimidated by the way his voice cracked, but it wasn't as though he could control that. Fear might not have been strangling him, precisely, but it had apparently caused his throat to revert to puberty.

Somewhere nearby, a centurion bellowed something that went completely unheard in all the noise. Fortunately, the *legionares* knew their work well enough without any such command. As the enemy closed, an Aleran-borne shadow passed over the ground before the wall, and more spears than a body could count in a week flew out to come sailing down into the front ranks of the vord. The spears weren't particularly deadly, in and of themselves. They might have scored one kill in fifty, by Ehren's estimation, one kill in thirty, tops—but every vord struck by one of the heavy weapons staggered in pain. Even if the wound was not fatal, the vord's pace faltered, and it was swiftly trampled by the warriors rushing along behind.

The volley was devastating to enemy cohesion, and an old standard Legion tactic.

But, this being a battle plan Tavi had a hand in, it didn't stop there.

The artisans of the Calderon Valley hadn't been able to provide every single *legionare* on the wall with one of the modified javelins—only the most skilled man of each spear of eight had been given the new designs. More often than not, the spears that had killed a vord outright had been thrown by those men—and every single one of the new spears contained a small sphere of glass, nestled into the cup of the javelin's iron head, where the wooden shaft joined it. Whether the javelins missed and struck the earth or hit home, thousands of tiny glass spheres shattered, unleashing the furies that had been bound within.

Ehren himself had field-tested the firestones, furycrafted devices developed from the coldstones used to keep food chilled in restaurants and wealthy households around the Realm—another innovation sprung from the tricky, twisty labyrinth Octavian had for a brain. The glass spheres could contain even more heat for their size than the first generation of stones could, and they were far easier to make.

Destruction was almost always easier to manage than something useful, Ehren reflected.

The fire-javelins exploded together in a roar, each bursting into a sudden sphere of flame the size of a supply wagon. It wasn't the white-hot fire of a Knight Ignus's attack, but it didn't have to be. The fire engulfed the front two ranks of the enemy and sucked so much air in to feed its short-lived flame that Ehren's cloak was drawn up against his back and legs, snapping as if he stood with his back to a strong wind. Greasy black smoke billowed out, the smell indescribably foul, and for a few instants, the vord line was thrown into complete disarray.

Ehren cried out and slapped Lord Antillus on the shoulder. There was no need for the signal. The large, athletic man was already throwing himself forward along with the Placidas and Phrygius.

The most powerful and dangerous High Lords of Alera rose together in a sudden column of wind and plunged through the black cloud and out over the enemy force, moving almost too quickly to be seen, and vanished behind a wind-crafted veil as they went. Ehren clenched his hands into fists and stared after them, trying to see through the mass of *legionares* in front of him. Their mission had been his idea. He bore a measure of responsibility for its outcome.

The vord recovered their momentum in seconds, those coming behind the first wave leaping over the slain and wounded. Their scythes gouged the stone of the wall, creating pitted spots that their insectlike legs could use to climb, and they swarmed fearlessly up the wall and into the swords of the Legions.

Men and vord shrieked and howled. Swords flashed in the sun. Vord scythes plunged. Blood, both red and dirty green, spattered the wall, which might have been a fallen log for all the attention the vord paid to it—but it did prevent them from employing their reach or their downward-stabbing scythes to the best effect. They came on in endless pressure, while the *legionares* fought on, with men forward on the wall fighting with shield and sword, their comrades behind them thrusting with longer spears. The vord would gain the wall, in places, only to be pushed back savagely by the Legions.

More and more of the creatures poured in, like a deadly, living tide, rushing in over the ground to wash against the wall. Wave after wave broke upon the low siege wall, upon Legion steel and Aleran blood. And, like an oncoming tide, the pressure only grew. The vord were climbing over one another in their eagerness to reach the *legionares*, and the growing number of bodies below the wall were forming ramps up to the top.

The breaking point was near. Within a few moments more, the vord would gain a foothold on the wall, somewhere, and would begin pouring over it in the thousands. The enemy sensed it as well. More and more of the vord pressed closer to the wall. Ehren could have stepped off the wall and walked a mile without touching the ground.

It was time.

He turned and nodded to the armored old Citizen on his left. "Now?"

Lord Gram had been watching the attack with his helmet off. His hair had been bright red in his youth, but was now mostly grey, with only a few lone, defiant sprigs showing a ruddy hue. He nodded and took his helmet from beneath his arm and settled it onto his head. "Aye. Pack them in any closer, and they'll overflow the wall."

"Should we send up the signal?" he said. Once a signal went up, it would propagate along the wall from one firecrafter to the next.

Gram grunted, scowling. "Wait for the order, boy. All we're looking at is what's right in front of us. That's our job. Bernard is looking at the whole picture. That's his job. He'll give the order when it's time."

A vord gained the wall not twenty feet away, a screaming *legionare* skewered on one of its scythes. It batted away a second *legionare* like a toy, then died under the massive maul wielded by a Knight Terra who rushed to plug the breach—but three of its companions had reached the top of the wall in the time that took to happen and drove outward. More vord would join them in a few seconds.

"Lord Gram?" Ehren called. His voice cracked again.

"Wait!" Gram thundered back.

Count Calderon would wait to signal the next phase of the plan until as many of the enemy as possible were in position. Ehren knew that. He also knew that as a commander of a battle this critical, Calderon would be willing to sacrifice the lives of some of the defenders if necessary. He had to be. That was the entire reason to have battle commanders in the first place—so that one man could balance the advantages of logic and reason against the emotional, insane demands of close battle.

It was just that, at the moment, with three vord having mounted the wall and with, oh dear, one of them looking directly *at* him, it did not seem to Ehren like a sound approach to warfare. He also suddenly thought that it would have been a fine idea to have accepted the set of lorica he had been offered yesterday. Thirty or forty pounds of steel over his fragile flesh (which had seemed impossibly cumbersome for the use of a man who was essentially a glorified rapid-messenger boy, a few hours before) suddenly sounded splendid.

A fourth vord appeared at the top of the wall, and Ehren realized that it was too late for the Aleran counterstroke to save them, even if it happened at that instant. They had to retake the wall, and right now, or the vord would kill the men all around him—and quite likely Ehren himself. Worse, they would kill Gram, one of only a few firecrafters with the capability to craft a flame hot enough for the counterstroke. His death was unacceptable.

A block of *legionares* followed the Knight Terra in an attack on the first two vord to reach the top, but the third swept a *legionare* from the wall and into the sea of scythes below it. The man's screams were swallowed as abruptly as if he had fallen into water. The vord's glittering eyes locked onto Ehren, and the mantis-form warrior scuttled forward, scythes flashing.

One of the deadly weapons plunged down at Ehren, who hopped back out of reach, and shouted, "Gram, watch out!" He put a shoulder into Gram's hip and shoved him roughly back from the oncoming warrior.

The movement cost him precious instants and inches. He did not quite evade the mantis warrior's reach, and a darting scythe plowed a bloody furrow down one shoulder blade, skipped a bit where his body arched in instinctive pain and reaction, then bit into him again as it sliced along one buttock.

Ehren staggered and went to one knee, knowing instinctively that he could not possibly remain there and sure that he could not escape the reach of the mantis. The *legionares* were coming, as eager as he had been to close the breach, but they were an endless second away.

Ehren flung himself *backward*, toward the vord, tucking his body into a roll as he went. He felt the scythe flash down at him and miss, digging into the stone of the wall.

Ehren stopped underneath the body of the vord, which began dancing about, trying to thrust its scythes beneath it, but unable to reach him. Ehren reached out a hand toward a fallen *legionare's* spear, which lay nearby. His wood-crafting was nothing to write home about, but it was more than sufficient to bend the haft of the spear a little, and when he released it, to allow its elastic spring to send it clattering into the reach of his hand.

He seized the spear, rolled to one side very quickly, and barely dodged the scythe that plunged down at him from the vord now mounting the wall beside his opponent. Scuttling like a limping crab, Ehren stayed beneath the vord warrior, grasping the spear and once more reaching out for his woodcrafting, until he had bent its shaft into a quivering bow that would have enclosed most of a circle. Then he took a second to decide where to strike and how to aim, grounded the spear's butt against the stone of the wall, and released the woodcrafting.

The spear straightened again, with vicious energy. The sharp tip of the weapon skittered along the vord's armored underbelly—but then the tip bit into the joint between two plates of chitin and plunged into the vord with such force that it lifted its forequarters off the ground. Dirty green-brown blood geysered from the wound, and the vord fell off on the Aleran side of the wall, thrashing in its death throes.

Ehren let out a whoop—but it turned into a scream as something that felt red-hot slammed into his lower back. There was a thumping sound, and his body jerked, and a muscle behind his right shoulder blade went into a sudden, vicious cramp. He tried to move, but something held him fast to the ground. It might have been gravity. He felt very heavy.

He looked over his shoulder, itself an agonizing motion, and saw that the next vord up the wall had leapt onto him as its less fortunate relative fell to the ground. He couldn't see the scythes or where they had pierced him. Thinking about it, he decided, he really didn't *want* to. The pain was bad enough. He didn't need a visual image to go with it.

He couldn't breathe. He just wanted to take a good, deep breath. But he couldn't inhale at all. That didn't seem fair. He laid his cheek on the stone.

There was a bright light, and something warm passed over him, and a vord shrieked.

"Healer!" bellowed Gram.

Ehren blinked open his eyes and looked to the south. There, hovering in the air, was a single brilliant spark of bright red fire.

"No, you idiot, don't pull them out of him," Gram snarled at someone. "He'll bleed out right here."

"But they've got him spiked to the bloody wall," protested someone with a deep, resonant voice.

"Use your head for something besides finding things to smash with that maul, Frederick," Gram answered. "Earthcraft the wall enough to get them loose."

"Oh. Right. Just a second . . ."

Gram was leaning over him, and there were *legionares* back on the wall around them. They must have closed the breach. That was good. Ehren lifted his hand. It shook more than it should have, he thought. "Gram," he gasped, pointing. "Signal."

The old Lord looked back over his shoulder, growled, then rose. He looked up at the sky, took a deep breath, then lifted his hand and sent what looked like a small blue star blazing into the air.

All up and down the wall, other stars answered.

A second star pulsed out from the command post, this one burning white-hot, almost painful to look at even in broad daylight.

Up and down the wall, Ehren knew, firecrafters were doing precisely what Gram was. The old Lord had his eyes focused on the ground in front of the wall, and a pair of *legionares* was covering him from any enemy attack. He concentrated for a moment, then pointed a finger down at the ground below and spoke a single harsh, quiet word. *"Burn."*

A sphere of white fire leapt from Gram's fingertip to the ground below.

For a long minute, nothing happened.

Ehren closed his eyes and pictured it in his mind. Bringing siege walls up from the earth required the moving of quality, heavy stone. But that wasn't the only thing that could be moved. The earth was full of all sorts of interesting minerals. Gold. Silver. Gems.

And coal.

And oil.

Over the past months, the entire plain before the first wall had been seeded with the latter two. Coal had been raised to within inches of the surface—and the much more easily manipulated oil had been brought up to the surface layers of earth, until the ground fairly squelched with it. It was hardly noticeable, given how soft and damp the regular rains had left the ground in the past few days, except for the smell. And the vord did not appear to be bright enough to recognize it.

Oil-filled tubes had been crafted throughout the coal undersurface, with air holes made in them every so often. Then the crafters upon the Aleran walls dropped the fire directly down and into the mouths of those tubes, flames rapidly licking down them.

Thirty seconds later, there was a roar of sound, as the fire fed upon the oil and the air expanded dangerously, rupturing the earth and shattering the flaky sheets of coal into gravel.

Fire screamed and rose, and somewhere above there was the howl of wind, wind, wind. The four Citizens who had taken off were providing the fire with enough air to be born—a veritable cyclone, really.

When it finally did leap up, it was in a roar, and a small cloud of earth and coal and blazing droplets of oil flew up so high into the air that, even lying down, Ehren could see the highest crown of it.

"Bloody crows!" cried a *legionare*, half in terror and half in joy.

Ehren could see it reflected in the young man's eyes. A vast curtain of flame was being drawn across the entire width of the Calderon Valley. Vord were screaming. Vord were dying—hundreds of thousands of them, who had so willingly packed as closely into the wall as possible.

Ehren thought sundown had come remarkably early. Somewhere nearby, a horn was sounding the retreat.

They had never intended to hold the first wall. It was simply too long to mount an effective defense. But the sacrifice and courage of the men who had bled and died at the first wall had let the Alerans cut a gaping wound into the vord's advantage of numbers. Brave young *legionares*. The poor idiots. Thank goodness Ehren would never have passed muster for a Legion, between his size and his lack of useful furycraft. He'd been able to avoid all that nonsense. And he'd helped get some good work done today.

A little voice told him that the vord could afford the losses. Though many had just died, in numbers greater than those of all the Legions of Alera that remained, the vord still had an overwhelming advantage.

Which was why, he mused, there were more surprises waiting for them as they progressed into the Valley. Count Calderon was more than ready to welcome them. He might not be able to stop them—it was possible that no one could. But, by the furies, from listening to the man, they would pay for every breath they took of the Count of Calderon's air before it was over.

Ehren found himself smiling. Then someone was moving him. He smelled the pungent aroma of a gargant. People talked, but he paid them little attention. He was too tired. He thought to himself that if he went to sleep, he might die.

Then again, as tired as he felt, if death was like sleep, how bad could it be?

Perhaps he'd try it for a little wh—

◼◻◻◻◼CHAPTER 37

Amara watched the vord's first assault go up in flames.

It had all worked more or less according to plan. When the firecrafters had lit the oil-lined little tunnels, the flame had rapidly spread down them, out to a distance of about half a mile, creating a steady source of flame. Black smoke had begun oozing up through the air holes.

Then, when the concealed High Lords sent a vast gale of wind sweeping across the plain, they had exploded. The ground erupted with fire and gouts of shattered coal in long lines spaced about twenty yards apart. Oil had splattered everywhere, along with the coal, and within moments the whole plain had been devoured by fire.

Beside her, Bernard peered through the sightcrafting she held between her outstretched hands. He grunted with satisfaction. "Tavi did this at the Elinarch, only backward," he told High Lord Riva.

"How's that?" Riva asked.

"At the Elinarch," Amara said, to spare her husband's jaw, "he heated the

paving stones first, to drive assaulting Canim off them and into the town's buildings. Then he set the buildings on fire."

Riva stared out at the plain of fire before them and shuddered. "Ruthless."

"Indeed," Amara said.

"The boy finishes what he begins," Bernard said. His mouth quirked up at
one corner. "His Highness, the boy."

Riva turned to look at the two of them thoughtfully, frowning. "Do you think
he's really on the way?"

"Said he was," Bernard said.

"But he has so few men."

Bernard snorted. "Boy didn't have anyone but an unarmed slave with him
when he stopped the Marat at Second Calderon." He turned to face Riva and
met his eyes. "He says he's coming to fight, believe him."

Lord Riva stared back at Bernard, his eyes thoughtful. Out on the plain, the
fires had begun to die down—leaving half a mile of red-hot coals underfoot.
The air over the plain wavered madly in the heat. Burning vord chitin smelled
utterly hideous, she noted. There was a dull roar of windstreams overhead as the
High Lords, their task completed, returned to friendly lines.

"Bernard," Amara said quietly.

Her husband glanced out at the plain and nodded. He turned to Giraldi, and
said, "Sound the retreat. We fall back to the next wall."

Giraldi saluted and passed the order along to the trumpeter. Soon, the signal
was echoing up and down the length of the wall. Centurions began barking orders. Men began to withdraw down the stairs leading from the walls and form
into their units. Marat gargants had rolled up a few moments before, their long,
slow steps covering ground rapidly. The wounded were being loaded onto beasts
whose saddlecloths had been prepared to carry hurt men safely.

"Count Calderon," Riva said, his voice becoming somewhat stilted and formal, "I realize that our relationship has been . . . a distant one. And that you have
doubtless already worked very hard to prepare the valley's defenses. Nonetheless, I should like to volunteer my skills and those of my engineers to do whatever we can to help."

Bernard eyed him again.

"I'm not a very good soldier, Your Excellency," Riva said. "But I know about
building. And some of the finest architects and engineers in the Realm ply their
trade in my city."

Bernard glanced at Amara, who smiled very faintly and pretended to be
watching for the enemy.

"Be honored, Your Grace," Bernard said. "Giraldi, here, will show you to

Pentius Pluvus. He's kept books and schedules for us on this project. He'll know where you and your folks can help the most."

Riva offered Bernard his hand. They clasped forearms briefly, and Riva smiled. "Good luck to you, Count."

Bernard answered him with small, sad smile. "To all of us."

Riva and Giraldi departed. Bernard gave orders to the rest of the command staff to begin the retreat to the tower. Amara moved to stand beside her husband and twined her fingers with his. Bernard stared out at the fields of glowing coals. Grass fires had begun at the edges of the burning coal, where the heat had leached the water from the land nearby.

Beyond the curtains of wavering heat, the vord were massing, moving, flowing like a single being with a million limbs. It was impossible to make out any details, beyond the fact that they were there—and that more and more of them kept coming.

Amara shuddered.

"Shouldn't we go?" she asked her husband.

"There's a little time," Bernard said. "That's the beauty of this plan. It does two things at once. Kills the vord and gives us time to fall back to a stronger position."

He fell silent and resumed staring to the west.

Amara said, very quietly, "You're thinking about Isana."

"She's my sister," Bernard said.

"You heard what Ehren said."

Bernard's expression hardened. He clenched his fist and slammed it into one of the low merlons on the wall. A webwork of cracks shot through it. "The Queen has her."

Amara put her hand on his fist and squeezed gently. Bernard closed his eyes and made a visible effort to relax. His fist came unclenched a moment later.

"I hoped this would draw her out," he whispered. "She'd run from a confrontation, but she might lead us back to Isana."

"The vord Queen is anything but stupid," Amara said. "She must know that we plan to kill her."

Bernard grunted. "We've got to make her come out. Show herself. If we can't do that, this is over."

"I know," Amara said quietly. "But so does she."

Bernard rubbed at his jaw again. "How's Masha?"

"According to Olivia, she's frightened," Amara said. "She knows that there's something bad going on."

"Poor thing," Bernard said. "Too bright for her own good."

"For her own peace of mind, perhaps," Amara said. "Not necessarily the other."

He grunted an agreement. "Suppose we shouldn't waste any more time here." He put two fingers to his lips and let out a sharp whistle. The horses they were riding nickered and came trotting over to the stairs nearest them.

Amara eyed him, smiling a little. "How do you do that?"

"It isn't hard," Bernard said. "You just—"

He stopped talking abruptly as a plume of gaseous white vapor suddenly billowed up from the far side of the field of coal. Amara felt her breath catch in her throat as she watched. The plume thickened, doubling in size and doubling again. At its edges, it became translucent.

"Steam," Amara breathed.

"Watercraft?" Bernard murmured. He looked up. Only a few white, innocent clouds raced across the sky, none of them dropping rain. "How?"

Amara frowned, then said, "They must have diverted a river. Like Aquitaine did at Alera Imperia."

Bernard thought it over for a moment, then nodded. "The Little Goose is about a mile and a half past that last hill. Would it be possible to move it that far?"

Amara tried to picture the intervening terrain in her mind, especially elevation. "It shouldn't be," she said. "We must be thirty or forty feet higher here than at the river's nearest point."

The plume doubled and redoubled again, and the rising column of steam began to approach their position on the wall.

Bernard whistled. "Serious crafting. And they did it far enough out so that even if the Queen was in on it, we'd never come within sight of her. Invidia's idea, you think?"

Amara shrugged. "It would take several crafters working together to accomplish this. Water is heavy. To make it move against its nature that way—I'm not sure if even Sextus could have done it."

Bernard spat on the ground in frustration. "I make it maybe three-quarters of an hour before they can walk right on up to the wall again."

Amara shook her head. "Less."

"Figured we had two, three hours at least." Bernard clenched his jaw and turned to descend the steps toward the waiting horses. "We'd better get moving."

CHAPTER 38

Tavi had been tricked.

Kitai, of course, had been in on it.

He hadn't meant to sleep, not with so much work left to do securing the city. But between the recent bleeding for Marok and the enormous effort the fury-crafting of the Rivan gates had required, he had already been exhausted. And Kitai had been particularly . . . he searched his thoughts for the proper descriptive word. "Athletic" didn't seem to convey the proper tone. "Insistent," while an accurate description, fell somewhat short in any but the most objective sense. He decided that his language lacked entirely a word sufficient to the task of describing such hungry, joyous, utterly uninhibited passion.

There had been food, at some point, discreetly left on the wagon's seat. Tavi suspected, in retrospect, that it had been laced with a tiny amount of aphrodin, which would explain both his, ah, extreme focus on the evening as well as the nearly comatose state he'd found himself in afterward.

He looked down at Kitai's hair. As he lay on his back, she was pressed up against his flank, her head pillowed on his chest. Her fine white hair veiled her face, except for the softness of her lips. A strong, slender arm draped over his chest. Her leg was half-thrown over his thigh. She was sleeping heavily, occasionally emitting a sound that an uncharitable (and unwise) person might have called a snore.

Tavi closed his eyes in contentment for a moment. Or perhaps they had simply wanted one another that much. Either way, he couldn't find it in himself to be upset about being given a night's . . . sleep, however duplicitously it had been arranged.

She murmured something in her sleep, and Tavi felt a stirring of vague, flickering emotion from her, rapidly shifting from one feeling to another. She was dreaming. Tavi stroked her hair with one arm and spread his focus, trying to get a sense of the camp around him. If something had gone amiss during the night, there would be some sense of it. And the air itself, the general emotional ambiance in a Legion camp, could tell him a great deal about the state of mind of his soldiers.

There were half a dozen guards posted around the wagon at a distance obviously meant to be discreet, but they couldn't have helped but overhear everything, unless Kitai had remembered to put up a windcrafting. Or one of the men had. Tavi found that fact to be far less embarrassing than he would have a year before.

There were a great many bad things in the world, which perhaps helped put such things into perspective. There was nothing earth-shattering about others knowing that he and Kitai enjoyed one another's company.

The guards were on alert and calm. A pair of valets, nearby, had the sense of men going about routine tasks—making breakfast, then. The general air of the camp was one of anticipation. Fear blended with excitement, rage against the invaders mixed with concern for fellow Alerans. The men weren't stupid. They knew they were about to go to war, but there was not a trace of despair—only anticipation and confidence.

That, by itself, was very nearly the most valuable attribute a Legion could possess. Legion captains had known for years that the expectation of victory breeds victory.

He should get up and get moving, rousing the nearer men, playing the role of a Princeps with boundless power, confidence, and energy. But the simple bedroll felt extremely comfortable. He turned his attention to the warm, relaxed, sleeping presences beside him, and—

Presences?

Tavi sat bolt upright.

"You didn't tell me," Tavi said quietly.

Kitai looked sideways at him, then away. She thrust her arms into the steel-stained padded vest she wore beneath her mail and began to buckle it on.

Tavi pressed gently. "Why didn't you tell me, *chala?*"

"I should never have come here with you," Kitai said, her voice hard. "I should have remained in my own bedroll, alone. Crows take it, I knew you would sense it if we were together. I was weak."

Tavi heard his own voice gain an angry edge. "Why didn't you tell me, Kitai?"

"Because your people are insane about the birth of children," she snarled. "What may happen! What may not happen! When it must happen, and within what order of events! Circumstances over which they had no control whatsoever dictate how they will be treated for the rest of their lives!" She finished buckling the vest and glared at him. "You should know this. Better than anyone."

Tavi folded his arms and met her gaze. "And how did you expect things to be made better by keeping this from me?"

"I . . ." Kitai stopped speaking and slithered into her mail shirt, a task made awkward by the cramped space of the wagon. "I did not wish you to aim your further insanity at me."

"Further insanity?" he demanded. "Don't bother with the armor, Kitai. You won't be using it."

She lifted her chin as she began binding her hair back into a tail. "There? You see? Because I carry our child, you expect me to sit quietly in some stone box until it is time to give birth."

"No," Tavi said. "I expect you to keep our . . ." He tried not to choke over the word. ". . . child . . . *safe*."

"Safe?" Kitai eyed him. "There is no such place, Aleran. Not anymore. Not until the vord are put down. There are only places where it will take longer to die."

Tavi had no real answer to that. He leaned back on his heels and stared at her for a long moment.

"This is why you insisted on a courtship," he said. "On us sleeping apart."

Kitai's cheeks flushed. "It . . . is another reason, Aleran." She swallowed. "There were many reasons."

Tavi leaned forward and offered her his hand.

She took it.

They held hands for a quiet moment.

"Our child," Tavi said.

She nodded, her eyes wide and difficult to read.

"When did you know?"

"Toward the end of the voyage back from Canea," she said.

"How long?"

She shrugged, and for one of the few times in Tavi's memory, failed to look calm and confident. "Six months. If the father was Marat. But our people and yours . . . this has never before happened." She swallowed, and Tavi thought that she looked, in that instant, fragile and beautiful, like a flower coated in ice. "I do not know what will happen. No one knows what will happen."

Tavi sat in total silence for a long moment, trying to get his head around such a simple and enormous truth.

He was going to be a father.

He was going to be a *father*.

A little person was going to come into the world, and Tavi would be his father.

Kitai's fingers stroked over his hand. "Please tell me what you are thinking."

"I'm . . ." Tavi shook his head, at a loss. "I'm thinking that . . . that this changes things. This changes everything."

"Yes," Kitai said in a very small voice.

Tavi blinked, then seized both her hands in his. "Not between you and me, Kitai. This doesn't change that."

She searched his eyes, blinked twice, and a tear rolled down each cheek before she remembered her watercrafting and closed her eyes.

Tavi suddenly drew her hard against him so that he could put his arms around her. "Don't," he said quietly. "Don't you dare think you need to hide them from me."

She turned her face against his chest, and her slender arms suddenly tightened on him. He was abruptly reminded that she was very nearly as strong as he was, despite the difference in their sizes. And she was wearing chain mail. Very chilly chain mail. Tavi winced but didn't move.

Kitai left her face against his chest for a time, and her tears, warmer than his ever were, made his skin damp.

"I did not know what you would do," she said a few moments later, her arms never loosening. "What you would think. We didn't do things in the right order."

Tavi was silent for a long moment. Then he said, "You were worried about our child being thought of as a bastard?"

"Of course," she said. "I've seen Maximus's scars. I saw how mad Phrygiar Navaris became. I've seen others who are . . . who are outsiders. Abused. Because they are not legitimate. As if simply by being born they are guilty of a crime. I did not know what to do."

Tavi was quiet for a time and stroked her hair with one hand. Then he said, "There are two things we could do."

She made a sniffling sound and listened.

"We could arrange things so that the child was not thought of as a bastard," he said.

"How?"

"Oh, we lie, of course. We get married at once and simply say nothing else, and when the child is born we marvel that he—"

"Or she," Kitai interjected.

"Or she must have come early."

"Will that not be found out? A truthfinder would realize that was a story immediately."

"Oh," Tavi said, "everyone would realize it was a story. But no one would say anything about it. It's what is called a 'polite fiction' among people who care about such things. Oh, there might be some sniggering, some remarks made behind our backs, but it wouldn't be seriously challenged."

"Truly?"

"Happens all the time," Tavi said.

"But . . . but it would still be used against the child. Laughed at behind his back. Used to taunt him— "

"Or her," Tavi interjected.

"Or her," Kitai said. "It will forever be a weakness that someone else will be able to exploit."

"That's up to the child, I daresay," Tavi said.

Kitai considered that for a moment. Then she said, "What other thing might we do?"

Tavi gently tilted her head up to look at him. "We do as we please," he said calmly, "and dare anyone to disagree. We give our child all of our love and support, ignore the law where it could hurt him, and we challenge to the *juris macto* anyone who tries to do us harm over the issue. We do something for all the bastard children of the Realm, starting with our own."

Kitai's eyes flashed a brighter shade of green as something fierce kindled to life in them. "We can do this?"

"I don't see why not," Tavi said. "I'm going to be the First Lord, after all. Anyone who is going to turn against me will do it regardless of what excuse they use. Anyone who supports me will do so regardless of what order we did things in."

Kitai frowned at him. "*Chala*," she said quietly, "I do not care about other Alerans. I care about what *you* will think."

He took her hands between hers, and said, "I am told that a Marat woman's custom is to offer a potential mate a trial by contest before The One."

She smiled slowly. "You've been asking about it?"

"The professor who gave me the assignment was most insistent," he said drily. "I have drawn a few conclusions from this fact."

"Yes?" Kitai asked.

"That since the woman chooses the contest, she has ample opportunity to reject her suitor. If she doesn't care for him, she simply selects a contest at which he is unlikely to prevail. Say, a young woman of Horse doesn't care for the attentions of a Wolf suitor, she challenges him to a horseback race."

Kitai's eyes danced, but her tone and expression were both serious. "The One witnesses the contest. The Marat most worthy prevails. This is known, Aleran."

"Of course," Tavi said. "I doubt that The One cares for his children to be forced to mate with those whom they do not desire."

"Many young Marat males would disagree with you quite loudly. But in this, you are very nearly as wise as a Marat woman," Kitai said solemnly. "Not quite. But very nearly."

"I seem to recall a trial by contest between a certain beautiful young Marat woman and a foolish Aleran youth. It was quite a number of years ago, and the trial was held in the Wax Forest near the Calderon Valley. Dimly though I recall such an ancient time, I seem to remember that the young man was victorious."

Kitai opened her mouth to reply hotly, then seemed to think better of it. She let out a rueful chuckle. "Only because the young woman willed it so."

"How is that any different from any other young Marat woman who wishes to accept a young man as a mate?"

Kitai arched an eyebrow at him. "It . . ." She tilted her head. "It . . . is not."

"Well, then," he said. "According to the laws and customs of your people, for which I have the deepest respect, we have been married for a number of years. The child is perfectly legitimate."

Kitai narrowed her eyes, and a smile haunted her lips. "We are *not* wed. That was not a proper mating trial."

"Why not?" Tavi asked.

"Because it was not intended as such!" Kitai said.

Tavi waved a hand airily. "Intentions count for far less than the consequences of the actions born from them. You are my wife."

"I think *not*," Kitai said.

"I know," Tavi said solemnly. "But in this, you are less wise than an Aleran male. Still, one must tolerate occasional fits of irrational passion from one's wife. So in your judgment, what needs to happen to make this a proper mating?"

"A proper challenge!" she replied. "You cannot dare think that . . ." Her voice trailed off, and she said, "Oh."

Tavi arched an eyebrow at her this time and waited.

"You . . ." She looked down. "You truly think the child is . . . that this is all right?"

"Why shouldn't it be?" he replied quietly. He dropped the playful, bantering tone. "Kitai, what does it matter what excuse we use to accept the child? So long as the child is welcomed and loved? Isn't that the important thing?"

"Yes," she said simply. She closed her eyes, and said, "Thank you, Aleran."

"There's nothing to thank me for," he said. Then he touched her chin and lifted her eyes to his. "If our child is to be born, Kitai," he said, in little more than a whisper, "I've got to do everything in my power to protect it. I've got to. I can't do anything else. It is who I am. Do you understand?"

"I understand that you mean to leave me behind," she said softly. "To go into this war alone."

"I must," he said. "Kitai, it would kill me if I lost you. But now, it would kill someone else, too."

She shook her head slowly, never blinking. "I will *not* stay behind, Aleran."

"*Why* not?"

She was quiet for a moment, thinking. Then she said, "Do you remember when I said that the vord could do nothing to us?"

"Yes," he said.

"Do you know why I said it."

"No," he said.

She put her hands on his face, and whispered, "Death is nothing to me, *chala*. Not if we are together. Death is not to be feared." She leaned forward and kissed his mouth, very gently. Then she rested her forehead against his. "Being taken from one another. That terrifies me. It terrifies me. I will go to any wasted wilderness, to any horrible city, into any nightmare to keep you at my side, *chala*, and never flinch. I never have. But do not ask me to leave you. To send you into danger alone. That, I cannot do. That is who *I* am. And that is why I did not tell you. Because I knew who you were."

Tavi inhaled slowly, understanding. "Because both of us can't be true to ourselves. Someone has to change."

"How can we stay together in the face of that?" she asked. There was something desperate in the quiet words. "How can you respect me if I abandon my beliefs? How can I respect you if you abandon yours?"

"And how could either of us respect ourselves," Tavi said.

"Yes."

Tavi took a slow breath. Neither spoke for a long time. The noise of the camp around them was growing louder as it began to get ready for the day's march.

"I don't know what to do," Tavi said. "Yet. But there's time. I'll think on it."

"I've had weeks," Kitai said. "I haven't thought of anything."

"It'll take us another two days, maybe more, to reach Calderon. There's time."

Kitai closed her eyes and shook her head. More tears fell. Tavi could feel a nauseating fear in her he had never felt from her before.

"I'll think of something," he said gently. "Take off the armor."

She hesitated.

"It's all right," he said. "Take it off."

She did, very slowly. Tavi helped her unbuckle the vest. He slid it from her. Then he grasped the hem of her shirt and lifted it slowly. With his hands, he guided her lovingly down onto the bedroll again.

Then, very gently, as if he might shatter her to so many chips of ice if he moved without utmost caution, he laid his hand over her belly, spreading his fingertips over her pale skin until his palm rested against her. The child was too small yet to show to the eye. But he closed his eyes and once more could feel the small, contented presence there, within Kitai's own quiet, controlled terror.

"Can you feel? Have you tried?" he asked her.

"I can't," she said, her voice quietly miserable. "I overheard some mid-wives talking. They said that you can't sense the baby with furycraft when it's in your own body. It's too much like you. And the child is too little to have moved in me yet."

"Give me your hand."

Tavi took Kitai's hand and intertwined her fingers with his. He focused, and his sense of her presence suddenly leapt into something far more vibrant and de-tailed than simple proximity could accomplish alone. He concentrated on her, then upon the little presence, sharing its warmth and peace with Kitai.

Her green eyes went very wide. "Oh," she said. Her eyes filled with tears. "Oh, *chala.*" She suddenly broke into a smile, still weeping, and let out a quiet little laugh. "Oh, that's beautiful."

Tavi smiled at her and leaned down to kiss her very gently.

The three of them stayed like that, in the quiet, just for a little longer, trea-suring that moment. Neither of them said it, but they both knew. Such moments were swiftly growing rarer and rarer.

And, in the next few days, they might even become extinct.

CHAPTER 39

Bernard rode into the command center a few yards ahead of Amara and stopped to look slowly around him. Amara rode up beside her husband, and said nothing.

"Technically," he said, "the old place is still Isanaholt. Elder Frederic hasn't taken his oath yet."

Amara smiled at him. "I still think of it as Bernardholt."

Her husband shook his head. "I wasn't ever really comfortable with that name. Me-holt. Sounded ridiculous."

The steadholt around them was laid out like virtually every other steadholt in the Realm—with a large hall at its center, surrounded by an enormous barn and a number of workshops, homes, and other outbuildings. Unlike most of the Realm, which until recently had enjoyed a much less dangerous climate, every building was made of solid stone, proof against the frequent furystorms that plagued the Valley. It was also surrounded by a defensive wall—not a fortress wall, by any means, and it didn't feature battlements, but it was thick, solid granite and showed no signs of weathering or decay.

Now, the hall, the workshops, and even the barn were all changed. The holders and their stock had long since been evacuated, just as had the seven smaller, newer steadholts that had been founded to the west of them, in what was (or shortly would be) vord occupied territory. It was instead filled with armed and often armored men and women, *legionares*, Citizens, and volunteers. There were perhaps forty or fifty Marat in and about the steadholt as well. A gargant bellowed from the vast barn, where several of the wounded beasts had been quartered out of the weather, to be tended by their Marat handlers and by a trio of old farmhands from the Valley with a gift for husbandry.

Multiple broad staircases were new additions, and ran from the ground up to the steadholt's walls. From there, a number of stone walkways led from the steadholt to the wall proper, a crenellated Legion-standard defensive structure twenty feet high.

Already, *legionares* were pouring up onto the wall, readying the second line of defense. Their march to the wall had been a difficult one. The cohorts stationed nearest the causeway had been able to move rapidly down the Valley, outstripping the pace of their pursuers, who moved in a slow, enormous block that was being steadily compressed by the terrain. Those poor souls who had been on the northern or southern lengths of the wall had been forced to march overland the hard way, without any sort of furycraft to help them, until they had reached the causeway as well. Then they had raced ahead of the pursuing enemy, and they were slogging back out to their positions again. It couldn't have been an easy task for them, to make such a march after spending half of a furious hour in hand-to-hand combat.

But they were Legion. All in a day's work.

"Giraldi," Bernard said as he dismounted. "How much longer before our men are all in position?"

The old centurion saluted. "Within the next few moments, sir."

Bernard nodded. "Everything is prepared?"

"Yes, sir. Except . . ."

"What?" Bernard asked.

"The civilians, sir," Giraldi said, his voice softening. "A lot of them are too old or too young to make use of the causeway. There are a lot of sick and wounded. A lot of confusion. Crows, my lord, there's just a lot of *people*. We haven't been able to get them out of this section of the Valley and behind the last wall yet."

Amara spat a curse and got off her horse, passing the reins to the same valet who had come to take Bernard's. "How long before they're clear?"

"If it happens before midnight, it'll be a miracle."

"It's going to be one long afternoon and evening." Bernard spat. "That tears it. We can't go with the plan if we've got to hold the walls that long." He looked out to the west as if picturing the oncoming foe. "I need to talk to Doroga. Love, please inform the Princeps and ask if he has any suggestions."

From the north, a bright green signal arrow burned as it rose, then fell slowly through the air. A moment later, more of them fell, both in the north and to the south.

"They're here," Amara breathed.

Bernard grunted. "Get moving. Giraldi, sound assembly, let's make sure we're ready to deal with these things. Send runners to the firing lines and spread the word—load the mules."

Giraldi's fist rapped his armor, and he marched away, bawling orders in a voice that could be heard for a mile.

Bernard and Amara touched hands briefly, then each of them turned to their tasks.

Amara hurried to the command post in the great hall. Its doors were heavily guarded, albeit by an entirely different group of men. One of the men challenged her, and she answered him somewhat curtly. The vord's takers were deadly in their fashion, but they could not make the bodies they occupied emit intelligible speech. Amara was high enough in the councils of Aleran command that the challenge was essentially a formality, to ensure she hadn't been taken.

She entered the hall, a very large structure with a fireplace at each end of sufficient size to place an entire cow on a spit over the fire within it. At the far end of the hall, the fireplace had been blocked off by suspended cloths. Another pair of guards stood outside the makeshift chamber. Amara marched over, and said, "I have information for the Princeps. It can't wait."

The taller of the two guards inclined his head. "One moment, lady." He vanished into the chamber, and Amara heard voices. Then he emerged and held the flap open for her.

Amara slipped inside to be greeted by a wave of uncomfortable warmth. The fire in the huge fireplace was taller than she. A bed stood nearby the fire, and Attis lay in it, his face even more pale and drawn than before. He turned his head listlessly toward her, coughed, and said, "Come in, Countess."

She approached and saluted him. "Your Highness. We have a problem."

He tilted his head.

"The evacuation is moving too slowly. We still have a horde of civilians west of Garrison's walls. Our people estimate that it may take until midnight to get them all through."

"Hngh," Attis grunted.

"Furthermore," she said, "the vord somehow managed to divert a river onto the coal plain. The fire held them back for less than an hour. They've been sighted approaching this wall. Signal arrows are rising at all points."

"It never rains." Attis sighed. He closed his eyes. "Very well. Your recommendation, Countess?"

"Keep to the plan, but slow it down," she said. "Use the mules to grind away at them rather than trying to do it for the shock value. Hold the wall until the civilians are safe, then disengage."

"Disengage in the dark?" he asked. "Have you any idea how dangerous a feat that is? The slightest error could turn it into a complete rout."

"Ask Doroga and his clan to hold them off for a time and cover the retreat," she responded. "Those gargants of theirs are natural-born vord-killers, and they're fast enough to stay ahead of the enemy on the way back down to Garrison."

Attis thought about it for a moment, then nodded slowly. "That's likely the best we're going to get, under the circumstances. Make it happen, Countess, on my authority if need be."

"Yes, Your Highness."

He nodded wearily and closed his sunken eyes.

Amara frowned at him and glanced around the room. "Your Highness? Where is Sir Ehren?"

Attis's cheekbones seemed to become even starker. "He died on the wall this morning, while stemming a vord breakthrough."

Amara felt her belly twist. She had liked the young man and respected his skills and intelligence. She could hardly bear to think of him lying cold and dead on the stones of that wall. "Oh, great furies," she breathed.

"Did you know, Countess," Attis said, "whose idea it was for me to present myself as a target back at Riva? Alone and vulnerable to draw out Invidia or the Queen?" His exhausted smile still had a leonine quality to it. "Of course, he didn't phrase it like that."

"Was it?" Amara said quietly.

"Yes. Put forward so diffidently I had to think for a moment to recall that it hadn't been my idea." He coughed again, though it had no energy to it. "No one will ever be able to know for certain, of course," he said. "But I think the little man assassinated me. Barely a fury to his name and . . ." He coughed and laughed as he did it, both sounds dry with exhaustion. "Perhaps that was why he insisted on watching what would happen this morning, when he sent Antillus and the others out to be a bellows for the fire. Because he knew that his suggestion had such power." He waved a hand down at his own shattered body. "Perhaps because he felt guilty to see the results of his actions."

"Or perhaps instead of being a manipulator and assassin, he was simply a loyal servant of the Realm," Amara said.

A wry, bitter smile tugged at his lips. "The two are not necessarily mutually exclusive, Countess."

"He shouldn't have been there. He was never trained as a soldier."

"In a war like this, Countess," Attis said very softly, "there are no civilians. Only survivors. Good people die, even though they don't deserve it. Or perhaps we all deserve it. Or perhaps no one does. It doesn't matter. War is no more a respecter of persons than is death." He was quiet for a moment, then said, "He was more than I have been. He was a good man."

Amara bowed her head and blinked sudden tears away. "Yes. He was."

He lifted a weak hand and waved it at her. "Go. You have much to do."

The vord arrived perhaps a quarter of an hour after Amara emerged from the steadholt's hall. Trumpets sounded. *Legionares* stood ready as engineers finished closing the gates that had been crafted into the walls, until the walls presented a single face of solid granite, its front smoothed to a gleaming finish. She stood beside Bernard upon a tower ten feet higher than the wall. Defensive towers had been spaced every hundred yards down the length of the wall, here a little less than three miles long.

A courier put down upon the tower, briefly kicking up a small gale of wind, and saluted. "Count Calderon, sir."

Bernard didn't take his eyes from the field ahead of him. "Report."

The young man stood there, blinking uncertainly.

Amara sighed and beckoned him. He took a few tentative steps closer.

"There," Amara said, once he was past the windcrafting she was maintaining to keep Bernard's orders from being monitored by enemy crafters. "Can you hear now?"

"Oh," said the courier, flushing. "Yes, ma'am."

"Report," said Bernard in exactly the same tone as before.

The young man looked mildly panicked. "Captain Miles's compliments, sir, and there's a sizeable enemy force moving to the north, sir, to circle around the end of the wall!"

"Hngh," Bernard said. "Thank you."

The young man's eyes widened. "Um? Sir? Captain Miles is afraid that the enemy will turn our flank. There's nearly a quarter mile of open ground at the end of the wall before it reaches the flank of the mountain."

"And that's a problem?"

"Sir!" the courier protested. "The *wall isn't finished, sir!*"

Bernard bared his teeth in a wolfish smile. The leading wave of the vord was now dressing its ranks and preparing to charge. "The wall is exactly what it's supposed to be, son."

"But sir!"

Bernard paused to give the young man a hard look.

The courier wilted visibly.

Bernard nodded. "Return to Captain Miles, give him my compliments, and inform him that he is to stand fast. An allied contingent has been placed to support him should he need it." He paused and looked at the young man. "Dismissed."

The courier swallowed, saluted, then dived off the side of the tower. He managed to call up a windstream just before he hit the ground, then raced away to the north.

Amara looked at Bernard, and said, "Couldn't you have told him more?"

"The fewer who know, the better." He rested his hands on a merlon and nodded calmly as the vord began to move forward in unison. "Giraldi. Signal the mules to stand ready. Section leaders will give the command to begin."

Giraldi's voice bellowed down the wall as the ground began to rumble with the vord's charge. The order was picked up and relayed down the line.

Bernard lifted his hand over his head and watched the oncoming enemy. Once again, as the vord closed to within a few yards, they let out a vast shriek that shook the walls, and once again, their cries clashed with those of the *legionares* upon the battlements. Bernard stood watching the nearest *legionares* intently as they lifted their javelins, and when the first of them threw, he snapped his arm forward, and screamed, "Loose!"

The mules went to work.

Each of the contraptions was built around a boxlike frame. Wooden support struts rose above it, to support a long wooden arm with a shallow bowl at its end. Amara wasn't familiar with the details of the devices, but each arm was drawn back by a crew of two men, who used raw strength and very minor woodcrafting to pull the arm all the way to a horizontal position. A pin, placed in the device, locked the arm back—and when it was removed, the arm snapped forward with startlingly energetic violence. When it did, it carried so much power with it that the entire framework jumped up off the ground at one end, like a cantankerous mule kicking out with its hind legs.

When Bernard dropped his arm, a hundred mules placed in ranks behind the walls kicked up off the ground, sending the contents of their bowls, dozens and dozens of small glass spheres, soaring up over the walls. They leapt up into the air and spread out into a glittering cloud that caught the light of the lowering sun, throwing back sparkles of scarlet, orange, and gold.

Then the fire-spheres struck the earth and burst into globes of hungry fire, *hundreds* of them all at once, spread out over a wide swath of land.

"Bloody *crows!*" screamed a nearby *legionare*.

The fire seemed to ripple out in a long ribbon as each group of mules unleashed its projectiles. Each mule's deadly payload devoured scores and scores of the enemy in clouds of sullen flame, spread out over an area fifty yards across. Indeed, if anything, the mules had been spaced too near one another—there were ample areas of overlap, where the spheres from multiple mules detonated in the same area. Thousands of vord died in the flames, and thousands more were scorched and disabled, wailing and running in circles, mad with pain, lashing out at anything that moved.

Amara stared in purest shock as she realized that she had just watched the world change, radically and forever.

That overwhelming hammerblow upon the vord had not been delivered by an exalted High Lord. No group of Citizens or Knights Aeris had unleashed their wrath upon the vord. Crows, it wasn't even the result of standard Legion battlecrafting. The engines had been shaped here, in the workshops of the holders of the Calderon Valley. Most of the people on their crews were simple holders—nearly half of them were *children*, young men too young to have served their term in the Legions. The spheres, intended only for a single use, rather than the long-term function of the food-cooling coldstones, had been manufactured in the Valley as well, each of them representing perhaps an hour's effort by someone gifted with a modest affinity for firecrafting—and much more quickly by someone with a more substantial gift.

Whatever happened, if Alera survived its latest foe, it could not return to what it had been before. Not when the holders had wielded the power of Citizens. Alera's laws protected freemen to some degree, but they were clearly made to protect the interests of Citizens first and foremost. More than once, Aleran Counts and Lords and even High Lords had faced rebellions from angry freemen—rebellions that were inevitably put down by the superior furycraft of the Citizenry. That was a constant, an immutable fact of Aleran history. The Citizenry ruled precisely because they had access to greater power than any freeman, or any group of freemen.

But that all changed the instant the holders of the Calderon Valley dealt the enemy a blow worthy of the assembled High Lords themselves.

And, less than a minute later, they did it *again*.

The vord warriors came hurtling forward, shrieking their brassy cries and hammering at the base of the wall. Their scythes slashed down onto the smoothed granite, but unlike the stone of the first wall, this wall's material resisted their assault tenaciously. *Legionares* upon the walls took ruthless advantage of the enemy's inability to scale it to meet them. Great cauldrons of boiling oil, water, or scalding-hot sand were poured down onto the mantis warriors. Where such containers were not available, the *legionares* resulted to a more primitive and reliable measure: They simply dropped large rocks onto the enemy.

After the first three massive volleys, the mules began lighter work. Their loads were smaller, and they threw less often. It was the only way they could make the limited supply of fire-spheres last. The resulting attacks were smaller, if no less devastating to the vord hit by them.

It took several minutes for the vord to rush over the havoc the mules had caused in the field before the wall. At first, they arrived in scattered, irregular bunches, easily focused on and destroyed by the wall's defenders. It didn't last. Though an ongoing slaughter was being wreaked upon the vord by Octavian's mules, the vord's strength of numbers seemed undiminished. Soon, they were pressing against the wall again, and if they could not easily create footholds in the wall, their own dead began to pile up into ramps that grew closer and closer to the ramparts.

Bernard watched another flight of fire-spheres go sailing over the wall and nodded his approval. "Great furies, if it didn't work," he said. He shot his wife a quick, fierce grin. "Tavi said they would work when he sent me the plans."

"When was that, again?" Amara asked.

Bernard scratched at his chin, then leaned his forearms on a merlon, casually crossed, like a man gossiping over a stone fence. The pose was intentional, Amara knew. The men around him were looking at him for indications of his state of mind every so often, and he showed them a mask of calm, almost casual confidence. "Three, four months after the Elinarch, I reckon. But I didn't look at them again until he wrote about his idea to use the fire-spheres as ammunition for the mules. So I had Giraldi build one and test it and . . ." He spread his hands demonstratively.

"I know you said they'd be effective, but . . ." Amara shook her head. "I had no idea."

"I know," Bernard said.

"This . . . this is going to change everything."

"Hope so," he said fervently. "Means there's something left standing to change."

Amara looked steadily at him for a moment while his eyes shifted back to the battlefield. He knew. She could see it in his face. He *knew* what the mules represented. Not in and of themselves, of course, but as a symbol for the collective strength of the freemen of Alera—strength that could now be given deadly expression, if need be, now that someone had shown them the way.

The battle raged. Gargants fitted with huge baskets shambled up and down the walls, carrying more stones to the *legionares*. *Legionares* with spears began to fend off the vord as they came within reach of the longer weapons. Occasionally, a Knight Ignus would melt a corpse-ramp into a bubbling pool of slagged, stinking chitin, or a Knight Terra would simply cause it to sink into the soft earth. But they were holding. By the great furies, they were *holding*.

Another flight of fire-spheres went whispering overhead to bring down raging fire on the heads of the mantis warriors, when there was a sudden tremor in the ground, and a distant sound, a roar that rose up like some great beast voicing a warning.

Amara turned her face to the north and looked at the enormous, bleak grey mountain that loomed there, like some unimaginably huge bastion positioned to hold the Legions' flanks. As she watched, she saw clouds of dust billowing forth from the mountain. An entire face of the mountain's slope had apparently given way, causing a rockslide so enormous that it beggared the imagination.

The roll of the land kept her from seeing any details, but it wasn't hard to imagine what had happened. The vord had circled around the end of the second wall, probably hoping to come at the Legions from the rear, or even to proceed toward the civilians back near Garrison. Instead, they had discovered what anyone who lived in the Calderon Valley knew from the time they were old enough to understand speech—that the mountain's name was Garados, and that it did not tolerate visitors.

Amara had known the murderous fury was dangerous, but when she imagined what that meant, she hadn't gotten the right scope of its overwhelming, malevolent power. Clearly, it would seem that Garados was the next best thing to a great fury itself, if not a full-blown superpower in its own right.

"Unbelievable," she murmured.

"Bloody mountain has been a worry and an almighty trial to me for most of twenty-five years," Bernard growled. "About time the thing started pulling its weight."

A few minutes later, a new cry abruptly went up from the vord, a long slow wail that rose and fell in a steady cycle every few seconds. Amara tensed and leaned forward onto the merlon beside her husband, watching the enemy intently.

The vord rushed about, swirling in ranks past and through one another, falling into some sort of unthinkable, alien order and . . .

And *withdrew*.

"They're running!" screamed a *legionare*.

The men on the wall went berserk with defiance and triumph, screaming imprecations after the retreating vord and raising their weapons into the failing light of the sun. While they did, the vord continued to fall back, and within a few moments, they had all vanished back in the direction from which they had come. A minute later, the only movement on the open field consisted of the still-twitching limbs of slain vord and the black wings of crows swooping down to feast upon the fallen.

"Giraldi," Bernard said. "Sound stand down. Get a rotation going to get the men food, water, and rest."

"Yes, sir," Giraldi said. He saluted and went about his duties.

"That goes for the rest of you, too, people," Bernard said to his command staff on the roof of the tower. "Get something in your bellies and find a spot to get a nap."

Amara waited until they had all departed to say, "You did it."

Bernard grunted and shook his head. "All we did was make them take us seriously. Before today, the vord had never had much in the way of tactics. They just threw more warriors at every problem." He rubbed at one eye with his forefinger. "Today they tried to turn our flank. Tomorrow . . ." He shrugged. "They pulled back because someone over there is busy thinking of a way to bring us down. The next time we see them, they'll have something nasty prepared."

Amara shivered. He took a step closer and put his arm around her. The movement was awkward in his lorica, but Bernard managed.

"The important thing," he said, "is that we're still here. Once we fall back to Garrison, we should be able to hold out for weeks, if need be. We've successfully bought time."

"For what?" Amara asked.

"For the boy to get here," Bernard said.

"What good will that do us?" she asked. "No one's sighted the Queen yet."

Bernard shook his head. "He's got something tricky in mind. Count on it."

Amara nodded. "I hope so," she said. "Love, you should have some food and rest, too."

"Aye. In just a moment." His fingers absently stroked her hand. "Pretty sunset, isn't it?"

"Beautiful," she replied. She leaned her head on his shoulder.

The sun was nearly gone, its ruddy light glaring into their eyes. Shadows spread long across the Valley's floor.

And off in the distance, the shrieks of angry vord whispered from the Valley's walls.

CHAPTER 40

"Let me deal with this," Invidia snarled. "Give me our earthcrafters and the behemoths, and that wall won't last five minutes."

"No," said the Queen. She paced back and forth beside the pool of water, staring down at it. Her tattered old gown rustled and whispered. "No, not yet," she said.

"You saw the losses they inflicted."

The Queen shrugged a shoulder, the motion elegant, at odds with the stained finery she wore. "Losses are to be expected. Especially here, at the last. They revealed hidden capabilities without destroying us, which we will overcome in our next encounter. That is a victory." She looked up at Invidia sharply. "However, I do not understand why you did not warn me about the great fury in the mountain."

"Because I didn't know about it," Invidia replied, her voice tight. "Obviously."

"You said you had been here before."

"To pick up Isana in a wind coach," Invidia said. "Not to plan an invasion."

The vord Queen stared at Invidia for a moment, as though she hadn't quite understood the difference. Then she nodded slowly. "It must be another disparate Aleran experience."

Invidia folded her arms. "Obviously. It wasn't a part of the context."

The Queen tilted her head. "But you intended to conquer Alera."

"I intended to take it whole," she said, "by co-opting its system of governance. The use of military force was never a preferred course of action. Certainly, there was little probability that I would *ever* have a need to attack this remote little valley. With the exception of providing a convenient and predictable place for the Marat to attack, it's been of no historical importance whatsoever."

At that, Isana looked up from where she sat, near the imprisoned Araris's feet, and smiled.

Invidia's presence became suffused with sudden rage, only slowly gathered back under control. The burned woman turned to the Queen, and said, "Every moment we spend here with our forces doing nothing brings complications."

"They are not 'our' forces, Invidia," the Queen said. "They are mine. And you still think like an Aleran. My troops will not desert in the face of starvation. They will not cast their allegiance with another. They will not hesitate to obey nor refuse to attack an enemy at my command. Do not fear."

"I am not afraid," Invidia said, her voice coldly precise.

"Of course you are," Isana said calmly. "You're both terrified."

Invidia's cold eyes and the Queen's alien ones both swiveled to come to rest on her. Isana thought that such eyes looked like weapons, somehow, and dangerous ones at that. She further thought that by all rights, she should be frightened herself. But given the past days, she found herself having difficulty giving fear much credit. In her first days in captivity, perhaps fear would have moved her more strongly. Now . . . no. She was really rather more concerned with the fact that she'd not bathed in days than that her life might come to an end. Terror had worn into worry, and worry was an old companion to any mother.

Isana nodded to the Queen in mock deference, and said, "You've been dealt a harsh blow by the first Aleran force actually prepared to resist you. They didn't have it all their way, of course, because you are unwholesomely powerful. But even so, the valley stands, and thousands of your warriors are no more. And they are ready to continue fighting. The fight seems hopeless to you, and yet they stand and fight and die—which makes you think that perhaps the fight is *not* hopeless. Yet you cannot see how that would be. You fear that you have overlooked some detail, some fact, some number that might change all of your careful equations—and that terrifies you."

Isana turned to Invidia, and said, "And you. I almost feel sorry for you, Invidia. At least you had your beauty. And now even that is gone. The only haven left for you, your best hope, is to rule a kingdom of the childless, the aging, the dying. Even if you take your crown, Invidia, you know that you will never be admired, never be envied, never be a mother—and never be loved. Those who endure this war to live under you will fear you. Hate you. Kill you, I should imagine, if they can. And, in the end, there won't even be anyone left to remember your name as a curse. Your future, no matter what happens, is a long and terrible torment. The brightest end you can hope for is a swift and painless death." She shook her head. "I . . . *do* feel sorry for you, dear. I have good reason to hate you, yet you've served yourself a fate worse than any I would ever have imagined, much less wished upon you. Of course you're afraid."

She folded her hands in her lap, and said, calmly, "And both of you are now worried that I have realized so much about you both. About who you are. About what moves you. You're both wondering what else I know. And how else I might use it against you. And why I have revealed what I know here, and now. And you, lonely Queen, wonder if you have made a mistake in bringing me here. You wonder what Octavian inherited from his father—and what came from me."

Silence filled the hive. Neither of the two half women to whom she spoke moved.

"Do you think?" Isana asked in a conversational tone, "that it might be possible to have hot tea with our dinner tonight? I've always found a good cup of tea to be most . . ." She smiled at them. "Reassuring."

The Queen stared at her for a time. Then she whirled to face Invidia, and said, "You may *not* have the remaining crafters," she hissed. Then, the hem of her tattered gown snapping, the vord Queen stalked from the hive.

Invidia looked after the Queen, then turned to Isana. "Are you *mad*? Do you know what she could do to you?" Her eyes flickered with disquieting light. "Or what *I* could do to you?"

"I needed her to leave," Isana said calmly. "Do you wish to be rid of her, Invidia?"

The burned woman gestured in burning frustration at the creature clamped to her. "It cannot be."

"What if I told you that it could?" Isana asked, speaking in a calm, almost-toneless voice. "What if I told you that the vord possess the means to cure you of any poison, to restore the loss of any organ—even to restore your beauty? And that I know its name and can make a fair guess at where it might be?"

Invidia's head rocked back at Isana's words. Then she breathed, "You're lying."

Isana offered the woman her hand calmly. "I'm not. Come see."

The other woman took a step back from Isana, as though the offered hand contained pure poison.

Isana smiled. "I know," she said calmly. "You could be free of them, Invidia. I think it is very possible. Even against the Queen's will."

Invidia lifted her chin. Her eyes burned, and her scarred face twisted into what looked like physical pain. Terrible hope pulsed from her, and though she tried to hide it, Isana had been too near her, through too much, for too long. There was no more hiding it from her finely tuned senses. Though it sickened her to do it, Isana faced her calmly and waited for the pressure of that hope to drive the other woman to speak.

"You," Invidia rasped, "are *lying.*"

Isana shook her head slowly, never looking away from the other woman's eyes. "Should you wish to change your future," she said calmly, "I am here."

Invidia turned and stormed from the hive. Isana heard a roaring windstream bear her away—leaving her in the hive alone. Except, of course, for perhaps a hundred wax spiders, most of them motionless but not asleep. If she moved toward the exit, they would swarm her.

Isana smoothed her skirts again and sat calmly.

Waiting.

CHAPTER 41

Fidelias had watched Crassus run the Legions and manage the Canim in the retaking of Riva while Octavian rested from the rather spectacular display of furycrafting he'd put on. Fidelias was impressed with the young Antillan lord. He'd expected Crassus to behave quite a bit differently when he was the one in command. He'd expected someone much more like . . . well, like Maximus, from the heir of Antillus Raucus. Crassus had, it would seem, inherited the best traits of his mother's bloodline, House of Kalarus: cool logic, intelligence, and polish, seemingly without being infected with the megalomaniacal self-obsession in which most of those petty-minded monsters had reveled.

Granted, Crassus's levelheaded style wasn't necessarily a perfect one where the Canim were concerned. An officer of their corps, a young Shuaran, had dropped a challenge to Crassus's authority within hours, at which point his elder half brother Maximus had promptly brought one of Raucus's strengths of character to the forefront—the ability to make a decisive and unmistakable statement.

When the Cane went for Crassus's throat, Maximus threw him through a building.

It was a rather absolute form of diplomacy though Fidelias could only assume that Octavian had rubbed off on Maximus to some degree: It had been a wooden building rather than a stone one. The Cane in question was expected to recover from his injuries—eventually. Varg had denied the uppity Cane the services of Aleran healers, which Crassus had promptly offered.

Fidelias's grasp of Canim was still fairly rough, but Varg's comment had amounted to something like, "Your stupidity will get fewer good warriors killed if you have time to reflect on today's mistake before leading them."

Octavian dropped his head back at Fidelias's recounting and laughed. His voice came out sounding a little flat within the privacy windcrafting he had woven around them. "One-eared Shuaran pack leader? Tarsh?"

"Aye, Your Highness, the same."

Octavian nodded. The two of them were walking the perimeter of the camp's defenses as the sunset closed, after another day of hard marching, inspecting the work of the Legions and the warriors. "Maximus has wanted to have an excuse to take a swing at Tarsh ever since we met him in Molvar. And I can't imagine that

Varg would be sorry about being given a reason not to place anyone under Tarsh's command." Octavian nodded. "What of the survivors from Riva?"

The Legions had found a handful of folk clever or fortunate enough to have successfully hidden from the vord during the days of occupation. None of them were in what would be considered good condition though few bore any injuries. "The children are showing signs of beginning to recover," Fidelias said. "The others . . . some of them have family who might be alive. If we get them to someplace warm and quiet and safe, they have a chance."

"Someplace warm, quiet, and safe," said the Princeps, his eyes hardening. "That can be a rare thing even in times of peace."

"True enough."

The Princeps stopped in his tracks. They were a short distance from the nearest sentries. "Your best guess. Could Crassus command this force in . . . my absence?"

"In your absence, as your lieutenant, yes," Fidelias replied immediately. "In the event of your loss, Captain? Not for long."

Octavian eyed him sharply. "Why?"

"Because the Canim respect Varg, and Varg respects you. The Free Aleran Legion respects you—but if you weren't here, they would follow Varg's lead."

The Princeps grunted, frowning. Then he said, "Are you telling me that I should name a Canim the second-in-command of our forces?"

Fidelias opened his mouth and closed it again. He blinked, thinking it over. "I believe . . . that Varg would have a better chance of holding the force together than Crassus, or anyone else in the First Aleran's command structure."

"Except, perhaps, Valiar Marcus," Octavian mused.

Fidelias snorted. "Yes, well, that's not an option now, is it?"

Octavian regarded him steadily and said nothing.

Fidelias tilted his head as it slowly dawned on him what Octavian meant. "Oh, Your Highness. You couldn't possibly do that."

"Why not?" Octavian asked. "No one but my personal guard and Demos's crew know the truth about you. They can keep a secret. So, Marcus runs the force until it can unite with the Legions, passes along Crassus's orders, and is watched by the Maestro—who is, I believe, still uncertain as to why you aren't hanging on a cross being eaten by vord."

"I'm a bit unclear on that point myself, at times."

Octavian's visage hardened briefly. "I will do as I see fit with your life. It is mine to spend. Remember that."

Fidelias frowned and inclined his head slightly. "As you wish, my lord."

"That's right," Octavian said, some measure of bitter humor touching the tone.

Fidelias studied the young man for a moment and realized that . . . the Princeps was torn over some decision. Normally he was so confident, so driven; Fidelias had never seen him like this. There was uncertainty hovering behind his words, hesitance. Octavian himself wasn't sure what his next steps would be.

"Are you planning on leaving the force, sir?" Fidelias asked carefully.

"At some point, it's inevitable," Octavian replied calmly. "If nothing else, I will be obliged to make personal contact with the Legions in Calderon—and hope to the great furies whoever is in charge over there has had sense enough to listen to my uncle."

Fidelias grunted. "But . . . that isn't what you think will happen."

Octavian grimaced, and said, "Someone has to command the men, regardless of what happens to me. We have to take down the vord Queen—and her cadre of captured or treacherous Citizens. I will, by necessity, be in the center of that conflict. And . . . the odds seem to be long against me."

Fidelias debated on how to respond to the moment of vulnerability the Princeps was showing. He finally just began chuckling.

Octavian frowned at him and lifted an imperious eyebrow.

"Long odds," he said. "Bloody crows, sir. Long odds. That's bloody funny."

"I don't see what's so amusing about it."

"Naturally, you don't," Fidelias said, still chuckling. "The furyless boy from the country who stopped an invasion."

"I didn't really stop it," Tavi said. "*Doroga* stopped it. I just . . ."

"Completely demolished an operation backed by the most dangerous High Lord and Lady in the Realm," Fidelias said. "I was there. Remember?" The last words were not bereft of irony.

Octavian gave a small inclination of his head in acknowledgment of the touch.

"The boy who personally saved the First Lord's life in his second term at the Academy. Who took command of a Legion and fought the Canim to a standoff—and who then stole Varg from the most tightly guarded prison of the Realm and brokered the first truce in history with the Canim to get them out of the Realm. The young upstart Princeps who pitted himself against a continent full of vord and hostile Canim and won."

"I got my people and Varg's out alive," Octavian corrected sharply. "I haven't won anything. Not yet."

Fidelias grunted. "Sir . . . honestly. Suppose you defeat the vord here. Suppose you unite our people again, take Alera back. Will that be a victory?"

Octavian raked his fingers through his hair. "Of course not. It'll be a good start. But there will be severe repercussions for the balance of power in our society that must be addressed. The Canim will, probably, be settling here, and we'll have to reach some kind of mutual understanding with them, and the Free Alerans are never going to back the same set of laws that allowed them to be enslaved. Not to mention the fact that—"

Fidelias cleared his throat gently. "Young man, I submit to you that your standards of victory are . . . set rather high. If you continue that way, no matter what you do, it will never be enough."

"That is exactly correct," Octavian replied. "Are the men and women the vord have already killed only partially dead? Are they only technically dead? Only legally dead? Can a compromise be made wherein they are given back some portion of their lives?" He shook his head. "No. No compromise. My duty to them, and to those still alive, demands nothing less than everything I can give them. Yes, old soldier, my standards are high. So are the stakes. They're a matched set."

Fidelias stared at him, then shook his head slowly. Gaius Sextus had held an air of absolute authority, of personal power that arrested one's sense of reason, at times, to extract support and obedience. Gaius Septimus had been a vibrant figure, driven and intelligent, always looking to the future. He could have inspired men to follow him down any path of reason, no matter how winding.

But Octavian . . . men would follow Octavian into a leviathan's gullet if he asked it of them. And crows take him if Fidelias himself wouldn't be one of them. The headstrong lunatic would probably discover some way to lead them all out the other side draped in the rings and crowns of a devoured treasure ship and somehow emerge clean.

"I couldn't lead the Legions and the Canim," Fidelias said quietly. "Not alone. But . . . if you made your will known to Varg, then Valiar Marcus could serve as Crassus's advisor, his huntmaster. Varg would give him the chance to stand on his own merits in that case. And I would direct him as best I could."

"You know the Canim," Octavian said. "Better than anyone else I have." His eyes glinted. "You've spent time with Sha, I think."

"I've met the Cane," Fidelias said calmly. "He seems most professional."

"And have you ever met Khral?"

"I do not believe my duties as First Spear ever brought me into contact with him, my lord."

"Oh," Octavian said, smiling suddenly. "Very smooth."

Fidelias inclined his head, his mouth touched with amusement at one corner.

The Princeps turned to him and put a hand on his shoulder. "Thank you, Marcus."

Fidelias dropped his eyes. "My lord . . ."

"Whatever else you've done," Octavian said gently, "I have *seen* you. I have trusted you with my life, and you have trusted me with yours. I have seen you work tirelessly to serve the First Aleran. I have seen you give your body and heart to the Legion, to your men. I refuse to consider the idea that it was all a ploy."

Fidelias looked away from him. "That hardly matters, sir."

"It matters if I *say* it matters," Octavian growled. "Crows take me, if I am to be First Lord, we're going to establish that from the outs—"

The earthcrafting went beneath Fidelias so swiftly, so softly, that he hardly noticed it. He froze in place and narrowed his eyes, sending his own awareness into the ground beneath them.

A second passed by him. And a third.

They were all heading in the same direction—toward the command tent, the center of the camp.

". . . if I have to crack every skull in the Senate to . . ." Octavian frowned. "Marcus?"

Fidelias's hand went to his side, where his sword would normally be. It was, of course, gone. "Sir," he said, his voice tight, "there are earthcrafters passing beneath us at this very moment."

Octavian blinked. Powerful the young man might be, but he didn't have the subtlety, the awareness, that could only come from decades of experience. He hadn't sensed a thing. But once he closed his own eyes for a moment, frowning, he let out a blistering curse. "Friendlies would never attempt to enter the camp like that. The vord had a number of Citizens in their control."

"Aye."

"Then we can't send *legionares* against them. It will be a bloodbath." He "listened" for a moment more, then opened his eyes. "They're heading for command," Octavian said shortly. Only his eyes showed strain. "Kitai's there."

"Go," Fidelias said. "I'll bring the Pisces after you."

"Do it," Octavian snapped, and before he was finished speaking, he took a single bounding step and leapt into the air on a roaring gale of wind. Within another heartbeat, he had drawn his sword, and white-hot, furious fire burned forth from the blade.

Fidelias turned to sprint toward the center of the camp. As he went, he began bellowing orders that carried even over the hollow roar of Octavian's monstrous windstream.

He did not need to be doing such things at his age, but he tried to focus on the positive: At least he wasn't running in full armor. And, thank the great furies, the Princeps hadn't taken Fidelias *flying* alongside him. Even so, some part of Fidelias noted with amusement that he wasn't simply following Gaius Octavian, unarmed and unarmored, into the leviathan's mouth.

He was *sprinting*.

CHAPTER 42

Tavi didn't know how many earthcrafters the vord had collared and enslaved, but given how quickly Alera said that they had affected repairs upon the causeways, it was either a great many Citizens with lesser gifts or a few very powerful ones. Either way, Kitai was in the command tent, averting friction between the Antillan brothers and the Canim, and between the command staff of the Free Aleran and Maestro Magnus, and unaware of what was coming.

Tavi dived at the command tent, a dangerous maneuver when flying so low—but he managed to land perhaps twenty feet off without breaking his legs or ankles, then promptly redirected his windstream to catch the command tent and tear it neatly up off its posts and stakes like an enormous kite. A dozen people in the tent, staff and guards, Aleran and Canim, came lurching to their feet. Half a dozen of them, including Kitai, had already drawn steel before Tavi got a clear look at them.

"To arms!" he thundered, before either the guards or the people within the tent could react. He ran toward the tent, the sword in his hand sending out sparks that threatened to catch his own bloody cloak on fire, and shouted, "Enemy earthcrafters coming in low!"

"Oh crows *take* it," muttered Maestro Magnus in a positively offended tone. He had to gather up his long tunic to show pale, scrawny legs as he stepped up onto a wooden camp stool. "Of all the ridiculous nonsense."

"Where?" Kitai snapped, taking several rapid steps from the others, looking left and right at the ground beneath her.

Tavi focused his thoughts upon the earth beneath him. Subtle though such travel might be, his flight to the command tent had been far swifter, and he felt the foremost earthcrafting coming toward him, several yards away. Instead of answering, he stopped, took a quick pair of steps, and with the power of the earth itself behind his arms and shoulders, thrust the burning blade straight down into the soil beneath him. The blade struck home, though he could tell only from the sudden quivering jerks that ran through the steel to his hand, like the wriggling motion of a fish caught upon a hook that ran through the line and pole to the hand of an angler. He withdrew, the motion effortless with the burning sword, and struck again only inches from the first blow.

The earth beneath him suddenly collapsed downward in a circle perhaps ten feet across. One moment, he was standing upon solid ground, and the next it was falling from beneath him. One hand, formed into a stiffening claw, thrust up from the loose soil. Tavi tried not to take note of the fact that the hand was a woman's and not young, forcing the fact of what he had just done to the back of his mind.

"Aleran!" cried Kitai's voice. Her anxious face appeared at the top of the sudden pit Tavi found himself in.

"I'm all ri—" Tavi began.

The enemy earthcrafter following in the wake of the first suddenly stumbled out of the earth five feet from Tavi, abruptly finding himself standing in the open air at the bottom of the pit. Tavi stared at him for a motionless instant of recognition. He hadn't seen the massively muscled, lank-haired man who had appeared, a thug named Renzo, since commencement activities at the Academy. The enormous young man was perhaps a year older than Tavi and weighed two of him. An extremely accomplished earthcrafter, Renzo had been stupid enough to be a friend of Kalarus Brencis Minoris, which doubtless explained the steel slaver's collar about his mountainous neck. Tavi had beaten Renzo into screaming surrender before he'd had use of any furycrafting at all, and the act still shamed him in his memory.

The instant of hesitation gave Renzo a chance to react. He flicked a hand, and the earth surged up around Tavi, as if to bury him alive.

Tavi recovered his balance and immediately drew strength from the earth—specifically, from the earth trying to smother him, weakening the furies responding to Renzo's command. He waded forward, through the failing power of those furies, and, with an instant of razor-sharp focus, cut cleanly through Renzo's hastily raised blade, the steel collar about the huge man's neck—and the neck beneath it. Renzo's body dropped like a slaughtered hog's, still quivering.

Time slowed.

There was little blood. The blazing sword in Tavi's hand had cauterized the cuts even as he made them. The courtyard bully's broad hands twitched and spasmed. His head had fallen facedown, and Tavi could see his mouth moving for a few seconds, as if to spit out the dirt upon his tongue. That didn't last long. A heartbeat, two, then there was stillness.

Renzo had been an appallingly petty evil from the last days of Tavi's childhood.

Tavi felt sick at how easy it had been to murder him.

His thoughts and focus were, for a few seconds, entirely shattered, and so, when the vord Queen exploded from the earth behind Renzo's corpse, she nearly killed him in the first instant of their meeting.

Tavi seized upon a windcrafting, weak though it was down in the sinkhole, to speed his perceptions. Even with the crafting, there was time for no more than a bizarre, flash impression of a beautiful face, glittering black eyes, a tattered old dress—and then there was a flicker of motion as a shadowy blade darted toward his heart.

Tavi had enough time to think, *I didn't feel it coming, it's not made of metal.* Fortunately, his reflexes hadn't had any metalcrafting to rely upon when he first trained with a weapon, and they hadn't needed the advance warning. His own burning blade caught the dark weapon in the vord Queen's hand, defeated the Queen's disengage, then suddenly slipped and wobbled as the resistance of the other weapon vanished. The dark blade curled in her hand like a striking serpent and drove into his belly. It pierced his armor as though it were made of soft cloth instead of battle steel, and he felt himself thrown back hard against the layers of a stone shelf lining the pit wall behind him.

The vord Queen came at him, her eyes shining with a terrible intensity, but he responded with the instant, deadly reflexes of a man who had been wise enough to embrace the cold, insensible strength of his armor and weaponry, who felt no pain though his body was trapped against the rough wall, impaled upon a deadly blade. The vord Queen was swift enough to avoid having her head taken from her shoulders, but only just. Tavi's burning sword left a wound in her scalp and seared away a mass of thin white hairs. She blurred away from him, letting out a metallic shriek, and simply bounded up out of the pit.

An explosion of light and furious sound bright enough to hurt his eyes— odd, that metalcrafting didn't seem to offer any protection from *that* source of pain—made the shape of the disappearing Queen a silhouette and left her profile burned onto his eyes in bright color as the rest of the world went dark.

Every instinct in him screamed to get out of the hole, get into action, move, move, *move*. But he didn't. When the Queen had leapt from the pit, she hadn't been holding a sword. Whether he could feel the pain or not, given the rock at his back it was almost certain that there was a preternaturally sharp weapon still thrust into his belly, sunk into the stone behind him like a nail into wood. If he simply tore his way free, he could all but cut himself in half.

He held the blazing sword uncomfortably close to his own body, squinting down with his light-dazzled eyes, and confirmed it. There was a bar of gleaming, green-black material still thrust through the plates of his lorica. He touched a hand to it, lightly, and found that it was double-edged and as sharp as a scalpel. The lightest touch had opened flesh with a horrible, delicate ease. It looked like vord chitin and, for all that he knew, it was. When the blood from his fingers touched it, the weapon *quivered*, sending silver shocks of sensation through his body, though his metalcrafting kept him from experiencing it as pain.

Bloody crows. The thing was *alive*.

Outside the pit, the vord Queen shrieked again, the sound a brassy challenge. Explosions of fire thundered outside. People screamed. Steel rang on steel.

Tavi was having a hard time getting enough breath. It couldn't be the lungs themselves. The chitin blade's thrust had been far too low. He glanced at his fingers and saw them smeared with something tarry and green. It smelled vile. Lovely—poison, which must have been shutting down his breathing.

Tavi grimaced. The chitin blade didn't have a guard or a tang. It simply . . . segued, from a long, lightly curved blade to an oblong, rounded handle. He couldn't walk forward and off the impaling blade. The handle would never fit through the relatively small hole the blade had made, and widening the wound himself seemed . . . counterproductive.

Stars thickened in his vision. His body was running out of air.

Tavi debated simply striking the sword, snapping it with his own burning blade, but there were excellent reasons not to. The blow might *not* break the vordblade, in which case it would just cut through him with all the power of his own strike. If he tried to burn through, it would heat the blade and cauterize the wound, rendering it all but untreatable by watercraft. Simply seizing it and breaking it with earthcrafted strength was a fool's game as well—the blade would nip off his fingers all the more neatly because of the supernatural power backing the attempt.

More screams, human and vord, came from above. Incoming windstreams howled, and a Cane let out a furious roar. He began to feel dizzy.

The soil around him, all over his clothes, his boots, his armor, was loose, fairly sandy.

That would do.

Moving carefully, he gestured with one hand, and a long pseudopod of sandy earth rose up from beneath him. He scooped up a handful, and mused that his own blood had made it sticky and clumpy. He caked it around the vordblade. He did that twice more, until a thick clump of bloody, sandy mud clung to it.

Then he ground his teeth, held out his sword, and poured fire from the glowing blade down onto the mud, shaping it with his thoughts and will. It enveloped the mud in a swift, sudden, short-lived flash of fire that brought up blisters on his hands and face—and when the light had faded, the sand glowed dull red with heat, clinging gelatinously.

A second pass of the sword allowed him to draw the heat back *out* of the sand again, before it could spread up the blade and into his vitals, and the vordblade was suddenly encased in an irregular lump of glass.

Tavi seized it, took a steadying breath, and drew on the weapon. It didn't move at first, but he didn't dare turn this into an exercise of brute strength. He increased the pressure slowly, gently, until the weapon abruptly slid free of the stone behind him. It raised sparks from his armor as Tavi pulled it carefully from his flesh.

He gave the vordblade a little toss so that it landed on the far side of the pit. Then he focused on his own body, finding the wound, a narrow and reasonably minor injury in its own right. But the tissues around the wound, all the way through his body, were swelling as though they meant to burst.

Tavi ground his teeth, focused his will, and stopped them from growing any worse. To some degree, the swelling was an advantage—it kept him from bleeding too hideously, for the moment. But he could feel his body's own unwitting rebellion in progress, a toxin-induced physical frenzy in his blood that would kill him in minutes if allowed to run its course.

Minutes suddenly seemed an endless amount of time. If he could move fast enough, he could end the Vord War in *seconds.*

Tavi reached for more strength from the earth beneath him and used it to spring from the pit in a single leap, taking in his surroundings as he did. There was a circle of blackened, smoking earth around the top of the pit, the ground glazed to dirty glass, presumably from the firecrafting launched at the Queen when she appeared. There were dozens of other pits in sight, and the sounds of desperate struggle. Corpses, clad both in chitin and Legion armor, littered the ground. The earthcrafters had attacked like ant lions, opening a sinkhole beneath their targets and drawing them down into close combat, where the enslaved Citizens would have all the advantages. The loose soil would slow Tavi's people and make them vulnerable to the vicious physical strength of the attackers. Old Maestro Magnus stood on his wooden stool, beating frantically at his beard, which had somehow been set on fire—but, rendered invisible to the subterranean attackers by his precarious perch, he was thus far unhurt.

Tavi landed lightly, on his toes, just as a chitin-armored man wielding an enormously oversized sword swept it in a deadly arc toward Varg.

The Cane caught the fury-assisted blow with a perfect deflection parry, redirecting the vast power of the strike, sliding it away at an angle instead of pitting the raw strength of his bloodred steel directly against the Aleran's greatsword. The Cane flowed forward and to one side in the wake of the huge sword's passing, graceful for all his tremendous size and weight, and struck cleanly, once.

The enslaved Citizen dropped dead in his tracks, his head attached to his body only by a scrap of muscle and flesh. Varg continued the motion, never stopping, his blade coming up to a guard that stopped a fraction of a second before becoming an attack directed at Tavi.

"Where?" Tavi demanded, in Canish.

Varg pointed with one clawed finger, then whirled and threw his great curved blade with a smooth contraction of what seemed like every muscle in the Cane's lean body. It tumbled twice and buried itself in the back of one of two enemy earthcrafters attacking his son, Nasaug. The thrown weapon struck with so much force that it pierced the chitin-armor, but even if it hadn't, Tavi saw the target's head snap back at the violence of the strike, and clearly *heard* the brutal impact break the enemy's collared neck.

Tavi looked in the direction Varg had pointed and spotted the vord Queen, vanishing into the mists that still surrounded the camp, courtesy of the ritualists. Kitai was pursuing her. That much Tavi had expected. He just hadn't expected to see the two of them running along the *tops* of the standard Legion white canvas tents.

Legion tents were mostly of the northern design, made to shed water and snow. Two upright poles at either end supported a long cross-pole, which held up the line of the roof. The cross-pole was perhaps an inch and a half thick.

Kitai and the Queen sprinted along them as though they were as wide as the avenues of old Alera Imperia.

Tavi leapt into the air and roared aloft on a column of wind. Though Kitai and the vord Queen were moving more swiftly than any human could have without crafting, flight was faster still.

"Stay with the Princeps!" someone bellowed behind him, maybe Maximus.

A second roar of wind joined his, and Tavi glanced over one shoulder to see Crassus soaring after him, fresh blood dripping from his wetted blade.

Kitai bounded from one tent to the next, took a half stride from one end of the tent to the other, and leapt to the next tent, following the vord Queen. As Tavi began to close in, she narrowed the Queen's lead to only feet, and their next leap between tent poles came at nearly the same instant. Kitai's sword, seething with amethyst fire (how the bloody crows had she done *that*? Tavi's fire always looked like . . . *fire*.) licked out and struck the vord Queen low on one calf—only a last-second convulsion of the limb prevented the blow from striking the tendon at the ankle. Kitai had gone for a crippling blow to slow the Queen and allow the rest of the First Aleran's skilled furycrafters to catch up.

The Queen spun in midair, her body contorting with what could only have been the aid of windcrafting, and a clawed foot lashed out at Kitai's face as the two of them soared through their leap. Kitai was not caught unawares by the attack, and intercepted it with her left arm—but away from the support of any earthcrafting, she was no match for the vord Queen's sheer power. The kick broke bones and laid open flesh in a short spray of blood. Kitai cried out and lost her balance as she came down again, tumbling into the tent canvas and bringing the tent down. The vord Queen took a single, contemptuous step on the tent's cross-pole before it could fall and continued without slackening her pace.

She met Tavi's eyes for an instant, and her expression unsettled him. He had rarely seen any emotion at all displayed by a vord queen, and he had encountered several—but *this* Queen was not wearing a blank mask. She was smiling, a child's gleeful grin of excitement and joy, an expression seen only in the midst of favorite games and birthday celebrations.

Bloody crows. The creature was having *fun*.

Tavi let out a cry of rage and flew faster, blade held ready for a cavalry-style passing stroke, but Crassus was surging steadily past him, his years of experience surpassing Tavi's raw power at windcrafting. He had shifted his blade to his left hand, and was arrowing toward the fleeing Queen's right side. The young Tribune clearly intended to occupy the vord's attention and defenses while Tavi took the killing stroke on her left. Tavi altered his flight path slightly, the edges of Crassus's violent windstream ripping his cloak to shreds. He braced himself and closed half an instant behind Crassus's leading attack.

Before they reached her, the Queen spun between one step and the next, a neat pirouette, and one pale arm moved in a swath across her body, spreading a small, arcing cloud of crystals into the air.

Crassus never had a chance. The salt crystals struck him before he could have registered the threat, tearing his wind furies to useless shreds. He fell with a short, frustrated cry into the sea of white tents beneath them, heavy poles snapping, heavy canvas tearing under the bone-shattering force of his speed.

Tavi rolled over and over to his own left, barely avoiding the spray of salt crystals, nearly losing control of his flight. A desperate thrust of wind sent him arcing up into the air instead of down into entangling tents, and the harsh, metallic laugh of the vord Queen mocked him. A motion of her arm gave birth to a sphere of fire that wiped away half a dozen *legionares* as they came pouring out of their tent, and with each step she cast more fire to the left and right, killing men as easily as a child crushed ants. Screams of terror and agony followed in her wake.

Tavi stabilized his flight and shook his head furiously. He could not afford to let his emotions control him. The Queen was deadly, and deadly rational. She wasn't simply running along the tents for a lark. She had a goal in mind, a destination.

Tavi didn't need to look ahead to know what was coming—and neither, he realized, did the vord Queen. The layout of a Legion camp was standard from one end of the Realm to another, established by centuries of practice, and he realized with a sudden chill that he had given the enemy some margin of advantage by adhering to Legion rote.

She was heading for the healer's tents.

With a snarl, Tavi dropped his concentration on everything but his wind stream and shot past her. He gained a fifty-, sixty-, seventy-yard lead, then had to come down at the most oblique angle he could, on his side in the air, his feet leading. The instant his boots hit the earth, he called upon it to shape itself to the line of his motion, to guide and slow him rather than simply kicking his feet out from beneath him and seeing to it that he broke his fool neck.

His boots tore up a furrow of turf as wide as his foot and six inches deep, sending a spray of soil, pebbles, and spring grass flying up in front of him in a bow wave for better than fifty feet and bringing him to a stop in the entrance to the main healer's tent. He whirled, called fire back into his sword, and then the vord Queen slammed into his chest, driving him into the tent and *through* the large support post just inside the entrance.

Tavi slapped one speed-blurred, dark-nailed hand aside as the vord Queen swept it at his throat, dropped his sword, and seized her by the hair with his other hand, rolling as they both hit the ground and putting her in front as their momentum carried her into the side of a filled metal healing tub, slamming his own heavily armored body into her slender form.

Water exploded up out of the tub as their impact crushed its nearer side flat against the other. The Queen let out a huff of expelled air. The pain he'd been holding off with metalcrafting until perhaps five or six seconds ago suddenly smashed into him in a wave, and he remembered that he had let go of the crafting that was slowing the toxin coursing from the agonizing wound in his belly.

She came rolling to her feet, never stopping her motion, bounding on all fours like something more feline than human. Fire-spheres charred half a dozen healers and two wounded survivors of Riva to so much meat. A young woman in healer's garb and a silver discipline collar was the next target. But Foss threw himself in front of her, giving her a powerful shove that sent her tumbling head over heels away from him—and then he was enveloped in another blast that left little more than blackened bones and melted steel in its wake.

The vord Queen hissed and gestured again—but Tavi suddenly recognized the young woman Foss had died to protect as Dorotea, who, in another life, had been the High Lady of Antillus.

Collared by her own allies, commanded to do no harm, the woman had been serving as a healer in the Free Aleran since its inception. Her personal ambition had been a cancer that the collar had neatly amputated, and she had done more good in her months as a slave than she ever had as a Citizen. A watercrafter skilled beyond anything that a Legion could hope for, she had doubt-less been called in to treat some difficult or delicate harm suffered by one of the survivors.

Her lips spread in a snarl as another sphere of fire bloomed practically upon her, and the earth itself heaved and bucked into a dome that shielded her from the blast. A second motion sent the contents of two healing tubs abruptly hur-tling toward the vord Queen like two enormous, transparent stones. The blasts of water smashed the vord to the ground.

Dorotea cried out in sudden agony and clutched at the silver collar at her throat, her body contorting.

Tavi ground his teeth and forced steel into his limbs, his mind, dismissing the pain as something unimportant. The former High Lady had pushed the vord into an open, unoccupied space to one side of the tent. Tavi lifted his sword and sent a thunderbolt of seething fire, whiter than the light of the sun, writhing into the form of some vast and deadly serpent, lancing toward her.

The vord Queen's smile was gone. Her glittering black eyes widened as the sun-fire streaked toward her. She crossed her forearms in front of her with an-other brassy scream, and the blast of fire struck her, burning again at Tavi's vision with a furious light bright enough to blind him though he had closed his eyes to shield against it.

He opened them again, peering.

The entire side of the tent was gone in a great, gaping circle, the canvas charred to fine ash, cut as neatly as with shears. The ground all around the blast area was several inches lower than it had been a moment before and smoothed to glowing glass.

Except for one small circle around the vord Queen. She stood up slowly, uncrossing her arms, and that gleeful smile spread over her face again as she stood over Tavi. Though her tattered old gown was singed black over most of its surface, she was apparently unharmed.

He let out a panting snarl and fought his way up to one knee, sword in hand.

"I came here only to weaken you, Father," the Queen said in a purring voice. "This was more than I dared to hope for. Perhaps there is such a thing as good fortune, after all."

A movement sent a fire-sphere toward Tavi. He caught it on his sword, will-ing the weapon to absorb the heat, to make it burn all the more brightly—but the effort made his vision tighten down to a narrow tunnel. His heart was racing, faster than he'd ever felt it. He couldn't *breathe*. She was coming, so *fast*, faster than he could see, even clawing for the speed of windcrafting, and he couldn't get his sword to *move*—

Maximus slammed into the vord Queen with a roar of pure rage, his armored body hurtling into her, a self-contained avalanche of steel. He carried her past Tavi and through a second upright, shattering it to kindling, and bringing two-thirds of the remaining canvas of the large tent down upon them all like an enormous, smothering blanket.

Tavi lifted his sword and cut an opening almost before the canvas could settle. He stumbled upright, through the opening, only to see the vord Queen neatly duplicate his maneuver using her talons, drag a metal tub out with her, and slam it with savage force onto a thrashing lump beneath the canvas—one that sagged and abruptly went still.

The vord turned toward Tavi, a wild grin twisting her lips, showing him teeth that were very white, with threads of green-black running in crazed lines over their surfaces.

Tavi lifted his sword, calling more heat to it, more light furiously shining forth. He couldn't move. His body was shaking, too weak. He knew that he now stood nearer death's door than he ever had before, though his furycraft allowed him to stay on his feet.

"Your grandfather," the vord Queen said, "died just that way. Defiant to the last, his sword in hand."

Tavi showed her his teeth, and said, "This isn't a guard position. It's a signal fire."

The Queen tilted her head, her eyes narrowed, and a steel balest bolt hit her in the ribs, just below her left arm. It didn't pierce her pale, seemingly soft skin, but the sheer force behind the bolt struck her from her feet and sent her down. She was up again almost instantly. Thirty yards away, all but invisible in the dark and the mist, Fidelias dropped his balest—and swung a second such weapon, already loaded, from his back, lifting it to his shoulder to shoot as he shouted, "Go!"

Windstreams rose in a howl as the Knights Pisces came streaking past Fidelias, thirty strong, some of them passing only inches over his head. A solid wall of wind preceded them, slamming into the vord Queen, forcing her back and away from Tavi like a leaf driven by a gale.

She looked at them for an instant, unimpressed and unafraid, her smile undiminished.

Then she let out another brassy, mocking laugh and bounded away, toward the northeast. She leapt into the air, gathering up a windstream of her own that ripped every tent within fifty yards from the earth, vanished behind a veil, and was gone in a howl of cyclonic thunder.

Fidelias tracked the movement with the second balest but didn't shoot. He came sprinting toward Tavi after that, as the Knights Pisces streaked forward in pursuit—but the men didn't go far before pulling up and spreading into a defensive formation over the camp. Tavi sagged in relief. If they'd followed her out there, she would surely have torn them to shreds.

"Your Highness," Fidelias breathed as he reached Tavi. He set the Canim weapon down and began to examine Tavi's injuries. "Oh. Oh, bloody *crows*, man."

"Kitai," Tavi grated. "Crassus. Back behind me. Dorotea and Maximus under the tent. Foss is dead. I couldn't stop her."

"Bloody crows, hold *still*," Fidelias snarled. "Stay down. Stay down, sire, you're bleeding. Stay *down*."

"Poison," Tavi mumbled. "Poison. Check her trail. Think we went by the water tanks. She could have dropped something in."

"Be still," Fidelias snarled. "Oh, great furies."

Tavi felt the metalcrafting slip. A second later, he felt the agony of his wounds rush up as viciously as a rabid gargant.

And then he felt nothing.

CHAPTER 43

Amara felt rather awkward, truth be told, about being given Bernard's old room at Bernardholt-Isanaholt-Fredericholt, but Elder Frederic had insisted on yielding it to Count and Countess Calderon. She had only seen the chamber once, and that briefly, as Bernard had fetched her a pair of shoes that had belonged to his late wife, back during the hectic hours leading up to Second Calderon.

Her husband had lived a significant portion of his life in that room. It was hard not to feel uncomfortable here. It reminded her how much of his life she had not been present to share. He hadn't stayed at the steadholt long, after she had come into his life.

She walked around the room, slowly. It was spacious enough, she supposed, for a small family, if they didn't mind being close, though not nearly as large as the chambers they shared at Garrison. She tried to imagine the large fireplace in one wall, shedding the only light on a quiet winter evening, children sleeping on little mattresses in front of it, their cheeks rosy with—

Amara shook the thought away. She would never give him children, no matter how much she might wish it or fantasize about it. And in any case, the entire exercise was ridiculous. There were more important things she should be focusing on.

The vord had been driven away, and they had not reappeared in the hours of the afternoon, but they would surely not absent themselves for long. The evacuation of the easternmost half of the Valley, moving everyone behind the last redoubt at Garrison, was not yet completed. The vord would surely not wait much longer—which was why she had come to this chamber, to attempt to get some sleep in the time available to her before the enemy arrived. She hadn't slept in days.

Amara sighed and slipped out of her armored coat. If only the Elder Frederic, now the acting Steadholder, hadn't been the steadholt's gargant master. The great beasts were of unsurpassed utility on a steadholt, but they stank—not unpleasantly, but enormously. They smelled very, very large. It was not the sort of addition to the décor one could readily ignore.

Unless you worked with gargants every day, she supposed.

On the other hand, Amara *was* exhausted. She dropped her weapons and armor next to the large simple bed and cast herself down upon it with a groan. A genuine mattress, by the furies. She hadn't slept on anything but a bedroll or the cold ground since the fighting had resumed. But even so, she just couldn't shake her sense of discomfort. It had, in fact, progressed to a sense of absolute unease.

Amara sat up, lifted her boot to the bed, and bent over it to unlace it. She seized the handle of the knife concealed there and called upon Cirrus to lend her arm speed as she threw it at the empty space next to the gaping fireplace, not six feet in front of her.

The dagger flickered through the air with a hissing hum, and steel met steel in a sharp chime and a shower of green sparks.

Amara flung herself over the bed without waiting to see the outcome of the throw. She grabbed her weapon belt along the way, drawing her *gladius* and holding the belt loosely in her still-aching left hand. The metal-fitted sheath dangling near the end of the belt, next to its heavy buckle, would make as good an improvised weapon as she was likely to find in these quarters. She gauged the distance from the bed to the door.

"Don't bother," said a woman's voice calmly. "You wouldn't reach it. And I cannot permit you to flee." A windcrafted veil fell, revealing . . .

It took Amara a moment to recognize Invidia Aquitaine, and even then she only did it because she recognized the chitin-armor and the creature upon her breast. The woman's long, dark hair was gone. So was most of her lily-white skin, replaced by mottled red burn scars. The corner of one eye sagged beneath a scar, but they were otherwise the same, and her calm, implacable gaze was chilling.

"If you leave now," Amara said, her voice cool, "you might escape before the Placidas catch up to you."

Invidia smiled. It did horrible things to the scars on her face. One of them cracked and bled a little. "Dear Countess, don't be ridiculous. They do not know I am here, any more than you did. Count yourself fortunate that I have not come here to harm you."

Amara checked the distance to the door again.

"Though I will," Invidia said, "if you attempt anything foolish. I am sure that you are aware how little hesitation I would have should I need to kill you."

"As little as I will have when I kill you," Amara replied.

Invidia's smile widened. The blood tracked over her lip and one very white tooth. "Feisty little thing. I'll dance if you wish. But if we do, you're a dead woman, and you know it."

Amara clenched her teeth, seething—because crows take her, the woman was right. Out in the open, with room to maneuver, Amara had a real chance of surviving against Invidia. In this smelly chamber, surrounded by stone? She would be dead before her scream reached the nearest guard. There was nothing she could do to change that, and the knowledge terrified and infuriated her.

"Very well," Amara said a moment later, stiffly. "I'll bite. Why *are* you here?"

"To negotiate, of course," Invidia said.

Amara stared at her for a long moment. Then she whispered, "Murdering bitch. You can go to the crows."

Invidia laughed. It was a bitter, unsettling sound, made eerie by some strange convolution of her burn-scarred throat. "But you do not even know, Countess, what I have to offer."

"Treachery?" Amara guessed, her voice venomously sweet. "That's your usual service, after all."

"Precisely," Invidia said. "And this time it will work in your favor."

Amara narrowed her eyes.

"What's happening out there, Amara, is the end of everything. Unless the Queen is stopped, Alera is finished."

"And you're going to . . . what, exactly? Kill her for us?"

She bared her teeth. "I would, were it possible. I cannot. She is too powerful. By far."

"Then I'd say you have little to offer us," Amara replied.

"I can tell you the location of her hive," Invidia said. "Where you can find her. Where she is most vulnerable."

"Please do."

Invidia settled her fingers a little more solidly on the grip of her sword. "I'm desperate, Countess. Not an idiot. I won't give you that without guarantees."

"Of?" Amara asked.

"My immunity," she responded. "A full pardon for any actions leading up to and during this conflict. My estate on the northeast border of the Feverthorn. I will accept banishment to it and house arrest there for the remainder of my life."

"And in exchange," Amara said quietly, "you give us the location of the vord Queen."

"And I will participate in the attack," Invidia replied. "If every High Lord still under arms pits his strength against her, if she can be caught in her hive, and if the timing is properly arranged, it might be an even match. And that's the best chance you're going to have between now and the world's end, which I estimate will be less than a week from now."

Amara wanted to snarl her defiance and scorn at the burned traitor, but she forced herself to step back from the emotions while she drew in a slow breath. Millions of lives were at stake. She could not let her weariness, her fear, or her anger guide her actions. She was a Cursor of the Realm, by training and by service, and she owed her teachers—even Fidelias—more than to mindlessly toss out an angry reply like a furious child.

It took her more than a minute to calm her mind, to slow her breathing, to reach a state of clarity and *think* about the traitor's offer.

"There's an issue of credibility," Amara said. "Specifically, you have none. Why shouldn't we assume that this offer is a trap to lead our most powerful crafters to their deaths?"

"Can you afford skepticism at this point, Amara?" Invidia asked. "The Queen is no fool. She knows that you will do whatever you can to kill her. She and her kind have been playing this game for a long, long time. She has no intention of allowing you to *see* her, much less attack her—and even if you defeat this army, in weeks there will be another upon your doorstep. What power remains to Alera is insufficient to stop her. She already controls too much territory, and you do not have the manpower necessary to retake it. Can you afford *not* to trust me?"

"Absolutely," Amara said. "I am perfectly willing to take my chances with an honest enemy rather than place the fate of the Realm in your demonstrably treacherous hands."

Invidia tilted her head slightly, her eyes narrowing. "You want something."

"Think of it as earnest money," Amara said. "Show me the color of your coin, and there's a chance we can do business."

Invidia spread her hands. "What would you have of me?"

"The numbers and disposition of the horde, of course," Amara said. "Add to that the time and focus of the next attack, and any information you have regarding vord troops present upon the field whom we have not yet observed."

"Give you all of that information?" Invidia asked. "It would not take her long to realize that she had been betrayed. I would survive her wrath no better than I would the High Lords'."

Amara shrugged. "That does not, in my view, make the plan any less attractive."

Invidia's eyes flashed with silent anger.

"Give me that information," Amara said quietly. "If it is accurate, we can discuss further cooperative actions. Otherwise, go."

"Give me your word," Invidia said. "Your word that you bargain in good faith."

Amara sneered at her. "You . . . *you*, Invidia, are asking *me* for *my* word? Do you see the irony inherent in that?"

"I know what your word means to you," Invidia said quietly. "I know that you will keep it."

"You don't know what it means," Amara replied. "You have no idea. You might see integrity in others, see it function, see how it guides them. But you do *not* know what it is, traitor."

Invida bared her teeth. "Give me your word," she said. "And I will give you what you ask."

Amara narrowed her eyes for a time, then said, "Very well. Within the limits of my power and influence, I give you my word, Invidia. Deal with me honestly, and I will do what I can to make this bargain for you. Though I must caution you—I do not know what the Princeps' reaction to your proposal is likely to be. Nor can I control it."

Invidia stared at her intently while she spoke. Then she nodded slowly. "I do not think the Princeps is going to be of any concern to anyone for much longer."

"You mean your ex-husband?"

Invidia's expression twisted into mild surprise. "Is he still alive?"

Amara paused deliberately before she spoke, placing emphasis on that silence. "For now," she said, finally. "I assume that the First Lady is still being held by the Queen?"

Invidia curled her lips in a grim little smile, pausing for the exact same length of time before she answered. "She is being held in the hive, along with Araris Valerian. You see, Countess? We can do business."

Amara nodded slowly. "I am listening, Invidia. But not for long."

*　*　*

"She was right here? In the bloody steadholt? In this bloody room?" Raucus bellowed. "Bloody crows, why didn't you raise the alarm?"

"Perhaps because Invidia would undoubtedly have killed her?" Phrygius suggested patiently. "Which was presumably why she approached the Countess instead of one of us?"

Raucus scowled. "I mean after she left. We could have brought the bitch down before she got back to her cave or whatever."

"Perhaps you should let the Countess speak. That way, she'll be able to tell us," Lord Placida said mildly.

Lady Placida frowned and moved her hand as if to restrain her husband, but dropped it back to her side again. Old Cereus sat in a chair near the door, frowning.

"Thank you, Your Grace," Bernard said. "Love?"

"Invidia came here to try to make a deal."

Everyone simply stared at her in shock, except for old Cereus, who snorted. "That isn't surprising," he said. "It's stupid, but not surprising."

"Why not, Your Grace?" Amara asked. She knew, but if any of the High Lords in the room hadn't worked it out yet, it would better come from one of their own than from her.

Cereus shrugged. "Because for Invidia, life was always about pushing people around like pieces on a *ludus* board. In her mind, what's going on right now isn't that different from business as usual in Alera. More difficult, more degrading, more unpleasant, but she doesn't understand what losing a loved one . . ." He cleared his throat. The old man's sons had been killed during High Lord Kalarus's uprising and the initial offensive of the Vord War. "What it can do to a body. How it changes things. Woman's never loved a thing in her life but power."

Amara nodded. "She seeks a more favorable bargaining position. To use whomever she can and abandon whomever she can't."

Phrygius stroked a hand over his roan red beard, musing. "I thought you said that she was trapped in the vord's service. That big bug thing on her chest was the only thing keeping her alive."

"Yes," Amara says, "Which means that she knows or thinks she knows some way to overcome it."

"What did she offer, Countess?" Placidus asked.

Amara told them about the conversation with Invidia. "She said that when we wanted to speak to her, we should send up green signal arrows from her in groups of three. She'll contact us."

Heavy silence followed.

"Do you think she's serious?" Raucus asked. "Tell me you don't think that bitch is serious."

"I think she might be," Lady Placida said slowly.

Phrygius shook his head. "It's a trap."

"Bloody expensive trap," Lord Placida mused. "If that information she gave you is accurate, Countess, we can use it to hurt them badly."

"You aren't thinking like a bloody bug," Raucus said. "She can afford to throw away a million warriors if it means she breaks the back of our heaviest furycraft."

Lady Placida nodded. "And if we deploy our troops to take advantage of the enemy attack, and she's lying to us, the vord will be able to take advantage of *us*. They'll know where we'll have to put them to counter the attack. If Invidia is lying, they can use that to their advantage."

"Hah," Lord Placida said suddenly.

"Oh," Lord Cereus said, at the same time. "Oh, Countess. I see now. Well *played*."

"Thank you, Your Grace," Amara said quietly, nodding to each of them.

Raucous scowled, looking back and forth between them. "What?"

"Don't try to figure it out," Phrygius muttered. "You'll hurt yourself."

"You don't know any more than I do," Raucus shot back.

Lady Placida pinched the bridge of her nose between her thumb and forefinger and let out a slow, patient exhale. "Countess, please. For *my* benefit, please explain."

Amara gave Lord Placida a slight bow, and said, "Your Grace, if you would?"

Lord Placida returned her bow, and said, "The Countess has established a situation in which all roads but the last will end in our favor. We can't be sure about the confrontation with the Queen, regardless of what happens. But we *can* test Invidia's honesty by watching the next vord attack."

"And if she's lying?" Lady Placida asked.

"If she's lying, she's doing it for a reason," Cereus said. "She's doing it because the vord need to create a weakness that they can exploit. We trump her hand by *not* trying to take advantage of the enemy dispositions in the next attack. We maintain the strength of our defenses as they stand and withdraw to Garrison when the evacuation is complete, just as planned. We give them no chance to exploit us. The outcome of this war is going to hinge on killing the Queen in any case, not simply slaughtering warriors."

Lady Placida nodded slowly, one hand toying idly with the single, long braid of her scarlet-auburn hair. "If the vord come at us the way Invidia says they will, we won't be able to hurt them for it. We'll miss the opportunity."

"But we'll know she's telling the truth about something," Amara said. "We've lost nothing. And no matter what happens, we've gained one piece of what I judge to be reasonably reliable information."

"We know my sister and Araris are alive," Bernard rumbled.

Lady Placida's eyes widened. "You think Isana is behind this?"

"I think it is one possibility," Amara said. "But the story about Isana saving Araris from garic poisoning was widely told. If Invidia thinks that Isana could potentially save her from the poisoning as she did Araris, she might well plot to betray the vord. She is determined and very intelligent."

"Would Isana do such a thing?" Lady Placida asked.

"It doesn't matter," Amara said. "All that matters is that Invidia *believes* she can. Whatever the truth, it would appear that Invidia thinks she may have been cast a lifeline."

Lord Antillus managed to fit a profound portion of skepticism into his grunt.

"I know," Amara said. "She's a schemer. But it's possible that she thinks she can scheme her way out of this situation the way she's done so many other times. If that is the case—if she's telling us the truth about the next attack," Amara said, "then she's probably telling us the truth about taking us to the vord Queen."

She frowned. "And there's one other thing. Something she may have genuinely let slip. She said that the Princeps would shortly be of no concern to anyone—and she wasn't talking about Attis."

The room suddenly became utterly silent. The air thrummed with brittle tension.

"I think Octavian is close," Amara said.

"If Invidia or the Queen attacks him, he's as good as dead," Phrygius said. "He's had his full abilities for what? A year at the most? With no formal training? There's no way he could have learned enough technique to apply them. And how many others could he possibly have with him, given that he landed in Antillus . . . a week ago, give or take? How many Knights Aeris were in the First Aleran?"

"Twenty-six," Placida said quietly. "And your sons, Raucus."

Raucus said nothing, but his expression was bleak.

"He must be trying to make it through to us," Phrygius said. "A small, fast-moving group for immediate protection, maybe flying under veils, if he's good enough to do that. It's the only thing that makes sense."

Placida nodded. "And if they're talking about taking him down, then he's probably close enough for the Queen to attack."

"No," Bernard said in a quiet, firm voice. "She's close enough for *him* to attack *her*, Your Grace."

"If the Queen is beyond Invidia, she's beyond Octavian," Phrygius said. "Simple as that. He's barely more than a boy."

"He shut down the plans of Invidia *and* Attis when he *was* a boy," Bernard growled, his eyes on Phrygius's. "I doubt he's planning on facing her in a wrestling ring or a dueling hall. You'd be a fool to dismiss him, Your Grace."

Phrygius narrowed his eyes, and his beard bristled.

Raucus put a hand on his shoulder. "Easy, Gun. Don't make more of that than what he said. What if I'd spoken of your son that way, huh?"

Lord Phrygius was stiff for a moment more, then inclined his head toward Bernard. "He's your blood. I didn't think before I spoke. Please excuse me."

Bernard nodded.

"Stay focused," Lady Placida said. "We can't know what to do about Octavian until we find him, or he makes contact. It's possible that he wants it that way. We can't know if Invidia is going to betray us at the last moment. But. Assuming that she appears to be telling us the truth . . . the only question is whether or not we pit ourselves against her knowing that it could be a trap, and we could be walking to our deaths. For that matter, even if she is sincere, we might *still* die."

Raucus exhaled slowly. "Maybe we should bring Forcia, Attica, and Riva."

Cereus shook his head. "They've never been fighters, I'm afraid. In a close-quarters fight, they'd be more dangerous to us than to the vord."

"It's up to us," Lord Placida said quietly. "And I don't think we're going to get a better chance. I don't think we have a choice, even if it *is* a trap. I'm in."

His wife intertwined her fingers with his, silently.

Cereus rose, with either his armor or his bones creaking.

Phrygius eyed Raucus, and said, "Maybe I'll finally get to see you get knocked on your ass."

"When we get back, you and I are going to have a talk in which you lose your teeth," Antillus replied. "Because I'm going to knock them out of your head. With my fists."

"I think we all understood what you meant at the end of your first sentence, dolt."

"Boys, boys," Aria said, her voice warm. "It doesn't matter unless she's telling the truth about the next attack, in any case. Until then, we're not changing any plans, yes?"

"Correct," Bernard said. "We lie low and wait. We'll meet again in Garrison and talk about the next step after we see what happens. If she's telling the truth, we'll know it in about three hours."

The meeting broke up. The High Lords went back out to their positions on the wall, leaving Amara and Bernard alone in the room.

Bernard watched her with calm green eyes for several seconds before he said, "What were you holding back?"

"What makes you think I was holding anything back, love?" Amara asked

He shrugged. "Know you too well, I suppose." He tilted his head, frowning, then nodded slowly. "You talked a lot about the vord's next attack. Kept their focus on it. So it's going to happen later." He furrowed his brow in thought. "Invidia's going to betray us at the hive."

"Yes," Amara said quietly. "She is."

Bernard inhaled slowly. "What are we going to do about it?"

The room, Amara thought, felt positively cavernous without the presence of the High Lords there. She bowed her head and closed her eyes and tried not to think too hard about what she had to do. "We," she whispered, "are going to let her."

⌶⌶⌶⌶ CHAPTER 44

Tavi awakened smoothly, naturally, and free of pain. He was floating in a tub of warm water, his head and shoulders supported on an inclined board. He was naked. His toes poked out of the water at the far end of the tub. He lifted his head, which was an effort. There was an angry red puckering of his skin over his belly, to the left of his navel, where the vord Queen's weapon had stabbed him. Little, angry veins of red spread out from the injury.

Tavi looked blearily around him. A healer's tent. One of the ones that hadn't been destroyed, obviously. Furylamps lit it. So he'd been unconscious for hours, but not many of them. Unless it had been more than a day.

He hated being unconscious. It *always* interrupted everything he had planned.

He turned his head to the left, and found the tub beside him occupied. Maximus lay in it. He looked awful, though that was mostly bruises beneath the skin of his shoulders, neck, face, head . . . There seemed very little of his friend that was *not* bruised, in fact. And his nose had been broken—again. His eyes were closed, but he was breathing.

Tavi leaned up a little and eyed the next tub over. Crassus occupied it, in the same condition he and Maximus enjoyed. The young Tribune stirred, though he looked like he felt even worse than Tavi did.

"Crassus," Tavi rasped.

Though he blinked his eyes open, the young man was still clearly in pain. He looked at Tavi and lifted his chin very slightly in acknowledgment.

"Crassus," Tavi croaked. His throat felt dry. It hurt to talk. "Report."

"I hurt," Crassus said, his voice slurring and weak. He closed his eyes again. "End of report."

Tavi tried to get the young man to open his eyes again, but there was no rousing him. He sank back tiredly into the tub.

"He's very tired," said a quiet voice. "It's better if you let him rest, Your Majesty. The attack on the headquarters tent was defeated and most of the attackers slain. We lost twenty-two, all of them from among the guards stationed around the command tent."

Tavi looked up to see Dorotea sitting quietly on a camp stool near the tent's entrance. She looked terrible, her eyes sunken, her cheeks bloodless. The collar on her throat threw back the subdued light of the lamp with a silent, malevolent gleam. She held a blanket wrapped around her though the night was not cold.

"Your Highness," he corrected her gently. "I'm not the First Lord yet."

The slave smiled tiredly. "You just stood against the nightmare of our time, young man. You put your life at hazard for the sake of a slave who once tried to murder you. Thank you. Your Majesty."

"If you want to thank a hero, thank Foss," Tavi said wearily. "He's the one who saved you."

"My thanks won't matter to him now," she said quietly. "I hope his rest is peaceful."

Tavi sat up slowly. "Where's Kitai?"

"Sleeping," Dorotea said. "She was exhausted."

"What happened after I went down?"

The slave smiled faintly. "Several of us were unconscious and dying. You. Me. Maximus. Crassus. She was not in good condition herself, and did not have the strength remaining to attempt a healing on more than one person. She had to choose whom to save."

Tavi took a slow breath. "Ah. And she chose you. Someone to lead the less-experienced healers."

Dorotea inclined her head slightly, as if she was afraid something might spill out if she tipped it too far. "Our senior folk were all conferring when . . ." She shivered. "When you saw us. Kitai's was a remarkably rational decision, under the circumstances. Emotions tend to overrule reason when one is in pain and afraid for another. And her feelings for you are disturbingly intense. She could easily have let those feelings control her. And I, my son, and your friend Maximus would all be dead."

"She made the right call," Tavi said. He looked at Max and Crassus. "How are they?"

Dorotea tightened the blanket around her slightly. "I assume that you know that watercrafting does not simply make a subject whole again. It draws upon the body's resources to restore what has been made unwhole."

"Of course," Tavi said.

"There are limits. And . . . and my Crassus had so *many* injuries. Broken bones. Shattered organs." She bit her lip and closed her eyes. "I did all that I could, *everything*, but there are limits to what can be repaired. The body can only sustain so much of its own regeneration . . ."

She shuddered and shook for several seconds. Then suddenly Dorotea seemed to master herself and lifted her face, wiping tears briskly from her cheeks. Her voice was unsteady, but she attempted to use crisp, professional description. "Crassus's injuries were extensive and serious. I repaired enough damage that they should not shorten his life. Assuming that there is no infection—which is an acute danger when a body is so badly strained—he may be able to walk again. Eventually. His days as a Tribune are finished."

Tavi swallowed and nodded. "Maximus?"

"The vord Queen hit him on the head rather than anywhere vital," Dorotea said with tired, almost fond irritation. "He's fine. Or will be, when he wakes up. It could take a while."

"How am I?" Tavi asked.

"The priority was to restore you to complete function," she said. "The actual trauma wasn't bad. The poisoning was acute, but not as difficult to overcome as others might have been. The only issue was keeping you breathing, for a while. You should be able to enter battle if you need to."

Tavi nodded slowly. Then he sat up, and said, "You look terrible. Get some rest. Battle's coming."

Dorotea looked over at Crassus again. "I won't leave him."

"You've already said you've done all you can," Tavi said, gently. "And other lives are going to depend on you. You'll rest. That is an order."

Dorotea's eyes flickered back to him, hot for a half second, before her mouth turned up into a slow, tired smile. "You can't give me an order, sir. You aren't the captain of the Free Aleran. My orders come from him."

"But I can order *him*," Tavi said testily. "Bloody crows, what does a man have to do to get a little respect around here? Am I the First Lord or not?"

Dorotea's smile widened, and she bowed her head. "Very well. Your Majesty. There are guards around and over and quite likely under the tent. But speak, and they will be here."

"Thank you."

Tavi waited until she had left to ease himself out of the tub. He felt shaky, but no worse than he had any of a number of other times he'd endured a healer's attentions. He climbed out without help and found a clean set of clothes laid out for him.

Tavi got dressed, though it was painful to bend at the waist. The strange sword he had been stabbed with had left an equally strange scar, a stiff ridge of nearly purple tissue, and the area around it was exquisitely tender. He slid into his pants and belted his tunic on cautiously. A quick spike of pain went through him and made him clench his teeth over suddenly frozen breath.

The awareness of a gaze upon him made Tavi look back, and he found Crassus awake again, bleary eyes focused on him.

"M' mother," Crassus said. "She was alive. And you didn't t-tell me."

Tavi stared at his friend in pure shock. It was true. He hadn't. Antillus Dorotea had been a traitor to the Realm, along with her brother, High Lord Kalarus. She had been snapped up for her talents in the slave rebellion that had followed the destruction of Kalarus and the chaos in Kalaran lands, and no one had known or cared who she was—only what she could do. Had he brought her true identity to light, it would have forced him to bring charges against her as well. More importantly, she had all but begged him not to tell her husband or her son that she had survived. Trapped in a slave collar that could not be removed without killing her, it was, in a sense, true. The woman who had plotted against the Realm would never return.

She had saved Crassus once before, when he was unconscious, but he had never wakened during the procedure, and she had been gone before he was awake again. She never left the Free Aleran camp or train and had hidden virtually in plain sight for the past years.

But this time Crassus had seen her.

Crassus's eyes burned. "Didn't *tell* me."

"She asked me not to," Tavi said quietly.

Crassus squeezed his eyes shut, as if in agony. Given his injuries, there was every chance that he was—even without other considerations. "Get away from me, Octavian."

"Rest," Tavi said. "We'll talk, later, when this is all—"

"Get *out!*" Crassus snarled. "How could you? Get *out.*"

He dropped back down, wheezing, and was asleep again, or unconscious, within seconds.

Tavi sat down on the stool Dorotea had vacated, shaking. He lowered his head to his hands and just sat there for a moment. Crows take it. He had never wanted this. And yet, it had been such a small worry among so *many* others. Truth be told, he'd barely thought about it. And now, the lie he'd felt he had no other choice than to make might have cost him the love and respect of a friend.

"Such a small concern, for a man with your problems," said Alera quietly.

Tavi looked up to see the great fury, appearing as she usually did, but this time also covered in a misty grey cloak and hood that hid all of her features but her face. Her gemstone eyes were calm and gently amused.

"I don't have so many friends that I can't be worried about losing one," Tavi said quietly. He looked at Max, silent and still in his tub. "Or more."

Alera regarded him steadily.

"I saw Foss die. I saw what was going to happen seconds before it did, and I just wasn't fast enough. I couldn't stop the Queen. He died. She killed so many people. And they died for nothing. She escaped. I failed them."

"She is most formidable. You knew that."

"That doesn't matter," Tavi said quietly, his voice growing harsh. "It was my responsibility. My duty. I know not everyone survives a war, but by the furies, I will *not* see my men give their lives for *nothing*." His throat tightened, and he bowed his head. "I . . . I wonder. I wonder if I am the right man for this work. If I had . . . if I had learned more, if I had been given more time to practice, if I had practiced harder . . ."

"You wonder if it would have made a difference," Alera said.

"Yes."

She considered the question gravely. Then she sat down on the floor beside the stool, folding her legs beneath her. "There's no way to be certain of things that never took place."

"I know."

"You agree. Yet you still feel that way about it."

Tavi nodded. They were both silent for a time.

"Good men," she said quietly, "must feel as you do. Or they are not good men."

"I don't understand."

Alera smiled. "A good man, almost by definition, would seriously question any decisions he made that led to such terrible consequences for others. Especially if those others trusted him. Would you agree?"

"Yes."

"Would you agree that you are fallible?"

"I feel it is manifestly obvious."

"Would you agree that the world is a dangerous and unfair place?"

"Of course."

"Then there you have it," Alera said. "Someone must command. But no one who does so is perfect. He will, therefore, make mistakes. And, since the world is dangerous and unfair, it is inevitable that some of those mistakes will eventually have consequences like those today."

"I can hardly dispute your reasoning," Tavi said quietly. "But I do not see your point."

"It is quite obvious, young Gaius," Alera said, smiling, her eyes wrinkling at the corners. "The logic is indisputable: You are a good man."

Tavi lifted his eyebrows. "What has that to do with anything?"

"In my experience?" she asked. "A very great deal. Perhaps Kitai will explain it to you later."

Tavi shook his head. "You saw the battle?"

"Of course."

"Is the Queen as strong as you believed her to be?"

"Not at all," Alera said.

"Oh?"

"She is stronger," the great fury said calmly. "And she handles herself almost as well as you do. Someone has been giving her lessons."

Tavi nodded ruefully. "I noticed." He shook his head. "I . . . I can't believe anything could be so powerful. So fast."

"Yes," Alera said. "I warned you about that."

"Then you see why I must question my place here," Tavi said quietly. "If I can't outwit her, anticipate her, overcome her . . . why am I attempting to lead these men at all? Can I take them forward with me, knowing that . . . that . . ."

"That you quite likely take them to their deaths," Alera said.

Tavi closed his eyes. "Yes."

Alera's voice turned wry. "How many more would have died had you done nothing, young Gaius? How many more would have died had you perished with the Queen's first strike? Do you not see what this attack means?"

He opened his eyes and frowned up at her.

"She cannot have many Citizens left to her," Alera said. "Yet she attacked this camp with more than fifty strongly gifted earthcrafters, knowing that it was a suicide mission. She told you she'd only come to weaken you."

"That . . . doesn't make any sense," Tavi said. "To waste such a valuable resource merely to weaken an opponent? Why would she do such a thing?"

"Indeed, why?" Alera asked.

"Because she thought it *was* worth the sacrifice," Tavi murmured. "But that doesn't make sense. Our losses were . . ." His lips tightened bitterly. "Light."

"She didn't come here to kill you, young Gaius. Not yet. She came here to bleed you."

"But *why?*" Tavi asked. "If she'd waited until the Legion was closer, she could have hit us with overwhelming support rather than losing her collared Citizens. It isn't rational! It's . . ."

He suddenly stopped speaking. He blinked twice.

"It *isn't* rational," he said softly. "It's the kind of mistake a young commander makes when victory is threatened. He forgets to be disciplined. He decides that doing *anything* is a better idea than doing nothing." Tavi's eyes widened. "She was *afraid* of me."

Alera inclined her head and said nothing.

A moment later, Tavi snorted. "Well. I think I must have cured her of that mistaken impression."

"And yet," Alera said quietly, "she ran. You didn't."

"Of course she ran. It prevented us from concentrating forces on her. It allowed her to control the pace of the fight . . ." His eyes widened.

Defeating the vord Queen was not about simple bloodletting. It was not about tactics, about furycraft, about organization or technique or ranks of shining armor.

It was about minds. It was about wills.

It was about fear.

Tavi felt himself shoot up off the table. "The horde," he said. "Where is it now?"

Alera considered the matter for a moment, then said, "They are about to attack the second defensive wall of the Valley. I do not think there is a reasonable chance of the Legions holding the wall."

"They aren't supposed to," Tavi said. "The vord have no chance of overcoming Garrison unless they are directed. To control them, the Queen must be within twenty-five or thirty miles—*well* beyond the second wall. That's near Bernardholt. I know that region, and there are only so many places where she could set up a defensive position around her hive."

Alera tilted her head thoughtfully. "You'll have the advantage of knowing the terrain."

"Yes," Tavi said, showing his teeth. "And if she's afraid of me interfering, it means that I *can*." He nodded firmly. "Every important fight I've ever been in was against someone bigger and stronger than me. This is no different."

Alera's gemstone eyes glittered. "If you say so, young Gaius." And she was gone.

Tavi stalked out of the healer's tent.

Twenty *legionares* snapped immediately to attention. Another sixty, within

the immediate circle of light, came hustling off the ground, some of them rousing from (fully armored, fully uncomfortable) sleep to do it. Every *legionare* in
sight bore the symbol of First Aleran, the eagle upon the field of scarlet and
silver—but the design had been blackened and subtly altered into the shape of
a crow. The Battlecrows had been the cohort who had followed Tavi into the
horrible business at the end of the Battle of the Elinarch, and ever since they
had maintained a reputation for discipline, absolutely deadly efficiency on the
battlefield, and reckless disregard for danger. In most Legions, men sought to
gain promotion to the Prime Cohort, traditionally the cohort composed of the
Legion's most experienced (and highest-paid) soldiers. In the First Aleran, men
strove very nearly as hard to be accepted into the Battlecrows, the cohort that
most often followed the captain into the deadliest portions of the battlefield.

Eighty men slammed their armored hands into their armored chests at the
same instant, like a report of mortal thunder.

"Schultz," Tavi called quietly.

A centurion strode out of the ranks, a soldier younger than Tavi himself.
Schultz had come a long way since the Elinarch. He'd grown half a foot, for one
thing, and added sixty pounds of muscle to the frame of a youth. His face and
armor both bore scars, and he had discarded the helmet crest that denoted him
as something other than a *legionare*, but he walked with erect pride and carried
his baton beneath his arm in the best tradition of Legion centurions. He snapped
off a precise salute to Tavi. "Sir."

"We're leaving," Tavi said.

Schultz blinked. "Sir? Do you want me to round up the command officers
for you?"

"We're not waiting that long," Tavi said. "The vord Queen knows where we
are, and we're going to be somewhere else as soon as possible. I need runners,
Schultz, to go to each cohort's Tribune and bear my personal command to break
camp. I want to be on the road in no more than an hour. Anyone who can't be
ready to go will be left behind. Understood?"

Schultz looked dazed. "Ah. Yes, sir. Runners to each Tribune, your personal
command to break camp, moving in an hour or left behind, sir."

"Good man," Tavi said. He turned to the assembled century of men and
raised his voice. "The Legions have a long tradition, boys. You march hard and fast
and show up in places where no one expects you—and then you go to work." He
grinned. "And you do it all carrying a hundred pounds of gear made by whoever
did it for the least coin—but every one of those slives gets paid better than you!
It's tradition!"

A growl of laughter went around the group of soldiers.

"This march," Tavi said, "is different."

He let silence sit over the men for a moment.

"In a moment, you're going to go out and give the orders to move out. And you're going to tell the men this: No packs. No tents. No blankets. No spare boots. They don't matter anymore."

The silence thickened.

"We have to move, fast and hard," Tavi said. "There are millions of lives at stake, and the enemy knows where we are. So we're not going to be here. We're going to be in Calderon by tomorrow, a full day before we're expected. And then we're going to find the vord Queen and pay the bitch back for what she did tonight."

Eighty men raised their voices in a sudden, furious roar of approval.

"Schultz will give you your assignments," Tavi said. "Get it done."

Another roar went up, and Schultz began striding down the ranks, striking each man lightly on his armored shoulder with his baton and issuing the name of an Aleran or Canim officer he was to contact. The men went sprinting into the dark, and within minutes trumpeters were sounding the signal to prepare to march.

"Sir," Schultz said, after he'd sent the last of the men off, "we might make Calderon that fast. But the Canim can't, sir, nor their beasts. There's no way."

Tavi showed the *legionare* his most Canish smile. "Faith, Schultz," he said. "Where there's a will, there is a way. And my will is for us all to be in Calderon by the sunrise after next."

Schultz blinked. "Sir?"

"Get the rest of the 'Crows ready to move out, Schultz," he said. "That's your job. Getting all of us there? That's mine."

▷□▷□▷□▷ CHAPTER 45

The vord came precisely when Invidia said they would. Sunrise was still four hours away, and once the moon had vanished behind the mountains to the south, the night turned as black as the inside of a coffin.

Amara was on the wall, waiting to see if Invidia had spoken the truth. There was no warning whatsoever. In one moment, the night was completely silent and still. In the next, there was a single flicker of movement at the very edge of the ground illuminated by the wall's furylights, then the gleaming black chitin of the horde exploded from the night, rushing across the ground in the rumble of millions of feet striking the still-scorched earth.

They must have moved slowly and silently until they reached the edge of the lights, Amara thought. No Aleran Legion could possibly have moved stealthily in such vast numbers—but it hadn't done them any good. The *legionares* on the walls were ready and waiting.

Hundreds of Citizens brought up the flickering curtain of fist-sized firespheres that had first been used at Riva. It proved just as deadly to the foe here as it had at the great city. Vord surged into the burned zone before the wall and were slain in blasts of fire and superheated air, a million deadly fireflies barring their way. The horde died by the hundreds, then the thousands, but as they had at Riva, the weight of numbers began to let the vord grind their way forward, scrambling over the corpses of their fallen comrades, laying a road of death and twitching limbs for those coming behind them.

Within moments, the vord had paid the necessary toll, and the Aleran firecrafters who lined the walls began to crumple down, exhausted. As they did, they were replaced with every Knight Flora in the Legions, and every Citizen with the necessary skills to join them. Arrows began to leap from bows, their fury-enhanced limbs sending the shafts leaping forward with supernatural power.

Deadly arrows hissed through the night, with the Knights Flora working in teams of ten and twenty, sharing targets with shouts of coordination, each archer loosing as fast as he could. Hundreds of streams of arrows slewed back and forth across the vord lines, like the sprays of water used by fire wardens in cities all across Alera.

In many ways, Amara supposed, fighting the vord was a great deal more like battling a fire than an enemy. They rushed forward with the same implacable need to devour and spread. The streams of arrows would beat back the vord where their deadly skill touched them, but wherever a stream hadn't swept for a few seconds, the vord surged forward again, like a blaze chewing through an old wooden building—just as determined, and just as unstoppable.

Amara licked her lips, her heart beating faster, as the first vord mantis reached the wall and began gouging out fresh climbing holds. Archer teams began withdrawing, leaving heavily armed *legionares* to take their places.

Standing beside her, Bernard nodded judiciously. "About now, I think."

Amara nodded and turned to the trumpeter next to her. "Signal the mules."

The man saluted and immediately began blowing a quick signal on his horn. In the dark on the ground behind the wall, the mules went to work again. Their arms made a creaking sound, followed by a distinct report of wooden arm striking wooden crossbeam, followed by a rattling, thumping sound as the mule rocked wildly back and forth before settling down again. A few seconds later, the ground outside the walls was illuminated by a blossoming wall of flame, incinerating hundreds more vord.

But they never slowed down.

Bernard watched a while more, until every archer team in sight was down from the walls and in their second position. The *legionares* fought on doggedly, throwing down the enemy with sword and shield, spear and fury. "Any sign?" he asked Amara.

Amara swept her eyes over the sky. It was impossible to see even the stars of the moonless sky outside of the radius of the wall's furylamps. "Not yet," she reported.

Bernard grunted. "What about that reserve force?"

Amara looked up and down the walls for the telltale colored furylamps they were using to send messages. A flashing blue light would have indicated that someone had spotted the specialized troops Invidia had described. "Not yet," Amara said.

Bernard nodded and continued watching the battle, unmoving, apparently unconcerned.

Amara knew it was a facade, for the benefit of the troops, and she tried to support it by appearing just as calm and steady as her husband—but despite her efforts, she bit her lip when she saw a young *legionare*, barely more than a boy, seized by a mantis's scythes and tossed screaming into the swarm below. His companions in arms cut the vord responsible into quivering chunks—but they were too late for the youth. Wounded were being carried from the wall by field medicos every few seconds. Once more, the Marat and their gargants stood by, patiently waiting while dozens of wounded were loaded into their carrying harnesses, then turned to begin striding toward Garrison.

"This is getting tight," Bernard muttered. "They're pushing harder than they did before."

"Should we sound retreat?"

Bernard stood calmly, looking down at the battle and giving no indication of his concern on his face or in his body language. "Not yet. We've got to know."

Amara nodded again and struggled to control her outer self once more. It was difficult. Calm and composure in the face of personal danger was something she had been trained for, something she had mastered. Watching others carried away, screaming in agony—or worse, dying in perfect silence—in support of the plan she'd helped to shape and create was something else entirely. She hadn't been ready for this. She'd had no talent whatsoever for watercrafting, and could barely make water roll across the bottom of a shallow pan, back at the Academy, when she'd been practicing hard. Now she wished she'd done even more. She would give anything to be able to let herself feel the horror that was hammering down on her without fearing that the sight of tears on her face might make things even worse.

She clenched her fists instead, forcing away the emotion. Later. She could let herself feel it later, she promised, when signs of panic among the command staff wouldn't deal gaping wounds to the *legionares'* morale.

She didn't know how long she held herself there, rigid and still. Only moments, surely, but they felt like hours—hours of nightmare, suddenly broken by distant, crackling reports from the night sky overhead.

Amara snapped her gaze up to see fire-spheres blossoming there in balls of grass green, arctic blue, and glacial purple. Black shapes like swarming moths flickered near and around the flaming spheres—vordknights, thousands of them. "Bernard!"

Bernard glanced at her, then up, then grinned suddenly, and the explosion of another massive salvo from the mules cast his face in a feral, almost bloodthirsty combination of light and shadow. "Trying to sneak over the wall to take out the mules in the dark, when we couldn't see them coming," he said. "But the Placidas and the northerners found them first." He pursed his lips for a moment, then said, "Glad they aren't directly overhead."

As if to punctuate Bernard's statement, the corpse of a vordknight, missing its head and two-thirds of the surface of its wings, plunged down and landed on the ground beside one of the crewmen of the mules. The crewman jumped and let out a shriek of surprise, before falling onto his rear, earning a round of frantic-edged belly laughs from his crewmates.

More vordknights appeared, beginning to dive upon the crews of the mules—but each team of Knights Flora had retreated from the wall to its assigned war engine, and they began providing their mule crews with a deadly shield of withering archery. Vordknights fell from the skies and smashed to the earth like rotten fruit. One of them came down on the small ammunition wagon of fire-spheres behind one of the mules, and it exploded in a sudden angry bellow of fire that roared out and consumed the vordknight, the wagon, the mule, its screaming crewmen, and the archers who had been protecting them. Deadly shards of wood from the shattered wagon flew out in every direction, wounding more men on either side, and Amara saw one shard no less than four feet long completely transfix one *legionare's* thigh, sending the man screaming to the floor of the battlements.

Amara made a gesture to the trumpeter, and the man sounded the call for an aerial attack. With a roar, hundreds of Citizens and Knights Aeris rose into the skies to do battle with the enemy in the darkness overhead. The sound of their windstreams was like the roaring of the sea crashing against stone cliffs. Each unit of Knights was led by Counts and Lords, many of them gifted in multiple disciplines of furycraft, and the number of exploding firecraftings overhead doubled and redoubled, a soaring panoply of brief-lived, swollen stars in every color imaginable. Roaring windstreams rose and fell in pitch and tone, making oddly musical harmonies amidst the flashes of chromatic fire.

Every eye in the whole of the Calderon Valley not being used to fight for survival was glued to the beautiful, deadly display.

"And now that our attention is on the sky," Bernard said, "it's time for the surprise attack. Your Lordship, if you would be so kind as to light the field."

Lord Gram stood nearby and grunted acknowledgment. Though the Princeps had put Bernard in charge of the defenses, Amara's husband had also served Gram for many years as one of the first Steadholders placed in the then-Count's service. Now Gram was a Lord (granted, his lands had been overrun by the enemy, but he was still a Lord), and her husband had made an extra effort to show Gram courtesy, despite his pained jaw. Gram didn't need it, Amara thought, and would have been perfectly comfortable following a simple order—but even in the face of ruin, Bernard had the presence of mind to be considerate. She supposed that, in a way, that sort of grace was symbolic of a great deal of what they were fighting for; the preservation of unnecessary beauty.

Gram stepped forward, lifted his hand, and casually held it out, palm up. Fire kindled in his cupped fingers, until a moment later a tiny form hovered there, just above the surface of his hand—a little feathered figure, its wings blurred into invisibility with their speed. The hot wind washing from them stirred Amara's hair. Gram whispered something to the little fire fury, and flicked his wrist. The fiery hummingbird shot off into the night, gathering speed and brightening in intensity as it flew.

It swept over the battlefield, a globe of white daylight several hundred yards across. It zipped over countless mantis warriors, and at one point blew entirely through the torso of a vordknight that had flown down to intercept it, not even slowing down.

"Bad idea," Gram said, shaking his head, "getting in Phyllis's way like that."

"Phyllis?" Bernard asked.

"Keep those teeth together, Calderon," Gram said testily. "Named her for my first wife. Hotter than any torch, couldn't sit still, and you didn't want to get in her way, either."

Amara smiled at the exchange and tracked Phyllis's progress—and within moments, she spotted the oncoming special units, exactly where Invidia had said they would be.

"Bloody blighted crows," Gram breathed, as if barely able to summon enough wind to speak.

Amara understood the feeling.

The oncoming vord were huge.

They weren't huge on the same order as a gargant. They were huge on the same order as *buildings*. There were half a dozen of them, each the size of three or four of the largest merchant ships. They moved on four legs, each thicker than the trunk of any tree Amara had ever seen. Their vaguely triangular heads ended in a jagged, black chitin beak that rather reminded her of that of an octopus, except large enough to hold three or four hogshead barrels. The creatures had no eyes that she could see, and their beaks simply seemed to flow up into their skulls, and from there into enormous arching fans of the same material, spreading around the titans' heads like shields. Every stride carried them a good twenty feet, and though they looked ponderous, their pace was, like a gargant's, swifter than one would expect. Dozens of mantis warriors could run beneath them at a time, and though a mantis could run faster than some horses, they passed the enormous bulks of moving black chitin only slowly.

A word from Gram halted Phyllis above the nearest bulk, and everyone on the walls who could be spared from fighting could only stare. Centurion Giraldi stepped up to the battlements beside Bernard and Gram. He stared at the bulks for a moment, and breathed, "Sir? I'd like a bigger wall now."

In the same instant, all six of the bulks raised their opened maws and let out basso bellows. They did not sound loud, precisely, but the sound shook the wall and Amara's bones with unnerving intensity.

The mules loosed another volley, which landed all around the leading bulk, exploding into fiery destruction. The great beast did not react. It just kept coming on, as vast and unstoppable as a glacier. As the bulks passed through the fires, Amara saw vord behemoths and mantises crouched upon their glossy, armored backs, as tiny as parasite-birds on the backs of gargants.

Amara could see the idea behind the creatures at once. They would roll forward and smash through the wall like so much rotten fencing. Anyone that attacked them would be forced to deal with the defenders riding upon them.

Amara started as a sudden presence intruded close upon her, but looked over to find that Doroga had arrived and made his way to them on the wall. The slab-shouldered Marat looked calm and interested as his eyes traveled along the walls, through the skies, then down to the field out in front of them. He, too, stared at the bulks for a slow count to seven before pursing his lips, and saying, "Hungh." After a moment, he added, "Big."

"Bloody crows," Gram said. "Bloody crows. Bloody crows."

"We got a problem, Count," Giraldi said.

"Bloody crows."

Bernard nodded. "Possibly."

"Bloody crows," said Gram. "Blighted bloody crows."

Giraldi's hand was resting on his sword. "I'd say get some archers and go for the eyes. But they ain't got any eyes."

"Mmmm," Bernard said.

"Bloody crows," said Gram.

"Sir?" the centurion asked. "What do we do?"

"We be quiet for a moment, so that I can think," Bernard said. He stared at the oncoming bulks. They were bellowing almost constantly, and signs of panic had begun to spread along the wall. A nervous gargant, somewhere nearby, let out its own coughing roar, and Bernard glanced over his shoulder in irritation— and then his eyes locked onto Doroga. They narrowed once, and the wolfish smile reappeared.

"We don't go for the eyes, centurion," Bernard said. "We go for their *feet*."

Doroga looked at Bernard, then barked out a harsh laugh, one that sounded rather remarkably like the one that the gargant, probably Walker, had just loosed.

Amara looked at Doroga, blinking, and suddenly understood. Years before, during the first vord invasion in this very valley, they had spoken with Doroga after a battle, while the Marat took care of his gargant's enormous padded paws:

"Feet," the Marat had rumbled. *"Always got to help him take care of his feet. Feet are important when you are as big as Walker."*

It made sense. Those creatures, whatever they were, had to be of fantastic weight—all of it settling upon four relatively small feet. Something that large could not easily manage its own mass, Amara was sure. A crippled foot might prevent the beast from moving at all.

Of course, the thousands of mantises running in a living river around and sometimes upon those feet could make it a bit difficult to reach the target. One of the High Lords might make short work of it, but they were mostly engaged above, and the Legion firecrafters had already exhausted themselves.

Of course . . . one didn't really *need* to hurt the bulks. They only needed to stop them, before they breached the wall and left gaps into which the vord swarm would pour, running down the retreating Legions before they could reach Garrison.

"Bernard," Amara said, her own voice thready. "Riva."

"Hah," Bernard said. He turned to Giraldi. "Centurion, signal arrows. One: Lord Riva to report to me. Two: General call for engineers at this location."

Signal arrows were bright enough to be seen for miles. The message would get to Riva within a moment. It would take him little longer to fly back to the front, but Amara was not sure how much time they actually *had*.

It seemed to take forever, and the bulks pressed ever closer. The mantises seemed to go mad with eagerness as they did, as if the bulks were pushing out some kind of psychic bow wave. One breach appeared atop the wall, and another, and Bernard dispatched reserves to reinforce the weakened areas.

There was the roar of a nearby windstream, and Riva, dressed in trousers and a loose, unbuttoned shirt, his hair a wildly tossed mess, looked blearily around the wall. He spotted Bernard and moved to him, lifting his fist in a salute and glancing out at the bulks as he did. He froze. "Bloody crows."

"Bloody crows," agreed Gram.

"We need water," Bernard said to Riva. "My lord, we need to water that ground, and we need to do it now."

Riva opened and closed his mouth a few times, then seemed to shake himself. "Oh, of course. Bog them down. We'd need a river to do it in time."

"The Rillwater," Bernard said. "It isn't far from here. Maybe a quarter mile southwest."

Riva lifted his eyebrows and nodded. "Possible, perhaps. Engineers?"

"Assembled below."

"Aye, aye," Riva mused. "Just like irrigating a field. Only more so. Excuse me."

Riva leapt from the wall to the courtyard below, braking his fall with windcrafting, and turned to the engineers. He began issuing rapid orders. The men gathered in ranks and knelt to place their bare hands against the earth. Riva, at the front of the group, did the same, and several hundred experienced engineers, led by Riva, began to make the earth quiver.

It didn't take long. There was a moment where nothing changed, then the charging mantises began to appear with their lower extremities covered in mud. The mud splatters began to go farther and farther up their legs—but the ground before the walls had been superheated several times over the last day, and had baked into something almost like hardened clay.

"More!" Riva shouted. "More, crows take you!"

The strain upon the furycrafters was enormous. One of the engineers let out a strangled squeak and abruptly fell onto his side, thrashing and clutching at his left shoulder. Two others simply collapsed, dead or unconscious.

Rushing water abruptly spread over the ground beneath the walls, rolling across it like a vast mirror that reflected the deadly glory of the ongoing aerial battle.

They waited, while the engineers kept up the effort of redirecting the little river. Men collapsed every few moments. Lord Riva's face became strained, with blotches of color on his pale cheeks. The water rose.

Then one of the vordbulks let out a higher pitched bellow as one of its feet slid out from beneath it, sliding on the smooth clay surface made slippery by water and by the dust and grains of dirt churned up by the passing of so many mantis feet. It listed far to one side, like a ship wallowing between swells, but then slowly, slowly righted itself. A moment later, it took another step and resumed its advance

"Close!" bellowed Bernard back toward Riva over his shoulder. "Can you give them a shake?"

"Aye!" Riva panted, his jaw set. Then he closed his eyes again, speaking to the engineers, and suddenly the earth itself groaned. It jerked and quivered once. Then it lurched abruptly to one side, and Amara staggered against Doroga, who caught her and prevented her from falling.

Out on the field, two more vordbulks, no more than two hundred yards from the walls, screamed and slipped, falling awkwardly. They pitched over toward their sides in motions that were rendered slow-looking by sheer scale. It took them what seemed like seconds to fall, letting out bone-shaking basso calls of distress as they did. They hit the ground hard, driven by their own vast weight, sending tons of water and mud flying into the air with the impact. Dozens, if not hundreds, of vord were crushed beneath each of the monstrous creatures, whose weight was sufficient to leave a deep impression even in the baked clay. They thrashed, their limbs crushing more vord, and moaned out low calls that made the surface of the shallow water around them quiver.

"Good enough," Bernard said. "Good enough. It'll have to be." He looked at Giraldi, suddenly sweating. "Centurion, the stone."

Giraldi reached into his pouch and retrieved a smooth, oblong stone of the same color as the wall. He passed it to Bernard, who placed it upon the ground, and said, "Prepare to sound retreat."

The trumpeter looked nervously out at the field and licked his lips.

Bernard took a deep breath, then drove the heel of his boot down onto the stone, shattering it.

A pulse of cold wind seemed to flow out from the broken stone, raising dust and smearing fresh blood into new streaks. Seconds after it did, one of the merlons, the large blocks of stone atop battlements, suddenly quivered and groaned, its form twisting into a new shape. What looked like a Phrygian sled dog seemed to come shuddering out of the block of stone as if digging its way from a snowbank.

It promptly turned, lunged forward, and crushed a vord warrior against the opposite merlon, splattering the mantis to shards of broken chitin and smears of green-brown blood.

All along the walls, the canine gargoyles came to life and began smashing into the vord with implacable ferocity—and once all of them were free of the merlons, the stone *beneath* that recently vacated place began to quiver and heave, and more gargoyles began to emerge.

"Sound retreat!" Bernard ordered.

The trumpet began sounding the signal, and the Legions moved back instantly, as if Bernard's voice had carried to each and every one of them. Amara joined her husband and the rest of the command staff as they turned to abandon the walls, while all around them more and more canine gargoyles tore their way free of the stone that made the wall and began killing vord with what looked like ferocious glee, their upcurved stone tails wagging.

The mules and their teams were already on the move, and as Amara reached the Valley floor again, she noticed—the ground was growing soft even on this side of the wall. Riva stayed where he was, gasping, both hands on the ground.

Amara rushed to Riva's side, and said, "Your Grace! We've got to go!"

"In a minute!" he panted. "Ground on this side of the wall is all loose earth. Watering it will slow them down even more."

"Your Grace," Amara said, "we do not *have* a minute." She turned to the engineers and snapped, "You men heard the signal. Retreat."

Exhausted, only a few of them had enough energy to salute, but they all groaned to their feet to begin shambling away from both the steadily shrinking wall and the steadily growing numbers of gargoyles.

Amara looked wildly around her. Everything was flashing colored lights and screams and confusion. Here and there, vord broke through the living wall of angry gargoyles. Knights Terra and Ferrous would close in on each of them, slowing their progress to give the tired *legionares* more time to retreat. Men dragged the wounded toward safety. Horses screamed in panic. Vordbulks continued their vast, deep bellowing while the mantises shrieked and screamed fit to pierce Amara's eardrums.

She couldn't see Bernard and the command group.

"My lord!" she screamed. "We must go! Now!"

Riva let out a short, hollow-sounding gasp and sagged to one side, throwing out an arm to catch himself. It was too weak to hold him up, and he crumpled to the steadily dampening ground.

"Get up!" Amara shouted. She knelt and pulled one of the man's shoulders over hers. "Get up!"

Riva blinked and stared at her with glazed eyes.

Amara wanted to scream in frustration, but she managed to get him mostly upright. The two of them began staggering away from the wall, lurching like a pair of drunks. Faster. They had to move *faster*.

There was a whistling shriek behind her, and Amara turned to see half a dozen mantises rushing her.

Fighting would be impossible. Instead, she flung up a veil around herself and the disoriented High Lord. The charge of the mantises slowed abruptly as it lost a focus, and they began to turn this way and that, each of the six darting forward after the first moving thing it saw.

Unfortunately for mantis number three, the moving thing it saw was Walker the gargant. Though the mantis charged with berserk aggression, Walker barely took notice of it. Instead, he simply lifted one big paw and brought it down in a simple, smashing arc that ended the vord's offensive with abrupt and absolute finality.

"Amara!" boomed Doroga from Walker's back. A pair of gargoyles went hurtling by in pursuit of the vord who had broken through. Walker tossed his head and snorted as Doroga continued to call out. "Amara!"

Amara dropped the veil. "Doroga! Over here!"

The Marat leaned forward, and said something to Walker, and the gargant began striding toward her. Doroga grabbed the saddle rope and swung partway down Walker's side, holding out a hand. Amara guided Riva's arm into the Marat's grip. Doroga hauled the man up with a grunt and dragged him onto the saddle. Amara swarmed up the braided leather rope after them, and Doroga shouted something to Walker. The gargant whirled, both front paws coming up off the ground, and turned to the east. It started forward at a pace Amara had never seen in a gargant before—a kind of lumbering gallop that nearly threw her off its back every couple of steps and covered ground with impressive speed.

Doroga threw back his head in a howl of triumph, and Walker answered him. Amara looked over her shoulder. The wall of gargoyles was holding, but not perfectly. Hundreds of mantises were slipping through, and one of the vordbulks had reached the space where the wall had been, despite the treacherous footing. Walker was moving quickly, but not quickly enough to outrun the oncoming mantises.

But then, he didn't need to.

A chorus of answering bellows came from ahead of them, and a moment later a long line of gargants came lumbering toward them out of the dark—Doroga's tribesmen. Gargants, moving in trios and pairs, went smashing into the vord that had leaked through the gargoyles, crushing them before they could mount an effective pursuit of the fleeing Aleran Legions. The sound of battle began to recede behind them, and Amara felt herself shivering in reaction.

She wasn't cold. She wasn't even reacting to the fear though she'd certainly been afraid.

The chill that went through her did so because of what had happened.

Invidia had told them the truth. They hadn't expected the sheer size of the vordbulks, but Invidia had certainly tried to tell them they were larger than gargants.

She'd been telling the truth.

If there was even a *chance* that she might actually be able to deliver on her promise of taking them to the vord Queen, of ending the war, they would have no choice but to take her up on the offer.

Amara looked overhead. The battle was winding down up there, and the fliers were coming down to support the Marat in holding off the oncoming vord. They would be the last troops to leave the battlefield—their speed meant that even if they kept fighting for two or three hours, they could potentially reach Garrison before some of the Legions.

Invidia had told the truth.

The one thing Amara did *not* need was to lose perspective on the situation, but she couldn't help it. Hope fluttered in her chest: hope that perhaps Invidia really was sincere. That perhaps all the horrors she had seen and committed had changed who she was. Though every reasoning fiber in Amara's brain told her otherwise, foolish hope continued to dance in and out of her thoughts.

A dangerous emotion, hope. Very, very dangerous.

She felt her smile bare her teeth. The real question was this: Whose hope was the more foolish? Her own?

Or Invidia's?

⋈⋈⋈⋈⋈ CHAPTER 46

"You realize, of course," Attis said weakly, "that she's going to betray you."

The Princeps lay in the bed in the quarters normally reserved for Amara and Bernard, and he was dying. Attis had forbidden anyone to enter the room, apart from Aria or Veradis, his physicians—or Amara.

With good reason. He looked horrible, wasted from a magnificent specimen of masculinity to a starving scarecrow within days. His hair was beginning to fall out. There was a yellow tinge to his skin, and a horrible stench surrounded him. No amount of incense could conceal the smell. It could only dull its edge. It even defeated the room's pungent scent.

"Is it not possible," Amara asked, "that Invidia has had a change of heart?"

"No," Attis said calmly. "A heart would be prerequisite. As would the ability to admit her mistakes."

"You're certain of that?" Amara asked. "Without a doubt?"

"Absolutely."

"That was my assessment as well, Your Highness," Amara said quietly.

Attis smiled faintly. "Good." His eyes fluttered closed, and his breath caught for a second.

"My lord?" Amara asked. "Should I send for a physician?"

"No," he rasped. "No. Save their strength for men who might live." He panted for a moment before opening his eyes again. They were glazed with fatigue. "You're going to use her," he said.

Amara nodded. "Either she will lead us to the Queen and betray us to her. Or she will not lead us to the Queen and betray us. Or she will lead us to the Queen and assist us as she said. Two of three possible outcomes result in an opportunity to remove the Queen. We can't pass up a chance like that."

"And she knows it," Attis said. "She can do the math as well. She knows you have no choice but to try. And your figures are fallacies, really. I would make it seventy percent that she intends to lead you to the Queen and betray you. Another thirty percent that she simply intends to take you to a trap without ever revealing the Queen."

Amara shrugged. "By your argument, we have a seventy percent chance, instead of sixty-six. Regardless, it's still a better opportunity than we've ever had or will ever have again."

Attis said nothing. Outside, trumpets blared. It was nearly noon, and the vord pursuing the fleeing Legions to their final fortification had begun their attack by midmorning. Crushed into the relatively small frontage of the final redoubt at the outskirts of Garrison, the vord were making little headway against the determined *legionares*. Mules operating from town rooftops and squads of firecrafters brought blazing death to the enemy. The air was filled with the grotesque stench of internal fluids and burned chitin, even here, inside the little citadel. The incense didn't help with that smell, either.

"I think you know what she intends to do," Attis said.

"Yes."

"You're willing to pay the price this could entail?"

"I have no choice," she said.

Attis nodded slowly, and said, "I do not envy you. When?"

"Four hours after midnight," Amara said. "The team will meet Invidia and strike just before dawn."

"Bother," Attis said. "I hate not knowing the end of a story."

"Your Highness?"

He shook his head. "You didn't need to consult me, Amara, and yet here you are. You must want something of me."

"I do," she said quietly.

His weak voice turned wry. "All things considered, it is probably best if you do not dawdle. Out with it."

She told him what she wanted.

He agreed, and they made the necessary arrangements.

Not long after noon, Gaius Attis, High Lord Aquitaine, fell quietly unconscious. Amara sent for the healers, but they only arrived in time to see him take his last slow, quiet breath.

He died there, his expression that of a man with few regrets.

Amara bowed her head, and wept a few silent tears for the man Gaius Aquitainus Attis had become in his last weeks, for all the lives she had seen lost, the pain she had seen in his last days.

Then she dashed the tears from her face with one fist and turned to leave the chamber. This night would see the most important mission of her life. There would be time for weeping soon, she told herself.

Soon.

Durias, First Spear of the Free Aleran, rode beside Fidelias, looking back over his shoulder at Octavian's forces. They had stopped for water, the first such rest in six hours, beside a small, swift-flowing river. Thousands of men and Canim, taurga and horses, drank thirstily.

"This is mad," Durias said, after a moment. "Absolutely mad."

"And it's working," Fidelias pointed out.

"You can't think that anyone is *pleased* with it, Marcus," Durias pointed out. "The men are puking their guts out."

"As long as they don't do it where everyone is drinking."

Durias smiled and shook his head. "The Canim resent it, you know."

Fidelias smiled. "They'll resent it a lot less when Legion shieldwalls and Legion Knights are holding their flanks."

Durias grunted. "You think we can win this fight?"

"No," Fidelias said. "But I think we can survive it. In the long term, it's probably the same thing."

Durias frowned thoughtfully and eyed him. "How are you feeling? Word is your heart started acting up."

"Better now," Fidelias told him. "I feel like a new man."

"I had hoping you'd stop moping it, slacker," Durias said. "You're going to miss that armor tomorrow morning."

Fidelias grinned easily. "That's a long time from now. Besides, I don't see you walking and letting some poor *legionare* have a turn on horseback."

Durias sniffed. "Rank has its privileges," he said piously. "I go letting some random *legionare* ride while the First Spear takes his place, I'm upsetting the natural order of the Legion. Bad for morale. Totally irresponsible."

"Good, kid," Fidelias said. "You'll make officer yet."

Durias grinned. "Take that back."

A Tribune of the Free Aleran rode up to them and threw Durias a salute. His armor, though standard Legion lorica, was old and worn, if obviously currently in good maintenance, and scoured free of any insignia whatsoever. "First Spear."

"Tribune," Durias said, returning the salute. "Report."

"Four more contacts with the enemy, all of them with the wax spiders. We also burned out another half a dozen patches of the *croach*. They like to start it around the edges of a pond whenever they can. They're getting easier to find."

"That means that the well-hidden patches will be that much more difficult to spot," Durias said. "Don't ease up on them."

The officer let out a rueful laugh. "Not bloody likely." He eyed Fidelias. "How's he doing?"

"He feels like a new man," Durias said.

"He *looks* like a lazy man." The officer leaned a bit to one side to peer around Durias at Fidelias. "Story is you shot at the vord Queen."

"Didn't shoot *at* her," Fidelias said. "I *shot* her. With a balest, no less. The bolt bounced right off her."

The officer lifted his eyebrows. A balest bolt could pass through a horse and fatally wound an armored *legionare* on the other side. "How far out were you?"

"Twenty yards, maybe," Fidelias said.

The officer stared at him for a moment. Then he fretted his lip and eyed Durias. "And we're chasing *that*? This is pointless. This Princeps is going to get us all k—"

Durias dug one heel abruptly into his horse's flank, and the beast lurched forward and to one side, slamming its shoulder against the Tribune's mount. Durias's hand flashed out and seized the man by the plates of his lorica, half-dragging him from the horse.

"*Legionares* complain," Durias said in a harsh, low voice. "Officers lead. Shut your bloody mouth and lead. Or if you can't do that, have the balls to resign your commission and let someone who isn't a bloody coward do your job." He didn't give the officer time to respond. He just shoved him, stiff-armed, away.

The officer recovered his balance and control of his horse, his face chagrined. "Aye. Aye. We'll get back to work."

Durias grunted and said nothing. The officer saluted and turned to ride away. Durias turned to Fidelias, a belligerent gleam in his eyes. "Well?"

Fidelias pursed his lips and nodded. "Not bad."

From the head of the column, not far away, trumpets began to blow assembly. The water break was over.

Men and Canim began to return to the causeway, walking in pairs of one Cane to one Aleran, moving wearily. They assembled into a column.

"We're going to get there exhausted," Durias said quietly. "On open ground. No fortifications."

Fidelias took a slow breath, and said, "If the Princeps must sacrifice us all to give him a chance to take down the Queen, he should do it. I would. In a heartbeat."

"Yes," Durias said, even more quietly. "I suppose that's what is bothering me."

"First Spear," Fidelias said. "Shut up and lead."

Durias let out a snort of bitter amusement. "True enough." The two exchanged a salute, and Durias turned to ride back toward the Free Aleran's section of the column.

The second trumpet signal came—the normal cavalry call to mount up. Fidelias stopped to watch the nearest *legionares*. Each of them carried a pair of long, wide canvas straps, cut from the cloth of their tents. A loop in the cloth had been tied in one end. The *legionares* stepped behind their Canim partner and slipped their boots into the loops. Then they passed the straps to the Cane before them.

After that, there was a bit of scrambling as the Canim slid the straps over their own shoulders, wrapped their other ends about their paw-hands, and crouched as their Aleran partners clambered up onto their backs, the straps becoming makeshift stirrups, the Alerans taking on the role of human backpacks. Men occasionally fell. Canim occasionally were kicked in inconvenient (and unarmored) places. Several tails, particularly, seemed to be put in harm's way in service to the Princeps' novel concept in transportation.

Other *legionares*, Fidelias knew, were now mounting up behind taurg cavalry riders, and doing just as much complaining. But when the trumpet sounded again, the Canim began to work up to their loping overland pace, then even faster, running without difficulty as the Aleran partners bid the furies of the causeway to help them. Not a single Aleran was touching the causeway with his own feet. The Canim's greater natural speed meant that they could use the causeway to move almost as swiftly as a good horse. Within minutes, the entire column was on the move again, miles vanishing beneath Canim feet. They were making faster progress than any Legion would have made marching alone.

Fidelias began to guide his horse back toward the front of the column as they marched, trying very hard not to think about what the Free Aleran Tribune and its First Spear had said about their prospects for surviving another day.

"Shut up, old man," he breathed to himself. "Shut up and face it head-on."

He pursed his lips and thought about a different portion of the previous conversation. Then he barked a short laugh to himself.

Whatever might happen in the next day or so, one thing remained true: Fidelias *did* feel like a new man—and it would not be long before the scales of his life were finally balanced.

Soon, he told himself.

Soon.

Isana sat at the silently entombed Araris's feet, her hands folded in her lap, watching the vord Queen command her brood. The Queen stood in the alcove, staring up at the green-lighted ceiling, her eyes seemingly unfocused and far away. The light of sunset added the barest hint of yellow to the *croach* that grew near the entrance to the hive.

"The defenses at the final position are quite cohesive," the Queen said abruptly. "They are very nearly as formidable as those in Shuar, and the counterstrikes far more effective."

Isana frowned, and asked, "Shuar?"

"The hive of a subspecies of the Canim. A particularly tenacious strain of the breed. Their fortifications had withstood siege for more than a year when I left Canea."

"Perhaps they withstand it still."

The vord Queen looked down at Isana, and said, "Unlikely, Grandmother. The presence of Shuaran Canim in your son's expeditionary force would suggest that they are refugees, cooperating because they have no other choice." She turned her face back up to the ceiling. "Though it is far too late, at this point. A unified resistance might have stopped us several years ago, but you were all quite busy exhibiting the most glaring weakness of individuality: self-interest."

"You see self-identity as a weakness?" Isana asked.

"Obviously."

"Then one cannot help but wonder why you have one."

The Queen looked at Isana. The vord's alien eyes were narrowed. She was silent for a long moment before she looked back up, and answered, "I am defective." Green light flowed down over her upturned face for a time before she said, "I ran a poisoned sword through your son's intestinal tract yesterday evening."

Isana felt her breath stop.

"He seemed well on the way to death when I left him."

Her heart pounded very hard, and she licked her lips. "And yet, you do not say that he is dead."

"No."

"Why did you not kill him, then?" Isana asked.

"The risk-benefit ratio was far too high."

"In other words," Isana said, "he ran you off."

"He and approximately forty thousand troops. Yes." She flexed her hands, finger by finger, black nails sliding out like claws, then retracting. "It doesn't matter. By the time they arrive, the fortress called Garrison will be gone, the Alerans there scattered to the winds. They fight upon the walls as if anchored to them. Do they expect me to simply permit them the advantage?"

Isana folded her arms over her chest. "What are you doing to defeat them?"

"You are familiar with the fortress?"

"Somewhat," Isana said. Technically, that wasn't actually a lie. Her knowledge of the new defenses was positively sketchy compared to that of many others.

"You know, then, that it straddles a natural choke point—a steep cut in a stone shelf. There are no practical routes to move large bodies of troops from this continent to the next except through the fortress."

"Yes," Isana said.

"Practically impassable is not the same thing as impassable," the vord Queen said. "My children think little of vertical land barriers. They have already overcome them in significant numbers on both the north and south sides of the fortress. They will approach and enfold the fortress from either side, and as they do, my juggernauts will pound the walls to rubble. And then, Grandmother, I will be free to concentrate upon Octavi—"

There was the howl of a windstream, practically at the entrance to the hive, and the Queen's black faceted gaze snapped to it. Dozens and dozens of wax spiders seemed to come from nowhere, flowing out of the *croach* upon the ceiling, floor, and walls.

Invidia entered, striding fast. A nervous spider leapt at her, fangs extended, and she swatted it out of the air without slowing pace. "Stop the flanking maneuver. Do it now."

The Queen let out a feline hiss, lips peeling back from her teeth. There was a blur of motion, and suddenly Invidia's shoulders were pressed against the back wall of the hive, seven feet off the ground. The vord Queen held her by the throat with one hand, and Invidia's heels waved and drummed against the wall.

"Where have you *been*?" snarled the vord Queen.

Invidia kept choking, her face going redder. The vord Queen tilted her head to one side, staring at her, and hissed again, more quietly. "The fortress. Why were you at the *fortress*?"

Invidia's eyes rolled back into her head, and her face turned purple.

Isana cleared her throat gently. "You may receive a more coherent answer if you release her."

The Queen glanced back at Isana, then at Invidia again. Then she simply let her go, and the Aleran woman crumpled to the floor. Invidia lay panting for a moment, her hand at her throat, and Isana could actually see the crushed dents in her windpipe being pushed back into the proper shape by Invidia's watercrafting.

"I was," she croaked, a moment later, "securing our future."

"What?"

"It was too easy. They deliberately left you an obvious approach." She swallowed, grimacing. "I went to scout out the tops of the bluffs. It's a trap."

The Queen eyed Invidia, then stalked to the edge of the pool. She passed a hand over it, and light and color began to flow up from its tranquil surface.

Isana rose and walked over to join the Queen at the pool. Invidia came over, too, and the women watched the images flowing there.

Several hundred mantis warriors flowed along the top of a bluff, one of the ridges overlooking Garrison. Several hundred yards before they could possibly threaten the fortress was a heavy stand of evergreens. The vord poured into them without hesitation.

Distant brassy screams echoed up from the pool. The pines and the ferns that grew up around them shook violently.

Then they went still.

Another group of mantises rushed the trees, this one twice the size as the one before, raising their scythe-limbs in anticipation—but just before they reached the timber line, the trees exploded with howling pale forms that came bounding out to meet them, clothed in hide with thick mantles of black feathers. At their sides came the enormous, nearly wingless predator birds, the herdbanes. They were taller than a man, thickly muscled, their feet tipped with razor-sharp claws to complement their deadly, hooked beaks. They fell upon the mantis warriors beside their Marat companions, each and every one of them armed with a heavy axe, decorated with carved handles, fringe, and feathers, but made of Aleran steel.

The two forces clashed together in mindless ferocity, but the Marat had the weight of numbers on their side, and the tremendous strength and speed of the herdbanes allowed them to wreak havoc among the mantis warriors, snapping off scythes, limbs, legs, and heads with thoughtless, primal ferocity, crippling them so that the axes, powered by barbarian muscle, could finish them off.

The Queen hissed and threw her hand to one side. The image in the pool blurred, then resumed itself—this time on the opposite side of the valley. There, though, the attacking mantises were being torn apart by thousands of warriors clad in grey hides and fighting beside enormous, shaggy wolves, some of them nearly the size of ponies.

The wolves and their barbarian companions were all wearing some form of armor—what looked like aprons fitted with steel plates. Moving swiftly, these Marat and their companions fought in tightly coordinated groups, all working to cut single mantises out from their companions, where they would be surrounded and brought down. Though Clan Wolf wasn't inflicting the sheer, savage amount of harm Clan Herdbane had, their efforts were bogging down a much larger number of mantises, and their cooperative tactics seemed to Isana to be doing a very great deal to keep their fighters from being severely injured: Wolf had made their battle into a contest of endurance.

"Withdraw them," Invidia urged quietly. "Wait until we can build a greater mass of troops atop the bluffs. Then we can remove the Marat and take the fortress."

The vord Queen looked distant. "It will take until nearly dawn to build up such a concentration."

"What matter?" Invidia said. "It still leaves us nearly a day to prepare for Octavian's force."

"You," the vord Queen said slowly, "are treacherous."

Isana looked hard at Invidia, and said, "Yes. Because she is a slave to her own self-interest."

"Mmmm," said the Queen thoughtfully. Then she waved a hand and turned from the pool. The image faded, but before it did, Isana saw the mantises within it begin to break off combat with the enemy, withdrawing. "You will proceed to the deployment areas and do all in your power to expedite the buildup of forces. Earthcrafting a number of ramps over the worst terrain should be sufficient."

Invidia bowed and turned toward the exit.

"And, Invidia," the vord Queen said in a very soft voice. "Do not make another covert departure until after the fortress has fallen."

The creature on Invidia's chest let out a hiss, and its limbs stirred. Invidia made a choking sound and fell to her knees. She kept her teeth clenched over a scream that lasted for several heartbeats, then sagged down to the floor.

She pushed herself up slowly, a moment later. She nodded to the Queen and departed, her expression a mask—one Isana had often seen her use to hide her anger.

The Queen ignored Isana and went back to the alcove, staring up into the green light above her.

Isana turned and walked slowly over to Araris, her heart beating quickly. She stared into his eyes through the murky translucence of the *croach* that held him and mouthed the word, *Soon.*

For an instant, one of his lips quivered, baring his teeth in the smallest of wolflike smiles.

Isana nodded and settled back down onto the floor. Waiting. But not for much longer. The time to act would be soon, she told herself.

Soon.

Gaius Octavian rode his horse at the head of the rather unusual column behind him, shivering as Acteon pounded steadily down the causeway, through the cold hours of midnight and beyond. He had never traveled the roads outside the Valley on foot, but when the moon had risen, he had been able to *see* the lofty peak of Garados, rising above the other mountains like an enormous, surly, dangerous drunk on the fringes of a harvest festival.

He was nearly home.

Beside him, Kitai rode with the same easy grace she brought to every endeavor—and if she looked weary, Tavi could hardly blame her. He was more than tired enough to suit himself, as was every man and Cane there with him. But he had made better time than even he had expected. They would reach the western end of the Valley well before sunrise. And then . . .

He shivered.

And then he would cast them all into harm's way beside him. With any luck, he would be able to coordinate with the Valley's defenders, cooperate in a mutual attack from either direction. Though badly outnumbered, the Alerans might still be able to use furycraft and the terrain to overwhelm their foe—and force the vord Queen to appear and intercede.

And then he would learn whether or not a lifetime of uphill battles would save his Realm and people—or see them both smashed to pieces and devoured. Either way, everything he had ever been and done would be justified or found wanting soon, he told himself.

Soon.

CHAPTER 47

Isana meant to stay awake all night, but found she couldn't. The continuous, unchanging lighting of the hive had made it impossible for her body to be certain whether it was night or day. She had slept fitfully, here and there, for what she suspected had been two weeks. Here, at the end, when she most needed to be alert, she found sleep creeping up on her—and by the time she realized what it was up to, it was too late to do anything about it.

She started awake with a small jerk, and swept her gaze silently around the hive without moving her head, careful to do nothing else to draw attention to herself.

All was quiet. The vord Queen stood in the alcove in that awful old gown, staring steadily up into the green light, her long white hair spilling in a fine sheet down her back and over her breasts. She paid no attention to Isana, though that was hardly unusual.

Still . . .

Something was different. Something she could neither identify nor define pressed upon Isana's senses. A shiver went down her spine.

There was death in the air.

Invidia entered the hive. The burned woman looked exhausted. She strode across the hive with a nod in the Queen's direction and was ignored as thoroughly as Isana had been.

Invidia walked straight to Isana and crouched. A slight motion of one finger and a tightening of the pressure around Isana's eardrums warned her that there was a very small, very subtle windcrafting in effect.

Invidia wanted this to be a private conversation.

"In moments," Invidia whispered, her back to the Queen, "things will change."

Isana's eyes widened. She glanced past Invidia to the Queen and nodded very slightly.

"She's hearing something different than I'm saying," Invidia said. "So far as she is concerned, I am gloating over your predicament."

Isana schooled her expression and made no motion, watching Invidia's face.

"Tell me what and where this cure is," Invidia said. "And I give you my word that I will do everything in my power to take you and Araris out alive."

Isana studied her quietly, then asked, "And if I do not?"

One of her eyelids twitched. "Neither of you will get out of here alive, Isana. Not without my help."

Isana took a slow breath. It had worked—at least, she had given Invidia enough hope that she had taken action of *some* kind, perhaps during her unsupervised scouting mission the day before. Isana felt her heart begin to pound. Had she truly gone to the High Lords?

"Once I give them to you," Isana whispered, "what is to stop you from seeing to our deaths?"

"I told you. My word."

Isana met her eyes and felt a swift, brief stab of pity for the woman as she slowly shook her head. "You don't have that anymore, Invidia. You cannot give me what you do not have."

Invidia stared at Isana without expression. Then she said, "What would you have of me, then?"

"Your sword," Isana said calmly.

Invidia's head tilted slightly. "Why? You're hardly a threat, Isana, even armed."

"If I have it, you don't," Isana said.

The burned woman's eyes narrowed suspiciously.

"Does it matter?" Isana asked. "You said there isn't much time. After any sort of battle, your cure won't be left whole. Do you really have time to debate with me? Do you have any choice?"

Invidia pressed her lips together. Then she started unbuckling her sword, and said, "A certain amount of drama will be required."

"The means in question is a mushroomlike growth found in hives like this one," Isana said. "The Marat call it the Blessing of Night. Unlike most fungus, it apparently has thorns. I would look for it concealed around the edges of the pool or within the Queen's alcove."

Invidia took her sword, in its scabbard, in hand, and asked, "How is it used?"

"Eaten, according to Octavian, or squeezed, and its juices applied to wounds."

Invidia stared at her for a moment. Then she frowned, and said, slowly, "I cannot tell if you are lying to me."

"Things are never true because we want them to be, Invidia," Isana said. "Or because we don't want them to be. They simply are."

Her spine stiffened. "And what is that supposed to mean?"

"That it is not surprising someone who has so thoroughly deceived herself about the truth can't recognize it when it is spoken to her."

Invidia's face turned cold. She drew back her hand and struck Isana's face with her palm. Quick, sharp pain expanded and dissipated almost immediately, leaving a harsh tingling in Isana's cheek. As the blow landed, the windcrafting concealing their speech vanished.

Invidia threw her sword at Isana's chest. "So pleasant to be lectured by a self-righteous camp whore who has stumbled into power." She sneered, and Isana felt the lash of Invidia's hatred against her skin like an unseen riding crop. "If you're so convinced of your cause, draw it. Challenge me to the *juris macto*. If you can take me, perhaps you will be allowed to rule a Realm of ashes and graves."

Isana gathered in the slender sword and held it against her stomach without ever looking up at the burned woman. The fire of her emotions was no act—and Isana knew with a sudden chill that while Invidia may have been manipulated into action against the Queen, she had no intention of letting Isana leave alive. "I never wanted a struggle with you, Invidia. All I ever wanted was for my family to be left in peace."

"Keep it," Invidia spat. "In case you change your mind."

Isana looked past the other woman to the vord Queen. Black, alien eyes had focused upon them both. They stayed there for a long moment, then, without comment, returned to the ceiling above.

Invidia literally spat upon Isana. Then she turned and began walking toward the exit. "There have been no troubles moving enough troops onto the bluffs, I trust?"

The vord Queen ignored her.

Isana felt a horrible suspicion begin to grow in her thoughts. The Queen had said nothing about Invidia's giving her the weapon. At the very least, she would have expected some sort of comment along the lines of how irrational the act was.

But the Queen said nothing.

Evidently, Invidia had been struck by a similar impression, but she seemed to brush it aside. Her steps slowed for an instant, and she slowed in midstride, perhaps poised on the precipice of some decision. Then her eyes narrowed, and her steps quickened. She went to the hive's entrance and, with a flick of her hand, sent a ball of stuttering red-and-blue light into the world outside.

The hive exploded into motion and violence.

Isana simply couldn't believe how *fast* everything had suddenly become. It seemed that for an instant, she could focus on absolutely everything in her field of vision, all at once, no matter where it was.

The hive's walls vomited forth a horde of wax spiders, the ones that were constantly in attendance, yet managed to remain all but invisible most of the time. She had expected that. It made their sudden appearance, all leathery, translucent bodies and legs and fangs and faintly luminescent eyes no less hideous, no less terrifying—and it certainly made the venom on their fangs no less poisonous. But, at least she had expected them.

She had *not* expected the four creatures that came dropping neatly out of the ceiling—what looked at first like . . . she wasn't sure what. Some kind of bizarre furylamp fixture, perhaps. They were spheres, essentially, with blades of gleaming steel standing out in ridges from the inner surface of each sphere, smoothly beautiful—until the bodies of the forms began to unfold with delicate grace into the long legs of creatures that resembled wax spiders—but which were ten times the size, and whose limbs were graced with blades of what was obviously fury-crafted steel.

Vord. Made of steel. Isana felt fairly sure that didn't bode well for whatever Invidia had planned.

Invidia turned as the initial wave of wax spiders leapt at her. Her hand twitched, as if to move toward her sword, then reversed itself, sweeping in an arc with her fingers spread. Blue-white fire slewed forth in a liquidlike spray from her open hand, splashing upon leaping spiders and clinging to them like hot oil, causing them to curl up into lumps of flaming, withered flesh. In an instant, two dozen of the leaping figures were destroyed—but there were far more than two dozen surging toward the burned woman. She swept one leg easily into the air, kicking a leaping spider aside, and brought her heel and foot straight down with a cry, a furycrafting movement that sent a violent jolt through the earth in a wave that spread out from her foot, knocking small and large spiders alike into one another, sending them tumbling over the floor and bringing dust and gravel falling from the holes in the ceiling where the great spiders had landed.

Except for one. One of the large, bladed spiders had already flung itself into the air before the shock wave could shake it, and two of its bladed legs snapped forward from its body, striking with the speed and precision of serpents.

Even then, the former High Lady was not to be undone. One of her hands moved with impossible speed, her chitin-covered forearm catching the blades, sliding them aside—almost. One of the swordlike limbs plunged through the chitin-armor covering her other arm, and emerged from the back of it in a small fountain of blood.

Invidia cried out, seized the weapon-limb, and tore it free of her arm by dint of pure, furycrafted strength, ducking aside as another half dozen weapons flashed toward her from different directions. She fell back toward the entrance, seized another leaping wax spider, and flung it at the blade-thing with such strength that it was slammed several feet back across the floor, staggering under the impact.

Isana could only remain in place, motionless, hoping to avoid any attention, stunned at the display. Invidia's power had, for an instant, stemmed the tide of hostile vord.

That instant was all that was required.

Blue-white lightning streaked through the entrance to the hive, twin lances arching around Invidia and converging upon the blade-thing in front of her. They struck in a hideously bright flash of light and a roar of sound that was physically painful. Isana felt the breath sucked from her lungs at the sudden change in air pressure. When she could see again a few seconds later, a blackened patch of ground remained where the first blade-thing had been standing, scorched free of vord and *croach* alike. Scattered pieces of sharp steel littered the ground, all that remained of the creature.

There was a roar of wind and two armored figures rode in on windstreams, miniature gales that carried them down the incline, growing weaker as they descended into the hive, and let both men land on their feet, blazing swords in hand. One weapon burned with cold blue fire, the other blazed with scarlet heat—High Lords Phrygius and Antillus, respectively, Isana thought.

Once more, wax spiders leapt forward, trilling their cries—but this time they faced master metalcrafters with steel in their hands. Quivering, scorched pieces fell to the floor as the two men strode forward, untouched, through the rain of screaming wax spiders.

"In the alcove!" Invidia cried.

Phrygius spun toward the alcove just in time to raise his blade and intercept the dark weapon of the vord Queen. Her sword, a weapon of gleaming dark green-black chitin, met the blazing steel of the High Lord and flexed with un-natural tensile strength, not so much blocking the weapon outright as catching it and flinging it back. The motion surprised Phrygius, who recovered swiftly, but not before the Queen's sword had left a deep slice in the steel plates of his lorica, the split steel bubbling with frothing green poison. They exchanged a series of blows too swiftly for Isana to keep track of them, circling around one another, darting through short passes. Neither seemed able to gain an advantage.

The three remaining blade-beasts rushed forward through the crowd of wax spiders at Antillus. He met them boldly—and within seconds found himself driven back. A dozen blades came darting in at him from every angle, and when his sword met one of the beast's limbs, there was an explosion of scarlet sparks against vord green.

Furycraft. By the furies, Isana thought, these things could use *furycraft*.

"Placida!" Antillus choked out. His sword became a blur of scarlet light, his steps as light as a dancer's despite the steel that encased him, as he weaved and dodged before and between the blade-beasts. "Bloody crows, I need a hand here!"

High Lady Placidus Aria darted in from outside the hive, cut several approaching wax spiders from the air without seeming to notice, and sized up the situation with a sweep of her eyes. Her nostrils flared as she tested the air in the hive and apparently found it suitable. She lifted her hand, and a spark leapt from her fingers to kindle into the familiar form of her fury, a fierce, fiery falcon. She gestured with one hand and let out a sharp whistle, and the fire fury streaked forth to slam into one of the blade-beasts fighting Antillus. There was a blast of intense flame no larger than the mouth of a steadholt's milking pail, but the force of it ripped the blade-beast off of the ground and slammed it into the wall not seven feet from Isana's head.

Aria lifted her hand again, and the falcon was reborn upon her wrist, its flaming wings already raised and eager to fly. Aria's mouth lifted into a chill little smile as she sent the thing flashing forth again, and in another roar of intertwined fire and wind embedded the broken remains of a second blade-beast into the far wall of the hive.

"Thank you!" called Raucus in a calm, workmanlike tone, and suddenly shifted his motion, darting forward under the last blade-beast's weaponry and striking its two foremost limbs from its body where they joined the trunk and were nothing but smooth chitin. The blade-beast recoiled, but Raucous took a spinning, dancelike step forward, to stay in close and build momentum for a thrust of his blade that struck into the unguarded area of the vord's head and upper body, plunging deep into both. The High Lord's mouth split into a ferocious, snarling grin, and he let out a sudden cry of effort.

For an instant, light seemed to pour from the joints of the blade-beast, from where its limbs joined its body, then the creature quite literally exploded, the red fire of Antillus's burning sword expanding into a firecrafter's sphere within the beast's body. Pieces flew everywhere, and an instant later, the High Lord of Antillus stood alone, scorched ichor plastered all over his armor. He whipped his head around and winked at Aria.

"Show-off," Aria sniffed. She turned to Isana, and said, "Isana. Are you well?"

Isana managed a brief and jerky nod. "Aria, this isn't right!"

"Stay down and out of the way! We'll talk about Invidia after," Aria responded, and fell into step with Raucus as he turned to approach the battle in the alcove. The two of them moved lightly up to the edges of the fight, hesitated like a pair of dancers looking for the beat before they stepped onto the crowded floor, then flung themselves into the battle against the vord Queen.

"People!" bellowed a voice from outside—Lord Placida. There was the boom of a nearby firecrafting. "The bitch has called in her pets! Hurry!"

Isana looked up to see Placidus Sandos backing down the incline, step by step, his legs spread widely, anchoring him to the ground like tree trunks. That enormous sword was in his hands—in fact, often he wielded it in a single hand—whipping back and forth. He looked like a man hacking his way through under-brush: black chitinous . . . parts, for Isana could identify them no more specifically than that, scattered to the floor with each swing. Only in this case, the under-brush proved to be pursuing him. Isana could see a thicket of mantis limbs on the ground above Lord Placida as he backed step by step away from the pressure of the attack.

Isana's eyes went back to the alcove, where the three Citizens had trapped the vord Queen between them. Blades darted and bodies moved, all almost too quickly to be seen. Each combatant was little more than a blur—the result of windcrafting, it had to be. Sparks raged in blinding clouds. Isana had no idea how the participants could even *see* through them, much less continue the bat-tle. She tried to scream to them over the chorus of miniature explosions and vord shrieks coming from outside, but to no avail.

Then there was a brassy, metallic scream that cut over everything, shocking the world into an abrupt silence.

Isana's eyes widened as the battle in the alcove froze in place. The vord Queen stood pinned against one wall, with the hilt of Antillus's sword standing out from her heart. She let out another scream and swept her sword in a futile slash at the unarmed man, but Aria caught the blow on her own sword in a last, feeble cascade of sparks, and as she did, the cold fire of Phrygius's sword struck the Queen's head from her neck.

"No!" Isana screamed. *"That—"*

Invidia was moving, after having hovered in the background during the whole of the battle. She reached out with one hand, and the scattered bits of steely blade-beast, all around the hive, abruptly rose up from the floor.

"—is not—"

The former High Lady of Aquitaine flicked her hand—and a cloud of bro-ken, deadly blades hurtled toward the alcove, a lethal storm of steel.

"—the true vord Queen!" Isana screamed.

Aria's head whipped around just as hundreds of bits of razor-sharp flying metal hurtled into the alcove. Her sword flashed up and steel chimed, but no one could have defeated every single threatening blade with nothing more than a sword in hand. Their armor offered some protection, but it was far from perfect.

Antillus managed to lift an arm to shield his face and neck, but Phrygius was too slow. Metal fragments slashed into his face, and Isana now, with sickening clarity, the way his eyes were sliced from his head. Antillus reeled against the wall, his face bloodied. Scarlet droplets scattered the wall.

The true vord Queen, naked but for her dark cloak, plummeted from the roof of the alcove. The first stroke of her blazing green sword echoed Phrygius's own strike with sinister irony, and the High Lord's head flew from his neck. Raucus reached for his sword, trapped in the wall, but the second motion of the Queen's attack struck his arm from his body at the shoulder. The third strike shattered his armor in a burst of ugly fire, slicing through his body just below his ribs and sweeping almost all the way to his spine. Never stopping, the Queen whirled, her sword describing a deadly arc aimed at Aria's neck as Raucus crumpled to the floor.

Aria's face was cut to bloody ribbons, and one of her eyes was shut with flowing blood. She did not even attempt to block the attack, but threw herself to one side in a roll and came up on her feet, the motion smooth and swift—but not swift enough to prevent the vord Queen from altering the sweep of her blazing sword to slash through the back of Aria's left thigh. Lady Placida let out a cry as her left leg buckled. She caught herself with her empty hand and began scrambling toward Isana, her leg dragging uselessly. She shook her head left and right, trying to clear her eyes of blood as she went. "Sandos!" she screamed.

The vord Queen's head snapped toward the entrance, and she made a gesture with one hand. The entire mouth of the hive suddenly fell, as abruptly as if it had been a nail driven down by the blow of a titan's hammer. One moment it gaped open, showing them Lord Placida's wild-eyed, panicked face, and the next it was a wall of granite.

Aria continued retreating, until her fingertips touched the hem of Isana's filthy gown. She swiped at her eyes a few more times, then hoisted herself to lift her sword into an awkward guard position, her left leg hanging lifelessly beneath her.

There was a quiet rustle of sound—and no fewer than *eight* more blade-beasts dropped from the ceiling all around the vord Queen and slowly rose. Their gently glowing eyes focused on the Alerans, and the vord creations lifted their sword-limbs, ready to strike, as they rustled closer.

"Crows take you," Aria choked, her voice shaking. "Crows take you, Invidia."

Invidia stared at the vord Queen from one side, her face bloodless. It made her scars stand out purple and hideous. "I didn't . . . I thought that . . ."

"You thought," the Queen said, "that you would allow the High Lords to exterminate me. Then you, in turn, would exterminate them—disposing of nearly every Aleran still alive who could match your power." She shook her head as she looked at Invidia. "Did you think me a fool?"

Invidia licked her lips and took a step back. Blood ran down her wounded arm and dripped to the *croach* in a quiet, steady patter.

"You have no need to fear me," the Queen told her. "It is a weakness over which you have no control, Invidia. I simply planned to take your shortcomings into account. It was not difficult to remove a junior queen's higher functions and reshape her into the lure for the trap. I regard your treachery as a minor shortcoming of character, in the greater scheme."

Invidia stared at the vord Queen, and whispered, "You aren't going to kill me?"

"I do not condemn a slive for its venom, a hare for its cowardice, an ox for its stupidity—nor you for your treason. It is simply what you are. There is still a place for you here. If you wish it."

"Traitor," hissed Lady Placida.

Invidia bowed her head. She shook silently for a moment.

"Invidia," Isana said gently, "you don't have to do this. You can still fight. You can still defeat her. Aria will help you. Sandos will find a way in, soon. And my son is coming. *Fight.*"

The woman shuddered.

"Isana was not lying about the Blessing of Night," the Queen said. "Serve me until Alera has been put in order, and I will grant it to you when I release you to rule what remains."

"When, Invidia?" Isana said urgently, leaning toward her. "When is the price too high? How much innocent blood must be spilled to slake your thirst for power? *Fight.*"

The Queen looked at Isana, then at the former High Lady. "Choose."

Invidia's eyes flicked to the two unmoving forms in the alcove, then to Lady Placida. She shuddered, and Isana saw something in her break. Her shoulders slumped. She bowed forward slightly. Though nothing about her changed, her face, Isana thought, suddenly looked ten years older.

Invidia turned to the vord Queen, and said, her voice bitter and weary, "What would you have me do?"

The Queen smiled slightly. Then she gestured with a hand, and a trio of wax spiders came walking over the *croach*, carrying with them the sword of the fallen Phrygia. They stopped at Invidia's feet.

"Take the weapon," the Queen said quietly. "And kill them all."

CHAPTER 48

"Bloody crows, Frederic," Ehren complained, as they moved into the hall. "You don't have to carry me. I can walk."

The hulking young Knight Terra grunted as the little Cursor elbowed him and stepped a bit away. "I'm sorry," he said, "It's just that Harger said—"

Frederic was interrupted as Count Calderon rounded the corner at a brisk walk and slammed into the young man. Frederic let out a grunt at the impact and fell backward.

Count Calderon scowled ferociously. "Frederic! What the crows are you doing in the citadel?" He looked at Ehren. "And you. You're . . ." His eyebrows went up. "I thought you were dead."

Ehren leaned on his cane and tried not to let too much wince leak into his smile. "Yes, Your Excellency. And so did Lord Aquitaine. Which was the point."

Bernard drew in a slow breath. "Get up."

The young Knight Terra hurried to obey.

"Frederic?" Bernard said.

"Yes, sir?"

"You're not hearing any of this."

"No, sir."

Bernard nodded and turned to Ehren. "Amara said that he suspected you had manipulated him into that stunt at Riva."

Ehren nodded. "I didn't want to be within reach when he figured it out. And the best way to do that was to be tucked safely into a grave." He shifted his weight and winced at his injuries. "Granted, I hadn't intended my exit to be quite that . . . authentic. The original plan was for Frederic to find me at the end of the battle."

"Wait," Frederic blurted, his eyes almost comically wide. "Wait. Count, sir, you didn't *know* about this?"

Count Calderon narrowed his eyes and eyed Ehren.

Ehren smiled thinly. "Sir Frederic, Tribune Harger, and Lord Gram may have been operating under the impression that they were acting under your direct and confidential orders, sir."

"And what would have given them that impression?" Calderon asked.

"Signed orders!" Frederic said. "In your own hand, sir! I saw them!"

Calderon made a rumbling sound in his chest. "Sir Ehren?"

"When I was learning forgery, I used to use your letters to Tavi for practice, Your Excellency."

"He *gave* you those letters?" Calderon asked.

"I burgled them, sir." Ehren coughed. "For another course."

Calderon made a disgusted sound.

"I—I don't understand," the young Knight said.

"Keep it that way, Frederic," Calderon said.

"Yessir."

"Leave."

"Yessir." The brawny young Knight saluted and hurried away.

Calderon stepped closer to Ehren. Then he said, very quietly, his voice hard, "You're telling me, to my face, that you conspired to murder a Princeps of the Realm?"

"No," Ehren said, just as quietly, and with just as much stone in his voice, "I'm telling you that I made sure a man who absolutely would have killed your nephew could never hurt him." He didn't let his gaze waver. "You can have me arrested, Your Excellency. Or you could kill me, I suppose. But I think the Realm would be better served if we sorted it out later."

Count Calderon's expression didn't waver. "What," he said finally, "gave you the right to deal with Aquitaine that way? What makes you think one of us wouldn't have handled it?"

"He was ready for any of you," Ehren said simply. "He barely looked twice at me until it was too late." He shrugged. "And I was acting under orders."

"Whose orders?" Bernard demanded.

"Gaius Sextus's orders, sir. His final letter to Aquitaine contained a hidden cipher for me, sir."

Calderon took a deep breath, eyeing Ehren. "What you've done," he said quietly, "orders from Sextus or not, could be considered an act of treason against the Realm."

Ehren arched an eyebrow. He looked down at the stone floor of the fortress beneath him and tapped it experimentally with his cane. Then he looked up at Calderon again. "Did *you* have orders from Gaius Sextus, sir?"

Bernard grunted. "Point." He exhaled. "You're Tavi's friend."

"Yes, I am, sir," Ehren said. "If it makes it easier for you, I could just vanish. You wouldn't have to make the call."

"No, Cursor," Bernard said, heavily. "I've reached the limits of my tolerance for intrigue. What you did was wrong."

"Yes, sir," Ehren said.

"And smooth," Bernard said. "Very smooth. There's nothing to link his death to you but a dying man's bubbling suspicions. And only Amara and I know about that."

Ehren waited, saying nothing.

"Sir Ehren," Bernard said, slowly. He took a deep breath, as if readying himself to plunge into cold water. "What a relief that your injuries were less serious than we believed. I will, of course, expect you to resume your duties at once. Right beside me." He growled, beneath his breath, "Where I can keep an eye on you."

Ehren almost sagged with relief. The only thing that prevented it was that it would have hurt a very great deal. The injuries to his body had been closed and stabilized, but it would be weeks before he could move normally again. "Yes, sir," he said. He found his eyes clouding up, and he blinked them several times until they were clear again. "Thank you, sir."

Bernard put an arm on his shoulder, and said, "Easy, there, young man. Come on. Let's get to work."

The view of the battle from the little citadel's tower was spectacular, even at night. Large furylamps, on the walls and towers of both the defensive ramparts and the citadel, illuminated the Calderon Valley for half a mile. Originally, the Valley's trees and brush had grown up to within a bowshot of the old fortress at Garrison, but they had long since been cleared, for the expanding little city, then cleared back more, to the edge of the range of the mules. It left the ground utterly devoid of features an attacking force could use for cover.

The vord covered that ground like a turbulent black sea. Despite the efforts of the firecrafters and the crews of the mules, which had been spread out on rooftops behind the first wall, the vord had finally covered the ground and were fighting their way up the walls, hacking out climbing holds and coming up in lots of a dozen creatures at a time, until the Legion engineers could earthcraft the holds out of the wall's surface, returning it to unbroken smoothness. Men fought and bled atop the wall, but nowhere near so ruinously as they had only a day or two before. The frontage of the entire fortification was less than three-quarters of a mile, and the sides of the Valley were no wider, there. The vord had to pack themselves in to reach the walls, to the point where their advantage of numbers did them the least amount of good.

Though, Ehren reflected, *that was quite a bit different than counting for nothing.*

Even though the Legions could face the vord at a point of maximum concentration, where the firecrafting of the Citizens and the freemen's mules could do the most harm, the Aleran Legions remained badly outnumbered. Ehren

watched as one segment of the wall rotated weary *legionares* out for a fresh cohort. The vord needed no such cooperation. They simply kept coming, an endless tide. Ehren counted, out of habit, noting that only six men of the eighty-man
century had been lost during their hourlong rotation on the walls. And yet it was
entirely possible that their losses, proportionately, were *worse* than those being
inflicted upon the vord.

The hollow booms of firecraftings continued to rumble irregularly through
the night, accompanied by the scattered popping sounds of the occasional
launch of fire-spheres from a mule, but even those were infrequent. Ehren asked
Count Calderon about it.

"The firecrafters are resting in rotation," he said quietly. "They're exhausted.
There are just a few of them on duty to prevent any breaches of the wall. And
we're running low on ammunition for the mules. Right now, there are workshops
being established in the refugee camp east of the city to manufacture more fire-
spheres, but it isn't coming along as fast as we'd like."

"How fast would we like it?" Ehren asked dubiously. A stray sphere from the
last mule launch had come down inside the ramparts, and a supply wagon was
burning enthusiastically.

"Twelve million of them an hour would be ideal," Calderon replied.

Ehren choked. "Twelve mil—An *hour*?"

"That would be enough for one hundred mules to loose two-hundred-shot
loads at their maximum rate of fire, nonstop," Bernard said. He squinted out
at the battle. "With that, I could kill every vord in this swarm without losing a
man. We're going to have to figure out a way to manufacture these things more
quickly."

Ehren shook his head. "Seems so unbelievable. When Tavi showed me the
sketches for this idea, I thought he'd gone insane." He paused. "More insane."

Two more mules launched their payloads, and a column of fire brought
more vord screams to the predawn darkness.

Suddenly there were sharp, high-pitched whistles drifting down from the
bluffs on either side of the little city. Bernard looked up sharply and swallowed.
"There. Here it comes."

"Here what comes?"

"The enemy's flanking attack. It's the weakest part of this position, defending against an attack from the west." Bernard gestured at the two bluffs. "The
vord are going to try to take the heights, then come down on us."

"The Marat are stationed there, I believe," Ehren said.

"Yes," Calderon said. "But if the vord have reinforced their flankers . . ." He
bit his lip and beckoned Centurion Giraldi. "Signal the Marat."

Giraldi saluted and stomped off to dispatch a messenger as the battle upon the bluffs resumed, with the screams and howls and cries of the Marat, their beasts, and their foes echoing down into the Valley.

"It would be nice to be able to see what's happening up there," Ehren said.

"Probably why they did it at night," Calderon replied. "Show up with a much larger force and try to hammer through before anyone realizes there are a whole lot more of them this time." He shook his head. "Did it ever once occur to whoever is in charge over there that they aren't the only ones who can furycraft a decent trail up onto the bluffs?"

Ehren turned with the Count in time to see three bright white signal-fire arrows launched into the air over each bluff. There was a brief pause, then the sounding of horns somewhere out on the plains.

And then there was a low, rumbling thunder.

As Ehren listened, it began to grow closer—and much, much louder. He hurried to fumble a farseeing into existence between his hands, to let him look out east onto the plains beyond Garrison. And there he saw, surging toward the west, an enormous mass.

Horses.

Thousands and thousands of horses, and pale barbarians armed with spear and axe and bow and sword riding upon their backs.

"Hashat would have killed me if I hadn't let her in on the fun," Calderon confided. "And it was something of a challenge to work out a battle plan that included a reasonable use of cavalry in a bloody wall battle."

The horses split into two columns, flowing around Garrison like a river, then surged up what sounded like plank-lined earthworks leading onto the bluffs on either side of the city. Moments later, Marat cavalry horns caroled brazenly through the dark, and the sounds of thundering hooves and fighting continued on the heights. For a few moments, there was nothing but noise and confusion, but then the trumpets started calling more excitedly and from farther west upon the bluffs the Marat were again driving the enemy back.

Bernard nodded once in satisfaction, and said, "My Valley."

And then a low, throbbing bellow rolled through the air and made the soles of Ehren's feet vibrate. A second one, from vaguely the other direction, rose and slowly fell again as the first call died away.

"Bloody crows," Bernard snarled. "Signal Knights Aeris," he called to Giraldi. "I need lights on those bluffs!"

It took only a few moments for the orders to be relayed and the Knights Aeris and Citizens to overfly the bluffs, dropping spherical firecraftings in clusters of blazing light. Count Calderon stood watching as they fell, and the light illuminated the vast, shadowy mass of vordbulks, one of them upon each section of high ground, so heavily surrounded with vordknights that they resembled animated carcasses surrounded by buzzing flies.

Ehren stared at them for a second, unable to believe his own eyes. "Those," he heard himself say through a dry mouth, "are quite large."

Giraldi spat. "Bloody crows. But those things can't attack us from up there, can they?"

"They don't have to attack us," Bernard replied. "They just have to walk up and *fall* on us."

"Oh, dear," Ehren said.

"We have to hold them off," Bernard breathed. "Slow them down. If we can slow them down . . ." He gave himself a shake. "Giraldi. Tell Cereus to concentrate his forces on the northern bluff. Set the trees on fire, create spines of stone to wound their feet—whatever he can think of. Kill them if he can, but he is to slow that bulk *down*."

"Yes, sir!" Giraldi snapped, and went about carrying out Bernard's orders.

"Slow them down?" Ehren said, bewildered. "Not kill them?"

"It'll be worse if they arrive simultaneously. And they're so heavily armored—and just so crowbegotten *big*—that I'm not sure if we *can* kill them," he replied. "But I think we just have to hold a little longer."

"Why?" Ehren asked, blinking. "What difference is it going to make if they're here in half an hour instead of ten minutes?"

"Because, Sir Ehren," Calderon said, "like your own demise, not everything here is as it seems."

⬡⬡⬡⬡⬡ Chapter 49

Gaius Octavian's host dismounted at the mouth of the Calderon Valley, much to the relief of riders and mounts alike. Fidelias watched the entire process, bemused. How different would the role of cavalry be if horses could talk?

And draw swords.

And eat their riders.

He thought there might be a great deal less running about.

Fidelias shook his head and struggled to focus on the task at hand. Such wandering thoughts might perhaps be natural in the face of exhaustion and near-certain death, but they wouldn't help accomplish the mission.

The captain came riding in from a nearby patch of woods on his big black, his *singulares* trailing at a slight distance. Though the trees had been a quarter mile away, he had insisted. It would never do, after all, for the Legions to see their Princeps beholden to the call of nature just as they were.

Fidelias swung down from his own horse and walked over to join the captain.

" know you aren't used to performing in this role," Octavian was saying to two young men—a cavalry centurion named Quartus and Sir Callum of the First Aleran's Knights. Both were the right arms of Maximus and Crassus, respectively, within the First Aleran. "But you've been trained well," Octavian continued. "You'll do fine "

Both young man replied in the affirmative and, Fidelias thought, tried to look more confident than they felt. But then, the captain was doing the exact same thing. He was just a lot better at it than the other two. It also said something about him that, even here, at the last, the captain had arranged matters so that he could have a moment to bolster their spirits before the rest of the commanders of the host arrived.

It took only moments for the command staff of both Legions to reach them, along with Varg, Nasaug, and Master Marok in his vord-chitin mantle. To Fidelias's surprise, Sha was there as well, clad in Hunter grey, pacing along in Varg's shadow.

"Gentlemen," Octavian said. There were no murmurs to be quieted—everyone was tired, though only the Cane didn't look it. Their fur simply seemed a bit limper than was usual. "Let's get right to it. There are two and a half million enemy troops packed into the next fifty miles or so. There are about forty thousand of us. So there are plenty of vord to share. Let's not be stingy."

A rumble of laughter went around the group. Nasaug looked amused, though Varg didn't. Varg looked patient.

"Garrison is about fifty miles from here, on the causeway. They've still got almost a hundred and fifty thousand *legionares* and support from another hundred thousand Marat."

"That isn't enough to face the vord directly," Nasaug said, his deep voice resonant.

"No," Octavian said. "It isn't. Somewhere between here and Garrison is the vord Queen. Once we kill her, we aren't facing an army anymore. We kill her, we have a chance."

Sir Callum lifted his hand. "Sir . . . ? Um, how are we going to find her?"

Octavian gave him a wolfish smile. "Well, Sir Callum. It appears that some blackhearted villains destroyed the vord's food storehouse at Riva, then proceeded to burn out the *croach* that was supposed to be their supply line."

Another rumble of laughter went around the group.

"As a result, there are more than a million vord thirty miles east of here, at the site of an old steadholt called Aricholt. They're completely motionless—asleep, in some kind of hibernation."

"How do you know this?" Varg asked.

"Sorcery."

Varg eyed Octavian, an expression far more intimidating on a Cane's face than an Aleran's, then flicked his ears in acknowledgment.

Marok let out a thoughtful growl. "Some of my monastic brethren once pursued similar disciplines. If the vord can do that, they will not need as much food to survive."

Octavian nodded. "I think they must be the vord reserves. And I think the vord Queen will be nearby." He looked around the circle. "Gentlemen, we are going to come down on them in force and annihilate them."

Silence fell on the circle.

"Sir," Sir Callum said slowly. "Attack a million with . . . sir, that's . . . the odds are . . ."

"Twenty-five to one," Varg said quietly.

"Shall we wait for them to wake up and come to us?" Octavian asked, his mouth spread in a wide, confident grin. "No, Sir Callum. The time for being cautious is long past."

"What if they wake up?" Callum asked.

"What if they don't?" Octavian countered. "What if the vord never need them? What if we do nothing while the vord at Garrision overwhelm the Legions?"

Callum frowned and bowed his head. Then he nodded.

"We're going to hit them as fast and as hard as we can," Octavian continued. "And we're going to inflict a crowbegotten lot of harm on them. While that's happening, I will lead a strike team after the Queen. As the most experienced Aleran present, Valiar Marcus will be in command once I am gone."

Fidelias felt his stomach drop out. He began to say something, but Octavian shot him a level look, and he subsided.

"Varg will be his second," Octavian continued. "Our objective is to eliminate the vord reserves at Aricholt, then fortify our position. Questions?"

No one spoke.

"All right, then, gentlemen," Octavian said, smiling. "Let's get to work. Oh, Master Marok. Would you be willing to speak with me privately for a moment? Thank you."

Fidelias watched the assembly break up as the captain moved over to one side, speaking quietly with Marok. The Cane listened and made short replies. He nodded once, then he and the captain exchanged bows.

The captain strode over to him after speaking to Marok. "Marcus," he said, "That's me."

Octavian's mouth tugged up at the corner. "With any luck," he said, "I'll be busy elsewhere once the music starts."

"I heard," Fidelias said.

"I'm not going to ask you if you can handle it. I'm telling you that you bloody well *will* handle it."

"Yes, sir."

Octavian nodded, and said, "We're going all out. Maximum damage to the enemy. Everyone, *everyone*, including me, is to be considered expendable." He looked back down the column. Hundreds of men and Canim were visible even within the ritualists' concealing mist. There was pain in his eyes. "We can't let the Queen escape us. And we can't allow those reserves to be used against Garrison. No matter the cost."

"I understand, Captain," Fidelias said quietly. "I'll get it done."

Tavi rode at the head of the column the rest of the way to the engagement. Moving down the causeway, it took them a little more than an hour to make the trip, and his mouth was dry the whole time, no matter how many times he drank from his water flask. Scouts and outriders reported infrequent contact with the enemy. They wouldn't have been able to see much—the host was still riding veiled beneath Master Marok's misty cloud. Of course, the reverse also held true. It was difficult for the host to see *out*. They had to rely heavily upon their scouts to be their eyes and ears.

They turned off the causeway to cover the last three or four miles to Aricholt upon a nonfurycrafted road. In the darkness, the ride was an eerie one. Vord cries drifted up and down the valley. Garrison was only another half an hour or so away upon the causeway, but that was plenty of distance to muffle all but the most piercing cries of the vord, who must have been laying siege to the place. The distant crackles and booms of firecraftings came through clearly, though. From the sound of it, there were still plenty of Citizens standing up to the vord— either that, or the idea he'd shared with his uncle by letter, about the mules and the fire-spheres, had actually paid off. If that was true, he'd be a little startled, he'd admit. He never thought that one would work out.

A scout from the Free Aleran appeared out of the mist ahead of them, riding his horse back at an easy lope. He pulled up next to the command group and saluted Tavi.

"Report."

"Sir, the steadholt is up ahead. It's covered in the *croach* and . . ." He shook his head. "The reserves you talked about are there."

"Asleep?"

"Maybe," the man said. "They weren't moving."

Tavi looked over his shoulder at Fidelias, and said, "Signal the halt. Quietly."

Fidelias nodded. Signals were passed by hand gesture and lowered voice back down the column.

"I want to see this for myself," Tavi said. "Everyone else, remain here."

"I am going," Kitai said.

Tavi eyed her. He had no desire whatsoever to expose her—expose *them*—to danger, but he gave in to the inevitable on the lesser risk. "Fine. But we're only going up to look, and we're doing it under sound, sight, and earth veils."

Kitai shrugged her shoulders. "As you would, Aleran."

They rode out together, and Tavi pulled up a windcrafted veil around them as they did. Without being told, Kitai managed the crafting that would hide the sounds of their passing and another that would make the earth more pliable beneath the hooves of their mounts, greatly reducing the amount of vibration they sent through the earth as they walked, in an effort to avoid detection by enemy earthcrafters who might be standing sentry duty.

They rode about half a mile before leaving the protective mists around the host—and were immediately bathed by the light of a waning moon. Predawn hovered in the east, a cold blue light that was only barely brighter than the darkness of night.

They went off the road, and approached the steadholt from the southwest, walking their horses carefully through the thick woods. A murmur from Tavi, and a low, constant effort of will made the trees bend back their limbs, and the new growth of briar and brush allow them to pass without sound or inconvenience. It took them only moments to come within sight of Aricholt.

Tavi had only heard it described by his uncle, and that had never been in great detail. The steadholt had been an average example of the breed—a barn, a great hall, some living quarters and workshops, all of them made of stone. A stone wall circled the place, though it had crumbled in multiple locations.

Standing in the fields were row after row of large, egg-shaped forms, which Tavi suddenly realized were the bodies of the vord warriors. They stretched for a square mile, easily, even with each one curled into a ball and stacked up touching the mantises beside it. None of them moved—it would appear that they were indeed asleep, at least for the moment.

Glowing green *croach* spread out from the barn and had already begun to creep outward. There was a crowd of mantis warriors sitting around the far side of the barn, a hundred or more. Further sentries crouched around the exterior of the barn, one every ten feet or so. Wax spiders rolled in and out, vomiting out fresh patches of *croach*, then trundling back inside to pick up more.

"Remind you of anything?" Tavi asked Kitai quietly.

She nodded. "The Queen's hive under Alera Imperia."

The high-pitched howl of windstreams bearing Aleran fliers screamed far overhead. Tavi looked up and saw a flier glide smoothly down to the barn entrance—a slender woman clad all in black, whose head had been badly scarred with burns. She passed through the crowd of mantises, shoving them out of the way like unruly lambs, then glanced over her shoulder and up before vanishing into the barn.

"She's there," he heard himself whisper. "Bloody crows, the Queen is right there in that barn."

Kitai's hand went to her sword. "Should we attack?"

He shook his head. Together they turned their horses and began moving slowly and stealthily back to the host.

Kitai stared at him, visibly furious, as they reentered the mists, and stopped her horse. "That was an opportunity. Perhaps the best one we are going to have. It was foolish of you to cast it aside out of some harebrained need to protect me."

"That wasn't what I was doing, Kitai."

"The crows it was not," Kitai said. "And if you think for a moment that you are going to hunt this Queen by yourself, Aleran, you are mistaken. I will *not* permit you to face her alone."

"Kitai—"

"I don't know who is on this strike team you mentioned, but I am hereby assigning myself to it."

"You're not on the team. You are the team. I've already decided that the safest place for you is next to me."

Her eyes narrowed suspiciously. "You have?"

He nodded. Then he stopped his horse and turned to her. "I wish you to become my mate," he said, duplicating her own accented Aleran flawlessly. "Set the challenge of your choice."

She tilted her head. "What?"

"You heard me," he said.

Kitai stared at him for a moment more, then said, "Let the winner of the trial be the one who slays the vord Queen."

Tavi huffed out a laugh. "If I didn't know any better, I'd say you didn't want me to marry you."

She smiled at him. "No, fool," she said. "I most certainly do. Kill this creature, my Aleran, and make our world a place where we might live again, where our child might grow up in safety. Kill her, and I will be yours until death parts us."

Tavi stared at Kitai and thought that he'd never seen a creature so beautiful. He leaned over to her and kissed her hard on the mouth. When it was through, they rested their foreheads together, until Kitai's horse sidestepped, and they both nearly plummeted off.

They shared another smile, righted themselves, and returned to the host.

Tavi rode up to Fidelias, who stood talking with Varg. "All right," he said. "It's just ahead. Give the order to get us under way and prepare to sound the attack."

⋈⋈⋈⋈CHAPTER 50

Invidia stared at the vord Queen, transfixed.

"Do not make a fatal mistake, Invidia," the vord Queen said, her voice calm. "One more dead Aleran means nothing to me. Nor should a few more matter to you, at this point. Kill them. I will keep my word to you."

Invidia bit her lip. Then she bent forward, slowly, her fingers outstretched for the sword's hilt. Once she touched it, something in her seemed to solidify, some resolution that made her expression as smooth and as cold as glass in winter. Her hand seemed to gain strength as she touched the blade. Then she lifted it and turned toward the two Alerans, her eyes hard, the mad, bitter rage pouring off her like smoke from the scorched carcasses around them. "You brought this upon yourselves."

It happened so swiftly. One instant, Invidia was beginning to take a step forward, a dead man's sword in her hand.

The next, there was a hiss of rushing air, the sound of a whip crack, and the jagged point of what looked like a spear tip carved from bone erupted from Invidia's chest, just below her breast, to the left of her sternum. The spear transfixed the burned woman and the creature clutching her body in a single blow, and she arched her back in agony, her eyes flying open wide, her mouth stretching into a breathless scream.

A hand gripping a stone knife emerged from a fraying windcrafted veil, swept around Invidia's body, and with a swift, sure motion, cut her throat from ear to ear.

Invidia Aquitaine fell to the *croach*, her blood pouring out like a fountain, her eyes wide with shock and terror and rage and pain. She turned her head to stare, bewildered, at the woman who had killed her.

Countess Calderonus Amara stood over her with the bloodied bone knife in hand, and whispered, "Thus are you served in Alera, traitor."

Invidia's eyes rolled back into her head, and her breath rattled in her throat. She sank very slowly to the ground, the legs of the beast upon her breast quivering madly, uselessly. Her own legs twitched and kicked several times, as if she believed herself to be running away from something.

Then her bloodless face fell to one side, staring sightlessly, and she went still.

Isana stared at Amara in shock. The Cursor had been in the hive all along. She must have entered when Antillus and Phrygia did, concealing her presence with a veil—doubtless intending to strike down the vord Queen. But the Queen was surrounded by a wall of blade-beasts, and Invidia had been a perfect target, fully focused upon her own self-conflict and pain.

Amara bent and wrenched the bone spear from the body, bracing one boot against the dead woman's shoulder blades. It was a short weapon, no more than three or three and a half feet long, and thicker than her wrist, decorated with Marat-style carvings. A bone spear, Isana thought, and a stone knife—neither of which would have been sensed by Invidia's metalcrafting. Amara took the primitive weapons in hand and turned to face the Queen, her stance casually arrogant.

The Queen narrowed her black, glittering eyes, and Isana felt a surge of deep, hot anger pulse from her in a single wave, then vanish again. As it happened, the blade-beasts parted, rippling smoothly out of the space between the Queen and Countess Amara.

"That," said the Queen, her diction precise, "was inconvenient."

"In what way?" Amara asked, her tone flippant.

The vord Queen answered, but Isana had realized what Amara was doing. She bit her lip and placed her hand on Aria's calf, her fingers clutching hard. Without the waters of a healing pool to work with, she couldn't tell precisely what shape Aria was in. It was like trying to read a book underwater, with her vision blurred and the ink running—but she could feel it well enough to know that Aria knew precisely what was injured, and that she was, in fact, making an effort to heal it. Silently, Isana threw her support behind Lady Placida's efforts, and she could feel it as the other woman's pains began to recede, as her wounds began to close.

"She was . . . uniquely useful to me," the Queen said.

Amara flicked some of the blood off the tip of the spear with one finger, and said, "She's still useful. You can eat her."

"Her," said the Queen, her eyes narrowing. "And you."

Amara lifted her spear in silent invitation and gave the Queen a mocking bow.

Isana clutched Aria's leg even harder, pouring all her energy into assisting her.

The Queen and the Cursor both called upon windcrafting to give them speed and abruptly rushed toward one another, streaks of motion. At the last instant, Amara flung the stone knife, and the vord Queen had to intercept it with her blade. Amara dropped into a slide and went by her, barely avoiding the sword's backswing. The Cursor came up onto her feet, rolled beneath another blow as the Queen pursued her, then reversed her facing in midleap and flung the bone spear at the Queen with unearthly speed.

The Queen's blade snapped out and shattered the bone weapon into hundreds of shards, and the frantic pace stilled again. Amara came to her feet weaponless, wearing only light clothing, not even a plated coat. The vord Queen stared at her with glittering black eyes, and said, "I had a bond with her. Why was such a thing so difficult to notice until it was gone?"

She tilted her head, still staring at Amara, and said, "This isn't fun anymore."

She flicked her wrist, a distracted motion, and there was a sudden high-pitched, hissing hum. Amara gasped, jerked, and twisted several times, driven back half a pace by some kind of impact.

Isana wasn't sure what had happened until she saw half a dozen creatures, like unthinkably large wasps, writhing on Amara's chest, belly, shoulders, arms, and legs. Each of them sported a stinger as long as a woman's finger, made of serrated and gleaming vord chitin.

Amara looked down at herself, at the enormous wasps, shocked. And then her eyes rolled back in her head, and she toppled to the ground, her back arched into a rigid bow, her limbs thrashing.

"Countess!" Aria cried, her face a mask of blood—but no longer bleeding, at least, no longer blinding her. She took a step forward, and her wounded leg buckled beneath her, nearly throwing her down.

The vord Queen looked over her shoulder and made the exact same gesture. Aria lifted her sword in a vain defensive motion, but there was the hiss-hum of more wasps flashing from some gaping orifice within the *croach*, high up on one wall. Where they struck steel, they hit with a heavy thump—it sounded like a hailstorm as literally hundreds of wasps lashed at Lady Placida. She shielded her eyes, but several of the creatures struck her cheeks, her neck, including one spectacular impact where the wasp's stinger pierced her left earlobe and all but tore it off her head.

Aria fell to one knee, gasping for breath. The little wounds frothed with poison, and the stream of wasps was merciless and unending. One struck her thigh, below the hem of the skirt of plated leather straps hanging from her belt. Another pierced her boot. Seconds later, the wasps had simply pounded her balance from her, and she toppled as well, letting out a high-pitched moan of agony and despair as her own body began to thrash like Amara's.

Isana felt her fingers tightening helplessly on the sheathed sword in her hand. Though she had some rudimentary training with such a weapon, she was in no way fit to compare herself to violent professionals such as Amara and Lady Aria—and even if she had been, neither of them had managed to defend herself. Her eyes flicked to the pool of water, but it was simply too far away. She would never be able to use what was in it in time.

The vord Queen's dark eyes focused on Isana.

She lifted her hand—and then her black eyes widened in surprise.

A gleaming metal hand reached out from behind Isana and gently took the late Invidia's weapon from her grasp. She twisted her head up to see Araris, stepping clear of the *croach* like a man walking through a field of grain. And yet, it was not Araris, as she had last seen him. Every inch of visible skin gleamed like polished steel. The mail he'd been wearing was gone, and Isana realized with a start that the master metalcrafter had, somehow, incorporated it into his very flesh.

He took two steps forward, each one falling with more sound and force than any being of flesh and blood should have possessed. He flipped the sword through several calm circles, evidently testing its weight and balance. Then Araris Valerian squared off against the vord Queen, and said, quietly, his voice strangely roughened, burred, "You will not touch her."

The Queen bared her teeth and flung her hand toward Araris, hissing. A sudden storm of wasps leapt through the air in three distinct streams. They hammered into Araris, hundreds of them in the space of seconds, each impact making its own sharply distinct pinging sound—and each and every one of them rebounded from his steely flesh, landing on the floor amidst the remains of his shredded shirt, their legs and stingers thrashing.

The streams of wasps died down and stopped, and Isana could clearly hear her own swift breathing in the silence that followed. The impotent wasps were littered into a pile halfway up Araris's thighs.

Moving very slowly, very calmly, his living-steel hand drifted up and lightly touched the hilt of his sword, settling the grip one finger at a time. "All right," he said in a soft, quiet voice. "My turn."

And suddenly one of the deadliest swordsmen in Alera was rushing across the distance separating him from the vord Queen, his weapon still sheathed.

The Queen let out a shriek of challenge and darted forward to meet him. In the very last instant, before the two reached each other, both of their swords leapt out, little more than blurs of green *croach* light on steel, and a thunderstorm of sparks erupted in the center of the hive.

The chiming sound of steel on steel from within the continual cloud of sparks sounded like twenty swordsmen were fighting, not two. It lasted for two seconds, three, four, then the sparks washed away over the floor, revealing a tableau: Araris stood facing the vord Queen, his sword before him, gripped in both hands. She stood facing him, sword arm extended down and to the side. Her pale cheek was marked by a thin line of green-brown blood.

Her eyes were slightly wide, and they flicked down to the cut on her face in disbelief. Her lip lifted in a snarl, and she made a hissing sound, pointing her sword at him.

Instantly, two of the blade-beasts bounded forward, menacing him with their weapon-limbs. They rushed Araris, unbelievably swift and strong. Blades descended toward the man Isana loved, and her heart flew up into her throat.

But Araris Valerian was their match.

The first two blades to come sweeping at him were shattered entirely in fountains of white and green sparks. Another blade struck his chest and rebounded in another shower of sparks, even as he caught a fourth in a literal steely grip and calmly drove the blade down through the limb of the other vord before him, slamming it through the vord and into the bedrock below, trapping one blade-beast in place with the piercing limb of the second. His sword flashed once, dispatching the trapped beast—and then he spun and drove his left fist forward, through the second beast's guard and into its head. His metallic fist smashed through the blade-beast's skull like a warhammer, until he had sunk his arm halfway to the elbow in the creature's skull. He withdrew his arm with a calm, smooth motion, and the blade-beast collapsed.

He had barely moved his feet.

The vord Queen's eyes narrowed, and she streaked toward Araris again, her sword flashing. Again, sparks flooded the hive, and Isana had to lift her hand to shield her eyes against them. By the time the two had parted once more, a second cut, almost precisely parallel to the Queen's first injury, but an inch closer to her throat, also graced her cheek.

"Speed isn't enough," Araris said in a gentle voice. "Not by itself. Your technique is sloppy. You haven't drilled enough."

The vord Queen's mouth spread into a very slow smile. Her eyes raked Araris, moving up and down his gleaming form, as she said, "Metal skin. Impressive. Painful?"

"Quite," said Araris.

The Queen made a quick gesture of her left hand, and the temperature in the hive seemed to drop. Crystals of ice formed upon Araris's steely skin, first here and there, then in a thick, spreading blanket. Isana felt the surge of agony in Araris as the torment of the frozen steel began to gouge at him even through a metalcrafter's insulation against pain.

"And now more so," the Queen said, and launched another attack.

Araris made his first defensive movement, and there was the peculiar sound of squealing metal. He screamed in sudden agony, a pain so great that it broke through his metalcrafting and left him at its mercy, raking against Isana's senses like frozen claws. He reeled back before the Queen, howling in pain with every tormented movement. He parried the first two blows, and the third, but missed the fourth, and the Queen's sword struck his shoulder.

There was a peculiar, hollow sound, and a webwork of cracks abruptly spread over the surface of his metallic skin.

Araris choked on another scream, his eyes wide and round, as the agony drove him down to one knee before the vord Queen.

"You cannot stop me," the vord Queen said. Her sword kindled to green-white flame as she loomed over Araris. "None of you can stop me."

Isana reached out a hand and seized upon the water in the little pool. She bade it leap up toward the Queen, but the vord was far too swift. She sensed the column of water speeding toward her and took a single step back as it washed by. As it went past her, the Queen stretched out a hand and Isana felt her rip control of the water from her as easily as Isana might have torn it from a child. The Queen sent it crashing into Araris, where it promptly began freezing on his armor, drawing even more pain from the battered man.

The Queen turned to look at Isana, and said, "Grandmother, you have one chance to live. Agree to govern the postconflict Alerans and to assist me in my current efforts, and I will spare your life and your mate's."

Isana straightened where she sat. She faced the vord Queen. And, very slowly, she shook her head.

"So be it," said the vord Queen.

Isana closed her eyes, and it was just then that trumpets began to blare, high and clear, from somewhere outside. Their voices were not the braying deepness of the Canim horns, nor the higher silver sound of the navy's bugles. These were genuine trumpets played by real Legion musicians, and their high-pitched, clarion call sent a shiver down Isana's spine.

The vord Queen's head whipped around to one side, and she hissed, "No. No, he cannot be *here*. Not *yet*."

The trumpets called again. The ground rumbled under the weight of many feet. The mantis warriors outside began to screech a warning—and all of those sounds proclaimed a single, unmistakable fact:

Gaius Octavian had come to do battle with the vord Queen.

"Kill them," the Queen snarled. "Kill them all."

The Queen crouched, then leapt skyward, clawing her way up through the holes in the hive's ceiling that had held the blade-beasts, and with a shriek passed out into the countryside.

Six blade-beasts turned toward Isana, Araris, and the wounded survivors of the failed assassination.

CHAPTER 51

Tavi and Kitai waited with the aerial contingent of the attack. Sir Callum and the other members of the First Aleran's Knights Pisces were restless. They couldn't lift off until the ground forces had begun their assault, for fear that the hollow roar of two dozen windstreams would alert the vord to their presence.

Then someone, probably Fidelias, let out a bellowed command to move out, and the host was on the march. It took them less than half an hour to reach the ruined steadholt, then, at another signal, the trumpets sounded the charge, and Aleran and Canim cavalry went roaring down onto the steadholt while the infantry marched at double speed in their wake.

"Right!" Tavi said. "Let's go!" He summoned up his windstream and lifted off. He was clumsier about it than most of the Knights Aeris there, but at least he managed it without hurting himself or fouling the efforts of the man beside him. Kitai took up position beside him on his left, while Sir Callum flew on his right, and the other Knights Aeris spread out into a v-shaped wing behind him.

Tavi led them forward, soon overflying the Aleran infantry, the slowest troops on the field. Their goal was the ruined steadholt itself, the nearest target, while their Canim peers, being much faster on their feet, swept to the east and around the steadholt, to strike into the fields of sleeping vord.

The other side included the cavalry, Canim and Aleran alike. The taurga were at least twice the weight of a horse, and they couldn't outrun one. As Tavi cruised up, the first Aleran cavalrymen were starting through the vord field, sabers lowering to flash left and right, in almost exactly the same motions and timing as their practice drills. They rushed down the columns of hibernating vord, wreaking havoc. Nearly eight hundred horsemen running at full speed through the field dealt the vord hideous wounds.

But they didn't hold a candle to the slower taurga.

The Canim beasts were enormously powerful, individually speaking—bigger and stronger than any beast Tavi knew of short of a gargant. But the taurga were omnivores with vicious tempers. Even if they hadn't been urged by their riders, they would have smashed vord left and right as they ran through them—while upon the beasts' backs, the Shuaran warrior Canim struck lazy-looking blows with long-handled axes that simply sheared through whatever they hit. They wreaked four or five times the damage the Aleran cavalry had done—which was only reasonable, since there were nearly five thousand of the bloody things.

Shrieks began to go up, here and there, the warning trills of wax spiders who had recognized that something wasn't right. The mantis warriors in the steadholt began streaking about, a couple of hundred of them at least, as the battle lines of the Aleran Legions closed on the steadholt.

Then a single alien voice rose over the noise of battle, a bone-chilling shriek that made Tavi feel cold to the bottom of his belly. For a second, he felt as if he had simply forgotten how to think, as if such civilized frippery as logic and the ability to form words had become deadweight he needed to cast off. His flight faltered a bit.

Beside him and below him, Tavi saw exactly the same reaction from all of the host, from Alerans, Canim, and their beasts alike—sudden hesitation, flashes of panic, wildly rolling eyes. Even Kitai shuddered. Worse, the sleeping vord seemed to have heard that voice and responded to it. Starting with the nearest vord, the mantis warriors slowly began to stir.

Tavi had heard cries like that before, and knew what they meant: The vord Queen had taken the field.

"See!" Kitai hissed, pointing. "There she goes!"

A shadowy form, hardly visible behind a windcrafted veil, burst through the thick stone wall of the barn as though it had been made from rotten wood. It shot off along the ground, visible only through the disturbance its violent wind-stream raised from the ground. As it passed over the hibernating vord, it screamed again, and more of the warriors began to stir.

The Aleran command sent out signals by trumpet, but not signals to re-form the ranks or to retreat. The trumpets rang out in pure, clear defiance of the sleeping swarm: attack, attack, attack.

"Go high!" Tavi snarled, and flung himself after the Queen. He dived for the ground to pick up speed and pulled himself out of the dive only seven or eight feet above the earth. He dodged around two Narashan warriors and half a dozen joyously destructive taurga before streaking out ahead of the entire host, closing distance on the fleeing, shrieking disturbance. As he went, even more warriors began to stir, and once a reaching scythe-limb came near to ripping his belly open more or less by pure providence. He batted it aside with his sword, closing to within a few yards of the Queen, and hit upon an inspiration. Concentrating intently, he reached forward with a windcrafting and closed it around the vord Queen in a bubble—a simple privacy crafting. Her voice cut off in midscream.

It took her several seconds to realize what Tavi had done to her. He thought he knew what tactic she would use next, and readied himself for it. Not two seconds later, the vord Queen suddenly shot twenty feet up, and her veil and windstream vanished altogether. She whirled, clearly visible in the predawn light, flinging open a small leather bag of fine salt.

But Tavi had anticipated the maneuver, and as the Queen shot up into the air, he did as well, dismissing his windcraftings an instant later. He sailed through the air and the cloud of fine salt on pure momentum, and didn't call back his windstream until he was sure he was past the salt.

He and the Queen regained their windstreams at almost the same instant, and she let out a shriek of frustration—cut off midway by another privacy windcrafting. She whirled on him, naked but for a cloak, her sword in hand, her eyes glittering. Then she reversed the direction of her windstream, slowing her forward momentum.

Just as her velocity came to an instant's standstill, there was the hiss of an arrow loosed from a bow in the darkness above Tavi. The sound gave the vord Queen more than enough time to react, and her sword rose to cut the arrow from the air. The missile splintered upon her blade.

The impact shattered the salt-crystal head of the arrow, and the Queen screamed as her wind furies were ripped and shredded by the weapon. Her windstream collapsed. She fell to the ground and landed on all fours, falling into an instant, inhumanly flexible roll that saved her from the swift sphere of white-hot fire Tavi called forth at the point of her impact.

Kitai and the Knights Pisces swept down and began strafing the Queen in twos and threes, flashing past and loosing arrow after arrow. She dodged with contemptuous speed and began shrieking once more to awaken the sleeping warriors—Kitai's arrow had disrupted Tavi's privacy windcrafting with the same vicious efficacy it had the Queen's windstream.

The nearby warriors stirred at once.

Tavi ground his teeth in frustration. If they allowed the Queen to fly, she would almost certainly waken all the sleeping vord, and odds were good that she might escape entirely—but using salt to keep her grounded also prevented Tavi from using the windcrafting that would prevent her from waking the other vord. If she managed to rouse enough of them, she could disappear into the swarm, and they might never be able to find her, much less bring lethal amounts of power to bear upon her.

Tavi glanced back. They hadn't flown for long, but it had taken them a mile or more away from the cloud-shrouded host. No help would be coming from there in time to do him any good.

She shrieked again, and, out of pure frustration, Tavi threw another fire-sphere at her. She darted out of it easily and slapped aside another arrow from one of the strafing Knights as she went. Tavi's strike missed her but caught half a dozen mantis warriors in its blast, charring them to twisted, skeletal shapes.

The vord Queen whirled to look at him, and Tavi felt the last thing he had expected: His watercrafting senses were pounded with an emotional assault—pure rage, the rage of a mother whose children are endangered.

Yes, he thought. *This is what I needed.*

"Aleran!" Kitai screamed.

He whipped his head up to see Kitai pointing toward the east. The sky, now the pale blue harbinger of sunrise, was thickly dotted with hundreds or thousands of dark shapes moving toward them—vordknights, they had to be. They would reach them in moments, and if that happened, there would be no way to bring enough power to bear upon the Queen.

The fliers of the First Aleran could not possibly stand against so many vordknights. Though their discipline and furycraft might make each Knight Aeris the equal of a dozen vord fliers, there were more than enough of the enemy on the way simply to overwhelm them. If he ordered them to stand against that, they would not survive. Their deaths would serve only to buy time.

But he needed the time.

He flashed the orders to Sir Callum by hand signal: Engage and hold the incoming enemy to the east.

By then, it was just light enough for Tavi to see the expression on Callum's face. He looked to the east and saw what was coming. He became pale, his expression twisting into a grimace of fear. He closed his eyes for a second and turned to Tavi. He banged his fist against his armored chest, meeting his gaze, and nodded slightly—whether in agreement or farewell, Tavi did not know. Then Callum began passing orders to the fliers, gathering each of them up as they finished their runs on the Queen.

As they did, Tavi continued hurling flame into the ranks around the vord Queen, killing dozens of mantis warriors, each blast earning him a fresh flash of her pure rage. Kitai took up the slack of the Knights as they ceased shooting at the Queen, her hand flying from quiver to bowstring, her arrows flashing with the supernatural speed and accuracy of a woodcrafter. The Queen was an elusive target—many arrows missed altogether, and those that stayed on their mark inevitably met with her blade. The Queen kept on shrieking, and several thousand mantis warriors were on the move, gathering up around her.

There was an enormous roar of collected windstreams as Callum and his men streaked out to engage the incoming vordknights, and a moment later Kitai switched to firecrafting as well. Bright spheres of blue-white light exploded beside Tavi's scarlet-white firecraftings, chewing a pair of broad holes in the ground. Mantis warriors screamed in agony and died in dozens as they were engulfed in the flames.

The Queen let out another howl of rage and turned toward Kitai, one hand raised and gathering a fistful of flame. As soon as Tavi saw that the Queen's attention was off him, he altered course to soar around behind her and, even as she sent the firecrafting at Kitai, Tavi hurled one of his own at the Queen.

The vord's spectacular reflexes saved her from Tavi's attack, though the warriors immediately around her were scoured from the face of the land. But the dodge had cost her—her own firecrafting exploded yards and yards short of Kitai.

The Queen shifted her aim to attack Tavi, only to have Kitai emulate the tactic Tavi had just used. As the Queen threw, Kitai's fire blast tore into her, forcing her to dodge and ruining her aim. Tavi felt his mouth turning up into a wolfish smile. If they could keep the battle moving this way, they would have her—and the vord Queen had to realize that every bit as much as Tavi did. Which meant that any second now she would . . .

The Queen shrieked again in anger and flung herself airborne. For a moment, Tavi thought that her wind furies were still in a state of disruption and that she wasn't going to have enough lift to fly—but then a vortex like a small tornado abruptly gathered beneath her, tossing her own brood about like toys, and she came rushing up at them at terrible speed, a wave of raw anger pulsing through the air before her as she flew straight toward Kitai.

Kitai set another salt-headed arrow to her bow, drew, and calmly waited until the last instant to loose it. The arrow leapt from the bow.

The vord Queen snatched it out of the air with her left hand, turned her wrist in a sinuous movement too swift to follow, and drove the tip toward Kitai's throat. Kitai lifted an arm in a desperate block, and the salt-crystal tip drove through her forearm and began to emerge from the other side before the arrow's slender shaft snapped. The blow still drove her forearm up against her mail, and the protruding portion of bloodied salt crystal was powdered to grains against it.

Kitai dropped like a stone.

Tavi sheathed his sword and altered his course smoothly, pouring on the speed, and hoped that Kitai had the presence of mind—even as she plunged through a lethal fall—to realize what the Queen was almost certain to do next.

Even as Kitai fell, she drew her third—her *last*—salt arrow from the specially designed quiver and loosed it at the Queen in an instinctive snap shot. The vord Queen had to swerve to one side to avoid the arrow, even as another fire-crafting blossomed forth from her dark-nailed hand.

Tavi rolled so that his body was to the sky as he intercepted Kitai, his shoulder blades slamming into his belly, her head whiplashing against his armored chest, even as he made a greater effort of furycraft to bear both of their weights. The Queen's firecrafting boomed deafeningly, exploding less than ten feet away from them with enough intensity to char Tavi's eyebrows and fill his nose with the reek of burned hair.

Tavi had caught Kitai perhaps twenty feet from the ground, and his back actually bounced off a hibernating mantis's head before their fall stopped, and he started gaining altitude again. He let out a grunt, made sure his arms were around her solidly, and poured on all the speed he could, running for the cloud of mist that had enveloped the abandoned steadholt.

"Kitai?" he called. "Kitai?"

She did not answer.

Thunder rumbled across the face of the Valley, a threatening, growling sound from the thunderheads gathering around Garados's snowcapped peak, colored a deep orange by the first rays of the rising sun—Thana, the wind fury known to the Valley's holders as Garados's wife, was preparing a battle force of her own.

"Kitai!" Tavi screamed.

She was limp in his arms.

The vord Queen let out a shriek of triumph and shot after them in deadly, intent pursuit.

Amara woke up with something foul in her mouth. She tried to spit it out, only to feel someone pushing it back in. She let out a weak grunt of protest and lifted a hand.

"Countess," said the First Lady's calm, quiet voice. "You must leave them in your mouth. Thanks to your wardrobe, you received considerably more poison than Aria, and if you spit them out before it has been neutralized, I fear you could relapse."

Amara shivered and blinked her eyes open. She was lying in a pool of shallow water, her head resting on Isana's crossed legs. Whatever the stuff in her mouth was, it tasted musty and vile—so much so that it almost completely neutralized the pain throbbing steadily through her cut and bruised body.

Which meant that she was alive. Which didn't make sense. One moment, she'd been about to sell her life for an extremely unlikely chance to combat the vord Queen—in fact, as she remembered it, she had taken that gamble and lost, handily, even before the wasp-things had slammed into her.

"Here comes another one," said a rasping, oddly metallic voice. She turned her head to see what looked like a gargoyle fashioned of steel in the image of Araris Valerian. It took her a second to realize that it truly *was* Araris, employing a form of metalcrafting they had only heard about Gaius Sextus performing.

Even as she tracked the thought, a vord mantis dropped from the ceiling of the hive—and landed on the ground in two essentially equal-sized pieces. Araris flicked the blood from the sword in his hand and kicked them to either side to clear the space beneath a pair of holes in the ceiling. He was building up quite a pile of remains. There were the various parts and pieces of half a dozen mantis warriors and what must have been eight or ten blade-beasts.

They were still in enemy territory.

That thought pushed another one to mind. She fumbled for her waist pouch and opened it. She reached around inside it with her fingers until she found the stone she was looking for, a smooth river rock the size of her fist. Then she started pushing at the vile mass in her mouth, trying to get it to move to one side.

Gentle hands pushed hers away from her mouth and Amara slapped lightly at them, letting out an irritated, mush-clogged growl.

"She's trying to talk," said a thready, exhausted voice. "Let her. See, the stone in her hand? She must have had some kind of plan for getting us out of here if things went bad."

Amara looked up to see Aria Placida sitting with her back against the wall, beside the pool. Her face was sunken and pale, and she looked as if she could barely hold up her own head, but her eyes were clear. To Amara's surprise, High Lord Antillus Raucus lay beside her, stripped of his armor, with an enormous, ugly purple scar wrapping around his waist like a belt, and the cauterized stump of his arm ending obscenely a few inches from his shoulder He was breathing unsteadily and clearly unconscious.

Isana's hands withdrew, and Amara pushed the mush in her mouth mostly into one cheek. "Firecrafting," she said, holding up the stone. "Signal flare. Need to get it into the open. I convinced Aquitaine to give me the Windwolves' contract. They're up high, waiting to get us out of here."

"Windwolves?" Aria asked.

"Mercenaries in service to the Aquitaines," Isana said. "They're mostly Knights Aeris."

Amara nodded. The movement made her a little dizzy. "Followed us, far enough back and high enough up that they wouldn't be detected by Invidia.

They'll know where we are, generally, but we have to signal them our exact location."

"No good," came Araris's voice. It sounded as if his words were rattling around the interior of a metal pipe before they left his mouth. "Those holes were where the blade-beasts were being kept for a rainy day—but they don't open beneath the sky. There's some kind of structure above us. If we threw the rock out, it might not be visible outside—"

Three wax spiders abruptly plunged down through both holes. Araris cut them all into quarters before they touched the ground.

"—the building," he finished, never altering the cadence of his words. Then he turned to look at Isana, and Amara noted that the metallic surface of his skin seemed cracked, rusted, and pitted over the right side of his chest and his right shoulder. She realized, with a shudder, that the "rust" was blood seeping out through the cracks. Evidently, the crafting did not make him entirely impervious to harm. He met Isana's eyes for a moment, then said, to Amara, "Give me the stone."

Amara felt the First Lady stiffen. "No. Araris, no."

"Only way," he said quietly.

"I forbid it," she said. "They'll *kill* you."

"If we all stay, we all die," he said in a quiet, firm voice. "If I go, there's a chance some of us will live." He turned his right hand palm upward, and said, "Countess."

Amara bit her lip—and tossed the stone toward him.

He caught it and rolled his shoulder, wincing. Then he went to stand beneath one of the holes and look up at it. It was ten feet or more to the ceiling. "Hmmm."

Aria pushed herself unsteadily to her feet. She walked over to Araris, bent over, and made a stirrup of her interlaced fingers. Araris hesitated for a moment, then put his booted foot upon her hands. "One," she counted. "Two. Three."

Aria straightened with fury-assisted strength and tossed Araris upward as if he'd been a small sack of meal. He went through the hole with his arms held straight up above him, then slammed his elbows down on either side of the hole when he reached the other side. Amara saw his legs kick several times as he hauled himself out, and heard a fresh round of wailing vord cries.

And beyond those, faint but clear—trumpets. Aleran Legion trumpets, sounding the attack, over and over and over again. Firecraftings crackled and boomed in the near distance, and Amara sucked in her breath, sitting up in the pool. "Do you hear that?"

"The Legions," Aria breathed. "But the whole horde lies between here and Garrison. How?"

"Tavi," Isana said, her voice suddenly fierce. "My *son*."

They fell quiet, and everyone listened to the distant sound of trumpets and firecrafting. Each sounded both near and far away by turns. Minutes crawled by in which nothing changed.

Then the exhausted Lady Aria, still slumped beneath the holes in the ceiling, drew in a sharp breath, and staggered back, crying, "Vord!"

And, as quickly as that, half a dozen mantis warriors came flooding into the hive.

⋈⋈⋈⋈CHAPTER 52

Fidelias sat upon his horse, keeping pace with the weary infantry of the Legions, and watched the most desperately aggressive military action he'd ever witnessed begin to play out.

The enshrouding mist complicated matters. The knot of Canim ritualists who kept pace with the command group muttered and snarled to themselves constantly. Every so often, one of the Canim would slice at himself with a knife and fling droplets of blood into the air. The drops vanished as they flew, presumably to maintain the misty shroud that would hide their precise location from the enemy.

Of course, it also meant that Fidelias couldn't see his own bloody troops once they were a few hundred yards away. They'd had to work out several chains of couriers to relay signals between the units that had traveled out of sight of the command group. Even now, signals were coming in: *Attack under way, light enemy resistance.* Apparently, the vord Queen had left a few alert guardians among her sleeping brood—probably posing as sleepers. At least, that was how Fidelias would have done it.

The front ranks of Legion infantry had reached the old steadholt, and the most experienced cohort of the Free Aleran, together with the First Aleran's Battlecrows, reached the gates and a broken-down section of the wall, respectively.

"Now," Fidelias said to the trumpeter behind him.

The man raised his horn and sounded the charge. Other horns throughout both Legions took up the same call, and the sudden roar from nearly four hundred throats joined the voices of the trumpets as the two assault cohorts rushed the old steadholt, while the rest of the Legions moved up to support them. As they did, windstreams roared behind him, and Gaius Octavian and the First Aleran's Knights Aeris took to the air.

A second later, there was an earsplitting cry, metallic, alien, and furiously hostile. It froze Fidelias's throat and locked his limbs into place for an instant. His horse shuddered and danced nervously, nearly knocking him from the saddle. All around him, he could see the same expression of dread and confusion marking the faces of the officers and the men. Even the Canim's mutterings had slowed to a trickle of soft sounds that fell from between their teeth.

"Sound the charge," he rasped. It was hard to force himself to make that much noise, so intent were his instincts to avoid attracting the attention of whatever had made that sound. He looked over his shoulder at the dumbstruck trumpeter, whose face was as white as everyone else's. Fidelias had played the role of Valiar Marcus for far too long to be stricken silent. He drew upon Marcus's strength, stiffened his spine, drew in a deep breath, and bellowed, "*LEGIONARE!* SOUND THE CHARGE!"

The soldier stiffened as if Fidelias had slapped him and jerked his trumpet to his lips. He puffed out a weak breath of sound, and Fidelias turned to him and broke his centurion's baton over the man's helmet. Shocked by the blow, the man dragged in a deep breath and blasted out the trumpet call, loudly enough to hurt Fidelias's ears.

Other trumpets took it up, and the momentary pause in the advance was over. Forty thousand infantry and cavalry resumed their motion, as a windstream larger and more powerful than any Fidelias had ever seen erupted from behind the old steadholt's walls and rushed out over the fields of sleeping vord, bearing a pale figure in a dark cloak, already vanishing into a windcrafted veil.

The Queen shrieked again, farther away, and Fidelias ordered the trumpeter to continue sounding the attack. Reports started flashing in from the courier lines: *Battlecrows heavily engaged. Horse cavalry light resistance. Taurg cavalry inflicting heavy casualties with no resistance.* And the last had come with the signal he'd been dreading. *Canim infantry heavily engaged by mobile enemy.* And, only a moment after that, *Enemy aerial forces in Legion strength, inbound.*

That tore it. Against a sleeping enemy, they'd had a chance. But if the enemy was waking, and if, as Fidelias dreaded, the Queen had summoned reinforcements, they could be in for it. He was willing to die, if it was necessary to save Alera—but as far as his experience had taught him, a living, fighting solider was almost always more valuable to his Realm than a dead one.

The Aleran infantry had been tasked to take the steadholt. He would simply have to expedite matters. They couldn't have fitted a fraction of the forces there into the steadholt, but at least it would provide a solid object against which the other forces in the field could put their backs—if it could be taken quickly enough.

Fidelias signaled for the Prime Cohort to move, sending them in after the first two, along with a pair of Knights Terra and Ferrous attached to the unit, with orders to support the Battlecrows and secure the steadholt with all due speed. Then he turned to the Canim.

"Master Marok," he said. "There are significant enemy forces inbound. We need to secure the steadholt immediately. Are you willing to help?"

Marok flicked his ears in the affirmative and began loping calmly toward the steadholt. Fidelias and the command group followed him. Fidelias unlimbered the Canim balest from its holder upon his saddle, more a gesture of habit than of any real intent. He was unused to ordering things done at this level rather than doing them himself.

The interior of the steadholt was chaos. Vord rushed and darted everywhere, wax spiders and warriors alike, boiling out of windows and doorway, skittering across rooftops, rushing along the walls. The Battlecrows had formed into two separate squares with iron-hard discipline, defending themselves from attackers and moving, step by step, closer to what was obviously their objective—the mouth of the large stone barn. A furycrafted ramp sloped down into the earth below its flooring. It was often an area used for cool storage on a steadholt. The barn's interior was shadowed, but a steady green glow emerged from two holes in the barn's flooring.

The cohort from the Legion of ex-slaves hadn't done as well as the veteran Battlecrows. Through whatever fortunes of war, they had not been able to lock into a defensive formation when swarmed by the vord. Half of them were dead, or isolated in odd corners of the steadholts, desperate rings of half a dozen men fighting a remorseless enemy. The other half had managed a defensive square, but it was a ragged one—the mantises were steadily picking it apart.

"Master Marok!" Fidelias called. He pointed at the rapidly disintegrating formation of the Free Aleran. Sensing weakness, the vord were attacking more ferociously and in greater numbers. "If you please!"

Marok stepped forward with four other Canim wearing vord-chitin mantles rather than those made of human leather. He snarled something in a language Fidelias did not understand, and the five ritualists drew their daggers in a single, simultaneous motion. A similar movement laid open a long cut upon each of their forearms, bloodying the bright steel of the daggers. They all threw their arms up, scattering droplets of blood to the sky, where they flickered and vanished—until with a single unified howl they lowered their arms—and the misty sky suddenly boiled with dark clouds and fell in time with the ritualists' arms.

Something like a thundercloud fell over the beleaguered Free Aleran cohort, a mass of dark grey. Fidelias thought he could see things writhing within it, sinuous shapes and flickering tentacles.

The vord within the cloud began to shriek and wail in distress.

Marok watched the cloud intently for a moment, then threw his bleeding arm out again, scattering droplets of blood into the darkness of the cloud, crying, "It is enough! The demons are not for you!" in Canish.

The cloud went still. The brisk spring wind soon began dispersing it, and when it had all washed away a moment later, the Free Aleran *legionares* stood entirely alone, with confused, stunned looks on their faces, their chests heaving for breath.

There was no sign whatsoever of the vord who had been attacking them.

Marok turned to face Fidelias and took on the posture of a Cane waiting for the answer to a question.

"Impressive," Fidelias said.

"Clouds of acid are for amateurs," Marok replied. He glanced over his shoulder at most of the other ritualists, who continued their steady chant and occasional self-bloodletting. None of them looked at him. Marok growled in unmistakable satisfaction.

The four Knights attached to the Prime Cohort broke with their unit and crossed the courtyard to join the first square of the Battlecrows. Centurion Schultz, supporting a dazed-looking young Tribune with blood sheeting over half his face, saw them coming and brought them into the lines at once. Then he put the four men at the "point" of the square's corner, wheeled it into a diamond relative to the second square, and began a steady march forward, using the devastating power of the Knights to cut a path through the vord. Within a moment, the two blocks of Battlecrows had rejoined, and they turned their efforts toward advancing, an implacable block of steel and swords that hacked and chopped its way step by bloody step into the barn.

There was a shriek and a sudden rush of pressure as dozens of warriors flung themselves at the Battlecrows in wholehearted, berserk determination to cut the invaders down, and for a moment the Battlecrows slowed. But then, abruptly, an apparition materialized from the darkness of the barn, a black shadow against the green light in the form of a man. The figure began to move, and suddenly strode out into the light, a completely metallic form the likes of which Fidelias had never seen and only once heard about. Fidelias recognized him at a glance— Araris Valerian, one of the deadliest blades in the Realm, a man whose sword had made him a legend before he'd gotten out of his mid-twenties.

Fidelias had *never* seen a furycrafter do what Araris had done, though.

The first vord warrior he approached never knew he was near. Araris's sword clove the legs from one side of its body, then swept its head from its trunk before it could finish falling.

The next vord spun to face the steel swordsman. Its plunging scythe struck Araris on his left shoulder and shattered like a length of desiccated wood. Araris parried the second scythe aside, split the creature's head with his sword, and kicked the vord's corpse, still thrashing dangerously, into the crowd of its brethren trying to stop the Battlecrows.

The vord broke, then, rushing back into the barn—but their flight took them within reach of Araris Valerian's blade. The swordsman never seemed to move with any particular speed—only a fluid, delicate grace entirely at odds with his statuelike appearance. And yet, his sword always seemed to move swiftly enough, no matter how quickly the vord might attempt to evade him. He dropped the first several, it seemed, merely to slow the escape of the others, and his blade and those of the Battlecrows took a heavy toll of the remaining vord. No more than half a dozen of them had survived to flee back into the barn.

Araris nodded at Schultz and looked wildly around him. "Marcus!" he called, his voice buzzing oddly. He tossed a stone from his hand into a long arc, and Fidelias snatched it out of the air. He could feel the tingle of a firecrafting in it—a signal flare, most likely. "The First Lady, and three others are trapped in the hive, wounded. They need to be taken to the stronghold at Garrison immediately. There's the flare for their escort. Lord Placida may be down at the bottom of that ramp. Find him."

Then he spun on one heel and began a heavy run back toward the green-lighted holes in the barn floor.

"Schultz!" Fidelias barked, tossing the stone to the centurion, who caught it handily enough. "Get that to some open ground and set it off!"

"Yes, sir!" Schultz said. He looked around the havoc within the courtyard a bit blankly, then seemed to be struck by an idea. He muttered something to the stone and hurled it up to fall onto the flat stone roof of the barn. A few seconds later, there was a loud hissing sound, and brilliant blue-white light blazed from the flare.

"Fine," Fidelias said. "Get a detail to the bottom of that ramp."

"Aye, First Spear," Schultz said, and began bawling assignments to his men.

Fidelias watched it happen and shook his head. "Never rains but it pours."

Between the mopping-up combat in the courtyard, the ongoing trumpet cries to attack, and the sound of the bloody flare all but burning a hole into the flat stone roof of the barn, Fidelias didn't hear the approaching windstream until Princeps Octavian had all but slammed into him. Flying backward and upside down, Octavian was hauling Kitai through the air, her back against his chest as he came in to land in the courtyard. His heels struck first, digging a furrow in the hard soil, then slipped out from beneath him. He slid across the ground on his back until he fetched up against the inner side of the steadholt's wall with a grunt.

"Marcus!" Octavian bellowed. "She's hurt! Get a medico over here, now!" He thrashed his way a bit awkwardly to his foot, lowering Kitai gently to the ground as he went. He spun and threw his right arm up, dragging with it a sheet of earth and stone more than a foot thick, raising it up into a shielding dome just as a flash of green-white lighting ripped out of the mists. It struck the improvised wall and shattered it, but when the debris settled, Octavian remained standing over the wounded Marat woman. "Bloody crows, Marcus!" he bellowed. "I'm a little busy here!"

Marcus kicked a team of *singulares* and a Prime Cohort medico to rush over to Kitai. As soon as Octavian saw that, he took two steps and leapt off the ground and into flight, vanishing into the mists. A second windstream, far larger and more violent, swept over the courtyard, clearly in pursuit.

"Marcus!" bellowed Araris in an iron voice from within the barn. "I need more men here!"

"First Spear, First Spear!" said a young *legionare* frantically. He made a series of frantic gestures.

"Bloody crows, boy, I'm standing right here!" Marcus snapped. "Tell me!"

"Enemy infantry," the boy panted. "At least thirty thousand, here in two minutes. Enemy airborne troops have been delayed by the Knights Pisces, and will arrive at the same time, approximately seven thousand. Sir, what do we do?"

Two minutes?

Two minutes?

Nearly forty thousand vord were inbound—and his own troops were scattered all over the terrain, out of sight of each other in the fog. They would be swallowed whole in detail.

Bloody crows, what had Octavian gotten him into?

If both he and that young man survived the day, which was looking increasingly unlikely, Fidelias thought, he might be forced to kill him on general principles.

CHAPTER 53

"Count Calderon," Ehren said, "I know not everything is as it seems. But I would truly love to know why the fact that we're about to get crushed by that pair of vordbulks is not as it seems. I mean, I thought it would have been obvious by now."

"Crows," Bernard breathed quietly. His face was tight with tension. "They must have missed the Queen."

"What?" Ehren asked.

A seventy-pound boulder went whizzing past them, hurled by one of the hulking behemoths accompanying the vordbulks. It missed them by no more than a foot and smashed into the wall of the tower behind them, sending a webwork of cracks into the stone.

"Bloody crows!" Ehren cried.

"The High Lords and . . ." He swallowed, and seemed to ignore the near miss. "And my wife learned where the vord Queen was."

"Oh," Ehren said quietly. The obvious move would have been to attempt to end the war immediately—a decapitating strike. Had it happened, the vord would not now be operating with such focus and direction. It was, therefore, reasonable to assume that the strike had failed. Given how critical it was, Ehren judged it unlikely that the High Lords would have done anything but fight to the death. And Countess Amara, while a skilled windcrafter, had been by far the person least able to defend herself against a threat like the one the Queen represented.

"I see," Ehren said quietly. A moment later, he added, "I think it's more likely that the Queen escaped than that they were all killed, Your Excellency. I'm sure your wife is all right."

Bernard shook his head. "Thanks for lying, son."

Ehren grimaced.

"Well," Bernard said. He turned to look at the damage the boulder had done to the tower. "If the High Lords haven't done the job, we'll just have to handle it ourselves, won't we?"

He disappeared inside the tower and emerged a moment later with a great, black bow as long as he was tall, its staves thicker than Ehren's forearms, and a war quiver packed with arrows. Count Calderon took a deep breath. Then he grunted and bent the great bow, leaning into it with the whole of his body. He strained with fury-born strength to bend the bow far enough to set its string—which was more like a cable as thick as Ehren's smallest finger.

Calderon let up on the bow gingerly and let out a huge exhale. The veins on his neck were standing out, and his face was red with the exertion. Ehren looked around nervously as Count Calderon readied the weapon.

The battle on the outer wall was still going well, as battles went, the *legionares* holding steady. The fight on the northern bluff had slowed the vordbulk dramatically—Cereus and the Citizens he led had been steadily assaulting the monstrous beast with every form of furycraft imaginable.

Dozens of square yards of its chitinous hide had been burned away. Trees swayed and bowed, lashing out with their limbs like enormous clubs, but the black chitin-armor seemed to absorb the impacts readily. Spikes rose from the ground to pierce the vordbulk's feet, but the beast had begun dragging its feet forward, shattering the stone spikes before they could pierce it—and anyone coming close enough to the enormous creature to attempt to bring up the spikes beneath one of the monster's planted feet was viciously assaulted by the vord protecting it.

Though it bled from scores of wounds, the vordbulk had not been killed, only slowed; and the furycrafters working against the beast were growing tired. It was an incredibly durable creature, and not simply because of its size. Despite the massive furycraft being brought to bear against it, it simply hunched its shoulders until the surges of power waned and took another giant's step forward. But this much had been done: The Citizens had stalled the creature for the moment, ruining the notion of a simultaneous assault on both sides.

On the south bluff, the vordbulk had not even been slowed down. Within moments, it would be in position to fall and crush the outer walls, simultaneously breaching the defenses and creating a fleshy ramp that the vord mantises could use to enter.

Bernard slung the war quiver over his shoulder, in a gesture that seemed like ritual to Ehren, something practiced so many times that the Count probably wasn't aware that he'd done it. Count Calderon reached up and selected a single arrow. Its head was oddly heavy, a set of four steel blades that reminded Ehren more of a harpoon than anything else. It was only at the last moment that he noted a sphere of gleaming black glass that had been trapped within the steel blades, like a jewel within its setting.

Bernard stared up at the nearest vordbulk, the one on the southern bluff. As both beasts had been doing periodically since they appeared, the vordbulk let out one of its enormous, bone-shaking basso roars.

"Clan Herdbane," Bernard sighed. "Those fools never did figure out how to stay out of a fight they couldn't win."

As Ehren watched, he saw barbarians and their beasts attacking the vord-bulk, hurling spears up at its belly, hoping to hit the vitals, as their deadly pred-ator birds clawed their way several yards up the vordbulk's legs, ripping and tearing to no appreciable effect. Perhaps if given a week, they might eventually nibble the great beast down—but they didn't have that kind of time.

"You might want to back off a ways, Sir Ehren," Bernard said. He brandished the arrow. "I'm not entirely sure this thing won't explode the second I release the string."

Ehren swallowed and took a couple of steps back. "I . . . see."

"Bit more," Bernard said.

Ehren walked twenty feet, to the far side of the citadel's balcony.

"Suppose it'll have to do," Bernard said. He set the arrow to the great bow's string, faced the vordbulk, and waited.

"That's . . . a long shot," Ehren noted. "Three hundred yards?"

"Range isn't a problem," said Bernard through his stiffened jaw. "Angle is a bit odd, though."

"Ahem, yes," Ehren said. "But honestly, sir . . . there must be some other way for you to . . . Your Excellency, it's *one* arrow. What could you possibly think it will do?"

The vordbulk's vast flanks expanded as it drew in a breath.

Bernard drew the black bow, and its staves groaned like the mast of a ship in high winds. Muscles knotted in his shoulders, back, and arms, and again his teeth clenched, and his face turned red with effort. There was a faint trembling in the earth as Bernard pulled the arrow back to his ear. The grain of the black bow writhed and quivered, even as it was bent, and Ehren realized that the Count was putting an enormous amount of earthcrafting into bending the bow and would be using even more woodcrafting to straighten its staves, to impart all the power he could to the missile. When he released the string with a short cry of effort, the reaction of the bow nearly took him from his feet. There was a thundercrack in the air before him, and the arrow leapt into the night so swiftly that Ehren would not have been able to follow it had not the morning light gleamed on the steel head.

The vordbulk opened its mouth to roar again, just as the arrow angled up-ward, into the creature's vast maw. The roar went on for a moment, then there was a flash of light, a whumping sound, and a burst of smoke and little licks of fire that poured from the vordbulk's mouth. It stopped in its tracks and roared again, this time at a higher pitch, and a veritable fountain of green-brown vord blood spewed from its mouth and fell to the earth in a disgusting miniature waterfall.

"Hngh," Bernard said. He sagged visibly, his chest heaving in slow, deep breaths, and he leaned against the railing to stay upright. "Guess . . . Pentius Pluvus . . . was right."

"Eh?" Ehren asked, watching the vordbulk with fascination.

Bernard sagged until he sat down on the bench against the outer wall of the tower, behind them. "Pluvus said an explosion is a very different thing when it starts off surrounded by flesh instead of occurring in the open air. Much more devastating. Apparently a crow ate one of our little fire-spheres one day, and a boy tried to knock it out of the air with his sling before it could escape. Normally, one of the little ones we used at first would only singe some feathers if they went off nearby. This time they found feathers and bits two hundred yards away."

"I see," Ehren said. "How very . . . very nauseating."

The vordbulk let out another distressed cry. It staggered like a drunkard.

"This bow can put an arrow right through a couple of sides of beef," Bernard said. "I wouldn't practice on live cows, of course. Cruel."

"Mmm," Ehren said faintly.

The vordbulk shook its head. Fluid slewed out and splattered in great, sickening arcs.

"So I shot at the roof of that thing's mouth," Bernard said. "I figure the arrow stopped three or four feet past that. Somewhere up in its brain, maybe. Then . . ." Bernard made an expanding motion with his hands and settled down to watch the vast creature in silence.

The vordbulk gradually listed to one side and fell. It was a motion more akin to a tree's toppling—to *several* trees' toppling—than any animal's movement. The ground shook when it landed, and dozens of stones were jarred loose from the side of the bluff, to come crashing down among the buildings of the town. Dust and dirt flew twenty feet into the air around the creature. The vordbulk let out one last slow, gasping cry that trailed off from an earsplitting roar to gradual silence.

Ehren turned his eyes to Bernard and just stared at the man.

"Anybody could have done it," Bernard said wearily.

Wild cheering, faint by contrast, rang up from the city below, and from the reserve positions behind them.

The Count of Calderon closed his eyes and settled back against the wall of the tower, clearly exhausted, and winced as his shoulders moved. "It was a crow-begotten big target." He opened one eye to squint at the second vordbulk. "Now. If only I had another one of those arrows. And a sphere to match it. And a night's sleep." He shook his head. "We're all just so bloody tired. I don't know how Cereus keeps going."

Ehren sat down beside Bernard, frowning up at the second vordbulk. "Count? What are we going to do about that one?"

"Well, Sir Ehren," Bernard said philosophically. "What do you suggest? My weaponsmith says it will be the day after tomorrow before he has another arrow like that one ready. I could send in the Legions, but they'd just get stomped flat by the hundreds. Our Knights and Citizens are all either on the wall fighting the horde, or they're already up on the bluff."

He ran a broad hand back over his short hair. "We can't bog them down like we did at the last wall, because the whole bluff is a rock shelf, and toying with that could collapse the entire bluff and kill us all, including our refugees. I don't have any more of those arrows, or the high-grade firestones, or the strength to shoot that bow. Think I tore something. My back is on fire." He grimaced. "So we hope the Citizens and Lord Cereus can wear it down before it gets here, and I'm forced to ask Doroga and his gargant riders to make a last-ditch attempt, which is likely to get them killed for no good reason."

"We can't just sit here." Ehren protested.

"No?" Bernard asked. "We've got nothing left in reserve, Sir Ehren. Nothing has been held back. It's coming down to old Cereus and the Citizens up on that bluff. If that thing makes it all the way here, this war is over. It's as simple as that."

They were both silent for a moment. The cries and calls of battle, and the distant report of furycraftings hurled in vain at the vordbulk wound around them.

"Sometimes, son," Count Calderon said, "you have to acknowledge that your future is in someone else's hands."

"What do we do?" Ehren asked quietly.

"We wait," Bernard said, "and see."

High Lady Placida Aria stumbled back as the vord rushed into the hive through the holes in the ceiling, and Isana had to roll rapidly to one side to keep from being trampled upon. The mantis warriors landed and rushed about in short, darting motions for a moment, clearly disoriented.

Aria fell back against the wall with a short cry. Isana's eyes widened in alarm. Lady Placida's system had been badly strained by the poison and her injury. Isana had healed the broken bone, and the Blessing of Night had countered the poison, but the High Lady had been utterly exhausted.

"I c-can't," she panted, and shook her head. "That last e-earthcrafting . . . I can't."

Isana's eyes went to Amara, who was in worse shape than Aria was. The Cursor had only just managed to lever herself up to her elbows.

Which meant . . .

"It's up to me," Isana breathed. She fumbled for a proper phrase to express the feelings that realization inspired, and settled upon, "Oh, bloody crows."

Then she steeled herself, reached for Aria's belt, and drew the High Lady's slender dueling sword from its sheath. She turned to face the six vord warriors, bouncing the sword in her right hand a few times, testing its weight and balance. Then she extended her left hand to the pool of water and narrowed her eyes. A bathing tub's worth of liquid abruptly leapt out of the water and gathered upon her left arm. Isana concentrated on it for a few ferocious seconds, and the water formed into the shape of a round disc several inches thick, resting upon her left forearm. The disc then began to stir and spin in emulation of a current, whirling faster and faster.

The whirling disc pulled on her upper body oddly, but Isana managed to take a few steps to place herself between the vord and the survivors of the assault on the hive, sword and improvised shield in hand.

One of the warriors noticed her and leapt at her with an unsettling hiss, like a teakettle boiling over. Isana saw the scythe-limbs of the mantis sweeping down toward her head and lifted her arm to interpose the watery shield.

The razor-sharp weapons pierced the water easily—and were both flung to Isana's left with such violence that the entire body of the mantis was hauled several steps in the same direction. Isana swept the long, narrow dueling blade in a nearly vertical slash, and the razor-sharp steel bit into one of the mantis's legs, laying open a wound more than a foot long. The vord let out a sharp whistle and reeled away.

Three more mantises turned their heads toward Isana and came scuttling forward. Isana saw that she could not simply try to interpose the water shield between herself and every single scythe—but she picked the mantis on the far right, stepping that way, creating an extra fraction of a second in which her target would attack her, but the other two could not. Once again, she raised the whirling shield of water, and once again the mantis's weapon-limbs were hauled violently to her left, tugging the mantis with it. The creature stumbled into its companions, fouling their attacks, and Isana had time to slash twice at the vord, inflicting two more obviously painful but less-than-fatal wounds.

She shuffled her feet to get between the vord and the wounded again, panting hard, her whole body trembling with painful fear. This was hardly her forte. Where was Araris?

Twice more she was rushed by single mantis warriors, and both times she defeated them the same way she had the others, though on the last attempt she nearly dropped the sword, her hands were shaking so hard.

The vord whistled and hissed at one another, their bodies beginning to bob up and down in unified agitation. And then, moving together, all six of them spread out into a half circle around her and began to close in with slow, certain confidence.

Isana felt her eyes grow enormously round, and she heard herself saying, in a completely level tone, "This is just ridiculous."

The vord plunged forward, all at the same time.

Isana wasn't sure exactly when she decided to do what she did. It simply happened, coming forth from her as naturally as if she'd planned and practiced the crafting for weeks. Again, she lifted the spinning water shield to the horizontal, but this time she cut the whirling wheel of liquid into slices, as one would a wheel of cheese. At the speed the watery shield was rotating, this had the effect of releasing a series of blasts of water, each consisting of several gallons of liquid.

The flying bursts struck the vord with flawless accuracy, one after the other, the sound of it a rapid *slap-slap-slap-slap*. And, as soon as the bursts of water had hit one of the vord, Isana locked it there through Rill, surrounding the mantises' rather tiny heads with globes of water.

The vord went mad, bounding about, leaping, clawing uselessly at their heads with their grasping claws, only to have them pass harmlessly through the water. Isana had no love for the vord, but she hated to see any creature suffer. Though they had no emotions readily identifiable with humanity, they felt fear as well as anything else that walked the surface of Alera—and Isana pitied them for their fear.

They collapsed, one by one, quivering still on the ground. Isana stepped forward, to finish each off as mercifully as she could, when another shadow blocked the ceiling above, and a steely figure dropped to the *croach*-covered floor, crushing the *croach* with his weight as he fell.

Araris's blade flashed through one vord, then a second, before it slowed and the steel-skinned Knight looked slowly around the hive at the six dead or dying mantises. Then he straightened, his sword dropping rather limply to his side as he turned to stare at Isana.

"Pardon, love," Isana said, rather whimsically. "I regret that you had to see me do anything so unladylike."

Araris Valerian's mouth spread into a slow, calm, and very pleased smile. Then he shook himself a little and dispatched the rest of the mantises as men in the armor of *legionares*—in the armor of the *First Aleran*, by all the furies, piled down the hole in Araris's wake.

"Come with me, my lady," Araris said. "There's little time. There's a team coming down to get you and the wounded out and back to Garrison, and another trying to find Lord Placida, but it's going to be close."

Amara pushed herself awkwardly to her feet. "Why? What's happening?"

Araris walked over to Lord Aquitaine, sheathing his sword. "The First Aleran is about to be overrun."

"The First Aleran," said Isana. "If the First Aleran is here, Araris, *where is my son?*"

From the hole above them came a screech of fury of such pure malice and scorn and raw, seething hatred that Isana had to flinch away from its intensity. The scream made her feel as though someone with long, dirty fingernails had shoved them beneath the skin of her back and drawn them slowly, spitefully over her spine.

Isana became aware that the men around her had gone very still, staring up toward the origin of that hideous sound.

"Where do you think?" Araris asked quietly, his voice still buzzing with that metallic edge. The swordsman indicated the ceiling with a flick of his sword's tip, and said, "He's fighting *that*."

⊃⊂⊃⊂⊃ Chapter 54

Tavi rolled to his right on pure instinct, and an instant later the Queen's sword sliced through the empty space he had occupied. Her windstream was enormous, violent, and the vicious turbulence that followed her was nearly enough to send him spinning from the sky.

By the time he regained his balance, the Queen was not in sight. The Canim-wrought mist had long since cloaked the ground from view, and at the speeds they were traveling, they would only be visible to one another for a flashing instant through the haze. But Tavi could hear her, or at least her presence. The dull, empty howl of her overpowered windstream was rendered directionless by the mist and seemed to come from everywhere. But Tavi knew she was out there, somewhere, circling him.

Excellent.

Tavi drew himself into a steady hover, reached out a hand, and summoned three fire-spheres in rapid order. They appeared with a disproportionately loud boom and were followed by the hiss of mist being turned to steam. They never came anywhere close to the vord Queen. They weren't supposed to.

The vord Queen let out another spine-shuddering shriek of hostility and rage—which grew louder as it went on. She was coming straight at him. Tavi swept his sword in a couple of swift circles and checked his pocket to be sure he was ready.

The Queen appeared: a sudden blur of white hair, glittering black eyes, and windblown cloak spreading like dark wings. She accelerated toward him with astonishing rapidity, and Tavi lifted his sword as though he meant to meet her blade to blade.

At the last second, he threw a firecrafting at her—even as she did exactly the same thing. The two craftings intercepted one another, and there was a deafening explosion of red and green flame. The vord Queen came plunging through it, the vanishing remnants of the explosion setting the edges of her cloak on fire in both colors. Her blade swept at his throat, but Tavi's sword intercepted the strike neatly. A red, blue, and vord green explosion of sparks the size of a city market flew out from the impact, and the vord Queen shrieked again in furious disappointment as she shot past him and banked immediately, coming around to rush him again.

From somewhere below, Tavi heard the weird, ululating howl of a Cane, and the bloodstone in his pocket suddenly felt almost warm enough to blister his skin. Marok had heard his signal.

The mist all around them thickened, congealed, and dark shapes stirred within. Long, twining tendrils of reddish flesh lashed out from a dozen different directions, and Tavi's heart lurched into his throat. No less than three of the Canim-called horrors had appeared all around him, and their questing tentacles slithered toward him, dripping a slime Tavi knew to be deadly acidic and poisonous to boot. He found himself all but holding his breath as the tendrils snaked all around him for several endless seconds . . . and abruptly withdrew. The protective power of the bloodstone talisman he carried had been enough to turn the beasts away—or at least enough to make them seek other prey.

The vord Queen had been swarmed by a dozen of the things.

Tentacles lashed out at her, flailing and grabbing. She eluded most of them but not all, and she shrieked in pain and anger as half a dozen dripping limbs left mild burn marks upon her seemingly vulnerable skin. The Queen spun madly in place, and her sword burst into flame as she began cutting her way free of the mist beasts.

Tavi didn't give her a chance to get loose. He focused his concentration upon her and crafted the hottest and most violent fire-sphere he'd ever attempted. It burst upon the vord Queen in a brilliant flash of light and a deafening roar of thunder.

Tavi wasn't trying to conform to the standards of a duel. He certainly had nothing to prove to anyone. And he'd seen too many battles to have any illusions about an honorable struggle; if he had his way, he would never engage in a fair fight ever again.

So he hammered the Queen with another fire-sphere. And another and *another*, as swiftly as he could throw them. The sound of her furious shriek provided a melody to the brutal percussion of the firecrafting.

He had her dead to rights for perhaps three or four seconds—but it couldn't last. His firecraftings might have been scorching the Queen, but they were wreaking havoc on the mist beasts, burning away the tentacles that held the Queen in place. The second she was free of them, the Queen dropped her windcrafting and plummeted into the mist. Tavi had a quick glimpse of a naked body, white hair burned away, half-covered by black scorch marks, like a steak left too long over the fire. Then she vanished.

Tavi turned and streaked after her. He could not afford to let her escape.

Fire rose from nowhere as he dived, and he realized with a start that the Queen had veiled herself and slowed her fall. He lifted his sword as the flame enveloped him, drawing the heat into the blade and away from his flesh, igniting the sword once more. Then the Queen was diving toward the ground beside him, an apparition half-hidden behind a veil, only the green fire of her sword truly visible. Their weapons flashed and chimed a dozen times, and suddenly the ground was rushing toward them.

Tavi pulled up first, terrified for a second that he was already too near the ground to manage it, but he was able to turn his motion from vertical to horizontal, just above a stretch of open field. Tall weeds and bits of the previous year's bracken scratched and hissed upon his armor, and he looked over his shoulder to see the vord Queen in pursuit, apparently none the slower for the damage wrought upon her flesh.

Crows. He'd been sure the Queen would be worse off than that after tangling with the Canim's pet horrors. Still, it had to have taken something out of her. She wasn't closing the distance on him nearly as quickly as he'd expected her to.

How many times had he been in this position, in front of someone much stronger than he was, knowing that only his wits would keep his skin in one piece. As a child in the Valley, and one who had never learned the knack of fading into the background, it had happened frequently with his playmates. But he had also dealt with thanadents and snow cats—crows, even the bloody sheep had been a great deal larger and stronger than he was, and the flocks' rams had frequently chased him up trees. And all of that *before* he'd left the Calderon Valley.

He found himself grinning.

Though worry and terror and rage all burned away at his guts, Gaius Octavian was smiling.

This was a game he knew how to play.

He altered his course abruptly, shooting straight up into the air. The Queen came after him, her windstream a howling, cyclonic roar.

It took him only a moment to clear the ritualists' mist, and he climbed out of it to find the sun coming up red on the eastern horizon under a heavily clouded sky, painting the Calderon Valley in the colors of blood. To his right, the Canim cavalry was engaged in wholesale slaughter of the sleeping vord, though Varg and the infantry were loping swiftly toward the vast bank of mist that hid the two Legions. Awakened vord ran amok by the thousands, and the comparatively small Aleran cavalry force was hitting any group of vord who thought they might attack the Canim infantry from the flanks while they marched. The sound of battle and the hollow coughs of medium-sized firecraftings drifted up to him, oddly attenuated by the mist.

The Queen emerged below him after several seconds. The unblackened part of her body sported fresh black-edged acid marks, and her speed seemed to have dropped even more, but her eyes glittered coldly, focused on Tavi and Tavi alone.

Tavi felt the grin spreading wider across his face. "All right. If you want the Calderon Valley so badly, the least I can do is give you the tour."

He poured all his concentration and will into his windstream and shot off to the northwest, toward the thunderstorm-shrouded peak of Garados.

Chapter 55

Fidelias struggled to pull some semblance of order out of the battle's chaos. Granted, battles were *never* orderly, tidy, or easily managed—but this one was worse than most.

With only minutes to prepare, and his army broken into separate elements, each of them too small to challenge the main body of the vord alone, he had done the only thing he could do. He'd marched the First Aleran out of the ruined steadholt and deployed them in an arching line around the steadholt's exterior, while ordering the healers, wounded, and medical personnel into the relative safety of the steadholt's great hall. He'd placed the Free Alerans on the stead-holt's flanks, intending to let his veteran troops take the brunt of the coming assault, while the less experienced freemen handled any stragglers or enemy probes. While he was screaming those orders and getting his *legionares* into position—at times laying about him with his fists rather than a baton—the Windwolves had nonchalantly swept down with their wind coaches as if this was simply another day in Alera Imperia.

Fidelias directed Aldrick ex Gladius to the hive and left him to get the First Lady and company out of this disaster before the vord swallowed them whole. He had just returned to the improvised command post on the roof of the great stone barn, when someone screamed, "Vord!"

They came rushing along the ground and buzzing through the sky, all of them moving with an unsettling, sinuous sort of rhythm.

Fidelias immediately appropriated every single Knight Aeris from the Free Aleran—all three of them—with instructions to, "Keep those bloody bug men off my roof." The Legions, without the defenses to which they were accustomed when fighting against such odds, locked shields in tight formation and waited to receive the mantises' charge. The vord flung themselves forward, filling the air with their whistling shrieks.

Men started dying.

The vord all but climbed over one another in a desperate need to attack the Aleran forces and showed none of the hesitance they generally did before attacking a shieldwall. They simply rushed forward, one vord paying the price to break the cohesion of the lines while two others took advantage of the disruption to strike. The First Aleran was giving at least as well as it got, Fidelias thought, but that was a ruinous rate of exchange in the current market.

Footsteps made him look over his shoulder, and he found the First Lady approaching with an escort of hard-bitten types wearing mail and the black sashes of the Windwolves. Aldrick ex Gladius, a large, brawny man with cold eyes and a black beard, walked on Isana's left, opposite the gleaming figure of Araris Valerian. Aldrick's madwoman, Odiana, trailed along behind him with one finger hooked into the back of his belt. She was beaming at the battle all around them.

"My lady," Fidelias said, scowling, "you need to leave the area at once. I insist that you take to your wind coaches now."

"We cannot," Isana replied steadily. "There are too many enemy fliers over-head. They'd swarm the coach before it could pick up speed if we tried to leave."

Fidelias glanced up at the sky above. It was filled with vordknights, more of them than he could easily count. For the most part, they seemed willing to hover overhead, though a few score were harassing the infantry, streaking down to rake at them with their scythe-limbs when they thought they had an advantage. At least two dozen kept trying to sweep down onto the rooftop, but the Free Aleran Knights Aeris were handily swatting them off target with blasts of wind, working with excellent coordination.

He considered the idea of passing them over to the First Lady to cover her escape but dismissed it. The Windwolves already had more than enough Knights Aeris to manage that trick. Men blasting away with wind from solid ground was one thing. Hurling extraneous windstreams around while Knights Aeris were trying to keep a wind coach aloft was something else entirely.

"How can I help?" Isana asked.

Fidelias grimaced and looked from her to her two immediate escorts. Aldrick ex Gladius looked completely unconcerned. The big swordsman was one of the most unreadable individuals he'd ever met, and it was entirely possible that the man wasn't sane. He might actually *not* feel any genuine anxiety about to-day's outcome. Araris, though, was scowling and eyeing Fidelias as though he expected him to Do Something About That Woman.

On the ground below, the vord broke open an enormous hole in the shield-wall, and only the efforts of the First Aleran's Knights Terra managed to close it again. Crows, but he didn't need another problem to solve. "You can get out alive, and take my wounded Citizens with you. They might be needed."

"I told you . . . Marcus, isn't it? There are simply too many vord in the air."

"Take Antillus Crassus," Fidelias said. "He can probably veil the whole lot of you, if you flew in close enough formation. He can't walk, but he can sit in a coach. Antillar Maximus and Ambassador Kitai are down there, too, unconscious."

"First Spear," Isana said. "You need such talents *here*. Or better yet, helping my son."

"They *were* helping your son," Fidelias growled. "That's how all of them wound up in healing tubs in the first place."

A trio of vordknights came zipping in from one side, with the risen sun be-hind them, and the Knights Aeris on the roof didn't redirect their windstreams in time. Fidelias moved on pure instinct, grabbing the First Lady and taking her down to the stone of the roof with as much speed and as little harm as possible. He stayed there, shielding her body, as the swords of Araris, Aldrick, and half a dozen Windwolves leapt clear of their scabbards.

Bits and pieces of vordknight, divided in perfectly neat lines, scattered to the roof around them.

Fidelias lowered his voice for Isana's ears alone, and said, "My lady. We can-not hold the position. We do not have much time. Do you understand?"

Isana's eyes were a little wide, but her expression was controlled. She took in a deep breath as Fidelias rose and Araris helped her up.

"Captain Aldrick," she said.

Aldrick gave a slight bow of his head, "My lady?"

"This Legion is short of their company of Knights. I wish you to deploy your men to support them."

Aldrick said nothing for a moment. His eyes shifted, left and right, toward the waiting wind coaches and the vord outside the steadholt, respectively.

The fingers of his right hand, his sword hand, flexed slowly, as though being loosened up for action. Fidelias had a flash of insight. Though Aldrick might be a mercenary, he wasn't inhuman. None of them were. And no Aleran could look at the vord destroying their world without realizing that there was no way to remain safely out of this fight. You could only decide whether to make a stand beside your fellow Alerans—or delay the moment of reckoning until you faced the vord alone.

"Say yes," Odiana said, her lovely eyes eerily bright. "Oh, say yes, my lord. I've been waiting ever so long to see you kill vord."

The mercenary glanced over his shoulder at Odiana, then turned to Isana with a second bow of his head. "Aye, my lady," Aldrick growled.

Wolfish smiles spread through the men behind him, along with growled words of agreement.

Aldrick stepped forward to overlook the battle below, and Araris went with him.

Aldrick grunted. "Earthworks?"

Araris nodded. "Little elevation will make a big difference."

"Odiana," Aldrick said.

She was still hanging on to his belt. "Who?"

"Antillar and his brother. We need them."

The woman turned and hurried from the roof.

"Where is she going?" Fidelias asked.

"Wake up your sleepers," Aldrick replied.

Fidelias shook his head. "You can't watercraft someone back to consciousness."

"She can."

Isana stepped forward. "It is possible. But it's somewhat insane."

Aldrick almost smiled. "Sanity. Huh."

Isana frowned after Odiana. "It's dangerous. For patient and healer alike."

Aldrick shrugged. "Dangerous for the vord to run those scythes through you a few times while you're lying there unconscious, too."

Isana's mouth compressed, and she nodded once. "I'll go with her."

Fidelias touched her arm as she began to turn. "Lady," he said quietly, "you need not do this."

She blinked at him as if surprised. "Of course I must. Excuse me, First Spear."

She left the rooftop to follow Odiana, and Fidelias turned to Aldrick. "The Antillan brothers could get us a ditch around this place—it's mostly soil here. I assume that's what you had in mind?"

Aldrick nodded. "Get your best seven or eight engineers, too. We'll give them each a Knight Ferrous escort to cover them."

Araris nodded. "It would be best if there was some way your Knights could drive them back for a moment," he added. "Buy the earthcrafters a few seconds in the clear."

Fidelias nodded slowly. Then he turned to the courier stationed on the roof near him, and said, "Ask Master Marok if he would please come speak to me."

In the five minutes it took to line up the desperate plan, the First Aleran suffered more losses than it had during the entire campaign in the Vale and Canea combined. Men screamed and were dragged back to badly overworked healers. Men fell and were dragged out into the horde. Swords shattered. Shields were rent asunder. Vord died by the hundreds but never relented.

On the flanks, the Free Aleran fared little better, for all that they were in what amounted to a backwater, in terms of enemy presence. Perhaps a double tithe of the vord in the battle wrapped around to the sides of the beleaguered Legions, but the Free Alerans' inexperience meant that they were hard-pressed. The only thing that kept some of the cohorts from bolting was the certain knowledge that there was no escape. Only victory—or death.

And victory was nowhere in evidence.

Marok stood with Fidelias calmly, looking out over the battle. Then he said, "You never asked me to lower the mists. I expected you to do so."

"Nothing to be gained by it," Fidelias said. "Except to show us exactly how many of the bloody vord are out there. The men fight better when it isn't hopeless."

Marok nodded. "As do our own warriors. But if I lowered the mists, the Canim units would see our plight."

"The mission wasn't for them to come rescue us. It was to kill sleeping vord. All of them. As long as we have the vord coming for us here, there are that many fewer in the field to oppose the others. They can kill twenty helpless vord in the time it takes to down one of the things while awake. It's worth it."

"Even if it means the death of everyone here?"

"That's right." Fidelias glanced aside as the courier waved a hand at him. The man gave him a thumbs-up. "They're ready."

Marok nodded slowly, and said, "The more vord attack your people, the fewer attack my own. Let us keep their attention."

Then he lifted his dagger and cut deeply into his left forearm. Blood began to patter to the stone roof. The Cane growled, then began chanting something full of snarls and coughing growls. A moment later, Fidelias saw the mist about five feet in front of the first rank of *legionares* begin to thicken. As he watched, it darkened, becoming opaque, and a moment later the shrieks of dying vord began to echo across the Legions. A hideous stench filled the air.

Teams rushed out in pairs, each with one of the Legion's best earthcrafters. Antillar Maximus looked hungover, but he wore his armor and moved under his own power. Beside him, the silver-skinned Araris Valerian kept pace, his eyes alert. Aldrick ex Gladius came after them, escorting a burly medico who had strapped Antillus Crassus to his back. Other Windwolves paced beside the engineers of the First Aleran, as they all hurried to spread themselves out equally within the defensive ring.

Marok kept on snarling and muttering to himself. The old Cane's eyes were closed. His blood ran steadily.

Even before the earthcrafters all reached their positions, those who had gotten there began their work. The earth swelled and heaved like an ocean before the wind. Then it began to fold upon itself. Fidelias was reminded of the way a sheet would ripple and fold when one snapped it to get it spread out over a mattress.

Within moments, the crafting was complete. The earth rose slightly in a short ramp before the Legion lines, rising perhaps eighteen inches—but the far side of the ramp sloped down sharply, to a ditch seven or eight feet deep and twice as wide. Centurions began to shout orders to their units, and the Legions advanced to the lip of the ditch, dressing their ranks and changing out weaponry, to ply their spears against the vord as they tried to climb out. It was not by any means an ideal defensive structure—but it was also far, far better than nothing.

"They've got it," Fidelias said.

Marok let out a slow exhale and allowed his snarling chant to trail off. The bloodspeaker slumped down to the stone of the roof and dropped heavily onto his side. His left arm was still extended, blood running from it. Fidelias turned to him with an alarmed intake of breath.

"Do not concern yourself for me, demon," Marok said. "Bandages. My pouch."

Fidelias found the bandages and began wrapping Marok's arm to stanch the flow of blood.

"I thought you said clouds of acid were for amateurs," Fidelias remarked.

"That was not a cloud. It was a wall." He closed his eyes, and muttered, "Whining demon. You are welcome."

Fidelias was about to order Marok taken to the healers when Ambassador Kitai stormed out onto the roof, looking around wildly. She spotted Fidelias and stalked toward him. "Where is he?"

"Not here," Fidelias replied. "He dropped you off and left. The Queen went after him."

Kitai ground her teeth, and said, "I might have *known* he would do something like this."

Fidelias arched an eyebrow. "The healers said you had a bump the size of an apple on the back of your head."

Kitai waved her hand impatiently. "I must go to him."

Fidelias leaned toward her. "He's alive?"

Kitai glanced aside, her eyes focused on nothing. "Yes. For now. And . . . pleased with his own cleverness, may The One help us." She blinked and looked back at Fidelias. "Quick. What is the absolute worst place in this Valley one could go? The most insanely suicidal place to be found? The place where only a great fool would venture—and only an *insane* fool would follow?"

Fidelias responded at once and found himself speaking in chorus with the Ambassador as they both said, "Garados."

"He is there," Kitai said. And without another word she turned, leapt into the air, and vanished behind a veil as she raised a windscreen and shot off into the open sky. Half a dozen vordknights dropped into her flight path, hoping to intercept her even though they couldn't see her.

Their wings burst into flame, and they went plunging to their deaths on the ground below.

Fidelias exhaled slowly. Then he turned back to the business of battle, redeploying their new assets, though he knew that their position could not long be held against such numbers, not for more than a few hours.

But he had a feeling he had done all that he could.

His eyes drifted in the direction of Garados. Somewhere on the cold, hard slopes of that mountain, a young man was pitting all the strength and cunning and brilliance of a thousand-year dynasty against the intelligence and remorseless power at the heart of the world-eating vord.

And, like everyone else, all Fidelias could do was wait to see what happened.

CHAPTER 56

From a distance the mountain was undeniably beautiful: tall and imposing, crowned with snow and ice. But the closer one got to it, the more a sense of malevolent, hostile presence seemed to grow. Tavi had encountered the mountain's ire once before—and what he had felt that day had been nowhere near this oppressively bleak. Garados wasn't simply surly and resentful this time.

The vast fury was absolutely enraged.

The thunderclouds gathering around its peak were growing darker by the moment, as though they had drawn the night into themselves as it waned. Thana Lilvia, the vast wind fury that came sweeping down off the Sea of Ice and over the Calderon Valley, was making a show of force today, gathering her herds as usual near her husband. Flashes of lightning in wildly varying colors lashed constantly through the clouds, and even from miles away, Tavi could see the gliding, looping, sinister forms of windmanes, windmanes by the *score*, prowling the mountain's slopes.

A low thread of fear ran down Tavi's throat, and he swallowed it as manfully as he could. He had seen windmanes kill, and it had been terrifying. But for a stroke of good luck, they would have torn him to shreds as they had that luckless deer.

He ground his teeth. He didn't need to be rehashing his life's closest calls. He needed to be focused on the enemy behind him, a being more dangerous than a cohort of windmanes. He checked over his shoulder. The vord Queen had closed his lead to a scant two hundred yards or so.

Tavi plunged into the thunderclouds gathered at Garados's summit and let out a quick bark of mocking laughter.

A pulse of anger strong enough to destroy worlds flashed through the mist, and Tavi winced at the intensity of it. That wrath belonged to the vord Queen, and was being directed entirely at him. He banked left and reduced his speed, aware that the mountain was near but not sure of its precise location.

He almost found it with the end of his nose. The grey mist occluded the frosty grey stone of the mountaintop near perfectly, and Tavi had to shift course frantically to keep from smashing against it. He avoided disaster, steadied himself, and settled down to light gently upon a slope near the mountain's peak, crouching. The vord Queen's windstream roared on by. She had apparently lost track of him in the mist.

Tavi waited for a moment, but nothing happened. He stomped on the rocky ground beneath him a few times. Then he jumped up and down, feeling exceptionally foolish.

If that didn't provoke the enormous fury, he wasn't sure what would.

Without warning, the vord Queen's voice called through the mist, disassociated from any particular direction. "Where are you, Father?"

Tavi blurred the obvious direction of his own voice with a windcrafting over his mouth. "Why do you keep calling me that?"

"Because your blood gave me birth. Yours and that of my mother."

"So that was you," Tavi said. "You were the thing Doroga dropped that big rock on."

The Queen's voice buzzed with steely undertones. "Yes."

"Grampa Doroga," Tavi mused. "I am not your father. It means more than blood."

"You are close," the Queen said, her words clipped and sharp. "For all practical purposes, it is a fact."

The stone beneath Tavi's feet quivered. He focused some of his attention downward. Though Garados was deadly dangerous, it was not swift. He should be able to leap clear if he was paying attention.

"Not quite," Tavi said. "If I were your father, you'd be the heir to the Realm."

"I am already the heir of this Realm, and after that, this world," came her answer, from the mist. "All that is left is for you"—her voice suddenly changed, coming from immediately behind him—"is to die."

He spun and barely got his sword up in time. Steel rang on steel, and again sparks bellowed forth in a thundercloud of their own, illuminating the mist around them with flashes of red, blue, and green light.

Her speed was incredible. Even without furycrafting, the vord Queen moved with blinding swiftness. Tavi had drawn upon all the windcraft he could to expand his perceptions, and it was barely enough to allow him to defend himself. Similarly, her strength was unbelievable, easily greater than a large Cane's, and Tavi found himself forced to draw strength from the earth simply in order to meet her attacks with enough power to stop them.

In retrospect, he thought, it probably wasn't one of his most insightful tactical decisions.

Within seconds of Tavi's drawing upon the earth for strength, the mountain was wrenched with a spectacular thundercrack of sound, so loud that it

knocked both Tavi and the vord from their feet. In front of Tavi's widening
eyes, the peak of the mountain abruptly *split*, a sudden crack running from the
summit down to Tavi and beyond him. Within a heartbeat, the crack had widened, with rock and stone grinding and screaming. Tavi rolled rapidly to one
side, an instant before that crack—well on its way to becoming a crevasse—
swallowed him whole.

The mountain groaned with an enormous basso voice, and rocks began to
fall around them. Most of the falling material consisted of pebbles, but among
many of those were other stones, more than large enough to kill a man if they
fell on him. Tavi regained his feet and dodged a falling rock. From the corner of
his eye, he saw the vord Queen simply bat a stone the size of an ale keg away
with her free hand.

A red glow suddenly suffused the walls of the crevasse, the light welling up
from within, and Tavi sucked in a sharp breath of surprise. He had not realized
that Garados was a fire-mountain.

A medium-sized stone clipped his ribs, and though the armor absorbed the
blow, he staggered and barely got out of the way of the next bounding stone. On
the other side of the crevasse, the vord Queen turned toward him and crouched
to leap, her sword held up and ready to strike—when a fountain of liquid fire
shot forth from the crevasse, sending molten stone high into the air.

Tavi turned from that at once, bounded into the air downslope as strongly
as he could, called up a windstream . . .

. . . and realized, an instant too late, that he was covered in a layer of dirt
and dust.

The wind furies he managed to summon were far from strong enough to lift
him into the air, and after an extra second or so of hanging at the apogee of his
jump, he was on his way back to the ground—to the steeply inclined, stony
ground of Garados. His heart leapt into his throat. If he should lose his balance,
there was virtually nothing to stop him from bouncing all the way to the base of
the mountain, while falling boulders and rocky outcroppings conspired with
gravity to grind him to paste.

He planted his right boot on a stable bit of rock and pushed himself up into
another leap, frantically calling the wind—not to bear him aloft this time but
merely to nudge him a foot or so to one side, so that his left boot could land on
the next piece of stable shelf he spotted. There was no time to think, only to
react, and so Tavi found himself running at full speed down the precipitous
slopes of the mountain, bounding like a mountain goat and accelerating with a
rather alarming ease. It wasn't until a few seconds later that he realized that he
was actually beginning to outrun some of the falling stones, and he rather felt

that the entire situation was shaping up to be quite exciting all the way up to an abrupt, ugly sort of end.

Behind him, there was a sound. A sound so deep and enormous that he did not hear it so much as feel it shaking his teeth. It rose and rose until it topped out in a gargantuan, basso brass horn sound, and Tavi risked a glance over his shoulder to see what had made the noise.

It was Garados.

The mountain's entire top had lifted, rocks melting and collapsing and re-arranging into the features of an enormous and ugly humanlike face. Burning red pits substituted for eyes, and its mouth was a great, gaping maw without visible lips or teeth. The entire mountain shook, and Garados twisted left and right, its vast, broad shoulders tearing free of the mountainside. Tavi's brain seemed to stutter and trip as he saw the great fury in motion. He simply could not believe he was looking at something so unthinkably large.

He barely turned back around in time to make his next step. A falling stone the size of his fist hammered his calf, and he cried out in pain—and kept bound-ing, guiding his leaps with his weakened windcrafting.

Garados lifted one leg clear of the mountain, and Tavi had to scramble to leap off what looked like a kneecap the size of a steadholt. A few steps later, a broad foot rose out of the mountain and came sweeping down toward Tavi as if he had been an annoyance, an insect to be smashed and never considered again.

Tavi bounded frantically down the slope, trying to get out from under the enormous foot, and suddenly felt that he had an entirely new appreciation of the word *hubris*. He heard someone laughing hysterically as a vast shadow fell over him, and recognized that the voice was his own and that he had an impos-sible half mile of ground to cover, at least, to be clear of the enormous fury's descending power.

He realized with a cool and practical certainty that he simply wasn't moving fast enough. There was no way he was going to get clear in time.

Ehren stood up slowly from his seat beside Count Calderon on the citadel's bench at Garrison. He watched as a mountain—as *the* mountain—rose from its resting place in the form of man, twice as tall as the mountain itself had been, unthinkably huge. Sheer distance clouded its features into haze, though Ehren could see that it was built heavily, disproportionately, a being of ugliness and spite and horrible power.

"Bloody crows," Ehren breathed, as he watched that far-distant form move, raising a foot as a man might to crush an insect. "What is that?"

Bernard stared at it and shook his head slowly. "Great furies, boy," he muttered. "Are you mad?"

The ground shook hard enough to slop water out of the improvised healing tubs that had been crafted from the stone floors in the old hall of the ruined steadholt. Amara steadied herself against a wall and hoped that the earthquake wouldn't bring the hall down on their heads. After a moment, the tremors subsided, but did not quite stop, and startled, incredulous cries were added to the din of cries of pain and agony.

Amara glanced over to where Isana and Odiana and the healers of Octavian's Legions labored on the wounded, too far gone into their own battles and crafting to take any note of their surroundings. Then she staggered to the door and met Lady Placida there. Placidus Sandos had been found beneath a mound of dismembered vord nearly eight feet deep, badly wounded but alive. Even now, he lay on the ground nearby, and this was the first time Aria had left his side.

She and Amara both stared out, at the incredible form rising from the mountain to the northwest, its brow crowned with thunder and lightning, its shoulders cloaked in storm clouds and rain, its vast and terrible shape blotting out miles of blue sky. Something like a mouth gaped open, and its roar shook the ground again. The two women had to grab at the frames of the doorway to stay standing.

"Great furies," Amara whispered.

"Aye," Lady Placida breathed, her eyes wide, her face pale. "*Two* of them."

Tavi managed his next bounding leap, useless as he knew it would be, frantically calling the wind for all that he was worth—and was suddenly hit in the back by something moving at incredible speed. Pale arms twined beneath his shoulders, preventing him from falling, and Kitai shouted, "Hold on!"

They accelerated as the mountain's foot fell toward them, blotting out the sky, darkening the morning to twilight. Kitai's windstream drove them faster and faster toward the rapidly dwindling strip of trees and sunlight at the mountain's base—and as they grew near, that passage to survival suddenly filled with a small legion of windmanes, their inhuman faces stretched into eerie howls, their claws reaching.

"That's *cheating!*" Kitai declared hotly—even as their forward pace increased in proportion to her outrage.

"Mind your eyes!" Tavi shouted back.

He lifted his right hand, noting with a touch of surprise that he still held his sword. An effort of will let the weapon burst into flame. He lifted the weapon awkwardly, still being held under the arms by Kitai, then shaped the familiar blade-shaped firecrafting into an elongated, white-hot lance, reaching out in front of them. The terrible speed of their passage didn't simply blunt the end of the lance; it spread the fire out into a concave disc a dozen feet across. The heat from the fire flooded back to them, distinctly uncomfortable, a hot wind that scorched exposed skin—and sent its own wind flowing out and upward from it.

As the fire-lance met the first of the windmanes, it bowled the feral furies aside—doing them no harm, but sending them wailing and spinning from Tavi and Kitai's path. Trees at the base of the mountain began to crack and shatter as that vast weight came down, and the darkness grew until only the lance of fire lit their way. Hundreds of terrified birds flew with them, darting shapes in the sole light of the fire-lance.

They shot into the open sky as the mountain smashed down onto the ground below, trees snapping and popping as they were crushed to splinters, stone grinding upon stone. A vast cloud of dust billowed out after them, and Kitai accelerated and climbed to avoid being engulfed by it and having her own windstream suffocated.

Tavi released the fire from his sword and looked down at himself. The high-speed passage upon Kitai's windstream had scoured much of the dust from him, and a second's experimentation brought up more than enough wind to sustain his own flight. He tapped Kitai's fingers, and she released him to fly on his own. He steadied himself, then pulled up beside her, flying with his body almost touching hers, their windstreams merging smoothly.

"Did you kill her yet?" Kitai called, her voice high and tight with excitement and fear.

"Not quite," Tavi said. He jerked a thumb back at the monstrous form behind them. "I was doing that."

She gave him a look that managed to blend respect, disgust, and a touch of jealousy. "This is how you show me you want me to be your mate?"

"It's a big decision," he returned blandly. "You can't expect me to make it in an hour."

Kitai stuck her tongue out at him, and added, "Watch out."

They both rolled away to the left as Garados's vast hand swept down at them, as if to knock them from the air. They evaded it by yards, but the wind of its passage was almost more dangerous to them. They were spun violently about and in different directions. Tavi actually watched as a windmane was spawned from the swirling vortexes the blow created.

"Where *is* she?" Kitai called to him.

"Last time I saw her was up near the . . . chest, I think."

She nodded, and without speaking the pair altered their flight paths to begin soaring up the enormous, slow-moving mountain fury. More windmanes came at them, these seeming to be random attacks rather than results of some deliberate malevolence—but there were so many of them around the vast earth fury that it hardly mattered. Each windmane had to be countered with windcrafting, driven away, and Tavi found himself thinking that it had really been a great deal less strenuous for him to deal with windmanes when he hadn't had any furies and had relied upon a pouch of rock salt to discourage them.

Of course, using salt while maintaining his own windstream was problematic in any case—and he didn't think he'd care to find a spot to land on Garados and craft some salt out of the ground. So he gritted his teeth and concentrated on swatting windmanes out of his path, discouraging the sinister furies from coming too close.

Vast sound shook the air around them twice—Garados, roaring in frustration or simple anger or some other emotion completely alien to such ephemeral beings as Tavi and Kitai. Perhaps he could ask Alera about it later. If there was time. The great fury's arm swept by, this time much farther away. Pine trees stood up on the forearm like a mortal man's hairs, and on the same approximate scale. Rain began to fall, heavy and cold.

They soared up past a distorted belly and over the great fury's chest without seeing the vord Queen—but as they reached the level of Garados's shoulders, they entered heavy storm clouds. Thick grey haze settled over them, and lightning flickered through the darkness. The wind surged and howled, then died away to a whisper at random—but as they kept going, Tavi was sure he could hear an actual voice in those whispers—a voice that promised torment, pain, and death.

There was another vast sound—and abruptly, the great fury stood completely still. The change was startling. Rock stopped grinding against rock. Tons and tons of earth and stone ceased their rumbling, and only the sound of a few falling stones, bouncing their way down to earth, remained behind. Almost simultaneously, the howling wind within the storm clouds died. The air went still, until they and the raindrops were the only things moving. The flickering lightning began to come less frequently, and the colors changed from every wild hue imaginable to one color: green.

Vord green.

"Aleran?" Kitai called, her eyes flicking around them.

"Bloody crows," Tavi whispered. He turned to Kitai, and said, "She's trying to claim them. The vord Queen is trying to claim Garados and Thana."

"Is it possible?"

"For you or me?" Tavi shook his head. "But Alera told me that her power has a broader base than ours does. Maybe. And if she does . . ."

Kitai's face turned grim. "If the Queen claims two great furies, it won't matter who remains to stand against her." She eyed Tavi. "And you led her to them."

He scowled at her, and said, "Yes."

They both increased their speed.

"And you woke her up in the first place."

Tavi clenched his teeth. "Yes."

"I simply wished to be sure I correctly understood the way things are."

Tavi suppressed a sigh, ignored his growing fatigue, and pushed ahead harder, until the roar of their windstreams precluded conversation.

They found the vord Queen atop the frost-coated crown of Garados's head. She simply stood there, half-burned and naked, her head bowed and her hands spread slightly apart. Above her was what looked like a motionless vortex, where terrible winds had borne up crystals of ice and snow into a glittering spiral.

The vord Queen opened her eyes as they came into view of her. Her lips curved up into a smile that no longer looked like a mimicked expression. It contained as much bitterness, hate, and malevolent amusement as Tavi had ever seen on anyone.

"Father," the Queen said. "Mother."

Kitai's spine stiffened slightly, but she didn't speak. Moving in time with Tavi, she touched down on the rocky ground facing the Queen. The three of them made the points of an equilateral triangle.

Eerie silence reigned for several seconds. Heavy, cold drops of rain fell upon stone. Their breaths all turned to steamy mist as they exhaled.

"You're here to kill me," the vord Queen said, still smiling. "But you can't. You've tried. And in a moment, it won't matter what kind of forces you might be able to—"

"She's stalling for time," Tavi said, and reached for his windcrafting to speed his movements. His own voice sounded oddly stretched and slowed as he continued to speak.

"Hit her," he said, and slung out the hottest firecrafting he could call.

The Queen began to dart to the left—but the Marat woman hadn't needed Tavi's direction to begin the attack with him. The Queen slammed into the sheet of solid rock Kitai had called up in a half circle around her. The vord smashed through, but not before Tavi's firecrafting had scored on her, driving a shriek of pain from her lungs.

The ground trembled and lurched as she screamed.

Tavi darted forward, sword in hand. The Queen flung a sheet of fire at him, but again he trapped the blaze within the steel of his blade, heating it to scarlet-and-sapphire flame. Somewhere behind him, Kitai wrought the stone beneath the Queen into something the consistency of thick mud. One foot sank ankle-deep into it, pinning her in place. Her blade swept out as Tavi closed, and their swords screamed as they crossed, a dozen times in the space of a heartbeat, a blizzard of sparks filling the air—so thickly that Tavi didn't see the Queen's foot lashing toward him until it was too late.

The kick hit him in the middle of his chest and threw him twenty feet, to fetch up against an outcropping of rock. His head slammed against it, and he bounced off to fall to the ground, his arms and legs suddenly made of pudding. He couldn't breathe. There was a deep dent in the frontal plates of his lorica.

Kitai closed on the vord Queen in a blur of shining mail and damp white hair, wielding a *gladius* in each hand. She waded into the fight with an elemental brutality and primal instinct that was nothing like the formal training Tavi had received, but which seemed no less dangerous. Violet and emerald sparks warred with one another as the Marat woman met the vord Queen's steel.

"This is pointless," said the Queen calmly, her alien eyes bright as she parried and cut, repelling Kitai's attacks. "It was too late when you arrived. Kill me now, and Garados and Thana both will be entirely unleashed upon the land. Do you think what Gaius Sextus did at Alera Imperia was destruction? And he had but one great fury to unleash. I have two, and more ancient, less tamed ones at that. Garados and Thana will kill every living thing on half a continent. Phrygia, Aquitaine, and Rhodes will be laid waste—as will Garrison, and the gathering of refugees there, and the barbarian tribes who have raised their hands against me."

Kitai bared her teeth, stepping away for a moment. "Better that than to let you live, let you claim them as your own."

"That presumes you have a choice, Mother."

"I am not your mother," Kitai said in a precise, cold voice. "I am nothing to you. You are less than nothing to me. You are a weed to be plucked from the earth and discarded. You are vermin to be wiped out. You are a rabid dog, to be pitied and destroyed. Show wisdom. Bare your throat. It will be swift and without pain."

The vord Queen closed her eyes for a second and flinched from the words as she hadn't from any of the blows. But when she opened them again, her voice was calm, eerily serene. "Odd. I was about to say the same thing to you." She twisted her hips and casually ripped her foot from the earth, the rock screaming protest. "Enough," she said quietly. "I should have dispatched you both at once."

There was a blur in the air, and the two came together in a fountain of sparks amidst the chiming of steel.

Tavi ground his teeth. The feeling was starting to come back to his arms and legs, but it was apparently a slow, slow process. His head hurt abominably.

This wasn't the answer. The Queen was simply too strong, too fast, too intelligent to be overcome directly. They'd had a small enough chance of killing her. Taking her alive, in order to prevent the great furies from being unleashed, was an order of magnitude closer to "impossible" than Tavi cared to attempt.

But how to beat her? With that added advantage, there was simply no way.

So, he thought, *take that advantage away.*

The Queen had begun to create a bond between herself and the great furies of Calderon, a task that Tavi felt was surely well beyond his own abilities. But in furycraft, like in everything else, it was far more difficult to create than it was to destroy.

"Alera," he whispered. He had no idea if the great fury could hear him, or if she would appear if she did. But he pictured her intensely in his thoughts, and whispered again, "Alera."

And then the great fury was simply there, appearing silently and without drama, the hazy shape of a woman in grey, blending into the cloud and mist, her face lovely but aging, weary. She looked around at the situation, her eyes pausing upon the motionless vortex longer than upon the spark-flooded battle raging between Kitai and the Queen.

"Hmmm," she said calmly. "This is hardly going well for you."

Tavi fought to keep his voice calm and polite. "Has the Queen truly bound the great furies to herself?"

"To a degree," Alera replied. "They are both held motionless, fury-bound, and are . . . somewhat upset about it."

"She can control them?"

"Not yet," Alera said. "But the house of her mind has many rooms. She is accomplishing the binding even as she does battle. It is only a matter of time." She shook her head. "Poor Garados. He's quite mad, you know. Thana does all that she can for him, trying to keep your folk away, but she's scarcely less psychotic than he is, the past few centuries."

"I need to break her link to Garados and Thana Lilvia," Tavi said. "Is it possible?"

Alera lifted her eyebrows. "Yes. But they are not mortal, young Gaius. They will take vengeance for being bound, and they will not show you the least gratitude."

"Binding can be done even by someone like me," Tavi said. "I mean, I could make Garados sit still if I had to. That's what happened at Kalare and Alera Imperia—and with you, to a degree. Someone like me bound them not to act."

"Correct," Alera said.

"Then show me how to break the bond."

Alera inclined her head and reached out her hand. Like the rest of her, It, too, was covered in opaque grey mist that one could mistake for cloth if one didn't look too closely. She touched his forehead. Her fingertip was damp and cool.

The means simply appeared in Tavi's mind, as smoothly as if it had been something remembered from his days at the Academy. And, like much of fury-craft, it was quite simple to implement. Painful, he suspected, but simple.

Tavi touched the stone with one hand and stretched the other up to the motionless sky. The principal furycraft used in the binding was watercrafting. It formed the foundation of the effort, while the appropriate craft related to the fury was added atop it: earth for earth, air for air, and so on. But water was the foundation. He had to cancel the watercrafting with its opposite.

Tavi bowed his head, focused his will, and sent fire, fire spread so fine that it never came to life as flame, coursing down deep into the rock of Garados and up in a broad, slewing cone into Thana Lilvia's misty presence. There was a flash of pain as the two forces collided, a kind of cognitive acid that felt like it was chewing clean the inner surface of his skull.

The Queen's head snapped toward him as she backpedaled lightly from Kitai.

The reaction from Garados and Thana was immediate.

The ground shook and swayed, and the Queen and Kitai both staggered several steps in the same direction, their bodies slamming against a rock shelf as the mountain tipped back its head and let out a bone-shuddering roar. An instant later, the darkness grew until it was nearly as black as night, and a storm blew up that made the worst weather Tavi had ever seen feel like a gentle shower. The wind screamed through the rocks, howling in mindless rage. Sleet fell from the sky in half-frozen, stinging sheets. Lightning writhed everywhere, a dozen bolts coming down around them in the space of a few seconds.

Worst of all, Tavi's watercrafting senses were abruptly overloaded with a single mindless, boundless, endless emotion—rage. It was an anger more vast than the sea, and it made the very air in his lungs heavy, hard to move in and out. And, he thought, it wasn't even being directed at him. There was a bladed point to that spear of anger, and he had only been grazed by it.

"Are you mad?" cried the vord Queen, staggering before the onslaught of the great furies' wrath. "What have you done? They will destroy us all!"

"Then we will have chosen our deaths!" Tavi screamed back, struggling through the horrible pain and confusion in his thoughts, through the unbearable rage of the great furies. "Not you!"

The Queen let out a shriek of frustration and terror and flung herself into the air. For a second, the wind of the storm seemed to rise to oppose her, only to relent. She hurtled forward, and in a flash of lightning, Tavi saw her pass into what looked like a great, fanged maw made of clouds of rain and sleet. The jaws of Thana Lilvia closed with a roar of wind, and Tavi saw the Queen spinning, spinning out of control, whirling down miles and miles of cloudy gullet lined with rings and rings of windmanes, their claws flashing and slashing.

Kitai struggled to reach him in the rocking fury of the storm and the mountain's anger, finally throwing herself down next to him as a bolt of lightning hit a rocky ridge not twenty feet away. He gathered her in close, and said, "I'm going after her."

Her head snapped up, and her green eyes were wide. "What?"

"We must be sure," he said. "Alera is here. There must be a way to soothe the great furies, or at least to direct them somewhere else. Talk with her."

"*Chala*," Kitai cried. "You will be killed in this!"

He caught her hand in his, squeezing tight. "If she is not finished, there will never be a better time. And too much is at stake. It must be done. And I am the First Lord." He drew her hand to his chest and kissed her mouth, swift and heatedly. Then he rested his forehead against hers, and said, "I love you."

"Idiot," she sobbed, her hands trembling as they framed his face. "Of course you do. And I love you."

There was nothing else he needed to say. Nothing else he needed to hear.

Gaius Octavian rose and flung himself up and into the teeth of the storm.

Later, he would never remember that final flight as more than bits of frozen imagery, painted onto his eyes by flashes of lightning. The vord Queen as a tiny and distant dot, spinning in the fury of the storm. Windmanes, their eyes burning with unspent lightning, slashing at his armor, their claws like thunderbolts. Pain as the wind and water of the storm cut at him like knives. The great and terrible face of the fury, its anger lashing out at the Queen, hardly brushing him—and all but killing him even so.

Tavi found himself grasping at watercrafting to close cuts and soothe burns, even as he continued to fly on. The air around him seemed more water than not, in any case, and it was easier than he had thought it would be. He wondered idly, as he flew onward, pursuing the distant form of the Queen, if he could somehow watercraft the portion of his brain that had advised this idiotic course of action. Clearly, it was defective.

And then a great blackness came rushing up at him—the ground. He slowed enough to land with a great shock of impact to his legs, as opposed to his spine, and rose, fighting the blinding wind and sleet. Though he knew it was full morning now, the storm had left it as black as night.

There was a hole gouged in the ground nearby, where the Queen had been flung to earth. She had climbed out of it, clearly. Windmanes in Legion strength scoured the land nearby. Lightning raked at the ground, each bolt lasting several seconds, carving great, long trenches into the soil. When the strike would fade, the land would be almost as dark as a moonless night.

And in that darkness, Tavi saw a flash of light.

He struggled toward it, noting signs of passage on the ground being swiftly obliterated by the rain. The markings, then, were fresh. Only the Queen could have made them. Tavi followed the trail, turning aside dozens of windmanes with windcraftings of his own, finally resorting to the use of a vortex that he set spinning about the blade of his sword, substituting windcrafting for the usual firecrafting that would ignite his blade. Once that was done, a single stroke was enough to send the deadly furies wailing away from him into the night, and he plodded forward, sinking ankle deep into the cold, muddy earth, struggling up a slight incline.

The warm light of furylamps spilled out onto the ground in front of him, abruptly, and Tavi sensed the presence of a structure, a great dome of marble the height of three men. Its open entryway glowed with a soft golden light, and above it, writ into the marble in gold, was the seven-pointed star of the First Lord of Alera.

His father's grave, the Princeps' Memorium.

Tavi staggered inside. Though outside the storm still raged behind him, within the Memorium, those sounds came only as something very distant and wholly irrelevant. The vast scream of the storm was broken here to near silence. Here in the dome there was only the slight ripple of water, the crackle of flame, and the sleepy chirp of a bird.

The interior of the dome was made not of marble, but of crystal, the walls of it rising high and smooth to the ceiling twenty feet above. Once, the scale and grandeur of the place had instilled in Tavi a sense of awe. Now, he saw it differently. He knew the scale and difficulty of furycraft it had taken to raise this place from the ground, and his awe was based not upon the beauty or richness of the structure but upon the elegance of the crafting that had created it.

Light came from the seven fires that burned without apparent fuel around the outside of the room, simulated flames that were far more difficult to create than the steady glow of any furylamp. That irregular, warm light rose through the crystal, bending, refracting, splitting into rainbows that swirled and danced with a slow grace and beauty within the crystal walls—crystal that would have long since cracked and fractured had it been wrought with anything less than perfection of furycraft.

The floor in the center of the dome was covered by a pool of water, perfectly still and as smooth as Amaranth glass. All around the pool grew rich foliage, bushes, grass, flowers, even small trees, still arranged as neatly as though kept by a gardener—though Tavi hadn't seen the place since he was fifteen. The woodcrafting needed to establish such a self-tending garden was astonishing. Gaius Sextus, it seemed, had known more about the growth of living things than Tavi did, despite the differences in their backgrounds.

Between each of the fires around the walls stood seven silent suits of armor, complete with scarlet capes, the traditional-style bronze shields, and the ivory-handled swords of Septimus's *singulares*. The armor stood mute and empty upon nearly formless figures of dark stone, eternally vigilant, the slits in their helmets focused upon their charge. Two of the suits were missing weapons—Tavi and Amara had taken them for protection on that night so long ago.

At the center of the pool rose a block of black basalt. Upon the block lay a pale shape, a statue of the purest white marble, and Tavi stared at the representation of his father. Septimus's eyes were closed, as though sleeping, and he lay with his hands folded upon his breast, the hilt of his sword beneath them. He wore a rich cloak that draped down over one shoulder, and beneath that was the worked breastplate of a somewhat ostentatious Legion officer rather than the standard-issue lorica Tavi had on.

Slouched at the base of his father's memorial bier was the vord Queen.

She was bleeding from more wounds than Tavi could count, and the water around her, instead of being crystalline, was stained the dark green of a living pond. She slumped in absolute exhaustion. One eye was missing, that side of her once-beautiful face slashed to ribbons by the windmanes' claws.

The other eye, still glittering black, focused upon Tavi. The vord Queen rose, her sword in her hand.

Tavi stopped at the edge of the pool and waited, settling his grip on his own blade.

The two faced one another and said nothing. The silence and stillness stretched. Outside, the storm's wrath was a distant thing, impotent. Light flickered through the crystalline walls.

"I was right," the Queen said, her voice heavy and rough. "There is a strength in the bonds between you."

"Yes," Tavi said simply.

"My daughter who lives in far Canea . . . she will never understand that."

"No."

"Is it not strange, that though I know her failure to see it is a weakness, though I know that she would kill me upon sight, that I want her to live? To prosper?"

"Not so strange," Tavi said.

The Queen closed her eye and nodded. She opened it again, and there was a tear tracking down her face. "I tried to be what I was meant to be, Father. It was never personal."

"We're beyond that now," Tavi said. "It ends here, and now. You know that."

She was still for a moment, before asking, very quietly, "Will you make me suffer?"

"No," he said, as gently as he could.

"I know how a vord queen dies," she whispered. She lifted her chin, a ghostly shadow of pride falling across her. "I am ready."

He inclined his head to her, very slightly.

Her rush sent out a spray of water, and she came at him with every ounce of speed and power left in her broken body. Even so badly battered, she was faster than any Aleran, stronger than a grass lion.

Gaius Octavian's blade met that of the vord Queen in a single, chiming tone. Her sword shattered amidst a rain of blue and scarlet sparks.

He made a single smooth, lightning-swift cut.

And the Vord War was over.

CHAPTER 57

The wind had picked up so sharply that the Knights Aeris Fidelias had borrowed began to run out of work. The conditions were simply too harsh for the vord-knights to stay aloft, especially when a mix of cold rain and sleet began sluicing down. The changing conditions had ripped the Canim's sorcerous mist apart even earlier than that, and Fidelias, from his vantage point on the barn's roof, had gotten an excellent view of the size of the force attacking them.

There weren't thirty thousand vord. There were more like fifty thousand.

No simple ditch could have given the Legions any real hope against a force that outnumbered them so badly. Oh, had they been fighting Marat, Icemen, even Canim, there might have been a straw of hope. Legion discipline in the face of overwhelming odds was less a professional practice than it was a form of contagious insanity, especially in a veteran unit like the First. They might be killed to a man, but they would never break. That fact alone was enough to grind the determination out of any rational foe.

But the vord weren't rational.

So the First Aleran would be killed to a man—and Fidelias with them, if it came to that. Perhaps that was the specter of Valiar Marcus inside his thoughts speaking, but if so, Fidelias had no intention of countermanding him. He wasn't leaving these men.

The rain came down harder, and harder still, until it was almost like one of the typhoons that sometimes visited the southern coast. Fidelias watched his men fighting grimly on against impossible odds and found himself weeping in silence, his face stony. It was raining. No one would see. But even so, force of habit made him reach for the modest watercrafting talents he possessed, which were at least suitable to stop tears.

His head whipped up abruptly, and he snapped, to the nearest courier, "Bring me the First Lady!"

Isana's cloak and dress were soaked through by the time she reached the barn's roof. Thank goodness. It was the closest thing she'd had to a bath in weeks.

The ground continued to quiver and shake at odd intervals. Vast sounds, deep and unearthly, reverberated through the night, passing over the screams and cries and drums and trumpets of battle, the roar of wind, the slap of heavy rain. They reminded Isana of the calls of leviathans in the open sea—only a great deal more expansive. She couldn't see a hundred yards in the rain, and she had a feeling that she should be glad of it.

She hurried across the roof with Araris and Aldrick trailing behind her, to where Valiar Marcus stood with his command staff. He saluted her as she approached, pointed at the ditch the *legionares* were defending, and said, without preamble, "My lady, I need you to fill that ditch with water."

Isana arched an eyebrow. "I see," she said, and stared thoughtfully at the ditch. Puddles were already collecting in its bottom, thanks to the rain. She closed her eyes, touched upon Rill in her thoughts, and sent the fury out into the land around the steadholt, where it appeared as a barely noticeable ripple in the downpour. It didn't seem favorable. The steadholt was located upon the local high ground, such as it was, so that any floodwaters would pour around it. Making that much water run uphill would be a terrible strain, possibly beyond her strength.

Instead, on an inspiration, she sent Rill up. The fury flowed into the air

above the steadholt, leaping from raindrop to raindrop, and then began to spread
out like a wide, unseen umbrella above the steadholt. Ah, much better. She
spread Rill's presence out as widely as she possibly could and murmured to her
to begin redirecting the rain as it fell.

For a long moment, nothing happened. Then, all at once, a waterfall appeared out of nowhere, the collected rain of several acres worth of ground all
funneled to the same spot. It splashed down into the trench, knocking several
mantises from their feet, and within seconds had begun to fill it.

Exhausted men lifted their voices in ragged cheers, and the surge of hope
that arose from all of them struck Isana like a cleansing fire. The *legionares*
began pushing harder, their spirits lifted, slamming the vord back into water that
grew deeper and deeper as Isana's crafting continued.

A good start. But she could do more. Once the improvised moat had been
filled, she sent Rill down into it and, with another effort of will and a faint circling motion of one hand, the water began to spin. It was not long before it had
become a current, circling the steadholt, strong enough to take a mantis from
its feet and send it spinning off downstream. She pressed it faster and faster,
then withdrew Rill wearily from the stream. It would continue circling on momentum for a good while, she judged, long enough to give the *legionares* a few
moments to breathe. Vord after vord splashed into the water, only to be swept
helplessly around the steadholt, over and over and over—and the current had
the added benefit of slowly eroding the ditch deeper. By the time the water
did calm enough for them to ford it, the vord would find the defenses higher and
more difficult to attempt than they had been before.

She turned wearily to the First Spear, and said, "Is that sufficient?"

Marcus pursed his lips and watched one luckless vord, which was on its
third trip around the steadholt. "Entirely, my lady. Thank you."

Isana nodded, and said, "Eventually, I think they'll bridge it, as ants sometimes do. Or simply choke it with enough bodies to create a crossing."

"Probably," Marcus said. "But even so, this buys us time, my lady. And—"

A brassy, blaring, groaning horn call sounded out in the rain-lashed dimness.
Then another, and another, and another. A few instants later, the ground shook,
and the taurg cavalry burst out of the murk, the huge beasts smashing through
the vord gathered around the steadholt. Five thousand strong, their blue-armored
Canim riders wielding their axes with deadly skill, they simply sliced off a portion
of the vord army. It was, Isana thought, oddly like watching a limb hacked off a
body. The cavalry drove through the vord in a wedge-shaped formation, cutting
out a portion of the enemy. Then they whirled on those mantises who had been
isolated from the main body and crushed them. The entire business took less

than two minutes, then the taurga were gone, bounding off into the grey haze of rain and storm. Acres of dead and dying vord were left in their wake.

Marcus let out a low whistle and shook his head.

"I take it that was impressive?" Isana said. "Beyond the surface appearance, I mean."

"In weather like this? Crows, yes, my lady. They took a tithe of the enemy force in a single pass. They won't gain the advantage of surprise again—see there, at the back, where the rearmost vord are facing out now?—but if the vord stay on that ground, the taurg riders will nibble them to death one bite . . ."

The air suddenly went silent and still. The ground stopped shaking. The only sound was the patter of rain.

". . . at a time," Marcus finished, his voice loud in the sudden hush, before closing his mouth himself.

No one spoke. No one moved. Even the vord seemed to recognize that something was happening, for they fell into a restless near stillness. Hushed expectation made the air heavy. Lightning flickered somewhere far overhead, pulses of vord green light. The grumbling sound of their thunder didn't reach Isana's ears for several seconds.

"What is happening?" one of the nearby Knights whispered.

Valiar Marcus glanced from the man to Isana. His expression flickered with a tiny, questioning frown, swiftly hidden.

Isana shook her head. "I'm not sure."

The sky to the northwest flared with irregular flashes of light. Blue, red, vord green, and instants later, the deep purple of an amethyst. Each burst of colored light would fade slowly, only to be replaced by newer brilliances. And the whole time, it was silent. No thunder rolled out to accompany the flashes.

"That's metalcrafting," Araris said with quiet certainty, his voice still ringing with steely undertones. "Three swords. The red and blue—that's Octavian."

Isana drew in a sharp breath. "Tavi."

For several moments, the flashes went on, green against purple. And then the ground suddenly shook again. That incredibly vast sound, laden with pure rage, filled the air once more. The storm returned in an instant, the wind rising to such a howl that, combined with the shaking ground, it knocked Isana from her feet. Araris caught her before she could fall to the stone, supporting her with one cool metallic arm as the earth trembled, and the tempest raged.

The vord warriors let out shrieks of their own and turned to fling themselves at the defenders with fanatic energy once more. Little was accomplished by the attack. The still-running waters of the moat swept them from their path. The shaking earth prevented the ones who managed to reach the other side of the moat from exploiting the vulnerability of the defenders—who were similarly incapacitated by the shaking earth and screaming sky. Lightning began to burn down from the storm, running along the ground like great, grasping fingers digging trenches in the earth for seconds at a time. There was a great wrenching snap of strained stone, and one section of the barn's roof caved in, only a few paces from where they stood.

"What is happening?" cried the Knight again, panic stretching his voice high and thin. "What is happening?"

Isana shivered and clung to Araris, feeling terrified, powerless, and small in the face of such raging, destructive forces. She wasn't sure how long it went on. It felt like hours, though it could only have been a few moments, or they would all have been slain. Then, the earth slowly began to grow calm again. The storm began to wane, the winds and rain dying down until they were no more severe than any springtime gale.

"The vord," Marcus choked. "The *vord!*"

Isana looked up and saw . . . utter confusion among the enemy. Mantises hissed and let out sharp shrieks and ran in every direction. Hundreds, if not thousands, of the creatures were locked in battle with one another—battles that seemed to end mostly in gory mutual destruction. Other mantises ripped at the bodies of their own dead, devouring them as though they were starving.

Again, the brazen horns of the Canim blared, only this time there were twice as many—Varg and the Canim infantry came out of the rain at the rangy lope of a Canim warrior, closing with the enemy from south of the steadholt, even as the taurg cavalry came rushing in from the northeast—accompanied by the bright clarion calls of the Aleran cavalry, who rode on the flanks of the main body of taurga, running down any stragglers who had separated from the main body of the vord . . . mass, Isana supposed, for it surely was no longer an army.

The Canim assault did not shatter the mantis horde so much as smash it to dust. Isana saw one of the lead taurga bounding a good six feet off the ground to come down with both of its front legs touching together, so that they drove into the vord before it like a sledgehammer, killing it instantly. It seized the next vord with its broad, blunt teeth and flung it into a cluster of other vord, so that four of them were tangled and unable to evade the next rank of taurga, who simply crushed them under their broad, pounding feet. Most of the attacking vord died in the first moments of the engagement, and many fled, only to be run down by teams of Aleran horsemen in position to do precisely that.

"He did it," Isana breathed, and found tears in her eyes. "He did it. My son did it."

The First Spear looked at her and spun to bellow in his parade-ground voice, "The captain's taken the vord Queen! He's done it!"

The cheers of the Legion shook the air, louder than the thunder they'd replaced.

Ehren would never have believed that anyone could be tired enough to sleep through the end of the world—but apparently he was wrong. Still recovering from the horrific wounds he'd taken in the battle, he supposed he hadn't fallen asleep so much as rejected consciousness.

"Ehren," Count Calderon said, shaking him by one shoulder. "Ehren!"

Ehren looked up, squinting down at the battle, then up at the northern bluff. The second vordbulk had almost reached them, and the vord were massing heavily against the defenders, ready to assault the second the bulk had breached the walls.

Though the sky had darkened and cold rain had begun to fall, there was still enough light to see. The sky to the west was absolutely black with storm clouds. The vast form of the great fury Garados could be seen intermittently through the overcast, though there was far less lightning playing through the distant clouds than there had been before. In fact, the bursts of light that colored the layers of cloud were . . .

"That isn't lightning," Ehren said, yawning. "We'd hear thunder. At least a little. Even this far away."

"What else could it be?" Bernard asked.

Ehren peered at the lights, then sat bolt upright. "Metalcrafting. Up near the head of Garados."

Bernard grunted in the affirmative. "The green flashes are the same color as the *croach*."

"Someone's taking on the Queen?" Ehren asked. "If they bring her down . . ."

"It still won't be in time for us," Bernard said calmly.

Ehren looked up at the northern bluff. While he had been unaware, the vordbulk had waded forward through everything that had been thrown at it. It was only yards from being in position to crush Garrison's defenses. The vordbulk let out another bellowing roar.

And a Citizen, bearing a sword that blazed with emerald fire, suddenly streaked from the ground toward the vordbulk. Ehren and Bernard both came to their feet. Both of them recognized the armored, white-haired form of Lord Cereus. The nimbus of light around the old High Lord's sword grew and grew, until it was almost violently bright. Ehren made himself watch, but just as it seemed the light's intensity would force him to avert his gaze, High Lord Cereus plunged completely into the vordbulk's roaring maw.

The vordbulk smashed its jaws shut, and they came together like a pair of city gates closing.

And an instant later, a brilliant green fireball replaced the vordbulk's head and the spreading shield of bone around it. Fire tore at the torso and limn of the vordbulk, incinerating tons of chitin and muscle in one supremely violent blast.

Incredibly, the vordbulk's mangled left front leg quivered and began to take another step, as if the limb had no idea that the head had been destroyed—but then the creature sagged to its left. Lord Cereus had, clearly, timed and directed his attack to achieve that very outcome, and the vordbulk toppled like the one before it, falling away from the fortress. It fell in seeming deliberation, because of its sheer size, but the impact when it came crashing down crushed fully grown trees to splinters.

Ehren stared in shock at the fallen vordbulk for a full minute, hardly able to comprehend the incredible courage and sacrifice of the old High Lord. But then, Cereus's daughter Veradis was behind the walls, employing her considerable talents as a healer, and his grandchildren were in the refugee camp. Of course her father would be willing to lay down his life to protect his sole surviving child and his sons' orphans; or at least, a man of Cereus's character would. It was one thing for a man to say he was willing to lay down his life for his child—but quite another for him to actually *do* it.

Count Calderon exhaled heavily, and breathed, "Thank you, Your Grace."

Ferocious battle ensued on the northern bluff, between the Wolf tribe and the vord who had been guarding the vordbulk, but it was no longer a hopeless fight for the Wolf, especially with the support of the Horse. Cereus's brigade of Citizens came flying back into the fortress in a state of total exhaustion.

Bernard looked up from a message brought by a courier and grunted. "That's it, then. We're out of firestones, and the rain is keeping the workshop from making any more."

"We can hold them with steel alone if they don't bring us any more surprises," Ehren said.

"I'd like to think that the vord are straining their limits as much as we are," Bernard said. "But our experience with them thus far does not fill me with confidence." He shook his head. "Well. We can only do what we can do. We'll stand for as long as our legs hold us. Sir Ehren, I wonder if you would please inform High Lady Cereus of her lord father's passing. Let her know exactly what happened."

Ehren sighed. "Of course, my lord. Better to hear it now than in rumor half an hour from now."

Bernard nodded and rubbed at his jaw—then froze and peered to the west.

Far down the valley, the storm clouds veiling Garados had apparently gone mad, spewing a thousand colors of lightning like spray at the bottom of a waterfall. Ehren stopped in his tracks and watched, as well, as the distant storm raked the land with lightning bolts. He was sure he imagined it, but for a moment it almost looked like one enormous windmane, miles and miles across, was raking the ground with claws of living lightning.

Then the vord all began to shriek, screaming as one creature. The wail put the hairs up on the back of Ehren's neck, but he stepped forward and gripped the edge of the balcony's railing, staring.

The seething, pulsing rhythm of the mass of vord, that sense of underlying organization and purpose that made them all seem like the various organs of a single body, began to fray. Over the next several minutes, Ehren watched the vord attackers change from an army driven by purpose and perfect discipline to a mob of hungry, dangerous predators. Though the sheer pressure of numbers crammed into limited space forced the vord at the leading edge of the mob to continue the attack on the walls of Garrison, farther back was a different tale.

Ehren brought up a sightcrafting and stared as the vord to the rear of the immediate combat began to turn upon one another, apparently driven by desperate hunger—and those farthest back began to depart altogether. It would take a long time, hours perhaps, for the pressure on the leading edge of the vord to relent enough to allow them to retreat, but it would happen. It would happen!

"What can you see?" Count Calderon asked, his weary voice anxious.

"They're breaking," Ehren said. He recognized that his own voice was thick with emotion he had neither expected nor approved. "They're turning on one another at the back of the mob. They're breaking." His vision was blurred by something. "They aren't holding together. They're *breaking*."

"They did it," Count Calderon breathed. "By all the furies, they *did* it. They killed the Queen!"

Ehren couldn't hear what Calderon said next. Months of horror and despair had all come down to this moment. He found himself sitting on the stone floor of the balcony, sobbing and laughing at the same time. He had never believed, never really believed, that the vord could be defeated. Not after so many retreats, so many deadly surprises.

But here, in the Calderon Valley, they had finally done it. They had endured the heaviest blows the enemy could deliver and survived. The Realm had survived. The Realm *would* survive.

It would survive thanks to the sacrifice of Cereus, and to the rather unassuming backcountry Citizen who now knelt beside him, putting a brawny arm around Ehren's shoulders. "Easy there, son. Easy. Come with me. I could use a drink. I've given orders to the Legions to keep rotating fresh troops in. Now all we have to do is wait this out."

Ehren nodded several times. "A drink," he said, his voice thick. "I don't think very well." Then he added, "But if you can't drink to this, what *can* you drink to? Let's go."

EPILOGUE

History will eventually claim that the appearance of the vord was a watershed moment, that it was the best thing that ever happened to Alera. The vord forced us to exceed our limits, to grow after centuries of stagnation and to look beyond ourselves. It is certain that because of the vord, we have gained a host of new enemies, in the Canim sense of the word. May we keep them and meet many more.

But history is a cold and distant observer. Those of us who must face today have goals far more finite: We must mend our wounds, mourn our dead—and survive the winter. Crows take what the historians think.

History will attend to itself.

—GAIUS TAVARUS MAGNUS, 1 AV.

"It's too tight," Tavi complained, tugging at the neck of the tunic. "And it's ridiculously overdone. Honestly, people are starving, and they're trying to deck me out in gems and cloth of gold?"

"No one is starving," Max said. "They just wish they were." He wore his new suit of armor, marked with the black crow of the First Aleran Legion upon a field of red and blue, and his dress uniform beneath it, including a captain's cloak of red velvet. "Bloody clever way to get rid of the *croach* if you ask me. Let people eat it up, especially as we're short on food and all."

"A bit too clever. I'm sick of the stuff."

Max snorted, slapped Tavi's hands out of the way, and started fastening the collar. "Stop eating it, then."

"I can't tell half the people in the Realm they've got to eat bug wax until next spring and not eat it myself, Max."

"Sure you can. You're the First Lord." Max arched an eyebrow. "You must not hate it all that much. This tunic fit you at your confirmation, you know."

Tavi grunted in discomfort. "It might taste terrible, but it's apparently good for you. Plus I'm not wearing armor around every day, now."

"And it shows," Max said cheerfully. He got the collar fastened with one last, hard tug, then eyed Tavi carefully. "Why is your face turning red?"

Tavi idly slid an effort of will into the cloth of gold, metalcrafting its strands to stretch out a bit. Once the collar had loosened, he was able to exhale without making an effort. "There. How's that?"

"Oh, ah," Max said, looking him over judiciously. "You look like . . . a First Lord."

"How descriptive. Thank you."

"Anytime, Calderon," Max said, grinning.

"Max," Tavi said. "Have . . . have you heard from Crassus?"

Max's grin faded. "He's . . . not coming. Officially, he's helping his father and mother get the situation in Antillus under control. But he's still upset about . . . well. Everything."

Tavi nodded, frowning. "I'm glad Antillus took Dorotea back."

Max grunted sourly. Then said, "She's gotten almost human over the past couple of years. I suppose she might do some good up there."

"Certainly, Crassus is in good hands, as far as healing is concerned. I . . . I wish I knew what to do to make it right."

"Stop thinking you can fix everything," Max said bluntly. "Give it time. That might help. Or not. But you'll only make things worse if you push."

Tavi nodded. "Thanks."

"Always happy to explain the obvious to you, Calderon. Now if you'll excuse me? Nothing makes a girl want to be seduced more than a wedding. I've got plans. I'll see you at the ceremony."

"Veradis is here, isn't she?" Tavi asked. "Do you honestly think she's going to change her mind about you because of the social environment?"

Max grinned. "No telling until I try, is there?" He paused by the door, and said, more seriously, "I've been looking in on her, since her father died. Making sure no one's been giving her a hard time, or anything. I might have spoken a few words into the ears of some of Cereus's clients who were not, shall we say, appreciative of the sacrifice he made."

Tavi smiled at his friend and inclined his head to him, not saying anything. Back in the Academy, he'd listened to Max describe beating the owners of crooked gambling houses in the same terms.

"You look fine, Calderon," Max said.

"Thanks."

Max saluted, giving the gesture more formal precision and grace than he usually did. He winked and departed.

No sooner had he left than there was a knock at the side door to the chamber, which was the largest suite of the largest private home in Riva. Its previous owner had died in the battle to cover the retreat from the city. Tavi had felt somewhat ghoulish moving into the house, but he'd needed the room. There was an absolutely astounding need for staff and support for the First Lord, and all of that help needed somewhere to work and sleep. The Rivan style tower proved more than roomy enough, though Tavi felt somewhat conflicted about residing on the top floor. With his windcrafting, stairs weren't really an issue which he was sure was part of the point of Rivan Citizens residing in towers. There was a real temptation to feel somewhat smug about that.

"Enter," Tavi said.

The door opened, and Ehren came in, looking much as he always did—neatly and plainly dressed, smudged with ink stains, and carrying a quill and a stack of paper. Even then, though there hadn't been a vord sighted within a day's march of Riva in months, Tavi could sense that Ehren still carried half a dozen knives on his person, out of sight.

"Good morning, sire," Ehren said. He plopped the stack of papers down on Tavi's desk. "I've brought the daily reports."

"I'm getting married in an hour," Tavi said. He crossed the room to sit down behind his desk and gestured for Ehren to sit in the chair across from him. "Summarize anything new?"

"You're going to love this," Ehren said, settling down comfortably. "We've got no less than three steadholts who have objected, violently, to our Knights attacking 'their' vord."

Tavi's eyebrows went up. "Excuse me?"

"They're communities that surrendered when the Queen gave them the option. Apparently, the *croach* just grew up around the perimeter of their fields and moved on. It's guarded by a crew of warriors and tended by spiders, apparently operating under orders to protect the holders as well as guarding them—and they've kept doing it, up to and including defending them from the rogue vord who scattered when the Queen died." Ehren shook his head. "The holders have painted their vord in various colors, so they can tell the difference."

Tavi frowned. "They want to *keep* them?"

"So it would seem. They're all deep inside occupied territory, but the holders declined an offer of transport out."

Tavi mused over the situation. "If the vord were given instructions, they would follow them to the exclusion of all others unless the Queen changed them."

Ehren blinked. "You want to let them stay?"

"No. But I can't blame them. The Realm didn't protect those people's homes and lives. The vord did. If they want to stay where they are, fine. This is a problem we'll deal with when we've killed enough of the *croach* to reach them. File them under secondary priorities."

"Very good," Ehren said. "The siege at Rhodes has been officially broken now, sire. The Legion Aeris and her Citizens arrived two days ago and made short work of it."

"Excellent," Tavi said. Rhodes had been the last city to be held prisoner within her own walls by large numbers of vord. Once sent running into the countryside, the vord tended to disperse as naturally as any predator. They were ill suited for life in the wild, though. After six months, most of the feral vord had starved to death. Some of them, though, seemed to have learned to survive on their own. Tavi imagined that they would continue to be a threat to travelers in the wild places for a good long while, despite the Legions' success at finding and destroying the underground warrior gardens, where new vord ripened and were born.

"We'll start breaking them into fire teams, then," Tavi said "We'll be able to handle twice as much *croach*-clearing in the Vale with the extra hands, as long as the vord don't get any more uppity than they already have."

Ehren nodded. "Without the Queen to drive them, they aren't much more than animals. They'll break at strong resistance, like they did at Garrison."

Tavi grunted. "You haven't talked about that much."

Ehren looked away and was still for a moment. Then he said, "I was there when Lord Cereus died. It was the most courageous, saddest thing I've ever seen. He deserved a better death."

"If he hadn't done it, that vordbulk would have crushed half of Garrison's walls. The vord had numbers enough that, even undirected, they would have killed everyone—his family included."

"That makes his death worthwhile. But not good. He deserved better." Ehren shook himself and went to the next page. "Ahem. The Academy Novus is officially under construction now. Magnus reports that he's building the lecture halls with enough windows and vents to keep them from baking all the students to sleep in the spring and summer, and setting up boundaries around the ruins to protect them from progress.

"And, in related news . . ." Ehren turned another page. ". . . Senator Valerius has lodged an official protest regarding the new College of Romanic Studies and the admittance of freemen without patronage. He has fourteen distinct arguments, but what it all amounts to is 'we've never done it that way before.'"

"Senator Valerius's protest will in no way disturb my digestion," Tavi said.

"Or mine. But Valerius has become a focal point for everyone who objects to your policies."

Tavi shrugged. "They don't want to admit to themselves that the war has changed things. If we don't look to the future, we'll never be able to manage it. Someone's always upset about something."

Ehren thumbed through the next several pages. "The good Senator opposes . . . the Slavery Ban . . . the recognition of the Canim State . . . the recognition of the Marat State . . . the recognition of the Iceman State . . . giving the Shieldwall to the Icemen . . . the enfranchisement of freemen, and, last but not least, relocating the capital to Appia."

"He has a point on that last one," Tavi said, somewhat wistfully. "There's a perfectly good volcano going to waste at old Alera Imperia. We could throw all the idiots in and be rid of them."

"I'm not sure if the entire Senate would fit inside, sire. In other news, the repair of the causeways is progressing reasonably well. We should have most of the old ones finished by next autumn, but . . ."

"But they all led to Alera Imperia, before," Tavi said. "What about the plans for the new routes?"

"Lord Riva thinks that a ring-shaped causeway circling about forty miles out from the old capital could be completed in three to five years—the hub of a wagon wheel, as it were."

Tavi nodded. "It will take us that long to clear all the *croach* around there in any case. What did he say about a more efficient map of new causeway routes?"

"Twenty-five years, minimum," Ehren said. "You don't want to know the cost estimate."

Tavi grunted. "Well. Nothing's ever easy, is it? Ask him to draft a more complete proposal, and we'll see if we can't start the groundwork while we're laying out this new hub."

"Very well, sire," Ehren said. "I'd like to suggest that the next time you watercraft to the Realm, you mention the need for those Citizens still in *croach*-covered territory to continue killing spiders whenever possible. In fact, I'd suggest that you place a bounty on them."

Tavi frowned. "Interesting. Why?"

"The spiders are responsible for the rapid spread of the *croach*, sire. The *croach* seems to generate enough spiders to support it, spontaneously, and the more of them we kill, the harder the *croach* has to work to replace them, and the slower it grows. The spiders are relatively weak, and should prove a capable testing ground for our younger Citizens—and for our Romanic scholars to test whatever new devices they create."

"You've been reading Varg's books again," Tavi commented.

Ehren shrugged and smiled faintly.

"What's happened to us, Ehren?" Tavi asked, bemused. "Last year we were marching with Legions and saving the Realm. Now we're negotiating treaties, planning roads, and implementing policies. What we're doing now isn't really fighting a war. We're just pioneering our way back to places we've already been."

Ehren rose and neatened the sheaf of papers in his hand by rapping them gently on the desk. "We've passed through the interesting parts of history, sire. May we never see them again. I'm completely in favor of a nice, long, boring stretch."

"Seconded," Tavi said fervently.

Ehren inclined his head. "Oh. Congratulations, by the way."

"Thank you," Tavi said, smiling. "You'll join us for dinner sometime soon, I hope."

"Of course, Tavi. My best to Kitai." Ehren departed as quietly and efficiently as he'd entered, and Tavi stretched out in his chair for a moment with his eyes closed. Outside, sleet mixed with early snow clicked and whispered against the windows, though it was only midautumn. This winter looked like it would be a bad one. He'd been spending most of his focus—and money—on making sure the Realm was ready to face a long, cold season.

Actually, it had come more easily than he'd expected. It was much like managing a Legion, save that in the Legion there was an absence of dissension. (Though upon thinking about it, Tavi decided that one little fact made for quite an astounding difference.) Still, the basic principles applied—recruit reliable subordinates and delegate authority in accordance with their talents. Help them when they needed it and stay out of their way when they didn't. Make absolutely clear what you expect from the people working for you and make sure rewards or discipline were consistent and fair.

So far, he thought, things could have been worse.

There was a knock at his chamber door, which opened a breath later. "Sire?" asked his valet's quiet voice. "Are you ready?"

"As I can be, I suppose." Tavi rose and checked his appearance in the mirror. His hair was short and newly trimmed, his beard likewise. The cloth-of-gold tunic was heavy, and all the gems didn't make it feel any lighter. Still, it didn't weigh as much as armor.

Fidelias, still wearing Valiar Marcus's face, entered the chamber and shut the door behind him.

"Sire," he said. "The guests have all arrived. No one has attempted to gut anyone. Today."

Tavi glanced over at him and showed his teeth. "Well. We didn't expect forging the Alliance to be simple."

"Naturally not," Fidelias said, setting down a tray that doubtless had a collection of light snacks on it. Tavi had been insisting on avoiding it for weeks, and it had become a kind of game for the sentenced man to provide Tavi with appetizing temptations. Tavi ignored them. Almost always. "What has most of the Citizens upset is how you handled the land grant for the Canim."

Tavi shrugged. "They're welcome to Parcia if they can take it for themselves. It's the city deepest in vord-held territory. It's our premier seaport, and the Canim have forgotten more about shipbuilding than our own shipwrights know." He shrugged. "Besides, if we didn't give them someplace to call their own, they'd take it anyway—and they wouldn't be inclined to be terribly friendly afterward. They'll be taking Free Alera with them, I'm certain—and any holders there who don't want to operate under Canim rule are free to seek another steadholt under a different lord."

"High Lord Varg." Fidelias sighed. "You know why they're truly upset about it, don't you?"

"Because someone without furycraft has been made a High Lord," Tavi replied. "My heart bleeds for the poor lambs." He took the cover off the tray and found it stacked with small meat pastries. They smelled heavenly. He gave Fidelias a murderous look. "Mark my words. The day is coming when anyone who wishes Citizenship will be able to work for it and get it. When brains will get you further than any fury ever could. And when we overempowered engines of destruction will be a quaint reminder of the past, not masters of the future." He put the lid back down with a sharp clang. "Someone should write that down. They can quote me later, the way they do all the other First Lords."

"I believe they'll save that for your words upon being dragged away to be locked in a tower as a raving madman," Fidelias replied.

Tavi burst out into a quick belly laugh. "No, I'm not quite mad yet. How are the plans for the new program coming along?"

"Covert plans for the covert training of covert operatives? If I told you, I'd have to kill you, sire."

Tavi grinned at him. "I'll take that to mean 'well enough.'"

Fidelias nodded. "Sha has been most helpful. I enjoy working with him. Though his ideas of teaching methods are rather different than mine." He cleared his throat, and asked, "Sire? Do you really intend to wait before taking the battle to the vord in Canea? Senator Valerius—"

Tavi threw up his hands. "Augh. I am sick of hearing that man's name. He wants me to lead an expedition to Canea to find the last queen, does he?"

"Exactly."

"Thus getting rid of me, which should make his campaign to frustrate everything I'm trying to build somewhat simpler." Tavi shook his head. "If we have

taken all of Alera back in ten years, we'll be doing well. And that's vital. We absolutely cannot leave the vord supply caches lying all over the place. And I don't
like our chances in Canea anytime in the next thirty years or so. It's *huge* over
there. We don't have enough bodies to get the job done."

"But you do acknowledge that it must happen."

"Probably," Tavi said. "Eventually. But for now . . . the vord in Canea are just
too bloody useful."

Fidelias frowned. "Sire?"

"Right now we've got something the world has never seen before: a working
alliance among the Canim, the Marat, the Icemen, and Alera. Over the past
century or three, how many Alerans have been killed fighting them, hmm?"

"Using the vord to hold the Alliance together. Risky."

Tavi spread his hands. "The fact of the matter is that none of us can stand
up to the vord on our own. The only way we have a chance is together. And the
only way we'll ever be able to take the battle to them in Canea is to live in peace
with one another now and build something capable of defeating them."

"Build something. Like this universal Academy you've been talking about."

"That's one element, yes," Tavi said. "Our peoples have a lot to teach each
other. The Academy is an excellent way to do that."

"I don't see what we can teach the Canim or the Marat, Captain. It's not as
though we can give them lessons in furycraft."

Tavi suppressed his own grin. "Well. You never know when some furyless
freak is going to develop talent. Do you."

Fidelias eyed him for a moment, then sighed. "You aren't going to explain,
are you."

"It's a First Lord's sacred right. I get to be cryptic whenever I want. So
there."

Fidelias huffed out a short laugh. "All right. That's an argument I'm not
going to win." His face sobered. "But . . . sire. Given my sentence . . . I thought
you'd have settled my account by now."

"Haven't I?" Tavi asked him. "Fidelias ex Cursori is dead. His name is black
and ruined. He betrayed a dead First Lord for the sake of a High Lord and Lady
who are also dead. All that he wrought for either patron has been destroyed. The
labor of a lifetime, gone."

The man who wore Valiar Marcus's face looked down. There was bitterness
in his eyes.

"I sentence Fidelias ex Cursori to death," Tavi continued quietly. "You will
die in service to me, laboring under another name, a name that will be heaped
with well-deserved honor and praise. I sentence you to go to your grave knowing
how things might have been had you never strayed from my grandfather's ser-

vice. I sentence you to die knowing that the First Lord who should have crucified you six months ago is instead granting you trust, a staff, and an expense
account that a fictional man deserves far more than you do." He leaned forward.
"You have too much talent to throw away. I need you. You're mine. And you're
going to help me build the Alliance."

Fidelias grunted. Then he asked, very quietly, "How do you know I won't
betray you?"

"The question is," Tavi replied, "how do *you* know I won't betray *you*?"

Fidelias looked a bit taken aback by that logic.

"I'm arrogant sometimes, but I'm not a fool. Don't think that I'm not watching you very carefully. I'm simply willing to invest in the paranoia it takes to make
sure I get full use out of you. The Realm needs it." He lowered his voice. "The
Realm needs heroes. The Realm needs *you*, Marcus. And I have no intention of
letting you go to waste."

The other man blinked his eyes once, and nodded. "Crows," he said quietly.
"If only Sextus had your courage."

"Courage? He was no coward," Tavi said.

"Not physically, no," Marcus answered. "But . . . the courage to look at the
truth and admit to himself what it was. The courage to strive for something that
was right even if it seemed impossible. He never walked out of the bounds set
for him by his father's fathers. Never even considered that our future might be
different than our past."

Tavi smiled slightly. "Well. He didn't have the benefit of my fine education
and upbringing."

"True."

Marcus squared his shoulders and faced him. "For what it's worth, I'm
yours, Captain. Until death takes me."

"That's been true since the Elinarch," Tavi replied quietly. "Please return to
the party below and tell them that I'll be down in a moment."

Marcus saluted Legion style, despite his lack of uniform, and departed
quietly.

Tavi sat down on a chair and closed his eyes for a moment. Now that the
day was upon him, this entire notion of marriage seemed a great deal more . . .
permanent than it had before. He took some slow breaths.

There was a ripple of water in the little pool in the room, and a ghostly voice
whispered, "Young Gaius?"

Tavi rose and hurried to the pool. It was the only way Alera could still appear
to him. Over the six months since Third Calderon, she had continued fading
away, appearing less frequently and for less time. Tavi leaned over and smiled
down at the water, where the ghostly reflection of Alera's face had appeared.

"You are to be wed," Alera said. "That is a significant moment. You have my warmest regards upon this day."

"Thank you," Tavi answered quietly.

She smiled at him, the expression kindly, and somehow satisfied. "We shall not speak like this again."

A little pang went through Tavi's chest at the words—but he had known that the day was coming. "I will miss speaking with you."

"I cannot say the same," Alera responded. "For which I find myself . . . somewhat grateful. It would be awkward." She inhaled slowly, then nodded. "Are you sure you wish to continue on the path you have begun?"

"Well. You say I introduced you to Kitai, without realizing it, because of our bond. That's why you can speak to her."

"Indeed."

"Then you should trust me. Interaction with the other Marat will be just as rewarding, on some level. As it will with the Canim. And the Icemen are already watercrafting, whether they realize it or not. It's hardly any change at all."

"I somehow do not think that the lords of your ancestral line would agree. Nor would they agree with the concept of . . . how did you phrase it?"

"Merit-based furycraft," Tavi said. "Those who want more of it should be able to work to get it. It's only fair. We're losing the contribution of talented minds in every generation simply because they were not born with enough fury-craft for their ideas to be respected. If that doesn't change, we won't survive."

"I quite agree," Alera replied. "And I'm willing to implement your plan before the end. I'm just . . . surprised to find the attitude in a mortal."

"I've had everything," Tavi said, gesturing at the room. "And I've had nothing. And I've made my peace with being in either place. That's not something many of my ancestors can say."

"Your people will look at this year, in the future, and they will call it a great marvel. They will call it the day your kind stepped from darkness into light."

"Provided such ridiculously arrogant know-it-alls actually survive to do so, I will be content," Tavi replied.

"You have a century and a half, by my estimation. Perhaps two. And then the Canean vord queen will come for you."

Tavi nodded. "Then I'll make us ready. Or get us part of the way there, at least."

"Strange," Alera said. "I feel a certain empathy for you, knowing that great events are to come, but that I will not be there to see them. I feel more like a mortal now than at any time I have existed in this form."

"That's to be expected. You are, after all, dying."

Alera smiled, the expression warm. "True," she whispered. "And not true.

Some part of me, young Gaius, will always be with you, and your children after you."

"What do you mean?" Tavi asked.

But the reflection in the water was his own.

He stared down at the pool for a few moments more, just to be sure. Then he rose and firmly watercrafted the tears from his eyes and marched off toward his fate.

Tavi met Kitai outside the Rivan amphitheater, where the Senate, the Citizenry, and anyone else who could squeeze into the building were waiting. The young Marat woman was wearing a white gown that left one shoulder bare and draped across her rather fetchingly. Trimmed in gold and studded with pearls and gems, her gown was easily a match for his own tunic. Granted, the Horse Clan hairstyle she wore would have scandalized the Realm, even if she hadn't dyed her pale hair in brilliant colors. He'd pointed it out gently to her a few days back, and she'd responded that her mane was dyed in the royal colors of vibrant red and blue, and so what did anyone have to be scandalized about?

Isana and Araris were there as well, both dressed in the green and browns of Lord Calderon's House, standing next to Bernard himself. Isana embraced Tavi when he appeared, and said, "What happened to your collar? It looks . . . stretched."

"I stretched it, in the interests of breathing," Tavi replied.

His mother smiled at him, her eyes wrinkling at the corners. "Well. It will do, I suppose. You've always looked too thin, the past few years."

Tavi turned to Araris and offered his hand. The swordsman took it, his sun-browned skin rough and warm, then embraced him in a brief, tight hug. "Your father would be proud of you, Tavi."

Tavi grinned at him. "Thank you, Count and Countess Rillwater."

"For goodness' sake, Tavi," Isana said. "You didn't have to appoint us to the Citizenry."

"I'm the First Lord," Tavi told her, smiling. "That's what you get for having a quiet, private ceremony when I'm busy fighting vord. Suffer."

Bernard let out a rumbling laugh and embraced Tavi hard enough to make his ribs creak. "Watch it, boy. There are enough folk around who remember how to let the air out of your head if it swells too much."

Tavi returned the embrace, grinning. "Look how much good it did me when I was young, eh?"

Bernard snorted and put a hand on Tavi's shoulder. He looked him up and down and nodded. "You've done well, boy."

"Thank you," Tavi said quietly, "Uncle."

"Lord Uncle," corrected Amara, her gold-brown eyes sparkling as she appeared from behind her husband. She held a bundled infant over her swelling belly. "You both look wonderful," she said to Tavi and Kitai. "Congratulations."

"Hah," Kitai said, staring at Amara. "You are as big as a house. How did you hide behind him?"

Amara flushed and laughed, clearly both embarrassed and pleased. "Endless practice."

"When are you due?" Kitai asked.

"Another three months or so," Amara said. She glanced over her shoulder, evidently an instinctive movement, and said, a bit plaintively, "Bernard."

Tavi's uncle glanced over to a nearby fountain, where a young girl was apparently leading two even younger boys on an expedition walking around its narrow rim. "Masha," Bernard called, and started walking toward them. "Masha, stop trying to get your brothers to fall in."

"Brothers?" Kitai asked.

"Adopted," Amara said. She looked down again, her expression both pleased and demure. "There were so many children in need of a home, after Third Calderon. We weren't expecting me to . . . to be expecting. Isana says it was the Blessing of Night that repaired the damage the Blight did to me."

"Oh, aye," Kitai said, nodding. "It was used for that among my people once, back before my Aleran woke up its sleeping guardian and nearly destroyed the world."

"Will you never let that rest?" Tavi asked, grinning.

"One day. When you are old and toothless. I promise."

"We'd best go on in," Isana said. "Tavi, do you want someone to hold him?"

"No, thank you, Mother," Tavi replied. "We decided that he's coming with us."

Kitai nodded firmly and accepted the infant from Amara. She settled him against her, fussed with his blankets, and told the child, "It is foolish, but we must endure this Aleran nonsense. It will make your father happy."

"It's a necessary formality," Tavi said, nodding to the other four as they went on into the amphitheater. "That's all."

Kitai ignored him to continue speaking to the baby. "Like many Alerans, he places undue value upon acts performed in front of witnesses in which all manner of ridiculous things are done that would be much more simply done at a desk or table than here. But we love him, so we will do these things."

"You love him, do you?" Tavi asked.

Kitai smiled up at him, then stood on tiptoe to kiss him. "Very much."

Tavi put his hand on the warm head of the little person who had entered the world scarcely a week before. His other arm slid around Kitai's shoulders. They stood like that for a moment, not moving, both of them looking down at the sleepy face of Gaius Desiderius Tavarus, their son.

Desiderius. The desired one. Let there never be a doubt in his mind that he was welcome in their family and in their world.

Tavi felt . . .

Complete.

"I love you, too," he said quietly. "Ready?"

"Remind me of the ceremony?" Kitai asked as they started walking.

"We go down the aisle to the podium and table. We'll stop in front of Varg, who will do the reading. Maximus will vouch for my identity and your father for yours. Then we'll each sign the marriage contract."

Kitai nodded. "And then what?"

"What do you mean? And then we're married."

She stopped in her tracks and looked up at him. "You . . . are quite serious, aren't you?"

Tavi blinked and tried not to sound as baffled as he felt. "That's . . . the wedding ceremony. I mean . . . granted there's no swordplay or arson or rock climbing, but what were you expecting?"

Kitai exhaled patiently, composed herself, and began walking again.

They entered the amphitheater, and as they did they came into view of forty thousand Citizens and freemen, Canim and Marat, and even one of the Icemen, who wore a coldstone around his shaggy neck like an amulet. To the "First Lord's March," that clanking and lurching piece of attempted music, they walked slowly down the aisle toward the center of the amphitheater. By the time they'd gone a third of the way, the amphitheater was already erupting into cheers.

"We both sign a contract," Kitai said from between her teeth. No one in the crowd would see anything but her smile. "We scribble on a page."

"Yes," Tavi replied the same way.

She looked up at him, her warm green eyes merry as she rolled them, and said, as though mouthing a curse, "Alerans."